E. V. THOMPSON OMNIBUS

Becky
The Restless Sea

E. V. THOMPSON OMNIBUS

Becky
The Restless Sea

E. V. THOMPSON

timewarner
paperbacks

A *Time Warner* Paperback

This omnibus edition first published in Great Britain by
Time Warner Paperbacks in December 2005
E. V. Thompson Omnibus Copyright © E. V. Thompson 2005

Previously published separately:
Becky first published in Great Britain by Macmillan London
Limited in 1988
First published in paperback by Pan Books Ltd in 1989
Published by Warner Books in 1999
Reprinted by Time Warner Paperbacks in 2002
Copyright © E. V. Thompson 1988

The Restless Sea first published in Great Britain in 1983 by Macmillan
Reprinted in 1985 by Pan Books
Published by Time Warner Paperbacks in 2002
Copyright © E. V. Thompson 1983, 2002

The moral right of the author has been asserted.

A CIP catalogue record for this book
is available from the British Library.

ISBN 0 7515 3787 X

Printed and bound in Great Britain by
Clays Ltd, St Ives plc

Time Warner Paperbacks
An imprint of
Time Warner Book Group UK
Brettenham House
Lancaster Place
London WC2E 7EN

www.twbg.co.uk

Becky

To Celia
for her help and understanding

CHAPTER ONE

WHEN FERGUS VINCENT first saw Becky she was lying amidst accumulated rubbish on the cobbled footway of Lewin's Mead, the worst slum in the busy port of Bristol, and he could not decide whether she was alive or dead.

No road-sweeper wielded broom or shovel in these streets, nor were there house-servants to clear a space in front of each tall half-timbered house. Prosperous merchants had once lived here, but that had been in the early years of the eighteenth century, more than a hundred years before. Now the tall unsymmetrical houses leaned drunkenly towards each other across a maze of narrow dingy thoroughfares, hiding the dank rubbish-strewn alleyways from the revealing light of the sun.

Stooping, Fergus prodded the rag-clad figure. It sat up immediately.

'Here! What d'you think *you're* doing? Leave off!'

'I didn't expect to find anyone sleeping in the street at this hour. It's hardly evening yet.'

'What's it to *you* when I sleep?'

The girl's voice carried a broad Bristol accent, and Fergus had an overpowering urge to sketch her as she sat scowling, surrounded by rubbish. The girl's pinched face was as dirty as any he had ever seen, but dirt could not hide the wary expression in her eyes. It was an expression Fergus had seen in the slums of half a hundred cities.

'Do you know Back Lane?'

Rising to her feet, the girl peered up at him suspiciously.

The light was poor, but Fergus could see she was older than he had first thought. Small for her age, she was probably about thirteen.

'What do you want in Back Lane? If you're looking for a tart, I know a young dollymop who'll serve you well – or you can have me for a guinea.'

Fergus had met younger girls than this one selling themselves and he was more amused than shocked.

'If I had a sovereign to spend on a woman, I'd want more for my money than a bundle of skin and bones wrapped in rags. That's not why I'm here. I'm seeking a friend.'

'A friend of *yours* in Back Lane?' The girl studied Fergus from head to toe. She saw a slim thin-faced young man with unfashionably long hair who must have been in his early twenties. From the way he moved it was evident he limped quite badly. His clothes were hardly those of a gentleman but, like Fergus himself, they were *clean*. This alone set him apart from the residents of Back Lane.

'What's your friend's name?'

'Henry Gordon.'

'*Jock* Gordon? The artist?'

'That's right. You know him?'

Fergus was both delighted and relieved to know he had found the right place. In the letter received by Fergus some months before, Henry Gordon had been overflowing with enthusiasm for the many subjects just waiting to be painted in Lewin's Mead. But Henry Gordon was a man of rapidly changing moods. It would have been in character for him to move on only a few days after telling Fergus of all he hoped to achieve in Lewin's Mead.

'I *did* know him.'

'He's gone? Damn! I wrote and told him I'd be here soon. . . . He couldn't have got my letter.'

'It wouldn't have made any difference.' The girl spoke almost nonchalantly. 'He's dead. It was probably the drink, though some think he caught something that came in on one of the foreign boats, down at the docks. Couldn't really say, myself. One day when I spoke to him he seemed as right as rain. The next, he was dead.'

Fergus felt deep shock. Henry Gordon had been his best friend – his *only* friend in earlier days, when Fergus had no one else to whom he could turn. He had known Henry Gordon for as long as he could remember. The artist had been more of a father to him than Fergus Vincent senior.

When Fergus had returned to Edinburgh from one of his sea-trips and learned his dying mother had been taken to an asylum for the chronically insane, it was Henry Gordon who helped Fergus to have her moved. Fergus still had nightmares about those terrifying nights when he had sat beside his mother's bed in a locked ward, as demons in every conceivable guise moved in to torment the unfortunate inmates of that uncaring and degrading place.

It was Henry Gordon who stood with Fergus at the graveside while his mother was lowered into the ground of a chilly and fog-shrouded churchyard, while Fergus's own father was accepting consolation – and drinks – from friends in the smoky warmth of an Edinburgh tavern.

From early childhood days, too, it had always been Henry Gordon who encouraged Fergus to sketch, offering his own artist's materials when there was no money in the Vincent household to indulge what Fergus's father scathingly dismissed as his son's 'nonsense'.

Even in later years when Henry Gordon developed a liking for the bottle and lost his teaching post at the Edinburgh academy, he had always worked hard to encourage the young sailor-artist.

'You won't be wanting Back Lane now?' The girl broke into Fergus's unspoken grief.

'What? No. . . . Not unless Henry's left any of his work behind. But it will be long gone by now, I expect. When did he die?'

'Must be a week ago. Ten days at the most. But if you're talking about his paintings they're still in his room.'

'The room hasn't been let?'

'Whores who work the docks are the only ones with money in Back Lane, and no drunken sailor's going to risk a broken neck climbing stairs to Ida Stokes's attic in the dark. Give me a penny and I'll take you there. For two I'll carry your bags.'

Fergus had a small kitbag slung over his shoulder and a large slim canvas satchel tucked beneath his arm. The two bags contained all he owned in the world. He had no intention of trusting either to an unknown Bristol street-urchin.

'What's your name?'

'Becky.'

'Becky what?'

She shrugged. 'I ain't never had no other name.'

For a moment Fergus softened. It was a fleeting emotion. Children who begged for a living were convincing liars.

'I'm Fergus Vincent. I'm an artist, too. Show me where Henry Gordon lived. If his work is still there, I'll give you *three* pence. If it's gone, you get nothing.'

'All right.' If Jock Gordon's belongings were still in the house, Becky would be three pence better off. If they weren't – well, the cobbles were no harder in Back Lane than here. 'His stuff will be there. Ida Stokes gives away nothing that comes her way, and no one with any money's come to Back Lane since Jock died.'

Fergus did not doubt her words. Little would happen in the closely packed Lewin's Mead slums that did not quickly become common knowledge. Much of the city's crime originated here. Any one of the residents of the narrow streets could have quoted time, place and the villains responsible for every unlawful incident. But none would. It was the same in the slums of every city in the land. Such close-mouthed silence had nothing to do with loyalty. A poor man lived by his own laws. Often crude, they were always effective. The secrets of a slum were kept where they belonged.

Becky led Fergus through narrow streets and narrower alleyways that became progressively dirtier as they climbed the hillside away from the quays and docks of the city centre.

As they neared a cheap beer-house which had more sacking than glass at its windows, Fergus could hear the sounds of a noisy argument. He and Becky had almost reached the door when a woman's screams rose above the din. Suddenly women and children spilled out of the beer-house doorway into the cobbled alleyway. In their midst was a scowling thickset man whose face was black with coal-dust and streaked with rivulets of perspiration. The man's fists were flailing, and he drove a woman ahead of him.

The crowd parted, and Fergus saw that the object of the coal-heaver's attentions was a thin scarecrow of a woman, no more than five feet tall. It was she who was screaming as she staggered back before the assault of the angry bully. Around them other women shouted obscenities at the man, while a couple of small children tugged at his clothes and begged him to stop.

Halted by the crowd, Fergus watched in growing horror as the coal-heaver hit the woman yet again. She fell backwards, her head striking the cobblestones with a sound that reminded Fergus of a hen's egg falling on a hard surface.

The woman lay on the ground unmoving, but her angry assailant had not finished with her. He began to kick her with heavy-booted viciousness, each kick accompanied by an angry oath.

Fergus had seen enough. He was too slightly built to be a fighter, but he would not stand by and watch a woman being kicked to death. Pushing through the futilely shouting crowd, he charged at the coal-heaver just as he aimed yet another powerful kick at the woman.

Caught off-balance, the coal-heaver slipped on the cobble-stones and fell heavily to the ground. He was up in an instant, looking to see who had the temerity to take him on. His glance found Fergus, and with a roar of anger he lunged forward, big coal-blackened fists swinging.

Most of the wild punches missed – but not all. One caught Fergus in the mouth and knocked him to the ground, and now it was his turn to be on the receiving end of the heavy-booted kicks.

As Fergus tried desperately to roll away, a small ragged figure leaped at the coal-heaver and clawed his face, jumping clear before he could retaliate. Taking heart from such unexpected support, the screeching women in the crowd began pummelling at the coal-heaver, the sheer weight of their numbers forcing him to back away along the cobbled alleyway.

Fergus climbed awkwardly to his feet and found Becky standing waiting for him, holding his bags.

'Come on!'

'The woman. . . . She might be badly hurt.'

'Her friends will take care of her. It's best to mind your own business when you're in Lewin's Mead.'

Fergus dabbed at the corner of his mouth, and his fingers came away sticky with blood. His lip was cut, and it felt as though one of his teeth was loose. But things might have been a great deal worse.

'Yet you stopped that coal-heaver from giving *me* a hiding.'

'If he'd knocked you out, your pockets would have been emptied in seconds. I wouldn't have got the three pence you've promised me.'

Becky thrust the bags at him, then turned and walked away. Smiling wryly, Fergus limped after her.

Minutes later they reached a cul-de-sac that was over-shadowed by tall leaning houses. This was Back Lane. The cobblestones here were broken and uneven, and there was more accumulated rubbish than they had encountered in any street or alleyway through which they had passed. It would have been far worse had Back Lane not been on a hillside. As it was, rain pouring from the roofs washed much of the household filth into lower, less fortunate thoroughfares.

Becky led Fergus to a house at the very end of the narrow lane. A nondescript mongrel dog lay inside the door, feebly scratching at a tattered ear with a rear paw. It paused to growl when Fergus stepped over the threshold, but at an admonishment from Becky the sound died in the animal's throat, its tail beating a tattoo on the stone floor.

Their arrival had not gone unnoticed. Fergus had seen a shadow behind the dirty glass and brown paper of a down-stairs window as they came in from the street. Now a door off the hall opened and a woman peered at them through the gloom.

'Who's that? If it's a catchpoll, you're too late. Irish Molly's gone back to Ireland. Sailed yesterday from the docks.' The old crone's voice was cracked and hoarse.

'It's not a constable, Ida. His name's Fergus. Fergus Vincent. He's a friend of the artist. The one who died.'

Ida Stokes advanced across the hall. She was an untidy, heavily overweight woman with indifferent eyesight. When she leaned closer to peer into Fergus's face he smelled cheap gin on her breath.

'He's bloody. What happened to him?'

'He tried to stop Joe Skewes beating his woman.'

'Joe Skewes? That man will kill someone one day, you mark my words.' Ida Stokes shook her head disapprovingly. She suddenly snapped at Fergus: 'Are you here to pay the rent your friend owed when he died?'

'No. I've come to see if he's left any paintings.'

'You're taking nothing until I'm paid what's owing to me. It's the law. I'm within my rights. . . .'

'I'm here because I'm Henry Gordon's friend, not his executor. Anything I take will be paid for. Where's his property?'

Fergus's manner was curt. The news of Henry Gordon's death had come as a great shock, and he was fighting hard to hide the grief he felt. He had no intention of wrangling with this woman about his friend's effects.

Surprisingly, Ida Stokes's manner underwent an immediate change. The Back Lane landlady had an ignorant woman's respect for learning – and Fergus's words branded him as an educated man. He had also mentioned he would pay for anything he took away. . . .

'The things are in his room at the top of the house. Wait here. We'll need a candle; the stairs are dark.'

When Ida Stokes disappeared into her room, Fergus dipped inside a pocket and produced a silver fourpenny piece. Handing it to Becky, he said: 'Here, use it to buy some food to fill that skinny belly.'

Becky snatched the money as though she feared Fergus might change his mind. The coin disappeared beneath her raised skirt a moment before Ida Stokes reappeared, the landlady's hand protecting the flame of a candle-stub against the draught coming through the open street-door.

Ida Stokes set off up the stairs without a word, and Fergus followed, Becky coming with them.

Three young women stood talking together in a doorway

on the first-floor landing. They looked curiously at the candlelit procession, and one of them, a thickset, dark-haired girl, hooted with mirth.

'Will you look at this! Ida's showing Becky and a young gent to a room. Becky's finally realised she's been sitting on an untapped fortune all these years.' The woman spoke with a strong Irish accent.

Rounding on the speaker, Ida Stokes snapped: 'Becky's doing nothing of the sort. She brought this gentleman to the house to check the belongings of his poor dead friend. So start showing some respect – and if any of you idle slatterns have laid your thieving hands on anything from his room you'd better return it now. Then you can get dressed and go out to earn some money; especially you, Irish Molly – you owe me a fortnight's rent. If I've had no money from you by the morning, you'll be out on the street.'

'You wouldn't do that, Ida. You know the beaks are after me because of the misunderstanding about that sailor's purse. . . .'

A loud and derisive snort from Ida Stokes interrupted the lament, but only for a moment.

'If they find me and bring charges, it'll be Australia this time for sure. Transportation, and me not a well woman.'

'And I'm not a *rich* one. Pay your rent tomorrow or there'll be someone else in your room by nightfall.'

Leaving the Irishwoman grimacing after her, Ida Stokes led the way up another flight of dark stairs. Wheezing laboriously, she said to Fergus: 'I should never have let that girl inside my house. She's trouble. All these Irish girls are alike. I'm too soft-hearted, that's what I am. Always been the same.'

There were several rooms off the next landing, but only one had a door. In one of the rooms a low fire was burning in the grate and a smell of unwholesome cooking pervaded the air. By the light of the fire Fergus could see a motley collection of men, women and crying children, sitting or lying on the bare floorboards. To Fergus's surprise Becky entered this room and was greeted with a shrill-voiced flow of Irish invective from a woman crouched by the fire.

'Does Becky live here?' Fergus asked the question as the landlady gathered herself to tackle yet another flight of stairs, this one narrower and more uneven than the previous two.

'Live here?' Ida Stokes echoed his words. 'Only when she has money to pay for a place in the room. I let it to an Irishwoman, O'Ryan. Never told me her first name. Not that there's any reason why I *should* know, not as long as she pays her rent regular. The less I know of them as stays here, the better it is for everyone. If I don't know names, I can't tell 'em. Can't be stood up before the magistrate for what they call "harbouring", neither. Becky comes here when she can pay her way, like the rest of 'em in there. When she can't she's out on the street. There's no shortage of company for her *there*, I can tell you.'

'Has she no family?' Fergus asked the question even as he was telling himself that Becky was none of his business.

'None as would admit to being "family". One of the sailor's women was once pointed out to me as her mother, but she's been dead these six or seven years – could even be longer.'

The wheezing old landlady's words conjured up memories for Fergus of his own childhood. He, too, had lived in a slum – an Edinburgh slum, where families were crowded into tenement buildings, as many as forty people occupying a flat originally built for two.

The cramped overcrowded conditions had bred disease, depravity – and frequent violence. There had been times when Fergus had gone hungry, too, but the one thing that had never been lacking in his life was the love of his mother. This was the thing he remembered most of all about those childhood days. It had provided him with the strength to fight free of his surroundings when an opportunity arose for him to join the Royal Navy.

Ida Stokes laboured up the last few protesting stairs and shook a key free from the jangling bunch worn on a cord about her neck. Inserting the key in the lock of the door at the head of the stairs, she turned it and said: 'Here you are, young sir. Everything's exactly as your friend left it – may God rest his poor soul.'

The attic room was long and narrow, with a sloping ceiling and a deep alcove at the far end. It also had two windows and was surprisingly light, even at this hour of the evening. The old house was taller than most of its neighbours, and there was a view from the windows over the adjacent rooftops. Fergus began to understand why Henry Gordon had been content to live in such an insalubrious area. Fergus wondered why the money-conscious landlady had not relet the room. When he put the question to her Ida Stokes was momentarily discomfited.

'Some mischevious gossip put word about that your friend died of cholera. It's a wonder I didn't lose *all* my tenants. There was no truth in the tale, but I'll not be able to let the room again until all such foolish talk's ended.'

'What *did* cause Henry's death?'

Ida Stokes kicked one of the many bottles strewn about the floor. 'Here's your answer – but as his friend you'll know all about his drinking habits. He reached for a bottle as soon as he opened his eyes. Mind you, he never woke before noon on most days. . . . But that was *his* business, as I often told him. I don't go prying into other folks' affairs. You'll find his paintings and the like in the alcove, just around the corner.'

Crouching on the floor in the small extension to the room, Fergus sorted quickly through the paintings leaning haphazardly against the wall. One or two had been painted on canvas, but most were on stiff pasteboard. There were portraits of sailors and dockside workers, one or two of inns and taverns – and a number of Becky.

'Well, what are they worth to you?'

Fergus shook his head. 'Very little, and I know of no one who'd buy them.'

He looked around the room as he spoke. Paint and pencils lay in untidy profusion on the single grubby table and also about the floor. There were paint-stained rags lying among them, and brushes were crammed inside an old pot on the window-sill. There was also an unfinished portrait on an easel standing close to the window.

'You might get a pound or two for everything, but no more.'

Fergus did not see Ida Stokes's disappointment. He was thumbing through a sketchpad which had been thrown carelessly on to the floor. There were many sketches here. Realistic *live* scenes drawn inside inns, or on the quays of the busy port. There were more sketches of Becky, too. Some were good.

'Will you give me two guineas for the lot?'

Fergus shook his head. 'I do my own sketches.'

He looked about him at the room. The walls were grubby, and the bed sagged in the middle like a first-day sailor's hammock. The bare floorboards were warped and rotten, and the floor sloped at an alarming angle. Above him dark mould-patches on the lath-and-plaster ceiling indicated where rain came in. But the light during the day would be exactly what an artist needed.

'If I decided to stay in Bristol, how much would you charge me for this room?'

Recovering quickly from her depression, Ida Stokes's expression resumed its natural cunning. 'It's a good room. Folks in Bristol are falling over themselves for places like this. I'd a mind to let it to a ship's bos'n, or a mate, perhaps.'

'How much?'

'I could get four and sixpence for it, easy. Five shillings if I let it to the Irish. They'd sleep twelve here with room to spare. . . .'

'I'll give you two shillings.'

'Two? That will hardly pay for the wear on my stairs. *Four* shillings – and I'll wash your bed-linen once a month, free of charge.'

'Two and sixpence, paid in advance – and my bed-linen washed once a fortnight. Agree now and I'll give you a guinea extra for the bits and pieces lying about the place.'

'I should know better than to dicker with a Scotsman – and mad to consider having another artist in my house. Make it *two* guineas for the things and the room's yours when you show me the colour of your money.'

Five minutes later Fergus was alone. Opening the windows to clear the smell of cooking that seeped up from the floor below, he sat on the sagging bed and looked about him with mixed feelings. Henry Gordon had spoken to him many times of living in just such a place as this and of using his talents to show how so many of the subjects of Queen Victoria lived in the mother country. Both men had agreed it was far more worthwhile than painting the dull and overweight wives and children of the more 'solid' citizens, as did so many artists of the time.

From the bustling port of Bristol, Henry Gordon had written to tell Fergus he had discovered a slum where he could put his ideas into practice. From Lewin's Mead he would produce a true and enduring record of the life and times. Not for the first time, he had suggested Fergus should leave the Navy and use his own considerable talents to help in Henry Gordon's self-appointed task.

The suggestion had raised a smile at the time. The letter had arrived while Fergus was serving on board a British man-of-war in the Mediterranean, with a promising naval career ahead of him. Taught by his mother to read and write, Fergus spent his off-duty hours studying in the narrow confines between decks. He was already an 'upper yard man', one of the lower-deck élite, and he had a thirst for learning.

Then Fergus's career was brought to an abrupt end. Boarding a suspected Arab slave-ship in rough seas off the North African coast, he slipped, and his ankle was crushed between the two vessels. At first the ship's surgeon feared he would need to amputate the foot, but fortunately decided Fergus should be taken instead to hospital in Gibraltar.

Hospital surgeons were able to save Fergus's foot, but he would have a serious limp for the remainder of his life. His sea-going days were over.

Convalescing, Fergus transferred the energy he had given his studies to his sketching. He wrote to tell Henry Gordon he would come to Bristol as soon as he received his discharge.

Fergus had limped down the gangplank of a small naval frigate in Bristol's docks only an hour before, with money and a discharge certificate in his pocket, and his sketchpad beneath his arm – only to learn he was ten days too late. Fergus felt like crying his anguish out loud. Henry Gordon was dead – but his dream could live or die with Fergus.

Reaching out, Fergus picked up his late friend's sketchpad again. It fell open at a sketch of Becky.

Fergus wondered whether she and the other residents of Lewin's Mead would accept him if he moved in and painted them as they went about their daily lives. He remembered something Henry Gordon had once told him.

'A good artist is accepted *wherever* he chooses to work, but in a slum an artist must observe the rules of the people who live there. *Their* code. Break it and he might as well pack up his things and leave. . . .'

CHAPTER TWO

FERGUS WAS AWAKENED by sunlight streaming in through the windows of the attic. Easing himself from the uncomfortable bed, he pulled on some clothes and made his way across the room to a window. A number of sparrows were chirruping happily on the roof outside, and Fergus watched them for a while as he planned the day that stretched ahead of him. He would start by checking how much work Henry Gordon had done. He picked up one of the sketchpads and looked through it yet again, marvelling at the enthusiasm which escaped from Henry Gordon's pages.

Fergus was still examining the pad when the door opened and Becky walked in. She asked no permission. Did not even greet him. Crossing to where he squatted on the uneven floor, she stood at his shoulder and looked down at the pad in his hand.

'I'm in there.'

'I know.'

He allowed the pages to fall back slowly, stopping when he came to a sketch which showed Becky peering in at a bakery window. Looking up at her, he said: 'It doesn't look as though you've washed since this was sketched.'

Becky ignored his comment. 'Can you draw as good as Jock?'

'He taught me.'

'Let's see *you* draw me, then.'

'Go and stand over there by the window.'

As Fergus picked up his own pad and a pencil, Becky

walked to the nearest window. She struck a stiff self-conscious pose – and then suddenly her attention was captured by three baby sparrows. Perched on the guttering of a nearby roof, they were noisily demanding food from their attentive but overworked parents.

'Look! Come and look at this.'

Fergus moved to the window and pretended to take an interest in the birds. His pencil moved swiftly over the paper as he worked to capture Becky's expression. He sketched the face of an innocent young girl, far removed from the product of the slums who had offered to prostitute her body to him for a guinea.

Enthralled, Becky watched the sparrows for many minutes, until a flock of pigeons arrived to take over the gutter in rapidly increasing numbers, their strutting and cooing eventually causing the protesting young sparrows to take to the air in nervous unpractised flight.

When Becky returned her attention to Fergus the moment of uncomplicated innocence had passed – but he had captured it on his sketchpad. Fergus continued sketching for some minutes more, perfecting the shape of an ear, shading in Becky's high cheekbones, and correcting the angle of her jaw. But the *essence* of the portrait had been transferred to paper in those first few moments.

Fergus put down his pencil, and Becky looked at him questioningly.

'It's done. It's a sketch, not a full-size portrait.'

Doubtfully, Becky left the window and took the sketch from his hands. She looked at it intently for a long while.

'Is that me? *Really* me?'

'*I* think it is.'

Becky looked back at the sketch. When she spoke again there was a strangeness in her voice.

'Jock never painted me that way.'

'Perhaps he never saw that particular expression on your face.'

She looked up at him again, and there was something in her eyes that made him want to paint her again. Then she shook her head. 'It's more than that. You've drawn the me that's *inside*. Not the me that other people see.'

'It's what an artist *should* do.'

'I'm not sure I like it.'

Handing back the sketchpad, Becky walked to the door. Pausing with her hand on the latch, she looked back at Fergus. 'But you're a good artist. *Better* than Jock.'

Then she was gone, the door swinging shut behind her.

Fergus spent the remainder of the day tidying the attic room and examining more closely the paintings and sketches produced by Henry Gordon during the last months of his life.

There was a small grate in the room, and Fergus found kindling and coal at the bottom of a nearby cupboard. He lit a fire and at noon stopped to make himself a brew of weak, sweet, but milkless tea, using ingredients he had brought with him in his bag. Afterwards he removed his own drawings and materials from his bags and laid them out on the table.

By the time evening began darkening the room Fergus was feeling hungry. He needed to eat. He would also have to earn some money. He had cash in his pocket, but it would not last for ever. Paying for the room and for Henry Gordon's effects had made a hole in the money the Navy had paid to him.

Arming himself with pencils and a pad, Fergus made his way down the rickety stairs. They seemed steeper and even more dangerous today. On the first-floor landing he stood aside to allow Irish Molly to pass. Behind the Irish prostitute a middle-aged sailor laboured up the stairs, his face dark-tanned. The Irish girl gave Fergus a cheerful wink, and he knew she would soon have the money to satisfy her debt to Ida Stokes.

It was almost dark outside, and Fergus did not see Becky standing in the deep shadows beside the doorway until she spoke.

'Where you off to, Fergus? Had enough of your new ken already?' She used a slang word to describe Ida Stokes's disreputable house.

'I've a living to earn. I'm off to the quayside. If I'm lucky, I'll find a few homecoming sailors willing to pay for a sketch to take home with them.'

'I'll take you to the Hatchet inn,' Becky said eagerly. 'Jock went there sometimes. He made good money, too . . . but he drank it all.'

Fergus shook off the thoughts her words conjured up of his friend's lonely death.

'Lead on, Becky. If I do well, I'll pay for your supper tonight.'

Fergus fell in beside his ragged companion and they walked in silence for a while. Becky seemed to be deep in thought and suddenly she said: 'You don't need to pay me for doing things for you. You're living here now. You're one of us.'

Thinking of those residents of Ida Stokes's house he had seen so far, Fergus was by no means certain he wanted to be 'one of them', but he kept such thoughts to himself.

'That's very generous of you, Becky. But, then, you don't need pennies from me when you can command *guineas* from fine gentlemen.'

Becky looked at Fergus quickly and caught the tail-end of his smile. 'I *could* get a guinea. More, if I wanted. There's one girl I know who's taken to the houses of posh gents and earns *three* guineas a time.'

'But not you?'

'No.'

The admission was given after only the slightest hesitation.

'What would you have done had I taken you up on your offer?'

They had left Back Lane behind. The houses they passed were still part of the slums, but some showed lighted oil-lamps in their windows, casting a yellow light on the cobbled footway. As they passed through one of these pools of pale light Fergus glanced at his companion. Her clothes were more ragged than he remembered from their morning meeting, and he was quite certain no water had touched her face since then.

Becky intercepted his glance and, as though reading his thoughts, she pushed a strand of hair back from her forehead.

'If you'd said you wanted me, I'd have asked to see your money, of course. Then I'd have snatched it and scarpered quick.'

Fergus did not doubt her. Becky had already impressed him as being a straightforward child, even in her dishonesty.

Suddenly the lighted windows were behind them and they were passing through a narrow arched alleyway. When they came out on the other side Becky led him across a steep and narrow street before plunging into yet another maze of dark alleyways.

When they emerged the next time they were in a busier thoroughfare, indifferently lit by an insufficient number of gas-lamps.

Fergus stopped and looked about him. The cries of street vendors vied with the rattle of carriage wheels on the cobble-stone road surface, and here and there a few bold pedestrians took their lives in their hands as they ventured across the busy street.

Suddenly Becky put her hand on Fergus's arm and pointed to a figure standing a little way back from the nearest gas-lamp, his face barely discernible.

'Who's that?'

'It looks like a constable. . . .'

Before Fergus could say more Becky had gone, darting back into the maze of alleyways from whence they had just come.

The man who had caused Becky to take to her heels crossed the circle of gas-lit footpath and approached Fergus. Exceptionally tall and powerfully built, he wore the high black hat and blue frock-coat of a police constable.

'Good evening to you, sir. I think we're in for a surprisingly cold night.'

'I hope you're wrong, Constable. I've come out without my coat.'

'Few folk hereabouts own a coat. But they don't have far to go before they're home. You'll be a stranger here?'

'I arrived yesterday – on discharge from the Royal Navy.'

'Ah! Then, you won't have had time to learn about the places where it's wiser for an honest man not to walk alone. The Lewin's Mead rookery is one of them.'

' "Rookery"? I'm sorry, Constable . . . I don't understand.'

'The area from where you've just come, sir. Thieves,

vagabonds and cut-throats all have their nests there. It's as bad a slum as you'll find in any city – and I should know. Before coming here I was a constable in Whitechapel, in London. A nasty incident occurred in the rookery only yesterday evening. A young woman was viciously assaulted and had her head broken. She'll be lucky to live.... But didn't I see a young companion with you a minute ago? She darted back to the rookery a bit quick when she clapped eyes on me.'

'It was just a young ragamuffin,' Fergus lied. 'She was guiding me to the Hatchet inn. Yes, she did go rather quickly.'

'Then, you'd best check you've still got your purse, sir. There are some clever young dips in the city, and young girls is the worst of 'em.'

'My purse is hidden away safely at home, Constable. I've no more than two pence in my pocket. It's hardly worth the attentions of a pickpocket.'

'Indeed, sir.... But you said you was going to the Hatchet inn. I'm acquainted with the landlord. Charlie Waller's not a man to serve ale to young gentlemen unless they've money to pay for it.'

Fergus smiled ruefully. He was being subjected to a polite but insistent inquisition by this constable.

'I'm hoping to *earn* money at the inn, not spend it. I'm an artist. I want to sketch a few of the Hatchet inn's customers.'

'Ah!' The constable released a satisfied sigh, leaving Fergus with the distinct impression he had just passed some form of test. 'Well, seeing as how I've frightened off your guide, the least I can do is show you the way to the Hatchet inn.'

Limping along beside the other man, Fergus felt very small. The police constable was a big man and, with his top-hat, he towered almost two feet above Fergus. The constable was also talkative.

'There was another artist painting in these parts recently. As I recall, he was a Scotsman, like yourself.'

Fergus explained about Henry Gordon and of his own reason for coming to Bristol.

Clicking his tongue sympathetically, the constable

declared: 'It's always sad to lose a friend, especially one who's been kind to you in the past. But did you say you'd taken his room? That would be in Ida Stokes's house, along with Irish Molly and some of her friends?'

Remembering his first meeting with Ida Stokes, and her conversation with Irish Molly, Fergus believed the big constable was questioning him again, albeit rather cleverly.

'Mrs Stokes is my landlady. I don't know who else stays in the house. Mrs Stokes seems to have a great many lodgers.'

It was the second lie Fergus had told to the constable, without quite knowing why. He owed no loyalty to anyone living in the house in Back Lane.

The constable did not pursue his line of questioning. Instead, he said: 'There are houses in the rookery more crowded than Ida Stokes's. The whole place is like a stew, bubbling away in a great cauldron. Every so often I and my colleagues need to skim some of the scum off the top to stop the whole thing going bad, if you understand me. But I don't think I caught your name, sir.'

'Vincent. Fergus Vincent.'

'I'm Constable Ivor Primrose. If you ever need help, or have anything you think I might like to hear about, call on me at the police station opposite the Bridewell. Here we are at the Hatchet inn, now. Charlie Waller is the landlord; tell him I've sent you – but whatever you do don't offend him. Charlie was once a prizefighter, and his temper's a bit uncertain at the best of times.'

Fergus arrived at a rapid decision. Constable Primrose could prove to be a great friend in the future. In the light from one of the inn windows Fergus made a rapid sketch. Holding it closer to the light, he added a couple more details, then tore out the page and handed it to the constable.

'You mentioned a girl who was badly beaten yesterday. I witnessed the incident. I'm reluctant to give evidence while I'm living in the "rookery", as you call it, but this is a fair likeness of the man who did it.'

Constable Primrose held the sketch up to the light. 'Joe Skewes! I thought as much. He's never far away when there's violence in the rookery.'

Folding the paper carefully, Constable Ivor Primrose unfastened two of the buttons on his coat and carefully placed the sketch inside. When his jacket was buttoned again, he said: 'You can leave this with me, Mr Vincent, but I won't forget your help.'

Touching a finger to the brim of his tall black hat, the policeman turned and walked slowly away.

It was still early in the evening, but the main tap-room of the Hatchet inn was crowded. There were many sailors here, and a number of women – women like those Fergus had seen talking together on the first-floor landing of Ida Stokes's house in Back Lane. One of them accosted Fergus as soon as he stepped inside the tap-room door.

'Hello, my lover. You a sailor? Looking for a good time ashore? I'm just the girl for you. What's your name, then?'

Fergus shook his head. 'I'm not a sailor any more, and I'm not looking for a girl. I just want to find a quiet corner, near a lamp.'

As the girl walked away across the smoke-hung room she passed a broad-shouldered bald-headed man. He had just deposited a number of overflowing pewter mugs on a table occupied by four sailors and two untidy women. The man jerked his head in Fergus's direction and spoke to the girl. She shrugged and gave a brief reply.

Wiping the palms of his hands on the short leather apron tied about his waist the bald-headed man frowned and made his way across the room to where Fergus stood.

'Can I help you, sir? Fetch you a drink?'

'Are you Mr Waller?'

The man's frown deepened. 'I'm Charlie Waller. Who's asking?'

'Fergus Vincent. I'm an artist. I'd like to sketch your customers . . . sailors.'

'So long as you're buying my ale you can do what you like – if it doesn't annoy my other customers. Now, what can I get you to drink?'

'I'll have a porter . . . but I won't be drinking much. I'll be sketching – and selling to your customers, I hope.'

'So that's your game! I thought it might be something like that. Well, you're not welcome in my inn. One of your sort was in here a while ago. I let him stay at first because he spent good money. Trouble was, when he'd had too much he'd start making sketches that my other customers objected to. I put up with him for a while – like I said, he spent money – but he had to go in the end. If you've no intention of spending, you'd best leave now. It'll save us both trouble. Out you go.'

Backing towards the door with the burly landlord in close attendance, Fergus managed to say: 'I'm a *good* artist. I might prove an attraction. . . .'

Charlie Waller seemed unimpressed, and Fergus continued to retreat. He was convinced that, should he come to a halt, the landlord would throw him out. Then, as his feet found the step that led to the street, Fergus spoke in desperation: 'Constable Primrose said I should tell you I'm here on his recommendation. . . .'

The menacing advance of Charlie Waller slowed, then stopped altogether. 'Ivor Primrose sent you?'

'That's right.' Fergus moved aside to allow three noisy sailors to stumble in through the door at his back. 'I left him outside your door only a few minutes since.'

'Why didn't you say so in the first place, instead of wasting my time? I'm always happy to do a favour for Ivor Primrose. Have you seen him fight?'

Fergus shook his head.

'Likely you will if you come here often enough – especially when there are Yankee sailors around. It's sometimes necessary to crack a few heads at such times – and there's no one does that better than Ivor Primrose. He'd have made a dandy prizefighter had he taken to "the fancy". Personally I can see no sense in putting on a constable's uniform and becoming a target for anyone with a mind to punch a Peeler. But Ivor seems to enjoy it. He's honest, too, and that's more than I can say for some other constables we've had about here. A quart of ale and some meat pie in the back room when they come on duty, then they disappear before trouble starts, in case they're asked to do anything about it. Here. . . .'

The landlord jerked a thumb at a painted-faced woman who was seated at a small table beneath an oil-lamp which hung from a dark-wood beam. She rose without a word, and Charlie Waller motioned for Fergus to take her place.

'This is the best-lit seat in the place. It's not much, but you'll find there's enough light to work by. How much do you charge for a sketch?'

'A shilling. Less if I find someone with a particularly interesting face and he'll let me make a sketch for my own collection.'

'I'll expect a penny ha'penny from each shilling, for the house. You can begin by sketching me, so I can see how good you are.'

Charlie Waller had features to delight any artist, but Fergus took care not to reproduce too many of the symptoms of advancing age he saw there. The landlord was elated with the resulting sketch, and the exercise aroused much interest among the customers. Soon there was a pint of porter on the table before Fergus and he was working on his first paid commission of the evening.

Fergus returned to Back Lane that night with his evening's work. He had sold eleven sketches and there were more in his sketchpad. Two would one day be transferred to canvas. It was a good beginning to his work in Bristol and boded well for the future.

A noisy quarrel was going on in one of the first-floor rooms of Ida Stokes's house; but the door was closed, and Fergus passed by to climb the complaining stairs that led to his own room.

Moonlight shone through the attic windows, and Fergus had no difficulty in finding a candle and putting a light to it. He was placing it on the table when he caught a movement in the shadows at the far end of the long narrow room.

'Who's that? Who's there?' He held up the candle and peered into the gloom.

'It's me. . . .'

A small figure sat up from the floor. It was Becky.

The candlelight fell on her face. There was a bloody graze at the corner of her left eye, and the skin about it was beginning to discolour. There was a bruise lower down on her face, too, and the ragged dress had been ripped from one shoulder.

Crouching beside here, Fergus asked: 'What's happened to you, Becky? Who did this?'

'Joe Skewes.' Becky mumbled the name, and Fergus saw there was blood on her lip, too. Becky had taken a beating. 'He came to the house. Told me to keep my mouth shut about the fight he had with his woman.'

'*Told* you? Joe Skewes has a strange way with words. Come over here.'

Leading Becky to the table, Fergus soaked the corner of a thin threadbare towel with water from a chipped jug and dabbed it on her dirty injured face. She tried to pull away from him, but he made her stand still and persisted in his efforts.

'I know you're a stranger to water, but your face needs cleaning.' There was a deep scratch on Becky's cheekbone, as though Joe Skewes had been wearing a rough-surfaced ring on one of his fingers.

Becky winced when the area about her bruised eye was touched, and Fergus felt sudden anger well up inside him. 'Joe Skewes ought to be put away. The man's worse than an animal. First his own woman, and now you.'

To his surprise, Becky shook her head. 'She deserved a drubbing. She spends time in beer-houses with sailors while Joe's at work. She must have known what he'd do when he found out.'

Gently, Fergus began to dry her face. 'That doesn't excuse what he's done to you.'

'It's said his woman will die. If she does, and Joe Skewes is taken, he'll be topped, sure enough. He's protecting himself.'

'I doubt whether the hanging of Joe Skewes would stop the world,' retorted Fergus. 'I'm surprised he hasn't tried to find *me*.'

Becky's sudden silence expressed more than words. Pausing in his task, Fergus said: 'He *was* looking for me, wasn't he? Did you take a beating for not telling him where *I* was?'

'He was more interested in knowing *who* you were,' replied Becky. 'I told him you were some gent from Clifton way who'd come to Lewin's Mead looking for a woman. I said I was taking you to Irish Molly, but that you'd run off after the fight.'

'Did he believe you?'

'He didn't ask me again. Just hit me around a bit, then left.'

'If he went away again, what are you doing up here now?'

'He'll be drinking again tonight, and I *know* Joe Skewes. When he's got enough ale in his belly he'll be looking around for someone to beat. Folks keep clear of him then. His woman isn't at home, so he might come looking for me again. Can I stay here tonight?'

'Stay as long as you like. If it hadn't been for me, you wouldn't be in this mess now. Have you eaten? I've brought back some ale and half a pie from the Hatchet inn. The landlord gave it to me for sketching his wife.'

'I haven't eaten all day.'

Fergus looked at her disapprovingly. 'What have you done with the four pence I gave you?'

'I had to give it to Mary O'Ryan. She lives in the room downstairs. I owed it to her. She guessed you'd given me a few coppers to bring you here. She said if I didn't give it to her she'd get her latest man to strip me to the skin and look for it. He'd have done it, too. He's tried before now – and he wasn't looking for money then.'

Fergus shook his head despairingly. 'God! What sort of place is this I've come to?'

'It's Lewin's Mead, Fergus. I don't suppose it's any different from anywhere else. Not that I know. I haven't ever *been* anywhere else.'

CHAPTER THREE

WHEN FERGUS WOKE and heard breathing in the room it startled him. Then he remembered that Becky was sharing his attic.

She had been wise not to spend the night in the overcrowded room rented by Mary O'Ryan. Joe Skewes *had* returned to the house in the middle of the night. Fergus and Becky had listened in apprehensive silence as the bullying coal-heaver lurched from room to room, shouting for Becky to show herself. Once it seemed he might climb the stairs to the attic, but the steep stairway defeated him and he made a noisy descent, much to the relief of the two listeners.

This morning Becky slept as though she did not have a care in the world. She lay spread-eagled inside a folded blanket, much of the top half thrown back to reveal her thin arms and upper body. Her head was lying to one side, hiding the bruising around her eye. Fergus stood looking down at her for a few minutes before reaching for his sketchpad.

He was on his sixth sketch before Becky stirred. Opening her good eye, she saw him standing over her and she showed a brief moment of fear before realising what he was doing. Then she smiled and made a move to rise, but Fergus said hurriedly: 'Not just yet. Don't move for a few minutes.'

'Why . . .?'

'Don't ask damn silly questions. Just stay still while I finish this. . . . No! put your arm back where it was.'

Becky pouted, but did as she was told.

Frowning in concentration, Fergus worked for another ten

26

minutes while from her makeshift bed Becky studied him with great interest.

When he was satisfied, Fergus relaxed and placed his pencil and pad on the room's small and unsteady table. Smiling at Becky, he said: 'That's enough to be getting on with. I'll not be paying you a model's fee, but I promise that you'll have the first canvas I paint of you. For now, you'll have to make do with a cup of tea. Start the fire while I fetch some water from the yard.'

The pump was in a dark yard hemmed in on all sides by tall buildings. It was shared by at least fifty families, and Fergus joined on the end of a line of bucket-carrying men, women and children, all shuffling towards the pump. There was little conversation. Most of those in the line appeared to be suffering from the excesses of the previous evening. Fergus wondered how they earned the money they spent on drink.

By the time Fergus returned to the attic room Becky had a cheerful fire crackling in the grate and a soot-blackened kettle was already rattling noisily on the coals. When Fergus asked Becky where she had obtained the water, she grinned.

'From the O'Ryans', downstairs. They were cleaning up after Joe Skewes's visit. He fair took the room apart. Fifteen of 'em was in there when he arrived, four of 'em men. Joe had every one out in the street for an hour – except for the one he put to the wide in the hall.'

The smile suddenly left Becky's face. 'It's a good thing I wasn't there, though. Mary O'Ryan said he'd have killed me for sure.'

'Is he likely to come looking for you again?'

Becky shrugged. 'No one knows what Joe Skewes is likely to do next. He ain't like other men. He's got a son who lives in Lewin's Mead, too. The pair of 'em have terrified the place for years.'

'I think you'd better stay up here with me for a while.'

Becky's face lit up with pleasure. 'Can I . . .?' She hesitated and the smile left her face. 'You know what the others will think?'

'They can think what they like. As long as I'm paying the rent for this room I'll do as I wish here. Can you cook?'

Becky shook her head. 'I've never learned.'

'Then, it's about time you did.' Fergus flicked a bright silver florin through the air towards her, and Becky caught it instinctively. 'Go out and buy some things. Eggs, bacon, bread – tea and sugar, too.'

Becky tested the coin between her teeth before replying: 'You must have had a good evening's work at the Hatchet. But there's no need to spend your money. I can pinch what you want. It might take me an hour or two —'

'I'll not have you stealing for me. You'll *buy* what we need. It'll be a unique experience for you.'

The proprietor of the first shop Becky entered chased her out through the door without giving her time to prove she had money. It would have been a similar story in the second shop, too, had Becky not opened her hand quickly and showed the proprietor the silver coin clutched in her palm.

Only partly satisfied, the suspicious grocer grumbled that he'd had girls like Becky in his shop before. If he hadn't turned them out promptly, he would swear they'd have stripped his shop of goods in no more than ten minutes. Indignantly, Becky informed the grocer that just because *she* had ragged clothes it did not mean she was dishonest.

Unimpressed by her indignation, the grocer kept Becky under close scrutiny while he weighed and wrapped her purchases. Even so, she managed to slip a two-ounce packet of tea into the pocket of her ragged dress without the grocer seeing.

Her shopping completed, Becky handed over the two-shilling piece with a degree of pride. She had never spent so much money at one time before. The grocer was not an unkindly man and he was aware that this was an unusual occasion for her. The purchases totalled one shilling and tenpence halfpenny. Before handing her the penny halfpenny change the grocer took down a sweet-jar from a shelf behind his wooden counter. From inside he lifted out a large, striped, pumpkin-shaped sweet. Handing it to her, he said seriously: 'Here you are, miss. I always like to give something a little extra to my best customers.'

If Becky felt any pangs of conscience in respect of the two ounces of stolen tea in her pocket, she did not allow it to spoil this moment.

'I expect you'll remember me next time I come shopping here,' she said, with all the ragged dignity she could muster. The shopkeeper held open the door, and she swept from the shop without a backward glance, clutching the groceries tightly to her.

Becky's feeling of self-importance lasted until she turned the last corner leading to Lewin's Mead. Not thirty yards ahead of her she saw two men talking. One looked uncomfortably like Joe Skewes. Becky never waited to confirm the rapid identification. Clutching the groceries even more tightly, she turned and ran.

Becky's intention was to enter the Lewin's Mead rookery by another alleyway, farther along the street, but her luck ran out when she was halfway there. Passing a doorway, she cannoned into a burly, black-hatted, blue-coated figure. The next moment her thin arm was taken in a strong and painful grip.

'Not so fast, young lady. Who are you a-running from?'

'No one. I . . . I'm in a hurry to get home.'

'I don't doubt it. Anxious to get this little lot tucked out of sight, I'm sure.'

The constable lifted a packet of sugar from the pile of groceries. Weighing it in the palm of his hand, he asked: 'Where did you steal this lot from?'

'It isn't pinched. I bought it.' Her cry was half indignation, half pain as the constable tightened his grip on her arm.

'Oh, yes?' There was heavy sarcasm in the constable's voice. 'No doubt you pawned the family silver to get the money. You'd better tell me which shop it's come from, my girl.'

Becky was about to tell him when she remembered the two-ounce packet of tea hidden inside her pocket. 'I don't remember.'

'Now, there's a surprise,' said the constable with heavy sarcasm. 'All right, young lady, you come along to the police office with me. Perhaps your memory will return along the way.'

'No!' Becky screamed the word, at the same time kicking out at the constable. Had she been wearing shoes, her struggles might have been effective. As it was, the constable tightened his grip on her arm until she cried out in pain.

'Struggle as much as you like, you're coming along with me, young lady. . . .'

A loaf of bread fell to the ground, and as the constable stooped to retrieve it Becky's thin bony knee came up and struck him on the nose.

'You little trollop! I'll see to it you're charged with assault as well as with thieving.' Tucking the loaf beneath his arm, the constable pulled out a handkerchief and held it to his nose. It came away stained with blood, and the constable hooted in anger. 'You'll regret this, you mark my words. No one makes my nose bleed – especially some ragged urchin who ought to be thrown in gaol and forgotten.'

His words only made Becky struggle all the more, but the constable retained his tight grip on her arm and Becky was handicapped by the groceries, which she was determined not to lose.

By the time they passed through the doorway to the Bridewell police station Becky was sobbing with anger and frustration, but she was more upset by the thought that she had failed Fergus than by the predicament she was in.

Fergus had found a new canvas among Henry Gordon's possessions. Setting it up on the easel, he began a painting of Becky, based on the sketches he had already made of her. While he was working, time had no meaning for him. Not until his stomach began to complain of hunger did Fergus put down his brush and wonder for the first time what was keeping Becky.

Squinting out of the window. Fergus looked up at the sky. It was overcast, but as far as he could tell it must have been early afternoon. Becky should have returned long ago.

He frowned as he wiped paint from his hands with a cloth kept by his late friend for the purpose. Becky must have found something to do that was more interesting than shopping. She was a young girl, and time would mean little to her.

She was probably using her visit to the grocer as an opportunity to see what the other shops had on display. He would go to the Hatchet inn and have something to eat while he worked.

Before leaving the attic Fergus moved the partially completed portrait closer to the window and gave it a critical appraisal. It was going to be good. *Very* good. Probably the best painting he had ever produced. Becky's sleeping pose was entirely innocent and natural. The thought made him smile ruefully. Here he was, living in the heart of one of the most notorious slums in the country, earning a precarious living sketching sailors and their women – and he had found innocence! Taking a last look about him, Fergus closed the door of the attic and set off for work.

The smoke-filled interior of the Hatchet inn quickly brought Fergus down to earth. Three large ships from the West Indies had entered the Bristol docks that day. The inn was crowded with sailors, all of whom had money burning holes in their pockets. Charlie Waller, perspiring heavily, suggested Fergus should forget his sketching and return when business was not quite so hectic. Just then one of the prostitutes saw Fergus and called for him to come to the table where she sat and 'do a likeness'. Shrugging his shoulders in resignation, Charlie Waller hurried off to fetch another order for the noisy and thirsty sailors.

Fergus had sketched the prostitute the previous day, but now she was with a new 'friend' and insisting that he pay for another.

It was the beginning of a busy but lucrative few hours for Fergus. When he eventually left the inn and gratefully gulped in comparatively pure, cold air there were twenty-seven shillings jingling in his pocket and he had drunk more than he was used to.

Entering Ida Stokes's house, Fergus found Irish Molly arguing with a man in the ground-floor hallway. The Irish prostitute was insisting that her prospective client pay for his pleasures in advance. The man was reluctant, but he grudgingly agreed to part with the Irish girl's fee as Fergus pushed past the couple and began to climb the stairs.

He had almost reached the first-floor landing when Irish Molly called after him.

'Have you heard about the po-lice arresting Joe Skewes?' She pronounced 'police' as though it were two words.

Fergus replied that he had not heard the news, but he was relieved for Becky's sake and he promised to tell her.

'I'm thinking she'll know all about it already. She was seen this morning being taken off by a constable.'

'This morning . . .?' Fergus had been so busy at the Hatchet inn it had slipped his mind that Becky had not returned with the shopping she had gone out to buy. He hurried upstairs much speedier than was prudent. His crippled ankle failed him on the uneven attic stairs, and he received a skinned shin for his foolhardiness.

'Becky?' He called her name in the darkness of the attic room, but there was no reply. When he found and lit a candle its pale yellow light showed him that the room was exactly as he had left it that afternoon.

Fergus sat down for a few moments to gather his thoughts. Irish Molly's news might mean nothing at all. Becky could be anywhere. Perhaps she had lost the money he had given to her – or even had it stolen. She might have spent the money and was afraid to return to Ida Stokes's house and tell him. If so, she could be sleeping anywhere. He knew she did not always spend her nights in the crowded house.

All these possible explanations for Becky's absence went through Fergus's mind as he sat in the attic room. Finally he admitted to himself that he believed none of them. The answer to Becky's whereabouts lay in the news Irish Molly had so casually imparted to him.

It was some minutes before Irish Molly responded to the insistent banging on her door. When she did appear she stood in the doorway, having dressed hurriedly, her lank untidy hair hanging about her shoulders. She carried a lighted candle in one hand and there was fear on her face before she recognised Fergus.

'What the hell d'you think you're doing hammering on my door like that at this time of night? Are you wanting to wake the whole house?'

'You said someone saw Becky with a constable this morning. What exactly did they see?'

'You got me out of bed to ask about that little urchin? Look, here Whatever-your-name-is, I've got a man in my bed and a living to earn. If you're feeling lonely upstairs by yourself, try Iris in the next room. She's only had a short-timer tonight. She'll be free by now....'

'Who's that out there? Get rid of him! I've paid you good money....' The grumbling voice of the seaman Fergus had seen arguing with Irish Molly came from inside the room.

As Irish Molly began to close the door Fergus said hurriedly: 'I believe Becky's been arrested. She might be sharing a prison cell with Joe Skewes right now. Where would the police take her?'

'Becky arrested ...?' Irish Molly opened the door wide again, at the same time turning back to shout at her unhappy client: 'Will you shut your gob for a minute! You'll get your money's worth when I'm good and ready!'

Returning her attention to Fergus, Irish Molly asked: 'Why would the po-lice want to arrest Becky?'

'I don't know, but I'm certain that's what's happened. I sent her out to buy groceries for me this morning and I haven't seen her since. Where would a constable take her?'

'To the police station opposite Bridewell prison. Oh, the poor girl. It's a terrible place. Haven't I been there myself – and more than once? A child like her shouldn't be put inside such a place as that – especially if Joe Skewes is there, too.'

'How do I find the Bridewell?' Irish Molly's words had alarmed Fergus.

'It's hardly more than a few hundred yards from here, but in the darkness –'

'Will you take me?'

'I'm sorry.... I'm too well known to go poking my head inside a police station, and there's a little misunderstanding about a sailor that's not cleared up yet. But I'll tell you how to get there....'

By the time Irish Molly had given Fergus directions to the Bridewell the sailor in her bed was grumbling once more.

'I must go now. Do what you can for Becky. She's a good

girl really. . . . Oh, for goodness' sake stop your bleating, man. I'm coming back to bed now — and you'd better have something to be making such a fuss about. . . .'

The door closed, and Fergus was left standing alone on the draughty landing.

CHAPTER FOUR

FERGUS FOUND HIS WAY to the Bridewell police station, but not before he had run the gauntlet of pimps, prostitutes and would-be pickpockets who lurked around the fringe of Lewin's Mead's alleyways even at this hour of the night. At the police station he needed to convince the watchman who sat outside that he had a good reason for entering the building.

There was a sergeant on duty in the police office, and behind him the police gaoler sat making a laborious entry in a huge cloth-bound ledger. Fergus quickly established that Becky *was* being held in the cells, but he was less successful in ascertaining what crime she was supposed to have committed.

'We're keeping her in custody pending certain enquiries,' declared the sergeant enigmatically. 'May I ask the reason for your interest? Are you a relative of this girl? If you are, perhaps you'll be kind enough to supply us with her surname. All she'll tell us is that her name is "Becky". Short for "Rebecca", no doubt.'

'Probably, but "Becky" is the only name she's ever known, and I doubt if there's anyone left alive who knows any more about her. As for the rest – I'm a friend, I sent her out to buy groceries for me this morning and I haven't seen her since.'

Just for a moment Fergus thought the sergeant looked disconcerted, but the policeman recovered quickly. Crossing the room, he returned carrying the huge ledger. Turning back a couple of pages, he studied one of the entries. Eventually he looked up at Fergus and said: 'The young lady *did* have certain victuals in her possession when she was arrested, but she refused to tell us the name of the shop where she obtained them.'

'*Wouldn't* tell you – or *couldn't*?' queried Fergus. 'She doesn't read.'

'That will all be looked into, sir, don't you worry. But she couldn't give us an acceptable address, so we had to keep her in the cells. There's also the matter of her assaulting Constable Fitzpatrick, of course.'

'Assaulting a constable?' Fergus was incredulous. 'She's a *child*. A mere scrap of a girl. The very idea is laughable!'

'I doubt if a magistrate would share your view, sir. But since you're here perhaps you'll be kind enough to give me *your* name and address. It seems you might be a material witness in this matter.'

When Fergus gave the address of Ida Stokes's house in Back Lane, the police sergeant frowned. 'It's the address the young lady gave.'

'It's a lodging-house. A great many people live there. How do I set about having Becky released?'

'There's no question of her being released just yet, Mr Vincent. Unless she appears before a magistrate in the meantime, I suggest you call again in a couple of days. I might be able to allow you to the cells to see her then.'

'But she's done nothing! Why should she have to remain locked up?'

'If she's done nothing, you can rest assured she *will* be released, Mr Vincent. No one is held in custody without due cause. Now, I have a busy police office here. If your business is over . . .?'

'Is there a chance of seeing Becky tonight?'

'She'll see no one until it's been decided what will happen to her. Good night, Mr Vincent.'

The sergeant's impatience was beginning to show, but Fergus had one last question that needed an answer.

'I believe you arrested someone else from Lewin's Mead today – Joe Skewes? I hope he's not in the same cell as Becky. He's already given her one beating.'

The police sergeant gave a sigh. 'Mr Vincent, most of our prisoners are from the Lewin's Mead area and most have fought each other in the past, or will do so in the future. As it happens, tonight we have both Joe Skewes and his son Alfie in the cells. Alfie's in the cells with this girl and some others, but his father isn't. Joe Skewes is likely to face a murder charge if his victim dies. In view of the seriousness of the charges against him he's been placed in a cell on his own. If that's all, I must ask you once again to leave. *Now*, if you please.'

Outside the police station Fergus felt both angry and helpless. Becky was still incarcerated in the police cells, and no one seemed anxious to establish her innocence. Just then someone walked between Fergus and the gas-lamp attached to the wall of the police-station entrance. Glancing up, Fergus saw the figure of Ivor Primrose looming above him.

'Well, well, if it isn't the young artist. What are you doing here at this time of night? Are you sketching policemen instead of sailors now? Charlie Waller tells me you've been doing good business at the Hatchet. He also says you're a fine artist.'

'I came here to get a girl released from custody. She's been wrongly arrested.'

Ivor Primrose's eyebrows drew closer for only a moment. 'Why, bless you, sir, I doubt if anyone's ever been shut away in a cell without someone coming along and saying the very same thing. It's all part of the game, you might say. But liberty is a very precious thing and it's neither given nor taken away lightly, I can assure you. What has this young lady-friend of yours done?'

Fergus repeated what the sergeant had said to him, adding his own explanation.

'Well ... mistakes *can* be made, but if it has in this case you can rest assured it will be righted when she comes before a magistrate.'

'But she's only a child. She shouldn't be locked away with *criminals*.'

'I doubt that any more harm will come to her there than has already been done during a lifetime spent in the rookery.'

Constable Primrose hesitated and appeared to be trying to make up his mind about something. Eventually he said: 'I owe you a favour for the sketch you gave me, Fergus. I can't do anything about having this young girl released from custody – or even help you to see her – but there's someone I know who *can*, if she's a mind to. She's a Miss Tennant. Miss Fanny Tennant.'

'Where can I find her?'

'Nowhere at this time of night. But tomorrow morning she'll be at the ragged school, in St James Back.'

' "Ragged school"? What's that?' The expression was new to Fergus.

'It's exactly what it sounds to be. A school for children who are too shabbily dressed for them to be accepted elsewhere. It's early days to say whether or not it's working, but the youngsters from Lewin's Mead are better off there than wandering the streets getting into mischief.'

'Thank you. I'll call on Miss Tennant first thing in the morning.'

'You do that, Fergus. Meanwhile I'll make it my business to visit this little friend of yours in the cells. She'll come to no harm, don't you worry.'

For Becky, the hours that followed her arrest were a nightmare. Inside the station she complained bitterly and loudly about being arrested 'for nothing'. When the constable who had arrested her cuffed her ear and ordered her to be quiet, Becky promptly grabbed his hand and sank her teeth into the fleshy part of his thumb.

Howling with pain, the constable shook Becky off as though she were a tenacious terrier. He cuffed her again and might have gone further had not the station inspector put his head round the door of his office and demanded to know what was happening.

'It's an urchin from the rookery,' replied the constable. 'I've brought her in for stealing. She's just bitten me.'

'Put her in the cells,' ordered the inspector. 'She'll soon quieten down there. Don't take her yourself; I want to speak to you in my office.'

Becky was relieved at the departure of the constable who had arrested her, but the feeling was short-lived. The constable whose task it was to search her was coarse and foul-mouthed. When he found the two-ounce packet of tea and a penny halfpenny in the pocket of her ragged dress he forced her to strip and seemed to enjoy the sight of her standing naked before him.

When she was eventually allowed to slip her dress on once more the police gaoler led her down a narrow corridor to a heavy iron door which had a small steel-barred grille for a window. Peering inside first, the gaoler turned a large key in the lock, then swung the door open with some difficulty. Grasping Becky by the shoulders, he propelled her roughly through the doorway.

'Here you are, Alfie. I've brought you something to keep you warm. There's not much of her, so keep the others away or there'll be nothing left for you.'

With this the constable gave Becky a violent shove that sent her sprawling in the straw covering the cell floor, and the door clanged heavily shut behind her.

There was a sudden movement in the straw not far from where Becky had fallen. Suddenly a shadowy form rose from the ground, grotesque and malformed in the scant light that shone through the grille of the iron door. A woman's voice screeched in anger, and the figure launched itself at Becky.

It seemed nothing could save her from the clutches of the demented woman, but as Becky tried to scramble clear there was the sound of a chain snapping taut and the woman jerked backwards and fell heavily to the ground.

As Becky sat up, hardly more than an arm's length from the woman who now lay moaning at the end of a stout taut chain, she became aware of laughter in the cell about her. There must have been upwards of twenty prisoners, of both sexes, in the cell.

Suddenly someone was kneeling beside her, and she smelled stale alcohol. 'Now you've met Annie come on over here with me. I've got a jug of good porter and I'll share it with you if you're a good girl.'

A hand reached for her arm and began caressing her skin.

'You need friends in prison, young 'un, and none will serve you better than Alfie Skewes.'

As Becky flinched back in sudden fear, a woman's voice called from across the cell: 'Don't you take no notice of him, dearie. Alfie Skewes has never given nothing but trouble to anyone. Him *and* that father of his.'

The hand stopped stroking Becky's arm, and Alfie Skewes jabbed a finger in the direction of the unseen speaker.

'Keep that gin-trap mouth of yours shut, woman, or you'll part company with your tongue long before you can perjure yourself in a courtroom.'

Becky took advantage of the diversion to scramble clear of Alfie Skewes. Giving the moaning madwoman a wide berth, she made her way towards a group of women who sat with their backs against the far wall of the cell. As Becky reached the place a woman moved over to make room on the straw beside her.

'What you in here for, dearie?'

'Nothing. I've done *nothing*.' Becky spoke indignantly.

'Of course you haven't. None of us here has done anything.'

In the gloom someone tittered nervously, and the woman asked: 'What will *they* say you've done? When you're brought up before the magistrate?'

'Pinched some groceries – and I *didn't*. I bought 'em with money that was given to me by Fergus. He's an *artist*. He's drawn pictures of me.'

'You don't draw pictures of *ordinary* people. Who'd want to see pictures of the likes of *us*?' The question came from across the dark cell.

'He probably mistook 'er for the bleedin' queen.' The sarcastic comment ended in a coughing fit.

As the laughter subsided, another voice said: 'Can't be much of an artist if he can't tell who he's painting, I says.'

'He's a *good* artist,' declared Becky defensively. 'He draws sailors in the Hatchet, and they pay him for doing it.'

'*I* draw sailors in the Hatchet,' retorted the sarcastic voice of another woman. 'That's what I've been brought *here* for.'

Again there was laughter, and the woman who had first spoken to her put a hand on Becky's arm. 'Take no notice of her, dearie. She'll not be laughing when she stands up in court tomorrow. Her and her ponce robbed one sailor too many. She'll be for the boat this time. For life, I don't doubt.'

Soon after midday there were the sounds of activity in the corridor outside the cell, then the door was opened and a constable stood in the doorway, calling out names.

When 'Rose Cottle' was called the woman next to Becky struggled heavily to her feet. 'That's me, dearie. Brought here for buying a handkerchief from a poor starving child like yourself. How was I to know it was stolen?'

'Will you be sent to gaol?'

'Bless you, no, dearie. It'll be a fine at the most – but they'll have to prove me guilty first. Come and see me when you get out of here. You and me could do business together. I've got a dollyshop on the corner of St James Street. You might know it.'

Becky *did* know the dollyshop. Unauthorised pawnshops, where the poor and thieves parted with goods for no more than a fraction of their value, dollyshops were recognised outlets for stolen goods. Becky had seen a dress she admired inside the dollyshop owned by Rose Cottle and was in the habit of returning to the shop time after time, merely to look at it through the window.

Rose Cottle was talking again: 'Watch that Alfie Skewes, dearie. He does some little favours for me sometimes, but he and that father of his are both "bludgers" – footpads. They're not above poncing, cheating, or anything else that might pay a shilling or two. Alfie's no respecter of young girls, either. Keep clear of him and come and see me when you get out of here.'

The constable standing in the doorway called her name again, impatiently this time, and Rose Cottle waddled to the doorway, grumbling for the gaoler to 'show a bit of consideration for an old lady what's shaky on her pins'.

It proved to be a long day for Becky. She expected someone to take her to the police office and ask her questions about the groceries, but no one came for her. Whenever the door opened it was to call someone else or, on more than one occasion, to admit new prisoners.

By evening there were only five prisoners left in the cell — six, if the madwoman was included in the number.

Three of the prisoners were men: Alfie Skewes and two men who might have been sailors. The other prisoner was an old woman who had been found with a number of forged coins in her possession. She claimed to be as baffled as the police by their presence in her purse.

Late in the evening a pot of weak soup and a mound of bread was brought to the cell and placed just inside the door, together with a pile of pewter bowls and spoons.

The men and the old woman were the first to help themselves, each doing their best to elbow the others out of the way. Becky waited until the others had left the pot before serving herself. Then she saw the madwoman looking at her. The woman was not old; she could not have been more than twenty-three or twenty-four, but there was something in the crazed eyes that made Becky shudder. However, she could not see the chained woman starve. Filling a bowl with soup, Becky pushed it cautiously across the floor to the mad-woman.

'You're wasting your time, girl.' The observation came from Alfie Skewes, but Becky ignored him. Pushing the bowl closer to the chained woman, she suddenly jumped back in alarm as the madwoman screamed and sprang at her.

Becky avoided the outstretched arms, but the soup was a casualty. The bowl spun across the cell, its contents lost among the straw.

Alfie Skewes hooted in merriment. 'What did I tell you? You should have listened to me, girl. Here, this is how you feed a lunatic. . . .'

Picking up a chunk of the hard bread, Alfie Skewes hurled it with considerable force at the tethered woman. It hit her on the head and bounced off into the straw. The woman screamed and put up an arm to defend herself as another rock-hard crust came her way.

Alfie Skewes and his two companions continued the barrage until their missiles were exhausted. All the while the madwoman's screeches brought hilarious laughter from the three men, while the old woman cackled with laughter at the 'fun'.

The whole incident made Becky shudder. It reminded her of something that had happened when she could have been no more than six years of age. A gang of boys had cornered her in a muddy gully where the River Frome flowed into Bristol's harbour. Pelting her with mud and stones, they had shouted and taunted her, driving her before them into the water. Before a passer-by came to her aid she was waist-deep in mud and filth and quite hysterical.

The one-sided barrage over, the madwoman scratched about among the straw, seeking the bread. When she found a piece she sat crunching it and growling like a dog with a bone whenever one of the men pretended to dispute her possession.

The cruel tormenting continued for almost an hour until two more diversions occurred in quick succession. The first was the arrival of another prisoner. Loud-voiced, boastful and half-drunk, he informed his fellow-prisoners that he had been arrested for attempting to rob a sailor in the yard of a dockside alehouse and had 'changed the face' of the first constable who tried to arrest him. He claimed it had taken four constables to subdue him and bring him to the Bridewell police station.

The next diversion was the arrival of a great pewter jug filled with porter for Alfie Skewes. When the newcomer commented with envy on Alfie Skewes's good fortune he was invited to join Alfie in a drink and informed slyly that it was the price paid by friends for his silence.

Becky was also invited to drink with them, but she preferred her own company on the far side of the cell and sat dejectedly with her back against the cold stone wall. She had hoped Fergus would come looking for her when she did not return to his attic studio. There was no reason why he *should*, she told herself, but he must have wondered what had become of her. Gloomily she admitted he was probably the only one who could extricate her from the mess she was in.

Sunk deep in her thoughts, Becky was not aware that the old lady on a counterfeiting charge and Alfie Skewes were having a long whispered conversation, casting frequent glances in her direction. When the furtive whispering came to an end the old woman crossed the cell and crouched in front of Becky, holding out a tankard of porter towards her.

'Here, child. Have some. It'll cheer you up. Alfie sent it across specially for you. We all need to help each other in here. It's the only thing that makes life bearable. . . .'

'I want nothing from Alfie Skewes. Give it to *her*.' Becky jerked her head in the direction of the madwoman, who rocked back and forth in the straw in the centre of the cell, her knees drawn up to her chin. As she rocked, the woman made a noise that might have been either singing or weeping.

'You should be grateful that someone's taking an interest in you, girl. Many a time in here I'd have given my soul for an important friend like Alfie Skewes.'

'Important? Because someone brings him a jug of porter? Or is it because he throws stale bread at a madwoman? Alfie Skewes can keep his porter and his "importance". I've got a friend who'll come looking for me soon. When he finds me you'll learn that importance is more than a threepenny jug of porter.'

Her voice carried clearly to where the men squatted close to the doorway, drinking. Alfie Skewes scowled his displeasure then rose to his feet. Making his way to where Becky sat, he stood above her for almost a minute. When Becky refused to look up he kicked the sole of her outstretched foot none too gently. She drew the foot back.

'Why are you being so rude to me? What have you got to be so stuck up about, eh? You say you're sorry and be nice to me, you hear?'

When Becky did not reply Alfie Skewes reached out towards her. Taking a fistful of hair, he jerked her head back painfully, forcing Becky to look at him.

'I'm talking to you. Answer me. . . .'

When Becky still said nothing the man released her hair. Straightening up, he drew back his leg to kick her. This was the moment for which Becky had been waiting. Reaching out, she pushed him, utilising all her strength.

Caught off-balance, Alfie Skewes staggered backwards.

Halfway across the cell he tripped over the softly crooning madwoman. Her transformation was as sudden as it was frightening. Screaming incoherently, she leaped upon the fallen man and looped her chain about his neck. Then, leaning back, she pulled the chain tight.

The ensnared prisoner tried to shout, but only succeeded in mouthing strangled sounds that were lost in the madwoman's fury. The other prisoners watched in silent horror until suddenly Alfie Skewes's arms dropped to his side and his heels began to beat a muffled tattoo on the straw-covered floor.

'The mad hag's killing him.' One of the sailors was the first to recover his senses. Snatching up the quarter-full pewter jug, he ran to where the struggle was taking place and brought the jug crashing down upon the madwoman's head. She dropped to the floor without a sound, and as she lay motionless her attacker removed the chain from about Alfie Skewes's neck.

Enough porter remained for some to be poured down the throat of the near-strangled man, but it served only to make his choking worse. However, it was soon apparent that the madwoman's victim would not die, although it was by no means certain he would ever recover his voice.

When the gasping man had been propped against the cell wall his rescuer rose to his feet and glared at Becky. Meanwhile the madwoman began to twitch spasmodically and moan, for all the world like some wounded animal.

'She's the one who caused all this trouble. She pushed Alfie. . . .'

There were growls of agreement from the other prisoners, and the second seaman said: 'She ought to be taught a lesson.' The men looked across the cell towards Becky, and she suddenly felt very, very frightened.

'You should have listened to Alfie. He said you needed a friend in here. I ought to know; I've been in here often enough. . . .' The old woman's cackling ceased to register with Becky as the men prisoners advanced upon her, skirting the moaning madwoman.

With her back against the cell wall Becky looked desperately about her for a means of escape. There was nowhere. She saw the slop-bucket in a corner. If only she could reach it, she might use the bucket as a temporary weapon.... Even as she prepared to dart across the room one of the seamen lunged forward and grabbed her by the arm. Before she could fight him off her other arm had been taken.

'What shall we do with her?'

The question was asked by the sailor who had saved Alfie Skewes. It was answered by his companion.

'You've been to sea for a twelvemonth and you ask a question like that? Keep a tight hold of her and I'll *show* you what to do with her. The rest of you can have a turn when I'm finished.'

Fumbling with his trousers, the sailor advanced upon Becky. When he was no more than a pace away from her she screamed and kicked out with all the force she could muster.

There was sudden bedlam in the cell. Shouting in pain, the sailor staggered away. Doubled over and holding his groin, he tripped on the madwoman's chain. The sudden jerk brought her to her knees screaming. Meanwhile Becky fought with all her young strength against the man who held her, while the old woman screeched advice to him.

The only one to see Constable Ivor Primrose enter the cell was Alfie Skewes, but he was unable to warn anyone. The others became aware of his presence only when one prisoner was sent reeling by a backhand blow from the fist of the giant constable. Then he grasped each of the men holding Becky. As they released their hold on her Constable Primrose brought their heads together with a crack that sounded painfully loud in the sudden silence that fell upon the cell.

It took Constable Primrose no more than two minutes to ascertain the cause of the rumpus. After satisfying himself that none of the injured parties was actually dying, he turned his attention upon the male inmates of the cell. He warned them in no uncertain terms of the consequences should Becky be molested again, promising each man a flogging, with the maximum number of lashes allowed by the harsh laws of England.

Whether or not Constable Ivor Primrose had the power to

ensure that such a punishment was meted out did not matter. The imprisoned men believed he would carry out his threat.

Satisfied that no harm would befall Becky for the remainder of her time in the cell, Constable Primrose told her of Fergus's visit to the police station and his attempt to secure her release.

'He'll be back again tomorrow. Likely he'll be able to see you then. Don't you fret, my girl. If you've done nothing to break the law, that young man will have you out of here in no time at all.'

When the door slammed shut behind Constable Ivor Primrose, Becky lay down in a corner farthest away from the others and covered herself with straw. There was a warm glow inside her that even the squalor of her surroundings could not extinguish. The other prisoners had heard what Constable Primrose had said to her. They had heard him say that Fergus would soon have her out of the cell.

Even more important to Becky was the knowledge that Fergus *had* come looking for her, after all.

CHAPTER FIVE

FERGUS MADE HIS WAY to St James Back as soon as he thought there was likely to be someone in the ragged school. He had no problem finding the premises. So much noise emanated from a disused and neglected chapel that it had to be a school.

It was a surprisingly large building, and Fergus wandered around inside for many minutes before meeting someone who looked as though she might know what went on there. He approached her intending to ask where he might find Miss Fanny Tennant, but the girl did not wait for *his* question.

'Who are you? What is your business here?' Her manner was as brisk and crisp as her appearance. No more than five feet two inches tall, she was about Fergus's own age and was dressed in a neat white blouse and a long coarse-weave brown skirt. But it was her hair that attracted immediate attention. Had Fergus been painting it, he would have used more red than yellow, but no doubt she would have preferred to have it called 'tawny'. Obviously very long, it was drawn back severely and pinned up with great care at the back of her neck.

'There's a back door for tradesmen, but if you are seeking Miss Carpenter you'll need to return another day.'

Her clothes might have been those of a servant, but servants were rarely allowed to keep their hair quite so long. Fergus finally decided she was probably a lady's maid to an indulgent employer.

'I'm looking for one of the teachers here. Fanny Tennant.'

The girl's manner changed from brisk officiousness to cold hostility. 'I am *Miss* Tennant. Do I know you? I can't recall meeting you before.'

'You haven't....' Aware that use of her first name had offended her, Fergus did his best to rectify his grave error. He had need of her. 'My name is Fergus Vincent. I was told you might be able to help me.'

'Indeed?' Fanny Tennant was unbending. 'If you have a child you wish to attend our school, you need only bring him, or her, along. We will expect you to contribute to the child's education if you have the means. If not ... We rarely turn needy children away. The same applies to the provision of a meal. We only provide soup and bread – but for many of our children that is the bridge between starvation and survival.'

'I'm not here to discuss a child's schooling. I've come to ask your help for a friend. A young girl who's been arrested by the police.'

Fanny Tennant's manner remained one of uncompromising disapproval. 'We are not here to provide a prison visiting service for wayward girls, Mr Vincent. There are other organisations who involve themselves in such activities. I don't doubt that your church will provide you with details to assist your lady-friend.'

'She's not a lady. She's a mere child. An orphan.'

Fanny Tennant succeeded in looking more disapproving than before, and Fergus added hurriedly: 'The child befriended me when I arrived a couple of days ago. I'm new to Bristol, and she guided me to the house where my friend had died. I sent her out yesterday with money to buy groceries, and she never returned....' Fergus shrugged sheepishly. 'At first I thought she'd probably spent my money on something she wanted – she has *nothing* of her own – but last night I discovered she'd been arrested. She's in the cells at the Bridewell police station. I've been there, but the sergeant won't allow me to see her. Constable Primrose suggested I should find you and ask your help.'

'Ivor Primrose made such a suggestion, after his sergeant said you *couldn't* see her?'

'I assisted him soon after I arrived in Bristol. I think it's his way of saying "Thank you".' Fergus found encouragement in the fact that Fanny Tennant knew Constable Primrose's first name.

Fanny Tennant studied Fergus for a few moments. She saw a slightly built young man with overlong hair and a face dominated by a pair of alert and intense eyes. She had also observed his limp.

'Are you in employment, Mr Vincent?'

'I'm an artist. I make a living.'

Fanny Tennant raised her eyebrows in surprise. 'Are you a *good* artist?'

Fergus grinned. 'Becky thinks I'm the best.'

'Becky?'

'That's her name. The girl who's been arrested.'

Once again Fanny Tennant gave Fergus a searching stare. 'Do I have your assurance there is nothing improper in the relationship between you and this young girl?'

'Of course. She's a mere child.'

'We have children in this school who have earned a living by prostitution since they were old enough to be taken on the streets by their mothers. I try not to pass moral judgements. My duty is to teach and try to show them there *is* a better way of life. However, I would be failing in my duty were I to help this girl to return to immorality.'

'You have my word there's nothing like that between us.'

'Very well, I'll come to the Bridewell police station with you and we'll learn why the girl is there. But I am no miracle-worker, Mr Vincent. If the girl is guilty of dishonesty, she will have to suffer the consequences — no matter how much I disagree with sending children to adult prisons. Now I must ask you to wait outside the building while I fetch a coat. I fear some of our impressionable young girls find your presence a distraction.'

As Fergus made his way to the door he passed a knot of giggling bold-eyed young girls who could not have been any older than Becky. A few minutes later he was joined by Fanny Tennant.

It was not far to the Bridewell police station, but as they walked along together Fanny Tennant questioned Fergus closely about his previous life and his reason for coming to Bristol. He told her about the Royal Navy, and Henry Gordon, and explained his reasons for living in Lewin's Mead. By the time they arrived at the police station Fergus felt he had satisfied the ragged-school teacher that he did not intend leading Becky into a life of debauchery when she was released from police custody.

Fanny Tennant marched into the police office and demanded imperiously to see the inspector in charge. Much to Fergus's surprise the sergeant on duty hurried away immediately to find his superior officer. Fergus was even more surprised when the inspector appeared a few moments later. After greeting Fanny Tennant respectfully by name, the senior policeman invited Fanny and Fergus to his office.

Pulling out chairs for his two guests, the inspector enquired first after Fanny Tennant's father, and then her uncle.

Replying that both men were well, the ragged-school teacher made it clear she had not come to the police station on a social visit.

'You have a young girl in your cells. She's called Becky. I don't think she has another name.'

'The urchin from Back Lane? Yes, she's in the cells on suspicion of stealing groceries. Is she one of your pupils?'

'No.' Fanny Tennant looked quickly at Fergus. 'Not yet. But Mr Vincent can throw some light on the matter. He gave her money to buy groceries for him. Your constable arrested her before she could return with them.'

The inspector frowned. 'I have a report here from Constable Fitzpatrick . . .' He shuffled through a pile of documents and pulled out a single sheet of paper filled with neat handwriting. Scanning through it quickly, he said: 'Constable Fitzpatrick reports that the girl behaved in a highly suspicious manner. She tried to run off when she saw him, and then refused to say where she'd purchased the goods. She also kicked and bit Constable Fitzpatrick when she was arrested and faces a secondary charge of assault on police.'

'Have you *seen* Becky? There's no more meat on her than on a slice of belly pork. A charge against her of assaulting a constable will be laughed out of court. She was *frightened* of your constable, as all the children from Lewin's Mead are. *That's* why she ran.'

The inspector maintained a dignified silence, but Fergus felt his response would have been very different had Fanny Tennant not been present. Fergus wondered why she was treated with such cautious respect here in the Bristol police office.

'You must agree there is a possibility the girl has been unlawfully arrested, Inspector. I would like to see her.'

After only a brief hesitation the inspector said: 'Of course, Miss Tennant. I'll have her brought here. Would you like some refreshment while you wait?'

Before Fergus could reply, Fanny Tennant said: 'I have work to do at the school. I wish to waste no more time than is absolutely necessary.'

'Of course.'

The inspector rose from his chair and hurried out. When he had gone, Fergus said: 'You seem to have a great deal of influence here, Miss Tennant.'

When Fanny Tennant smiled her whole face relaxed, making her look years younger, and far less formidable. '*I* have no influence. In fact, the inspector and many of his constables would be delighted to see the ragged school closed down. However, my father is a city alderman and chairman of the Watch Committee, which controls the police force. I take unashamed advantage of the fact that I am his daughter.'

'And your uncle – the one mentioned by the inspector?'

Fergus was treated to the smile again. 'Oh, he's a Member of Parliament for Bristol.'

Fergus was still speechless when the door opened and Becky was ushered into the room. The neatness of the police inspector's office served to accentuate her dirty unkempt appearance, but the delight on her face when she saw Fergus made those in the room forget her raggedness and Fanny Tennant looked sharply at Fergus.

'I knew you'd come to get me out. I told them in the cell you'd be here before long.'

'We'll have you out of here soon,' promised Fergus. 'Just as soon as one or two small matters are cleared up. Miss

Tennant has come with me to help you.'

It was a moment or two before Fergus's words sank in, and Becky's new-found happiness changed to dismay. 'I'm *not* going off with you? I've got to go back to that cell again?'

'Not for long.'

'But I've done nothing – and I don't want no help from *her*.' Becky jerked her head defiantly at Fanny Tennant. 'She's a busybody who tries to run other folks' lives for 'em.'

'You need someone to help run *yours*, that is quite certain,' snapped Fanny Tennant. 'Inspector . . . leave us alone for a few minutes, if you please.'

It did not please the inspector at all, but he obediently backed out of the room, closing the door behind him.

When he had gone, Fanny Tennant turned her attention to Becky. 'Now, young lady, Mr Vincent has been to a great deal of trouble on your behalf, and *I* have many other things I should be doing, so we'll have no more nonsense. The inspector says you refuse to say where you purchased the groceries you were carrying at the time of your arrest. If we are to secure your release, we *must* know where they were bought.'

Becky looked from Fanny Tennant to Fergus uncertainly, then her mouth clamped tight shut.

'I see. Such reluctance can mean only one thing. You *did* steal the groceries. All the same, I suggest you tell us the name of the shop immediately. The police will find out sooner or later, and I would rather *we* spoke to the shopkeeper first.'

'I *didn't* pinch 'em,' declared Becky vehemently. 'I paid for everything with the money Fergus gave me. . . .' She hesitated a moment before adding reluctantly: 'There might just be a couple of ounces of tea extra.'

'Is that all?'

Becky nodded, meeting the ragged-school teacher's stern look which dared Becky to lie to her.

'That's all. Honest.'

Fanny Tennant's nod of acceptance surprised Fergus. She surprised him still more when she spoke again.

'I know when a girl is lying to me and I'll not see a child thrown into prison for a few pennyworth of tea. Which shop did it come from?'

'The one in Broad Street.'

'That's only just around the corner from here. We must waste no more time. It's probably one of the first shops the police will visit.'

Fanny Tennant rose to her feet, and Fergus followed suit.

Becky's face registered dismay. 'Can't I come with you? I don't want to go back to the cells again.'

'You'll need to stay here a while longer, Becky. Don't worry, we'll have you out of here just as soon as we can — probably by midday. I promise.'

Fergus took hold of Becky's hands in a bid to reassure her, and once again Fanny Tennant's questioning look encompassed them both.

'There will be a condition attached to your release, Becky.'

Fergus dropped Becky's hands, and they both turned towards the speaker.

'A condition?' Fergus was puzzled. 'I don't understand. . . .'

'I intend keeping an eye on Becky. She'll commence classes at the free school — the ragged school — on Monday.'

'I don't see why I should . . .!'

'Becky! Miss Tennant's been a great help. Without her I wouldn't have been able to *see* you, let alone secure your release. The police might yet bring charges against you. I agree with her. You *should* go to school. It's a wonderful opportunity for you.'

'School is for *kids*.'

'We have older children than you, Becky. Anyway, I *insist*.'

Becky would not look at Fanny Tennant. Her eyes went to Fergus, and he nodded.

'Oh . . . all right, then. But I don't see why I *should*. I've not done nothing. . . .' Becky's voice faltered as she remembered the two ounces of tea.

Fergus had to resist an urge to hug Becky to him. She looked more childlike and vulnerable than at any time since he had first met her.

'Good girl. Don't worry about anything now. We'll have you out of here just as soon as we can.'

*   *   *

Walking from the police station with Fanny Tennant, Fergus brought up the question of the assault charge being made against Becky. The ragged-school teacher shrugged the matter off.

'Given the circumstances of her arrest, the police will not want to proceed with any other charges. I'll see to that. I only hope the grocer will be equally accommodating.'

Fortunately the grocer had no wish to press charges against Becky. He remembered her well and even suggested that *he* might have included the extra tea in the purchases, by mistake. The grocer recognised the alderman's daughter as soon as she entered his shop, and Fergus had no doubt this accounted for much of the man's generous and forgiving manner. It was a great relief. Now there was no reason why Becky should not be released from police custody before the day was out.

Fanny Tennant agreed with him. She had work to do at the ragged school in St James Back, but she suggested Fergus should return to the police station and tell the inspector what they had learned.

When Fergus tried to thank Fanny Tennant for her assistance, the teacher silenced him immediately, saying: 'I wouldn't be working in a ragged school if I didn't care about children like Becky. There are far too many of them. We *all* need to do everything we can to help them.'

Fergus murmured polite agreement – and immediately regretted such unthinking rashness.

'I am pleased to know you are equally concerned. The children I teach are not as amenable to discipline as children from more – shall we say *stable* home backgrounds? In order to teach them anything at all we need to make their lessons *interesting*. To hold their attention. You can be of very great assistance to us in our work, with your sketches. It need only take up a couple of hours of your time each week. Shall we say Wednesday afternoons, about two o'clock? Good. Now I can return to the school with a clear conscience and tell Miss Carpenter it has been a very satisfactory morning's work.'

CHAPTER SIX

IT WAS THREE O'CLOCK in the afternoon before the police inspector released Becky. A constable had checked Fergus's story with the grocer, but then the inspector had to listen to a complaint from the disgruntled Constable Fitzpatrick, his red and swollen nose a testimony that Becky's assault was a determined one.

By this time Fergus had spent some hours in the police station, and his patience was wearing thin. When he announced he was going to fetch Miss Tennant to help settle the matter, the inspector ordered that Becky be brought up from the cells.

The inspector gave her a stern warning about running from constables when ordered to stop, but Becky did not even pretend to listen. Instead she grinned happily across the office at Fergus.

'Do you understand what I'm saying to you, young lady?' The inspector was aware his warning had fallen on deaf ears.

Becky nodded, not shifting her gaze from Fergus.

The inspector gave up. Shrugging his shoulders, he said to Fergus: 'Take her away. I hope she pays more attention to Miss Tennant than she has to me.'

In the busy street outside the police station Becky took Fergus's hand in a spontaneous gesture of relief and happiness. 'I *knew* you'd come and get me out, Fergus. Even when the others said no one would want *me*, I knew you'd come.'

Becky's happiness was contagious, and passers-by smiled at the young cripple and his ragged companion.

'Who else was in the cell with you?'

The happiness left Becky, and her hand dropped away from his. 'I don't want to talk about them. For all I care, they can all "get the boat".'

Fergus wondered what had happened to Becky while she was in police custody, but her face had assumed the stubborn expression he had seen there before; he knew better than to question her right now.

When they arrived at the house in Back Lane, Becky had to run the gauntlet of well-wishers who crowded around to offer their congratulations on her release from police custody. It was rare for a resident of the Lewin's Mead rookery to be arrested by the police and released without having served a prison sentence.

As it happened, not one but *two* Lewin's Mead dwellers had been freed from the cells of the Bridewell police station.

Irish Molly was among the well-wishers, and while Becky was chatting to the numerous occupants of Mary O'Ryan's room the prostitute took Fergus aside. In a low voice she said: 'Try to keep Becky with you as much as you can. Joe Skewes also got out of gaol this morning.'

'You mean . . . he's escaped?'

'No, he was released. His woman died, but before she did she gave the police what they called a "dying declaration" and swore her injuries were the result of an accident. She said Joe Skewes had been trying to *help* her after she'd fallen downstairs.'

'But I *saw* what happened. So did Becky, and a couple of dozen others.'

'We *all* know what happened. The fact remains that Joe Skewes is free and he thinks Becky narked on him.'

'But she *didn't*. Becky would run a mile the other way rather than talk to a constable. That's what got her in this lot of trouble.'

'It's what Joe Skewes *thinks* that matters. Just be careful for a while. Joe Skewes is celebrating his release right now and in another day or two he'll probably not even remember Becky. Until then he's dangerous.'

When they eventually reached the attic room, Becky

started a fire in the hearth while Fergus prepared something for them to eat. Afterwards, as Fergus cleared away, Becky looked through the sketches he had made for himself at the Hatchet inn. One of them made her chuckle, and in answer to his question she held up the sketch. It was of a sailor dancing a 'hornpipe' with one of the women at the inn.

'This is good, Fergus. What will you do with it?'

Fergus shrugged. 'I'll turn it into a proper painting one day – but there's a painting over there that's much better.' He pointed to the canvas resting on the easel, close to the window.

Becky crossed the room and when she saw the incomplete painting her eyes opened wide in delight. 'It's *me*, when I was sleeping the other morning.'

Fergus stood beside her and looked down at the canvas. 'It's probably the best thing I've done, and I have other sketches of you that will one day make even better paintings. You're an inspiration to me, Becky.'

Becky beamed happily, but at that moment the lid of the kettle began rattling noisily as steam set it dancing and they both rushed to move the kettle to one side of the fire.

Becky asked suddenly: 'You going to paint that Tennant woman?'

The question took Fergus by surprise. 'I haven't thought about it. I doubt if she could spare the time to sit long enough for me to paint her.'

'Would you like to?'

Fergus thought of Fanny Tennant's face with its high cheekbones and her long, unusually coloured hair. 'Yes, I think I would.'

Becky pouted. 'She's *bossy*.'

'Fanny Tennant was a great help to you, Becky. If it hadn't been for her, the story of your arrest might have had a very different ending.'

'Oh, it's *Fanny* Tennant, is it? Perhaps *you* ought to go to her old ragged school, instead of me.'

Fergus grinned. He knew how the thought of having to attend school rankled with Becky. 'I *am* going to the ragged school. She's asked me to spend a couple of hours each week teaching there.'

Becky did not share his amusement. After glaring speechlessly at Fergus for a few long moments, she turned away and headed for the door.

'Where are you going?' Fergus remembered Irish Molly's warning about Joe Skewes.

'Not that it's any of your business, but I'm going downstairs to talk to Mary O'Ryan and the others. *They* don't try to run my life for me.'

Becky had not returned to the attic by the time Fergus gathered together his sketchpad and pencils and set off for the Hatchet inn, but as he passed the door of the Irish family's room on the next floor he could hear her voice dominating the conversation.

The sound gave Fergus a sad pleasure. There could not have been many occasions in Becky's young life when she had done something to warrant so much attention. It was a pity it had come as a result of being arrested. He shrugged off the thought. The reason did not really matter. Everyone needed to feel important occasionally.

It was another busy evening at the Hatchet inn, and Fergus did not return to his attic room until the early hours of the morning. Although tired, he was well satisfied with his evening's work. Sketching sailors and their women was proving a profitable business. Nevertheless, Fergus realised the port of Bristol would not always be as crowded with ships as it was at present. He needed to take full advantage of the situation for as long as it lasted.

Becky was not in the attic room, but Fergus was not unduly concerned. She lodged with the Irish family when she had money – and her credit would be good in view of her current popularity.

Fergus was awakened earlier than he would have liked by the sound of a crackling fire and the smell of frying food.

Sitting up in bed, he saw Becky crouched by the hearth. One hand was holding a skillet over the flames while with the other she tried unsuccessfully to push back a recalcitrant tress of hair which hung dangerously close to the fire.

Becky gave Fergus a sidelong glance and she said defensively: 'I'm making you breakfast.'

'I thought you couldn't cook.'

Her chin came up defiantly. 'I watched Mary O'Ryan doing it this morning. It's easy.'

'Hold that pan straight,' said Fergus hurriedly. 'If you tip the fat on the fire, you'll burn the house down.'

Becky levelled the skillet hurriedly.

'It smells delicious,' Fergus volunteered, hoping he had not offended her.

Her delighted smile gave him his answer. 'Does it really?'

'I've never smelt a better meal.'

Reluctantly rising from his bed, Fergus pulled on shirt and trousers and walked the length of the room to stand beside Becky's crouching figure.

'Do you think it's nearly done?' Becky looked up at him anxiously.

Fergus gazed down at rashers of streaky bacon foundering in a sea of broken-yoked eggs and grubby dripping, all evidently placed in the skillet when the fat was still cold.

'It looks delicious,' Fergus lied. He wished he had drunk less at the Hatchet the night before. 'But it might need a few more minutes' cooking. I'll have a quick wash while I'm waiting.'

Breakfast looked no more appetising when it was transferred to a plate, together with most of the melted dripping, but a thick chunk of bread soaked up most of the greasy excess, and a glass of water helped wash the whole meal down.

'Becky, you're a wonder.' Fergus's gratitude was tinged with relief at having successfully cleared the plate. He only hoped his breakfast would *stay* down. 'I hope you're as quick at learning school lessons.'

Much of the happiness escaped from Becky's face. 'I don't want no schooling. Do I *really* have to go?'

'Yes.' The breakfast lay in Fergus's stomach with the weight of a cannonball. 'You've promised, and a promise should always be kept.'

'All promises – or only those made to Miss Tennant?'

'*All* promises.'

'Did you go to school?'

For just a moment Fergus forgot the rebellion in his stomach as he thought about the lessons given to him by his mother. It all seemed a lifetime ago.

'I bet you went to a *proper* school, one chosen by your mum and dad.'

'No, my mother taught me to read and write.'

'Is she still alive?'

'No, she died a few years ago.'

'Your pa, too?'

Fergus nodded. His father *had* probably drunk himself to death by now.

'So we're *both* orphans?' It put an immediate bond between them.

'Yes, Becky. We're both orphans – but I can read and write.'

'All right, then, I'll go to her rotten old ragged school.'

Suddenly the breakfast he had just eaten began an assault on Fergus's stomach, and he winced. Fortunately Becky did not notice.

'Do you fancy her?'

'Fancy who?' Turning away, Fergus placed a hand to his stomach. He felt very peculiar.

'*Her*. Fanny Tennant.'

'I've hardly spoken to the woman. If you hadn't got yourself arrested, I'd never have met her.'

'Honest?'

'Honest. Now, run off and find something useful to amuse yourself. I have work to do.'

Becky smiled happily, unaware of Fergus's discomfort. 'I didn't *really* believe you fancied her. Jock used to say that painters prefer their women with some meat on 'em.' She hesitated. 'I ate with Irish Molly last night. She said that the way I eat she don't doubt I'll be bigger than her in *no* time. She put on a special spread because I'd not been sent to prison. Got it from the butcher in St James. His wife's away with her sick mother, and Irish Molly calls in there at night. We ate more'n two pounds of belly pork between us. . . .'

Fergus groaned. 'Becky. . . . Go away now. Come back and talk later.'

'All right, I won't keep you from your work any longer. I'm glad you ate a good breakfast. Irish Molly says you're the sort who'd probably starve to death if no one fed you. At least I know you've got something in your stomach today.'

Becky's statement was not accurate for long. From the doorway of the attic room Fergus waited until Becky entered the room occupied by the O'Ryan family. The moment the door closed behind her he fled down the stairs and just made it to the communal privy in the yard behind the house before he was violently ill.

When Becky returned to the studio in the early afternoon Fergus was working. He feared she had come to offer to cook him lunch, but much to his relief she made no mention of food. After she had wandered about the attic in a desultory manner for some minutes he wiped his brushes on a rag and asked: 'What have you been doing this morning?'

Becky shrugged her shoulders carelessly. 'I went to St James Back to see who went to the ragged school. It's like I said before, they're all *kids*.'

Fergus smiled wanly. His stomach had not yet returned to normal. 'Then, you can feel superior when you're with them.'

'No, I can't,' Becky rounded on him fiercely. 'It may be called a *ragged* school, but there's no one there as ragged as *me*. I'm not going, Fergus. I won't go there to be laughed at.'

Becky turned to run from the room, but Fergus caught one of her arms and pulled her around to face him.

'No one is going to laugh at you.' Even as he spoke Fergus was looking at Becky's dress. Dirty and torn, it was in reality little more than a tattered piece of rag. It was also much too short for her. Designed as an ankle-length dress, it hardly covered her knees.

'Come here a minute.' Leading Becky to a chair by the table, Fergus sat her down. She looked up at him wide-eyed, as though fearing he might be about to strike her.

Releasing her arm, Fergus said: 'You're quite right. The dress you're wearing is a disgrace. Do you know any place nearby where you might buy a dress that's half-decent?'

Becky remembered the dress she had admired so much.

'There's a dollyshop in St James Street. I've seen a dress there – but it costs three and six.'

Fergus withdrew a soft-leather, draw-string purse from beneath his shirt and took out a bright silver coin. 'Here's a crown. Go and buy it. Then I want to hear no more about not going to the ragged school. Is that clear?'

Becky looked up at Fergus in an awed silence. He had given her a *crown* – a *whole crown* – and asked for nothing in return. She frowned. There *had* to be a catch. No man gave a girl so much money for *nothing*.

Returning to his painting, Fergus had picked up a paint-brush before he looked up and saw her indecision.

'What are you waiting for? Go and buy the dress before it's sold, or before I change my mind. Get some ribbon while you're there, too, and I'll wash your hair when you come back. By the time I'm finished with you you'll be the *best*-dressed girl in Fanny Tennant's school, not the worst.'

Clutching the silver coin, Becky left Ida Stokes's house with mixed feelings. She was on her way to spend more money on herself than she had ever possessed before. She should have been the happiest girl in Bristol. She *would* have been, had she been certain Fergus was doing it for *her* and not in order to impress Fanny Tennant.

CHAPTER SEVEN

ROSE COTTLE'S 'DOLLYSHOP' was an ordinary house on the corner of St James Back – and the dress was still there, hanging from a pole placed inside the window, where it could be seen by passers-by. A grey woollen dress with red tape edging, it had probably been stolen from a washing-line in one of Bristol's more fashionable suburbs.

Becky thought it the most beautiful dress she had ever seen, but she walked past the house three times before venturing in to spend the coin that lay warm and safe in the palm of her hand.

'What do you want?' In the passageway of the dollyshop a big woman wearing a faded black dress emerged from the shadows and blocked Becky's path. It was Rose Cottle, the dollyshop-owner. 'If you've been dipping, I don't want to know about it, or you ... unless you've got a fine fogle or two.'

'I'm no pickpocket, and I'm not here to sell anything.'

Rose Cottle moved closer and peered into Becky's face. 'Why, bless my soul! It's the child from the cells. Come in, girl, come in. So you got off, too, eh? Good. I knew you was a bright girl as soon as I clapped eyes on you. A girl like you can earn a lot of money with some help from me. *Easy* money.'

'I've not come to work for you. I'm here to buy a dress. The red and grey one hanging in the window.'

Taken aback, the dollyshop proprietress looked suspiciously at Becky. '*You*? Buy a dress? Let's see the colour of your money first.'

Becky opened her hand to reveal the large silver crown given to her by Fergus. The suspicious attitude of Rose Cottle underwent an immediate change.

'Well, who'd have believed it! Come inside, child. You've got good taste. At five shillings that there dress is a bargain. I bet there's not another like it in the whole of Bristol.'

'It was a bargain at three and six when I last looked at it,' retorted Becky. 'A young gent gave me this crown to buy more than just that old dress.'

Rose Cottle looked again at Becky. She was as dirty as any young urchin the dollyshop-owner had ever seen, and the dress she wore was no more than a filthy rag, yet there *was* an appeal about the girl. Enough, it seemed, to captivate a young man who could afford to spend a crown on clothes for her. Well, she might as well spend it in the St James Street dollyshop as elsewhere.

One day the 'young gent' would tire of her. Rose Cottle had seen it happen to young girls many times before. When it occurred Becky would not want to return to a cold hard bed among the rubbish of Lewin's Mead. She would be desperate for money – and there was only one sure way for a girl from the rookery to earn a living. When this day arrived Rose Cottle wanted to be the one to whom Becky would turn for help.

The signs would be easily read. When a young mistress was abandoned by her lover the first things to go were her clothes, bought back by a dollyshop-owner at a greatly reduced price, and then . . .?

Rose Cottle received a considerable income from ragged young prostitutes who came to her for nice clothes with which to entice sailors and the young men of Bristol. The dollyshop-owner hired out clothes to them and also rented out 'short-time' rooms above the shop, thus ensuring that most of the young girls' earnings came her way.

'If you think the dress should be three and sixpence, then three and sixpence it shall be, dearie. Rose Cottle ain't one to go back on her word, even if it means I make not a farthing profit because of it. The dress is yours. What would you like to go with it? A shift? Some ribbons? How about shoes for those pretty feet? I've got a lovely pair at the back of the shop. If they've been worn at all, I swear it must have been by a lady who 'ad a carpeted floor. There's hardly a sign of wear on 'em. She had them made at a cost of *guineas*, I don't doubt. For you, four *shillings*. No, because you're such a pretty little thing, *three*. You tell your gentleman friend about them – but don't forget to tell him they're *five* shillings, you understand me, dearie?'

The advice was accompanied by a wink and a chuckle, both lost on Becky. She walked past the dollyshop-owner to where the dress was hanging. Quite unselfconsciously she shrugged her own dress from her shoulders and allowed it to fall to the floor about her ankles. Stepping out of the ragged circle, she reached down the red-trimmed grey dress and slipped it over her head.

Becky had trouble fastening the unfamiliar buttons, but she refused Rose Cottle's offer of assistance and eventually succeeded. Standing in the centre of the room with the dress on, she hardly dared to breathe.

'*Lovely*, dearie. You look *lovely*.'

For once Rose Cottle meant what she said. The ankle-length grey dress had transformed Becky. Hugging her slim body, the red-trimmed bodice hinted at budding maturity.

From the rear of the shop Rose Cottle produced a badly stained and dirty dressing-table mirror, and she held it so that Becky might see her new dress from every angle.

Fearing that at any minute she might burst from pride and sheer delight, Becky nodded and held out the crown.

'I'll have the dress. But I'm not paying more than three and six, so I'll have some change, if you please.'

Becky's pride was, if anything, heightened by the time she returned to Ida Stokes's house. With her new dress on she had been able to go in shops without the proprietor coming out from behind his counter and chasing her off, or hovering nearby to ensure she stole nothing.

She had bought ribbons for her hair – and soap. Real 'lady's' soap. She had also bought a present for Fergus. A beautifully shaped clay pipe, and three pennyworth of tobacco. The fact that Becky had never actually seen Fergus smoking a pipe caused her a moment's pause for thought, but she quickly shrugged off her faint misgivings. *All* the men she had ever seen smoked pipes. Fergus had probably not had an opportunity to buy one for himself since his arrival in Bristol.

Clutching both happiness and purchases close, Becky entered the house in Back Lane. She needed to lift her long dress well clear of her ankles in order to climb the stairs, and it delighted her.

When she reached the first landing Becky became aware of the aroma of cheap gin. It became stronger as she crossed the large dark landing – and suddenly a figure rose from the shadows beside the second flight of stairs and loomed over her.

'I've been waiting for you. . . .' The man's voice was slurred and thick with the effects of heavy drinking, but Becky recognised it immediately as belonging to Joe Skewes.

Becky turned and made a dash for the stairs leading to the ground-floor hallway but, drunk as he was, Joe Skewes was too fast for her. He grabbed and caught her by the collar of her new dress. Screaming as a number of buttons parted company with the front of her dress, Becky dropped her purchases to the floor.

The scream owed as much to fury as to fear and, twisting in his grip, she kicked out, her foot catching Joe Skewes in the groin.

Grunting in pain, the drunken man released her, but he still barred Becky's escape. He recovered quickly, and for some minutes the relentless pursuit continued, with Joe Skewes crashing into doors and walls, and Becky shrieking loudly whenever he had her cornered.

By now all the doors leading off the landing had been thrown open and the occupants were adding their voices to the din, shouting for Joe Skewes to leave Becky alone.

Working beside an open window in the attic, it was a couple of minutes before Fergus realised that the din he could hear came from somewhere *inside* the house. He recognised Becky's voice and, putting down his palette and brush, he set off in search of the source of the noise.

He pushed his way through the gathered residents of the second floor in time to see Joe Skewes corner Becky yet again on the landing below.

As Fergus gained the stairs to come to Becky's aid, Irish Molly ran from her room brandishing a heavy iron skillet. The Irish prostitute swung the pan in an awkward backhanded swipe that threw her off-balance, but the result was quite spectacular. The flat bottom of the heavy iron pan struck Joe Skewes on the side of his head and knocked him back to a sitting position at the top of the stairs leading down to the ground floor.

Irish Molly swung the skillet again. This time she missed, but the result was no less effective than before. In contorting to avoid the blow Joe Skewes leaned too far backwards. Fergus watched in speechless awe as the violent coal-heaver executed a series of backward somersaults down the steep stairs.

By the time Fergus reached Becky, Joe Skewes was lying spread-eagled on his back in the hall at the foot of the stairs. Coming from the doorway of her room, Ida Stokes stood over him, shrieking abuse at the prostrate man.

Fergus's concern was for Becky. She kneeled on the floor of the landing making strange, unintelligible, animal-like noises that resembled the whimpering of a small hurt puppy.

Dropping to his knees beside her. Fergus asked anxiously: 'Becky . . . are you badly hurt? Where . . .?'

Becky put her hands to her throat, and her wail of anguish was directed at the skillet-wielding Irish Molly.

'He's torn the buttons off me new dress. I've only just got it. . . .'

Irish Molly lowered the skillet and put a comforting arm about Becky. 'It's all right, my love. You come with me. We'll have it fixed up in no time at all.'

As she helped Becky to her feet, Irish Molly spoke to the bewildered Fergus: 'Don't worry yourself; I'll take good care of her. Go and look at Joe Skewes. God forbid I've killed him – although, so help me, no man deserves it more.'

Irish Molly led Becky away, her head close to the younger girl's, talking comfortingly to her. Moments later the door to

Irish Molly's room closed behind them. Still baffled, Fergus turned his attention to Joe Skewes as the haranguing from Ida Stokes reached new heights.

The coal-heaver was on his hands and knees. Looking up at Ida Stokes, he shook his head and tried to gather his scattered wits. The effort was too much. Giving up the task, he crawled on hands and knees across the hallway and out through the open door, pursued by Ida Stokes's shrill voice.

The O'Ryan family was carrying out a loud-voiced conversation entirely in Gaelic as Fergus made his way past them and climbed the stairs to his attic room. He was concerned about Becky and was hurt that she had turned away from him to Irish Molly when she was in trouble. He tried to shrug off the feeling. After all, he had come into Becky's life only a few days before. Irish Molly had been around for a long time. No doubt there had been other occasions when Becky needed help. All the same, he wished he had been successful in his clumsy attempt to comfort her.

Fergus had been painting for an hour when he heard footsteps on the creaking stairs outside before the door opened. He was completing a detail of a sailor he had sketched the previous day and did not look up immediately. When he did, his brush fell slowly away from the canvas, all thoughts of painting gone.

Becky stood in the doorway wearing her new dress, the buttons sewn back into place. But Irish Molly had not stopped with the buttons. Becky's hair had been washed and brushed, the dark tresses tied back with a red satin ribbon. Her face had been washed, too, and at her throat she wore a narrow chain, from which dangled a cheap red glass pendant, loaned to Becky by Irish Molly in a moment of generous understanding.

Becky entered the attic room in shy anticipation of Fergus's reaction to her new image. Irish Molly had told her she looked 'positively ravishing'. Not entirely certain of the meaning of 'ravishing', Becky had some qualms. As Fergus gazed at her in silent open-mouthed astonishment, Becky's uncertainty grew.

'My new dress . . . you don't like it?'

As Becky's face began to crumple, Fergus gathered his wits together rapidly.

'Like it? Of course I like it. . . . *More* than like it.'

Fergus meant every word. The dress could have been made for her, and Fergus made a rapid mental reassessment of Becky's probable age.

His reaction delighted Becky. She was watching his face closely, and his changing expression revealed far more of his thoughts than Fergus would have wished.

'I've brought *you* a present, too.' Handing him a small package, Becky added an apology: 'The pipe got broken by Joe Skewes.'

Opening the package, Fergus held the tobacco and broken-stemmed pipe in his hand. 'That's all right, Becky. It's still usable – and the thought is more important than anything else.' Fergus's face screwed up as though he was in pain, and then he leaned forward and kissed her on the cheek. 'I can't remember the last time I was given a present. Thank you.'

Suddenly Becky was clinging to him, her cheek against his chest. 'It's me who ought to be thanking *you*, Fergus. I've never had a present from *anyone* before. It's a *lovely* dress. Irish Molly says she thinks it's the best she's ever seen. I *know* it is.'

Becky's hair smelled of the 'lady's' soap she had bought. When he brought up his hand to touch it Fergus felt the hair still damp beneath his touch.

Suddenly Becky pushed away from him, concern on her face. 'I've been so busy thinking about my dress I've forgotten to get you something to eat.'

'It doesn't matter,' Fergus said hurriedly. 'I have to go to the Hatchet now. I'll get something to eat there.' He lifted a hand to touch her hair again, but dropped it to his side uncertainly. 'You'd better sleep up here tonight. . . .'

Fergus deliberately avoided meeting Becky's eyes. Somehow it had seemed so natural for her to sleep in his room before. Something – the dress, her hair, or perhaps her new-found cleanliness – had come between them. 'We don't want to risk having Joe Skewes spoil your new dress again.'

70

Fergus smiled, hoping that if he treated the ugly incident as a joke he might be able to break down the barrier of awkwardness that had suddenly come between them.

'If that's what you want.' Becky, too, sensed the barrier, but she was more puzzled than embarrassed.

'I think it would be the most sensible thing to do.'

Becky nodded agreement. 'I'll walk to the Hatchet with you.'

Becky walked as far as the main road where they had seen Constable Primrose on an earlier occasion. Ivor Primrose was not here this afternoon, but posted to the door of a deserted house nearby was a large coloured poster on which was a drawing of a paddle-steamer, and Fergus stopped to read it.

'What does it say?' The question from Becky reminded Fergus that she was unable to read.

'It's advertising a boat-trip from the docks tomorrow. It's to give people a chance to have a trip on a real ocean-going paddle-steamer. It says there will be a band and refreshments on board as well.'

'Can we go and watch it set off?' Suddenly Becky was a child again. 'I *love* boats.'

After only a moment's hesitation, Fergus said: 'We can do better than that. I'll take you on the trip. It should be fun.'

'You'll take me for a trip on a paddle-steamer? Honest?'

'Honest.'

Her enthusiasm was contagious, and Fergus found himself grinning. '*And* I'll buy you some of those refreshments.'

Suddenly Becky was hugging him again. 'It sounds wonderful! Can I tell Irish Molly?'

'After a hugging like that you can tell the whole world – but be sure to get to bed early tonight. You don't want to be late rising. The paddle-steamer sets off at nine o'clock sharp.'

Becky did as Fergus suggested and went to bed early – but she did not sleep. Covered by a single blanket she lay on the straw-stuffed mattress in Fergus's bed, her new dress neatly folded on a chair nearby. The room was warmed by a low-burning fire, and Becky lay drowsily gazing through the windows as a sickle moon harvested the star-spangled sky.

She felt thoroughly contented. In the space of less than a week her whole life had undergone a dramatic change. Gone was the ragged urchin, kicked from underfoot by every drunken man who staggered along the footways where she lay most nights, or reviled by 'honest' traders when she lingered near their shops and stalls.

Becky felt she *belonged* – belonged to Fergus Vincent. She gave herself a mental hug. It pleased her merely to think about him. Fergus made her feel safe – and he *cared* about her.

For as long as Becky could remember she had never considered anyone but herself. Selfishness was an essential requirement for life in the Lewin's Mead slum. Every day was a new and desperate battle for survival, especially for a small abandoned child. A *constant* battle. Winners took all in the rookery. Losers rarely had a second chance.

There *had* been good days, of course. Days when a woman might include Becky in a family meal, or allow her to sleep among her own children. But such occasions had been infrequent, and they never lasted for long. A day would come when generosity was forced to give way to expediency, and Becky would return to pick over rubbish in the street with a steadily growing band of fellow-urchins. Sometimes she would join a group of them to follow a drunken man, hoping he might fall in the gutter where his pockets would be emptied in seconds.

Later, as Becky grew older, she received more frequent offers of victuals and a night's lodgings – but there was always a price to be paid for such 'benevolence'. It was a price Becky had not been prepared to pay.

Caught between thinking of Fergus and of the boat-trip he had promised her for the next day, sleep seemed a long way off, yet suddenly Becky started up, disturbed by a sound, and she realised she had been sleeping.

At first Becky thought it might have been Fergus's return that had woken her, but then she heard the sound again. There was an argument going on in the room occupied by Mary O'Ryan, and Becky remembered it was Saturday. It was the night Mary O'Ryan's man was paid and returned home. The latest in a long string of men who had lived with the Irishwoman before moving on, this one was a navigator — a 'navvy', employed on a railway line being built to link up with Brunel's 'Great Western'.

Becky was glad she was not in the downstairs room tonight. This latest man became argumentative after a bout of drinking. If another of Mary O'Ryan's many lodgers was similarly inclined, it usually led to an hour or two's dangerous violence.

Rising from the bed, Becky made up the dying fire. It was late spring, but the nights were still cold. She wondered what the time was. She had heard a church clock strike a great many times, but had not thought to count the chimes.

Pulling the blanket about her again, Becky snuggled down and nurtured her thoughts of Fergus. She hoped he would not be too long in returning home.

CHAPTER EIGHT

'COME ON, SLEEPY HEAD. The boat will be long gone if you don't move yourself. This is what comes of taking over my bed while I'm out working for a living.'

Becky woke with a start and sat up. She tried to focus on Fergus through heavy-lidded eyes but gave up and let her head fall back to the pillow.

'What time did you get home . . . and where did you sleep? I stayed awake waiting for you as long as I could.'

'Three ships came in on the evening tide, and the Hatchet was full of sailors. It seemed as though every one of them wanted me to sketch him. When I came in I slept on the floor by the fire. If things continue as they are, I'll be a rich man by the year's end. Come on now, out of that bed. It's a lovely morning, and we need to be at Cumberland Basin before nine o'clock.'

Cumberland Basin was part of the Bristol dock complex almost a mile from Lewin's Mead, and they would have to walk there.

Forty minutes later they were at the quayside and Fergus was paying their fares to a crewman who stood at the foot of the gently sloping gangplank that linked ship to shore. The sailor frowned when he saw Becky approaching with Fergus. Barefoot and hatless, she contrasted greatly with other young girls boarding the ship. Well shod and wearing hats, most had come pale-faced and newly-freed from sin, direct from celebrating Communion at one of Bristol's many churches.

But Becky's obvious delight and anticipation when she

reached the gangplank and gazed wide-eyed at the sheer bulk of the paddle-steamer brought a smile to the face of the sailor, and the shortcomings of her attire were immediately forgotten.

'This your first voyage, missie?'

Becky nodded, overawed by the size of the great steamer which Fergus was hastily sketching on the pad that was his constant companion. Smoke trickled from the vessel's two tall yellow funnels, and dirty brown water was being gently churned to froth by the huge paddle-wheels, one on either side of the vessel.

'Don't you worry about a thing. By the time we get back here this evening we'll have made a sailor of you.'

Becky smiled at him and then reached nervously for the comfort of Fergus's hand as they stepped from the quay to the gangplank.

Once on board, Becky gripped Fergus's hand even tighter. The deck stretched away for a seemingly vast distance both fore and aft of the gangplank. There were ample green-painted seats, but most of the passengers were promenading along the deck, the ladies enjoying the opportunity to show off their Sunday-best dresses.

Fergus led Becky to a seat by the guard-rails, close to the stern of the paddle-steamer. Unusually subdued, Becky's eyes missed nothing that was going on around them. After a while she whispered: 'Fergus, why does everyone look at me all funny-like as they walk past?'

'There's nothing "funny-like" about their interest. They're looking at you because you're the prettiest girl on the ship, and they're envious of me because I'm sitting with you, holding your hand.'

Becky squeezed his fingers gratefully, and all her doubts were forgotten when loud orders were shouted from the canvas bridge spanning the long deck. Sailors hurried all about them, and minutes later the gangplank was heaved ashore. Mooring-ropes followed, and with the paddles beating the muddy water to a frenzy the steamship edged away from the quayside.

This was the signal for the red-uniformed band assembled

near the bow of the ship to strike up a catchy tune. In that moment Becky became a child again. Dragging Fergus to his feet, she hurried him to where other passengers were gathering about the bandsmen. Displaying a determined energy, Becky forced her way between them. Dragged along in her wake, Fergus mumbled apologies to surprised and indignant fellow-passengers.

Not until she had an unobstructed view of the band did Becky come to a halt. Releasing Fergus's hand at last, she absentmindedly cuffed her nose as she stood watching the musicians.

During a brief lull between tunes, Fergus asked: 'Have you ever heard a band playing before?'

' 'Course I have!' Becky looked at him scornfully, before adding: 'I've never *seen* one, though. Not close like this, I haven't.'

Becky continued to watch the band long after most other passengers had drifted away, men to the below-decks saloon with its alcoholic comforts, women and children remaining on deck. Soon young girls were squealing in mock-terror as small boys on the high cliffs beside the gorge lobbed balls of mud towards the paddle-steamer as it navigated the river flowing through the gorge, far below.

Becky did not tire of the band until the paddle-steamer had successfully negotiated the last bend in the River Avon and was gathering speed towards the Severn estuary.

Meanwhile Fergus had gone to the rail to watch a large sailing ship being positioned for its trip up-river by a diminutive and fussy little steam-tug. As Becky joined him at the rail two children, a young boy and a girl of about Becky's own age, moved along to make room for her. As she took her place the two children tittered and, in a loud whisper that carried to both Fergus and the object of their amusement, the girl said scornfully: 'She has no shoes on. . . .'

The boy made a sound for his companion to be quiet, then he, too, giggled.

Fergus saw the blood drain from Becky's face and he gripped her arm, fearing she was about to faint.

In a strained voice, she said: '*That's* why everybody's looking at me. It's because I've got no shoes on.'

'Take no notice, Becky. They're just unthinking children. . . .'

His words were wasted. Becky's eyes were searching among all the passengers on deck.

'I'm the *only* one with no shoes.'

'It doesn't matter, Becky. I doubt if anyone else has even noticed. You're wearing a prettier dress than any other girl on the boat.'

Fergus silently cursed the insensitivity of the two young children, but they had already moved off to rejoin their mother and an older woman who might have been a grandmother.

'I want to sit down, Fergus. Let's go and sit down.'

'All right, but you mustn't let the foolish chatter of a young girl spoil your day.'

Becky made no reply, and Fergus followed her to a seat that faced outwards on the starboard side of the ship. Here Becky sat down with her feet tucked beneath her, hidden under the seat.

As the paddle-steamer heeled over to make the turn into the wide waters of the Severn estuary, Fergus pointed to the far side of the estuary. 'See that land over there? That's Wales.'

Fergus had last looked at this view when he was on his way to Bristol on board a naval frigate, a week before. The realisation startled Fergus. It seemed he had known Becky for years.

'Enjoy your day, Becky. Tomorrow I'll take you out and buy you the best pair of shoes in Bristol. I promise.'

Becky turned her head to look at Fergus, and for a brief embarrassing moment he thought she would cry. Instead her hand sought his once more. 'You don't have to buy no shoes for me, Fergus. You've spent too much of your money on me already. But I'll make it up to you. Honest.'

'That's better. Now, you just sit here and enjoy the view and the fresh air. I'll go and find some of those refreshments we've been promised.'

Fergus returned carrying a tankard of ale and a glass of ginger beer in one hand, and balancing a plate piled high with a variety of cakes and pastries in the other. Unused to such rich fare, Becky temporarily put the misery of having no shoes behind her, but she did not go unnoticed.

Becky's eating habits reflected the environment in which she had fought a fierce battle for existence for as long as she could remember. Each cake she ate was snatched from the plate, crammed in her mouth whole and swallowed in the manner of a puppy bolting a stolen delicacy.

Among the passengers who watched her in horrified fascination were the boy and girl who had called attention to her bare feet. When Becky looked up and saw them watching her she quickly drew her feet back beneath the seat, at the same time giving them such a fierce look of crumb-embroidered ferocity that they scuttled away and went in search of their mother.

When the last cake had vanished from the plate, Becky mumbled through a mouthful of pastry that they had been 'lovely'.

'They should keep you going until lunch-time,' observed Fergus. 'Come on now, there are guides all around the deck pointing out landmarks and taking parties on guided tours of the ship. Neither of us has ever been on a paddle-steamer before. Let's make the most of it.'

Still self-conscious about her unshod feet, Becky was reluctant to leave the seat, but Fergus insisted. Soon they were in the midst of a crowd of passengers gathered about one of the sailors who pointed out landmarks in the Somerset countryside, on what he insisted upon referring to as the 'larboard' side of the paddle-steamer.

They remained with the same group as the sailor moved to the starboard side of the vessel and gave a vivid and probably inaccurate description of the industries of Cardiff, whose smoking factory-chimneys could be seen on the Welsh coast.

There followed a tour of the ship, from the cramped officers' quarters to the boiler-room, a hot hissing hell-hole filled with coal-dust, escaping steam and gleaming brasswork. In the engine-room they both watched in silent fascination as oiled steel rods that drew their power from the heart of the steam-powered engine elbowed great wheels into perpetual motion.

When they returned from the heat of the engine-room to the chill of the deck it was immediately evident that a change of weather was in the offing. Fergus had been aware of increasing movement in the ship while they were below decks. Now he could see the horizon heaving and falling, and the waves about the paddle-steamer carried white lace on their curling crests. The vessel had emerged from the Severn estuary into the Bristol Channel. There was no land between here and America to hold back the vast power of the Atlantic Ocean.

At first the passengers treated the movement of the ship as a huge joke, laughter greeting each roll of the ship which caused them to stagger drunkenly about the deck.

As the paddle-steamer ploughed on its course and the uncomfortable motion continued, the laughter died away. Passengers sought a place to sit in silence, pretending not to notice the pale drawn faces of their neighbours. Soon the band stopped playing and the musicians filed below deck, carrying their instruments with them.

When a white-coated steward came on deck and called in a loud voice that a midday meal was being served from a buffet in the ship's saloon his announcement provoked groans and hardly anyone moved. Becky was an exception. Turning eagerly to Fergus, she asked: 'Does it mean *we* can eat now?'

Fergus was also unaffected by the ship's movement and he looked at Becky with new respect. 'Of course. Come with me and choose what you want to eat.'

In the saloon Becky worked her way along a long table, pausing at each white-hatted chef for more to be added to the increasing pile of food on her plate. The steward spoke to Fergus in an awed whisper: 'Bless me, sir. It's a good job there aren't too many like her on board. We'd be out of food before we fed half of you.'

'There's not much fear of that today,' commented Fergus. 'Most of the passengers seem to have lost their appetite.'

'Can't say as how I blame 'em, sir,' confided the steward.

'I've no stomach for food myself when the weather plays up. Mind you, there's really no need for us to be out here at all. It's not as though we're going anywhere in particular. Cap'n Clegg could have kept everyone happy by staying close to the Welsh coast instead of coming out here. But "Let 'em get some good sea air in their lungs," he says when the mate suggested we should turn back. "Do 'em good and put colour in their cheeks." He should come down from the bridge and have a look at some of them up on deck now. Not much colour on *their* faces. . . . They ain't breathing any too well, neither. But you can't tell Cap'n Clegg anything. Not when he's had a few drinks, you can't. Begging your pardon, sir, you'd better help your young lady. She'll never carry that lot up on deck by herself – and if she eats it all someone ought to give 'er a bleedin' medal!'

Fergus followed Becky up on deck. She had helpings of every kind of meat – pork, ham, roast beef, boiled beef, chicken, game pie and tongue – all buried beneath mounds of mashed potato and salad, heaped with pickles and topped with a hunk of fresh bread.

A few passengers followed the progress of Becky and her gargantuan meal with unconcealed amazement. For most, food was the last thing they wanted to think about and they turned their pale faces in other directions.

Impervious to the misery of her fellow-passengers, Becky attacked her huge lunch with the same gusto she had shown towards her morning snack. It was more than many of her observers could bear. Among those who rushed for the guard-rail was the girl who had commented upon Becky's lack of shoes.

By the time Becky was ready to sample a dessert, some of the male passengers were beginning to gather in small angry groups, their glances turning frequently towards the canvas-enclosed bridge where the captain stood surrounded by a number of his officers. The buffeting of ship and passengers had gone on for long enough. What had begun as a pleasurable Sunday outing had become a miserable uncomfortable ordeal. It was time to bring the voyage to an end. The ship's captain must be asked to turn his ship around and return to calmer waters.

By the time Becky had consumed a sizeable portion of plum pudding and another glass of ginger beer the conferring passengers had elected three men to approach the ship's captain and ask him to turn his ship about and return to calmer waters.

Seated beside the now replete Becky, Fergus watched with interest as the three gentlemen appointed by their fellow-passengers climbed the ladder to the ship's skeletal bridge and put their request to the black-bearded captain. Fergus could not make out the words used in reply, but no one on the long deck of the paddle-steamer missed the captain's bellow of anger. With the irate commanding officer pointing the way, the passengers' deputation beat a hasty retreat down the ladder to the deck.

Now the knots of passengers grew larger, women making themselves heard among them now. When one of the ship's officers left the bridge he was immediately surrounded by noisy gesticulating passengers, and soon they were joined by another of the ship's officers. Meanwhile, on the bridge, the bearded captain stared straight ahead, ignoring the altercation on the deck beneath him.

Eventually the two ship's officers returned to the bridge, and now it was their turn to experience their captain's anger. He ranted and raged at them while the crowd of passengers beneath the bridge grew larger. Then other officers came to stand beside their colleagues in open opposition to the captain.

Suddenly, with a final dramatic gesture the paddle-steamer's captain pushed the other officers aside and clattered down the ladder to the deck below. Walking with an unsteady gait for which the movement of the ship was not entirely to blame, he strode along the deck pushing passengers aside with the same disdain he had shown for his officers.

When he reached a companionway at the stern of the paddle-steamer the heavily bearded captain clattered noisily down the ladder and disappeared from view.

'What's happening?' Becky had been so engrossed with her meal that she had missed the whole drama involving captain, officers and passengers.

'I think we're about to turn back.'

'So soon? I thought we was out for the whole day.'

Her loudly voiced dismay was overheard by one of the three passengers who had been in the delegation to the bridge. Pausing briefly beside their seat, he said pompously: 'There is no need to upset yourself, child. We are only returning to calmer waters. There is no reason why we should return to Bristol just yet.'

Dropping his voice to a far from confidential level, he addressed his next words to Fergus. 'The captain should never be in command of a passenger-vessel. He's been *drinking*! One of the officers told me in confidence that he is more often drunk than sober during a voyage. It's *disgusting*. I intend taking the matter up with the ship's owners tomorrow. . . .'

At that moment the ship heeled over and began a wide turn in the rough waters. The movement caused the man to side-step away from them, and he continued his progress at an unsteady angle along the long wooden deck.

'Why do we need to turn around? I'm quite happy out here.' Becky spoke indignantly. The rough weather did not trouble her, and it meant that the other passengers were far too preoccupied to concern themselves with the way she was dressed.

'Everyone doesn't have your wood-lined stomach. Come here a minute; you've got gravy streaked halfway to your ears. . . .'

Becky obediently thrust her face forward and allowed Fergus to wipe it clean with his handkerchief.

When he had done she beamed at him. 'I *am* enjoying myself today, Fergus. It's the best day I've ever spent. Can I have another ginger beer now?'

'You're just a belly on legs. If you're not very careful, you'll be bursting out of that dress. All right, stay here and I'll go and fetch you another drink.'

Looking back as he made his way to the hatchway leading down to the saloon, Fergus saw Becky anxiously examining the seams of her dress. Fergus smiled. Becky was a confusing mixture of worldly-wise young woman and innocent child. He had grown very fond of her.

CHAPTER NINE

TWO HOURS AFTER TURNING BACK, the paddle-steamer splashed its way into calmer waters in the lee of the Welsh coast and an anchor was dropped. Soon afterwards the band came on deck once more and colour began to return to the wan faces of the paddle-steamer's passengers.

Before long the crew began to gather children for a game of Musical Chairs. Becky refused an invitation to join in, even though it looked as though it might be fun. She likewise refused to be drawn into a game of charades, or any of the other games being organised for the passengers, declaring she was quite content to sit and watch the merry-making.

Fergus knew it was because Becky had once more become conscious that she had no shoes, but he made no comment. Instead, he sat beside her making sketches of the passengers as they enjoyed themselves.

The games and music continued until a ship's officer announced it was time for the paddle-steamer to get under way and return to Bristol. The announcement was greeted with howls of disappointment. The outing that had so nearly foundered in uncomfortable misery had become an experience the passengers were reluctant to have brought to an end.

So loud and prolonged was the passengers' reaction that the ship's officers had a brief consultation among themselves. A few minutes later it was announced that the games could continue for another hour. The passengers were also reminded that drinks were still being sold and snacks were available in the ship's saloon. This last piece of information caused Becky to brighten considerably and she prevailed upon Fergus to fetch more food for her.

Commenting that the sea air was turning her into a greedy seagull, Fergus set off for the saloon. There was so much happening on deck that he decided to use the nearest hatchway in a bid to find a short-cut there.

Once below decks he could hear the sound of raised voices along a passageway leading towards the stern of the ship, in the opposite direction to the saloon. After listening for a few moments, Fergus set off to find out what was happening.

The noise came from the part of the ship where the officers' cabins were situated, and Fergus turned a corner in the passageway in time to see the black-bearded captain trying to force his way past four seamen. After a violent but unsuccessful attempt, the captain began cursing his men.

'You'll regret this, every one of you. If ever you get out of gaol, I'll make damned sure you never work in a ship again. This is mutiny, you hear me?'

'Sorry, Cap'n. The mate has taken command of the ship now and he says you're not to go to the bridge. Go and lie down, sir. You'll feel better by and by, I dare say.'

'Don't you tell me what I should do, mister. Dammit, twenty years ago I'd have strung you up from the yard and made an example of you. . . .'

At that moment two officers hurried along the passageway behind Fergus. When they reached him he recognised them as having been on the bridge when the captain's authority was unsuccessfully challenged.

One of the officers paused to ask Fergus to leave the officers' quarters, adding: 'Don't worry about what's happening down here, sir. Everything is in hand. If you care to go forward to the saloon, you'll find food and drink there.'

Murmuring his thanks, Fergus moved away, but only a few paces. He was curious to see what would happen next.

One of the officers took hold of one of the captain's arms and tried to lead him away, but the deposed commanding officer shook the hand off angrily. In so doing he staggered and fell heavily against the bulkhead.

'Keep your hands off me. You've taken over my ship; don't

add assault on your captain to your crimes – and crimes they are, as you'll find out soon enough. You can be sure of that, mister. I'll have you in court before you're a day older.'

'You've been drinking, Captain Clegg. Please return to your cabin and remain there until we're back in Bristol.'

'Until . . .? We're never going to *get* to Bristol. It's seven o'clock now, time we were entering the Avon and riding a rising tide to Bristol. Leave it any later and all the pilots will be engaged. I suppose you damn fools have forgotten it's Sunday? Half the pilots are Wesleyans. They won't work Sundays. It's first come, first served to get to Bristol today, mister – and *my* ship ought to have been first in line.'

There was enough logic in the captain's words to concern the officers, but the mate who had assumed command said: 'You let *me* worry about that, Captain Clegg. You return to your cabin peaceably now, or I shall have to ask these seamen to take you there forcibly.'

'Forcibly? *Forcibly?* Why, I'll have your guts for halyards, so help me if I don't. . . .'

At a signal from the mate the seamen closed in upon the furious captain. After a brief scuffle he was bundled away, shouting oaths after the man who had assumed command of the paddle-steamer in his place.

Fergus did not wait to hear any more. Hurrying back along the passageways, he located the saloon and took another heaped plate on deck for Becky.

The paddle-steamer weighed anchor and set off across the Severn estuary no more than half an hour after the incident witnessed by Fergus, but it was another hour before Gibbet Isle at the mouth of the River Avon was reached. It was immediately apparent that, drunk or sober, Captain Clegg had been right. Many ships were gathered here and there was a noticeable dearth of tugs and pilot boats.

With steam-whistle shrieking, the paddle-steamer eased its way into the tidal river before it was brought to a halt by three sailing vessels anchored in the main channel. Then there began a battle of words between the acting commander of the paddle-steamer and the masters of the sailing ships.

The argument ended when the officer on the bridge of the

paddle-steamer telegraphed 'slow ahead' to his engine-room. Paddles thrashed the water to foam as the steamer nosed forward. Only now did the master of one of the sailing ships order his seamen to slacken the anchor chain and allow the sailing vessel to drift clear of the oncoming steamer.

There were other sailing ships anchored in the main channel of the river, and the paddle-steamer proceeded cautiously up the narrowing river until it was opposite Pill, the small steep-sided creek from which the pilot cutters plied. On most days the pilots would be waiting at the mouth of the River Avon, vying with each other for business, but not today. As Captain Clegg had reminded his officers, it was Sunday, and many of the pilots were men of strong religious convictions.

As an anchor rattled down from the paddle-steamer, the acting captain paced the bridge and waited for a pilot to come out to him.

He waited in vain. Pilots for excursion vessels were always arranged well in advance – but no arrangements had been made for the paddle-steamer. Captain Clegg was himself an ex-Pill pilot and he had no need of anyone else to guide his ship through the winding Avon gorge.

By now the tide was on the turn and darkness was approaching. Time was crucial. If the paddle-steamer did not set off up-river very soon, its acting captain would be stranded miles from Bristol with a couple of hundred irate passengers on his hands. He ordered the dinghy lowered in order that two of the ship's officers might be rowed ashore, their mission to find a pilot and persuade him to take the paddle-steamer up-river.

The officers were gone a long time, during which darkness fell. So did the tide. The ship's lights showed glistening black mud on either side of the narrowing channel, and the passengers became as apprehensive as the acting captain who paced the bridge incessantly.

The dinghy returned from Pill creek, and the passengers raised a hearty cheer when they saw there was an additional man in the boat. Their enthusiasm waned when the 'pilot' was helped on board. White-haired and frail, he was as stooped and gnarled as a stunted wind-sculpted winter blackthorn.

It seemed the paddle-steamer's acting captain also entertained doubts about the old man's ability to guide the big ship up-river. After some discussion on the ship's bridge the pilot turned away and was halfway down the ladder to the deck before he was called back again. Time had run out. Responsibility for taking the great paddle-steamer up-river to Bristol *had* to be given to the crippled old pilot.

With whistle shrieking the paddle-steamer was got under way, churning up mud as well as water before finding the centre of the channel. The band was ordered to strike up again, and the upper deck was festooned with lanterns, but the passengers had lost their festive spirit. Crowding the ship's rails, they peered anxiously into the darkness, and when they spoke it was in low nervous voices.

Becky echoed the fears of the majority of passengers when, caught up in the apprehensive mood of those about her, she asked Fergus: 'Do you think we'll make it to Bristol?'

'Of course we will.' Fergus put a reassuring arm about her shoulders. 'I don't doubt that our pilot is the most experienced man on the river. He's probably taken *thousands* of ships through the Avon gorge.'

Fergus was right. The old pilot had spent forty years guiding ships along the winding river that linked Bristol's docks with the Severn estuary. But he had rarely attempted the feat in the dark, and *never* with a ship as large as the paddle-steamer. What was more, he had been retired for eight years because of crippling arthritis. He had been taken on for this trip solely because he was the only man available who knew the river at all.

Even so, the old pilot might have succeeded where few younger men would have dared, had not a small sailing vessel being towed by a fussy underpowered little tug not also attempted to beat the falling tide and reach Bristol that night.

The two vessels were just ahead of the paddle-steamer at the notorious Horseshoe Bend when the sailing ship swung wide. In a bid to correct his course the coxswain of the sailing ship swung his wheel hard over. The vessel veered away from the northern bank – and promptly grounded on the other side of the channel. Straining at the other end of the tow-rope like a terrier on a lead, the tug did not have the power to pull the sailing vessel free and, swinging as though on a pendulum, it, too, grounded on the mud of the south bank of the river.

Faced with the unexpected double grounding, the ageing pilot of the paddle-steamer had to make an immediate decision. It was a bold one. By increasing speed there was a chance that the steamer might hold the channel and squeeze past the other vessels. The great bulk of the paddle-steamer would cause some damage to the rigging of the listing sailing vessel as it scraped past, but this was the least of the pilot's worries.

Calling for full speed, the pilot shouted instructions to the helmsman. The paddle-steamer churned past the sailing ship, snapping off spars and ropes. Moments later it ploughed past the grounded tug, too – but this was the last piece of good luck the pilot would experience. He was a product of the age of sail. His last few working years had brought him into contact with steamships, but never anything as large or as powerful as the passenger-carrying paddle-steamer. Before he could reduce the still increasing speed of the ship it was upon an acute right-hand bend. The sharp iron bow sliced into the mud as efficiently as a knife sliding through butter. The vessel rose in the air, tilting alarmingly, and came to an abrupt halt, scattering passengers in all directions.

The great wooden paddles were still turning at high speed, and above the violent juddering of the stranded vessel the passengers could hear the splintering of wood as one of the paddles fought a disastrous battle with the heavy Avon mud.

The paddles were eventually brought to a halt by the initiative of the ship's engineer, and the ensuing silence was broken only by the sound of steam escaping from a broken pipe.

As the passengers picked themselves up there was a babble of voices expressing anger, shock – and terror.

Half the lanterns had been thrown from their hooks by the force of the grounding, and in the gloom Fergus could not see Becky. He called her name repeatedly and felt great relief when she rose from a pile of sprawling passengers who had been thrown together against the guard-rails.

'Are you all right?' he asked anxiously.

'I think so.' She clutched his arm, seeking reassurance. 'What'll we do now?'

'Stay here and wait for someone to come and rescue us, I suppose. There's nothing else we *can* do.'

'But ... won't we sink, or something?' Becky's grip tightened on his arm. She was genuinely scared. Capable of coping with most things that happened in the rough harsh world of Lewin's Mead, she was lost outside the confines of its narrow streets and alleyways.

'I expect a tug will be sent to tow us back to Bristol when the tide turns. Until then we'll just sit firmly on the mud. . . .'

As though in determined contradiction of Fergus's words a sudden judder ran through the ship. Then a shout went up that the small tug had broken free of both tow and mud. As his small vessel wheezed past the stranded paddle-steamer, the tug-boat captain called out that he would send help from Bristol.

More lanterns were found, and the angle at which they hung indicated that the bow of the paddle-steamer was high on the mud, with the stern well down in the channel. But no one was in any immediate danger, and as their fear seeped away the passengers began to enjoy the unexpected experience of being 'shipwrecked'. Soon the band began playing once more and the ship's officers announced that food and drink were once more available in the ship's buffet.

The party atmosphere lasted for about two hours, until an ominous sound began to make itself heard. The paddle-steamer's structure began creaking and groaning as though bemoaning its own fate, and a whispered rumour went round that the ship was breaking up. The officers were quick to move among the passengers and reassure them, but uneasiness had descended upon the ship once more.

Some four hours after the grounding, lights were spotted on the bank between the ship and Bristol, and as they drew closer many men and horses became discernible. A rescue force was on the way.

A great cheer rose from the passengers – but they soon learned that rescue was still some way off. When the Bristol men reached the bank nearest to the paddle-steamer a shouted conversation began with the ship's officers, and the truth of the situation emerged for the first time.

The hull of the great ship was twisting under the strain placed upon it by the grounding and the angle at which it was lying. Water had flooded the after bilges, adding to the weight. Far from floating clear of the mud when the tide rose, it was feared the ship would sink!

The furore caused by this unexpected disclosure rendered further conversation between ship and shore impossible for many minutes. When he could once more make himself heard, the leader of the shore party assured those on board they need have no fears. He had sent for long ladders. These would be laid across the mud and up the side of the ship. All the passengers would be safely on dry land long before there was any danger.

The news was greeted with mixed reactions by the women, but the men agreed it was better to be *doing* something about their predicament than to remain on board all night in the hope that things *might* be all right.

It was close to three o'clock in the morning before ladders reached the stranded paddle-steamer. Large wooden rafts had been hastily constructed on the bank, and with the aid of ropes stretched between shore and ship the rafts were hauled into position on the mud. Then ladders were laid across them and lashed together, the final ladder extending up the side of the ship to the deck. A rescue could now commence.

Some difficulty was experienced by the women with their long and impractical dresses, but gradually more and more passengers reached the bank, loud in their relief at having safely negotiated the unusual gangplank on their hands and knees.

By the time it was the turn of Fergus and Becky to go ashore the wooden rafts had sunk deep into the mud, causing the centre of the long sagging ladders to touch the surface of the black evil-smelling ooze, and making them dangerously slippery.

By a coincidence, the two children who had commented upon Becky's naked feet were immediately ahead of Becky on the ladders. It had been Fergus's intention to cross ahead of her, but at the last minute Becky pushed in front of him.

When they were well out on the long sagging ladder the well-dressed young girl in front of Becky screamed and there was a heavy *plop* as she fell from the ladder in the darkness. All became immediate confusion as the girl's mother screamed and men from both ship and shore shouted conflicting advice.

It was Becky who saved the day by lying on her stomach and gripping the other girl's hands. Then, with Fergus helping, the girl was hauled back to the ladder.

Instead of being grateful, when the girl regained her breath she accused Becky of deliberately knocking her from the ladder.

'I did *not*!' Becky spoke indignantly. 'You'd stopped. If I'd knocked you into the mud on purpose, I wouldn't have stopped to pull you out again.'

'Come on, we'll get you to the bank and dry you.' The girl's father had crawled along the ladder from the shore to her assistance. 'If you fall ill because of this, I'll sue the steamship company. Why I agreed to bring you all on such a foolish adventure I'll never know. . . .'

'But I've lost my shoes. They're stuck in the mud. . . !'

'*Damn* your shoes. Come on, girl. My God! You stink like a dockyard sewer. Don't *touch* me. . . .'

Fergus smiled secretly in the darkness. For the sneering young girl to have lost her own shoes was an ironic twist of fate.

For a long time Becky lay on her stomach in the darkness, not moving forward. Realising she might have exhausted herself pulling the other girl from the sticky mud, Fergus let her rest for a while, but then the passengers behind him began complaining at the lack of movement on the ladder, and Fergus asked: 'Are you able to go on, Becky?'

'Just a minute.' Her voice sounded muffled, but not particularly weary.

'What are you doing?' Fergus spoke irritably, increasingly aware of the growing number of passengers waiting impatiently on the ladders behind him.

'I'm going now.' Becky sounded suddenly cheerful, and the ladder began shaking as she scrambled ahead.

There was much confusion on the river-bank. Rumour and counter-rumour swept the ever-growing crowd of rescued passengers. Transport to Bristol was being arranged.... Passengers were expected to make their own way home.... They were to await a boat from Bristol.... Fergus and Becky joined the steady trickle of passengers who decided to walk back to Bristol.

It was dawn by the time they reached the city, and Fergus was beginning to feel the strain of the last twenty-four hours. Not so Becky. With her arm linked through Fergus's she skipped beside him as he limped along. Chattering happily about the great adventure they had just experienced, she occasionally hummed some of the songs the band had played – and frequently reminisced happily about the food they had eaten.

As it grew lighter Fergus could see that Becky was covered from head to toe in black mud. He supposed it must have happened when she pulled the young girl to the ladder and he commiserated with her on the state of her new dress.

'Oh, *that* doesn't matter. It'll wash off easily enough.'

Fergus was surprised by her cheerful reply. He had expected her to be upset – angry even. Then he noticed a suspicious bulge beneath the dress, held surreptitiously in place by her free arm. Coming to a halt, Fergus demanded to know what Becky was hiding.

'Nothing!' Becky was indignant, but she tried to work the lump to the side farthest from him.

'Let me see what it is.'

Fergus put on his sternest no-nonsense voice. Reluctantly Becky reached beneath the muddy dress and pulled out a pair of lady's satin ankle-boots that were even muddier than her dress.

'Where did you get them?' Even as he asked the question Fergus realised he knew the answer. 'You *did* push that girl from the ladder!'

'No, I didn't,' Becky defended herself indignantly. 'I didn't pinch these shoes, neither. She left 'em there in the mud, too scared to search for 'em. I wasn't, though ... so that makes them mine.'

Fergus opened his mouth to argue with her – but closed it again without saying anything. Discussing the legal niceties of ownership with Becky would get him nowhere. 'Lewin's Mead Law' weighed heavily in favour of the possessor of disputed property, whatever else the laws of the land might suggest. Moreover, there was a certain wry justice in the situation.

Suddenly Fergus grinned. 'If their late owner is having to walk home, I doubt if she'll ever again mock anyone without shoes.'

CHAPTER TEN

FERGUS AND BECKY made their way quietly up the stairs of Ida Stokes's house and met Irish Molly in the act of letting an all-night client out from her room. Client and prostitute stared in amazement at the homecoming couple, Becky coming in for special attention.

'What the hell have you been doing? I thought you were away on a boat-trip down the river somewheres.'

'Looks like it was low tide and they've walked back. . . .' Even as he spoke the client was bundled down the stairs by Irish Molly, who quickly returned to Becky.

'You'd best come into my room and let me clean you up. You can tell me what's happened while I'm doing it.'

Becky hesitated, reluctant to leave Fergus, but Irish Molly snapped: 'He can clean himself up. I've had enough of sorting out the problems of men for one night. I haven't had an hour's sleep with him who's just gone. I should be looking for tired old merchants at my age, not healthy young sailors just back from six months at sea. Come on, young lady. In there with you and let's get you cleaned up. Holy Mother! You smell worse than the backyard!'

Fergus went up to the attic and cleaned himself up before lying down on the bed to wait for Becky. It had been a strange twenty-four hours. A day and night like no other he could remember. He grinned as he remembered Becky and the way she had behaved on the boat. He had enjoyed being with her. . . .

When Becky entered the room wrapped in a large dress

that belonged to Irish Molly, Fergus was sprawled on the bed snoring loudly.

Becky was disappointed. In her mind she had been practising a special 'thank you'. The boat-trip had been a wonderful treat, in spite of its disastrous ending. She wanted Fergus to know exactly how she felt.

Fergus did not stir when Becky covered him with a blanket. After laying her newly washed dress on the flat window-sill to catch the sun, Becky lay down in a corner of the room. Within a few minutes she, too, was fast asleep.

Heavy knocking at the door brought Fergus awake with a start. As he struggled from the bed the knocking was repeated.

'All right! All right! I'm coming.'

Few callers came to the attic room, and Fergus thought it must be Ida Stokes. Anyone else in the house would have knocked only once, if at all, before walking in. But what could the landlady want? The rent was paid up. . . .

He opened the door and was confronted by Fanny Tennant. Aware he was wearing no shirt, he stuttered: 'I . . . I'm sorry. I didn't know it was you. If you wait a minute, I'll finish dressing.'

'Don't bother, Mr Vincent. I came to find out why Becky hadn't come to school this morning, but I can see the ragged school has slipped *both* your memories.'

Frosty-voiced, Fanny Tennant was staring beyond Fergus. Looking round, Fergus caught a glimpse of Becky's naked body before it disappeared inside Irish Molly's loaned dress.

'You have been less than honest with me, Mr Vincent. I should know better, but I confess to being disappointed. Very disappointed. Nevertheless, I expect to see Becky at school tomorrow.' Turning away, Fanny Tennant started back down the stairs.

'Wait! Let me explain. I'll dress and walk through Lewin's Mead with you.'

'Explanations are unnecessary, Mr Vincent. I told you once before, I try not to pass judgements on people. As for walking with me through Lewin's Mead, I venture to suggest I am safer here than you.'

Having made this observation, Fanny Tennant lifted her skirts above her ankles and disappeared from view around an angle of the stairs.

'Damn!' Scowling furiously, Fergus turned back into the room. 'She's gone away with entirely the wrong idea. That woman is too full of her own importance even to consider she might be wrong.'

'Does it matter what she thinks?' Becky asked the question casually. 'What we're doing here is nobody's business but yours and mine.'

'That's not the point. I don't want her thinking . . . Oh, it doesn't matter!'

'You don't want Fanny Tennant thinking you might care enough to have me living with you. Is that what you were going to say?' Becky looked at Fergus defiantly, but there was just the hint of a tremor in her voice.

'That's *not* what I was going to say at all. She *knows* I'm fond of you. If I weren't, I wouldn't have gone to her for help in getting you out of the police cells. But before she would agree to help me I had to give her my word we weren't living together. I don't like her – or anyone else – thinking I'm a liar.'

Suddenly Fergus grinned. 'Although how anyone might believe I would fancy you in that dress, I don't know. There could be two of you in there without either one ever meeting the other. Get a fire going; I'll go out and buy some food for us.'

Becky smiled, but it had nothing to do with Fergus's humour. He had admitted he was *fond* of her. No one had ever told her that before.

That evening in the Hatchet inn Fergus saw a face he immediately recognised. It was the black-bearded captain of the paddle-steamer, the man whose removal from authority had indirectly resulted in the grounding of the vessel.

Fergus attempted to speak to him, but there was no sense in the man tonight. The only time he was briefly rational was when Fergus mentioned he had been on board the grounded vessel.

'*Grounded*, you say? *Wrecked* is what you mean.' The captain's voice boomed out above the sounds of the inn, and heads turned towards the speaker. 'My officers mutinied and then wrecked my ship. One of the finest vessels ever to sail out of Bristol – and what do the owners do? I'll tell you. They've dismissed *me*. Me who's never so much as lost an anchor in thirty years of command. Dismissed on the evidence of a gang of *mutineers*. It's *them* the owners should have dealt with. Strung 'em up, every lying mother's son. Made an example. Made an example. . . .'

Obadiah Clegg's voice dropped away to an incoherent mumble as he stared down into his tankard. Fergus backed away, leaving the befuddled former paddle-steamer captain alone with his drunken misery.

Returning to his seat, Fergus sketched a portrait of Captain Clegg as the seaman sat motionless, hunched over his tankard of ale. It was a good sketch and captured the utter dejection of the black-bearded man.

Soon afterwards Fergus was asked to make a sketch of an East India crewman for the man to take home to his family. When it was done Fergus looked across the room to where he had last seen Obadiah Clegg, but the sea-captain had gone.

It was not a very busy evening, and as he was still tired as a result of the previous evening's shipwreck Fergus left the Hatchet inn and returned home earlier than usual.

There was light showing beneath the attic door, and when Fergus entered the room he found Becky there. She was wearing the dress Fergus had bought for her, together with the newly scrubbed shoes she had 'acquired' from her unfortunate fellow-passenger on the paddle-steamer. She stood beside the table, her hands hidden behind her back. On the table was a bottle of brandy, a pewter tankard, a small ham and a loaf of shop-bought bread.

Fergus looked at the items on the table with some surprise.

'They're for you. For taking me out yesterday.'

'Where did the money come from?'

'I saved it . . . from the money you gave me to buy the dress.'

It was a lie, Fergus knew it; but Becky was happy, and he was reluctant to spoil the moment for her.

'It's a wonderful surprise, Becky. Just what I fancy right now.' This at least was the truth. Fergus was hungry, and bread and ham were a great improvement on Becky's fried eggs.

'I've got another surprise for you. Here. . . .' Becky brought her hands from behind her back, and he caught the gleam of gold. Then she was holding his hand and placing something in his grasp.

In his hand Fergus held a finely scrolled gold pocket-watch, complete with a heavy gold chain. Becky was watching him with eager anticipation, but the eagerness disappeared when she saw his expression harden.

'Becky, where did you get this?'

Her chin came up in a characteristic expression of defiance. 'It's a present. I bet you wouldn't ask Fanny Tennant where it came from if *she* gave you a present.'

'She's not likely to give me a present, Becky. Certainly not one like this. This is real gold. Where did it come from?'

'You don't *have* to keep it if you don't want to. There's lots of others I can give it to.'

Becky tried to snatch the watch back from him, but Fergus closed his hand about the extravagant present.

'I asked a question. Where has this come from?'

Becky tried to slip past him to the door, but Fergus was too quick for her. He was certain now that the watch had been stolen.

'You'll not leave this room until you've told me where it came from.'

'I thought you'd be pleased with the watch. You *need* one; you've said so more than once.'

Becky was close to tears, and for a moment Fergus weakened. Then he looked at the watch and hardened his heart. It was a valuable time-piece. Someone would report its loss.

'The thought that you *wanted* to give me a present touches me very much, Becky, but I'll not have you stealing for me — and there's no other way you could have got this.'

As he was talking Fergus flicked open the back of the watch. Engraved inside was the name 'Aloysius Tennant' and the date 'October 1821'. Fergus looked at Becky sharply. 'Where *did* you get this? The name in here is Aloysius Tennant. Could it be one of Fanny Tennant's relatives?'

'What if it is? Are you going to tell her I pinched it from him?'

'Of course not — but it will have to be returned to its rightful owner.'

Becky met his gaze unashamedly and shrugged her shoulders. 'Then, I've done you a favour, haven't I? Given you an excuse to go and talk to her. To make your peace.' Suddenly she said: 'I wanted you to have a present, Fergus. Something *special*.'

'You don't *need* to give me a present — and certainly not *steal* for me.'

Becky gazed at him in hot-eyed accusation. 'You don't understand, do you?'

Fergus moved across the room towards her, but with a sudden unexpected movement she slipped past him and reached the door. Flinging it open, she paused for a moment on the top stair.

'You're no different from anyone else. Whenever I try to do something nice it's always spoilt. I hoped you'd be different. . . .' Becky choked on her words, then turning she fled noisily down the stairs to the street.

Some time later Fergus enquired for Becky in the room on the floor below. Mary O'Ryan was drunk and aggressive. She informed Fergus that she had not seen Becky for days, and doubted if her life had lost any of its colour on that account. In the room behind the woman a man crooned tunelessly to himself while two companions quarrelled and a child cried monotonously and fretfully. It was easy to see why Becky was eager to find a place away from the overcrowded O'Ryan room, but it did nothing to help him find her.

It would have been foolhardy to go out and search the

maze of streets and alleyways that formed Lewin's Mead at such an hour, and Fergus returned to the attic, hoping she would return when her anger and hurt had worn off.

Becky did not return that night or the next day, and Fergus spent many of the daylight hours searching for her without success. She seemed to have disappeared off the face of the earth, and no one to whom he spoke would admit to seeing her.

Irish Molly listened sympathetically to his guarded explanation for Becky's disappearance, but she shrugged off a suggestion that Becky might have run off.

'Where would she go? Like most of the urchins around here she's lost outside the alleyways of Lewin's Mead. No, she's here somewhere, but if she doesn't want to be found, then she won't be. She knows this place better than anyone you'll ever meet. Go about your business, Fergus. She'll come back in her own time – if she wants to.'

CHAPTER ELEVEN

THE GOLD WATCH weighed heavily in Fergus's pocket on his way to the ragged school to give his first art lesson to Fanny Tennant's pupils. There was still no news of Becky, although he and Irish Molly had made enquiries throughout the rookery.

The cool reception Fergus received from Fanny Tennant did nothing to make him feel better. She met him at the entrance to the converted chapel, and her eyebrows rose in an expression of exaggerated surprise.

'Mr Vincent! This *is* an unexpected pleasure. I assume you *have* come to give an art lesson to our pupils?'

Brushing aside his mumbled affirmation, Fanny Tennant snapped: 'What of Becky? It was agreed she would attend school. . . .'

'You'll have to ask her yourself – if you can find her. She went out on Monday night, and I haven't seen her since. To tell you the truth, I'm very concerned for her.'

'For *her*, Mr Vincent? I doubt it. I doubt it very much.'

'I haven't come here to argue with you. I'm here to sketch for your pupils – and also to ask if you recognise this.' As he spoke Fergus pulled the gold watch from his pocket and handed it to her.

Fanny Tennant took the watch, and her expression told him immediately that she *had* seen the watch before. 'Yes. It belongs to my father.' She looked up at him suspiciously. 'How did it come to be in your possession?'

Fergus shook his head. 'That doesn't matter. Let's say I'm

pleased to be returning the watch to its rightful owner.'

Fanny Tennant was watching him carefully. 'Becky stole it, didn't she? My father missed it after coming here to inspect the school. He lost his purse, too. He said a young girl bumped into him outside. A girl wearing a grey and red dress.' Fanny Tennant held up the watch. 'Did she leave you because of an argument over this?'

'Becky has never lived with me. She stayed in my room when she had nowhere else, that's all.'

'Be that as it may, my father will be grateful for the return of his watch – but don't expect a reward.'

'None was asked for. Now that's over with . . . I came here to do some work.'

Fergus knew Fanny Tennant did not believe his version of his relationship with Becky, but it did not matter for the moment. It was far more important that she did not pursue the matter of who had stolen her father's watch. Aloysius Tennant was an alderman and chairman of the Watch Committee. A Bristol judge would ensure that Becky received the maximum sentence for the theft of *his* watch. She might even be transported. . . .

He became aware that Fanny Tennant was talking to him.

'You'll be teaching a class of older children, some of the first to attend our school. You'll find them surprisingly bright, but we haven't been able to instil a great sense of discipline into them. It might be better if I remain in the classroom with you for today.'

Fanny Tennant's caution proved unnecessary. The raga-muffins from the Lewin's Mead rookery maintained an air of indifference until Fergus sketched a couple of hastily executed but good likenesses of a few of them. Then the ragged youngsters clamoured to be shown how to sketch one another. Soon they were hunched over their tables, laboriously producing crude sketches. Fergus moved among them as they worked, guiding their primitive efforts and occasionally adding a few lines of his own to make a sketch appear more lifelike. A couple of the boys possessed a raw elementary talent, and Fergus spent extra time showing them a few basic techniques.

Thoroughly absorbed in what he was doing, Fergus was startled when a bell rang somewhere inside the school. Fanny Tennant said: 'That will be all for today, boys and girls. Mr Vincent will be here again next week to give you another lesson, and I'll see you all tomorrow morning. Try to be on time, if you please.'

As the last of the pupils disappeared through the classroom doorway, Fanny Tennant gave Fergus a rare smile. 'Your lesson was a great success, Mr Vincent. It's the first time I have ever been greeted with a groan when I have sent them home from school. I must congratulate you.'

Gathering up his materials, Fergus said: 'A couple of the boys show some talent. They should be encouraged.'

'I have never believed talent to be lacking in Lewin's Mead – only opportunities. But while we're on the subject of talent . . . Don't you think yours is wasted in Lewin's Mead?'

'No.' Fergus tucked his folder of drawings beneath his arm and took up the bag in which he carried his materials. 'We're both educators, in our own way. You're teaching the children about the present, in order to prepare them for the future. I hope that one day my sketches and paintings will show the children of the future what life is really like in Bristol during our lifetime. I want them to realise there's more to it than well-dressed men and women, and tidy Clifton street scenes.'

'You're a strange man, Fergus Vincent. Would these views you hold prevent your from *visiting* tidy Clifton? We're having an informal dinner-party at my home on Friday night. I would like you to be one of our guests.'

The unexpected invitation took Fergus by surprise. Since their first meeting he had felt that Fanny Tennant disapproved of him and his way of life, yet here she was inviting him to an informal dinner with her family.

Fanny Tennant realised something of what he was thinking. She smiled as she explained: 'Not all city aldermen are Tories. My father is a nonconformist in both politics and religion. He enjoys meeting those who choose their own path through life. You'll come?'

Fergus's first inclination had been to decline the invitation, but he surprised himself by nodding his head.

'Good. We will expect you at about seven-thirty.'

Not until he was in the narrow street outside the ragged school did Fergus realise he had not asked Fanny Tennant where she lived. Shrugging the collar of his coat up about his ears as protection against a heavy shower, he thought that the home of Alderman Aloysius Tennant should not be difficult to find. Certainly not as difficult as the present whereabouts of Becky.

Fergus had intended spending the evening painting in his attic studio, but the disappearance of Becky had left him strangely unsettled. The thought of keeping his own company held little appeal. He decided to go to the Hatchet inn and earn himself some money.

As it happened, the Hatchet inn was unusually quiet, and Fergus made only three sketches during the whole of the evening. Soon after ten o'clock he decided to return home. He was about to enter an alleyway that led to the rookery when a tall figure stepped from the shadows of a nearby doorway. It was Constable Ivor Primrose.

'It's a little early for you to be heading home, Fergus.'

'There's no business about. The Hatchet's so empty the "girls" are buying their own drinks. Even the regulars seem to have gone elsewhere tonight.'

'They'll be at the Chartist meeting up on the Downs, together with all but three of the Bristol police force. Tomas Casey's come down from the north to make a speech, and trouble has a nasty habit of travelling with him.'

'Tomas Casey? I don't think I've heard of him, but I must confess I know very little of Chartism.'

Ivor Primrose snorted. 'Ask twelve Chartists what it is they're seeking and you'll have twelve differing answers. For Dr Tomas Casey it's just another means of stirring up trouble for the Government. He's been imprisoned in Ireland for his views, but it hasn't prevented him from being elected to Parliament by his countrymen.'

'He sounds an interesting man.'

'He's an agitator – a *dangerous* agitator. We can do without his kind here in Bristol. . . .'

The tall policeman changed the subject abruptly. 'You must have well-nigh filled your sketchpad by now. Mind if I have a look at what you've done?'

Fergus passed over the sketchpad and waited patiently as Ivor Primrose leafed through the pages, chuckling when he found sketches of characters he recognised and occasionally putting a name to a face.

'You have many drawings of that young lady who got herself into trouble a while back. Is she behaving herself now?'

'She ran off a few days ago. I haven't seen her since.'

Still turning over pages, Ivor Primrose gave Fergus a shrewd glance. 'She's a product of the rookery, Fergus. Expect too much of her and you're doomed to disappointment.'

Suddenly the constable stopped talking and stared down at one of the sketches. Jabbing a heavy finger down on the paper, he demanded: 'Where did you draw this?'

Moving with the pad closer to the gas-light that illuminated the entrance to the alleyway, Fergus stared down at the portrait of Captain Clegg.

'He was in the Hatchet a few nights ago, drinking to drown his sorrows.'

'He drowned more than his sorrows. Someone saw him jump into the dock, but by the time we got to him he was dead. He'd had his pockets rifled at some time, too, and there was nothing left to identify him. He's in the mortuary now.'

Visibly shaken, Fergus said: 'His name was Clegg. *Captain* Clegg. He was in command of the paddle-steamer that ran aground coming up the Avon. At least, he *should* have been in command. His officers relieved him and put him under arrest in a cabin for being drunk.'

'It would seem he got drunk once too often.' Handing back the sketchpad, Ivor Primrose pulled out a pocket-book and began writing. 'I'm obliged for your help, Fergus. If I see or hear anything of your young waif, I'll get word to you.'

CHAPTER TWELVE

FERGUS'S ORIGINAL INTENTION had been to go to dinner at Alderman Tennant's house dressed in his 'everyday best', but at the last minute he gave way to his own misgivings and bought a suit from a tailor's shop not far from the Hatchet inn.

He felt uncomfortable in his stiff new clothes walking the alleyways of the dockside slum. Fortunately the residents of Lewin's Mead had come to accept his presence among them and were even showing proprietary pride in his talents.

So wrapped up was Fergus in thoughts of his appearance that he failed to observe a small figure who watched him intently from the shadows of a Back Lane doorway. When he turned the corner from Back Lane, Becky slipped quietly into Ida Stokes's house. Had he seen her, Fergus would have happily forgone the uncertain pleasure of an evening in Bristol's most fashionable suburb.

The spacious and elegant houses of Clifton were far removed from the crowded slums of Lewin's Mead. Each house stood in its own gardens, occupying a space that might have housed a thousand rookery residents. Built on a hill high above the city they also commanded an attractive view over the surrounding countryside. Having grown accustomed to the narrow streets of Lewin's Mead, Fergus felt uncomfortably conspicuous.

A neatly dressed maidservant opened the door to Fergus, and a moment later Fanny Tennant came into the hall to take him to meet her father and the other guests.

Fanny was a very different girl from the one Fergus had last seen at the ragged school in St James. Gone was the neat austere look. Her long hair hung loose, reaching almost to her waist, and she wore a long pale green dress that was deceptively and expensively simple.

The change in her appearance was accompanied by an apparent shift in her attitude towards Fergus. After greeting him warmly she led him along a high-ceilinged corridor towards a room from which there came a loud buzz of conversation. It seemed a great many other guests had been invited to the 'informal' evening at the Tennant home.

At the doorway to the room Fanny Tennant paused. 'Don't be overawed by my father. He occasionally forgets he's at home and not in the council chamber. You and I are probably the youngest people here, so I will be looking to you for support.'

Fergus realised immediately they entered the crowded room that he was underdressed for the occasion. In spite of the wording of Fanny's invitation most of those present wore formal evening wear – including the host, Alderman Aloysius Tennant.

When the two men were introduced, Aloysius Tennant shook Fergus's hand enthusiastically, saying: 'So you are Fanny's young artist friend. She's told me a great deal about you.'

As Fergus tried to digest this surprising statement, the city alderman's eyes were searching the crowded room. Finding the guest he sought, Aloysius Tennant took Fergus's arm and led him towards a curtained alcove, explaining as he went: 'There's someone here who's dying to meet you. You'll get on well together. Lady Hammond is a great supporter of the arts, as well as being a well-respected expert in her own right.'

Alderman Tennant pushed his way through the crowd gathered in the alcove, murmuring polite apologies along the way. At their centre was a large-bosomed lady of advanced years dressed in a brown velvet dress with a stole to match. Perched on the edge of a hard-padded settle, she turned lively blue eyes on the newcomer.

'Lady Hammond, I would like to introduce a young man to you. Mr Vincent is an acquaintance of Fanny. He's an artist.'

Fergus took the hand that was extended to him and bowed over it, acutely aware that Lady Hammond was casting a critical eye over his clothes.

'What do you paint, young man? Landscapes? Portraits?'

'Portraits, mainly.'

A cynical half-smile crossed the face of the seated woman. 'But of course. Clifton has become a Mecca for portrait-painters seeking commissions.' Her comment brought a ripple of amusement from some of the guests behind Fergus. 'Very well. Bring some of your work to my house and leave it with my butler. I can't guarantee a commission, but you'll have an honest criticism of your work, at least.'

Painfully aware of the amused derision of his fellow-guests, indignation welled up inside Fergus.

'I doubt if my portraits would be of any interest to you, Lady Hammond. I don't paint flattering portraits of Clifton society – or any other society. I live and work in Lewin's Mead, sketching drunken sailors and their women, and dirty-faced urchins who grub in the gutter for food. I paint *life*. Real down-to-earth life as it's lived by thousands of people in your city.'

Inexplicable anger had replaced indignation, and the shocked expressions on the faces of his fellow-guests told Fergus his outburst had gone too far.

As he pushed his way from the alcove someone started applauding and a loud voice called: 'Bravo! Bravo, sir! That's telling them what they should hear, and no mistake.'

Looking up, Fergus saw a diminutive figure dressed as casually as himself elbowing his way across the room towards him. Reaching Fergus, the beaming and perspiring newcomer grasped Fergus's hand in both his own. 'I'm delighted to make the acquaintance of such an outspoken young man.' The Irish accent and his disdain for the company about him gave the man away even before he introduced himself. 'Tomas Casey at your service, young sir. Tell me, are *you* a Chartist? If not, why not?'

At that moment Fergus saw Fanny Tennant hurrying

towards him. Freeing his hand from the Irishman's strong grasp, he braced himself to meet his hostess.

'I'm sorry if I upset Lady Hammond, but —'

'Upset her? My dear Fergus, you've made her evening. I should never have allowed Father to make the introductions. He's dedicated to making money and he thinks everyone else is the same. He believes people only have parties to meet those who might prove useful to them. He forgets some people come to parties simply to enjoy themselves. He honestly thought he was doing you a favour by introducing you to Lady Hammond. She is a very generous patron of the arts. Were you to take some paintings to her house, she would give you an honest appraisal of them and probably buy some, too, even if she didn't really like them.'

'I don't need anyone's charity.'

'*I'm* aware of this; so, too, are my father and Lady Hammond — now. Please, come back with me. Lady Hammond really does want to speak to you.'

'Don't you retract a single word, my boy. Remember those "real" people you were talking of — the ones you and I know all about.'

'No political speeches, Tomas. Lady Hammond has been very generous to you and your cause.'

'That's because she recognises it as a *just* cause. She hasn't bought my soul with her money.'

Fanny Tennant led Fergus back to the alcove, the guests making way for them. Lady Hammond was aware of their approach but she did not look up until Fergus had halted before her. For a moment her glance held his, but he could read nothing in her eyes. Then she patted the empty seat beside her.

'Sit down, young man. Come along, I won't attack you.' She shifted her position slightly as Fergus obeyed her command.

'That's better. I don't know why today's young men feel they have to be rebellious in order to be noticed. Tell me something of your work. Do you *really* live in Lewin's Mead?'

Gradually, with patient and sympathetic questioning, Lady

Hammond drew Fergus's story from him, while Fanny Tennant listened with many of her interested guests.

After hearing details of Fergus's proposed series of paintings about the men, women and children who frequented the rookery, Lady Hammond asked: 'Is it really necessary to *live* in this slum in order to complete this "record of life", or whatever it is you intend calling your sketches? Could it not be carried out just as well from Clifton?'

'No. By living there I become one of them. They behave naturally when I'm around. I also see what's happening and *feel* it for myself. It's important if I'm to put real *life* into my sketches and paintings.'

Some of the intensity of Fergus's feelings came out in his explanation. Lady Hammond was watching him with great interest and she asked: 'How good are your sketches, young man?'

Before he could reply, Fanny said: 'He's very good, Lady Hammond. Very good indeed.'

Fanny Tennant's remarks took Fergus by surprise. He had not realised she had studied his work in any detail.

'Then, I must see some for myself. You have taken on a noble project, young man, but not one to make your fortune. Certainly *not* while you're living in Lewin's Mead.' She gave a faint shudder. 'Bring some of your sketches to my house and we'll discuss the matter further.'

Fergus realised he was once more dismissed, but Lady Hammond had expressed a genuine interest in his work and suddenly it seemed everyone wanted to talk to him. It was a long time before he was able to break away and find a drink.

Tomas Casey was standing at the drinks-table. The Chartist leader had not been without a glass in his hand for many moments during the course of the evening.

'Well, well, well! So they've made you the "belle of the ball" after all, eh? Beware of sudden fame, my young friend. It's no more enduring than a butterfly in a rainstorm. If Lady Hammond hadn't called you back when she did, all you'd have been given would have been the toe of someone's boot kicking your backside through the doorway. But now it'll be "No, Mr Vincent," and "Yes, sir, Mr Vincent," and "You're a bloody genius, Mr Vincent". Hypocrites, every one of 'em. Soft over-privileged hypocrites.'

'Aren't you worried the "hypocrite's" gin you're drinking will choke you?'

Tomas Casey lowered the glass from his mouth and smiled ruefully at the clear liquid there. Swirling it about and allowing the fumes to escape from the tiny alcoholic whirlpool, he said thoughtfully: 'Since I became a Chartist I've choked on far worse. I used to love my fellow-men, Mr Vincent. It's only since I began fighting half the world on behalf of the other half that I've become a cynic.'

'Why do it?'

Tomas Casey shrugged, and then grinned. 'I'm an Irishman, Mr Vincent. I was *born* fighting.'

'Is that all Chartism means to you? A fight?'

Some of the fire that had made Tomas Casey a formidable leader of men cut through the alcoholic barrier he had put between himself and the world, and the Chartist leader became suddenly serious. 'If that were *all* it meant, I could spend a happy life in any dockside town. No, Mr Vincent, what Chartism means to me is fighting to give a working man the dignity that God intended he should have. After all, *he's* made in God's image, too. He should have the dignity to decide his own future. The dignity to play a part in that future and be treated as a man. But before he can achieve any of this he must be given the vote. The *vote*, Mr Vincent, the all-important vote.'

'I know little of Chartism.'

'That's a sad admission from a man who claims to be recording the life of the working classes for posterity.'

'You're right,' agreed Fergus. 'I'll come to your next meeting. When is it?'

'We'll be meeting on Durdham Downs on Thursday evening at about six o'clock. You'll have no problem finding us. Just follow the constables. They'll all be there. If I visit Lewin's Mead in the meantime, where will I find you?'

Fergus gave Tomas Casey his address in Back Lane; then, after thanking Fanny Tennant for inviting him to the party, Fergus left.

On the way home he stopped for a moment on the heights of Kingsdown and looked down at the jumbled moonlit roofs of Lewin's Mead. Huddled close together they seemed to shut out the world about them. He could not help comparing the abject poverty of its residents with the luxuries he had just enjoyed. Champagne and fine foods, consumed in vast quantities by the families of plump and complacent merchants who dressed in expensive clothes and bedecked wives and daughters with a fortune in jewellery.

Then his thoughts turned to Becky. She was somewhere in the crowded slum below him. But where . . .?

CHAPTER THIRTEEN

NOT UNTIL HE WOKE THE NEXT MORNING did Fergus notice that Becky's few miserable possessions had disappeared from the attic room. He clattered down the uneven stairs, and his persistent knocking brought a bleary-eyed Irish Molly from her bed.

'Oh, it's you.' Irish Molly's fingers made a futile attempt to bring some order to her tangled hair. 'I thought it might be.'

'Becky's been back. Her things have gone. Did you see her?'

'I did. Now you've woken me you'd best come in. Get the fire started, and I'll brew a cup of tea. What time is it? It feels like the unholy crack of dawn.'

'It's after nine – but Becky? Where is she? What's she doing? Why didn't she stay?'

Irish Molly groaned. 'Will you keep your tongue still between your teeth for a while? I have trouble thinking of the answer to *one* question at this time of morning. Me poor head's reeling. Make a start on that fire, will you?'

'Tell me of Becky.'

'The child's all right. She's not happy, but there's nothing in the Good Book to say the poor are entitled to happiness. My mother used to tell me that – and there's nothing happened in *my* life since to teach me any different.'

'Where is she staying?' Fergus stood back as flames attacked dry tinderwood in the grate and smoke rolled into the room from an unswept chimney.

'She wouldn't tell me, but she can't have left Lewin's

Mead. She knows too much of what's been going on here.'

'Damn!' Keeping his face turned away from the billowing smoke as much as was possible, Fergus used his foot to push the blackened kettle farther into the fire. 'If only I'd been here to speak to her.'

'She only came to the house because she knew you'd gone out.' Irish Molly eased a grubby slip down over her large hips. 'I told her you'd searched everywhere for her. Said you wanted her back.'

'What did she say?'

'She snorted loud enough to drive the cork back in a bottle of Hollands. She'd watched you going out all dressed up like a dog's dinner and guessed you was off to see your fine fancy-girl at Clifton.'

'Where do *you* think she's staying, Molly?'

The Irish prostitute's head emerged from a rough-spun dress that covered the grubby slip. 'There's a hundred places to hide no more than a stone's throw from this very house. My guess would be that she's in one of the old houses backing on to the river. I've heard that a boat-load of my people came in from Ireland this week and have moved in there. . . . Hey! Aren't you even stopping for a cup of tea?'

But Fergus was gone. Irish Molly shrugged at the closing door and picked up a dirty cup. Flinging the previous night's grouts in the fire, she ran a finger round the rim to remove a couple of tea-leaves, then spooned sugar into the cup.

The area adjacent to the River Frome was avoided even by the unfastidious residents of Lewin's Mead. The river was little more than a sluggish open sewer, and the stench from it was overpowering. The houses backing on the river were a hotchpotch mixture of Tudor and early Georgian, all in an advanced state of decay. They were occupied by the city's vagrants, their numbers recently swelled by the arrival of immigrant Irish families, driven from their homeland by unemployment and yet another failure of the potato crop.

The Irish reacted with suspicion when Fergus began asking after Becky. Few spoke English, and those who did were reluctant to admit to it. Fergus persisted in his questioning until a large number of ragged and silent men joined the group about him. No one made an overt move against him, but they were becoming suspicious, and their very hopelessness posed a threat. Uprooted from their homes by a combination of outdated feudalism and unbalanced husbandry, starvation had brought them to the brink of despair. They had fled from their homes with death never more than half a pace behind them, and the restraints of a law-abiding society meant little to them. Fergus deemed it wiser to end his futile questioning and leave them to their misery.

It was doubtful whether Becky was here and, settling down at a safe distance, Fergus spent a while sketching the listless Irish children who sat in silent misery about the houses.

When Fergus returned to the attic he sat looking at the sketches. He wanted to commit them to canvas immediately, yet somehow he could not bring himself to begin. In some way the children still *lived* while they were on his sketchpad. Re-creating them on canvas seemed in some strange way to be an acceptance of the fate that would inevitably overtake them in their squalid surroundings.

Fergus was fighting his indecision when Irish Molly came up the stairs to the attic. She entered the room without knocking and saw him hunched in his chair in front of an empty canvas.

'Did you find her?'

Fergus brought his mind back to thoughts of Becky and shook his head.

'You came back more quickly than I expected. I hoped you might have had some luck. . . . Holy Mother! Where have you seen children like these?'

Irish Molly was looking down at a sketch of two young children, one sitting, the other lying. Surrounded by filth and rubbish, both had dull dark eyes too large for their pinched skull-like faces. The prostrate child had bones that seemed intent on breaking through his taut skin.

'They're Irish children. I saw them at the houses by the river. . . . Molly, are you all right?'

The Irish girl had suddenly begun to shake, as though she were about to fall in a fit. 'I'm all right. . . .' Irish Molly's voice was hoarse with the emotion she was feeling. 'But *they're* not. They're dying. I . . . I've seen it all before. We were put out of our cottage when I was ten, and came here, to Liverpool, with some others. My father thought he'd find work to do in England. There was no work, and we were all of us moved on from one place to another, even when the smaller ones began dying. Every place we went to the folks were concerned that we'd become "a burden on the parish". They wouldn't feed us and they didn't want to have to bury us. They just wanted us to move on, to go somewhere else. Their consciences could stay untroubled so long as they didn't have to *watch* us die. I had two brothers die just outside Liverpool, and a sister is buried right here in Bristol. My father disappeared somewhere on the road in between. Ma thought he'd run off to look for work. I didn't. I believe he threw himself in the river because he couldn't bear to watch his family starving to death before his eyes.'

'You were the only survivor?'

'Survivor? Oh, yes, I'm a "survivor". I was ten years old when I became a whore – but I survived. I thought times had changed since then – until I saw these sketches.'

Abruptly Irish Molly turned away and ran from the room, clattering at a dangerous speed down the uneven stairs from the attic.

Fergus felt he should follow her. Then he looked again at the sketch that had upset the Irishwoman so much. He stared at it for a long while. Then, standing before the empty canvas, he picked up a brush and began to paint.

CHAPTER FOURTEEN

BECKY WAS DEEPLY HURT and bewildered by Fergus's refusal to accept her 'gift'. True, she *had* stolen the watch, but *everyone* in Lewin's Mead was a thief when the opportunity arose, and she had stolen the watch especially for *Fergus*. He had been kind to her, and she was desperate to give him something in return. She had no money, so the present *had* to be stolen. How was she to know that the man from whom she had taken it was a relative of that Tennant woman? It would not have made any difference to anyone had Fergus *accepted* the gift.

Becky felt that life was unfair. All she had succeeded in doing was to give Fergus an excuse to go and see Fanny Tennant. All right, *let* him go to her. They could have each other. He didn't belong in Lewin's Mead, anyway. He was more Fanny Tennant's kind, whatever he said to the contrary.

Becky spent that first night in a doorway. There was one ugly moment when a drunken man fell into the doorway and landed on her. He made a nuisance of himself when he realised she was a young girl, but she sank her teeth into one of his exploring hands and then used a bony elbow to great effect on his face.

Cuffing a bleeding nose, the unhappy drunk staggered to his feet and weaved his way homewards. Behind him Becky drew up her knees and rested her forehead on them. She was very unhappy — but stubbornly refused to contemplate returning to Fergus and his attic studio.

The next morning Becky was abroad at daybreak. She stole a loaf of newly baked bread from a basket inside a bakery doorway, then wandered about the dockside until it grew busy.

By mid-morning she was hungry again. She returned to the bakery, but the proprietor was more alert now. He told her to 'clear off', emphasising his words with a menacing broom. Becky felt better after giving him some cheek, but she was still hungry.

She passed close to the ragged school and heard the monotonous sound of a lesson being repeated, parrot-like, by a class of children. Perhaps the lesson was being given by Miss Fanny Tennant. The thought reminded Becky of Fergus, and she felt more miserable than ever.

Becky wandered aimlessly round a corner looking down at the ground when a voice said: 'Hello, dearie. It's Becky, isn't it? I thought I recognised that dress. It suits you, dear.'

It was Rose Cottle, the dollyshop-owner, standing in the doorway of her premises. She had seen Becky turn the corner and noticed immediately the dirty downcast face, the unbrushed hair, and the creased dress stained with dirt from the doorway where she had spent the night.

'You're looking tired, dearie. It's this spell of hot weather we're having. Makes us all hot and irritable. What we need is a good storm to clear the air. Come inside the shop: I've got a nice hot cup of tea, fresh made. You look as though you can do with one.'

It was just what Becky needed. Her mouth felt as though she had been eating dry sand. She followed Rose Cottle inside the dollyshop.

'Sit down and take the weight off your feet.'

Rose Cottle knocked a mangy-looking cat with ragged ears from a chair. Taken by surprise, it crashed heavily to the floor, registering an indignant protest. The dollyshop-owner's response was to hook her toe beneath the animal and send it on its way to the door, at the same time saying to Becky: 'Another of me strays. Animal or human, they all find their way to Rose Cottle. I'm a soft touch, dearie. My husband always used to say: "You'll never be a rich woman,

Rose. Never have a penny, you won't, 'cos you're all heart." I don't mind. We're on this earth to help one another, I say. Ain't that the truth, Becky?'

The tea was stewed and barely warm, but it was wet and sweet. Swallowing a large mouthful, Becky nodded. 'Is your husband still alive?'

'Him? No, he was dead before you was born, I dare say. They strung him up outside the New Gaol, down in Cumberland Road. Drew as big a crowd as any of the rioters. There was hardly room to move between the river and the gaol that day.'

Becky looked at Rose Cottle open-mouthed. 'He was hung? What had he done?'

'He'd done *nothing*, dearie. Nothing at all – and I should know. I lived with him long enough. He'd barely got enough "go" in him to get out of bed for his dinner. But they said he'd been waylaying gentlemen riding into Bristol, down Stokes Croft. He was still swearing his innocence when they gave him the drop and he was just as dead as if he'd owned up and told me what he'd done with all the goods he'd pinched. Talking about menfolk, them's a fancy pair of "runners" you're wearing. Did that gentleman of yours buy 'em for you?'

The sudden tightening of Becky's expression confirmed the dollyshop-owner's suspicions. Becky was once more fending for herself.

'I got the shoes myself.'

'That's best, dearie. Look after yourself and you're beholden to no one. I says it all the time to the young girls who come to me for advice when they're in trouble. I've always got a spare bed for them as needs it. Nice little room it is, too. Small enough to feel cosy, but large enough to entertain a gent if you need to earn a shilling or two. It would just suit you.'

'I don't entertain no gentlemen.'

'I never thought for one minute you did, dearie. I was just letting you know as how I'm broad-minded about such things, that's all. A girl needs to earn a living the best way she knows how, these days. Times are 'ard and no mistake – and there's worse ways of earning money. I should know; I've tried 'em all! Have a look at the room, dearie. You'll like it; I just know you will.'

'I've got no money to pay for a room, but thanks for the tea.' Becky stood up to leave.

'Who's asking for money? Have you heard me so much as mention *money*?'

Looking about her quickly, as though someone else might have crept into the room without being observed, Rose Cottle leaned towards Becky and dropped her voice. 'As a matter of fact I was hoping you would take the room in return for a little favour.'

'What sort of favour?' Becky viewed the offer with suspicion, but the dollyshop-owner chose not to notice.

'All the girls around here aren't as trustworthy or high-minded as yourself. They come begging me to let 'em have nice clothes to catch the eye of young dandies in the arcades. Of course, I can't loan 'em such fineries for nothing now, can I? So, to make sure I get my money and the return of my clothes, I make 'em bring the young gents back 'ere. It's only fair, I'm sure you'll be the first to agree. But some of the girls are *greedy*. They're taking men to *other* places, then coming back telling me business is bad and they've had no customers at all. It's not the money I'm concerned about, you understand. But one of these days a girl will meet a careless young man who has a purse full of gold. He'll lose his money, and I'll never see her or my clothes again.'

'What could *I* do to stop it happening?'

'Follow the girls around for me. Make sure they don't take their young gents off somewhere else. You'll be doing us *both* a favour, really. Stopping them from getting into trouble, and looking after my interests at the same time.'

'That's all I'd need do to have a room of my own? Nothing else?'

'Nothing at all, dearie. Of course, if you wished to do some "business" yourself, start earning money, I'd expect you to pay me *some* rent. That's only fair.'

Rose Cottle's wheedling manner was not in keeping with what Becky knew of her character, but she could see very little wrong with such an arrangement. The opportunity to sleep with a roof over her head – in her *own* room – appealed to her.

'Show me the room.'

'Of course. You'll love it, I know. It's one of the best rooms in the house.'

The room was somewhat less than the dollyshop-owner had claimed. Tucked beneath the eaves at the back of the house there was no ceiling between the occupant and the tiles of the roof, and Becky had room to stand upright only within an area an arm's length from the door. She would have rats for company, too. One scampered across the room as Becky entered with Rose Cottle, but rats were nothing new to her. Rats and mice abounded in the gutters and doorways of the narrow streets outside. The room was dirty and had no window, but it had a mattress, a table and chair, and a fireplace – and Becky would not be sharing it with *anyone*. It was undreamed-of luxury.

'Well, dearie, what do you think?'

Becky nodded. 'All right, I'll come and live here.'

'Good! First time I clapped eyes on you I knew you had a wise head on your shoulders.'

For just a moment Becky wondered why Rose Cottle was so pleased, when it was the dollyshop-owner who was doing *her* a great favour.

'When do you want me to start watching the girls who borrow your clothes?'

'This evening. Young Maude Garrett will be along here for certain. Always works the arcades on a Tuesday. Spends all her money over the weekend, I expect. Mind you, she's working most other evenings as well, these days. But you settle in, dearie. Make yourself at home. I'll call you when I want you.'

Becky's call came at seven o'clock that evening, when her stomach was complaining noisily about being empty. Rose Cottle came swiftly and quietly to the small room. 'Maude Garrett's downstairs now, getting dressed. Go outside and wait for her to come out, then follow her – and don't lose her.'

Becky had never seen Maude Garrett before. Had Rose

Cottle not come to the doorway of the dollyshop and gesticulated wildly in the girl's direction, Becky would never have taken her to be a part-time prostitute. Dressed in a ground-length gingham dress, with a light shawl draped just off her bare shoulders, and a demure poke-bonnet covering her mousy-coloured hair, Maude Garrett could have passed herself off anywhere as a respectable middle-class girl.

Others were not so easily misled. Maude Garrett had sauntered half the length of Bristol's upper arcade, not far from the dollyshop when a smartly dressed young man stopped and engaged her in conversation. Minutes later the couple were returning to Rose Cottle's establishment.

Fifty minutes later Maude Garrett 'hooked' another client in exactly the same spot. Once more they returned to a room above Rose Cottle's dollyshop.

On this occasion Maude Garrett did not emerge from the dollyshop until some twenty minutes after her client had departed. By now it was growing dark. Gas-lamps in the arcade were spilling their yellow hissing light on the pavements below, while in the shadows high up in the glass roof pigeons ruffled their feathers and cooed softly as they settled down for the night.

Maude Garrett found her next man in the lower of the two arcades. An older man this time, there was some discussion before Molly nodded her head and led the man away. But she did not take him in the St James direction. Instead, she took him to Broadmead, at the other end of the arcades. At a door beside a shuttered ironmonger's shop she paused, glancing along the street in both directions before ushering the man inside and closing the door behind them.

The young 'dollymop' catered for the needs of her latest client with astonishing speed. No more than fifteen minutes after taking him to the rooms above the ironmonger's shop Maude Garrett was back in the street. The man seemed disgruntled, but Maude Garrett wasted no time placating him. Leaving him standing in the street, she returned to the gas-lit shelter of the arcades.

Twenty minutes later Maude Garrett was leading yet another man up the stairs of Rose Cottle's dollyshop.

When Becky followed the girl through the door, Rose Cottle came out of the room that served as her shop.

'Maude says there was a constable patrolling the arcades and she needed to stay out of his way for a while. Is she telling the truth?'

Becky shook her head, feeling strangely guilty about informing on the other girl. 'She took a man to a place in Broadmead. She wasn't there long, though.'

'Long enough for her to earn a couple of easy shillings, no doubt. I *thought* this was happening.'

'Do you want me to follow her again when she goes out?'

'No, dearie. You go up to bed now. Maude won't be bringing any more men back tonight.'

When Becky hesitated, Rose Cottle said sharply: 'Off you go. I'll deal with Maude Garrett. You've done your part.'

'I'm hungry. I've had nothing to eat since this morning.'

For a moment Rose Cottle's expression might have been one of triumph. 'I've provided you with a room and bed, dearie. You can't expect me to *feed* you as well. Food costs money, and we all have to work for that. I've told you, I don't mind what you do in your room. I'll even lend you nice clothes to wear when you go out – on the same generous terms as I've given Maude Garrett, her as is abusing my generosity.'

Becky shook her head, and Rose Cottle said hurriedly: 'You don't need to make up your mind straight away. But if you don't want to go hungry . . .!'

As Becky turned away the dollyshop-owner said quicky: 'I can't see a young girl go to bed with a complaining belly. There's a tasty stew cooking over the fire in the back room. Help yourself to what you want. Take as much as you can eat to your room; you could do with a bit of fattening up. Think about what I've said. When you're good and ready, I'll find some gentleman who'll treat you nice – and put a gold coin or two in both our purses. Don't you forget now.'

Carrying a bowl filled with stew up the stairs to her room, Becky *did* think of what the dollyshop-owner had said. She had no qualms about getting money in any other way, but for some reason she had always drawn the line at allowing some man to make use of her body. It was the one thing no one had ever been able to take from her. It was also something she could offer to Fergus that had never belonged to anyone else.

CHAPTER FIFTEEN

FERGUS FOLLOWED UP Tomas Casey's suggestion that he attend his Chartist meeting. As the Chartist leader had predicted, the Bristol police were there in great numbers. 'The Downs' were a wide expanse of meadow and scrub overlooking Bristol city, and the police travelled there in black-painted enclosed vans, parking them close to the meeting-place.

There were a great many Bristol residents here. Men and women from Lewin's Mead, St Pauls, the Dings, and the sprawling unadopted suburb of Bedminster. Some had come out of curiosity, others because they had nothing better to do with their time. Very few were fired with passionate Chartism.

There were many women and children among the crowd, too. Fergus hoped Becky might have found her way here, but he was disappointed. However, there were many faces to fill the pages of his sketchpad, and he was soon sketching away busily.

There were a number of Chartist speakers, but it quickly became evident that only Tomas Casey had the ability to rouse the crowd to great heights. The theme of his speech was that every male in the community should be afforded the dignity that was rightly his – the right to *vote*. Using this as a stepping-stone, he went on to declare that a *working*-man was worth ten of those who grew rich as the result of his labours.

There were few 'working'-men among Tomas Casey's listeners. Most were shiftless petty criminals from the slum districts of the city, but they all accepted that Tomas Casey was talking to *them* – even though fewer than half knew what he was talking *about*. What mattered was that Tomas Casey was a brilliant speaker with the ability to reach and hold the interest of every one of his listeners.

Fergus was so busy catching the mood of the crowd on the pages of his sketchpad that he hardly heard a word of the arguments being put forward by Tomas Casey and his fellow-Chartists. Even when large sections of the crowd began chanting an enthusiastic 'Yes! Yes!' he was recording their eager perspiring animation and did not pause to question *why* they were becoming so excited. Not until the word being chanted by the crowd had become 'Fight! Fight! *Fight!*' did realisation come to Fergus that serious trouble was about to erupt.

A loudly chanting section of the crowd formed ranks to confront some two hundred frock-coated police constables, each of whom was armed with a long hardwood night-stick. Many of those opposing the police carried similar weapons.

Fergus worked furiously to sketch the scene of policemen opposing Chartists, but events were already moving too fast for him.

The superintendent of police had been forced to listen to a series of inflammatory speeches, all castigating a government he supported, and espousing the aims of an organisation he personally despised. When Tomas Casey made the waiting constables the target for his wrath, calling them 'tools of an oppressive State, bent on suppressing the just aspirations of the working man', the superintendent had heard enough. He called on his men to break up the meeting and arrest the Chartist ringleaders.

Some of the crowd tried to flee from the advancing policemen but others, seemingly eager for the prospect of a fight with the forces of law and order, forced their way against the tide of retreating onlookers.

Still attempting to record the increasingly hectic scene on paper, Fergus stood his ground for as long as possible – and suddenly discovered he had left it too late to escape the imminent clash.

A stone curved through the air, knocking off a tall black

hat worn by one of the advancing policemen. An instant later their ponderous ordered advance became a charge, and Fergus found himself trapped in the midst of a shouting, brawling mêlée, unable to fight his way clear. As staves and truncheons thudded with increasing frequency upon heads and bodies, Fergus clutched his sketchpad to him and tried to force his way clear of the fighting.

It was not clear whether the blow that felled him came from police or Chartist, but it was both heavy and deliberate. It knocked him to the ground and sent the world reeling about him. Then he was swallowed up in a roaring black void that exploded outwards from his brain.

The loud and insistent ticking of a clock intruded upon Fergus's unconsciousness. The sound was alien to his ears, and it was some minutes before it could be identified by his scrambled mind.

Gradually Fergus became aware of other sounds. Street noises from somewhere in the distance, a faint clattering of pans – and voices. Soft low-talking voices.

Opening his eyes required great concentration. His eyelids were heavy and unresponsive. Eventually he was successful – and became more bewildered than before.

He was in bed in a large unfamiliar room. It must have been dark outside because there was a low-burning lamp somewhere near. He could see the dull indistinct circle it cast on the sculpted ceiling above him.

The voices sounded close, and Fergus turned his head. He immediately wished he had remained still. There was just time to see two indistinct figures standing in the doorway before a headache such as he had never known before forced him to screw up his eyes in pain. When he opened them again an unfamiliar woman was staring down at him. Her face registered approval, but before he could ask any of the questions that were beginning to come together in his brain she had gone.

He heard a door open, and a voice called loudly: 'Miss Tennant ... Miss Tennant! Come quickly. His eyes are open.'

There was the sound of hurrying feet, and then Fanny Tennant was leaning over the bed looking down at him.

'Praise the Lord! I was beginning to believe you would *never* regain consciousness. You haven't even *moved* for three days.'

Suddenly Fergus remembered. The Chartist meeting on the Downs. The fight. But how had he got here? Presumably he was in the Tennants' house? He wanted to ask so many questions, but only managed to croak: 'My sketchbook?'

Fanny Tennant smiled and picked something up from a bedside table. He was afraid to move his head to see what it was.

'Still the dedicated artist! It's here, safe and sound. Ivor Primrose said it would be the first thing you would ask for when you came round.'

That was another of Fergus's questions answered. Constable Ivor Primrose had brought him here. Fergus had glimpsed the large policeman standing head and shoulders above his colleagues when they were lined up on the Downs. But why had he been brought to *this* house?

As though reading his thoughts, Fanny Tennant explained: 'Ivor didn't know where else to take you. He couldn't return you to Lewin's Mead. It was fortunate for you he was near at hand when you were clubbed down. Without proper care I doubt if you'd be alive now.' She saw him wince. 'Does your head hurt?'

'Yes.'

It came out as a painful gasp. Talk of Lewin's Mead had reminded him of a great many other things. Becky. Suddenly his head hurt worse than before.

'The doctor said you would have a very bad headache when you regained consciousness. Your skull isn't fractured, but you received a severe blow and suffered concussion. He's left something for you to take. I think it's laudanum.'

Fergus detested laudanum. It reminded him of the pain-filled weeks spent waiting for his injured ankle to heal. But he was in no position to argue; his head felt as though it might burst at any moment.

Calling on the maid to help, Fanny Tennant raised Fergus

to a sitting position and spooned a large dose of laudanum down his throat.

Fergus sank back on the pillow gasping in pain, and Fanny Tennant was concerned. 'The laudanum should take effect soon. Try to rest and I'll send a maid to fetch the doctor. It isn't right that you should be in such pain.'

Most of her words were lost on Fergus, and by the time the doctor hurried into the room he had drifted off into an opium-induced sleep.

After checking Fergus's pulse and breathing, the doctor straightened up and smiled at Fanny Tennant. 'His heartbeat would shame a drayhorse, and he's breathing well. I don't think you need worry, Miss Tennant. Your young man will suffer headaches for a while, but I don't doubt he'll make a full recovery. He'll need rest, that's all. It will be at least a week before I'll even consider allowing him out of bed, but with such an attractive young nurse in attendance it should prove no hardship for him. If he doesn't enjoy your attentions, then perhaps I should look for brain damage!'

Later that same evening Alderman Aloysius Tennant tiptoed into the room where his daughter sat reading a book by lamplight as Fergus slept.

'How is your young invalid?'

'He hasn't moved since I gave him his medicine, but he's breathing easily. Dr Harrison says all he needs now is rest.'

'He can stay here until he's well.' Aloysius Tennant shifted his glance to the sleeping figure. 'I know you're smitten with this young man, Fanny, but how much do you know of him – apart from the fact that he's living in the worst slum in the city?'

Aloysius Tennant's question was not put in an unkindly way. A self-made man who had worked very hard to earn his fortune and a place in Bristol society, his concern was solely for his daughter's happiness. Father and daughter had been very close since the death of Fanny's mother, some years before.

'I'm not "smitten", as you put it, Father. Fergus is a very talented artist who is working hard to achieve an ambition. I *admire* him. He's also an asset to the ragged school. I want to see him well again.'

'You and that school.' Aloysius Tennant spoke in mock despair. 'Charitable works are all very well, Fanny, but you can't wed a good cause.'

'I'm not looking for a husband, Father. I've told you so, many times.'

'So you have.' Aloysius Tennant looked pointedly at Fergus. 'But perhaps one will turn up when you least expect him. I'm off to a meeting now. Don't stay up all night. I pay servants to perform such duties.'

'You're a fusspot, Father.' Fanny Tennant stood up. After straightening her father's cravat, she gave him a kiss. 'But I love you for caring. No man will ever take your place.'

'I doubt whether there's a father in the land who hasn't been told the same thing by his daughters – but I love you, too. I don't want to see you hurt.'

Fergus's recovery was marginally slower than the doctor had forecast. It was ten days before he could stand, or even sit up, without feeling that his head was about to explode.

However, Fergus discovered it was possible to work in a prone position and he managed to sketch each of the servants who attended to his needs. He even made a sketch of the cook. Brought grumbling from her kitchen, she left the sick-room delighted with the likeness she clutched in pudgy hands. Word soon went around the servants' quarters of the Clifton houses that Alderman Aloysius Tennant's sick guest was a genius.

During the evenings Fanny spent much time in Fergus's room, and he made many sketches of her – far more detailed than those he had made of the servants. They talked a great deal, too. At first much of the talk was of Becky. Fergus had hoped Fanny might have learned of her whereabouts, but as time went on it seemed Becky must have left the Lewin's Mead rookery.

Whenever Alderman Tennant visited the sickroom the talk turned to Chartism, a cause with which he had a great deal of sympathy. Many of those involved in the meeting on Durdham Downs had been arrested. Some had been summarily dealt with and sentenced to periods of imprisonment ranging from one to six months. Others, looked upon as instigators of the violence that had erupted at the meeting, had been remanded for trial at the forthcoming assizes. Search was still going on for other ringleaders – chief of whom was Tomas Casey.

Aloysius Tennant declared the Chartist leader would do well to flee to the remotest hills of his native Ireland. The British government was determined to stamp out Chartist violence. If he were found Tomas Casey would face charges of sedition – a capital offence.

'*Has* he left the country?' Fergus asked.

The Bristol alderman shrugged. 'I don't know, and I must confess I don't very much care. I'm a firm believer in the aims of Chartism, but I won't countenance violence. It certainly hasn't helped the cause. By stirring up trouble at his meetings Tomas Casey has hardened official attitudes and set back Chartism by years.'

'Father, if you continue talking politics you'll have Fergus's head spinning and set back *his* progress, too.'

'You're right, my dear, of course. Quite right. But I *do* want to talk to this young man about his future.'

'Then, I'll leave you to talk for a few minutes – but don't bombard Fergus with questions. His brain has taken a severe shaking. Dr Harrison says he needs rest and *quiet*.' Fanny put down the book she had been reading and left the room.

'My daughter is very fond of you, young man. I hope you're aware of this?'

'Fanny's a very warm and caring girl. The children in the ragged school think the world of her.'

Aloysius Tennant opened his mouth to tell Fergus he had missed the point of his statement, but he changed his mind. 'I'm proud of her work in Lewin's Mead, of course, but there's more to life than what Fanny sees as "her duty". To be perfectly honest, I'd like her to spend less time in that part of the city.'

'But she's doing wonderful work. The children *need* her.'

'They need *someone*, certainly. It doesn't have to be my daughter. Fanny's proved her point. The school is a success.

There's no reason at all why she can't pass the responsibility on to someone else now. She needs to look to her own future. Most young girls of her age are married by now – or heading in that direction. I don't want to see her left behind.'

Fergus was puzzled. Aloysius Tennant was an alderman and Unitarian churchman. He preached the equality of all men, yet Fergus doubted whether he was about to suggest he would approve of Fanny being courted by a penniless artist.

But Aloysius Tennant was a man of many surprises. 'As I say, she's *fond* of you. I don't want you getting foolish ideas because of it, but folks who should know tell me you've got an exceptional talent. I'm willing to put up money to give you a studio here in Clifton. I can guarantee you'll never be short of people coming to have their portraits painted. No doubt Fanny will want to see you get on and will spend more of her time helping *you*. Time spent with you will be time away from Lewin's Mead. Are you beginning to understand me now?'

Fergus's head had begun to ache again, but he nodded.

'I thought you would. You're no fool, Fergus. You've been around – and you've got a God-given talent. Use that talent well and it'll make you a rich man, like me. Then, if you and Fanny are of a mind to wed, you won't find me standing in your way.'

Fergus's head was throbbing painfully now, but he tried to word his reply carefully. 'I think you're underestimating Fanny's commitment to the ragged school. She's —'

Aloysius Tennant held up his hand in a peremptory gesture and silenced Fergus. 'I don't want you to give me a reply straight away. Your brain's still addled from the blow you took, and I can tell by looking at you that I've been talking too long. I don't doubt I'm in for a scolding from Fanny. But I've spoken my mind because that's my way. Think on what I've said. I've made you a generous offer. You'd be a fool to reject it out of hand.'

When Fanny entered the sickroom she saw from Fergus's expression that his headache had returned. Ushering her father unceremoniously from the room, she drew the curtains and ordered Fergus to sleep.

Fergus lay back on the pillows and tried to follow Fanny's instructions, but his mind kept returning to the offer made to him by her father. It was an opportunity that most young artists would have grasped eagerly, and yet ... Fergus was still trying to make some sense of his thoughts when he fell asleep.

He woke suddenly, aware he was not alone in the room. Turning his head, he saw Fanny with a small lighted lamp in her hands looking guiltily at him from across the room. She was dressed for bed, a dressing gown over her nightdress.

'I woke you. I'm sorry. I was in bed when I remembered you had no light. I had instructed the maids not to come into your room for fear of disturbing you.' She shrugged apologetically. 'But that's exactly what *I've* done.'

Fergus struggled to a sitting position, his head temporarily free of pain. 'It's all right. I've had sleep enough to last me a lifetime since I was brought here.'

Fanny placed the low-burning lamp on a table and made a slight adjustment to the wick before turning back to Fergus. 'I am intrigued by the interest Father is taking in you. He refuses to tell me anything of your discussion, saying only that I'll know soon enough, once you have made up your mind.'

'He's offered to set me up in a studio, here in Clifton.'

Fanny's reaction was one of undisguised delight. 'That's wonderful! You'll accept his offer, of course.'

'He wants me to give the matter some thought. But I don't have to think about it. I have to remain in Lewin's Mead. For the time being at least.'

'Why? Father is offering you a wonderful opportunity. People from this part of Bristol would flock to you to have portraits painted once they saw your work.'

'Why don't *you* open a school in Clifton?'

'That's different. There's a great need for a school such as ours in Lewin's Mead.'

'There's also a great need to record the lives of the people forced to exist in such a place. To sketch them in their rags amidst the filth of their surroundings. To show the conditions in which they are forced to live by their appalling poverty.

Their work, their homes. . . . There are millions of people in the land – many right here in Clifton – who are blissfully unaware of conditions in the slums of our cities.'

'Do you think all these sketches of yours can shake the foundations of our society?'

'Ah! Now, that's where I *would* appreciate your father's help. I'll need a gallery to put my paintings on exhibition when they're completed. We might even have some of the sketches published in a magazine. Run a series, perhaps.'

'And in the meantime you'll continue to live in Lewin's Mead?'

'I must. If my sketches and paintings are to have any authority at all, I need to be on the spot to record life as it's lived there. The residents of the rookery won't come to Clifton to pose for their portraits.'

'Is that your only reason for returning to Lewin's Mead? Or does it have something to do with a young ragamuffin named Becky?' For just a moment in the dim light cast by the small lamp, Fanny Tennant looked strangely vulnerable.

'I shall continue looking for Becky, yes. But my plans were laid before I ever set foot in Bristol.'

'Then, I hope you'll soon be well enough to succeed in your crusade – if not in your quest. Good night, Fergus.'

He wanted to tell her once again that Becky was no more to him than a young orphan he had befriended, but Fanny had gone from the room before he could even respond to her 'Good night'.

CHAPTER SIXTEEN

BECKY HAD LITTLE WORK TO DO for Rose Cottle during the next few days. One evening she followed a thin nervous young woman who borrowed clothes from the dollyshop but she brought only two 'clients' to the premises before changing back into her old clothes and hurrying off into the night.

When Becky commented on the woman's brief foray into the world of the 'dollymop', Rose Cottle shrugged. 'You'll see many like her, dearie. Her husband's out of work and she's two babies to feed. Brought up a strict moral Wesleyan, she was. But morals don't fill hungry bellies.'

Maude Garrett was absent from the dollyshop for five days, and Becky received a shock when she saw the young prostitute's face. Maude Garrett had taken a beating. The skin around one of her eyes was bruised, and a cut ran half the length of her lower lip.

When Maude Garrett left the dollyshop Becky followed at a discreet distance. Maude Garrett turned into the higher arcade, and Becky gave her a few moments' lead before she, too, turned into the arcade – and stopped in disbelief. The young part-time prostitute was nowhere to be seen! She could not have reached the far end of the arcade during the brief time she had been out of sight; but Becky had been day-dreaming, more time might have passed than she thought. . . .

Becky began to run, but suddenly a foot was thrust out from a doorway and she measured her length on the hard stone paving.

Becky looked up to see an angry Maude Garrett glowering down at her.

'You bloody little nark! I ought to kick the stuffing out of you, just like Alfie Skewes did to me. How much is Rose Cottle paying you to follow me around? Or are you hoping to take my place? You're welcome to, any time Rose says so.'

'She's not paying me anything. I owe her a favour.'

'A *favour*? Rose Cottle don't do *favours*. She'd stop breathing if she thought there was a penny to be made from doing it. She did me a "favour" once; now I have to stay on the game to pay her off. She'll have you doing the same before you've finished saying "Thank you". What's she done for you so far – given you a cheap dress or something?'

'She's let me have a room.'

'Where? Above the dollyshop? God! I didn't know girls as green as you could still be found around Lewin's Mead. You're living in a knocking shop. Rose Cottle can do what she likes with you while you're there. Complain to a constable and he'll laugh his trousers off when you give him your address. The best thing you can do is run back to where you came from and keep well clear of Rose Cottle until she's forgotten what you look like.'

'Leaving you free to take men off somewhere else and tell Rose Cottle business is bad, I suppose?' On her feet again, Becky brushed grit from a grazed knee and looked at Maude Garrett sceptically.

'Do you think I *enjoy* what I'm doing? Having some slobbering man use me as though I'm a hired horse he's determined to get his money's worth from? You think I enjoy *that*? All right, so I sometimes take men to my own home to earn a few extra shillings. One day I might earn enough to get Rose Cottle off my back.'

Suddenly Maude Garrett's shoulders sagged. 'No, I'll never be free of her. Rose Cottle will keep her claws in me until I'm so poxed I'll be letting Lascars have me against an alley wall for the price of a drink. She'll do the same for you unless you get out now.'

When Becky made no reply, Maude Garrett shook her head. 'You'll learn the hard way, won't you? All right, come with me and see why *I'm* doing it.'

Without waiting for a reply Maude Garrett turned and walked away towards Broadmead. After a moment's hesitation Becky followed.

At the door beside the ironmonger's shop Maude Garrett paused. 'If we meet my pa inside, I'll say we've come from work to pick up something I left behind. You'll back me up, you understand?'

Becky did not understand, but she nodded.

The stairway inside the door smelt of dampness, and with the door closed it was dark, but Becky could hear her companion making her way up a flight of creaking uncarpeted stairs and she cautiously followed after her.

There was another door at the top of the stairs. When it opened it allowed dim light to show peeling paintwork and stained walls. It also released a confusion of noises and unwholesome smells.

A girl's voice, pitched low, spoke from somewhere beyond the doorway, and Maude Garrett replied: 'I've brought someone with me. It's all right, it's a friend. Is Pa home yet?'

'He was, but not for long. He said he was going out to look for work.'

'That means he'll come home drunk again tonight. Make sure Phoebe isn't crying when he comes in. He'll kill her if he gives her another beating. Is she any better?'

'She's been asleep most of the day. The only way we know she's awake is when she starts whimpering.'

There was a cry from somewhere behind the speaker. As Becky stepped inside the room Maude Garrett was overwhelmed by a deluge of children, their ages ranging from about two to fourteen. It was impossible to count them with any accuracy, but Becky put their number somewhere in the region of eight.

Turning to Becky, Maude Garrett said: 'These are my brothers and sisters. Lisa's the oldest and Victoria the youngest. She's two this week, I believe.'

'Where's your ma?'

'She died when Victoria was born.' Maude Garrett feigned indifference. 'We manage all right most of the time – except when Pa's on one of his drunks. They seem to be lasting longer lately. The last one went on for a month and cost him his job.'

'This one's gone on for three weeks and looks like lasting another three!' The information was volunteered by one of the small girls.

Maude Garrett spoke to Becky again. 'I hold down a job making pasteboard boxes during the day. The money doesn't go far among nine of us – and Pa. Lisa knows how I make a bit of extra money. She'll do the same when she's a bit older – but not for Rose Cottle.'

Shaking off the children who were clinging to her, Maude Garrett said: 'Talking of Rose Cottle . . . If we don't get back to her place with a client soon, she'll have her ferrets out for both of us.'

'I'll tell her there were a couple of constables in the arcades.'

Maude Garrett gave Becky a triumphant smile. 'No, you won't. You'll save that excuse for a night when I can make money out of it – I'll see you have a cut, too. But we'd better be off now. Take care of Phoebe, Lisa. If I manage to bring someone home tonight, I'll give you a couple of coppers to get something for her from the stall down the road.'

For four nights Maude Garrett took two clients a night to the crowded flat above the ironmonger's shop in Broadmead. On the fifth night she took only one there before returning with the next to the St James dollyshop.

When Becky came in after her, Maude had gone upstairs and Rose Cottle called Becky into the shop. 'Maude's been slow off the mark tonight.'

Becky shrugged. 'It's the constables. There must have been a new bunch started this week. They're being shown around Broadmead. It was half an hour before Maude dared poke her nose into the lower arcade. They'd have had her in Bridewell for sure.'

'Is that so? If that's the way it is, there's not much sense you following her around all night, dearie. Go upstairs and have an early night. You look as though you could do with a good night's sleep.'

Surprised, but grateful, Becky made her way upstairs and went to bed. She lay beneath the single threadbare blanket and thought about Fergus. She had seen Ida Stokes that day. The Back Lane landlady had told her Fergus had not been seen for some time. Ida Stokes also volunteered the information that his rent was paid up until the end of the month, so what he did and where he went were his own business.

Becky thought that if Fergus was not at the house in Back Lane, then Fanny Tennant would probably know where he was. The thought stirred an unusual emotion inside Becky. Had she been able to put a name to it, she would have called it jealousy, but Becky was aware only that it left her feeling empty and very unhappy.

Becky heard Maude Garrett go downstairs and leave the house with her departing client, then she closed her eyes drowsily. Tomorrow she would return to Fergus's room and see if she could find a clue to his whereabouts. Perhaps he was searching for her! The thought warmed Becky. It was time she made it up with him. She missed him. She must accept that Fergus did not look at things in the same way as other residents of Lewin's Mead and try to understand him. Perhaps ask him to help her. . . .

Becky came awake with a start. Some unusual sound had woken her. Then she saw that the door of her room was open and someone was standing in the doorway. She could see it was a man, and for a moment her heart leaped.

'Fergus. . . . Is that you?' Could he possibly have traced her here? To Rose Cottle's dollyshop? Then the unidentified man gave a chuckle, and Becky's hope became fear.

'I ain't no "Fergus", me dear. I don't even know who he be. But I promise you'll know as much about *me*, come morning, as you do of this Fergus.'

To her horror, Becky recognised the voice of Joe Skewes.

There was an echoing chuckle from another man, already in the room, and Becky sat up, deadly afraid as the man in the doorway entered the room and Rose Cottle's bulk took his place.

'I'm disappointed in you, dearie. You've cheated on me, just like Maude. Betrayed my trust in you. I gave you a good room, out of the goodness of me heart, in return for a small favour, and what happened? I'll tell you – you took advantage of my easy-going nature, that's what you did. Well, it's time you began to earn your keep. You're lucky tonight because I've found two old friends as your first clients. Treat 'em nicely, mind, or I'll be looking for men for you from that American ship that's just come up-river. Word has it that it's been slave-trading along the African coast. The men on there will know how to beat bad ways out of a young girl. They're more used to black girls, o' course, but I don't expect there's too much difference. Not in the dark there ain't, anyway.'

'There won't be no need for that, Rose. Me and Alfie know how to persuade a young girl to behave the way she should. We'll enjoy teaching this one. Alfie would tell you so himself, but he hasn't been much of a one for talking since that madwoman in the Bridewell cells choked him with her chain. You can close the door now, Rose; me and Alfie are used to working in dark places in coal-ships. We'll enjoy this more, I'll wager. Close the door now.'

Becky made a sudden bolt for the doorway. She reached it, but got no farther. A foot came out to trip her and then she was picked up bodily and carried back to the mattress. She fought for all she was worth, using fists, feet, nails and teeth, but she could not match the combined strength of the two coal-heavers. When her dress had been ripped from her body she escaped and made it to the door once again, but she was caught before she could lift the latch.

Maude Garrett heard Becky's cries when she came up the stairs with a client who was too drunk to take any notice of the noise in the room. Maude paused long enough to hear the sound of someone being slapped inside the small room, then her client pushed her ahead of him, grumbling at her tardiness.

By the time Maude left the dollyshop the only sound coming from Becky's room was indistinct low-voiced talking.

Rose Cottle was standing on the pavement outside the shop, and in a sudden burst of anger Maude Garrett said: 'Are things so bad you're having young girls raped to earn a living for you now?'

Rose Cottle's eyebrows rose very slightly. 'Oh, found some spirit at last, have we, dearie? I should save it for your clients, if I was you, they'll get a pleasant surprise – and I don't care for that word "rape". She's paying her rent, that's all. Just paying the rent. I'll have yours while we're about it, and if you don't watch your tongue you'll find the cost of renting a decent dress and a room is likely to go up. Come to think of it, I believe *you're* due another reminder that it don't pay to cheat Rose Cottle. . . .'

Becky was subjected to abuse and humiliation until the early hours of the morning, by which time her mind was registering the nightmare experience from a distance far removed from the sordid little room above Rose Cottle's St James dollyshop.

When both men left the sloping-roofed room, well pleased with their night's 'work', Becky rose to her hands and knees and crawled painfully to the door after them, only to find it securely locked. She collapsed sideways against the door-frame and rested her cheek against the door, painfully aware that Joe Skewes and his son had made free use of their fists in subduing her.

Crouching with her head against the closed door, Becky heard the sound of footsteps passing by outside. After the sound of whispered words, heavy footsteps moved away and Becky heard the stairs creaking beneath the weight of a man.

Suddenly there came a gentle tapping at the door. Fearing it was one of the Skewes men again, Becky sucked in a terrified breath and backed away.

The tapping was repeated, and this time a voice whispered urgently: 'Becky? Are you there?'

It was Maude Garrett.

'Can you open the door? It seems to be locked from the outside.'

Becky could hear Maude Garrett fumbling in the dark passageway, and then her voice whispered: 'Rose Cottle must have the key. There's no bolt or anything. I heard what was happening. Was it because you hadn't told on me?'

'Yes. I've got to get out of here. Can you help me?'

'How? Is there someone I can tell?'

Becky thought immediately of Fergus, but she could not tell *him* what had happened to her, even if he *had* returned to Lewin's Mead. She rested her forehead against the door and felt the hopelessness of her situation.

'Becky! Can you hear me? I can't stay here much longer.'

'Get word to Irish Molly. In Ida Stokes's house, in Back Lane.'

'Where's Back Lane?'

A wave of total despair swept over Becky. She had realised that by sending word to Irish Molly she was merely hoping that in a roundabout way she might bring Fergus to her aid.

There was silence outside the room, and a few minutes later Becky heard Maude Garrett's footsteps going away along the passageway and down the stairs.

CHAPTER SEVENTEEN

BECKY NURSED DESPAIR and an aching body all that day. By nightfall ravenous hunger added to her other problems.

When the sounds and movements in the passageway outside the room told her the evening activities were beginning in Rose Cottle's dollyshop, Becky crawled back beneath the sloping roof and waited for what she knew was in store for her.

She recognised many of the voices she heard passing by the room. Most belonged to older women who paid only for the temporary rent of a room, too worldly-wise to fall into Rose Cottle's dollyshop trap.

It must have been mid-evening before there was a knock at the door. Her heart beating faster, Becky crouched in the corner of the room farthest from the door and said nothing. The knock was repeated, and then Rose Cottle's voice came to her: 'I know you can hear me, dearie. It'll do you no good pretending you can't.' When Becky maintained her silence Rose Cottle adopted a wheedling tone. 'I've got food here for you. Bacon pie and taters. All you need do is show a bit of common sense. We can make a lot of money, you and me. You'll not find me greedy. Fair payment's all I'll ask for. No more, and no less. What do you say now, dearie?'

Becky wanted to shout defiance at the unscrupulous old procuress, but she remained silent, her fiercely clenched fists the only indication of the effort it cost her.

'All right, you please yourself. You'll come round to my way of thinking soon enough. Then it'll be "Yes, please,

Rose", and "No, thank 'ee, Rose". I've seen it all before. Girls like you come two a penny in Lewin's Mead, and without someone like me you'll never be worth anything more. Your friends Joe and Alfie Skewes'll be back soon to help you change your mind. I'll have words with Joe – tell him not to be so nice to you tonight.'

When Rose Cottle had gone away muttering angrily to herself, Becky looked about her in utter desperation. The thought of being subjected to another night's ordeal at the hands of the two coal-heavers filled her with terror. Joe Skewes and his son would not have her again. She would stop them somehow.

But it was as though Rose Cottle had deliberately furnished the room with the imprisonment of young girls in mind. There was nothing Becky could use in her defence. There was no ceiling in the room, only rough wood rafters to which the slates of the roof were nailed. As she turned around, Becky grazed her arm on one of the rafters – and then she saw the very thing she was seeking.

A number of slates on the roof were cracked or broken, and Becky suddenly saw a piece of broken slate about ten inches long and shaped like a dagger. It was low down where the roof touched the floor but, by lying flat and stretching out, Becky was able to work the piece of slate free.

When she finally held it in her hands, Becky felt elated. Her hope was that the two Skewes men would not return to the house – but, if they did, she was determined they would not use her again.

Becky must have dozed off for a couple of minutes before a sound from outside brought her awake with a start. She had no way of knowing what time it was, but light still showed through the gaps in the roof tiles.

When a key turned in the lock Becky gripped the piece of pointed tile tightly in her hands. Then the door opened, and Joe and Alfie Skewes entered the room. Behind them the ample figure of Rose Cottle blocked the doorway.

'Hello, me young beauty. Are you pleased to see us again, eh?'

When Becky made no reply, Joe Skewes turned to his grinning son. 'Where's that bottle you brought with you, Alfie? Offer the girl a drop of "blue ruin". That'll cheer her up. Rose says she's had no food or drink all day.'

Alfie Skewes pulled a bottle of cheap gin from a pocket of the jacket slung over his arm. Drawing the cork with his teeth, he held the bottle out towards Becky.

When she made no move to take it, Joe Skewes sighed, but his expression gave the lie to any implied sympathy. Calling over his shoulder, he said: 'She's a stubborn girl, Rose. You're right, Alfie and me must have been too gentle with her. Tonight we'll give her the full benefit of our experience. She'll be a different girl in the morning, I promise you. Away you go now; me and Alfie have "work" to do. . . .'

Becky knew she had to make her bid for freedom now. As Joe Skewes's hand reached towards her she lashed out with the slate 'knife'.

Joe Skewes let out a howl of pain and snatched his hand back, blood spurting from a gash that extended from wrist to knuckle.

Seizing her opportunity, Becky ran for the door, to find Alfie Skewes barring the way – and he was grinning at her.

Becky struck out at him with blind ferocity, her mind filled with the thought of escape. The piece of slate snapped off in her hand and she let out a scream of tormented frustration that filled the small room.

The sound remained after Becky's mouth snapped shut, and it was coming from Alfie Skewes now. He stood in the doorway with both hands clutched to his stomach, but already blood was staining a larger area of dirty shirt-front than two hands could cover. For a brief moment his hoarse screaming ceased as he took a hand away from his midriff and held it up close to his face. Seeing the blood, he began a hoarse shrieking again, and this time the sound conveyed terror as well as pain.

Rose Cottle, unable to see what was happening, entered the room and collided heavily with the wounded man. Before either could recover Becky was through the open doorway and running for her life.

She hurtled down the dark staircase, tumbling down the

last few stairs. Scrambling to her feet, she fled along the ground-floor passageway – only to be caught up in a pair of strong arms as a number of men rushed past her into the house.

Arms and legs flailing wildly, Becky was lifted clear of the ground. As she struggled and shrieked abuse a voice said: 'Well, now, I do believe we've found what we came looking for.'

It was Constable Ivor Primrose.

From the moment she dragged herself out of bed in the morning until she folded and glued the corners of the last pasteboard box in the sweatshop where she worked, Maude Garrett wrestled with her conscience.

Common sense told her it would be foolish to involve herself with the happenings at Rose Cottle's dollyshop. After all, Becky's 'spying' had resulted in a beating for *her*. On the other hand, Becky was in trouble now for turning a blind eye to Maude's more recent untallied clients. The arguments for and against raged in her mind all day.

Maude Garrett was still undecided as she made her way homewards that evening and found a crowd blocking a narrow road not far from the backstreet pasteboard-box factory. Pushing her way through, Maude Garrett came to where a knot of men were gathered about a brewer's dray. They were trying to lift the heavy wagon in order to extricate a small child whose leg had somehow become trapped between the heavy iron-bound wheel and a leather-faced brake-block. The child must have been trapped for some time, because her screams of pain had died away to a low despairing moan. The moaning reminded Maude Garrett of the sound she had heard through the door of the room above Rose Cottle's dollyshop.

Turning away from the wagon, Maude Garrett hurried away, heading for the narrow alleyways of Lewin's Mead.

When Irish Molly heard the urgent knocking at her door she was at first too frightened to answer. No client would knock that way unless he was drunk, and she did not encourage men to come looking for her here. She preferred to find *them* and bring them back to the house. Besides, there was already a man in her room. He was not a client, and Irish Molly feared the police had come for *him*.

The knocking was repeated, louder this time, and Irish Molly resigned herself to opening the door. If it was the police, they would break the door down and come in anyway. If it wasn't, it did not matter. However, it would be foolish not to take elementary precautions.

Waving the man to a place where he could not be seen from the doorway, Irish Molly called: 'Who is it?'

'You don't know me. . . .' At the sound of the voice, Irish Molly sagged in relief. It was a woman. 'I'm looking for Irish Molly with news of Becky. She's in trouble.'

Irish Molly threw open the door and saw Maude Garrett standing outside looking about her nervously. 'What sort of trouble? Where is she?'

'Can I come inside and talk?' Maude Garrett's glance went to where two Irish children from the O'Ryan room hung over the flimsy banisters looking down at them.

'You cannot. Whatever you have to say can be said as well out here as inside.' Jerking her head in the direction of the children, she said: 'You need take no notice of them. They don't understand a word of English.'

In spite of Irish Molly's assurance, Maude Garrett pitched her voice too low for the children to hear and told the older woman a somewhat garbled story of Becky's plight.

'What does she expect me to do?' Irish Molly asked the question angrily. 'If I go to Rose Cottle, she'll laugh in my face – and I can't go to the police, Becky knows that.'

'All I know is that you're Becky's only hope and it was your name she mentioned.'

Irish Molly knew well why Becky had got word to her, Becky was hoping she would send Fergus to her aid. It might have worked – had she known where to find the artist.

'Damn the girl! She should have more sense than to get herself in a mess like this. Will you be going to Rose Cottle's tonight?'

Maude Garrett nodded.

'Then, tell Becky not to do anything foolish. I'll get help somehow.'

Maude Garrett's immediate relief made Irish Molly realise this girl was herself not very much older than Becky. It was a disquieting thought. Irish Molly was only twenty-six years of age, yet she felt old and weary when confronted by Maude Garrett.

When the young 'dollymop' had gone, Irish Molly closed the door behind her and tried to marshal her thoughts. She had promised to help Becky, but where did she begin . . .?

'What was all that about?'

The voice, carrying the same accent as her own, momentarily startled Irish Molly. Thinking about Becky's problems, she had forgotten that this man, too, was in desperate trouble. Her 'lodger' was Tomas Casey, the hunted Chartist leader. Seeking temporary refuge in Lewin's Mead after the fight on Durdham Downs, he had come to Back Lane hoping to find Fergus. Hearing Irish Molly's accent, he had sought her help instead. It had not been difficult to persuade her to give him temporary sanctuary. Tomas Casey was an attractive and very persuasive man.

Irish Molly looked harassed. 'It's a young girl . . . a child, and she needs help. I know of only one person who can do anything. You stay here and read one of those books I got for you. I'm going to the ragged school to talk to Miss Tennant.'

CHAPTER EIGHTEEN

FANNY TENNANT was not one to hesitate when a situation called for prompt action. Within an hour of Irish Molly's visit to the ragged school a hurriedly assembled force of half a dozen uniformed constables led by the station inspector was on its way from the Bridewell police station to Rose Cottle's dollyshop.

Despite the inspector's protest that no genteel young lady should set foot inside a house frequented by the type of women he expected to find there, Fanny insisted upon accompanying the constables to the St James dollyshop.

She got no farther than the front door before Constable Primrose emerged holding the struggling Becky out in front of him as though she were a disgraced puppy.

Depositing his struggling burden on the pavement in front of Fanny, the tall constable retained a tight grip on her. 'I think this is what we came looking for, Miss Tennant.'

As though aware of her surroundings for the first time, Becky ceased struggling and looked up at Fanny before transferring her attention to the cobblestones beneath her feet, but she was unable to control her trembling.

Taking in Becky's wild-eyed expression, bruised face, and torn and dishevelled dress, Fanny spoke sympathetically: 'Shall I ask a doctor to come and see you, Becky?'

When Becky made no reply, Ivor Primrose shook her gently. 'It's thanks to Miss Tennant that we're here at all. You owe her – and the police – an explanation.'

'I didn't ask no one to fetch *you*. Neither of you.' Still held fast in Ivor Primrose's grip, Becky rounded on him. 'I don't want your help. All I want is to go home.'

'*What* home, Becky? Fergus said you'd run off. He searched for you for days.'

'What business is it of his? I don't have to ask him before I do anything.'

Fanny's nod conceded acceptance of the strength of Becky's argument. 'True ... but it might have helped his recovery had he not been so worried about you.'

'Recovery ...?' For a moment Becky forgot all her own troubles. 'What's wrong with him?'

'He received a blow on the head at a Chartist meeting. It would have had far more serious consequences had Constable Primrose not brought him to my house. Fergus is conscious now and will be up and about before long – but at this moment I'm far more concerned about you. What *has* been going on here?'

Becky only half-heard Fanny's words. Fergus was living under the same roof as Fanny Tennant! She remained silent.

The police inspector came from the house and paused to have a few words with a constable standing at the door. The policeman hurried away, and the grim-faced inspector came to where Fanny Tennant stood with Becky and Ivor Primrose. His first words were directed at Becky.

'I've some questions to put to you, young lady. There's a badly wounded man in a room upstairs. Likely as not he'll be dead before morning. What do you know about it?'

Becky stared silent defiance at the police inspector, and Fanny asked: 'What makes you think Becky can help you?'

'The wounded man is lying in the room where we expected to find her. He's been stabbed in the stomach. He's a nasty piece of work named Alfie Skewes, and I don't doubt he deserves all he's got – but that's not my business. I've sent for a doctor. If Skewes dies I'll need to know the truth of how he came by his wound.'

'Ask his old man – or Rose Cottle. They were both there.'

'I shall have words with them in due course. There's enough evidence inside the house to charge Rose Cottle with running a brothel, and Joe Skewes was a bit too free with his fists when my men entered the room, so I'll no doubt be charging him, too. But you'd better come to the station, young lady. There's a fair bit of explaining to be done.'

'You're not taking this child to the Bridewell,' Fanny said indignantly. 'I didn't ask for your assistance in order to have her locked in a cell. I'll arrange for her to be taken to Miss Carpenter's reformatory at Kingswood. You can question here there – but only if it is absolutely necessary.'

'It *is*. If Alfie Skewes dies, I'll need to question her in some detail.'

'She'll be better able to speak after a few nights in decent surroundings. I have told you where she'll be, Inspector. I would be grateful to have Constable Primrose accompany me. On the way I will try to learn more of what has happened here.'

It was doubtful whether the inspector would have allowed anyone else to dictate to him in such a manner, but he had been a member of the Bristol police since its inception in 1836. Long experience had taught him the dangers of arguing with close relatives of those in authority over him. He agreed that Fanny might take Becky to the Kingswood reformatory.

It was about four miles to Kingswood, and Becky and her companions travelled there in a hansom cab. Seated in the cramped interior, Fanny explained to Becky about the 'reformatory'. At the moment it was part of an experiment in the treatment of juvenile criminals. Magistrates possessed no powers to commit young people here, but many young offenders *were* being sent here with the permission of a parent or guardian.

When Becky indignantly reminded Fanny that she had done nothing wrong, Ivor Primrose said quietly: 'There's a man lying seriously wounded in Rose Cottle's dollyshop, Becky. He might well die. Inspector Treblett would be within his rights to put you in the Bridewell until he discovered what happened back there. I'd listen very carefully to what Miss Tennant has to say, if I were you.'

'Perhaps one day someone will listen to what *I* have to say.' Becky spoke with great bitterness.

'If you have something to tell me, I'll be happy to listen.

According to Miss Tennant's information, you were being held in Rose Cottle's house against your will. Is this so?'

When Becky fell silent again, Fanny said sharply: 'You must help the police in every way you can, Becky. Fergus would say the same. He *will* tell you so as soon as he's well enough to come and see you.'

'I don't want to see him!' Becky's cry startled the others, and the tortured expression on her face told Fanny that no one else would ever know what had occurred in the locked room above Rose Cottle's dollyshop. Whatever it was, Becky would not be ready to face Fergus until the memory had receded into the farthermost recesses of her mind.

Changing the subject, Fanny told Becky what she would find at the experimental 'reformatory' at Kingswood.

Becky said nothing more until they had almost reached Kingswood. Then, in a more subdued voice, she asked: 'If I stay here, it will be because *I've* said I'll stay? Not because I've been sent here like the others?'

'That's right, Becky. But there will have to be a written agreement that you'll remain for as long as it's thought necessary. You'll need to put your signature to such an agreement.'

'Will it say on this paper that I've done nothing wrong?'

Fanny looked at Constable Primrose for an answer, and he pursed his lips thoughtfully before giving Becky a reply.

'We'll word it to say you're in the reformatory because you're in need of care and protection. I think a magistrate will agree to that.'

Becky thought very hard. 'Will they teach me things? How to behave like other people? Like you?'

Fanny reached out and grasped Becky's hand. 'They'll teach you all you want to know, Becky. How to read and write, too. You'll get on well here. I *know* you will.'

When the formalities had been completed in the reformatory and Fanny Tennant and Ivor Primrose had gone, Becky was forced to take a bath, then given an ill-fitting dress of coarse grey material. She was allocated a bed in a dormitory already occupied by some fifteen young female 'criminals', most of them older than herself.

The moment the woman supervisor left the room the other girls crowded around Becky, bombarding her with questions. What had she done? Where had she come from? Had she witnessed the Durdham Downs Chartist riot? Did she know . . .?

Becky was no more communicative than she had been with Fanny and Ivor Primrose. She sat on the edge of her hard bed, unused to the company of so many other girls and feeling out of place in the unfamiliar surroundings. Gradually most of the girls lost interest in the newcomer and drifted away.

Those who remained were followers of a heavily built girl with close-cut fair hair. After a few more questions had gone unanswered, the girl came and stood in front of Becky, looking down at her belligerently.

'I'm Eva Tromp. My father was a sea-captain. He had his own ship. A Dutch ship.'

Becky knew the volunteered information was intended to impress her. It did not, and she said nothing.

'I'm in here for "rolling" seamen. I'd take 'em down some back alley, then when their trousers were about their ankles my man would come out and bludgeon 'em. We got dozens like that before we was caught. Charlie – that's my man – and me were a great team. As Charlie used to say, a bloke can't run after you when his trousers are about his ankles.'

There was polite laughter from Eva Tromp's companions, and Becky thought they had probably heard the same weak joke every time a new girl was admitted to the reformatory. She did not change her own expression.

'While you're here it don't matter how you behave with anyone who's in charge, but you'll do whatever I tell you, unless you want trouble. You got that?'

Becky glanced up briefly at the girl, then looked back at the floor, still without speaking.

'Do you hear me, Becky – or whatever they said your name was?'

The girl's manner was becoming more aggressive, but still Becky said nothing.

The Dutch girl was disconcerted by Becky's silence. Surrounded by her 'followers' the self-appointed leader of the dormitory needed to assert her authority over this uncommunicative newcomer.

'Perhaps she's deaf,' suggested one of the girls.

'Then, I'd better shout in her ear,' said Eva Tromp. She leaned over Becky to carry out her intention – and staggered back as Becky butted her in the face.

Eva Tromp shook her head stupidly and stared in dazed disbelief at the specks of blood the movement spattered on the blanket of Becky's bed. She put a hand to her nose, and it came away sticky with blood. *Her* blood.

'You poxy little drab. I'll teach you to lay one on me. . . .'

Eva Tromp fell upon Becky, and moments later the two girls were rolling on the floor, fighting furiously, spurred on by the other occupants of the dormitory.

The sound of the excited girls shouting encouragement to their champion brought an inevitable response from the staff of the reformatory. Running into the dormitory wielding canes, they swiftly broke up the ring of spectators, and Becky and Eva Tromp were dragged apart and hauled to their feet.

Esther Stott, the principal of the reformatory, had held the post for only ten days. This was the first major test of her authority. She knew the staff were watching to see how she would cope with it, and the knowledge did nothing to boost her confidence. It was all she could do to control the shaking that threatened to give away her uncertainty.

'Who began this?' Her voice, like the woman herself, was thin and high-pitched, and behind gold-rimmed spectacles her eyes blinked rapidly. She felt her nervousness must be apparent to her watching staff.

Becky, bloodied but silent, saw only a tall gaunt woman with hair drawn back in a severe style, who was looking at her as though she were something particularly loathsome.

'I asked who began this fight.' Esther Stott repeated her words, this time including the grinning bystanders in her enquiry.

Still no one said a word.

'We've never had fighting before today.' The information was volunteered by the member of staff responsible for the dormitory. 'Eva has always been particularly helpful in maintaining discipline.'

Her uncertainty gone, Esther Stott turned her full attention upon Becky. 'Did you hear that? We have never had trouble in this dormitory before, yet within an hour of *your* arrival there's a disgusting brawl. What do you have to say?'

Becky had no more to say than before.

'Very well, you'll be put in solitary confinement until you've found your tongue. Take her away, please.'

Looking about her at the faces of the staff. Esther Stott thought she saw approval there. She felt she had satisfactorily passed her first test.

Becky offered no resistance until the women escorting her took her down some stone steps and opened the door of what had once been a small coal-cellar. It had an earth floor and no window other than a small grille in the door. With the main door to the cellars closed the room would be in total darkness.

As the door slammed shut behind her, Becky felt a sudden surge of panic. She did not want to be left in the darkness alone.

'Please.... Don't leave me here. The fight was my fault. I'm sorry. Don't leave me....'

Becky was still shouting when the cellar door slammed shut behind the last of the departing reformatory staff. She shouted until far into the night, her cries faintly audible to those she had left behind in the dormitory.

At first the girls treated the matter as a huge joke, but as the night advanced the joke wore thin and most lay in sleepless silence, listening to Becky's pleas.

By morning the shouting had ceased, and a member of staff was overheard telling Esther Stott that Becky had neither moved nor spoken when bread and water was taken to her.

Expressing satisfaction, the reformatory head declared that a few more days on her own would give the girl time to accept the wickedness of her ways and reflect on the advantages of virtue.

CHAPTER NINETEEN

FERGUS DID NOT LEARN about Becky's committal to the Kingswood reformatory until two days after she had been taken there. Fanny deliberately withheld the news until the doctor had pronounced Fergus fit enough to leave his bed for a few hours.

His reaction was exactly what Fanny had anticipated. He wanted to go and see Becky straight away.

Fanny needed to explain that the reformatory was run on strict lines. Unauthorised visits were not allowed. They could only be sanctioned by Mary Carpenter, the founder and principal of the reformatory, who was ill at her recently acquired property known as the Red Lodge.

Fanny's words made little difference. Although it was already late in the afternoon, Fergus insisted that they call on Mary Carpenter immediately and obtain her permission to visit Becky. Fanny fell in with his plans when Fergus threatened to leave the house and walk to the Red Lodge to see Mary Carpenter.

By the time the Red Lodge was reached in the Tennant carriage Fergus's headache had returned, but he said nothing as he and Fanny were taken to a first-floor room and asked to wait. Unable to sit still, Fergus wandered to a tall window that offered a view over a steep-sloping high-walled garden towards the spires and chimneys about the city-centre dock area.

The light hurt Fergus's eyes and exacerbated the pain in his head. Turning from the window, he came face to face with

157

Mary Carpenter. A woman in her forties, she had a strong face, but it showed signs of a pain as great as his own, and borne for much longer. Yet it was *his* well-being that was her immediate concern.

'My dear young man, your head is troubling you? I have heard all about your dreadful injury. Fanny, my dear, draw the curtains a little. Come and sit down, Mr Vincent.'

'I'm all right.' Fergus's mission was more important than a little pain. 'I've come to seek your permission to visit a girl in your reformatory at Kingswood.'

'One of my girls . . .?' Mary Carpenter looked to Fanny for an explanation.

'She's a new girl named Becky. A young orphan from the house in Lewin's Mead where Fergus has a studio. A few days ago I received word she was being held against her will in a brothel in St James. I informed the police, and they raided the house. Becky was released, but a man in her room was found to have serious stab wounds. The police wanted to take her to the Bridewell . . .' Fanny hesitated. 'You were still ill, so I took it upon myself to have Becky admitted to Kingswood. I felt you would have wished it. . . .'

'Yes, yes.' For a few moments Mary Carpenter displayed a sick woman's irritability. 'You did the right thing – but it makes me wonder what *else* has been going on during my absence, both here and at Kingswood. There's a new supervisor there. How *old* is this girl? Why are you taking such an interest in her welfare, young man?'

Mary Carpenter gave Fergus a look that hinted at an immediate visitation of fire and brimstone should he dare lie to her.

'She has no one else – and I'm fond of her.' Fergus met her question with an honest aggression.

Mary Carpenter accepted his explanation without further questioning. 'Very well. We'll *all* go to Kingswood and visit your young orphan.'

'You're no more fit to make the journey to Kingswood than is Fergus. Neither of you has been out of bed for a full day yet.'

There was a faint glimmer of amusement in Mary Carpenter's eyes when she exchanged glances with Fergus.

'The Lord never intended me to be an invalid, Fanny – and Mr Vincent seems well on the way to recovery. We'll leave for Kingswood at eight o'clock tomorrow morning. I usually walk there, but if your carriage is available I shall be most happy to ride with you. Now you must excuse me. Owing to my "indisposition" the house has been neglected for far too long. There is much work to be done. . . .'

Once back inside the carriage, Fergus sank back in the seat gratefully, his head aching abominably.

'Your Mary Carpenter is a tough lady.'

'Not nearly as tough as she pretends to be. And neither are you. You should both be in bed for a few more days.'

'Time enough for that when I've seen for myself that Becky is all right. . . .'

Becky was *not* all right. When the visitors arrived at Kingswood and Mary Carpenter announced that they had come to see Becky, the school principal displayed such acute discomfiture that Fergus was filled with alarm.

'Has something happened to her? She's still here?'

'Yes . . . but she hadn't been with us an hour before she was involved in a fight with another girl. It was necessary to punish her.'

Esther Stott found it easier to direct her explanation to Fergus than to Mary Carpenter.

Fergus was bewildered. 'You had to *punish* her? But I thought she was rescued from a disorderly house and brought here to safety?'

'This is a *reformatory*. Punishment is an essential part of discipline. Without it we would be quite unable to cope with girls of the type we accommodate here.'

'Miss Stott! Need I remind you that this is *my* reformatory? *My* policy is dictated by principles I consider to be vital. To inflict punishment is to admit defeat – and there is no room for defeat here. *I* have never found it necessary to resort to punishment. I will have a full report on your actions. It will be on my desk tomorrow morning. Now you will be good enough to bring the child to us immediately.'

Esther Stott paled before Mary Carpenter's rebuke, and she had some difficulty in voicing her reply. 'She's still in solitary. I thought —'

'*Thinking* does not appear to be one of your attributes, Miss Stott. This child has been locked away in a room in a brothel, where she was no doubt subjected to all manner of unmentionable abuses. She has come here to be helped back to a normal life – and what do you do? You have her locked away again. No, indeed, *thinking* is something you should avoid, Miss Stott. Where is the poor child now?'

'In a cellar at the rear of the house.'

Mary Carpenter drew in such a deep breath it seemed she must burst. Then the air was expelled in an explosion of anger. 'Take me to her at once. *No!* Miss Hooper, *you* take me there. I don't think I want to look upon Miss Stott again. Quickly now. ....'

One of the reformatory staff who had been listening to the exchange between Mary Carpenter and Esther Stott hurried forward. Taking a bunch of keys from the ashen-faced principal, she led the way to the cellars.

It was dark in the cellar even though there was bright sunshine outside, and Fergus waited with growing impatience while a lantern was found and lit.

As a flustered Miss Hooper tried key after key in the lock of the heavy door, Fergus called through the grille in the door to Becky. When his calls went unheeded he rounded on the harassed reformatory official. 'Are you sure she's all right? When did you last speak to her?'

'No one has been allowed to speak to her. That's part of the punishment. . . .' The woman shook out yet another key. 'Food has been placed inside the cellar, but no one has spoken to her. She shouted a lot the first night, but she's been quiet since. I felt she should have been released. I would have said so. . . .'

A key finally turned in the lock, and Miss Hooper struggled with the stiff iron handle. Impatiently, Fergus stepped in front of her. Using two hands, he turned the handle and swung open the heavy door.

Inside the small cellar Fergus kicked over a full bowl of

cold watery gruel. Two bowls of untouched food stood nearby. Behind him someone brought the lamp to the doorway, and Fergus saw Becky.

She sat crouched against a wall, legs drawn up, her forehead bowed on knees. In spite of the commotion in the doorway she had not moved.

Fergus dropped to one knee beside her. 'Becky, it's me . . . Fergus. Are you all right?'

She did not move. Alarmed at her stillness, Fergus put a hand on either side of her face and raised her head. Her eyes stared back at him, but there was no recognition there. No emotion of any kind.

'Becky. . . . Everything's all right now. We've come to take you out of here. Can you stand up?'

There was no reaction from her and, standing behind Fergus, even Mary Carpenter seemed at a temporary loss as to what ought to be done.

Looking down at Becky's pinched face, as dirty as on the day he had first seen her, Fergus felt pity for her well up inside him.

'My poor, *poor* Becky.'

Fergus spoke in a whisper, but to Fanny it was as though he had shouted his feelings for the numbed little ragamuffin to the world.

Fergus gathered Becky in his arms. For a brief moment she tried to fight against him. Then she slid through his arms to the floor.

Mary Carpenter kneeled on the cold floor beside Becky, and her efficiency returned.

'The poor child's fainted. From lack of food as likely as not.' She nodded grim-faced towards the uneaten gruel in the bowls by the door. 'Bring the girl upstairs – Miss Hooper, send for a doctor, please. Tell him it's urgent.'

Fergus carried Becky from the cellar with ease, appalled at the lack of weight in her body, and Mary Carpenter led the way to a tiny bedroom situated behind the study. On the way they met with a wide-eyed and fearful Esther Stott. Mary Carpenter walked past the principal of the reformatory as though she did not exist. Esther Stott's brief period in charge of the wayward girls was over.

In the tiny bedroom Fergus laid his burden gently upon the bed and then he was dismissed from the room.

Fergus was in the study when the doctor arrived, but he had to wait for another anxious half-hour before he could question the physician about Becky.

'The child is suffering from severe malnutrition. It's a condition by no means uncommon among children brought here from the slums of Bristol.'

'She has also been grievously abused. . . .' Entering the study behind the doctor Mary Carpenter could not hide the anger she felt. 'Those responsible should be transported and forgotten.'

'Has Becky told you anything of what happened to her?' asked Fergus.

'No. She's conscious now, but she won't say a word.'

'Will you allow her to come back to Lewin's Mead? I'll look after her. . . .'

Mary Carpenter shook her head. 'She has agreed to stay in a reformatory. The commitment is not one to be entered into lightly by either side, and in view of her recent experiences in Lewin's Mead she's better off away from there for a while.'

Aware of Fergus's genuine concern, Mary Carpenter added: 'Don't worry, Mr Vincent, she'll recover in due course from *all* that has happened to her. I have seen similar symptoms shown by sensitive children subjected to solitary confinement. It's a barbarous punishment. That reminds me, I have something to say to Miss Stott. I don't want her here at Kingswood for one moment longer than is absolutely necessary.'

Mary Carpenter hurried from the room, her purposeful air boding ill for the reformatory principal. The doctor followed after her, leaving Fergus in the study with Fanny.

'Can I go in and see Becky?' Fergus's question broke the awkward silence that fell between them.

'She's better left alone for a while. It's been a bad time for her. Far worse than you know. Right now I would say you are the *last* person she wants to see.'

Fergus could not understand why Becky should not want to see him, but he bit back the question. Instead, he asked: 'What will happen to Becky now? She'll never settle here after what's happened.'

'Mary Carpenter is opening a new reformatory in Bristol, in the Red Lodge. She intends taking personal charge there. Becky will be the first girl to go there.'

'Will I be allowed to visit Becky?'

Fanny hesitated before saying: 'That's something you'll need to discuss with Mary Carpenter.' After a slight hesitation Fanny added quietly: 'You must not forget what Becky is, Fergus. Don't expect too much from her. She'll hurt you again – not because she wants to, but because she can't help herself.'

CHAPTER TWENTY

FERGUS RETURNED TO BACK LANE the next day. Calling at the Red Lodge *en route*, he was told only that Becky had arrived there but was not yet talking. His request to be allowed to see her was refused. The doctor had ordered strict rest and quiet. Mary Carpenter's staff would ensure his instructions were obeyed to the letter.

The brief reunion with Becky had put a strain upon Fergus's friendship with Fanny. Fergus believed that Becky's ordeal in solitary confinement might have been avoided had Fanny informed him at the time she was found and taken to Kingswood.

For her part, Fanny was of the opinion that Fergus's reaction was more emotional than mere friendship demanded. Nevertheless, she tried to persuade Fergus to remain at the Tennant house until he was fully well.

Fergus argued that it was time he began working again and declined the offer of the Tennant carriage to return him to Lewin's Mead. Arrival by carriage in the narrow streets would immediately set him apart from the other residents and destroy the *rapport* he had built with the suspicious slum-dwellers.

As he climbed the stairs to his attic studio, Fergus was inclined to question the wisdom of his own decision. The stairs were littered with rubbish and filth of every description; the stale, stomach-churning stench of cooked cabbage hung heavily on the air, and a noisy argument could be heard above the crying of children in Mary O'Ryan's room. The opulence of the Tennants' Clifton home and the squalor of the Back Lane house were worlds apart.

Thoughts of Becky were still foremost in Fergus's mind, and the first thing he saw when he entered his room was her half-completed portrait standing on the easel by a window. Fifteen minutes later he was working on the painting and the remainder of the world was temporarily forgotten.

Fergus was still painting when Irish Molly entered the attic room, an hour and a half later. She did not knock, and Fergus was so engrossed in his work that he was not aware of her presence until she stood beside him, staring at the portrait with awe in her eyes.

'What a *beautiful* painting. I've never seen anything like it. . . . But where *is* Becky? Is the child all right?'

Fergus looked at her with the abstract expression of a man woken from a particularly absorbing dream. Then he put down his brush.

'No, she's not all right – although everyone keeps telling me she'll improve with rest.'

Fergus told Irish Molly of Becky's experience after the police raid on Rose Cottle's St James brothel.

As he ended his story, Irish Molly exploded in anger. 'I knew it! All the time I was telling that Miss Tennant about Becky, something inside me was saying that no good would come of calling in the po-lice. It never does. All they're interested in is *arresting* people. Poor Becky, I should have minded my own business.'

'You did the right thing, Molly. Everyone did. Becky couldn't keep running. Things went very wrong at Kingswood, that's all.'

'Talking of people running . . .' Irish Molly dropped her voice as though they were surrounded by people. 'I believe you know Dr Casey? Dr *Tomas* Casey?'

Fergus's hand went to his head, and he said ruefully: 'Yes, I know him. Thanks to his brand of Chartism, I've spent the past couple of weeks laid up with a sore head.'

Irish Molly looked at Fergus in dismay. 'Does that mean you'd like to see him caught by the po-lice?'

Fergus shook his head. 'No. He's an honest enough man,

and he has a just cause. It's his methods I question. But what's all this about? I wasn't aware *you* knew Tomas Casey.'

Irish Molly ignored the question. 'What would you do if he came to you and asked for your help?'

'Molly, are you telling me you know where he is?'

'Would you help him?' Irish Molly persisted doggedly with her own line of questioning.

'Of course I would. If he's caught, he'll be hanged for sedition. He's done nothing to deserve that.'

Irish Molly sagged with relief, and Fergus said: 'You *do* know where he is! I think you'd better tell me what this is all about.'

'He's downstairs in my room.' Irish Molly was relieved to be able to share her secret with someone. Hiding Tomas Casey was proving a great strain for her.

Fergus could scarcely hide his disbelief, and Irish Molly added: 'He came here looking for you, but we discovered we're both from the same part of Ireland. He knew my father . . . in better days. Can I tell him you'll help him?'

After only a moment's hesitation, Fergus nodded. 'He'd better come up and see me. Tell him to wait an hour. It will be dark then and there'll be no risk of any of the O'Ryans seeing him.'

Halfway down the stairs, Irish Molly paused to call back: 'I'm sorry about Becky, truly I am. I'd hoped she might escape from the rookery through you. But there's no escaping, is there? Not for the likes of her and me, there ain't.'

Irish Molly's parting comments gave Fergus much food for thought. He would not argue that Becky was a product of the Lewin's Mead slum. It was something he had always accepted. But to suggest that she and Irish Molly had anything in common . . . He looked at the unfinished portrait and picked up his brush again. No, it was *not* true. He would not allow Becky to travel the same path.

Fergus was finally forced to accept that the light was too poor for him to continue painting any longer. After cleaning his brushes he lit a lamp and turned his attention to the fire.

Some twigs had just begun to crackle cheerfully when the door opened and Tomas Casey entered the attic studio.

The Chartist leader had not shaved since his escape from Durdham Downs, and a full red curly beard now hid his sharp features, but the bright intelligent eyes had not lost their humour.

'Well, well, well! It's nice to see you again, Fergus. It's a fine place you have here.'

'Not up to Clifton standards, perhaps, but it's home.'

'Ah, yes! I hear you've been nursed back to health by the delightful Fanny. That was a terrible blow you took on the head from a constable. Terrible. I saw it all. The way they laid into us, I swear they were out to kill someone, so they were. And you just standing there minding your own business! I hope you complained to Fanny's father, him being the chairman of the Watch Committee, and all.'

'I'm not certain it *was* a constable. It could just as easily have been a Chartist. Your men were wielding stakes with as much enthusiasm as the police.'

'It was the police, I'm telling you. Haven't I just said I saw it all?'

'Only moments before I was struck down I saw you busily engaged in sending some of your men to head off a band of constables. You weren't even looking in my direction.'

'Wasn't I now?' Tomas Casey grinned unashamedly. 'Well, I don't need to jump into the ocean to know it's wet; and tell me, why would any Chartist want to hit *you* over the head?'

Fergus ignored the question. 'Irish Molly says you have need of my help. What is it you want me to do?'

'Ah!' Tomas Casey appeared mildly embarrassed. 'Well, now, there are one or two small problems in my life at the moment – as you'll appreciate. The most pressing, and embarrassing, is a temporary shortage of funds. Molly's a good girl – figuratively speaking, of course – and more than willing to help a fellow-countryman when he's in trouble, but she's a working girl. I fear I've prevented her from pursuing her . . . "profession"? As she so rightly reminds me from time to time, she has rent to pay and food to buy.'

'Will five guineas help?' Fergus pulled out the money-pouch he kept hanging on a thong inside his shirt.

'Could you make it ten? I'll give you an IOU, of course. I'm not short of funds, you understand, but they aren't immediately to hand.'

Fergus counted out ten sovereigns and passed them to Tomas Casey.

'God bless you, Fergus. You're a gentleman.'

'Ten guineas might solve your immediate problems, but what of the future? You can't spend the rest of your life hiding in Irish Molly's room.'

'True, Fergus – but I'm hoping you might be of some assistance in this matter, too.'

Something of Fergus's misgivings must have shown, because Tomas Casey said hurriedly: 'It's only a little thing. It need hardly take any of your time at all.'

Fishing a folded piece of paper from his pocket, the Chartist leader handed it to Fergus. 'Here's a list of Irish ships trading into Bristol whose captains are known to me. If any of them is in harbour at the moment, I'd like you to take a message to the captain for me.'

'Don't you think a watch will be kept on the docks for you?'

Tomas Casey shrugged. 'Perhaps. But they'll be looking for a Chartist leader, not a bearded seaman.'

Fergus tucked the paper in a pocket. 'I'll have a look around the docks tomorrow. It will be safer than asking questions.'

'Good lad. Now I'd like to see some of these pictures of yours, and you can talk to me while you're showing them. Molly's a big-hearted girl, but she's no conversationalist. Comment on the weather, the cost of food, and how many prostitutes were arrested during the night and you've exhausted her conversation for the day.'

CHAPTER TWENTY-ONE

NONE OF THE SHIPS listed by Tomas Casey was in Bristol, nor did they visit the West Country port during the ensuing week. In the meantime Tomas Casey borrowed another five guineas from Fergus, while Irish Molly became increasingly unhappy about the effect her lodger was having on her trade. She complained she was losing regular clients to younger girls who were constantly swelling the ranks of Bristol's prostitutes, and who owed no loyalty to the loose-knit fraternity to which they belonged.

Molly suggested Tomas Casey should move to the attic room, but Fergus refused to consider the suggestion. The Irish Chartist leader was too garrulous to have in the tiny attic room. Fergus was working hard on his paintings; Tomas Casey would be a calamitous distraction.

Fergus also nursed a forlorn hope that Becky might be allowed to return to Ida Stokes's house in Back Lane, even though common sense told him Becky was likely to remain at the new Red Lodge reformatory for a long time yet.

Alfie Skewes was on the road to recovery now and had wisely refused to consider charges against Becky. However, the circumstances surrounding Becky's 'rescue', together with her mark on a magistrate's agreement, were enough to keep her in Mary Carpenter's care.

Fergus had still not been allowed to visit Becky. Mary Carpenter was in London for a few days, and on the two occasions when Fergus called at the Red Lodge he was told only that Becky was 'making satisfactory progress'.

However, she was still confined to bed and no visitors were being allowed.

Fanny, too, proved suddenly elusive. She was not at the ragged school when Fergus took his weekly art lesson, and her staff claimed not to know when she was likely to be available.

Then, nine days after Fergus's return to Lewin's Mead, he was checking the docks when he saw one of the ships on Tomas Casey's list. *Lady of Wexford* was berthed in the part of the docks that extended into the very heart of Bristol, hardly a stone's throw from Lewin's Mead.

According to the Chartist leader, the captain of the ship should be one Henry Kennedy. The vessel was moored outside two others, and Fergus boarded it with some difficulty. He could see no sign of activity on board, but when he was beginning to think the boat was deserted a man wearing a soft woollen hat, dirty corduroy trousers and a badly holed blue jersey emerged from a hatchway.

When Fergus asked whether Captain Kennedy was on board, the seaman's glance rested on Fergus for only a second before he asked: 'Who'd be wanting him?'

'A friend of mine – he's a friend of the captain, too, I believe.'

'Would this "friend" be having a name?'

Fergus looked about him quickly. There were men working on the other ships and on the quayside above them. 'It might be better if I spoke to Captain Kennedy.'

'I'm Henry Kennedy, and *Lady of Wexford*'s not in Bristol to entertain visitors. If your business can't be spoken of out loud, then I don't want to hear about it at all.'

Captain Kennedy picked up a heavy coil of rope and began dragging it towards the ship's stern. Moving along with him, Fergus tried again. 'This friend needs your help. He asked me *to find you. . . .'*

'It's surprising how many friends I find in foreign ports, and every one of them in some sort of trouble.'

Pulling a spliced loop from the coil, Captain Kennedy handed it to Fergus. 'Take this and put it over that bollard on your way ashore. My crew were so eager to go landside we're not even half-secured.'

As the Irish sea-captain handed the rope-end to Fergus, he said in a low voice: 'Name an inn where I can meet you this evening.'

In an equally low voice, Fergus replied: 'The Hatchet inn, Frogmore Street.'

Straightening up, the Irish captain said loudly: 'I'm sorry I can't help your friend.' With this he turned and picked his way across the deck of *Lady of Wexford*. Moments later he clattered down the steps of another hatchway and was lost from view. Limping slowly from the quayside, Fergus observed a small nondescript man taking a great interest in the dirty water lapping around *Lady of Wexford*'s bow. He remembered there were large rewards out for a number of prominent Chartists who had been present at the Durdham Downs meeting – and the largest reward of all was for the apprehension of Dr Tomas Casey.

Captain Kennedy came to the Hatchet inn soon after eight o'clock that evening. After watching Fergus at work for a while he said he would like to have Fergus make a sketch of him.

It was a quiet evening, and as Fergus sketched the two men were able to talk. Captain Kennedy wanted to know the name of their mutual 'friend'. When Fergus told him, the Irish sea-captain sucked air through his teeth noisily.

'I figured as much. I heard of the trouble at his meeting. It won't be easy. The authorities are set on bringing him to trial and making an example of him. Every Irish ship in the port of Bristol is being watched day and night.'

'So there's little chance of Tomas escaping by sea?'

'I haven't said that. The sooner Tomas returns to Ireland the better. He has more friends there than in England – yourself excluded, of course.'

'I'm no more than an acquaintance,' corrected Fergus. 'But I'll not stand by and see a man hanged for no other reason than to deter others from taking up a just cause.'

'We're more used to it happening in our land than you are, it seems.' Henry Kennedy spoke with no trace of bitterness in his voice. 'But I'm in agreement with your sentiments. A rope collar's an uncomfortable prospect for a sensitive man like Tomas. I'll do my best to see he never gets to wear one. Can you get hold of some seaman's clothes for him?'

'It shouldn't be too difficult. The local pawnshops carry on a good trade with sailors. Tomas has grown a handsome beard, too, but I'm not sure that will be enough to get him past the men who are watching your ship.'

'It won't be necessary. Only the Irish boats are being watched. My brother is captain of *Lucy*, trading between Bristol and Halifax, in Canada. His boat is lying in the dock about three ships behind mine. Tell Tomas to go on board after dark tomorrow. He'll be landed on the coast of Cork and able to take a gentle stroll home from there.'

'How much will his passage cost?' Fergus was aware that *he* would be required to foot the bill.

'Are you asking me to put a price on a man's life?' For a moment Captain Kennedy frowned angrily, then his brow cleared and he said: 'That's a fine sketch of me you're making. I'll take it as a gift and you can leave it to me to make the arrangements with my brother.'

Late the next morning Tomas Casey was in the attic with Fergus, drinking tea and chatting happily about the prospect of returning to his native land.

'You'll have to come visiting, Fergus. It's a grand country. There's no other place quite like it in the whole world.'

'Is that why so many of you live elsewhere?' Fergus's current opinion of Ireland and the Irish was coloured by the fact that Tomas Casey had just borrowed more money from him. Fergus now held Tomas Casey's IOUs for twenty-five guineas. It was more money than he could afford, and the prospect of having it returned to him looked decidedly bleak.

'I didn't say it was easy to *live* there, only that it's God's own country.' Tomas Casey refused to allow Fergus's remarks to dampen his good humour.

'Will you continue working for Chartism when you return there?'

Tomas Casey looked at Fergus scornfully. 'Can a bee stop buzzing? I'm committed to Chartism, and there's no going back. Mind you, I'll need to lie low for a while. I'll go to the west coast and set up in practice as a doctor again. I'll get by; you needn't worry about me. But the country . . .! It's green, with a smell about it as though the world is renewed every morning. A man's not afraid of breathing in and filling his lungs with air. . . .'

Tomas Casey's eulogy of his homeland was brought to a halt by the sound of footsteps hurrying up the stairs to the attic.

Even as the Irish Chartist looked about him for a place to hide, the door was flung open and Irish Molly stumbled into the room. Seeing Casey, she cried: 'Thank God you're still here. I was feared you might have already gone.'

Tomas Casey had told his countrywoman only that he would not be sharing her room for another night. She knew nothing of the ship that was to return him to Ireland.

'You must come with me, Tomas. Your skills are needed at the old houses down by the river.'

'*I'm* needed? I don't understand you, woman. No one knows I'm here. How can *I* be needed?'

'You're a *doctor*, aren't you? Or so you've been telling me all this time.'

'I'm a doctor right enough, but if there's someone sick you'll need to send for a Bristol doctor. I'll not risk being caught now, not when another twelve hours will see me on my way home to Ireland.'

'There's not another doctor would come within a mile of the poor souls I'm asking you to help. They're our people. Irish.'

'But they're not in Ireland now, so they've become the responsibility of the English authorities.'

'Responsibility, you say? No one will take any responsibility for these poor souls. They're outcasts. When they become a problem they're moved on somewhere else.

Anywhere else. These people – *our* people – are sick, Tomas. Desperately sick. Fergus . . . you sketched two of the children a couple of weeks ago. Show him.'

Fergus walked to the far end of his long room and picked up a canvas that leaned with its face to the wall. He handed it to Tomas Casey without a word.

Tomas Casey looked at the painting, and the faces of two undernourished and unsmiling children stared back at him from the canvas. Their eyes were sunk deep in fleshless faces, and twiglike arms protruded from tattered sleeves. It was a tragic and moving painting, but their story did not end on the canvas.

Jabbing a finger at the painting, Irish Molly said: 'I've seen both these boys this morning. One is lying dead and the other's dying on a bed of filthy straw, in a cellar that was flooded until two days ago. There are almost two hundred others who'll go the same way if they don't get help right now.'

'What's wrong with them? *Why* are they dying?'

'Have you no eyes? Look at the painting. They're starving to death. They were starving when they arrived from Ireland and they've stayed alive by scavenging. They're living in tumbledown houses down by the river. *River*, did I say? It's an open sewer. A disgrace to the city. A week ago the river rose in flood and poured inside the cellars of the houses. All those who'd been sleeping there moved upstairs to where they were already sleeping as many as twenty to a room. When the water went down many of them moved back to the cellars, even though the walls were streaming with filth and water. It's no wonder fever's broken out among them.'

'Fever?'

'Every one of them is ill in some way or another. The children especially.'

Tomas Casey's instinct for self-preservation was battling with the sense of duty he felt towards his countrymen and their children.

'How far are the houses where these people are living?' Tomas Casey put the question to Fergus.

'They're on the edge of Lewin's Mead. I doubt if you're

likely to meet up with a constable on the way. Even if you did, you wouldn't be recognised behind that beard.'

'All right, then, we'll go and see what can be done – but I'm not missing that ship, you understand?'

The stench from the river as they approached the houses was almost overpowering, and Tomas Casey wrinkled his nose in disgust. 'I'm not surprised that fever's flourishing hereabouts. Does the Bristol Council have no regard for public health?'

When they reached the derelict riverside houses, Tomas Casey's concern increased. The houses were in an advanced state of decay, and the recent floods had not improved matters. There was not a pane of glass in any of the windows, half the doors were missing, and the roof of one house had collapsed in upon the upper storey.

A cool wind was blowing by the river, yet a number of men, women and children sat or stood in the lane before the houses, or on adjacent wasteland. No one seemed to be *doing* anything. Even the children sat and stared at the ground. One or two raised their heads to gaze from sunken lacklustre eyes at the newcomers. Most did not bother. There were no comments about the arrival of the trio from Back Lane. Indeed, there was an almost total lack of conversation among the people here.

Tomas Casey stopped and looked about him in concern. 'I haven't seen people who looked like this since I was in Kerry during the famine of 'forty-five.'

'You're looking at the *fit* ones. Wait until you go inside. . . .'

Irish Molly took the lead, and the two men followed her inside the first of the broken-down cottages. The stench in here was more oppressive than outside, dampness and decay adding to other odours. They passed a number of men and women as they entered the house, but no one showed any interest in them. Then they entered a cellar, and Fergus was brought face to face with men, women and even children who had given up all interest in life itself.

He could only see those in the immediate vicinity of the stairs, the light from above penetrating no further than three or four feet into the cellar. It was enough. Bodies were packed so close together that it was almost impossible to pick a way between them, and the air in here was well-nigh unbreathable.

For a few disbelieving moments Tomas Casey just stared at the bodies lying at his feet. Then he took command, calling for a light so that he could assess the situation more fully. When nothing happened, the Chartist leader repeated the demand in Gaelic. Within a few minutes a lighted candle-stub had been produced and handed to him.

Treading carefully, Tomas Casey picked his way across the cellar floor, occasionally pausing to stoop over a still form. When he gained the far wall the Irish doctor turned, and Fergus saw the shock on his face.

'I can't believe it. Half these people are dead already!'

From the cellar steps, Irish Molly spoke with a choked voice. 'You'll believe it, Tomas. There are more of them upstairs – and it's the same in every house.'

'But . . . there are *ten* houses!' Fergus was horrified.

'That's right. *Now* do you believe these people are in desperate need of help?'

'They're all doomed unless we can do something for them right away.' Leaning over another still figure, Tomas Casey parted the front of a tattered shirt. As he did so the tiny scrap of candle disintegrated in his hand and left them in darkness.

'Unless I'm mistaken there's both cholera *and* typhus here – in epidemic proportions. It's a situation no town council can afford to ignore.'

Gingerly picking their way between prone bodies, Tomas Casey and Fergus returned to the steps. The Chartist leader stood in silence for a moment, deep in thought. Suddenly his shoulders straightened, and Fergus saw a return of the expression he had seen when the Chartist leader roused the passions of his followers at the Durdham Downs meeting.

'We can't do everything that's needed, but we can make a start. Molly, I'll need opiates, laudanum, peppermint water and flannel – lots of flannel, to make belts for those who are still free of cholera.'

'Oh! And will I be given all these things out of the goodness of someone's heart? Or do I offer them one of Tomas Casey's IOUs?'

Reaching inside the waistband of his trousers, Tomas Casey pulled out a small linen bag, and there was the dull clink of gold coins as he emptied the bag into Irish Molly's hand.

'Get as much as you can with this.'

'But it's all the money you have.'

'Don't stand here arguing, girl. Each minute you delay is costing life. Fergus . . . you know Alderman Tennant. Go to his house and tell him what you've seen here. Ask him to obtain doctors and medical supplies – and food. As much food as he can provide. Molly . . . on your way out try to bully some life into all the men you can find. I want them to help me clear this cellar. It's the only way to separate the living from the dead. If we leave them down here any longer, there'll be *no one* left alive. Go on, get moving, Fergus. What are you waiting for?'

'If the authorities become involved, they'll send constables. You're a wanted man.'

'I've always known what the consequences of my campaign might one day be, Fergus. I've controlled my own destiny as far as any man can. These poor souls have had to accept whatever fate doled out to them – and it's always been a loser's hand. If I were to walk away from them now, I'd be haunted all my life by something more relentless than the law of the land. I couldn't live with it. Go and fetch all the help you can muster. Get Fanny to help you; she's worth ten others when it comes to an emergency like this.'

CHAPTER TWENTY-TWO

ALDERMAN TENNANT WAS NOT AT HOME — but Fanny was. Fergus impressed the urgency of his mission upon the servant who opened the door to him, and minutes later Fanny hurried into the room where he waited.

'The servant said you needed urgent help. What is it? Have you lost another Lewin's Mead urchin?'

Fergus described what he had seen at the derelict cottages on the bank of the Frome river, and repeated what Tomas Casey had said about the situation.

'Tomas Casey is still here? In Bristol? But there's a price on his head.'

'He's well aware of it, and plans had been made for him to leave England tonight, but he's given all his money to buy medicines and is refusing to leave the sick families.'

After a few more brief questions, Fanny said: 'We must discuss Tomas's problems later. First we need to bring help to these poor people — doctors, food and clothes. If they have the fever, everything they own must be burned. How many of them do you think there are?'

'I don't know for certain. Probably about two hundred.'

'So many? You return to Tomas, and I'll do what I can, as quickly as possible. Take this and use it to buy anything Tomas feels he needs in the meantime.'

Fanny took Fergus's hand and dropped a number of gold coins into his palm.

Tomas Casey had been busy during Fergus's absence. The

cellars of the houses had been cleared, and their recent occupants lay on the waste land beside the houses. A few were on blankets, but most lay on the bare earth. Others, farther from the houses, lay shoulder to shoulder in neat rows, their suffering over. Most had died unnoticed in the dark and crowded cellars.

Irish Molly had bought what she could with the money Tomas Casey had given to her, and she and some of the Irishwomen were busily tearing flannel cloth into strips to make 'belts' for those not yet stricken with cholera to wear next to their skin. This was widely believed to be an effective means of keeping the disease at bay.

Meanwhile, Tomas Casey was doling out doses of a mixture of laudanum and peppermint water, all the time complaining that there was only sufficient medicine for a single dose.

When Fergus handed over the twenty guineas donated by Fanny Tennant the Chartist doctor called to Irish Molly and sent her off once more to procure all the medicine she could buy.

'How many of them are ill?' Fergus asked the Chartist doctor when Irish Molly had hurried away.

'Pretty well *all* of them, I'd say. As for a count. . . . There are people in some of the upstairs rooms I haven't seen yet.'

Wiping a dribble of medicine from the lips of a pathetically thin young girl, Tomas Casey rose to his feet and looked about him in despair.

'There are too many here for me to deal with alone. I've had seventeen bodies laid out over there, mostly young children. I'd say we're likely to lose three or four times that number before we're through.'

With a movement of his arm, Tomas Carey encompassed the people about them. With the exception of the few women who were making flannel belts they stood around in silent apathetic groups. 'Look at them. They've given up. They're so used to losing their battles with life they've stopped fighting. As they fall ill they just lie down and die.'

Gazing about him at the homeless Irish refugees, Fergus knew the bitter words spoken by his companion were true. There was an air of hopeless resignation among them that seemed to have passed beyond human help.

'Is there something I can do?'

'Go through the houses and make sure everyone is brought outside. The air here is far from fresh, but it's better than inside. Then gather the men together; I see a couple have shovels with them. Get them to clean the filth from the houses, from attic to cellar. When that's done I'll see if the money will stretch to lime-wash for the cellars. While you're about it, try to prevent them leaving this place. If cholera reaches Lewin's Mead, it will go through the place like the wrath of God.'

By the time Fanny Tennant arrived on the scene the house-cleaning operation was well under way. She brought a number of volunteer helpers and two light wagons loaded with food – and suddenly there was new-found hope among the sick and hungry immigrants. They crowded about the wagons, snatching greedily as food was offered to them.

Fanny undertook her own tour of inspection in a bid to ascertain the extent of the problem and she spoke at some length to Tomas Casey. By the time she reached Fergus she was visibly shaken by the desperate plight of the Irish families.

'It's appalling that people can exist in such conditions in the very heart of our city without anyone knowing.'

'I saw them here some weeks ago, when I was searching for Becky,' said Fergus guiltily. 'But I had no idea things would become as bad as they are now.'

Just then Irish Molly returned from her latest errand. She was accompanied by two youths from the apothecary who were helping her carry the medicines. Seeing Fergus, she made her way to him.

Nodding a brief greeting to Fanny, she said: 'I've got most of the things Tomas wanted. Where is he?'

'In the end house. I found a mother with a tiny baby in the top-floor rooms who refuses to come out. He's gone to see them.'

'I'll take some of this medicine to him there. He might be needing it.'

As Irish Molly walked away Fanny said: 'That's the girl who came to tell me Becky was locked in a room above the dollyshop. Is she a prostitute?'

'Yes.'

Fergus did not amplify his reply, and Fanny looked at him curiously. 'You have some peculiar friends, Fergus.'

'I suppose I have.' Fergus looked at her without humour. 'Some might include you among their number. It's not everyone who would come to the aid of people as sick and destitute as these.'

'It will become far worse before we see any improvement.' Fanny looked anxiously up at the clouds gathering in the sky. 'It will be raining soon. How long before the houses are thoroughly cleaned?'

'They won't be ready today. They are in a disgusting state.'

'Then I'll send someone to the barracks for marquees. Better still, I'll go myself. The Army will have doctors experienced in cholera, too. Tomas on his own can't do all that's needed here.'

'Tomas should leave if army doctors are being brought in. If he's taken by the police or the Army, he's as dead as any of those corpses over there.' Even as Fergus spoke another body was being carried to the line of corpses.

'I forgot. What should I do?' It was the first time Fergus had ever heard Fanny ask anyone for advice.

'Tomas will never leave until there's someone to take his place. Bring army doctors here if you can. Once they've arrived I'll try to persuade Tomas to leave.'

Fanny Tennant succeeded in obtaining three large marquees and the services of two army doctors by evening, but fortune did not smile upon Tomas Casey.

Fergus was upstairs in one of the houses when he heard a commotion outside. Looking from the broken window, he saw Irish Molly running. Holding her skirts high, she was already halfway to Lewin's Mead. Closer to the houses Tomas Casey struggled futilely against the three policemen who held him. One was Ivor Primrose.

Nearby, one of the army doctors was protesting angrily to a police inspector. Around them a number of Irishmen watched the scene with non-participating interest. There were town officials, too. Escorted by the constables, they had come to assess the situation on behalf of the Bristol authorities.

By the time Fergus reached the scene Tomas Casey had been handcuffed to Constable Ivor Primrose and the brief scuffle was over.

'Tomas . . . are you all right?'

The Chartist leader held up a manacled hand and shrugged. 'I'd be better if they took this off and gave me a half-mile start, so I would.'

Ivor Primrose frowned at Fergus. 'How long have you known the whereabouts of Casey?'

'Fergus knows nothing.' His voice loud and arrogant, Tomas Casey was no longer the solicitous doctor treating dying patients. He was a Chartist leader, holding the attention of a gathering. 'He wouldn't be here at all if I hadn't suddenly appeared at his door and asked him to enlist Miss Tennant's help on behalf of my poor suffering countrymen here.'

Ivor Primrose still looked accusingly at Fergus. 'You should have reported his presence to the police straight away. There's a warrant out for his arrest.'

'He's been responsible for saving many lives here today. If it hadn't been for his efforts, you'd probably have twice as many bodies lying over there.'

'I'll add my professional endorsement to that statement, Constable.' One of the army doctors spoke heatedly to Constable Primrose. 'But for Dr Casey – if, indeed, it *is* Tomas Casey – every one of these men, women and children would be dead within a week. I'll repeat my statement in open court, if necessary.'

'Your remarks will be noted, sir, and if you aren't able to attend the court I'll ensure they're passed on to the proper quarter. But I have my job to do. Tomas Casey has been recognised, and there's a warrant out for his arrest. He's now my prisoner.'

'He's desperately needed here, Ivor,' Fanny Tennant interceded on Tomas Casey's behalf. 'Can't you allow him to continue his work until all the Irish have been treated? There are more than two hundred of them – many are children, and most are desperately ill. If you release him, I'll take full responsibility.'

Ivor Primrose shook his head. 'I'm sorry, Miss Tennant. I'd be in serious trouble if I didn't take him into custody immediately. As for these unfortunate people . . . The Inspector of Health is here now, and they've become his responsibility. He'll provide all the medical care that's needed.'

Tomas Casey tugged at his curly red beard and attempted a weary grin. 'Don't worry yourself about me, Fanny. It will be a relief to have a shave and emerge from behind this foliage. I don't know why I grew the damned thing; it's fooled no one.'

Nearby, the Irish immigrants were crowded about a fire on which the contents of a huge soup 'boiler' were beginning to bubble, wafting an appetising aroma over a wide area. Tomas Casey tried to point in their direction, but the handcuffs prevented him. Lowering his shackled hands, he inclined his head towards them.

'Do all you can for them, Fanny. They're simple folk from Ireland's far west, but they feel pain, sorrow and humiliation as surely as the rest of us.'

Fanny and Fergus watched helplessly as Tomas Casey was led away, handcuffed between Ivor Primrose and another constable.

'What do you think will happen to him?' Fanny asked the question anxiously.

Fergus shrugged. 'He'll be charged, of course, but he'll probably get off. All he's done is to put into words what the rest of the country is thinking. All the same, he'll need plenty of support. I'll be visiting him in prison.'

'We'll *both* visit him. But we can do nothing for him at the moment, so I'll find out what is going to happen here.'

The pale-faced health inspector was surrounded by his officials, each of whom was compiling some form of inventory of the Irish immigrants. When Fergus asked the inspector what he intended doing, he received a curt reply.

'I'll do whatever is best for the citizens of Bristol – but what's your business here? Who are you?'

'I'm Fergus Vincent – and this is Miss Tennant, daughter of Alderman Tennant. We've been helping these people as best we could.'

Some of the belligerence left the health inspector, but he showed no inclination to be friendly. Touching his hat to Fanny, he said: 'Good day to you, miss. I don't doubt you've done much to relieve the suffering of these people – unlawful vagrants though they are – but I'm here as the official representative of the Town Council and will ensure that all necessary steps are taken.'

'Oh?' The scorn in Fanny Tennant's voice would have withered a more sensitive man. 'Have you brought doctors? Food? Medicine? And men to bury the Irish dead?'

His face reddening, the official said: 'I have only just arrived, Miss Tennant. I will do what's needed when I've assessed their needs. . . .'

'These people don't need "assessing". Any fool can do that with no more than a glance. They need food, clothing, blankets – and more doctors. When you've made all these things available I and my helpers will leave – but I don't doubt we'll still be here when darkness falls.'

Fanny was right. She and her volunteer helpers did not withdraw from the derelict houses until after dark, and there was still no aid from the Bristol Town Council. They left the Irish families in better circumstances than when they had arrived. All had been fed, and bread was left to break the night's fast. A few items of clothing had also been obtained, together with blankets. The newly cleaned rooms had been heavily whitewashed, and there was an air of cautious optimism among the Irish vagrants for the first time since the potato blight had driven them from their lands. It seemed that at last someone *cared* about their plight.

The two army doctors left at the same time, but they were less optimistic. They dismissed Tomas Casey's diagnosis of typhus among the Irish families. They identified the rash on the children as measles – just as much of a killer among the weak and emaciated children – but there was no doubt that many of the immigrants were suffering from cholera. The outbreak could be expected to worsen before it began to improve. The doctors promised to return with more medicines the next morning.

Fergus was exhausted when he returned to the house in Back Lane. He had declined an invitation to go to Clifton for a meal at Fanny's house. The emotional impact of the plight of the Irish immigrants had left him drained of energy. Even so, there were some faces that haunted his mind. Most were children. He wanted to commit them to paper before he slept.

On the landing where Irish Molly had her room, Fergus paused before knocking at her door. There was no reply, but he thought he heard a sound inside before he knocked again. This time there was utter silence. Hesitating for only a moment, Fergus lifted the latch and pushed the door open.

It was gloomy inside the room, light from a full moon barely penetrating the uncleaned panes at the small window.

At first Fergus thought he must have been mistaken and the room empty, but then he detected a slight movement in a chair across the room.

'Molly, is that you?'

'Who did you expect to find – a titled lady, perhaps? Of course it's me – and I don't remember asking you to come in.'

There was belligerence in Irish Molly's voice, but it was not as aggressive as it might have been. Crossing the room towards her, Fergus smelt the fumes of cheap gin.

'Are you all right, Molly?'

'And why shouldn't I be?'

A lamp flickered on in a window not six feet away across the narrow thoroughfare outside, and the light invaded the room. Irish Molly turned her head away, but she was not quick enough to prevent Fergus from seeing her face.

'You've been crying.'

'Prostitutes are too tough to cry. Surely you know that? Oh, what the hell! Yes, I've been weeping, I've been weeping for that red-haired idiot who'd be on a boat heading for

Ireland now if it wasn't for me. Did the po-lice take him?'

'Yes.' There was no gentle way of confirming what Irish Molly already suspected.

'Damn! Damn the po-lice. Damn those poor ignorant suffering people down there by the river. Damn you for letting me see the sketches you'd made of them in the first place. But if anyone needs to be damned it's me, for persuading poor Tomas to help them.'

She swung the bottle of gin towards Fergus. 'Here, pour some of this down your throat — but don't drink it all. I'll need more of it if I'm to go to work tonight.'

'You'll be bringing another man back here?'

'Isn't that how I earn my living? Pass me that bottle if you're not going to drink. I need it more than you.'

Irish Molly took the bottle. Raising it to her lips, she drank noisily. When she lowered the bottle again she saw Fergus silently watching her.

'What will they do to him, Fergus? What's going to happen to the poor dear man? Will they hang him, as he thinks they will?'

'No.' Fergus fervently hoped he sounded more optimistic than he felt. 'What's happened today will be taken into account. He'll be given transportation, but in a year or two the demands of the Chartists will be met and he'll be pardoned.'

'Do you honestly believe that, Fergus? Do you really believe he'll be all right?'

'I certainly don't think they'll hang him. All the other Chartists who were arrested on the Downs have been transported or imprisoned.'

'Thank you, Fergus. I'll always blame myself for causing Tomas to be caught, but you've made me feel better . . . about everything.'

Irish Molly stood up unsteadily and reached for her shawl. 'You're a kind man. I know you've been giving Tomas money during the time he's been staying here. I can understand why Becky thinks so much of you. Out of the way now; I've a living to earn. . . .'

Irish Molly paused in front of Fergus and breathed gin

fumes in his direction. Reaching out, she patted him drunkenly and none too gently on the cheek. 'If you ever feel lonely up in that room of yours, just come down and see Irish Molly. I'll find room for you in my bed any night, my love.'

CHAPTER TWENTY-THREE

FERGUS WOKE EARLY THE NEXT MORNING. Throwing off his blanket, he placed his feet on the bare-board floor and crossed to the window. It was grey and overcast outside, but at least it was not raining. He was able to fan some life into the embers of his fire, and while he waited for the kettle to boil he washed and dressed and put sketchpad and pencils in a canvas haversack. Fergus was going to check on the condition of the Irish vagrants, but this time he intended making a detailed record of their plight.

There was no sound from the remainder of the house. Few of the residents pursued occupations requiring them to rise early – and Irish Molly was unlikely to be abroad early today.

When Fergus left the house a sprinkling of men and women were making their way from Lewin's Mead to places of work outside the rookery. A light drizzle was riding the wind, and Fergus turned his coat collar up about his face and thrust his hands deep into coat pockets.

Leaving the narrow alleyways behind him, he crossed the waste ground that extended towards the river – and came to a sudden surprised halt. The area in front of the derelict riverside houses was filled with people milling about in apparent confusion. Most were Irish, but there were constables here, too – and the health inspector who had come to the houses the previous day.

Hurrying to the health inspector, Fergus demanded to know what was happening.

For a moment the health inspector could not recollect

Fergus. When he remembered, he immediately looked about him for Fanny Tennant. Failing to see her, his confidence grew.

'We're moving the Irish. They'll be on the road out of Bristol by the time most people are abroad.'

'On the road to where? These are homeless people – and they're desperately ill.'

'That's none of my business,' the health official said callously. 'The decision was taken at a special meeting of the Town Council last night. Hopefully we're in time to avoid a cholera outbreak in the city.'

'They would only have acted so swiftly upon your recommendations,' Fergus accused the official angrily. 'Did you tell the Council just *how* sick these people are?'

'My duty is to the city of Bristol. By your own admission these people are vagrants. They are also a very serious health hazard. They must go, and quickly, if an epidemic is to be averted.'

'These "vagrants" are men, women and children, driven from their own homes by starvation. They need help.'

'Then they must find a place where help is available. Preferably many miles from Bristol.'

'At least let them set off with a good meal in their bellies,' pleaded Fergus. 'Food will be here soon.' He knew Fanny Tennant and her volunteers had arranged to bring breakfast to the sick Irish families.

The health inspector shook his head stubbornly. 'I want them out of Bristol before people take to the roads. They'll leave as soon as the constables can round them all up.'

The Irish vagrants were almost ready to move off, those who had difficulty in standing being supported by others. Fergus made rapid sketches as he walked among them. Then he was attracted to one of the derelict houses by a commotion going on inside.

As Fergus reached the door a constable staggered out. His tall hat was missing, and blood flowed down his face from a gash on his forehead.

'Take care. . . . There's a madman inside!' The policeman gasped out the information as he pushed past Fergus.

The noise was coming from upstairs, and at the head of the broken stairs another constable lay on the floor, attended by his colleagues. Beyond them a number of constables crowded a narrow and gloomy passageway. Among them was the giant figure of Ivor Primrose, and Fergus pushed his way through to reach him.

'What's happening?' Fergus asked the question with difficulty as an angry and unintelligible bellowing filled the passageway and constables were forced back upon their companions.

Peering down at Fergus, the giant constable exclaimed: 'Oh, it's you. . . .' As he spoke, Ivor Primrose warded off a retreating policeman who was backing into Fergus. 'One of the Irishmen's gone beserk. He's got hold of a shovel and has downed four constables already. He's keeping us from going into the room at the end of the passage. I think his family must be in there.'

'Let me through. I might be able to reason with him.'

It was neither bravado nor a wish to aid the police in their distasteful task. Sooner or later the constables would be ordered to rush the shovel-wielding Irishman. Someone might be seriously injured, or even killed. If this happened, the Irishman and his family would suffer the penalty of the law.

Helped by Ivor Primrose, Fergus wormed his way forward, squeezing between the close-packed constables, most of whom were clutching heavy wooden truncheons.

The two constables in the front rank were hatless, and one had a bloody face. On the floor in front of them lay four tall black hats. No more than two paces away, filling a doorway, stood an Irishman, the sharp-pointed shovel balanced in his big hands as menacing as any medieval battle-axe.

The Irishman was one of those who had helped Fergus clean out the houses the day before, using the very shovel he wielded so effectively today. Fergus remembered something else. One of the smallest bodies laid out on the waste ground had been that of this man's young daughter. His wife and baby son were also ill. After they had been treated by Tomas Casey, Fergus himself had taken food to the woman. Fergus had also learned the man's name.

'Giraldus. Giraldus Reilly, is your wife in there with your child?' Fergus put the question to the Irishman quickly as the man raised his shovel threateningly, mistrustful of the movement in the police ranks.

The Irishman peered suspiciously through the gloom at Fergus. Then he moved slightly to one side, allowing more light from the room behind him to escape into the narrow passageway. Suddenly the spade was lowered to a more defensive position – and Fergus discovered he had been holding his breath.

The Irishman began talking earnestly, but unfortunately he spoke only Gaelic, a language understood by none of the men in the narrow passageway. Three times the unintelligible words were repeated in what was clearly a plea to Fergus.

When Fergus indicated that he did not understand, the Irishman eyed him uncertainly for a few moments. Then he side-stepped and signalled for Fergus to enter the room.

'Be careful!' As Fergus moved away from the assembled policemen and walked towards the room, Ivor Primrose took a pace forward to caution him. In an instant the shovel was raised menacingly once more.

'It's all right. You and your men stay here until I see what's happening inside. Nothing will happen to me.'

Having given this reassurance, Fergus ducked beneath the Irishman's raised arm – and immediately forgot the thought of any danger to himself.

A woman lay on the board floor, covered by a blanket. Her breathing was shallow and uneven, and her eyes were closed. She was undoubtedly dying, and Fergus thought she must be unconscious – until her eyes suddenly opened and she looked up at him.

Unable to endure the pain he saw in her eyes, Fergus broke off the visual encounter – and saw that the room had another occupant. There was a low fire burning in the grate, and close to this lay a baby wrapped in a ragged jacket that must have belonged to the man guarding the door. The child could not have been more than a month or two old.

The woman made a strangled sound in her throat. Turning back to her, Fergus saw she had turned her head and was also looking at the bundle that was her child. When the woman tried to speak the sound died in her throat, but there was no mistaking the plea in her dark expressive eyes.

Fergus was uncertain what to do until a shudder ran through the woman's body and he realised she did not have many minutes to live. Crossing to the fireplace, he picked up the baby, intending to place it beside the dying woman. The baby seemed unnaturally stiff, and when he looked closer at its face he realised why. The baby was dead!

Fergus almost dropped the child in that first moment of realisation, but he recovered in time. Carrying the dead child to the woman, he pulled back the blanket that covered her, laid the child by its mother's side and gently crooked her thin arm about the dead baby.

She tried to say something to him, but no words came and he found the gratitude in her eyes unbearable. Moments later a terrible tremor racked her body and Fergus crossed the room to the doorway. Touching the Irishman's arm, Fergus pointed back inside the room. The Irishman's glance went to his wife before returning to the waiting constables in an agony of indecision.

Stepping outside into the passageway, Fergus said: 'He has a wife and baby in there. The baby is dead and his wife has no more than minutes to live. I also happen to know he lost another daughter yesterday. Give him a few minutes and he'll come out quietly. He'll have nothing left to fight for.'

The uncomfortable silence that followed Fergus's words was broken by Ivor Primrose. Talking to the Irishman, he said gently: 'Go to your wife. We'll leave you in peace for a while.'

Shifting his gaze to Fergus, Ivor Primrose said: 'I'll come back for him later. We'll not have this lot moving for another half an hour or so anyway, whatever the health inspector says.'

The Irishman did not understand Ivor Primrose's words, but when the constables began to move back along the passageway towards the stairs he took a pace towards them.

Handing Fergus the shovel, he hurried inside the room to where his wife lay.

Kneeling beside the woman, the Irishman took her hand and began talking softly to her, although by now it was doubtful whether there was enough life left in her to understand what was being said.

It was this scene that Fergus committed to paper. He knew it was an intrusion on what should have been an unshared moment of tragedy, but Fergus believed it epitomised the whole sordid incident.

As Fergus sketched, Constable Ivor Primrose came to stand silently beside him and Fergus asked quietly what would happen to the Irishman.

The big policeman shrugged uncomfortably. 'Who knows? He and the others will probably tramp the shires until they die beside the road, or until there are few enough left for a workhouse to take them in.'

'What about his battle with your constables? His spade put a sizeable dent in one of them.'

'That was Tommy Cabot. He's got a wife and two young children himself. He'll not press charges.'

Fergus glanced up from his sketchpad in surprise, and Ivor Primrose said: 'Constables have feelings the same as anyone else, Fergus.'

'Of course. . . . I'm sorry.'

Fergus looked back at the tragic Irish family in time to see the Irishman gently close the eyelids of the woman. When he stood up tears were coursing down his face and he was so distraught he seemed not to know what to do next.

Ivor Primrose entered the room and took the Irishman by the arm. As he was led away the man stopped suddenly. Pointing back to the room, he said something in his own language and the big constable patted his arm reassuringly.

'I don't know what it is you're trying to ask me, but if it's about a decent burial, then you needn't concern yourself. They're digging a large plot in St James churchyard, and your wife won't be short of company. With those who died yesterday and her own child, she'll have twenty-seven companions.'

'There will be many more deaths along the road.'

'I don't doubt it, Fergus, but neither one of us can shoulder the burdens of the whole world.'

Fergus followed the other two men, and at the door the Irishman paused to grasp him by the hand before going outside to join the remainder of his people.

When Fanny Tennant and her helpers arrived at the derelict riverside houses, Fergus was sketching the macabre spectacle of the last of the Irish bodies being removed in an enclosed cart. Giraldus Reilly's wife and baby were the last to go and they were swung inside the van together in a single blanket.

One of Fergus's sketches showed the Irish vagrants being marched away, escorted by constables and health officials, and when Fanny demanded to know what had been happening Fergus handed her his sketchpad without an explanation. He wandered away to stand gazing morosely into the filthy waters of the Frome river.

It was some minutes before Fanny joined him. Handing back the sketchpad without a word, she stood beside him for a long time.

'How long is it since they were taken away?'

'Forty minutes. Perhaps an hour.'

Fanny looked to where the wagons she had brought stood loaded with foodstuffs.

'I'll try to catch up with them. They have need of food.'

'Why bother? They're doomed. They know it as well as we do.'

Fanny looked at Fergus sharply. 'You don't believe that any more than I do.'

Changing the subject abruptly, she asked: 'What do you intend doing with the sketches you've made?'

'Make paintings of some. I'm not sure about the others.'

'Show them to Lady Hammond. She'll arrange an exhibition for you.'

To have an exhibition of his works was the dream of every artist, and Fergus was no exception, but he showed no enthusiasm. 'I'm not sure I'm too interested in an exhibition right now. Besides, a lot of work needs to be done on them.'

'Then, *work* on them. You are not exactly overburdened with commissions.'

'I'll do it in my own time.'

'Will you, Fergus? Or are you enjoying living this dream of yours too much to make it anything *more* than a dream?'

Fanny waited for Fergus's reply. When none came she sighed: 'All right, tell me to mind my own business. But before you do I had better tell you of more of my meddling. I spoke to Mary Carpenter and told her how worthwhile your sketching lessons have been for my pupils at the ragged school. She would like you to hold similar classes for the girls at the Red Lodge reformatory, at a fee to be agreed. She wants to see you tomorrow morning.'

'Would I be teaching Becky?' Fergus's enthusiasm suddenly returned.

'There are no more than a dozen girls at the Red Lodge. You will be teaching them all.'

'When do I begin?'

'That's up to you. Go now, if you want to. Meanwhile I shall try to catch up with the Irish. It would be criminal to waste all the food I have collected for them.'

CHAPTER TWENTY-FOUR

FERGUS WAS PREPARING A MEAL for himself when he had an unexpected visitor. Maude Garrett entered the attic hesitantly after knocking and being invited to enter.

'Are you Fergus? Becky's friend?'

Puzzled, Fergus nodded. He did not recall having met this girl before. Drab and untidy though she was, there was a certain animation in the tired pinched face that an artist would have remembered.

'I'm Maude. It was me who came to tell Irish Molly about Becky – when Ma Cottle had her locked up in the dollyshop. I called to find out what's happened to her. Irish Molly's not in, so I came up here.'

'*You* were responsible for rescuing Becky? Come and sit down. I've just made tea. Will you have a cup?'

Maude Garrett hesitated. 'I'd really like to speak to Irish Molly. I want to ask her about . . . something. I'm on my way home from work.'

'You can spare a few minutes. I want to know exactly what happened to Becky. She's at the Red Lodge in Park Row. It was a choice of agreeing to go to a reformatory or being taken to police cells. They said she stabbed someone.'

'They've put her away for stabbing Alfie Skewes? She ought to have got a *reward*! It's a pity she didn't kill him. There's a lot of girls I know would have cheered if she had. Alfie *and* that father of his. Three months they gave Joe Skewes for assaulting a constable. They ought to have given him life for what he did to Becky.'

Her earlier reticence forgotten, Maude Garrett took the cup of tea offered by Fergus. 'Ta! I haven't had anything to drink since this morning. I upset the glue and had to work through dinner-time to pay for it.'

Taking a sip from the cup, her face lit up in sudden delight. 'It's got *sugar* in it. This is a rare treat and no mistake.'

'If you've had to work through your dinner-time, you'll be hungry. There's bread and cheese and cold meat on the table. Help yourself.'

Maude Garrett eyed the scant fare greedily, but said: 'I ought to be getting on home. My pa will be shouting for grub unless my sister Lisa's been able to earn some money. None of 'em usually has anything until I've bought it with my day's wages.'

'They'll wait for a few more minutes.' As he spoke Fergus cut off a slab of cheese, broke off a piece of bread from the loaf and set the food on the table in front of Maude Garrett. 'Before you go I want to hear all you know of Becky.'

Maude Garrett began to eat, speaking with difficulty as she did so. She glossed over her own involvement in Rose Cottle's establishment, but Fergus had no difficulty in filling the gaps in her narrative. By the time food and story had come to an end, Fergus knew exactly what had happened to Becky in the room above Rose Cottle's dollyshop.

Maude Garrett's knowledge was graphically supported by a vivid imagination, and Fergus was gripped by self-guilt. He ought to have tried harder to find Becky before she fell into the clutches of Rose Cottle. She had been out there in Lewin's Mead all the time. He should have carried on looking until he found her. Suddenly the brush he had unconsciously picked up snapped in two in his fingers.

'Are you all right?'

Maude Garrett had been looking at him curiously as he tormented himself with thoughts of what Becky had suffered. If only he had behaved differently when she had given him the stolen watch. . . .

'I'd better go now.' Maude Garrett stood up, studiously avoiding looking at the broken brush. 'If I'm not home soon, Pa will think *I've* been kidnapped. Not that he'd care about *me* overmuch. If it wasn't for the money I give him, he wouldn't notice if I went home at all. I used to think the kids would miss me, but since Phoebe died the rest seem to have been running wild. Still, Lisa's getting money most days now.'

Maude Garrett seemed to be talking largely to herself, but looking up at Fergus she asked: 'Do you know how long Irish Molly's likely to be?'

'No, but if you want her urgently she can usually be found in the White Hart when the docks are as quiet as they are right now.'

'Ta! When you see Becky tell her I hope everything goes well for her. . . .' She hesitated uncertainly for a moment, then nodded towards the painting on which Fergus had been working. 'Could you paint a picture like that of me?'

'I'd be happy to sketch you any time you have a few minutes spare.'

Maude Garrett beamed at him. 'Would you . . .? And let me take it away? I'll come in one evening, on my way home from work. . . .' She suddenly became serious. 'I can't pay for it. . . .' She looked at Fergus speculatively. 'Not with *money*, I can't.'

'The sketch will be a present because of what you did for Becky.'

'You don't have to pay me for *that*. Seeing Rose Cottle put away for six months is payment enough – even though it *has* left me short of money.' Maude Garrett shrugged. 'But that's *my* worry. I'll come and see you one of these evenings.'

Fergus presented himself at the Red Lodge the next afternoon. After being made to wait for some minutes he was taken upstairs to an airy wood-panelled study. It smelled of polish, and every speck of dust seemed to have been banished from the room.

Mary Carpenter was seated behind a large desk. Its vast polished surface was empty except for a slim vase containing three carnations, and a slim writing-folder.

The reformatory-school pioneer greeted Fergus unenthusiastically. It would be some time before Fergus learned that the stern austere spinster reserved her smiles and the hidden warmth of a caring personality for the girls sent to her by the courts.

'So you wish to share your talents with my girls, Mr Vincent?' She managed to make it sound as though he had come to the Red Lodge begging a favour.

'Fanny seems to think they would benefit from sketching classes.'

Mary Carpenter sniffed almost imperceptibly. 'Miss Tennant speaks very highly of your work. Have you brought any sketches with you?'

Fergus handed over his sketchpad and sat waiting as Mary Carpenter turned the pages. Occasionally the reformatory-school founder drew in her breath sharply and an expression of distress would come to her face. More than once she looked up at Fergus as though seeking the answer to an unasked question.

When she reached the last sketch Mary Carpenter closed the pad and placed it carefully on the desk before her. She sat in a deep brooding silence for long moments before fixing her gaze upon Fergus.

'You have a great talent, young man, but it carries with it an equal responsibility. These sketches provide a stark record of the plight of the more unfortunate members of our society. What use do you intend making of them?'

'When I've made paintings from the sketches I'll probably hold an exhibition. . . .'

'I'm not talking of the furtherance of your career. You are a young man; you can afford to wait for recognition. Many of the subjects of your sketches can*not*. The wretched Irish vagrants; the slum-dwellers right here in our own city; children like Becky. I see you have a great many sketches of the girl, including a number of her sleeping. . . .'

There was disapproval and a question in the statement, and Fergus found himself telling Mary Carpenter of his first meeting with Becky, and of her use of his room as a refuge. Mary Carpenter's eyes never left his face during the whole of the time he was talking.

'There are other sketches of her, too. On a ship?'

'For a treat I took her on a day-trip on a paddle-steamer. It ended in disaster when the ship ran aground on its return passage up-river.'

'I seem to have heard something of the incident.' Mary Carpenter's fingers tapped the desk in front of her abstractedly, but there was nothing abstract about her expression. 'What exactly is the relationship between you and this girl? The truth, if you please, Mr Vincent.'

'There is no "relationship". Becky is hardly more than a child. She was the first person I met when I came to Bristol. We became friends. She has no one else, and I suppose I feel a certain responsibility for her in a strange way. I am also rather fond of her.'

The movement of the fingers on the desk ceased, and Mary Carpenter stared hard at Fergus for some moments more.

She nodded suddenly. A short, sharp and positive movement. 'Becky is a young *woman*, Mr Vincent, but young women are as needful of the *right* kind of affection as are young girls – more so, perhaps. I'm happy to know Becky has *someone* to care for her. She's a strangely lonely young lady. You are aware of course that she has not said a word since coming to the Red Lodge? The physician assures me there is no medical reason why she doesn't talk. It is simply that she chooses not to.'

Rising to her feet, Mary Carpenter said: 'You may have a few minutes alone with Becky in the garden, if you wish. Perhaps she will talk for you. Then, as you're here, you can give the girls their first art lesson. I don't believe in wasting time. Becky is not well enough to take lessons yet, but she should be present at your next class. Shall we say the same time every week? A two-hour lesson at a fee of two shillings and sixpence. I will provide pencils.'

The tone of Mary Carpenter's voice ruled out all discussion of the matter, and there was nothing for Fergus to do but nod his agreement.

'Good. I'll have you shown to the garden while a room is prepared for your class. If you have trouble with any of my girls, you will discuss the matter with me personally. Good day to you, Mr Vincent.'

Mary Carpenter bustled from the room, and a few minutes later a maid arrived to show Fergus the way to the garden.

Surrounded by a high stone wall, the well-kept gardens sloped down sharply from the house to give a view across the rooftops and the masts of tall ships tied up to the quay in the heart of Bristol.

Fergus had to wait a while before Becky joined him in the garden. She came from the house alone, and Fergus stood up to greet her as she walked slowly down the steps towards him.

When she reached him the words of greeting died on his lips and he took one of her hands in his, greatly concerned at her appearance. Becky was clean – cleaner than he had ever seen her – and was wearing a neat grey frock of a serviceable coarse material. Her hair was pulled back and tied neatly behind her neck. She was painfully thin, but it was her eyes that held his attention. Dark dull expressionless eyes that dominated her pale drawn face and stared at him with a total lack of expression.

'It's good to be with you again, Becky. I've been worried about you.'

Still holding her hand, Fergus led Becky to a garden seat. Sited beside a bed of perfumed French roses, the seat was in full view of the house, as were all the other garden seats.

'I'll be seeing you quite often in the future. I've been asked to come and take a sketching class, once a week.'

Becky sat down, her hand still held in his. She had not tried to pull it away, but neither had she responded when he squeezed her fingers affectionately.

'Are you eating well? If there's anything you particularly fancy, I'll bring it for you when I come to take my sketching class. Miss Carpenter won't mind.'

It was a lie. Fergus never doubted that Miss Carpenter *would* mind. He was merely trying to provoke a response – *any* response – from Becky. It was possible she was being given something to calm her, but her total silence was unnerving. For a few more minutes Fergus tried without any encouragement to provoke a reply from Becky. Finally, aware he would be allowed only a few more minutes alone with her, he grew desperate.

Gently pulling her around, he forced her to face him.

'Becky, I know what happened at Rose Cottle's dollyshop. Maude came to see me. Maude Garrett. She's told me everything. What you were doing at Rose Cottle's, and why she went to Irish Molly.'

'She couldn't tell you *everything*. I'm the only one who knows that.' Becky's voice was low and strained, reflecting her long silence.

Overjoyed that she had broken her unnatural silence, Fergus said: 'None of it matters now, Becky. All that's important is for you to recover and begin looking towards the future.'

'It *does* matter. . . .' The words came out as a wail of anguish, and Fergus gripped her hands tightly until Becky pulled them free. Clasping them in her lap, she looked down at her tangled fingers.

'I'd never done it before. . . .' Suddenly she said fiercely: 'Did I kill Alfie Skewes? I wanted to. I wanted them both to die for what they did. . . .'

Fergus gripped her hands again. 'Alfie Skewes didn't die, and it's all behind you now. I'm so very, very sorry I didn't understand how much the present you offered me meant to you. I looked for you after you'd gone. I searched *everywhere*.'

'You weren't searching for me on the night I saw you going out dressed up to the nines. You were on your way to see Fanny Tennant, I expect.'

'Why didn't you speak to me then, Becky?'

'I told you, you was on your way to see *her* and her fine friends up at Clifton. You wouldn't have wanted anything to do with me. Not *that* night, you wouldn't.'

'Becky, if I'd seen you, I'd have given up all thought of going *anywhere*. I was worried sick about you.'

Becky looked at him doubtfully. 'Honest?'

'Honest. I'd have given a reward of everything I owned to have found you again.'

It was some moments before Becky spoke again. 'I've been stupid, haven't I? Running away, I mean. If I hadn't done that, I wouldn't have ended up in Rose Cottle's dollyshop.'

'It's all over and done with. You're on the mend, and everything is going to be all right again.'

Becky managed a wan smile. 'I'm glad we've had this talk, Fergus. Do you think they'll let me go home now? I mean, to Lewin's Mead? To your room? I'll be all right, honest I will. You can tell that Miss Carpenter —'

'I don't think you understand, Becky. You've signed an agreement before a magistrate that you'll stay here. There's no going back on that.'

Becky looked at Fergus, not comprehending. 'But I've done nothing wrong.'

'You stabbed Alfie Skewes nigh to death. You'd have been charged with attempted murder if you hadn't agreed to come here.'

'Attempted murder? After what he'd done to me and was trying to do again?'

'There were *two* of them to deny all you said about them, Becky — Rose Cottle, too. You *might* have got off, but more likely you'd have ended up being transported. Fanny Tennant thought this was a better way out for you.'

'*She* would. How long do I have to stay here? A month? Three months? How long?'

'I don't know. Until Mary Carpenter thinks you're ready to go out into the world again, I suppose.'

'How long is that likely to be? I could be here for a year. *Two* years, even.'

'It won't be that long — and you're better off in here for a while. You'll be out of the way of Alfie Skewes — Joe Skewes, too, when he comes out of prison.'

'I'll be out of *everybody's* way, yours included. Do you think a couple of years spent in this place will make me more like your precious Fanny Tennant? Well, it *won't*. I'm Becky, and I'll still be Becky, no matter how long they keep me in here.'

'I don't want you to change, Becky, and if it were possible to take you off with me this minute I'd be the happiest man alive, believe me.'

Becky's eyes searched his face for the slightest hint of a lie. 'Cross your heart?'

Fergus made the sign of a cross over his chest. 'Cross my heart and hope to die.'

Becky's glance fell from his face to her lap once more and remained there for a full minute. When she raised her head once more he saw she had reached a decision.

'All right. I'll stay here for as long as they make me, just so long as I know you really want to have me home with you. While I'm here I'll work hard at learning to behave more like your Fanny Tennant. When I come out you'll be able to take me anywhere, I promise.' Just for a moment her lip trembled. 'I won't shame you again by having to take me somewhere barefoot.'

Fergus's smile hid the pain he felt on her behalf. 'I wasn't ashamed of you on that day, Becky, and I never will be.'

'It's easy to say that now, Fergus Vincent, but one day you're going to be famous. You won't want a Lewin's Mead brat hanging round you. Mary Carpenter's right. I should stay here. There's no other way to shake off the dirt of Lewin's Mead. I'll learn everything she can teach me, and I'll learn it well. You'll never have to be ashamed of me, I promise you.'

'Cross your heart?' Fergus managed a grin, although he felt closer to tears.

'Cross my heart and hope to die.' Becky grinned, too, and it cost her even more.

The woman who had brought Becky to the garden was advancing down the garden steps towards them now. It was time for Becky to return to the house.

'I'll need your help sometimes, Fergus.'

'You'll have it, I promise you.'

Becky nodded briefly but she was unable to prevent tears from welling up in her eyes. Cuffing them away angrily, she said: 'It's all right. I don't cry ... never.' Then, as her eyes filled again, she whispered: 'But I still wish I was coming home with you.'

CHAPTER TWENTY-FIVE

TOMAS CASEY was never brought to trial to answer the charges laid against him. Forty-eight hours after treating his homeless countrymen he was himself struck down with cholera.

Irish Molly gave the news to Fergus when he returned from the Red Lodge to the house in Back Lane. Tomas Casey had sent word from the Bridewell that he wanted to see her.

'I'll come with you.'

Fergus realised guiltily he had been so preoccupied with Becky that the plight of the arrested Chartist leader had been pushed to the back of his mind.

'I can't go anywhere near the Bridewell. The po-lice are looking for me.'

Irish Molly sounded genuinely distressed, and Fergus remembered how quickly she had taken to her heels when the police arrived at the derelict riverside houses to arrest Tomas Casey.

'Why should they be looking for you?'

'I spent an evening in a beer-shop with a drunken seaman, then he complained I'd stolen his purse. He said it had his pay from a two-year voyage in it.'

'Was he telling the truth?'

'He was not.' Irish Molly spoke indignantly. 'There was no more than two guineas there. The man was a boastful liar.'

Feeling that Irish Molly's indignation was perhaps not entirely justified, Fergus asked: 'When did all this happen?'

'Almost a year ago.'

'And the police are still looking for you? Surely they could have picked you up at any time, had they wanted to?'

'I've kept well out of their way.'

'Well, we can soon find out the truth of it. Here, take these upstairs to my room. I'll be back in a few minutes.'

Fergus passed his sketching satchel to Irish Molly and hurried from the house. He had spoken to Ivor Primrose not five minutes before. The big constable was trying to sort out the traffic chaos on a steep hill just beyond Lewin's Mead, caused by a wheel collapsing on an overladen wagon. He would know whether Irish Molly was still wanted.

When Fergus found him Ivor Primrose was wiping perspiration from his forehead with a large spotted handkerchief, having just played a considerable part in manhandling the broken wagon off the road.

'Irish Molly wanted? No – but I remember the complaint well. The seaman in question tried to obtain money from the Sailors' Relief Fund on the strength of his loss, but they discovered he'd never been farther than Ireland on his "round-the-world" voyages. He was given a month's hard labour and then he disappeared from Bristol. Are you telling me Irish Molly's thought for all this time that we were after her?' The constable grinned. 'No wonder she legged it so fast when we arrested Tomas Casey.'

'It's because of Casey that she needs to know whether she's still wanted. He's gone down with cholera, and we want to visit him in the Bridewell.'

'I'm sorry to hear about Casey. He's worked hard to help his people. But it's probably for the best. There's been talk that he would swing for his part in the rioting on the Downs. That's no way for a man to end his life – especially an educated man like Tomas Casey.'

Fergus had learned what he wanted to know but, as he turned to go, Ivor Primrose asked: 'By the way, how is that young friend of yours? Has she told you what really happened in Rose Cottle's place?'

'Not everything, but the gaps have been filled in for me by one of her friends.' Fergus told Ivor Primrose all he had heard.

'I thought it must be something like that when Alfie Skewes refused to lay any charges, even though he was close to death. He and his father are bad villains, Fergus. Beware of them. They won't know Becky is in Mary Carpenter's reformatory, and one of these days they're likely to come to Ida Stokes's house looking for her. Don't let anger lead you into any foolishness. They'd as soon stick a knife in you as look at you.'

'I'll try to remember your warning – but I can't promise anything.'

The sight of constables entering and leaving the Bridewell police station, just across the road from the prison, reduced Irish Molly to a state of abject fear. She had yet to be convinced that Ivor Primrose's assurance was anything more than a trick to bring her out of the narrow-streeted safety of the Lewin's Mead rookery. She became doubly nervous when she entered the damp dark confines of the Bridewell prison and she clutched Fergus's arm fearfully every time a heavy iron-clad door clanged shut behind them.

'It's all right, Molly. We're just *visiting*. There's no need to be nervous,' Fergus reassured his companion for the umpteenth time.

'So you keep telling me. Just you make sure you don't leave here without me, that's all.'

Eventually they were led to a small dark-walled cell, the gloom relieved by the faint light from a lamp hanging from the ceiling. A wooden bench ran the length of one wall, and on this Tomas Casey lay covered by a coarse grey blanket. There was no one in the room with him, and the gaoler did not enter. Locking the door behind Fergus and Irish Molly, he remained outside in the corridor.

Tomas Casey's breathing was shallow and rapid. He still had his red curly beard, and above this his face was bathed in perspiration. Fergus thought the Chartist leader was either asleep or unconscious, but he had heard them enter the cell. In a cracked voice he begged to be given water.

Her own fears forgotten, Irish Molly lifted a battered pewter jug from a small rough-board table in a corner of the cell.

The jug was empty. Striding to the door, Irish Molly banged on it noisily, adding a few new dents to the jug.

When the door swung open she thrust the jug at the gaoler. 'Here, fill this – and make sure it's good sweet water, or you'll feel the weight of the jug about your ears. Quickly now, before I forget I'm a lady and give you what you deserve for leaving a sick man without water or attention.'

By no stretch of the imagination could Irish Molly have been mistaken for a 'lady', but her anger was real enough. The gaoler took the jug from her and, grumbling to himself, hurried off to do her bidding.

The floor of the cell was filthy, and Irish Molly hitched up her skirts before crouching by the side of the crude and uncomfortable bunk. Wiping Tomas Casey's face with a silk handkerchief, purloined for her by Becky many months before, Irish Molly asked gently: 'How are you, me darling? Can I give you something to eat? I've brought some ox tongue, and a couple of bananas, given to me by a sailor. . . .'

Weak though he was, Tomas Casey shook his head with enough vigour to silence her. 'No. Just a drink . . . and talk.'

'Save the talking until you've had some water. Your voice is rough enough to take the hide off a Belfast dog. Here, I've brought you a drop o' "blue ruin". I'll not have you saying "no" to it, neither. It's the best thing you can possibly have inside your belly in your state.'

Putting a strong arm beneath Tomas Casey's head, Irish Molly raised him without any visible effort. Pulling the cork with her teeth, she placed the bottle to Tomas Casey's lips and tilted it.

Not until the sick man began choking did she remove the bottle. Fergus looked on in alarm as the sick Chartist leader threshed about on the narrow bunk, fighting for breath, his body writhing and contorting as though he were having a fit.

Irish Molly looked up at Fergus and shook her head sadly. 'He's on his way out, poor soul.' She spoke in a 'whisper' that carried to the gaoler, approaching along the corridor. 'It's always been his favourite tipple. I've known him knock back a half-bottle with hardly a pause for breath before now.'

When the gaoler entered the cell Fergus took the jug from

his and hurriedly filled a cup. Taking over from Irish Molly, he fed water to the choking man while she berated the gaoler, demanding that he bring a bucket and mop and clean up the cell floor.

Before the gaoler left the cell Fergus slipped a half-guinea into the man's hand. It was sufficient to stop the man's grumbling, but Irish Molly voiced her disapproval loudly.

'Anyone who needs to be given money before he'll tend to the needs of a dying man is a robber. Away with you – and when you return bring something to make the poor man half-comfortable.'

As the door banged shut behind the hurriedly departing gaoler, Tomas Casey beckoned for his two visitors to move closer. Whether it was as a result of the gin, or of the water, his voice was stronger, although he was still breathless.

'Molly, you're a fine girl. You'd make a good wife for a man. I'd marry you myself . . . but I've nothing to offer a girl now. I've little to offer anyone.'

'You haven't brought me here just to listen to your old blarney, Tomas. If you've something to say, then let's be hearing it.' Irish Molly's brusque and businesslike words were tempered by the fact that she had taken his hand and was patting it affectionately as she spoke.

Instead of replying, Tomas Casey arched his back in sudden pain. For more than a minute his two visitors looked on helplessly as disease and Irish tenacity fought each other for control of the wasted body.

When the bout was over Tomas Casey needed to wait until he was breathing more easily before he spoke again.

'I've made a will. . . . The prison chaplain has drawn it up for me. He's sent it to my executors . . . in Dublin. I don't own much. A small cottage. . . . A few pounds in the bank. . . . They're all to be yours when I die, Molly. . . . All but the money I owe to Fergus.'

'Hush now, we'll not be having any talk of dying. While you've God-given life left in you there's always hope.'

'I'm dying, Molly. You know it . . . and so do I. If only I could have lived to see the Chartists win the day. They will. . . . Ah, Fergus! If only you could put some of the power you show in your sketches into Chartism. . . .'

Suddenly it seemed as though the effort of talking became too much. Tomas Casey fell silent. As his eyelids drooped slowly the noise of his laboured breathing filled the tiny cell.

For many minutes Tomas Casey's breathing was the only sound in the cell. Then the distant clanging of heavy doors heralded the return of the gaoler.

As the sound came closer, Irish Molly said to Fergus: 'There's nothing more you can do for Tomas. Go on home: I'll stay with him for a while.'

She still had hold of her countryman's hand, and looking down at him she added quietly: 'It won't be long now. I've seen too many like him to hope for a miracle. Once they've sunk this low they go quickly. It'll be the kindest thing, too. Tomas has lived his life as a proud man, but a man with cholera is better knowing nothing at all of pride.'

The gaoler's key rattled in the lock, and Irish Molly repeated: 'Go now, Fergus. I'll be all right. No man should die alone, especially in a place like this. I'll stay here with him to the end.'

Fergus knew he could do no good by remaining in the evil-smelling Bridewell prison. Tomas Casey had lapsed into a sleep that bordered on unconsciousness. If he ever recovered his senses, Irish Molly and her bottle of 'blue ruin' could provide such comfort as might help the Chartist leader.

Sadly, Fergus left the Bridewell prison.

It was midnight when Fergus heard footsteps climbing the stairs to his attic room. He knew who it must be, and by the time Irish Molly pushed open the door he was filling a tumbler with Hollands, a somewhat superior gin to the 'blue ruin' she had served to Tomas Casey – but it was no less potent. Fergus handed the tumbler to Irish Molly without a word. He had already been sampling the contents of the bottle.

'God bless you, Fergus. I have need of this. I stopped off at the White Hart, but I couldn't take the good humour there tonight. Not after those last few hours with Tomas, God rest his soul.'

'He's gone, then?' Fergus realised he must have drunk more than he had realised. His voice sounded unusually slurred.

Irish Molly appeared not to have noticed. 'Sure he's gone, but he fought it to the end. Tomas was a fighter, and I dare anyone to say anything to the contrary.'

She emphasised her words by banging her already empty tumbler on the table, causing everything else there to jump and rattle.

Fergus refilled the tumbler, adding a splash of gin to his own half-empty glass. 'He was a good man,' he agreed.

'Good? He was a *saint*, I tell you. A real, live, God-fearing *saint*. Didn't he give his life for others? He should have been sailing back to his home instead of tending to his fellow-men. Back to Ireland. . . . Have you ever been there, Fergus?'

Fergus shook his head sadly.

'You must. You must. It's a lovely land. You'd love it.'

Irish Molly downed another glass of Hollands and stared morosely down at the empty glass until Fergus leaned across and refilled it.

'I've got a house there now, you know? *He* left it to me. He was a dear man. A dear, *dear* man.'

'You'll be going back to Ireland now you have a house there?'

'It's something I dream about, Fergus. To return and live the sort of life I can hardly remember any more. But that's all it is. A dream. I know that.'

Fergus shook the last few drops of gin from the bottle into Irish Molly's tumbler, and she looked down at it with an expression of dismal resignation.

'My room feels empty, not having Tomas there at all hours of the day and night. He was a great one for chattering. Half the time I didn't understand him, but he never seemed to mind. It's going to be even worse next week when Iris leaves the house. She's getting married, you know?'

'She's what . . .?' Fergus could not hide his surprise. Iris was the prostitute who occupied the room next to Irish Molly. Older than the Irish girl, she would pass the time of day with Fergus whenever they passed each other on the stairs, but he had never held a conversation with her. She appeared to pursue her 'profession' quietly and efficiently. 'She's marrying a Dutch captain. He's taking her to Holland with him.' Irish Molly stood up unsteadily. 'I'll go back to my room now.'

She set off across the attic studio, walking as though she carried a heavy weight suspended from her left hand.

By the time Fergus intercepted her she had strayed well off course and was heading for the wall a few feet to one side of the doorway.

'I'll help you down the stairs. They're a bit cranky, even when a body's sober.'

Fergus held Irish Molly's arm and took her down the stairs with exaggerated caution.

Leaning heavily on him, she said: 'You're a good boy, Fergus. A good *man*. Becky was foolish to run off and leave you the way she did.'

They were still a couple of stairs short of the first landing when Irish Molly pulled him to a halt.

'Will you stay with me tonight, Fergus? I don't like being on my own at any time. It'll be worse than usual tonight.'

'I'll see you safely back to your room, that's all. I don't think you'll have any trouble getting off to sleep.'

'Are you thinking I'm too old for you, Fergus Vincent? Is that what you think? Ah, well, you could be right. Perhaps you'll be more interested in the girl who's taking Iris's room when she's gone. Her name's Maude and she's not much older than Becky.... But you already know her. Maude Garrett...?

CHAPTER TWENTY-SIX

THE FUNERAL OF TOMAS CASEY was well attended. The service was held in Bristol's Roman Catholic cathedral, and the large modern building was filled to capacity for the occasion. In spite of the events of the weeks preceding the Chartist leader's death, many civic dignitaries attended the service, as did numerous Chartist supporters. The large number of mourners overawed Irish Molly. She had been Tomas Casey's only visitor while he was in prison. Fearing his body was destined for a pauper's grave, she had made a tentative offer to pay for a simple funeral. To her surprise, she had been informed by the prison authorities that 'arrangements were in hand' for Tomas Casey's burial.

Fergus accompanied Irish Molly to the service and they occupied seats well to the rear of the building. At the graveside, too, they stood well behind the 'official' mourners, and Irish Molly's small posy was lost amidst the more ostentatious floral tributes contributed by the city elders.

Nevertheless, Fanny saw both Fergus and Irish Molly. Indeed, it would have been difficult to overlook the Irish prostitute, even in such a crowd. Irish Molly had put on her very best dress for the occasion, but the bright-green full-skirted velvet and silk creation had been purchased from a dollyshop to attract sailors, not for attending a funeral.

Aware of Irish Molly's way of life, Fanny disapproved of her easy familiarity with Fergus, even though she tried to keep things in perspective. Fergus lived in Lewin's Mead, Bristol's most notorious slum. It was hardly surprising if his friends were from there, too. She told herself that Fergus was pursuing a goal, one that no one else could achieve. Yet the nagging conviction persisted that it might as easily be achieved from Clifton.

When the Catholic priest began saying a prayer over the grave of Tomas Casey, Irish Molly broke down in tears. Fergus would have led her away, but the Irish prostitute refused to allow him to leave.

'Please stay, Fergus. Tomas would have wanted one of us to stay until the end. I always make a fool of myself at funerals. They're almost as moving as weddings. I'll go, but you stay. Please!'

The next moment Irish Molly had gone, slipping away easily through the loosely knit crowd.

Fergus remained until the ceremony was over. Then, with the others, he stood back respectfully to allow the official mourners to leave first.

Fanny would have walked past without acknowledging him, but Lady Hammond was with her, and the elderly philanthropist recognised him.

'Why, it's the young Scots artist – but of course you met poor Tomas at one of Fanny's parties. You should have joined us . . . Fergus – isn't that your name?'

'*Mister* Vincent came to the funeral with a friend from Lewin's Mead.' Fanny's voice was icy enough to cause Lady Hammond's eyebrows to rise in amused surprise. 'Where has she gone? Lady Hammond would have enjoyed meeting her.'

'Irish Molly was so overcome with grief she had to leave.' Fergus was puzzled by Fanny's unprovoked hostility, but he thought she deserved an explanation. 'She knew Tomas well. She was with him when he died. I believe she is also the sole beneficiary in his will. It was she who persuaded him to come out of hiding and treat the sick Irish families. Because of what happened, Molly feels responsible for his death.'

'Poor girl. I would have liked to meet her. It's time you and I met again, too, young man. Call on me some time soon – and bring your sketchbook with you.' With a smile and a nod of her head, Lady Hammond moved on.

Fanny remained behind for a moment longer and seemed

about to say something to Fergus. Instead, she turned and hurried after Lady Hammond, and the two women walked together to a waiting carriage.

A few nights later a large number of ships docked in Bristol from the West Indies. Fergus took advantage of the increased business at the Hatchet inn. There were more seamen in the inns about the docks than there had been for very many weeks and they were willing to pay for sketches. Fergus did good business, and it came as a great relief. Loaning money to Tomas Casey had left Fergus with little to spare after paying for rent, food and fuel.

It was about eleven o'clock at night when a man made his way to the table where Fergus had just completed a sketch of a black-bearded Welsh seaman. Fergus had seen the man earlier that evening. Seated at a table just inside the door, he seemed to be taking a great interest in Fergus and his work.

Setting his drink on the table, the man sat down facing Fergus. Looking up at him, Fergus smiled and turned to a fresh page of his sketchpad. 'Is it a sketch you're wanting? Well, you've come to the right place.'

'I'm in the right place all right, but what I want to know is the whereabouts of a friend of yours.' The man spoke hoarsely, as though he was suffering from a severe sore throat.

The smile left Fergus's face. 'A friend? If it's Tomas Casey, you're too late. He was buried today.'

'It's not Casey. I want to find a girl. Becky's her name.'

'Why do you want Becky. . . ?' Sudden enlightenment came to Fergus. 'I know you. You're the son of Joe Skewes.'

'Names don't matter. It's Becky I want. I've been told that if anyone knows where she is it's the crippled painter who works the Hatchet inn. I don't see any other crippled painter in here.'

'I'll tell you nothing – except that she's beyond your reach.'

Fergus felt a great rage growing inside him. This was one of the men who had brutally raped Becky. He felt frustration, too. He ought to give this man the beating he deserved, but Fergus realised he would be no match for Alfie Skewes. More than a head taller, the coal-heaver must have been at least four stone heavier, and his face bore the scars of a lifetime of fighting.

Ashamed of his inability to deal with Alfie Skewes as he deserved, Fergus gathered up his sketchpad and made a move to rise from the table. Alfie Skewes leaned across the table and, placing a great hand on Fergus's shoulder, pushed him back in his seat again.

'You'll go when you've told me where I can find the girl. I know she's not living in Back Lane any more. I've been there.'

Fergus struggled to break free, but the grip on his shoulder tightened painfully. In a sudden burst of furious desperation Fergus lashed out with his fist. The blow caught Alfie Skewes over his left eye. There was sufficient force behind the blow to cause Alfie Skewes to release his grip, but before Fergus could make his escape the bullying coal-heaver was on his feet and towering over him.

'I'll teach you to hit me. . . .' Alfie Skewes swung his arm in a backhanded blow and knocked Fergus from his seat to the floor.

As Fergus struggled to sit up Alfie Skewes threw the heavy table to one side. Moving surprisingly quickly for a big man, he leaned down intending to drag Fergus to his feet.

Alfie Skewes was brought to an abrupt halt when a hand as large as his own gripped the back of his jacket collar and hauled him upright.

'I'll have no brawling in my inn. If you've a difference with someone, you'll settle it with words or go elsewhere.'

'Keep out of this, landlord. This is between me and the crippled artist.'

Not until Alfie Skewes had tried unsuccessfully to shake off the hand gripping his collar did he turn around to look at the landlord of the Hatchet inn. He saw a bald-headed man, burly but past his prime. The sight reassured him.

Meanwhile, Charlie Waller was talking to Fergus. 'What's this all about? It's not like you to become involved in any trouble.'

'This is Alfie Skewes. He and his father take their pleasure attacking young girls. The last one fought back and left Alfie with a scar to remember her by. He's trying to make me tell him where she is, so he can teach her a lesson.'

'Oh, you'll tell me all right. By the time I've done with you you'll be singing like a lark.'

Once again Alfie Skewes tried to break free of Charlie Waller's grip, but the landlord screwed the collar tighter. 'It's not singing but *dancing* we'll have here tonight, my beauty — and *you'll* be dancing to *my* tune, make no mistake.'

Alfie Skewes dug back with his elbow, at the same time throwing all his weight behind an attempt to break the land-lord's grip.

Charlie Waller was ready for the ploy. The elbow missed him, and he released his grip on Alfie Skewes's collar. As the coal-heaver turned towards him the landlord of the Hatchet inn stepped in close. Two short vicious jabs landed flush on Alfie Skewes's jaw, dropping him to the floor, his senses thoroughly scrambled.

The brief action brought howls of glee from the patrons of the inn. Before the sound died away, Charlie Waller's big voice boomed out: 'I think he's a bit dazed, boys. He's more used to beating young girls who can't fight back. A good dowsing should bring him round. Will you give it to him?'

A loud chorus of 'Ay!' gave Charlie Waller his answer. Putting up only a feeble resistance, Alfie Skewes was picked up bodily. Encircled by a couple of dozen seamen, he was hurried out through the door to the street.

'You saved me from a beating.' Fergus spoke to the land-lord as he recovered some of his pencils from the floor beneath the upturned table.

'You ought to pick on someone your own size, me lad, otherwise you'll end up with worse than that — especially if the Skeweses are involved.' Charlie Waller touched a graze beside Fergus's eye, where a ring worn by Alfie Skewes had broken the skin.

'I'll need to watch my step,' agreed Fergus. 'The Skewes family are slow to forget a grudge.'

'You don't need to worry overmuch. When Alfie Skewes

climbs out of the dock he'll find Ivor Primrose waiting for him. Ivor was in the back room enjoying a drink when the trouble began. He'll warn Alfie what to expect if anything happens to you. Ivor's too well known around Lewin's Mead for anyone to want to cross him. Come into the kitchen now and let my wife put something on that cut, or you'll bleed all over your sketches.'

Becky was concerned when she saw the bruising on Fergus's face and learned he had come to blows with Alfie Skewes. However, it was necessary to keep her feelings largely to herself. Because the girls in the Red Lodge reformatory were of dubious morals, the authorities insisted that Fergus's lesson be conducted with the classroom door wedged wide open. Even with this precaution a suspicious official put her head round the doorway every five minutes or so. Yet it was still possible to conduct a conversation while pretending to be criticising a sketch, and occasionally Fergus would enclose Becky's hand in his and guide her pencil over the paper, aware of the knowing grins and elbow-digging of the other girls in the class.

Becky was less understanding when Fergus told her Maude Garrett would soon be moving to Ida Stokes's house in Back Lane.

'Why is *she* going to live there?' She hissed the question at Fergus. 'She's got her own place in Broadmead, and a family to look after.'

'Maude's sister has taken on more responsibility for the family so that Maude can branch out on her own.'

The statement needed no explanation. Becky knew well enough how young girls living alone in Lewin's Mead earned a living.

'You know a lot about it. Who told you?' Becky's quick guarded glance was filled with suspicion.

'Maude has been to the house to talk to Irish Molly a couple of times. I've thanked her for her help in rescuing you from Rose Cottle.'

Becky snorted. 'She's talked to you more than she has to me. Has she been up to your room?'

'Yes. She admired the sketches I've made of you.'

'Are you going to paint *her* picture?'

'I haven't thought about it,' Fergus lied. He was aware that the other girls were taking an increasing interest in the conversation between Becky and himself.

Fearing one of the staff might look into the room while Becky was in such a smoulderingly explosive mood, Fergus took her hand and attempted to move the pencil over the sheet of paper on the desk in front of her. 'We'll talk about it some other time.'

'When? After the lesson's over when I line up with the other girls for my tea? Or during the two hours afterwards when we're all having "religious learning" together? No, I've just remembered, it's *bath* night tonight. This is the night when the staff watch us undress and bath, and make us wash out our mouths with soap if we've been caught swearing during the week.'

Becky pulled her hand free angrily. 'There's *no* way you can talk to me in here. Not without someone listening to every word we say, there isn't. They even walk around our rooms at night to see if they can find out what we're *dreaming* about. I *hate* this place. I hate everyone in it – and I hate *you*, Fergus Vincent.'

Becky's voice became shriller as she gave way to her anger, and as two members of staff hurried into the room the class erupted in pandemonium. Fergus was bundled from the room clutching his sketchpad, and more members of staff arrived to help restore order.

Fergus was left in a small room by himself for more than twenty minutes before the uproar gradually subsided.

Eventually a tall grim-visaged woman entered the room and informed Fergus that Mary Carpenter wished to speak to him.

As he followed the tall member of staff up the stairs to Mary Carpenter's study, Fergus felt depressed. Coming to give sketching lessons to the Red Lodge reformatory inmates provided him with an opportunity to meet and talk with Becky. No doubt the riot in the classroom would put an end to such meetings.

Much to Fergus's surprise he found Mary Carpenter in a cheerful frame of mind. When he tried to apologise for the disturbance, claiming it was his fault, she waved him to silence.

'I have no doubt you *precipitated* the trouble, Mr Vincent, but we have been expecting something like this for quite a while.'

The pioneer reformer smiled at his bewilderment. 'It doesn't surprise you, surely. You are well acquainted with Becky. She's a lively spirited young girl, used to leading a life of almost total independence – as are most of my girls. Confinement in this house, with all the discipline it entails, is totally alien to her. We've been waiting for just such an explosion of temperament. It happens to *all* girls of her type who come here. It's a *good* sign, believe me.'

'But ... does it mean I'll be able to continue to come here teaching? That was a near-riot in there. . . .'

Mary Carpenter smiled once more. 'No, Mr Vincent. It was the pricking of a fester. The opportunity for some of the wickedness that's in all of us to escape harmlessly. It was a *noisy* incident, nothing more.'

Greatly relieved, Fergus asked eagerly: 'May I speak to Becky before I go?'

Mary Carpenter shook her head. 'I don't think that would be wise. Nor will she attend your next couple of lessons. This is not a punishment, I hasten to add, but Becky is very fond of you. She will feel foolish and ashamed of her behaviour today. She will not *want* to see you for a while. We'll keep her away until she asks if she can resume sketching again. I'm quite certain you understand. But I have much to do – I don't doubt you have, too. Good day, Mr Vincent. We will see you again at the same time next week.'

In spite of Mary Carpenter's reassuring words, Fergus left the Red Lodge with a feeling that he had somehow failed Becky.

He would have felt far worse had he known that from the window of a room, high in the Red Lodge, Becky watched him making his way home to Lewin's Mead. She hoped he might turn and see her, and yet she remained poised to dart away from the window if he *did* turn round. She could see by the set of his shoulders that Fergus felt miserable and the knowledge was a solid painful lump deep inside her.

CHAPTER TWENTY-SEVEN

BEFORE IRIS LEFT IDA STOKES'S HOUSE to marry her Dutch sea-captain the prospective bridegroom threw a party that would be remembered in Lewin's Mead for many months to come.

Fergus was busy painting in his attic studio when the drinks began to arrive. Hearing a noise, he went down the rickety stairs and peered over the banisters to the first floor. A number of firkins of ale were being manhandled up the stairs by cheerful Dutch sailors.

Not wishing to join in the celebrations, Fergus returned to his room and resumed painting. He was nearing completion of the series depicting the plight of the Irish immigrants, and it was an emotionally exhausting task. Committing the tragic figures to canvas conjured up many memories and mental images that he thought he had forgotten.

Fergus soon became totally engrossed with his painting. Although aware of an increasing noise in the remainder of the house, it had no part in his work and he was able to exclude it from his mind.

When the light was beginning to fade he heard footsteps on the stairs to the attic and then there came a hammering at the door. Before he had time to rise from his chair the door opened and Maude Garrett entered the room carrying two battered pewter tankards in one hand.

'I thought this was where you'd be. Aren't you coming downstairs to join in Iris's party? Everyone else in the house is there. I'm going to have a hell of a job clearing up when I move in tomorrow.'

Fergus shrugged apologetically. 'I've got a lot of work to do. I want to complete the paintings of the Irish. . . .'

'I knew you'd have some excuse for not coming down, that's why I've brought a drink up for you.'

'That's very thoughtful of you, Maude.' Fergus had been so engrossed in his work he had paused for neither food nor drink since breakfast. He took a full tankard from her hands and raised it to his lips, believing it to contain ale. The fumes that rose to his nostrils told him of his error, but by then he had already taken a deep gulp and was coughing out his mistake.

'I thought you was going at it a bit greedy.' Maude Garrett put down her own tankard and began thumping his back as she spoke. 'That's real good brandy, that is. Captain Gobius brought it in a barrel specially for his wedding.'

It was some minutes before Fergus could breathe normally once more and take another sip from the tankard. He nodded appreciatively. It *was* very good brandy.

Meanwhile Maude Garrett was inspecting the paintings lined up against a wall to dry. As she crouched down to look more closely at one of the paintings her thin dress was stretched taut across her back and Fergus saw that she was pitifully thin. Skinnier even than Becky.

Straightening up suddenly, Maude Garrett turned to look at Fergus with an expression of new respect. 'These are beautiful paintings, Fergus. But they're so *sad*. They make me want to cry.'

'That's exactly how I felt when I made the sketches.' Acutely aware of the brandy warming his empty stomach, Fergus studied a painting depicting the afflicted Irish families being escorted away from the derelict houses. 'They were a doomed people.'

'Do you always feel something for the people you're painting?' Maude Garrett had moved on and was examining a number of completed paintings, among them some of Becky.

'That depends on the subject.' Fergus made a guarded reply.

'I hope you haven't forgotten you've promised to paint me.'

'I've promised to *sketch* you,' Fergus corrected her. 'There's a difference.'

'All right – to *sketch* me, then. When?'

Fergus shrugged. The brandy was taking effect and he felt at peace with the world. 'Any time. *Now* if you like.'

'Yes, do it now. What do you want me to do?'

Fergus drained his tankard and handed it to her. 'You can go and get me another drink while I look out a good pencil.'

Maude Garrett's face had a fine bone structure, but she was not a good model. She insisted on adopting unnatural facial poses that could not be transferred to paper. Nevertheless, by persuading her to talk to him as he worked, Fergus caught her unawares often enough to produce a good likeness. However, Maude was not happy with the sketch.

'I don't look like *that*!'

The sketch showed a certain sharpness of expression that was not immediately discernible on Maude Garrett's face.

'The light isn't too good right now,' he pleaded. 'Besides, it takes more than a single sketch if I'm to get a true likeness.'

The explanation seemed to satisfy Maude Garrett. Still looking at the sketch, she suddenly smiled. 'I expect you're right. It isn't too bad really, although it looks as though I'm wearing what my sister Lisa calls my "someone's-going-to-suffer-for-this" expression.'

'How is your sister? Will she be able to care for the family when you've moved out?'

Maude Garrett's smile disappeared. 'She'll *have* to. Pa's giving her a hard time, but I've put up with him for long enough. It's her turn now.'

Her voice died away as they both heard someone noisily negotiating the stairs outside the room. There was a crash and mumbled cursing as the unseen visitor slipped. Then there was a noisy hammering at the door.

Fergus lifted the latch, and as he opened the door a large man with greying hair and an unkempt beard fell into the room.

The bearded man blinked in the sudden light of the oil-lamp, a luxury Fergus had recently acquired. Rising to his feet, he extended a large hand to Fergus. 'You must be the artist. I am Pieter Gobius. I am to marry Iris. You have not come to our party. Do you not wish us happiness together?'

Then the Dutch sea-captain saw Maude Garrett standing in the shadows at the far end of the long attic room.

'I am sorry. You have *other* reasons for not coming to my party. No matter, you will come. She will come, too. *Everybody* comes to my wedding party. You must bring this.' Captain Pieter Gobius picked up a sketchpad and waved it drunkenly in front of Fergus's face. 'You will make a picture of Iris and me.'

Fergus did not feel inclined to argue with the sea-captain. In any case, the brandy brought to the attic by Maude Garrett had put him in the mood for a party.

'All right. I'll give you a sketch as a wedding present. Lead on. You, too, Maude.'

Maude Garrett scowled as she left the attic. She had planned to spend much of the evening in Fergus's studio.

The party was in full noisy swing when the trio from the attic room arrived, but Captain Gobius's voice was capable of carrying to men in the rigging of a ship at the height of a North Sea storm. He needed to call for silence only once before the noise faltered and died away.

'You will clear a space for me and Iris to have a drawing made of us.' Turning to Fergus, Pieter Gobius asked: 'Where would you like us to be?'

As Fergus looked around the dingy overcrowded room, the voice of Irish Molly called loudly: 'Let Fergus sketch you both in bed together. It'll remind you of when you first met.'

When the ribald laughter had died down, Fergus said sheepishly: 'Actually, the bed *is* the best place in the room. If the two of you can sit on the edge together. . . .'

His words were greeted with cheers, and Irish Molly could be heard shouting jubilantly: 'There, what did I tell you? It's the natural place for the pair of 'em.'

Iris and her husband-to-be settled themselves self-consciously on the edge of the bed, but they grew more relaxed when Fergus brought them closer together. When he ordered Pieter Gobius to put an arm about Iris's shoulders the good-natured bantering began again.

Fergus sketched quickly, used to working in the Hatchet inn. When he eventually ripped the page from his sketchpad and passed it over, the not-so-young couple beamed their delight. Fergus had been kind in his portraiture, carefully playing down the defects of both parties.

'It is good. It is *very* good.' Pieter Gobius's voice boomed out his approval. 'Give the young artist a drink. A large brandy.'

Moments later Fergus had another huge brandy in his hand. It was his third of the evening, and things became increasingly hazy thereafter. He remembered repeated requests for sketches, and he executed them at a rapid rate, but his pencil could not keep up with the demand – or the amount of brandy being forced upon him.

He kept going until he suddenly found himself sitting on the floor, sketchpad and pencil gone, and with only a half-empty tankard of brandy for company, while the stamping feet of 'dancers' shook dust from the floorboards beside him.

'Come on, it's time I got you back to your room.'

It was Maude Garrett's coaxing words rather than her doubtful strength which brought Fergus to his feet after he had rescued his sketchpad from beneath the bed. She guided him through the crowd and past a couple embracing at the foot of the stairs to the attic. Fergus thought the woman looked like Ida Stokes, but he dismissed the identification immediately, attributing it to the poor light and the effects of the brandy he had consumed.

Fergus never knew how he negotiated the stairs, remembering only that at one stage he gave up the steep climb, declaring that if he had wanted to climb mountains he would have remained in Scotland.

He *did* eventually reach his room because he could remember unsuccessfully trying to focus his bleary eyes on the lamp. He also had a vague recollection of indignantly protesting when he lay on his bed as someone undressed him. . . . But he remembered nothing more of that night.

Fergus came awake with a sudden start. Opening his eyes he saw the ceiling above him and raised his head as he always did, to gauge the time from the light coming through the attic window. The move set loose the hammers held poised above their anvils by a dozen blacksmiths – all gathered and waiting in Fergus's head.

His head dropped back on the pillow, and a groan of self-pity escaped from between lips that felt like dry leather to the touch of his furred and bloated tongue.

The sound had an echo from nearby, and there was a movement in the bed beside him. Then a body came into contact with his own – and both were as naked as newborn babies.

Battling successfully against pain and the nauseous swinging of the room about him, Fergus struggled to a sitting position and peered down at Maude Garrett.

Fergus leaped from the bed, his self-induced ailments forgotten. By the time Maude Garrett stretched spindly arms above her head and opened one brown eye to gaze in his direction, he was hopping awkwardly in a clumsy circle, trying to thread a second leg inside a pair of trousers.

Maude Garrett sat up, and her skinny chest settled into an undernourished semblance of womanly form.

'What time is it?'

'Late. Past nine, certainly.' His voice emanated from deep within his throat.

'Christ! I'm hours late for work. I'll have the sack. . . .' Her urgency ebbed away as suddenly as it had sprung into being, and Maude Garrett lay back on the bed again. 'Oh, what the hell! I move into Iris's room today and begin a new life.' She turned both her brown eyes on Fergus. 'Do you think the party is still going on?'

Fergus groaned. 'I don't even want to think about it. I feel too ill.'

'Poor Fergus.' Maude Garrett threw back the blanket, exposing her thin body as far as her knees. 'Come back to bed. I'll make you feel better. . . .'

Fergus had his trousers on just in time. His stomach was heaving, and the communal privies were in the backyard. He fled barefoot down the stairs, determined to reach the yard in time.

When Fergus returned to the attic room, ashen-faced and wan, Maude Garrett was dressed and the kettle rattled merrily on the fire.

'Sit down. I'll make you some tea. Would you like any breakfast? No, I didn't think so.'

Fergus sat down shakily and followed Maude's movements about the room. When she put a mug of steaming tea on the table in front of him he put his hand around the mug gratefully, avoiding looking up into her face.

'Are you sure you know what you're doing? The life you intend leading . . . ?'

Maude Garrett snorted derisively. 'That's a funny question after last night. Yes, I know what I'm doing. Irish Molly's going to take me to the White Hart with her and show me the ropes. It'll be good to be working for myself and not having to hand over most of my money to the old man, for him to spend on drink. I'll make sure the kids don't go short, though.'

Fergus winced, not because of the life Maude Garrett intended leading, but because of her references to the previous night.

'Did anything happen last night? I mean . . . between you and me?'

'Don't you remember? I'll need to work harder if I'm to have my regulars, like Irish Molly.'

Fergus groaned. 'I'm sorry. . . . I was so drunk I don't remember a thing.'

'If you wanted to go back to bed again, I could remind you.'

Maude Garrett was enjoying his discomfiture, and Fergus rose to his feet unsteadily. 'I'm going out. I need some fresh air.'

'I expect I'll be in my own room when you get back. Call in and see me, Fergus . . . *any* time.'

Crossing the first-floor landing, Fergus thought Maude Garrett was being unduly optimistic. It looked as though a battle had been fought in the room she was to occupy. Bodies, bottles, barrels, tankards and all manner of rubbish extended as far as the front door of the house. There was even a man dressed as a seaman lying in the gutter in the street outside, the linings of his empty pockets ominously displayed to the world.

Fergus wandered disconsolately about the quays, watching ships being loaded and unloaded. The rattle of block and tackle vied with the creak and clatter of horses and wagons, and wagoners cursed their horses as shod hoofs slipped and slid on cobblestones wet from the light drizzle that fell on the city.

It was autumn cold, and Fergus shivered. He had come out without a coat, but he did not want to return to Back Lane just yet. He found a small coffee-house on the quayside and for twopence bought a large mug of weak but sweet coffee. He sat in the dismal coffee-house warming his hands about the mug.

Fergus wished he could remember more of what had occurred the previous night. There were brief recollections of tripping on the stairs while someone tried to steady him, and of lying on his bed while someone else undressed him. He cringed at the thought. He was very self-conscious of his crippled leg and rarely allowed anyone else to see it. Fergus tried to stretch his memory, but it was a total blank. He would never know what had happened after he had been put to bed by Maude Garrett.

Sitting in the coffee-shop feeling cold and ill, Fergus came close to abandoning his dream of recording the life of those who lived in the slums of Bristol. He could move on to London, perhaps. Begin again.

Just then a young urchin came into the coffee-shop wearing a dress consisting of a slip of sacking, stitched up the sides and with holes for head and arms. Her face was as dirty as he had once seen Becky's.

The urchin was begging, and the coffee-shop proprietor waved a cloth in the air, ordering her to get out. Expressionless, she had turned to obey when Fergus called her back.

Reaching in his pocket, he pulled out a fourpenny piece. He had once given a coin of the same value to Becky. The urchin's face lit up with delight, and she ran from the coffee-shop as though afraid Fergus might change his mind. Behind the counter at the far end of the coffee-shop the proprietor dried a cup with the dirty cloth and shook his head in disapproval.

Rising to his feet, Fergus limped to the door. Hunching his shoulders against the drizzle, he stepped outside on to the wet cobblestones of the quayside.

He would not leave Bristol. He would continue painting children like the one who had just left the coffee-shop and he would put together an exhibition that would bring their plight home to the world.

He owed it to Becky.

CHAPTER TWENTY-EIGHT

IT WAS THREE WEEKS before Fergus saw Becky again. Mary Carpenter had sent a message to him, suggesting that he cancel his lessons for the two weeks following the trouble at the Red Lodge.

When Fergus did return he found an unrepentant Becky who refused to apologise for her behaviour on the occasion of their previous meeting. Indeed, she hardly spoke to Fergus during the whole time he was there.

For the next few weeks Fergus showed great patience, and the rift between them healed slowly. Then, one late autumn day, when the first frost of the year had put a silver sheen on the grass of the park sloping away up the hill from the Red Lodge, Fergus entered the reformatory to a welcome from Becky that was warm enough to dispel the chill from the high-ceilinged room. The unsmiling classroom supervisor passed her charges into Fergus's care and had hardly left the room when Becky suddenly hugged Fergus and planted a happy kiss on his cheek.

Hastily waving her classmates to silence, Fergus asked what he had done to deserve such a welcome.

'It's because I'm happy to belong to you.'

'*Belong* to me? I don't understand.'

'Well, I do. Fanny Tennant said so. She brought a lady to see us. A *real* lady.... Lady Hammond, I think her name is. Fanny Tennant called me to the front of the class and said: "This is Becky; she's Fergus Vincent's *protégée*." ' Becky said the word slowly and carefully, as though she had been practising. 'I asked Selina what it meant, and she said it means you belong to someone.'

Selina was the brightest of the girls in the reformatory, placed there for her part in a banknote fraud that had netted hundreds of pounds and resulted in two counterfeiters being gaoled for life.

Becky looked at Fergus anxiously, afraid she had made a fool of herself. 'That *is* what it means?'

Fergus smiled. 'I guess it does – and, yes, you are certainly my *protégée*.'

'There you are, then!' Becky beamed triumphantly. 'If I'd known I was your *protégée* ... if you'd *told* me, I wouldn't have caused you half the trouble I have.'

She frowned. 'How did I become your *protégée*?' She was enjoying the use of her new-found word.

'It happened when I became fond of you and began to feel responsible for you.'

'Does that mean you're my *protégé*, too?'

'Not exactly. . . .' The other girls were following the conversation with great interest, and Fergus was aware that the lesson should have begun. 'We'll discuss it some other time. You'd all better begin sketching now.'

'All right, if you say so.' Becky smiled happily at him, and Fergus wondered whether Fanny Tennant had any idea how her simple introduction had brightened Becky's young life.

Fergus worked hard at his paintings until a shortage of money sent him back to the Hatchet inn. However, he still took his sketchpad about with him whenever he went out during the daylight hours. The cold weather heralded an early winter, and beggars, vagrants and the desperately poor had already donned their winter 'fashions'. Every available form of covering was utilised to protect thin bodies from wind and weather. Tattered blankets, sacking and even newspapers were brought into use, but even such primitive protection was beyond the means of a few orphaned urchins. Fergus sketched them as they sheltered in corners and doorways, angry red chilblains flourishing on their dirty hands and feet.

Fergus had seen little of Fanny Tennant since Tomas Casey's funeral. It was as though she was deliberately avoiding him, even when he gave his weekly lesson in the ragged school. It came as something of a surprise, therefore, when Fanny walked into one of his classes at the ragged school. After greeting Fergus politely she went to a corner of the room where pupils squatted on the floor sketching a quite ordinary pitcher. After inspecting their half-completed drawings she returned to stand beside Fergus and looked down at the sketch he was making of the class at work.

'We always seem to have a full class for your sketching, Fergus.' She spoke quietly, so as not to disturb the working children.

'It's warmer in here than out on the streets.' This at least was true. Through the high rounded windows the sky was a sullen snow-filled grey.

'I believe it's something more than that. Whatever it is, I wish we could bring it into our other lessons. The numbers of our pupils are dropping quite dramatically.'

'Perhaps the school is suffering as a result of your absence.'

'Because I don't often attend the school on the days *you're* here doesn't mean I am not here on the other days....' Aware of the possible interpretation of her words, Fanny explained: 'I help my father one day a week, but he is in London on business for a while.'

'I wasn't being critical, merely making an observation. I realise you lead a very busy life ... but I also believe the ragged school needs you.'

'I wonder. Indeed, I sometimes wonder whether it might not be better for everyone – especially for *me* – if I gave up the whole wretched idea. Perhaps I should take my father's advice and spend more time in London, or seeing something of the Continent.'

Fanny's words rocked Fergus. He had always looked upon her as being totally dedicated to her 'good causes'.

Fanny saw his bewilderment and she shrugged apologetically. 'I'm sorry, Fergus. I am feeling particularly depressed this morning. I was called to the Bridewell police station last night. One of our pupils is in trouble. She is involved with an

233

unsavoury young man who has been in and out of prison regularly since he was eight years old. Last night they entered a house, threatened an old lady and stole some silver. They ran from the house straight into the arms of two constables.'

Fanny shook her head sadly. 'I cannot understand her. She is such a bright young girl. One of the school's best pupils. I had great hopes of setting her on the path to a decent future, perhaps using her as an example for others to follow. Now she'll receive ten years, or more, in prison. When she comes out, thieving or prostitution will be her only means of earning a living. Before long she will be back in prison again – and that will be the pattern of her miserable existence. It's a tragedy.'

Fergus was about to make a trivial remark about life being simple were it not complicated by people, but he could see that Fanny was deeply upset.

'We mustn't expect too much of people, Fanny. Especially those brought up in Lewin's Mead. Things that seem everyday to us appear frighteningly strange to them – and, God knows, the familiar is frightening enough.'

'I seem to remember suggesting you should apply such splendid logic to your relationship with Becky.'

After only the slightest hesitation, Fergus said: 'I do, but I'm always willing to help her improve *herself*.'

Fergus's hesitation had nothing to do with the reply he made. He was wondering why, whenever he was talking with either Becky or Fanny, each seemed disproportionately interested in the other.

'That wasn't a fair comment, Fergus. I'm sorry. I really came here to remind you of your promise to show your sketches to Lady Hammond. I met her a day or two ago. She said if you don't soon bring her some of your work she will be forced to visit your studio, in Back Lane.'

For a moment Fergus contemplated the stir a visit from Lady Hammond would cause in the squalid and overcrowded slum. He dismissed the thought immediately. Ida Stokes's house was no place for Lady Hammond.

'I haven't forgotten. I'll show them to her.'

'When?'

'I have a lot of paintings to do that I haven't even begun yet. . . .'

'Lady Hammond isn't asking to see all your work. She would like to see a sample. Some sketches and one or two paintings, no more.'

'I do have *some* paintings completed. . . .'

'Good. When can I tell her to expect you?'

Fanny was forcing Fergus into making a decision. There was no way he could wriggle free without appearing churlish – and no *real* reason why he should. Ironically, the true reason for his prevarication was the one he had given to explain the behaviour of those who lived in Lewin's Mead. He was as reluctant to move on into the unknown as were they.

Fergus had spent many months sketching the Bristol slum and had built up a remarkable pictorial catalogue of its people and their way of life. There was still much work to be done before he would be satisfied with his self-imposed task. It would *never* be fully comprehensive, but the time was fast approaching when others would need to judge whether his work was worthwhile. Fanny was pushing that time closer.

There was some justification for Fergus's apprehension. Lady Hammond was an acknowledged art expert. Her comments about Fergus's paintings and sketches would be accepted by the art world, of which she was a formidable part. If she were to be critical of his paintings, his dream of showing them to the world at large would be over.

Fergus was not certain he would find Lady Hammond's approval any easier to accept. He would then come under pressure to complete his project. There would be exhibitions, discussions of his work, and no doubt commissions, too. The simple life he had been leading in Back Lane would be over. He would become part of the larger world once more.

'If you don't want to take your sketches and paintings to Lady Hammond, I will willingly take them for you. I'll come to Back Lane and collect them, if you wish.'

'No.' The word came out unintentionally abruptly, but Fergus would not entrust his completed paintings to anyone else, especially if they were to be carried through the narrow thief-infested alleyways of the Lewin's Mead rookery. 'I'll take them myself.'

'When?' Fanny was relentless.

'Next week, some time.'

'What day next week – and at what time? I'll come with you and show you the way.'

By the time Fanny left the classroom Fergus had committed himself to taking a sketchpad and two completed paintings to show Lady Hammond. He would bring them to the ragged school at six o'clock the following Tuesday evening, and Fanny would be waiting with a carriage to take Fergus and his work to Lady Hammond's Clifton home.

CHAPTER TWENTY-NINE

LADY SARAH HAMMOND'S HOME was sumptuous, even by Clifton standards. A liveried butler opened the door to Fergus and Fanny and escorted them to the room where Lady Hammond sat with a number of her friends. Fergus was disconcerted by the company. He had expected to be showing his work only to Lady Hammond. He was not dressed to meet the guests he found in her house.

Lady Hammond saw his discomfiture and guessed the reason immediately. Advancing across the room, she took his arm and led him to the large table where a servant had placed the paintings and sketches, waving for her other guests to follow.

To Fergus, she said: 'You can meet the others later. They're here because they have been *dying* to meet you and see your work. Actually, the only one you need take any notice of is Ferdinand. Ferdinand Lascelles. Of course, if he *really* likes them, he'll probably refuse to say anything at all, for fear you'll put up the price when he tries to buy them.'

Now Fergus was more certain than ever that it had been a mistake to bring his work here. Ferdinand Lascelles was a famous art critic and dealer. One wrong word from him this evening and any future Fergus might have had as a painter would be ruined.

They reached the table with the others close behind, and Lady Hammond released Fergus's arm. 'You can begin by showing us some of your sketches. Fanny speaks of them as though they depict life in another world, so let us inside this world of yours, young man.'

Fergus had brought his personal sketchpad, not the one he took to the Hatchet inn. It commenced with sketches of Becky and life in and about Back Lane. It also included sketches made on board the ill-fated paddle-steamer. The polite murmurs of Lady Hammond's guests turned to silence when the pages began to show ragged urchins seeking food amidst the rubbish piled in the Lewin's Mead alleyways.

The unfolding of the drama of the Irish vagrants on the pages of Fergus's sketchpad provoked gasps of horror, and Lady Hammond asked Fergus to explain the series of harrowing sketches.

The guests listened in shocked silence until Fergus revealed that the subjects of the sketches were Irish. One of the men snorted derisively: 'You should have told us that in the first place, young man, and we need not have wasted our sympathy.'

'Why? Does dying come easier to *Irish* children?' Fergus's voice was deceptively quiet as he tried hard to control the anger he felt.

'I think *I* would like to hear your answer to that question, General.' Support for Fergus came from Fanny.

The general looked from Fergus to Fanny and he smiled condescendingly. 'Ah! The innocent compassion of youth. Such sentiment is sadly misplaced where the Irish are concerned. As a race, they have scant regard for life. Why, I've known instances where women and children urged their menfolk to murder captured British soldiers, then fought each other to be first to strip the clothes from the murdered men's still-twitching bodies.'

'I could introduce you to a hundred women and children right here in Lewin's Mead who would do the same – and men who'd kill and rob an old woman for sixpence. *They're* all English. I can also name an Irishman who forfeited his own life to help others – and another who grieved as deeply for his wife and children as any Englishman. Fanny, will you hand me that top canvas?'

When Fergus had the wooden-framed canvas painting in his hand he turned it over and held it up to view. It was a painting of a dying woman lying on the rat-gnawed floor-boards of a room in one of the derelict riverside houses. Her arm was about her dead baby, and her tearful husband knelt helplessly by her side.

When Fergus eventually lowered the painting, only the general remained unmoved.

'It's an artist's business to use his imagination. He must paint a picture capable of moving prospective purchasers. It's something you do well, Mr Vincent.'

Fergus placed the painting back on the table. 'I wish I could say that scene existed only in my mind, General. Sadly, it was painted from life – and death – right here in Bristol.'

'Minutes afterwards that man was driven out of the city, leaving his wife and two children lying dead behind him. The order came from you, I believe, General?' asked Fanny.

'They were moved out of Bristol on my instructions, yes. As chairman of the Health Committee I still believe I made the correct decision,' the general bristled angrily. 'I've never been one to run away from a difficult decision, young lady.'

'What an interesting evening this promises to be.' Lady Hammond smiled disarmingly at her guests before moving closer to the table, where Ferdinand Lascelles was turning the pages of Fergus's sketchpad.

'What do you think of them, Ferdinand dear?'

'They are quite good,' replied the art critic cautiously.

'Come now, Ferdinand. You can do better than that. Give us an *honest* opinion – as an art expert, not as a prospective buyer.'

Ferdinand Lascelles seemed more amused than embarrassed by Lady Hammond's remarks. 'Very well. You are an extremely talented young man, Fergus. *Exceptionally* talented. Your paintings – the sketches in particular – display a rare sympathy with your subject. You also have the ability to transfer that sympathy to canvas. Technically, too, you are extremely skilful. If I were to make any criticism at all, it would be that the colours in your paintings are perhaps a little *too* delicate – although this does serve to make them quite distinctive. There, does that satisfy you, Lady Hammond? It should, it's more fulsome praise than I have ever given to an unknown artist before. As a result I have probably priced myself out of the market for this second painting – the young urchin looking out of a window. It is quite delightful.'

'That one's not for sale,' said Fergus hurriedly. The painting was of Becky looking out of the attic window at the family of sparrows. 'I've promised it to the model ... when she returns to Lewin's Mead.'

Lady Hammond peered at the painting. 'Why, it's that young *protégée* of yours. The girl in the reformatory. I hope she will appreciate such a gift.'

'I believe she will.'

'Good. Shall we dine now? You'll sit next to me, Fergus. I have a proposition to put to you. . . .'

In the dining room Lady Hammond sat at the head of the table, with Fergus on her right and Fanny beside him. Fergus was relieved to see that the general had been given pride of place at the far end of the table, where he happily dominated the conversation about him.

During the meal Lady Hammond unfolded her suggestions for the future of Fergus and his art. She would provide him with a studio and accommodation in Clifton where he could produce paintings from the many sketches he had made of Lewin's Mead and the people who lived and worked there. He would be free to accept commissions during this time and, as Fanny pointed out, Bristol 'society' women would flock to him when the comments made by Ferdinand Lascelles were repeated and it became known that Lady Hammond had become Fergus's patron.

'I'm not certain I *want* to paint portraits of society women,' asserted Fergus. 'I came to Bristol to paint the people of Lewin's Mead.'

'Nonsense!' Lady Hammond spoke sharply. 'You've sketched *hundreds* of characters from this dreadful slum. Do you want to sketch them all over again? Or do you wish to become a well-known and respected painter? Besides, what are you doing with the paintings of your slum-dwellers? Is your way of life a crusade to make Bristol's more fortunate citizens aware of the plight of their fellow-men? Very well, I will arrange an exhibition of your work – and I promise that every alderman and councillor in the city will attend. How long will it take you to produce enough paintings for such an exhibition?'

'I don't know....' The unexpected and generous offer took Fergus by surprise. 'Probably the best part of a year.'

'Ferdinand!' Lady Hammond's voice cut through the conversation around the table. 'If Fergus produces enough paintings of his precious slum-dwellers, could an exhibition be arranged in Bristol – say, in a year's time?'

'Of course. I know many men who would be delighted to be associated with such an exhibition. It will prove one of the most important for many years, you have my word.'

'There! Does that suit you, my young artist friend? Will you agree to have one of Ferdinand's friends make you famous?'

'You are most generous, Lady Hammond.'

'It is a wonderful opportunity, Fergus.' Fanny added her own quiet persuasiveness to the discussion. 'It's the chance to have your talent recognised, and the fulfilment of your dream. Why are you hesitating?'

'I don't know.'

Fergus tried to find words to explain his confused thoughts – words that would make sense to the others seated about the table. Becky would have understood. . . . And suddenly he knew the cause of his doubts. If he left the house in Back Lane, it would feel as though he was abandoning Becky. She belonged to Lewin's Mead. It was not the reason he gave to Fanny.

'Perhaps I'm worried that I won't capture the true essence of my subject if I live outside Lewin's Mead.' The excuse sounded feeble and ungrateful. 'If I moved away and things didn't work out, it would be a disaster for me.'

'Unless you give it a try you'll never know.' Lady Hammond's manner became suddenly brisk. 'You could keep your room in the slums – and return there occasionally if you found it necessary to recapture this "essence" you consider to be so important. I have offered you my patronage, Fergus. The decision whether or not to accept must be yours.'

Peremptorily dismissing the subject with a brief movement of her hand, Lady Hammond raised her voice to carry above the chatter. 'Shall we adjourn? Ferdinand has found a delightful new painting for me. I must show it to you. It's a hunting scene – rather more to your liking, I fancy, General.'

As they left the dining room Fanny walked beside Fergus. Without glancing at him, she asked: 'Have you thought of the effect any decision you make will have upon Becky's future?'

Fergus looked at her sharply. 'In what way?'

'Unless I and the staff of the Red Lodge have misread the situation, Becky is going to want to be near you when she is eventually released. Do you *really* want her to go back to Lewin's Mead and all that Mary Carpenter is trying to put behind her?'

Fergus was still pondering Fanny's words when he climbed the stairs to his room in Back Lane. Fanny was right, of course. Becky could never escape from her past here. Where would she live? *How* would she live? Sleeping in the overcrowded room occupied by Mary O'Ryan and her succession of 'paramours' had always been fraught with danger for Becky. When she left the Red Lodge she would be a couple of years older – and even the most innocent of observers could see she had already left childhood behind. To think of her sharing a room with Irish Molly or Maude Garrett was equally unthinkable. That left only Fergus. Becky had slept in his room before, and he knew she would expect to again, but was it only for this she was learning to read and write and to be 'more like Fanny Tennant'?

Clutching his paintings and sketchbook, Fergus pushed open the door to the attic room and fumbled for matches and a candle on the shelf where he kept them. As he did so his foot kicked against something on the floor. Fergus was puzzled. He had left the room tidy before going out. As he shifted his foot he trod on something that broke beneath his shoe. Reaching down, he felt the broken frame of a prepared canvas.

Groping in the darkness, Fergus finally located the candle. Striking one of the long matches, he produced a flame and applied it to the candle – but by then he had already seen the mess about him. Canvases and pages from the sketchbooks he had left in the room were strewn about the floor. His expensive lamp was smashed. So, too, was the easel made by Henry Gordon. There were paint-smears on the walls, and broken brushes were strewn about the floor.

The room was a shambles. Fergus stood amidst the debris and gazed about him in utter dismay. Whoever had wrecked the room had done so in an unsystematic manner. Many of his sketches had been screwed up, or torn beyond redemption. Others could still be used. Nevertheless, the damage caused to his prepared canvases and painting equipment was serious. If Fergus had not taken his most important sketchpad to Lady Hammond's house, the vandalism would have proved disastrous.

Outside the room one of the stairs creaked beneath a stealthy footstep, and Fergus looked about him for a handy weapon. He settled for the iron poker that stood in the grate. Snuffing out the candle, he took up a position in the shadows close to the door. If the destructive burglar was returning, he would receive a shock.

'Fergus . . .? Are you in there?' Maude Garrett's nervous whisper came through the door.

Fergus relit the candle, and Maude Garrett entered the attic room cautiously, gazing wide-eyed about her at the damage.

'Do you know anything about this?'

Maude Garrett nodded. 'It happened this evening, as me and Irish Molly were getting ready to go out. We'd left it late because there aren't many ships in —'

'Who did it?'

'Joe Skewes. We heard someone coming up the stairs and thought it was you. There was a bit of noise, but we thought you might have been drinking. But when we heard things being smashed up Irish Molly came up here and found Joe.'

Maude Garrett looked at Fergus and shrugged helplessly. 'He'd have made a better job of it if she hadn't stopped him when she did.'

'But why should Joe Skewes want to smash up my studio?'

As he asked the question Fergus remembered his first

encounter with Joe Skewes, and the sketch he had made for Constable Ivor Primrose. But that had been too long ago to provoke this.

'Joe Skewes was after Becky. He's been drinking since coming out of prison yesterday and came looking for trouble.'

'Where is he now?'

'Irish Molly took him off to the White Hart and got him so ginned up he couldn't remember his own name. She said to tell you he wouldn't be back tonight. She also said she'd expect you to foot the bill.'

Fergus began to pick up sketches from the floor. 'I hope she also told him Becky's not living here any more. There's months of work in these sketches, and most of them are irreplaceable.'

Maude Garrett began to help Fergus with his task. 'It's no good telling anything to Joe Skewes. When he's full of drink he'll not remember a thing he's told – but he won't forget that he's going to get even with Becky. He'll come here again. If he doesn't find her, he'll take it out on you instead.'

'He's mad. Someone ought to have him locked away.' Fergus's anger flared as he found a half-completed painting with a hole kicked through the canvas.

'He's not all there,' agreed Maude Garrett. 'And Alfie's no better, but it would take a brave man to try to have either of 'em put away. Oh, look at this beautiful lamp of yours. It's smashed to bits.'

Maude Garrett placed the pieces of broken oil-lamp on the window-sill and turned to watch Fergus for a while.

'Leave it until morning. Come down to my room and I'll make you a nice cup of tea. I'm not working tonight. . . .'

Fergus shook his head. He did not want to have to listen to Maude Garrett's chatter – or to go along with whatever else she might have in mind. He needed to think.

Maude Garrett's shrug did not hide her disappointment. 'Please yourself, I'm sure. I must be poor company compared with all your swanky friends.'

She waited a few more moments, hoping for a reply, but Fergus was lost in thought. He hardly noticed her departure, noisy though it was.

Fergus slept very little that night. He lay on his bed gazing up at the ceiling for a long time and he was awake when Irish Molly returned home. She was not alone, but the voice of the man with her was not that of Joe Skewes.

Fergus was still awake when the first dull grey light of dawn filled the attic windows. By then he had made up his mind. He would continue to pay rent to Ida Stokes for the attic. It would form a base for his sketching forays into the maze of the Lewin's Mead streets. But he would accept Lady Hammond's offer and move his studio to Clifton.

It was the only sensible thing to do. His sketches were too valuable for him to risk another visit from Joe Skewes. Sooner or later the Skewes men would go back to prison. When this happened he would consider returning to Back Lane.

Belatedly, Fergus dozed off. His last waking thoughts were of Becky. He hoped she would understand.

CHAPTER THIRTY

BECKY did *not* understand Fergus's decision to move away from Lewin's Mead, and she greeted his news with dismay and bewilderment. They were in the garden of the Red Lodge, Fergus having wrung permission from Mary Carpenter to pay Becky a private visit.

'But *why* do you want to leave Back Lane? I thought the attic was ideal for your painting. You've told me so yourself, many times.'

'It *is* ideal, and there's no question of my *wanting* to leave,' Fergus explained patiently. 'But from now on I'll be painting for an exhibition, and that costs both time and money. I can't risk having Joe Skewes or his son come there while I'm out and destroying everything I've done.'

'Joe Skewes was drunk when he went there. He won't have remembered a thing about it when he sobered up. It won't happen again.'

'Are you saying Joe Skewes won't be drunk again? Or that Alfie Skewes won't come looking for me when Constable Primrose's warning isn't quite so fresh in his mind?'

'This is all my fault, isn't it, you having to leave Lewin's Mead and being threatened by the Skewes family? If I hadn't been so stupid, everything would be all right. You'd still be in your attic – and I'd be there, too.'

'Things *would* have been different,' Fergus admitted, 'but you mustn't blame yourself. We all do foolish things and most of us get away with them. You were unlucky enough to fall foul of Rose Cottle and her friends.'

Becky sank into an introspective silence for a while, then she raised her head and looked directly at Fergus. 'None of it would have happened if I didn't care so much for you. When you took me on that boat you gave me the most wonderful and exciting day of my life. I *had* to give you something in return. That's why I took that watch for you. I wasn't to know I was taking it from Fanny Tennant's old man, was I? Anyway, he could walk into a shop and buy another; I couldn't − and neither could you. I wanted you to have a watch. When you said you didn't want it I thought it was because it was coming from *me*. . . . That you didn't want to feel . . . *beholden*.'

'Beholden' was another new word in Becky's rapidly expanding vocabulary. Fergus had seen it written on the blackboard in the classroom where he gave his sketching lessons.

Fergus was deeply moved. Becky was not given to expressing her true feelings. He took her hand in a sudden gesture of affection. 'Becky, you don't *need* to steal for me. There's no one in this whole world I would rather be beholden to. I'm more fond of you than of anyone else I know.'

'Honest? Even after what's happened?' Becky searched the recesses of her mind for the most sacred oath she could find. One to which Fergus would not dare lie. 'God's truth?'

'God's truth, Becky.'

'I think more of you than anyone else, too.'

From the corner of his eye Fergus saw one of the reformatory supervisors advancing determinedly down the steps of the house towards them. 'You won't do anything silly because I'm leaving Lewin's Mead?'

'I'll try not to. Where will you live?'

'Clifton.'

'At Fanny Tennant's house?' All the happiness disappeared from Becky's face.

'No. Lady Hammond is to become my patron. I'm to live in a studio in the grounds of her house.'

The smile returned. 'Then, I don't mind, and when you're famous I'll be proud of you. I'll make you proud of me too. . . .'

'*Mr Vincent!* You will release this girl's hand *immediately*. Physical contact of any kind is strictly forbidden between girls and their visitors – even their closest relatives. It disturbs them.'

'Miss Carpenter needn't worry. She'll not have a harder-working girl than Becky. One day she'll be more famous than any of them because I've painted a portrait of her that will live for ever.'

Leaning forward, Fergus kissed Becky on the cheek. Then he walked away, leaving the outraged reformatory supervisor glaring after him.

Lady Hammond was a generous patron. Fergus was installed in a small cottage in the grounds of her Clifton house, and she ensured he wanted for nothing. Although small by Clifton standards, the cottage was palatial compared with Fergus's Lewin's Mead room. The living quarters were on the ground floor, and the whole of the upper floor had been made into a studio that was in itself four times the size of the Back Lane attic. Fergus brought most of his surviving paints, brushes and canvases with him, but they were not necessary. Lady Hammond understood the requirements of a painter, and the studio was liberally stocked with equipment far superior to any he had used before.

Servants from the main house did his cleaning, washing and cooking, and Fergus was expected to take his evening meal in the main house. When Lady Hammond had dinner guests – which seemed to be most evenings – Fergus would end the evening by showing them his work. He also became used to Lady Hammond calling at the studio during the day, frequently accompanied by friends. Such visits were disturbing at first, but Fergus quickly learned he was not expected to join in their conversations and he would continue with his work, leaving Lady Hammond free to put her own interpretation on what he was doing.

At first, Fergus was embarrassed about accepting Lady Hammond's generosity, but when he mentioned it to her she brushed it aside as being of 'no consequence'. She suggested that, if he painted her portrait and presented the painting to her, she would consider it more than ample repayment for all she was doing for him.

Soon the weekdays fell into a regular pattern. On Monday he would spend an hour working on the portrait of Lady Hammond; on Wednesday afternoon he took a class at the Red Lodge, and on Thursday at the ragged school. On Saturday evenings it became the custom for him to dine at the Tennants' home – but always the paintings of Lewin's Mead and the tragic record of the Irish immigrants dominated each working day.

For the first few weeks Fergus paid a regular visit to Back Lane whenever he went to teach at the ragged school, paying the rent for the attic room with money given to him by Lady Hammond. On these occasions he renewed his friendship with Irish Molly, and sometimes spoke to Maude Garrett, but as winter settled upon the city Fanny would give Fergus a lift back to Clifton in her carriage after school, and his visits to Back Lane became less frequent.

During the worst of the weather Fanny's carriage was usually waiting for him outside the Red Lodge, too, and Fanny was a frequent guest at the home of Lady Hammond.

Meanwhile, Becky was keeping the promise she had made to Fergus. She could read tolerably well now and, although her spelling was atrocious, she would write long notes to Fergus in a bold even hand and pass them to him secretly during the sketching lessons. She seemed content with life at the reformatory and eager to learn all she could.

A few days before Christmas, Fergus was painting in his studio when a maidservant came to tell him he had a visitor.

'Is it one of Lady Hammond's friends?' Fergus was painting in details of Lady Hammond's portrait, hoping to have it completed as a surprise Christmas present. He did not want any of Lady Hammond's circle to have a preview of the painting.

'It's *not* one of m'lady's friends, sir. It's a . . . a "lady".' Accompanied by a loud sniff, the word was more polite than descriptive. 'The butler told her to go and wait by the garden gate, and he's sent me to inform you she's there.'

Fergus was intrigued. Servants were the most broad-minded of people, but clearly the maidservant did not approve of his visitor.

There was a thick frost on the lawns, and Fergus shivered as he walked to the gate. He wished he had slipped his coat on before leaving the warmth of his studio. However, when he opened the solid-wood door set in the high stone wall that surrounded Lady Hammond's garden, he found his visitor was very much colder than he.

Irish Molly stood as close to the door as was possible, taking advantage of what little shelter the shallow doorway afforded against the icy wind. Wearing a thin lined coat more suitable for warding off summer sunshine than the blast of a winter wind, she had forsaken warmth for 'fashion' on this her first visit to Clifton. She had also gone to a great deal of trouble with her heavy make-up, but her experience in this field was with sailors and not with the butlers of large Clifton houses.

'Molly! What are you doing here? Come to my studio and get warm.' Irish Molly was shivering violently, and Fergus bundled her through the doorway and hurried her to the cottage.

Although she was so cold, Irish Molly looked about her with great interest. She had not seen gardens such as this since her childhood days in Ireland and she had not imagined Fergus to be living in such surroundings.

Once inside the cottage Fergus led Irish Molly to the tiny ground-floor sitting room and pulled a comfortable chair close to the crackling log-fire.

'Sit down and warm yourself while I fetch you a drink. I've got some brandy here that I've been keeping for a special visitor. It was brought from France by one of Lady Hammond's dinner guests and is much to good too be drunk when I'm alone.'

By the time Fergus returned with two half-filled glasses Irish Molly had her shivering under control. She was holding chapped hands out towards the fire, rubbing them together occasionally to ease the pain of returning circulation.

Handing her one of the glasses, Fergus raised the other.

'Cheers! This will warm you from the inside, I don't doubt.'

Taking a swig of the brandy, Irish Molly belched appreciatively.

'This is a very pleasant surprise, Molly. What's brought you to Clifton? Is business so good you're thinking of moving up here now?'

Irish Molly snorted, and brandy fumes rose to the back of her nose. When her coughing and spluttering came to an end, she croaked:'I'd never get within a mile of a place like this if I stayed on me back for a hundred years.' She snorted again, more cautiously this time. 'I'm not so sure I'd want to, either. Is everyone as stuck-up as that feller in the house who's dressed up like an organ-grinder's monkey? Would he be the *Lord* Hammond, or something?'

Fergus grinned. 'He's the butler. But what's brought you here today, Molly? You haven't come to tell me that Ida Stokes wants to let my room to someone else?'

'No – although she could. Iris has come back.'

'Iris . . .? The one who got married?' Fergus was still embarrassed by the memory of the night of the wedding party in Back Lane. 'What's happened?'

'Her husband was lost on the very next voyage he made after taking her home with him. His folks in Holland were as kind as they could be, so she said, but Iris couldn't understand what they were talking about, so she caught a boat back to Bristol.'

Fergus was at a loss for words. Iris had left Lewin's Mead with the hopes and dreams of every Bristol prostitute nailed to the mast of her new husband's ship. She was proof that even the lowest among them could pull herself free of her profession and move on to lead an ordinary decent life.

Irish Molly, warmer now, was hauling something clear of the bodice of her dress. It was a small linen bag. Clasping Fergus's hand, Irish Molly poured the contents of the bag into his palm. Bewildered, Fergus looked from the pile of gold sovereigns to Irish Molly and awaited an explanation.

'There's twenty-five guineas there, and it's all yours.'

'For what?'

'It's the money owed to you by poor Tomas – God rest his

dear soul. I had a letter from a solicitor, right here in Bristol, asking me to go and see him – "in connection with the estate of the late Tomas Casey, Esquire", his letter said. Well, I went to see him and he told me Tomas had left me his house, as he promised, but there was some money, too – *a hundred and seventy-two guineas*, no less. I knew twenty-five guineas of it was yours, so here it is.'

Fergus was deeply touched, not only by Irish Molly's honesty, but by her willingness to sally forth from Lewin's Mead on a bitterly cold winter's day to bring the money to him.

'I thought you might have need of the money, you not being able to get down to the Hatchet to work. I thought that might be why you haven't been down to see me lately. I needn't have worried; you're doing all right here, Fergus.'

'Not for ready money, Molly. Lady Hammond gives me bed and board and pays all my bills, but I don't think she realises that people like to have money in their pockets – and I can't bring myself to ask her for any. She's already been very generous. I've even thought of sneaking off to the Hatchet some night to sketch sailors again.'

'Well, you won't have to worry about that for a while now. You're better off here, Fergus, I'm telling you. The weather's that bad out at sea we haven't had a ship in or out for a whole week. The sailors we do see have been in Bristol so long they've spent all their money. When I go to the White Hart these days it's *me* who's buying *them* drinks. I'm taking home men these nights just to warm up me bed. No, Fergus, you stay here – but I'll have another of those brandies, if you don't mind. It's putting a glow like summer inside of me.'

Fergus filled Irish Molly's glass and handed it to her. As he splashed some brandy into his own, she said: 'You know, I've never had so much money in all me life before, and it's all thanks to poor Tomas, who I talked into going to his death. It hardly seems right.'

'You mustn't think like that, Molly. Tomas was grateful to you for looking after him when he had no one else he could turn to. But what will you do with the money ... and the house?'

'I was hoping you might give me some advice, Fergus. What do *you* think I ought to do?'

'Where is the cottage?'

'County Wexford. Tomas would talk about it sometimes. It sounds beautiful there.'

'How far would your money go in such a place?'

'Far enough to let me plant the land with praties, buy a couple of pigs and a cow, and live like a queen with what I'd have left.'

'It's a wonderful opportunity for you, Molly. Any of the girls would give ten years of her life for such a chance.'

When Irish Molly made no reply, Fergus asked: 'What does the future hold for you here? How many years before you're reduced to beckoning to sailors from alleyways too dark for them to see what you look like? Or until you're performing in dark doorways with Lascar seamen?'

'You've got a cruel tongue, Fergus Vincent. Hurtful, too. Poor Iris had her first Lascar last night – and only a few months ago she thought she'd given up this life for good.'

'Tomas Casey has given *you* a chance now, Molly. Take it. Get out of Lewin's Mead as soon as you can. This week. *Now!*'

Irish Molly held up her glass again. As Fergus filled it he could not tell whether she was thinking of what he had said, or whether the brandy was having a dulling effect on her senses.

As though aware of his thoughts, Irish Molly said: 'I'm thinking, Fergus. Thinking that I'd likely die of boredom within six months.'

'There are worse ways to die, Molly. If you are in any doubt, then come with me. There's something I'd like you to see.'

Rising to his feet somewhat unsteadily, Fergus led the way up the stairs to the studio. Many completed paintings hung on the walls. Others, unframed or not completed, rested against the walls around the room.

Fergus went to a stack of unframed paintings and picked up one of them. Thrusting it towards Irish Molly, he asked: 'Do you remember her?'

Irish Molly took the canvas from him and gazed at the painting for some minutes. Suddenly her eyes filled with tears. 'It's poor old Meg. She worked out of the Hatchet years ago. Long before you set foot in Bristol. She's dead now, poor soul. Been dead this five weeks since.'

'Look again, Molly. She died inside *years* ago.'

Reluctantly, Irish Molly gave the painting a sidelong glance. It showed old Meg, diseased and filthy, sitting in the rain among the rubbish behind a dockside warehouse. She was dressed in rags, an old piece of sacking about her shoulders. With an empty 'blue ruin' bottle clutched in her hand she gazed open-mouthed and glassy-eyed at a world that had overtaken her, leaving her far behind.

'Is that how you want to end your days?'

Irish Molly thrust the painting away and shook her head. Turning away, she headed back towards the stairs. She was brought up short by a painting hanging on the wall. It was one of Fergus's Irish series and showed Tomas Casey kneeling on the ground beside a sick child.

'He was a good man.' Irish Molly spoke as though to herself. 'He tried to save them with his skills. Now he's trying to save me, with money and his own home.'

Turning to face Fergus, Irish Molly said: 'All right, Fergus. I'll return to Ireland. I'll go out in the mist every morning to weed the praties and drool over the size of the backsides of my pigs. I'll milk the cow and shake my head at the weather when I meet up with my neighbours. If that's what you think Tomas wanted for me, then I'll give it a try.' Her glance dropped to the empty glass clutched in her hand. 'But right at this moment I'll settle for another of those brandies. . . .'

When Fergus returned with the brandy-bottle Irish Molly was standing in front of a portrait of Becky. When her glass was full, she asked: 'Do you still see Becky?'

'Every week.'

'I was hoping you did.' Irish Molly produced a small wrapped package from within the sleeve of her dress. 'Give her this from me. It's for Christmas. It's only a handkerchief, but it's a silk one. I wasn't sure what they would let her have in there.'

Fergus took the present from her. He had been so involved with his paintings he had forgotten how near Christmas was.

Suddenly Irish Molly said: 'Do you know, Fergus, I must be the only one in the whole of Lewin's Mead who's never been sketched by you.'

'That's easily remedied. . . .' Picking up a sketchpad and pencil, Fergus sketched Irish Molly as she stood with a full brandy-glass in her hand, not daring to raise it to her mouth while he worked.

Fergus stopped working and shook his head. 'It's no good, Molly. Your expression's all wrong. Come back here and look at this painting of Tomas again.'

Irish Molly obeyed, and when she looked at the painting of the Chartist leader her expression softened immediately.

'That's better! *Much* better. This is the Irish Molly I want to remember.' Fergus worked furiously as he chatted. A few minutes later he led her to another painting. This one showed a dying Irish child, and here he sketched Irish Molly again.

For half an hour Fergus led her from painting to painting, sketching as he chatted ceaselessly. Occasionally he paused to refill her glass, usually topping up his own, too.

He sketched Irish Molly in tears. He sketched her laughing . . . angry . . . and sad. But not once did he sketch her as she appeared to Fanny when she came to the studio that evening.

Accompanied by a small, round-faced, middle-aged man Fanny entered the studio and saw a heavily made-up woman dressed in a gaudy outmoded dress, with strings of glass beads at her throat. Irish Molly's hair had been carefully pinned up for her visit to Clifton, but in moments of excitement or uncertainty she had a habit of putting her hands to her hair. The result was that during the course of the day it had become increasingly dishevelled. She had been drinking heavily, too, and was lying back on a sofa, urging Fergus in a loud voice to sketch her in an exaggerated posture of repose.

Belatedly aware of the two visitors, Irish Molly struggled to her feet. Her hand flew instinctively to her hair, but by now it was beyond redemption.

Fanny recognised Irish Molly immediately. Had they met in the vicinity of the ragged school, she would have engaged her in conversation, but Fanny did not approve of the prostitute's presence here.

Pointedly ignoring Irish Molly, Fanny spoke to Fergus in a voice as frosty as the lawns outside. 'I've brought someone to meet you. I wasn't aware you had ... *company*. We'll talk over dinner tonight.'

Fanny's assumption that he would be where *she* expected him to be annoyed Fergus almost as much as did the manner with which she had snubbed Irish Molly.

'I'm sketching. It will go on until late. When I've finished I'll probably take Irish Molly to an inn for a meal.'

Fanny Tennant paled. 'Fergus, this is Mr Stern. He's here at the request of Ferdinand Lascelles. He's travelled a long way just to see you. . . .'

'I'm an artist, a *working* artist, not some zoological specimen – and I happen to be busy right now.'

As Fanny and Fergus stood in the middle of the studio glaring angrily at each other Irish Molly struggled to her feet. Relying on the back of a sofa for support, she said: 'I must go now, Fergus. I promised to meet Maude in the White Hart. . . .'

'You're in no state to meet anyone, Molly. I'll get a hansom and take you home.'

'May I suggest a solution?' Unnoticed by the others, the man brought to the studio by Fanny had wandered over to examine the sketches of Irish Molly, scattered haphazardly on a table. Now, advancing across the room, he held out a hand to Fergus. 'I'm Solomon Stern, an art dealer and critic. Both occupations stem from a passion for art coupled to a sad lack of talent. I am pleased to make your acquaintance, young man – and I believe you called this charming lady "Molly"?'

'*Irish* Molly.'

Solomon Stern was not a tall man, and Irish Molly beamed down at his balding head as he bowed extravagantly low over her hand.

When he straightened up, the art dealer spoke to Fergus once more. 'I have a light carriage outside. May I instruct my driver to take the young lady home?'

'I'm going to the White Hart to meet Maude,' insisted Molly. Relinquishing her supporting grip on the sofa, her determined expression dared Fergus to suggest she was incapable of taking care of herself.

Fergus knew better than to argue with the Irish prostitute after she had been drinking. She had a sailor's vocabulary and could hold her own with any of her kind in the dockside taverns.

'As you wish. Don't forget to take your sketches with you.'

Solomon Stern said quickly: 'Not *all* the sketches, I beg you. I've just been admiring them.' He picked one from the table. 'This one is particularly good. If you hold it back for me, young man, I'll commission you to make me a painting from it.'

The sketch was one Fergus had made when Irish Molly was looking at a painting of the sick Irish children.

'You can have that one,' said Irish Molly generously. 'I don't need a picture to remind me of the times I've cried. I like these happy ones. I'll take them to show Maude and the others, to prove I really *have* been here today.'

She scooped up half a dozen sketches, leaving twice as many lying on the table.

'I am grateful to you, Molly. Now, if you two young people will excuse me, I will escort Molly – I beg your pardon, *Irish* Molly – to my carriage and give my driver his instructions.'

As they walked away across the studio, Solomon Stern held out his arm to Irish Molly. 'Perhaps you'll do me the honour of taking my arm, dear lady. I fancy the stairs are a trifle steep. . . .'

CHAPTER THIRTY-ONE

WHEN THE ILL-MATCHED COUPLE had passed from view down the stairs, Fergus smiled. 'Where on earth did you find *him*? He's an absolute charmer. He's got Irish Molly eating out of his hand. I doubt whether any man has achieved *that* before.'

'Fergus Vincent! You owe me an apology – or at the very least an explanation. Solomon Stern is a famous man in the world of art. Most artists would sell their soul for an introduction to him. I bring him here for you to meet over dinner and find you cavorting with a . . . a common *prostitute*. Did Lady Hammond know that creature was here?'

'That "creature" has just inherited Tomas Casey's estate. She came here to return some money I loaned to him. She's also the "creature" who told you Becky was being held against her will in Rose Cottle's house. Irish Molly also brought our attention to the plight of the families in the houses by the river – *and* helped them while the rest of the city quaked at the very thought of coming in contact with cholera. She was a friend to me while I lived in Lewin's Mead. A *good* friend. Now she's got a chance to return to Ireland and forget her past. I'm happy for her, and I wish her well. But if she were staying in Bristol I'd *still* be pleased to have her for a friend – *and* welcome her into my home. If I can't do it here, then I'll need to go back to Lewin's Mead.'

'Are you telling me you would give up a chance to establish yourself as a painter . . . for a prostitute?'

'I'm telling you more than that, Fanny. I'm grateful to you

and Lady Hammond for what you're doing for me, and I'll work like hell to succeed – but I'll not give up my freedom and my principles to do it. I'm vain enough to think my talent will be recognised eventually. I'll just go back to Lewin's Mead and wait for it to happen.'

At that moment Solomon Stern returned to the studio. He saw Fergus and Fanny standing facing each other. Neither had fists raised, but the art dealer was immediately reminded of two prizefighters shaping up to each other in a prize-ring.

Beaming benevolently at each of them in turn, as though unaware of anything amiss, Solomon Stern said: 'The young lady is safely on her way. My driver is a reliable man. He'll see she comes to no harm. "Irish Molly" . . . what a charming name.'

'No doubt Fergus is suitably grateful to you, Mr Stern, but we mustn't keep him from his work. "Working like hell", I think, was his expression. We must not stand between an artist and his destiny. I presume we *shall* see you for dinner, Fergus?'

'You might.'

'I sincerely hope we *will*, Mr Vincent. I look forward to talking to you.'

With a cheery and vaguely apologetic wave of his hand, Solomon Stern followed a stiff-backed Fanny Tennant from the studio.

'*Damn* Fanny Tennant. Just *who* does she think she is?'

Angry at what he considered to be Fanny's unpardonable arrogance, Fergus lifted the brandy-bottle from the table. There was no more than a spoonful remaining in the bottom of the bottle. Cursing his luck, Fergus raised the bottle to his lips, swallowed the brandy dregs, then flung the bottle petulantly at the far wall of the studio.

The sketch of Irish Molly chosen by Solomon Stern stared up at him from the table, beside the present she had given into his keeping. Fergus picked up the sketch and gazed at it for some minutes. Then he found a new canvas, set it up on his easel, and began painting.

Meanwhile, on the way to the main house, Fanny walked in silence until she and Solomon Stern were almost at the door, when she said: 'I really must apologise for Fergus's behaviour. . . .'

'Hush, young lady. Why should *you* apologise? Why should *anyone* apologise? You have just introduced me to a very nice young man. One who does not make excuses for his friends. He is also a very talented artist. Very talented indeed. You are fond of him, Fanny?'

The unexpected question caught Fanny off guard.

'Fond of him? I *like* him. I can recognise his talent. But he's a *difficult* man. Unpredictable, too. . . .'

Solomon Stern took advantage of the darkness to hide a smile. 'You have found a true artist, my dear. A rare animal indeed — and, like all rare beings, he needs more love and understanding than the rest of us.'

Fergus was late for dinner. It was not intentional. He became so engrossed in his painting that he was unaware of the passing of time until a servant came from the main house to tell him it was time for dinner — and Fergus had still to change.

Fergus murmured his apologies to Lady Hammond and the dozen or so guests seated about the table, aware of Fanny's disapproving look. Lady Hammond waved his apology aside. 'It doesn't matter a jot. Solomon has been entertaining us with his amusing stories. He tells me you are working hard, and even had a model in the cottage. A "lady of the streets", if my butler is to be believed. Was it the woman I saw at Tomas Casey's funeral?'

Fergus nodded, not daring to look at Fanny.

'How absolutely *fascinating*! You really should have brought her to meet me.'

'She is an interesting lady. Her face has a very attractive bone structure.' Solomon Stern came to Fergus's rescue. 'Fergus is going to paint a portrait of her for me.'

'I trust you're charging Solomon a hefty fee, Fergus. When Solomon Stern commissions a painting you can be quite certain he expects to receive a huge return on his investment.'

'I most certainly will,' agreed Solomon Stern. 'But in order to increase the value of a painting it is first necessary to bring the artist to the attention of the buying public. In the case of Fergus it should not prove difficult. But tell me, young man, why have you chosen the slums as the subject for your paintings? Have you made this your mission in life?'

Fergus skimmed over his own background in the slums of Edinburgh and told his listeners of Henry Gordon and how he had wanted to record the life about him. Gordon had chosen Bristol because the poverty of Scotland was too close to him.

Lady Hammond's guests fell silent when Fergus spoke of arriving in Bristol, only to learn that Henry Gordon had died friendless and alone in the studio flat at the top of Ida Stokes's house.

Embarrassed by what he saw in the eyes of his fellow-guests, Fergus tried to shrug off the emotion he felt when speaking of the man who had been his friend. 'When I first began painting in Lewin's Mead I thought I was doing it because I owed it to Henry Gordon. This isn't true any more. I'm painting the Beckys, the Irish Mollys and the old Megs, the sailors, beggars and urchins, because I believe others should know these people exist. A mission? Well, I didn't have that in mind when I began, but, yes, it has become that for me.'

Looking about him at the other guests, Fergus added apologetically: 'It sounds hypocritical to talk of people who have nothing, when I'm eating and drinking my fill in such pleasant surroundings.'

There were sympathetic murmurs from his fellow-diners, but with one or two exceptions it was a polite response, no more. However, he could see by Fanny's face that he had her on his side once more. Solomon Stern, too.

'Have you ever been to London, Fergus? We have slums there the like of which you will never have seen. Veritable warrens of vice, and pits of indescribable poverty.'

'I haven't been there, but Henry Gordon had. He described them to me many times.'

'It may interest you to know that many people of note in London are becoming aware of the shame of their slums, too. For years they have ignored the problem; now they accept that something must be done. Your paintings could help *them* to face up to their problems, too. If I arrange an exhibition, will you bring your paintings to London?'

'Of course!'

For Fergus the prospect of having his paintings exhibited in London was very exciting, and not only because it might help to improve the appalling conditions existing in the slums of Britain's cities. Such an exhibition would also establish Fergus as an artist of some stature.

'It's a wonderful opportunity for Fergus,' agreed Lady Hammond, 'but I want to see his paintings exhibited in Bristol before he goes off to London. Once he samples the flattery of your London friends he might never return.'

'Of course,' Solomon Stern concurred. 'And once the good people of London see his paintings he will find himself in great demand to speak of his experiences to the reform societies.'

'I'm a painter, not a speaker.' Fergus was genuinely alarmed at the prospect of facing an audience and telling them about Lewin's Mead. 'I couldn't do it. . . .'

'There is someone here who *can*.' Lady Hammond looked to where Fanny was sitting. 'Fanny, you've given talks on ragged schools and the effect of the slums on the young people who live there. How would you like to talk to London audiences supported by Fergus's paintings and sketches?'

'I would welcome such an opportunity.' Fanny spoke eagerly. 'But you'll need to ask my father whether I might travel to London for such a purpose.'

She spoke loudly enough for Aloysius Tennant to hear, and attention at the table immediately focused upon the Bristol alderman.

Aloysius Tennant had been enjoying Lady Hammond's hospitality and was in a genial mood. 'I've yet to meet the father who can prevent an only daughter from doing *anything* she really wants to do.'

There was general good-humoured agreement around the table, and Aloysius Tennant spoke to Fanny again.

'You can talk to whoever will listen. Something *has* to be done about the problem of our cities' slums – and it should be done quickly. I'll even help arrange some of the talks for you. A number of Unitarian societies are involved with such matters. When you have a date for the exhibition, I'll write and have them organise talks and meetings for you. While you're there you can stay with my sister – your Aunt Agnes. She'll be delighted to have you as a guest. Fergus, too, I'm sure.'

'It sounds a most satisfactory arrangement.' There was a note of triumph in Lady Hammond's voice as she rose from the table.

Leaving the dining room, beside his hostess, Solomon Stern said in a low voice: 'I do believe you are match-making, Lady Hammond.'

'Nonsense. I merely took an opportunity to bring two very busy young people together and give them the chance to learn more of each other. Doubtless you, too, were fully aware of Fanny's talents as a speaker when you suggested that a rather shy young man might enjoy public speaking?'

'True, but my motives lack the romance of your own. Your young artist associates too much with those he sketches. He feels their pain. True, his sympathy reaches out from the canvas of his paintings, but Fergus must learn to paint them seething in their miserable pit – and still be able to walk away from them at the end of the day. If he doesn't, he might one day slip into the pit with them and find there is no escape.'

'And Fanny? What of her?'

'Ah! She, too, is passionate in her championing of the poor, but she is a practical young lady – and fond of Fergus. She will not allow him to throw away his talent.'

'Then, we are working towards the same end, Solomon, but I fear they are both strong-willed enough to confound us.'

'Indeed, dear lady, so we must keep them busy. Give them no time to fall out with each other. Can you arrange the Bristol exhibition? Make it soon and keep Fergus working hard on his paintings. Shall we say . . . in the spring? Meanwhile I will plan a London exhibition for early summer. You have discovered one of the most exciting young artists I have met for many years, but he needs to be prised away from his conscience and brought into the *real* world.'

*   *   *

Christmas came around more quickly than Fergus wished. It was almost upon him before he realised he was expected to exchange presents with Lady Hammond, with Fanny – and with Becky.

The news that Becky had a present for him was given to Fergus when he went to Mary Carpenter's office to sign for the fee he received for giving sketching lessons to the girls of her reformatory.

As he was signing the scrupulously kept receipt-book, she said: 'I trust you'll be spending some of this on a small present for Becky?'

When he looked up in surprise, she said: 'It seems I was quite right to remind you. Christmas is only a few days away, Mr Vincent. It's a time when friends and family give small presents to each other. Becky has been working for weeks on a present for you. More than that I will not say. It is to be her surprise for you.'

'But what can I give her? I mean, what will you allow her to have?'

'Anything sensible, Mr Vincent. I have no doubt you will think of something.'

'How about a painting? A small one to hang on the wall by her bed, perhaps?'

'That will be splendid. But it must not be a portrait. A portrait of Becky would only encourage vanity, while a portrait of yourself would cause jealousy among the other girls. I don't doubt you will think of a suitable subject.'

Fergus painted Becky a group of sparrows standing on the roof outside an attic window of the room in Back Lane. He took it from the sketch he had made of the young birds that had so enchanted Becky. He was well satisfied with the small painting and put it aside to dry. He would take it to her on Christmas Day, when he had been invited with other staff to enjoy afternoon tea at the Red Lodge.

For Fanny, Fergus made a painting from a sketch she particularly liked. The sketch depicted a smiling child, one of the few 'successes' recorded in the tragedy of the homeless Irish immigrants. The child had been starving when Fanny first saw him, but a couple of good meals had worked wonders, as his smile and full rounded belly showed clearly.

For his third gift Fergus was obliged to paint well into the night of Christmas Eve to complete the portrait of Lady Hammond, but he was well pleased with his work. With the exception of a portrait of Becky it was the best painting he had produced to date. It was fitting it should be a present for his benefactress.

Because of his late night Fergus overslept on Christmas morning. He was awoken by Fanny when she made a noisy entrance to his cottage. He sat up in bed as she threw open the door of his room and strode purposefully to the window to pull open the curtains.

'Come along, Sleepy Head. It's Christmas Day and you've already missed your breakfast. Look what else you're missing by lying in bed all day.'

Large white snowflakes floated down outside the window and had already settled in a sloping white mass on the sill. In the dull grey light Fergus could see that Fanny's hair and the shoulders of her coat were sequined with slow-melting snowflakes.

'It looks cold out there.'

'Nonsense! It's marvellous. A merry Christmas, Fergus. I must return to the house now or I'll lose my reputation. Hurry and join us. Lady Hammond is impatient to see you.'

Despite Fanny's plea Fergus took his time dressing. He did not enjoy Christmas. Somewhere in the farthermost recesses of his mind he could vaguely remember seeing others enjoying good things at Christmas-tide, but could never recall sharing any of them. The Christmas days he remembered were bleak cold days when his father nursed a hangover. They grew worse with the passing of the years, despite all that his mother tried to do.

All these memories returned to Fergus as he washed, shaved and dressed, but he could not put off joining the others for ever.

Only the occasional snowflake drifted down outside as Fergus carried his two gifts to the house. The paint on Lady Hammond's portrait would not be fully dry for a day or two yet, but it would dry as quickly in the main house as in his studio.

The door to the house stood open. It was hung with a large holly wreath, and as Fergus stepped inside the rear hall he saw that holly also bedecked the paintings hanging on the panelled walls.

There was a great toing and froing of servants in the corridor. As the maids passed they dropped Fergus a curtsy and wished him 'A merry Christmas, sir'. A buzz of conversation came to him from the large drawing room, and as he drew closer he could see a great many people inside.

Fergus had expected only Lady Hammond, Fanny and perhaps her father to be in the house, but there must have been at least fifty others here. Taken aback, Fergus hesitated, reluctant to enter the room bearing his gifts.

The decision was taken out of his hands when Lady Hammond saw Fergus standing uncertainly in the doorway and advanced upon him, arms outstretched.

'My dear, we were all becoming concerned about you. We thought you must be ill. No one is *ever* tardy about rising on Christmas morning. Come along, poor Fanny is too excited to take a bite of food until she knows you approve of her present to you.'

Reluctant to admit he knew little of how people were meant to behave on Christmas Day, Fergus seized the opportunity to give his present to Lady Hammond, pointing out that the paint was not fully dry as he had been working on it during the night.

'So *that's* why you are late joining us this morning. My dear Fergus, that was very, very noble of you. I must see the portrait immediately.'

Calling to her butler, Lady Hammond had him hold the painting up for her inspection. Slowly she backed away until she felt she was viewing it to the best advantage.

She remained silent for so long that Fergus became concerned. 'Do you like it? I think it's rather good. . . .'

'Good?' The words came out as though Lady Hammond had been holding her breath. 'My dear boy, it's *marvellous*! This one portrait alone justifies *all* my faith in you. What can

I say but ... thank you! Thank you for a truly wonderful Christmas gift. It must hang in pride of place. . . .'

Lady Hammond led Fergus and the butler across the drawing room. Conversation gradually fell away, and by the time the small procession reached the fireplace the eyes of everyone in the room were upon them.

Acting upon his employer's instructions, the butler substituted Fergus's painting for one of an earlier Hammond dressed in the fashion of a courtier of Charles II, who struck a heroic pose above the fireplace.

Holding up her hand to still the sudden buzz of interest, Lady Hammond said: 'You are the first to see the portrait Fergus has painted of me. You will understand how privileged you are when you come closer and see it in more detail. You are looking at a major work by a young man who will one day be recognised as one of our foremost artists.'

The guests surged forward and crowded around the fireplace to view Fergus's 'masterpiece'.

Fergus himself backed away until he found Fanny at his side.

'Lady Hammond is right, Fergus. It is a wonderful portrait.'

'I've a painting for you, too.' Self-consciously, Fergus handed over his second painting. It was smaller than the one he had presented to Lady Hammond.

Fanny took the painting and held it up to view it better. An expression of great pleasure crossed her face as she recognised the subject. 'The Irish child. . . .'

Suddenly and unexpectedly her eyes filled with tears and she said in a whisper: 'Fergus ... it's beautiful, truly it is. Thank you.'

Before Fergus guessed her intention, Fanny kissed him on the cheek. Lady Hammond's eyebrows rose as she pushed her way towards them through the guests gathered about her portrait.

When she reached the couple, she said: 'I am pleased to see the Christmas spirit is reaching you at last, Fergus.'

'Fergus has just given *me* a painting. Look, isn't it wonderful?'

Lady Hammond looked at the painting critically and nodded agreement. 'It's a very fine painting, Fanny – but I am afraid I cannot look at any painting but my own today. I am *so* thrilled with it. . . . But what do you think of Fanny's present to *you*, Fergus?'

'I haven't given it to him yet.'

Fanny was clutching a small package tied with a thin blue ribbon. Handing it to Fergus, she said almost shyly: 'A very happy Christmas, Fergus.'

Fergus stripped off the wrapping clumsily, aware that both women were watching him with an almost proprietary interest. When the last of the paper fell away Fergus held a small draw-neck chamois-leather bag in his hand. As he turned it upside down a silver watch fell into his hand, the case heavily decorated with elaborate scrollwork.

He stared down at the gift for so long that Fanny asked anxiously: 'Don't you like it. . . ?'

Fergus shook his head as though he was emerging from a daydream. 'Of course I do – but it's far too generous.'

'Look inside. I've had something inscribed there.'

Fergus pressed a tiny catch near the top of the watch, and the back sprang open. Inside was inscribed: *Fergus Vincent from Fanny. Christmas 1854.*

'It is a lovely present, Fanny. Really lovely. Thank you.'

Others began crowding about them now, demanding to see the painting Fergus had presented to Fanny. Within minutes they were separated by Lady Hammond's Christmas guests.

Later, in a quieter moment, Fanny looked across the room to see Fergus gazing down at the watch in his hand and she smiled happily. She could not know that Fergus's thoughts were neither of Fanny nor of the watch he held in his hand. He was thinking of another watch. That, too, had been a gift – a gift that had resulted in disaster for the giver.

In one of Clifton's most luxurious houses, surrounded by Bristol's most influential citizens, Fergus stood at a window and his gaze shifted to the snow-covered garden. He saw neither watch nor garden. He was thinking of Becky, wondering what manner of Christmas she was enjoying at the Red Lodge.

CHAPTER THIRTY-TWO

FERGUS OUGHT NOT to have been surprised when he learned Fanny was also invited to tea at the Red Lodge. He knew she sometimes took classes of girls in the reformatory, but he was taken aback when she informed him they would both be travelling to the Red Lodge in her father's carriage and going on to the Tennant home afterwards.

'You *do* know you are dining with us tonight?'

Fergus shook his head.

'Lady Hammond should have given you my invitation. Fergus, you *will* come? I have told all my friends you'll be there.'

Fergus realised he had been built into something of a celebrity among Fanny's friends. This had become apparent when she introduced him to some of them during the morning.

He nodded. 'It's a very kind invitation.'

He would have preferred to spend the evening painting, but it *was* Christmas. It would be churlish to decline the invitation. Fanny's relief and delight told him he had made the right decision.

They set off together from Lady Hammond's house soon after three o'clock in the afternoon. It was snowing again, and the noise of the carriage and the horses' hoofs was heavily muffled in the snow-covered streets. Clifton was situated on a hill above the city, and enterprising ragamuffins had organised themselves into snow-clearing gangs. Armed with shovels, twig brooms and buckets of sand and cheap rough salt, they negotiated a deal for helping coaches down the steeper sections of the road into the city.

Fergus carried no money with him, and it was left to Fanny to find the wherewithal to guarantee their safe arrival at Mary Carpenter's reformatory.

The speed with which the boys worked was impressive. While some shovelled and swept away the snow, two boys strewed salt and sand in an economical ribbon in front of each wheel, thus enabling the coachman to drive his horses forward in cautious safety.

Meanwhile other boys worked equally hard behind the carriage. Fergus was not certain if they were trying to recover the salt and sand, or whether they were spreading snow over the tracks to prevent other coachmen from taking free advantage of their labours.

On a sharp bend the Tennant coach strayed from the narrow twin tracks. Immediately a great deal of shouting went up and a dozen or more youngsters clung to the carriage until it slid back to the hard-won safety of the wheel-width paths. Then a horse lost its footing on the hard-packed snow and went down. This time the boys called upon the help of passers-by, and with much slipping and sliding the snorting horse was raised to its feet.

The Red Lodge was decorated on a more modest scale than Lady Hammond's house, but a neat holly wreath adorned the door, and inside the building holly, ivy and mistletoe were tucked behind every picture.

Becky's face broke into a relieved smile when she saw Fergus, but her happiness was marred momentarily when Fanny followed him through the doorway.

'I was feared you wouldn't come ... what with all the snow we've had.'

'It would take more than a bit of snow to stop me coming to see you on Christmas Day. Here, I've brought a present for you.'

Becky took the small painting from Fergus. Memories returned to her as she looked at it, and her delight was evident. 'It's the sparrows outside the window ... when you sketched me, the first time I came up to your room.'

'That's right. I've finished the painting of you, too. It's the best painting I've ever done, Becky.'

Eyes shining, Becky shook her head. 'No, *this* is the best.'

Reaching inside the wide front pocket of her pinafore dress, Becky handed Fergus a small, badly wrapped package and just managed to maintain an air of exaggerated indifference. 'Here's something for you.'

It felt very light in Fergus's hand, and he said: 'You shouldn't have bought me a present, Becky. You can't get much money in here.'

'I didn't buy it. . . .' She grinned suddenly and was once more the cheeky young urchin he had first met only some eight months before. 'I didn't pinch it, neither. I *made* it.'

Fergus unwrapped his Christmas gift, wondering what it could be. Then it cleared the paper, and he saw it was a tapestry bookmark, embroidered with his name. The letters were somewhat uneven, but it was apparent that a great deal of effort had gone into its making.

'It says "Fergus". I did it all myself.' Becky's pride in her accomplishment overcame the air of indifference.

'Becky, you're a *genius*. It's a present I shall always treasure.' Fergus kissed Becky on the cheek, something he would never have dared to do in Mary Carpenter's reformatory had it not been Christmas.

There were other guests at the Red Lodge, and more were arriving all the time. Many were local dignitaries, councillors, teachers and preachers, and most had arrived on foot.

'Come along, girls; it's time we showed our guests what splendid cooks you are.'

Mary Carpenter marshalled her girls, and soon there was a steady stream of food arriving from the kitchen. Remembering Becky's earlier attempt at cooking, Fergus could not hide his astonishment when she passed him a plate of cakes and whispered: 'I made these.'

It was an afternoon of surprises. After tea the guests were entertained by a choir of the girls, Becky among their number. Four of the girls recited poems – Becky was one of these, too, and she glowed with pleasure at Fergus's enthusiastic applause.

Afterwards the girls were allowed to mingle with their guests. On their best behaviour, they earned the approbation of the reformatory founder and her guests.

When the assembly was beginning to thin, Fergus was talking to Becky when Fanny called to him: 'It's time we left, Fergus. I promised Father I would be home early to greet our guests.'

Unthinkingly, Fergus asked: 'Is it that late already?'

Fanny smiled. 'You have no need to ask such a question now. Look at your watch.'

With this parting remark, Fanny moved away to find Mary Carpenter and tell her that she and Fergus were departing.

Becky's face was ashen when she asked: 'You have a watch now?'

Fergus nodded.

'Did *she* buy it for you?'

'It came as a complete surprise. . . .'

'But you took it? You didn't ask *her* where it came from?'

'It isn't a stolen watch, Becky.'

'Have you asked *her*? No, of course not. *She* wouldn't need to steal to get you a present.'

'Becky, it's been wonderful to spend a couple of hours with you. Don't let's quarrel now.'

'Why? Will it spoil your dinner with her? I bet you never even think of me when you walk out of here. Well, that's all right. I don't think of you, either. So if you only come here because of me you don't need to any more.'

With fists clenched tightly by her side, Becky fought hard to prevent her hurt gaining ascendancy over anger. She succeeded, but the remaining guests were looking at her curiously.

Deeply hurt, Becky's whole being strained to rebel against the strict discipline of the reformatory. She hated the regimented routine and missed the independence she had enjoyed in Lewin's Mead. Above all, she fiercely resented the privacy that had been stripped from her when she entered the house in Park Row. Not for a moment was she allowed to enjoy the luxury of her own undisturbed thoughts or her own company. Even at night she had to endure the ribaldry, the whispered conversations and surprise inspections in the dormitory. Becky put up with all these things only because she believed she was becoming the sort of woman Fergus wanted her to be. Someone more like Fanny Tennant. But, while she was in here trying hard for Fergus's sake, Fanny Tennant was out there with Fergus and buying him expensive presents.

As Becky choked on her thoughts, Fergus took her arm and led her to a quiet spot close to the great fireplace. When she tried to pull away from him he gripped her more tightly – so tightly that, had she not been quite so determined to keep her feelings from him, she would have winced.

There were fewer people at this end of the room, and when he released her Fergus said quietly: 'You're talking foolishly, Becky. I'd swap all the fine things I have now for a breakfast cooked by you on the attic fire in Ida Stokes's house.'

In spite of her present mood, Becky found it hard not to smile. Now she had learned to cook she realised how dreadful had been the breakfast she had cooked for Fergus.

'What's more, I value the bookmark you've made for me above all my other possessions, including the finest painting I've ever made – a portrait of *you*.'

'Honest?'

It took a long time for the one-word question to come out. There was no anger in her now, but her feelings were more confused than before.

'Honest.'

'Why? Why does it mean so much to you?'

'Because *you've* worked hard to make it for me. I've told you before, Becky. I'm very fond of you.'

More used to expressing his emotions in paint upon a canvas, Fergus felt tongue-tied and awkward. But it did not matter. Becky was looking at him as though he had just made a dazzling speech.

'Fergus ... I *love* you. I really do.' Suddenly Becky was hugging him close.

The display of overjoyed affection was brief, for suddenly Mary Carpenter was standing before them.

'Any physical contact between the girls and their visitors is *strictly* forbidden, Mr Vincent, as well you know. Becky, Mr

Vincent is leaving now. Say goodbye, then go to the kitchen and help the other girls with the washing-up.'

Becky hesitated, rebellion welling up inside her once more, but Fergus said hastily: 'Go on, Becky. I'll see you again when I come for my next sketching lesson. Thank you again for a wonderful present – and hang the painting somewhere nice.'

Before reaching the doorway Becky turned twice to smile and wave.

When she had gone, Fergus said to Mary Carpenter: 'You mustn't blame Becky for what happened. . . .'

'Blame her? For what? For being happy? No, Mr Vincent, I am *grateful* to you. You have let Becky know she matters to someone. Today she feels she is a *special* person. This is the most wonderful Christmas gift you could possibly give to an orphan girl from Lewin's Mead. Unfortunately, it also burdens you with a heavy responsibility. A young girl's love is a very fragile thing.'

The new year was a week old when Constable Ivor Primrose came to the house to speak to Fergus. He was shown to the studio by a disapproving butler. Uniformed police constables were among the lower orders of a class-conscious society and not welcomed in the homes of the well-to-do.

Ivor Primrose was not a man to allow the butler's disapproval to upset him. Shaking snow from his cape, he hung the heavy garment behind the studio door. Then, warming a glass of Fergus's Christmas brandy between his hands, he wandered about the large studio admiring the paintings that adorned the walls and naming many of the Lewin's Mead residents portrayed in them.

'You didn't come here just to admire my paintings, Ivor. What can I do for you?'

'For me ... nothing. I'm here at the express wish of a friend of yours. She's landed herself in a spot of bother.'

'She?' Fergus could only think of Becky, and she was in the Red Lodge.

'Irish Molly. She and another prostitute named Iris were convicted of being drunk and disorderly in St James Square, yesterday. Unless she can find a surety of twenty pounds she'll go to prison for six months – with hard labour.'

'You must be mistaken, Ivor. I saw Irish Molly off on a boat from the Docks the day after Christmas. She went back to Ireland with more than a hundred and fifty pounds to begin a new way of life.'

Ivor Primrose shrugged his shoulders. 'All I know is that she's in the Bridewell now with not a penny to her name, and six months' hard ahead of her – unless she can find a surety of twenty pounds to guarantee her good behaviour for the next six .months. It's not necessary to produce the money right away. You need only satisfy the magistrate that you'll be able to pay the money if Irish Molly misbehaves again – as she probably will.'

'When do I need to see the magistrate?'

'The sooner you sign a surety, the sooner Irish Molly will be released. There's little comfort in the Bridewell in this weather. The river runs beneath the gaol, and last week it rose and flooded the cells. They haven't dried out yet.'

'Then, I'd better go now.'

Ivor Primrose downed his brandy and looked regretfully at the empty glass. 'It isn't every day I have a drink of such quality. You've come a long way from Back Lane, Fergus.'

'It was one of half a dozen bottles given to me by Lady Hammond.' Picking up the two-thirds-full bottle, Fergus handed it to the tall constable. 'Tuck this beneath your cape. You've had a cold walk up here.'

On the way to the Bridewell, Fergus tried to learn more about Irish Molly's unexpected return to Bristol and her subsequent arrest. Ivor Primrose knew little more than he had already told Fergus. He had not been the arresting officer, but he was in court when Irish Molly and Iris were convicted and sentenced. Iris had been convicted of a similar offence before and was given six months' hard labour without the option of being bound over.

After Fergus had signed the surety guaranteeing Irish Molly's future behaviour, a gaoler took him to the communal cell where the Irish prostitute was lodged.

Irish Molly looked dreadful. Usually clean and tidy, her clothes looked as though they had been worn day and night for weeks. Her hair was uncombed, and her face was mottled and bloated.

On the way from the Bridewell to Back Lane, Irish Molly told Fergus what had happened to her.

The ship carrying Irish Molly to Ireland had been beset by bad weather from the moment it cleared the Avon river. For three days the captain battled against storms in the Bristol Channel, being gradually forced far to the south of his intended course. Finally, with crew and passengers verging on total exhaustion, the captain turned his ship about and ran before the storm.

More by luck than by any navigational skill, the vessel arrived off the north Cornwall port of Padstow. Blissfully ignorant of the infamous 'Dumbar', the sandbank that barred the entrance to the port during all but the highest tides, the ship rode in with the storm and made the safety of the small harbour.

It had been a nightmare experience. As soon as the ship was safely moored alongside the harbour wall passengers and crew abandoned the vessel. Reeling as though already drunk, they made their way to the nearest inn. Here they quickly learned how lucky they had been to reach safety. On the first day of the storm a schooner had grounded on the Dumbar and not one of the crew had been saved. Not a single vessel had entered or left port since that time. The safe arrival of the Irish-bound vessel was declared to be a miracle.

Relieved to be alive, Irish Molly had bought drinks for the crew, most of whom had spent the money earned on their previous voyage. By the end of the evening Irish Molly was buying drinks for anyone willing to raise a tankard and drink to her safe return to shore.

The party lasted for three days and nights, until the wind dropped and the sea calmed. The vessel departed from Padstow leaving behind it memories of a riotous seventy-two hours – and Irish Molly.

Vowing she would not tempt the Devil again, Irish Molly returned to Bristol by coach, arriving with just enough money to secure her old room in Ida Stokes's house for two weeks and spend four nights celebrating her safe, if unexpected, return.

Having told the story of her adventures, Irish Molly ended lamely: 'The rest you know. Jesus! By the time the po-lice picked me up I hardly knew my own name. I've never been on such a glorious hooley in my life.'

'And now you're back where you started from.'

Irish Molly shrugged. 'Ah, well! Can you really imagine me living among the landed gentry, mistress of my own house?'

'You'd be enjoying a much better life than picking up sailors in the White Hart.'

'I doubt it. Some sailors are quite nice, really. Anyway, I don't expect too much from life here, so I shan't get disappointed the way I probably would if I were to return to Ireland.'

Irish Molly touched Fergus's arm. 'Besides, I've got some good friends here. Your twenty pounds is safe, Fergus. I'll have the lawyer sell the cottage and I'll give you the money to keep for me. Now, come up to my room with me. I've got a bottle of good stuff hidden away for a special occasion – if Ida hasn't found it already.'

CHAPTER THIRTY-THREE

FOR THE FIRST THREE MONTHS of 1855, Fergus worked harder than ever before in his life, producing a remarkable series of paintings from sketches he had made during the previous year.

As more and more paintings were hung on the walls about his Clifton studio, the number of interested visitors increased. Fanny was the most frequent, and with Lady Hammond's help hung the paintings in the order she felt would prove most effective in Fergus's forthcoming exhibition.

Solomon Stern also called in whenever he was in Bristol. His ideas did not always coincide with the views of Fanny and Lady Hammond, and they would argue about the relative merits of each painting as though Fergus was not there.

One day their arguments became so heated and distracting that Fergus put down his brush, cleaned his hands and walked out of the studio unnoticed by the three quarrelling art experts.

Fergus went to Back Lane. Here he found a pencil and pad and made his way to the Hatchet inn. He was greeted by landlord Waller as though he were a long-lost friend. After sketching a few patrons, Fergus returned to Back Lane with money in his pocket and a gait that was less than steady.

He spent the night in the attic room and was woken by Ida Stokes. Fergus had arrived back at the house from the inn during the early hours of the morning, but the landlady had heard him, and much of his earnings changed hands by way of rent for the attic studio.

Ida Stokes also told Fergus what was happening in the rest of the house. Mary O'Ryan, in the room beneath Fergus's own, had found yet another 'protector' for her large family. He was the fourth since Fergus's move to Clifton, according to the knowledgeable and garrulous old landlady.

He also learned that Irish Molly had taken to spending nights on board the boats in the harbour. It seemed her recent experiences had given her an even closer affinity with the men who earned their living upon the unpredictable seas.

'What about the latest of your tenants — Maude Garrett?'

Fergus had just found a half-full bottle of gin in the small cupboard where he kept his cups and plates and he asked the question as he poured some into a cup for Ida Stokes.

'I've a feeling in my bones that I'll rue the day I let *that* one into my house,' came the surprising reply. 'She's a wrong 'un, and no mistake.'

Accepting the cup from Fergus, the old landlady continued: 'She's mixed up with that Alfie Skewes. He's not a month out of prison and he'll be back there again before long — and her with him, I shouldn't wonder.'

'Why, what are they doing?' Fergus was surprised that Maude Garrett was involved with Alfie Skewes. If either Alfie or his father learned it was Maude who had tipped off the authorities about their treatment of Becky, her life would be worth nothing.

'That young girl's greedy. More greedy than most. She's not content to earn her living like Irish Molly and poor Iris — yes, and me, too, in my time. Encouraged by Alfie Skewes and his drunken father, she's found a way to get easier money. You'll find her up around Wine Street on most nights, dressed up to look like a child's nurse with a night off and looking for a good time. She'll pick up with a gent old enough to know better and lure him down some dark alleyway, to where Alfie Skewes is waiting. Afore he knows it the gent's bludgered over the pate. When he wakes up he's lucky if they've left him so much as a stitch of clothing. One day the gent won't wake up at all. Then it'll be the gallows for Alfie Skewes *and* Maude Garrett, make no mistake.'

'Have you tried speaking to her?'

'Not me! It's none of my business what she does – but I make sure she pays her rent on time every week, I can tell you!'

When Ida Stokes returned downstairs after a second cup of gin, Fergus wondered whether he should try to speak to Maude Garrett, but decided it would not be wise. She was unlikely to take notice of anything he said, and if Alfie Skewes happened to be with her Fergus would be walking into trouble. After cleaning and tidying up the attic room, Fergus set off up the hill to the very different world of Clifton.

Solomon Stern and Lady Hammond were apologetic for their part in driving Fergus from his studio, Lady Hammond generously declaring it was unforgivable that they should have carried on such an argument in his presence.

When Fanny came to the house that evening she was more hurt than apologetic. She pointed out that they all had Fergus's interests at heart and wanted to display his talents in the best possible manner. Fergus said nothing. When the time came, he was determined that he alone would decide the order in which his paintings should be displayed.

The Bristol exhibition of Fergus's work was held in Wine Street, in a fashionable enough part of the city, yet only a short distance from the slums which had provided inspiration for so many of the paintings on show.

Lady Hammond ensured the exhibition had a grand opening. The mayor attended with many aldermen and councillors, and a great number of the city's wealthiest citizens. Many expressed their reservations about the *subject* of Fergus's work, but none criticised his talent.

Fergus found the opening night a nerve-racking experience as he was introduced to one dignitary after another. Unused to being the centre of attraction in such company, he would have been totally overwhelmed by the occasion had Fanny not been at hand to support him. She succeeded in parrying the more difficult questions, guided the more important of the guests to particular paintings, and came to Fergus's rescue when an aggressive art critic tried to interview him.

At the end of the evening, Lady Hammond, Fanny and a few of their friends remained behind to congratulate Fergus on the great success of his first exhibition. It *had* gone well. Yet Fergus felt something was missing, although he was unable to put a finger on what it was.

When he expressed his thoughts to Fanny she smiled understandingly and patted his arm in a rare gesture of affection. 'It's a perfectly natural reaction, Fergus. Tonight you've become a celebrity. Everyone has wanted to talk to you. Now they've gone you feel deflated. That's all it is.'

'Yes, you're probably right.'

'Of course I'm right.' Fanny slipped her arm through his. 'But you can relax now. Lady Hammond and I have arranged a small champagne-party to celebrate your success. Come along. I think Lady Hammond is almost as proud of you as I am.'

The following day the exhibition of paintings was opened to the general public. Much to Fergus's delight and surprise, a sprinkling of Lewin's Mead residents were among the viewers, most wearing the clothes they usually kept for Sundays.

Fergus went out of his way to speak to them all, pointing out paintings of people and places he thought would be of particular interest to them. Without exception every one of them stopped before his first portrait of Becky, marvelling at the manner in which he had captured her rags and the pinched and dirty face – and suddenly Fergus realised what had been missing the previous night. Everyone there had come to meet him not because he was a painter, but because he was Lady Hammond's *protégé*. Some had recognised his talent, it was true, *but no one had expressed shock or sympathy for the subjects of his paintings*. It had been left to those for whom such conditions were a familiar part of their daily life to show compassion.

Looking about him, Fergus saw how the well-dressed viewers studiously avoided those paintings which attracted groups of chattering excited men and women from Lewin's Mead. Not all of Bristol's citizens viewed the city's less fortunate residents with the benevolence of Mary Carpenter or Fanny Tennant. The revelation should not have come as a surprise to Fergus, but it did.

'What thoughts are capable of bringing such a serious expression to the face of an artist with such a highly success-ful exhibition?' Solomon Stern asked the question as he moved to Fergus's side and shared his view of the crowded gallery. 'You should be beaming, my boy.'

'The only people who are really *seeing* what I've painted are those who live in the Lewin's Mead slum – and they can change nothing. Anyone with any influence is here solely because I'm being sponsored by Lady Hammond and they wish to be seen at my exhibition.'

'Ah, yes! I had forgotten that you are not content to paint the world as it is. You also wish to *change* it. My friend, you have a talent – a *great* talent – to paint the pathos and the sadness you see about you. Now these paintings are exhibited for all to see – and not everyone is here with a cynical motive. There is far more compassion in people than you seem to believe. Many women think as do Fanny, Lady Hammond – and this Miss Carpenter. Let *them* fight poverty and all that goes with it, while you continue to paint what you see. They can take your paintings to show to those who will never visit a slum and see the wretchedness for themselves.'

'No doubt you're right. But I need to feel *I'm* doing some-thing more for those I paint.'

Solomon Stern rolled his eyes to the ceiling. 'Artists! All my life I have either had to encourage good artists who are convinced they can't paint, or discourage bad ones who believe they are Michelangelo reincarnated. Now I find the best of them all – and he wants to be a social reformer! All right, I humour the others – why not you? Have you kept the sketches you made for these paintings?'

Fergus nodded. Except for those he had sold to sailors at the Hatchet inn, and some destroyed by Joe Skewes, he still had every sketch he had made since coming to Bristol.

'Choose the best and bring them to me. I have a friend who owns a magazine. He, too, is a reformer. Will it satisfy you for a while if he takes some of your sketches and uses them to illustrate his articles?'

'It will ease my conscience when I begin selling the paintings these people have made possible.'

'Good. But I need to talk to you about this. You must sell nothing until after your London exhibition. That will be the most important exhibition of your career.' With a movement of his arms, Solomon Stern dismissed the gallery in which they stood. 'This is merely a rehearsal. Your future depends upon your success in the capital, so any exhibition there needs to be carefully planned —'

Solomon Stern's words were interrupted by the sound of a loud voice coming from somewhere close to the entrance of the long art gallery. Then viewers were roughly pushed to one side and a burly figure lurched in through the doorway.

With a sudden chill of apprehension, Fergus recognised Alfie Skewes weaving his drunken way along the gallery towards them, causing men and women to scatter before him, all interest in the paintings forgotten.

Without taking his gaze from the unwelcome new arrival, Fergus spoke urgently to Solomon Stern: 'Send someone for a constable – *quickly*! We've got trouble.'

Alfie Skewes was stopping to examine the paintings now, pushing his unshaven face to within an inch or two of the canvases. Fergus broke into a limping run towards him. He thought he knew what the drunken bully was seeking.

Fergus was right. Pride of place in the exhibition had been given to the portrait of Becky. When Alfie Skewes reached the spot where the picture hung he stopped and peered at it for a while. Then, taking an unsteady pace backwards, an expression of drunken triumph crossed his face and he reached for the painting.

Fergus's shoulder slammed into Alfie Skewes before he could pull the portrait from the wall, and he was sent sprawling to the floor.

Alfie Skewes got up slowly, and the look he gave Fergus was more sober than it ought to have been – and it was filled with malice.

His glance flicked to the portrait of Becky, then returned to Fergus. 'What I did to her is nothing compared with what I'm going to do to you.'

Mention of Becky's ordeal at the hands of this man angered Fergus beyond all reason. Instead of retreating from Alfie Skewes he stood his ground and aimed a blow at the bigger man's face as he closed in.

Alfie Skewes brushed the blow aside as though it were a curtain and retaliated with a punch that knocked Fergus to the ground, his senses reeling.

Fergus had no defence against the larger man, but as Alfie Skewes closed in to boot him a small figure leaped between them. White-faced, Fanny tried desperately to reason with the Lewin's Mead bully.

Alfie Skewes pushed her aside as easily as he had blocked Fergus's blow, and she crashed heavily against the wall.

Fanny's plucky intervention gave Fergus time to climb to his feet. The sensible thing now would have been to flee to the street and shout for help. Instead, he delayed long enough to tug Becky's portrait from the wall, leaving Alfie Skewes between him and the door. Clutching Becky's portrait to him, he backed slowly away towards the rear of the long art gallery, occasionally stumbling over the feet of terrified onlookers who were slow to clear his path.

'Leave him alone, Alfie. He's done nothing to you.' The plea was made by a woman from Lewin's Mead, but she never expected her words to be heeded. When Alfie Skewes was dangerously drunk someone invariably suffered the consequences of his violence.

'Stand still and wait for me, cripple. There's no way out for you at the back. I should know, I've done more than one of these places in my time. I know every way in – and every way out. Stay still, and take what you've got coming.'

As he retreated, Fergus was fully aware of the danger he was in. Alfie Skewes was a dangerous man, violence a familiar part of his life. Fergus tried to think of a means of escape, but he knew there was none. Behind him there was only an office and, as Alfie Skewes knew well, there was no back door. But Fergus was more concerned for

Becky's portrait than for his own safety.

Behind Fergus someone was slow in moving from his path and he tripped, falling awkwardly to the floor. Alfie Skewes reacted swiftly, kicking Fergus's legs from under him as he tried to rise. Alfie Skewes kicked out again, but now the kicks were aimed at Fergus's body, and Fergus squirmed in pain, still attempting to keep Becky's portrait clear of the coal-heaver's boots.

Fergus was vaguely aware of the shouts of the onlookers, but no one dared tackle his assailant until the angry crowd standing behind Alfie Skewes suddenly erupted and men were flung aside. The man who carved a path between them took only two more paces to reach the unequally matched combatants.

When Alfie Skewes turned to deal with the unexpected threat he found himself wrapped in a massive 'bear hug'. As his arms were pinned to his side his breath escaped in a shout that was half pain, half anger. Then, still struggling in the powerful hold, he was propelled across the room and his head brought into violent contact with the wall, the force of the blow rattling Fergus's paintings against the plaster.

Alfie Skewes slumped in the arms of Fergus's rescuer, and his sagging body was dumped unceremoniously to the floor.

'Are you all right? By Jesus, he was wiping his feet on you as though you were an old piece of sacking. Have you been upsetting him at all?'

The words were those of a man unfamiliar with the English language. Looking up at the big man who had come to his rescue, Fergus searched his memory for a name. He came up with Giraldus Reilly, the big man who had once kept the Bristol police force at bay in the derelict house by the River Frome.

Helped to his feet, Fergus bit back a groan of pain and handed the painting of Becky to Solomon Stern.

'Is Fanny all right?'

'Yes, I'm all right. But *you* wouldn't have been had that brute not been stopped. He would have killed you. Who is he?'

'Alfie Skewes. He's the man Becky stabbed when she was being held in Rose Cottle's place.'

'So *that's* why he was after Becky's portrait. The man's insane, Fergus. You should have let him have the painting and made good your escape.'

'I'm safe enough now, and so is Becky's portrait – thanks to Giraldus Reilly.' Fergus gripped the hand of the large Irishman. 'I'm deeply in your debt.'

While they waited for the police to arrive and take Alfie Skewes into custody, Giraldus Reilly told Fergus he had been working on the railway, building a new branch line to the north of Bristol. By working hard he had made good money and learned to speak the language of the country.

The police station was close at hand, and in a matter of minutes three constables arrived with an inspector.

When the inspector had taken details of what had occurred, he declared: 'Alfie Skewes will be transported for certain this time, and Bristol will be a safer place. Had the Irishman not come to your aid, he'd have been on a murder charge. Where is Mr Reilly, by the way?'

Fergus inclined his head to where Giraldus Reilly stood before one of the paintings of the Irish vagrants. Oblivious to the admiring crowd about him, the big Irishman stood with tears coursing down his cheeks and occasionally shaking his head in anguish.

'I sketched his wife and child when they were in one of the houses down by the river. They both died shortly before you moved him and the others on.'

'We were merely carrying out the orders of the City Council, our employers,' said the police inspector defensively. 'If he's still here for the trial, I'll see that the city gives him a generous reward for his help in arresting Skewes.'

'If he *is* still here, you'll find him in Lewin's Mead. I've told him he can have the room I rent there for as long as he wants it.'

Alfie Skewes had regained consciousness by the time he was taken from the art gallery. Darkness had fallen outside, but as the Lewin's Mead bully was led away Fergus saw a face he recognised among the large crowd gathered outside. It was a pale-faced Maude Garrett. Fergus called to her, but by the time he reached the place where she had been standing she had gone. All that remained was the memory of the look she had given to Fergus just before he called to her. There had been an expression of sheer hatred on her face.

CHAPTER THIRTY-FOUR

INSIDE THE POLICE STATION Alfie Skewes went beserk when his handcuffs were removed. He floored two constables and was breaking up the furniture when Ivor Primrose entered the charge office. For the second time that day the Lewin's Mead bully met a man who was more than a match for him. Carried unconscious to the cells, Alfie Skewes was secured in heavy chains and leg-irons.

When he appeared before the Bristol magistrates, Skewes was committed for trial at the quarter sessions, charged with causing damage to the police station and assaulting Fergus and Fanny. All the witnesses, including Giraldus Reilly, were ordered to attend the hearing at the high court, and there was no doubt that the Lewin's Mead bully would be sentenced to a long period of transportation on board one of the prison hulks moored in various ports around the country.

Giraldus was quite happy to remain in Bristol, where his wife and children lay buried. Helped by the police inspector, the Irishman obtained work on the quayside, loading and unloading ships. It would prove useful to him when he decided to return to Ireland. No captain who watched him work would refuse the Irishman a place among his crew. As strong as two men, Giraldus Reilly seemed never to tire.

The big Irishman was in no hurry to return to his native land, and Irish Molly ensured he lacked nothing during his stay in Bristol. She would always be haunted by the memory of their first meeting, and when she visited Fergus's room and found Giraldus weeping over a sketch of his wife and baby son her big heart went out to him. She took upon herself the task of cooking his meals, even turning 'clients' out of her room at an unheard-of early hour in order to cook breakfast for her countryman before he set off for work.

In return, Giraldus Reilly treated Irish Molly with a quiet courtesy that no man except Fergus had ever shown to her. Sometimes in the evening he took her out for a drink or two – but he would never accompany her to the White Hart. That was strictly for her 'business'. Instead, he took her to the Hatchet inn, or to one of the smaller alehouses dotted around the dockland area.

On one occasion Giraldus remonstrated with some newly returned sailors who were singing bawdy songs in Irish Molly's hearing. Afterwards, as they walked towards Back Lane, Irish Molly asked him if he really knew how she earned her living.

'I do,' was his terse reply.

'Yet you stopped those sailors from singing a song to which I probably know twice as many verses as any man there!'

'Molly, how you earn your living is no business of mine – and certainly none of theirs. When you're out with me you'll be treated as a decent woman, or I'll want to know why.'

'You're a strange man, Giraldus – and a good one. You deserve more than life has given to you.'

'I can look back on very many happy years. To times when I've walked down a sweet-smelling lane at dusk, with a tiny hand holding tight to mine. We'd return to a snug little cot and a fine woman. She needed only to look at me to say more than all the words ever written by the Irish poets. . . .'

Giraldus Reilly's voice broke, and Irish Molly's hand gripped his arm in a gesture of silent sympathy.

'I've enjoyed all those things, Molly. They were good years. Wonderful years. Years that no one can ever take from me. Do *you* have such memories? How many good years have you known?'

Irish Molly was silent for a long while. When she did speak it was in a voice so soft her companion needed to lean close to catch her words.

'I've known poverty and shame . . . plenty of shame. There *have* been days when I've walked from an inn with cries of "Good old Molly" to warm me on my way – but, God knows, it gets cold again pretty quick when you sit down and ask yourself how much it all means.'

She fell silent again until, looking up at Giraldus Reilly, she asked: 'Will you stay with me tonight, Giraldus? I can't give you back what you've lost, but I *can* promise to make you forget for a while.'

'And what of tomorrow? Will you be back at the White Hart picking up sailors?'

'That's how I earn my living, Giraldus.'

'Then, I won't be coming to your room tonight, or any other night, Molly. I hope I'm man enough to accept what any woman has been forced to do, through no fault of her own, but once I take a woman I won't share her with any other man.'

'You're asking me to give up my living? For what? To share a dockie's money? Is this what you're asking?'

'I'm not asking anything, Molly. I'm telling you why I won't be sharing your bed.'

'You're a strange one, Giraldus. I can't ever remember meeting a man like you before.'

'Does that mean you'll come for a drink with me again, even though I won't share your bed or let you listen to bawdy songs?'

They had reached Ida Stokes's house now, and Irish Molly said: 'It means I'll be upstairs to cook your breakfast before you go out in the morning. Away with you now, before I'm tempted to come up there after you.'

Irish Molly waited outside her room until Giraldus reached the head of the next flight of stairs.

'Giraldus!'

'What is it?'

'You've given me a fine evening. One I *will* enjoy remembering. Thank you.'

Before Giraldus could think of a reply Irish Molly had gone inside her room, closing the door behind her.

*   *   *

The trial of Alfie Skewes was one of the shortest of the quarter sessions. Once the prosecution case had been presented, the recorder hurried impatiently through the evidence of the witnesses. He had made up his mind that Alfie Skewes was guilty, and there were many more cases on the calendar. Within thirty seconds of being pronounced guilty, Alfie Skewes was clattering down the steps to the cells to begin a sentence of ten years' transportation.

There was a disturbance in the courtroom as Alfie Skewes disappeared from view, and when the witnesses left the building they were confronted by Joe Skewes, incensed by his son's sentence. Joe Skewes made a lunge for Fergus but he was restrained by two constables who quickly bundled him inside the building. As he went, he shouted: 'I'll get you, artist. You've been nothing but trouble to the Skewes family since you came to Bristol. I'll get you and you'll leave – feet first. You *and* that ragged-arsed urchin of yours. I'll get you both, even though I take the drop for it. . . .'

'That one's a dangerous man,' commented Giraldus Reilly. 'Be careful of him, Fergus.'

'He's more likely to bother you than me. When he's stupid with drink he has a habit of pitching up in Back Lane.'

'He'll have a surprise when he finds Mr Reilly in your room,' commented Fanny. 'But you would be wise to keep well clear of the man.'

Fergus made no reply. He was remembering the menace in Joe Skewes's voice when he spoke of Becky as Fergus's 'ragged-arsed urchin'.

By the time Fergus's Bristol exhibition came to an end it was acknowledged that it had been a great success. Solomon Stern was well satisfied, Bristol's art critics had praised Fergus's talent, and the city's newspapers used such phrases as 'this exciting and greatly gifted young painter'. There had also been a few tentative enquiries from well-to-do Bristolians. If the London exhibition proved equally successful, Bristol society would flock to Fergus to have portraits painted.

Fergus now had a month in which to complete as many additional paintings as possible before setting off for the capital. In London he would first make a tour of Unitarian churches. A display of his sketches would illustrate Fanny's talks on the work being carried out among the children of Bristol's slums.

Solomon Stern's magazine-owning friend also wanted to select a number of the sketches for publication. It promised to be a busy time for Fergus.

Becky was very unhappy when she learned she would not see Fergus for at least six weeks. Her unhappiness turned to dismay when she learned Fanny would be with him for at least two of the six weeks.

'Why, Fergus? Why does *she* want to go to London with you?' Becky asked the question for the third time in as many minutes.

'Hush! Keep your voice down.'

They were talking during the only opportunity that would present itself before Fergus went away, their heads bent low over the sheet of sketching paper on the table in front of her. The special relationship that existed between Fergus and Becky was accepted, but it was an acceptance that depended entirely upon their own discretion and the goodwill of the staff.

'Then, tell me why you're taking *her* with you.'

'I'm not *taking* anyone. Fanny is going to London to talk to members of her church about the work she's doing in the Bristol slums. She wants to use my sketches to illustrate her talks – and at the same time help to promote my exhibition.'

'Couldn't she have gone some other time?'

'Not if she wants to use my sketches. I won't let them out of my possession, you know that.'

Becky was not satisfied, but lacking any argument that might effectively change the arrangements, she asked: 'Where are you staying while you're in London?'

'With one of Fanny Tennant's aunts. It's all perfectly respectable.'

Becky's derisive snort attracted the attention of one of the staff, who appeared in the doorway on one of the regular inspections. When the woman showed no sign of leaving, Fergus was forced to leave Becky scowling down at her sketch and return to his table in front of the class.

He did not have another opportunity to talk to Becky again until the end of the lesson, as the girls were preparing to leave the classroom.

Placing a sheet of paper in front of her, he said: 'Here, I've been sketching you as you worked. It's very different from the first sketch I made of you. You've grown into quite a young lady.'

Successfully hiding the pleasure his words and the sketch gave her, Becky asked stiffly: 'As much of a "young lady" as *her*?'

'If by "her" you mean Fanny Tennant, then the answer is yes.'

'Honest?'

Suddenly, by the use of that one word Becky contradicted all he had just said. She became the uncertain Lewin's Mead urchin once more.

'Honest.'

Becky screwed up her face, and for a moment Fergus feared she was about to dissolve into unprecedented tears, but with a visible effort she regained control of herself.

'Fergus, *I want to get out of here*. You must help me!' She whispered the fierce plea.

'Becky, I'm about to go to London for six weeks. It isn't a good moment to make a statement like that to me.'

Becky made no reply, but stood looking down at the floor at her feet.

'I'll write to you – and send you sketches of the things I see in London.'

Becky nodded, but she did not look up at him.

Fergus hesitated. He did not want to leave Becky while she was in such a dejected frame of mind, but anything else he said was likely to involve him in a commitment. A responsibility. He was not certain it was one he was ready to assume.

'Come along, girls, it's time Mr Vincent left. Becky, take the things from your desk with you, please.'

As Becky obeyed and gathered up the papers on the table, Fergus made up his mind.

'When I return from London I'll speak to Mary Carpenter

and discuss your release with her.'

The papers dropped back to the small table, a couple of them falling to the floor as Becky swung around to face Fergus.

'Do you mean that, Fergus? *Really* mean it?'

He nodded, aware of the tight-lipped disapproval of the member of staff.

Becky could not contain her excitement. 'I'll try very hard not to mind you going to London ... but I'll be counting the days until you come back. Oh, Fergus. ... Thank you!'

Suddenly, Becky kissed Fergus. Then she fled, before the scandalised class-supervisor could think of words strong enough to express her disapproval.

CHAPTER THIRTY-FIVE

FERGUS AND FANNY travelled to London by train, on the broad-gauge railway line constructed by Isambard Kingdom Brunel and his gangs of 'navigators' only a few years before. It was the fastest, but by no means the most comfortable journey Fergus had ever made.

It was a hot day, and by a majority decision the occupants of the carriage decided the windows should be opened. Unfortunately, they were close to the fussy little engine which belched a continuous stream of black smoke from its tall chimney. Twice Fergus removed small pieces of sharp cinders from Fanny's eyes with his handkerchief, and by the time the train jerked to an uncertain halt at Paddington station both their faces were heavily streaked with black.

They were still chuckling over each other's appearance when their horse-drawn cab drew up at the door of a tall narrow terraced house in a not-quite-fashionable street in Kensington.

The house might not have been as impressive as Fanny Tennant's Bristol home, but Agnes Spoure, widow of a Church of England clergyman, had inherited the same disconcerting bluntness as her brother.

Confronting her guests at the door, she stood with hands on hips and said: 'Before I show you to your rooms I want to know if there's anything between the two of you. Are you betrothed or do you have any . . . "understanding", I think, is the word you young people use today?'

'Aunt Agnes!' Fanny Tennant's face was scarlet. 'Fergus is

here to help me with a series of lectures I'm giving. In return I am helping to prepare his exhibition of paintings. We are *friends*, nothing more.'

'Is that the way you see it, young man?' Agnes Spoure turned such a fierce eye upon Fergus he doubted whether any mere mortal would *dare* to tell her a lie.

He nodded.

'In that case I'll put you both in rooms on the first floor. It will save me work, and you won't need to drag that lame leg of yours up an extra floor.'

Ordering the cab-driver to bring in their bags, she led the way inside the house, saying: 'I'll expect you both to make your own beds and keep your rooms tidy. Aloysius Tennant may be my brother, but *I* don't have the money to pay servants.'

As she walked up the stairs behind her 'no-nonsense' aunt, Fanny threw an apologetic glance at Fergus and he smiled his understanding.

Fergus's room was the first one they came to, and Agnes Spoure proved she was also a thoughtful woman. Throwing open the door, she said: 'You'll be comfortable enough in here. It's the room with the largest window in the house. It's south-facing, so you should have plenty of light if you wish to do any painting – but I'll not have paint spilled all over my carpets.'

Fergus tried to thank her, but she cut his gratitude short. 'What sort of paintings do you do? None of those nude women, I hope. They're disgusting, all of them.'

Before Fergus could reassure the straight-talking woman, Fanny said quickly: 'Fergus paints *life*. His exhibition will consist mainly of paintings of Lewin's Mead – the worst of the Bristol slums. There are some wonderful paintings, Aunt Agnes. You must come and see them for yourself.'

'Good gracious me, girl! I have better things to do than waste my time at art exhibitions. Besides, there's enough misery in this world of ours. I don't need to go to an exhibition to see it for myself.'

Fergus settled himself in his room before going downstairs, and for the remainder of that first evening most of the talk was of family matters. It seemed the Tennant family were indifferent correspondents, and the two women had a great deal of trivial news for each other. As soon as he felt it was polite, Fergus excused himself and returned to his room. Here he sat down and wrote a long letter to Becky, telling her of the journey and illustrating the letter with many 'thumbnail' sketches of people and places he had seen along the way.

Later that evening Fergus was looking through the many sketches he had brought with him, placing them in order for Fanny's talks, when there came a soft knock at the door. In answer to Fergus's call, Fanny entered the room.

'You're not working already? The journey itself is wearying enough for one day. I ache from head to toe. I *swear* I have ash and cinders ground into my skin. It will be at least two days before I'm ready to think of work. I was hoping I might show you something of London.'

Fergus had always regarded Fanny as being over-serious, but since leaving Bristol she seemed to have shed both years and her air of authority. He had never seen her so relaxed. The mood was infectious, and Fergus agreed to let her show him London.

The London weather favoured the two visitors, and they were able to enjoy many of the sights of the capital. Together they visited the Tower of London, the British Museum, the Houses of Parliament and the London palaces, and they explored the bazaars of Soho Square, Pantheon and Baker Street before going on to the more fashionable Burlington and Lowther Arcades.

Along the way Fergus sketched many of the London scenes, putting aside a couple of the more interesting sketches to send to Becky. Fanny proved herself to be a good companion. During the two days spent in her company, Fergus found himself growing increasingly fond of her. But as each new experience came his way he never failed to wonder what Becky's reaction to it would have been.

The two days of sight-seeing passed quickly and it was time to get down to the more serious side of their visit to London.

The talks arranged by Fanny were sell attended. The

audiences asked intelligent questions and seemed to take a very real interest in the problems of organising a ragged school in a slum area. Fergus's sketches came in for a great deal of attention, and he, too, was closely questioned about his subjects.

Meanwhile, arrangements for Fergus's exhibition were going ahead. Solomon Stern had found premises in Pall Mall where gas lighting would prolong the viewing hours into the late evening and show the paintings to best advantage. Somehow Fanny found enough energy to spare to help in the décor of the impressive gallery and take a close interest in the exhibition.

One evening, after a particularly happy day, Fanny returned to her aunt's house, leaving Fergus hanging the last of his paintings in the gallery. When Fanny entered the house Agnes Spoure was flicking imagined dust from the highly polished rosewood table in the hall, her expression as dour as ever.

Acting on a sudden happy impulse, Fanny planted a kiss on her aunt's cheek.

Startled, Agnes Spoure put a hand to the cheek and a number of conflicting emotions fought for possession of her face. 'And what was that for, may I ask?'

'Because you've made these last couple of weeks the happiest I have known for a very long time.'

'I can hardly take the credit for *that*. You'd be content to be locked in a prison cell if Fergus Vincent were there with you. And to think I believed you when you blushed and told me there was nothing between the two of you!'

'I just enjoy being with Fergus and seeing the exhibition of his wonderful paintings take shape. Solomon Stern says it's the most important exhibition of paintings seen in London for many years. It's all very exciting.'

Agnes Spoure snorted. 'There's a letter for you on the table. Take it to your room and read it. I'm busy down here.'

Refusing to allow her aunt's words to dampen her high spirits, Fanny picked up the letter from the table. She did not recognise the bold handwriting and, tearing open the letter, she read it there and then.

Looking up from the much-dusted table, Agnes Spoure was alarmed to see the blood drain from her niece's face.

'What's the matter? Is there bad news from home?'

Fanny read in silence for a few more moments before looking up at her aunt. 'No. . . . It's from Mary Carpenter.'

'Has something happened to her?' Agnes Spoure had once met the reformatory-school pioneer and took a keen interest in her projects.

'No, nothing. She's all right. Everything's all right.' Turning away, Fanny fled up the stairs to her room, leaving Agnes Spoure frowning after her.

The art gallery in Pall Mall was destroyed on the eve of the grand opening of Fergus's exhibition. Word of the calamity reached him soon before dawn, when a runner sent by Solomon Stern woke the whole household.

Fergus received the news standing shivering on the doorstep because Agnes Spoure refused to allow a stranger inside her house at such an unheard-of hour.

At first Fergus was unable to comprehend the scale of the disaster. 'What do you mean? Is the hall badly damaged?'

'There was a great explosion. It must have awakened half of London. I'm surprised you didn't hear it right out here. They say it was gas as caused it. My pa has always said he wouldn't have it in the house. . . . Mr Stern says you ought to come at once.'

'Of course. Tell him I'm on my way.'

At the top of the stairs, with rag curlers peeping from beneath a night-bonnet, Agnes Spoure sought to protect Fanny's nightdress-clad body from Fergus's gaze, but he had no eyes for Fanny or for anyone else. He was stunned by the news he had just received. It *couldn't* be true. All his work. . . .

'I mut go to the gallery. Solomon's there. . . .'

'I'll come with you.'

'You'll do no such thing. . . .'

Agnes Spoure's indignation was wasted. Neither Fergus nor Fanny heard her. As Fergus went into his room shaking his head in total bewilderment, Fanny hurried off to get dressed. She was determined that Fergus would not leave the house without her.

Agnes Spoure did not keep a carriage, and there were no cabs to be found at such an early hour. It was about two miles to the exhibition premises in Pall Mall, and Fergus and Fanny walked. So anxious was Fergus to reach there quickly that Fanny found it difficult to keep up with him, despite his limp.

'How much damage do you think has *really* been done to my paintings?' Fergus asked the question for the umpteenth time as they passed Green Park. He was convinced Solomon Stern's messenger had exaggerated the damage to the gallery. Surely nothing short of an act of God was capable of destroying a whole building?

'We shall soon know. It's only a couple of minutes now.'

Dawn was far enough advanced to silhouette London's buildings against the skyline, and there were all manner of illuminations in the city. Then, as Fergus and Fanny rounded St James's Palace they saw a great many lamps hanging about the premises where the exhibition was to have taken place.

The messenger *had* exaggerated – but only a little. The front of the building had been blown outwards, blocking the road. Inside, floors sagged crazily towards the ground floor. They had acted as funnels, carrying tons of rubble from falling walls and chimneys, sending it cascading towards the main exhibition room.

'Oh, Fergus, it's *disastrous!*' Fanny saw the shock on Fergus's face and she gripped his arm tightly.

He seemed not to notice. Without once taking his glance from the scene of devastation he freed his arm and limped towards the shattered building. In spite of the early hour a large crowd had gathered in the street, and Fergus had to force a way through them, Fanny staying close behind him.

At the front of the crowd a metropolitan constable extended an arm to prevent Fergus from advancing any farther.

'My exhibition is in there. My paintings. . . .'

'It's all right, Constable. Allow him through.' Solomon Stern was one of a knot of men standing amidst the rubble.

He gripped Fergus's hand and nodded a mute greeting to Fanny.

'My dear chap ... I don't know what to say to you. Nothing like this has ever happened before. It's a *tragedy*. An absolute *tragedy*.'

'What happened?' Looking about him at the devastation, Fergus felt numbed. Beneath the rubble lay not only the sum total of his Bristol works, but also his future. This was to have been the exhibition that would make him famous.

'It was the damn fool of a caretaker. It seems he spent much of the evening in a beer-house around the corner. He must have somehow blown out one or more of the gas-lamps without turning the gas off. Then, perhaps when he sobered a little, he probably took a candle to check whether he'd locked up properly. A constable standing in a doorway some distance along the road saw a small light in a bedroom window shortly before the explosion.'

'Where is the caretaker now?'

'Dead. He was blown to pieces.' Solomon Stern looked guiltily at Fanny. 'I'm sorry. It's not a subject that should be discussed before a young lady.'

'How many of Fergus's paintings have been lost?'

'All of them ... save one. I've got it here.'

Solomon Stern walked to the premises next to the picture gallery. All the windows had been blown in here, but the building was intact and the owners were inside, sweeping up glass and plaster.

Solomon Stern returned carrying a painting with a broken frame. 'If I'd had to choose one painting to save, it would have been this one. It survived because it was in pride of place, well back inside a deep alcove.'

Turning the picture towards him, Fergus saw it was the painting of Becky looking out of the Back Street attic window at the family of sparrows.

'I expect you had an insurance that will cover you for your loss ...?'

Fergus shook his head, not trusting himself to speak.

'Neither had the gallery. The paintings *would* have been insured, of course, but the insurance was due to take effect only from the time the exhibition was opened.'

'You still have your sketches, Fergus,' said Fanny. 'You can produce more paintings from them. Lady Hammond will allow you to keep the studio. It will be all right. You'll see. . . .'

Fergus could see nothing with any clarity. Almost all his work had been destroyed and his future placed in jeopardy. Yet he felt an absurd relief that the painting of Becky had survived. Fanny was right, he probably *could* use his sketches to produce the paintings again. They would not be the same, of course – but they *would* be good. Only the painting of Becky could never have been produced again – and it had survived. It was fate. . . .

So great was his sudden relief that he felt like breaking down and crying. Instead, he turned away from the scene of devastation. Still clutching the painting of Becky, he limped away.

He was fifty yards along the road before Fanny caught up with him.

'Fergus. . . . Where are you going?'

'Home.'

'That's very sensible. Go straight to bed. I'll have Aunt Agnes call in a doctor. He'll give you an opiate. This has come as a great shock to you.'

'I'm going home to Bristol. There's nothing for me in London now. I need to begin working again. My paintings have to be replaced.'

'You would do better to rest at Aunt Agnes's house for a few days. I'll send word to Lady Hammond and she'll have your studio ready for you when you return to Bristol.'

'I won't be returning to Lady Hammond's house. I'm going to Lewin's Mead. To Back Lane. It's the only hope I have of re-creating what's been lost. It *has* to be Back Lane.'

Fanny was silent for a long time, then she suddenly ran ahead of Fergus. Confronting him, she brought him to a halt.

'Are you serious? About returning to Lewin's Mead?'

'Absolutely serious.'

'Then, there's something I think you should know. It's about Becky.'

Fergus looked at her blankly, and Fanny winced. He looked so tired. Far too weary to hear the news she had to give him now.

'A friend of Becky's, a girl named Maude Garrett, was picked up by the police and sent to the Red Lodge reformatory. She and Becky had a dreadful fight, and afterwards Becky broke out of the Red Lodge and ran away. Mary Carpenter believes she's returned to Lewin's Mead.'

CHAPTER THIRTY-SIX

BECKY TRIED VERY HARD to come to terms with the knowledge that Fergus had gone to London with Fanny Tennant. She told herself he was an artist, a *great* artist, and his art must come before all other considerations. Becky looked at the painting of the sparrows he had given to her for Christmas and she felt little squiggles of pleasure inside her. Fergus *was* fond of her, she was certain of it, and he had promised to write to her. Very well, she would wait for his first letter and try not to think of what he and Fanny Tennant might be doing in far-off London town.

For three days Becky was a model of patient reasonableness to everyone about her. If she felt despair – as she frequently did – she had only to look at her painting and think of Fergus. Somehow nothing else mattered very much then, for a while.

On the fourth day, Maude Garrett was brought to the reformatory. Hers was not a serious offence. Stopped in the street by one of the new police 'detectives', who had seen her soliciting, she had hit him in the face with her shoe and attempted unsuccessfully to escape. The magistrates offered her the choice of prison or Mary Carpenter's reformatory. Having spent three nights in the Bridewell cells, Maude Garrett had no hesitation in choosing the latter option.

Becky expressed her sympathy with Maude Garrett at being committed to the reformatory, but she was secretly delighted to see her again. Maude brought with her a breath of Lewin's Mead. A reminder that a *real* world still existed beyond the walls of the Red Lodge.

Becky took it upon herself to guide the 'new girl' through the disciplined routine of the reformatory, punctuating her explanations with a barrage of questions.

Most of Becky's questions went unanswered. Others brought only short replies. Maude Garrett's churlishness was hurtful, but Becky made excuses for the girl she regarded as her friend. Maude Garrett's freedom had been taken from her, and she needed time to adapt to her new and strange surroundings.

In a bid to make her friend feel more at ease, Becky said: 'Don't worry, you'll soon get used to it here. It's not so bad really.'

'I won't be here long enough to get used to anything,' retorted Maude Garrett. 'I'm not having some bossy old spinster telling *me* what to do every minute of the day and night.'

Becky was about to say that every girl in the Red Lodge had expressed similar sentiments upon arrival, but she said nothing. Maude would learn for herself. Instead, she asked: 'How are your family. Do they still live in Broadmead?'

Maude Garrett shrugged her indifference. 'I suppose so, unless Pa's drunk himself to death. They're Lisa's responsibility now, not mine. I had to look after them for as long as I can remember. Now it's her turn.'

'But what of the babies?'

'They're both dead. Phoebe couldn't have lasted long anyway, and Lisa said Victoria died in her sleep. I expect the truth of it is that Pa smothered her one night when she was crying. She cried a lot after Lisa took to going out and earning money.'

'You don't really believe that? That your father killed her?' Becky was used to violence and brutality, but the thought of a father smothering his young daughter because she cried horrified her.

Maude Garrett shrugged. 'You asked about the babies, and I've told you. I don't suppose I'll behave any better towards mine when it's born.'

'You're having a baby? When?'

'I dunno. Probably about five months' time, I reckon, but

they'll let me out of here soon enough when they find out, that's for sure.'

'Who's the father?'

Maude Garrett threw a scornful look in Becky's direction. 'What sort of a question is that? I was one of the most fancied girls in the White Hart. I was kept busy, I can tell you, until I found an easier way of getting money – like taking old men who ought to know better down alleyways to where my man was waiting to tap them on the head and empty their pockets.'

Maude Garrett looked at Becky maliciously. 'The baby's father could be any one of hundreds. Sailors, gentlemen. Even a certain high and mighty artist – him who had my man thrown into gaol.'

Becky paled. 'You're not trying to tell me that Fergus knocked you up? You're lying.'

'Am I? Next time you see him, you ask him who he woke up in bed with the morning after Iris's party.'

'Liar! *Liar!*' Becky screamed the words at Maude Garrett.

'Call me as many names as you like. I'm telling you what happened. Not that it's worth remembering. I expect he's better at knocking women like that Miss Tennant who works at the ragged school. Women like her don't know what *real* men are like.'

Becky fell upon Maude Garrett screaming obscenities learned from a lifetime in Lewin's Mead, her fingernails raking the older girl's face.

The other girls quickly gathered round, shrieking encouragement, and within minutes the staff of the Red Lodge were struggling to contain the worst riot that had ever occurred in the Park Row reformatory.

When order was eventually restored neither girl would tell the reason for their fight and eventually both were sent to separate dormitories. They would be taken before Mary Carpenter the next day and their future decided.

That night Becky slipped out of the Red Lodge, scaled the high garden-wall, and disappeared into the darkness of the Bristol streets.

Fergus made the return journey to Bristol alone. Fanny

remained in London in the hope that more paintings might be salvaged from the ruins of the picture gallery. She had urged Fergus to remain with her, but the loss of his paintings had numbed his mind. He did not want to stay in London for one day longer than was necessary. There was also the problem of Becky's escape from the Red Lodge. Fergus was philosophical enough to accept that, given time, his paintings could be produced again. Rebuilding Becky's life was likely to prove rather more difficult.

Mary Carpenter's letter to Fanny had made mention of Becky's fight with Maude Garrett. Fergus believed it had been caused because of his part in the arrest and conviction of Alfie Skewes. Maude had been associating with the transported man and had been in the crowd outside the Wine Street art gallery when Alfie Skewes was taken away by the police.

Fergus was hopeful he could find Becky quickly. She had nowhere to go but Lewin's Mead. What he would do when he found her was another matter. It was a problem that occupied his mind for much of the bone-shaking train-journey to Bristol, taking his mind off the tragic London 'exhibition'.

On the platform at Bristol's Great Western Railway station, Fergus was cheered to see Constable Ivor Primrose. A visiting dignitary had travelled on the same train as Fergus, and the largest and most impressive member of the Bristol police force had been detailed to meet the visitor and escort him to a waiting carriage.

Waiting until Ivor Primrose's official duties came to an end, Fergus walked with the tall constable from the station to the centre of Bristol, a distance of almost a mile. Along the way they spoke of Becky.

Ivor Primrose was able to provide the answers to most of the questions Fergus had formulated on the journey from London, and in return Fergus told the constable of the decision he had taken.

They had reached one of the old toll-houses guarding Bristol Bridge, and Ivor Primrose stopped and looked gravely at Fergus.

'Do you think you have given this matter sufficient

thought? Wouldn't it be better to leave it to me to see Becky is returned to the Red Lodge? She won't be punished. Mary Carpenter doesn't believe in punishment, as well you know. Go back to your studio in Clifton and think things over for a while. The explosion in London and the loss of your paintings have been a great shock for you. This isn't the time to be making decisions.'

'I've made up my mind, Ivor. I know what I'm going to do. The only question is whether or not you'll help me.'

Ivor Primrose shook his head despairingly. 'I doubt whether Fanny Tennant will ever forgive me for this, but, yes, I'll help you.'

'Thanks. Now all I need do is find Becky.'

Clutching the painting of Becky, his sketches and a few personal belongings, Fergus made his way through the darkening streets of Lewin's Mead. A few loafers eyed him speculatively, wondering whether he carried anything of value in his bag. Many more recognised him and nodded a greeting.

By the time he reached Back Lane, Fergus had begun to think about the reception he would receive from Becky. She would no doubt be anticipating his disapproval. He had a lot to say to her. Away from the supervision of the reformatory staff they should be able to discuss Fergus's plans for her without any interruption.

There was a light showing beneath the door of the attic and the sound of someone moving about inside. Fergus threw open the door with barely concealed excitement – and was confronted by a startled Irishman holding a cup of steaming hot tea in his hand.

'Fergus!'

'Giraldus.'

Fergus had forgotten that he had turned the room over to Giraldus Reilly.

'What are you doing here? I thought you were finding fame and fortune in London.'

'It's a long story. I'll tell you about it some other time.' Disappointed at not finding Becky here, Fergus suddenly felt very tired.

'Here, have this tea. I was taking it downstairs to Molly. She enjoys a cup before going out to work.'

Fergus took the cup gratefully. He had neither eaten nor drunk anything that day.

'I was expecting Becky to be here. While I was in London I heard she had run away from the Red Lodge.'

'You must be talking about Molly's friend. A young girl. Pretty, but not a lot of flesh on her.'

'That's her. You know where she is?' The description was not altogether flattering, but it fitted Becky well enough.

'She's moved into the room next to Molly. The one that Maude used to have. But she's not in at the moment. I passed her on the stairs not half an hour since. She was on her way out to work.'

'Where would she be working at this time of night? I need to find her.'

Giraldus Reilly hesitated before replying. 'I think you'd best be asking Molly about that. She told Becky you'd not be happy with what she's doing.'

'What *is* she doing?'

'Come downstairs and see Molly. Bring your tea with you. I've another here for her.'

Carrying a cup of weak tea, liberally sweetened with sugar, Giraldus Reilly led the way to Irish Molly's first-floor room.

Irish Molly's pleasure at seeing Giraldus quickly gave way to dismay when she saw his companion.

'Fergus! We ... I ... thought you'd be away for much longer.'

'So did I. Where's Becky?'

Irish Molly sought support from Giraldus Reilly. From the corner of his eye Fergus saw the big man shake his head and shrug away any responsibility for answering Fergus's question.

'She's at the White Hart, working.'

Fergus frowned. 'That's dangerous. The police visit the inns. If she's found, she'll be taken back to the Red Lodge.'

'You don't understand, Fergus. She's picking up men and bringing them back here. Becky's on the game.'

For a moment the room seemed to reel about Fergus.

'Are you all right?' Giraldus gripped Fergus's arm anxiously.

Brushing the Irishman's arm away, Fergus spoke angrily to Irish Molly. 'I don't believe you. It's a trick to stop me from looking for her. It won't work. . . .'

'It's no trick, Fergus, so help me. I tried hard to stop her. I knew how you'd take the news when you found out. I begged her to think about that. She said you wouldn't care. She said you might even become one of her regulars, like you were with Maude Garrett.'

Fergus's mouth dropped open. So *that* was why she and Maude Garrett had fought. It had nothing to do with Alfie Skewes, after all. Suddenly all Fergus's other problems were forgotten.

Irish Molly watched Fergus struggling with his guilty thoughts and there was disbelief in her voice when she asked: 'You *didn't* cop with that little shabroon?'

'I don't know, Molly. I woke up the morning after Iris's wedding party and found Maude in bed with me, but I have no idea what *happened* there.'

'You poor soul. You mean that since that night you haven't known whether you gave it to her or not?' Irish Molly tried hard not to laugh, but she failed and for a full minute she was unable to speak.

When she eventually regained some control of her voice, Irish Molly said: 'No, you wouldn't have known – and Maude certainly wouldn't have told you. She'd *want* you to believe there was something between the two of you. But I *saw* you on your way upstairs to bed that night. You couldn't have had it off with her, or with anyone else, the condition you were in.'

'Do you really think so?'

'*Think*? I *know*. Many's the time I've listened to a man snoring his head off all night, then sent him on his way in the morning believing I'd earned every penny he gave me. I can tell by looking at a man whether or not he'll make it – and after Iris's party you couldn't have even raised a smile.'

'But Becky must think I did. That's why she fought Maude Garrett and ran away from the Red Lodge. I'm certain of it.'

'I know nothing about that, but if you think it will help I'll go down to the White Hart and tell Becky she's let Maude Garrett make a fool of her.'

'I'll come with you,' said Giraldus Reilly unexpectedly. 'It's time I was off to work, too – but first I'll bundle up my clothes and get them out of Fergus's room.'

'There's no need to do that. You can stay for as long as you wish.'

'No, I'd have moved earlier if I hadn't been so lazy. I'm working at the Hatchet as a cellarman now. A room goes with the job. Wait for me, Molly.'

When the Irishman had gone from the room, Irish Molly asked: 'What will happen to Becky? You know she'll be sent back to the reformatory if the po-lice get their hands on her?'

Fergus nodded, but the carefully thought out plans he had made for Becky were in total disarray. On the way from London he believed he had resolved Becky's future. Now he was more uncertain than ever.

'Becky's not a bad girl really, Fergus. She could have gone on the game years ago when she was a hungry ragged little urchin, but she didn't, and if it hadn't been for Rose Cottle she wouldn't have started now. I've done what I can for her since she's been out of the Red Lodge, Fergus. Kept her clear of men she might have trouble with. I couldn't do more.'

Irish Molly shrugged philosophically. 'After what happened with Joe and Alfie Skewes she had nothing to lose any more.'

Fergus said nothing, although he knew both he and Becky had a great deal to lose. He had returned to Lewin's Mead to ask Becky to marry him.

CHAPTER THIRTY-SEVEN

WHEN IRISH MOLLY AND GIRALDUS REILLY left the house Fergus returned to the attic studio and waited. It was not long before inaction became intolerable. He tidied up the studio, then began to sort through the sketches brought back with him from London, putting them in the order in which he intended making new paintings. When this was done he took the portrait of Becky, recovered from the London gallery explosion, and set it up on the easel, placing it where it would be immediately visible to Becky when she entered the attic room.

The painting stood in its place for two hours before Fergus finally accepted that Becky was not going to hurry home to see him.

He contemplated going to the White Hart and having a confrontation with Becky, but reluctantly discarded the idea. Becky was a very stubborn girl. If Irish Molly had not been able to persuade her to return to the house, it was doubtful whether he would succeed – and certainly not in the presence of others. She might also fear he would try to persuade her to return to the Red Lodge. Fergus was not prepared to risk another misunderstanding. This time everything had to be right.

Looking at the painting of Becky, Fergus had a sudden idea. Lifting it from the easel, he carried it downstairs to the room occupied by Becky. The room was sparsely furnished, and there were few personal belongings in evidence. There was nowhere to hang a painting on the bare walls and after some deliberation Fergus stood it on the mantelshelf above the fireplace.

Although it was not exceptionally large, the painting dominated the whole room, and Fergus was satisfied it would not be overlooked when Becky returned to her room.

Back in his attic room once more, Fergus left the door open and settled down to wait, hoping to hear Becky when she came back to the house.

He had forgotten the night noises of Ida Stokes's house. People seemed to come and go the whole time, and the many occupants of Mary O'Ryan's room contributed in no small degree to the traffic on the stairs.

Fergus had almost persuaded himself that Becky was spending the night elsewhere when he heard voices in the downstairs hallway. He was on his feet in an instant. There were two voices – and one belonged to Becky. The other was a man's voice, and his loud laughter and slurred words made Fergus feel physically sick. Fighting back an urge to go downstairs and confront Becky and her companion, he forced himself to remain in the attic room. Tackling her now would do far more harm than good. The very fact that Becky had returned to the house with a 'client', knowing Fergus was there, was an indication of her defiant mood.

When the sound of Becky and the man became unbearable Fergus closed the door. Walking to the farthermost window, he looked out at the night sky. He should not have come back. Everyone else was right, and he was wrong. There was no returning to the past. Too much had changed. Before he left London, Fanny had told him he was trying to live out a foolish dream. She was right. He had come to Lewin's Mead to recapture something that had probably never existed outside his own mind. The only certainty now was that he could no longer live here. He could not listen to Becky's voice on the stairs night after night, knowing what was happening in her room, in her bed. . . .

Fergus was bundling up the last of his sketches when he heard footsteps on the stairs to the attic. They were followed by a soft knock on the door.

Thinking it was Irish Molly coming to explain her failure

with Becky, Fergus called: 'Come in.'

He finished tying the tape on the last bundle as the door opened and looked up to see Becky standing in the doorway. In her hands was the painting he had left in her room.

He straightened up, and for what seemed long minutes they looked at each other in silence.

She looked tired, her eyes wide and dark in the pale face. She had grown since she was last in this room, but they had confronted each other then, he remembered.

'I heard you come in. . . .'

It was not what he had intended saying. It sounded as though it was an accusation. 'I'd hoped you'd come home earlier. To see me.'

'Why did you put this in my room?' She held up the painting.

'It's yours. I painted it for you.'

'I've still got the other one you painted for me for Christmas.'

Fergus had not seen the painting in Becky's room. Her next words provided the reason.

'I keep it hidden. It's the only thing I own that's worth anything.'

'You brought it with you when you ran away from the Red Lodge?'

Becky's chin came up. 'Should I have left it there for Maude Garrett? Yes, perhaps I should have. She's got more right to anything of yours than I have.'

'Maude Garrett has no claim to anything of mine, Becky.'

'Are you denying you slept with her?'

'No.' It was useless to try to evade the question. 'But sleeping was *all* I did. Ask Irish Molly. She saw the state I was in when Maude helped me up here to bed.'

'What about the other times?'

'There were no other times.'

Becky lowered the painting to the floor and held it upright with two extended fingers. 'That isn't what she says. She told me you're probably the father of the kid she's having.'

Fergus was startled. 'Maude Garrett's having a child? Well, she'll need to look elsewhere for a father; it's nothing to do with me. Is that why you fought with her?'

Ignoring the question, Becky looked to where Fergus had made bundles of his sketches. 'Are you moving your things out?'

'Yes, I'm leaving.'

For just a moment Becky looked vulnerable, but the moment passed quickly.

'I suppose you're going back to Clifton, to that Lady Something-or-other? I thought you were supposed to be in London with Fanny Tennant for some important exhibition. That's what you told me.'

'I'm not going to Clifton, and there'll be no exhibition. There was an explosion at the gallery. Your painting was the only one saved.'

'Oh! I'm sorry, Fergus, really I am.' Becky's sympathy was genuine. 'I know what the exhibition meant to you. And your paintings. . . . All the work you did on them.'

'I'll make other paintings, of other places. There will be other exhibitions.'

Turning away, Fergus began blindly stuffing the remaining sketches into his bag. He found Becky's sympathy harder to take than anger or indifference.

'You're leaving Bristol? Where will you go?'

'That's *my* business.' Fergus hoped abruptness would cloak the abject misery he felt. 'You've got a client in your room. Shouldn't you be down there looking after his needs?'

Becky winced as though he had struck her a physical blow, but it gave him no satisfaction.

'He's almost as drunk as you say you were the night Maude Garrett put you to bed. His money will buy him a good night's sleep, nothing more.'

Fergus was packed now. A few sketches protruded through the opening of his bag, but they did not matter. Nothing mattered very much any more. Fergus felt utterly defeated. Becky had achieved what an explosion and the loss of his paintings had failed to do.

Lifting the bag and tucking it beneath his arm, Fergus took a last look around the attic room. It was now part of the past. Only Becky stood between him and a new life.

Becky did not stand aside for him when he reached the doorway, and he was forced to stop and face her.

'Are you leaving because of me?'

He wanted to say no, but the lie would not come out. He said nothing.

'Why *are* you leaving?'

'There's nothing here for me now.'

This, at least, was the truth.

Becky had been watching him closely, and now she said: 'I've made a mess of things again, haven't I? Just like I did when I pinched that watch for you.'

She looked more like an abject and friendless waif than a prostitute who had a drunken man lying in her bed.

'Why did you run off from the Red Lodge and begin ... what you're doing now? You've never done it before. You were getting on so well at the Red Lodge. Everything was working out right for you.'

'Was it? Or was it what everyone *else* wanted for me?' Becky's aggression flared up for a moment, but it subsided as quickly as it had appeared.

'I tried, Fergus. I tried very hard because I knew it was what you wanted me to do. Then, when Maude Garrett arrived and said you might be the father of her baby, it all seemed a waste of time....'

Becky looked up at him, and he could only guess at the desperate struggle going on inside her. 'But I'll go back to the Red Lodge ... if you'll stay in Bristol.'

As Fergus looked at the unhappiness on her pinched face, some of the anger and frustration bottled up inside him bubbled over. 'Why the hell did you have to become a *whore* the minute you got back here? Why couldn't you have done something else? On the way from London I thought of a way to stop you *ever* returning to the Red Lodge....'

Becky's shrug hid the hurt she felt at his words. 'I was a whore *before* I went to the Red Lodge. Joe and Alfie Skewes saw to *that*. It wouldn't have mattered very much, but for you. I'd have ended up on the game one day. What else is there for a girl like me to do in Lewin's Mead?'

'You could have *married* me, Becky. That way I would be

responsible for you and could have had a magistrate rescind the order committing you to the Red Lodge.'

Becky did not even hear the second part of Fergus's statement. Looking at him open-mouthed, she gasped: 'You'd have *married* me? Why?'

'Because you're one hell of a worry to me and it's the only way I know of having some control over what you do.'

'You'd have married me . . . just for that?'

'Not entirely. I'm very fond of you . . . but you already know that. I have been since I tripped over you when I first arrived in Lewin's Mead.'

Becky's eyes filled with tears and, as though her legs had suddenly become incapable of supporting her, she sat down heavily on the top stair.

'I *have* made another mess of things. An even *bigger* mess this time.' The words came out as hardly more than a whisper. And then Becky, the girl who had once said she never cried, began to sob, and she sobbed as though her heart was breaking.

Fergus put out a hand to touch her head uncertainly. She knocked it away violently.

'Don't touch me. Go away. Just *go away*!'

Fergus brushed past her . . . then he stopped. He could not leave her like this. Putting down the bag, he sat beside her on the stair and put an arm about her, ignoring her protests. He turned her towards him, and suddenly all her resistance came to an end and she clung to him, scrubbing her eyes against the front of his shirt.

It was a long time before her sobbing subsided enough for Fergus to become aware of other sounds in the house. The murmur of Iris's voice from her room, a man's voice with her, laughing. There was a baby crying in the O'Ryan room and the shrill sound of Ida Stokes berating someone from the street-door.

When Becky spoke again it was in a voice so soft that he needed to put his ear close to her mouth before he could hear her.

'I love you, Fergus. I love you more than I ever thought I would love anyone.'

Fergus felt an absurd lump rise in his throat. He said fiercely: 'I think I love you, too, Becky.'

'Honest?'

'Honest.'

In the attic behind them a candle began spluttering as the flaming wick burned close to the hot wax, swimming in the saucer in which it stood. Downstairs another voice began hurling abuse back at Ida Stokes.

'What am I going to do with you, Becky?'

'Just holding me is enough for now. It's what I thought about you doing all the time I was in the Red Lodge. I'd listen to the other girls talking of what they'd done before, and what they'd do as soon as they got out. I'd say the same things sometimes, just to be like them, but really I just wanted *you* to hold me.'

Behind them the candle gave a final splutter. After a momentary flare-up of yellow light the attic was plunged into darkness.

'Fergus, can I sleep with you tonight? You don't need to do anything except hold me close, like this.'

'If that's what you want.'

'I do. Very much.'

Fergus stood up awkwardly. He had cramp in his lame leg. Forced to lean on Becky for a few moments he grimaced in the darkness as he suffered a moment of self-appraisal. He was a crippled artist with nothing to offer a bride but a sparsely furnished attic in the heart of Bristol's dingiest slum. He was hardly the most eligible man in the world.

CHAPTER THIRTY-EIGHT

FERGUS WAS AWAKENED in the morning by a commotion coming from somewhere in the house. He tried to move, but a weight was pressing down on his outstretched arm. When he turned his head he saw Becky looking at him ... and he remembered.

The commotion ended abruptly with the sound of footsteps clattering noisily down the stairs to the street. Then there was a noise outside the door, and Irish Molly entered the room. Dressed in a wrap, her heavy make-up was badly smudged, her hair was in disarray and she looked about her from bleary eyes.

'Fergus, have you seen ...? Oh, there you are!' Irish Molly answered her own part-spoken question as she saw Becky's head resting on Fergus's arm, half-hidden by the bedclothes. 'I wish you'd make up your mind which bed you were meant to be in. I've just had a seaman come barging into my room demanding to know where he was, and how he'd got here. Lucky for all of us the man in bed with me was the first mate from the same ship. He remembered they were meant to be sailing on the early-morning tide. Shall I be making up the fire and putting on the kettle for you?'

Becky looked at Fergus apprehensively, wondering how he would react to being reminded of her way of life. But he was looking at Irish Molly.

'Yes, put the kettle on, then Becky can get up and make us all some tea. She'll need to get used to it. We're going to be married.'

'That won't come as a surprise to anyone except the two of youse. I saw it coming the first day you walked into the house together, so did Ida Stokes. Don't tell *her* too soon. The minute she knows, she'll be putting your rent up – or will you be moving off somewhere else? Clifton, perhaps?'

'We'll be staying right here. I've a lot of painting to do and I work better in Lewin's Mead. Now, get that fire going while I dress.'

As Fergus donned his clothes he told Irish Molly about the destruction of his paintings, at the same time filling in some of the details for Becky's benefit.

Irish Molly clicked her tongue sympathetically. 'Now, isn't that a terrible thing? I've said many times that these new inventions will be the death of all of us. Gas, indeed. My grandmother raised ten children by candlelight, and my great grandmother twenty-two! What are we needing to see more for anyway? As you grow older you realise that darkness is one of the Lord's great blessings. We'd all be better off for not seeing so much of what's about us.'

Irish Molly used a foot to push the blackened kettle farther into the crackling fire. 'Mind you, I believe all these things happen for the best. If it hadn't been for the explosion, you might not have come back here and got together with Becky again. It was the same with me, when poor Tomas left me all that money. If I'd gone back to Ireland on me own, I'd have made a mess of me life for sure . . . and I'd never have met up with Giraldus.'

Fergus had finished dressing and he said: 'Do I scent romance in *your* life, Molly?'

Irish Molly turned around and peered at him from between puffy eyelids, the surrounding skin marbled from years of heavy drinking. 'Look at me! Would *you* marry me if you'd once been married to a decent woman and had children by her? No, of course you wouldn't. All the same, don't be surprised if I take Giraldus back to Ireland one day, to see what might be done with that cottage of mine. . . .'

The kettle slid sideways, sending a cascade of water hissing among the hot ashes, and once again Irish Molly used her foot to restore the kettle's balance.

When it was steady once more, she turned to Becky. 'Never forget how lucky you are, young lady. The "girls" in the White Hart may talk of marriage with scorn, but there isn't one of 'em who doesn't dream that the right man will come along and take her off, one day.'

The kettle had not boiled, but Irish Molly decided it was hot enough. Wrapping the trailing hem of her grubby nightgown about her hand in a manner that defied modesty, she lifted the kettle from the fire. Pausing to look across the room to where Becky had her feet to the ground, she said: 'Mind you, if I hear you repeating one word of what I've just said I'll swear you're out of your mind, you understand?'

The wedding of Fergus and Becky took place in a small Baptist chapel on the edge of Lewin's Mead. The venue had been suggested by Constable Ivor Primrose. The big policeman could not become personally involved with any of the wedding arrangements because Becky was still officially 'a wanted person', but he ensured that no obstacles were placed in the way of the young couple.

The Baptist preacher was a man who worked hard to ease the lot of those who lived in the poverty-afflicted streets about his church. He was concerned about Becky's youth and her lack of a surname, but when Fergus visited the chapel and explained the situation honestly and frankly the preacher set aside his doubts. He promised that nothing should put the wedding in jeopardy. After many years spent working for the poor he accepted that success and happiness were elusive goals. He would not stand in the way of a Lewin's Mead urchin who had the opportunity to improve her meagre lot in life.

The marriage took place three weeks after Fergus's return from London. It was a quiet affair, with only Irish Molly, Giraldus Reilly and, surprisingly, Ida Stokes attending from Back Lane. There were also a few curious members of the regular Baptist congregation in the chapel, and all added their loud Amens to the blessings called down upon the married couple.

Afterwards Fergus, Becky and their friends adjourned to a

private room at the Hatchet inn to enjoy a wedding breakfast provided for them by Charlie Waller. Fergus had resumed his evening work at the inn, and during the course of the celebrations many of the inn's regular customers looked in to wish the newlyweds health and happiness.

Later that night, as Becky lay in bed in the attic room in Back Lane she thought she had never been so happy in all her life. The moon cast a soft light into the room through the windows, there was a comforting glow from the low-burning fire in the grate, and Fergus slept at her side.

Fergus . . . her *husband*! She was now Becky *Vincent*. She had a surname for the first time in her life. Becky snuggled closer to Fergus. As the rhythm of his breathing broke, his arm reached out across her body and Becky warmed to his touch. At this moment she would not have changed places with anyone in the land.

Fergus met Fanny for the first time since returning from London when he visited the Red Lodge reformatory to speak to Mary Carpenter about Becky. Fanny was leaving the building as he entered, and her face lit up with pleasure at seeing him.

'I've been very worried about you, Fergus. Nobody here seemed to know where you were. Had I heard nothing by this weekend, I intended coming to Back Lane to look for you.'

She gripped his arm in a gesture of warmth. 'I realised you needed time to think about your future after the tragic loss of all your paintings. There is no chance of compensation, I'm afraid. Has Solomon told you? No, of course he hasn't. None of us has seen you since your return.'

'Fanny . . .' Fergus attempted to halt her chatter, but she seemed not to hear him.

'Why haven't you called on Lady Hammond? It's very naughty of you, after all she has done. But never mind. Come to dinner tonight. Lady Hammond will be there and she has a forgiving nature. She's certain to ask you to return to the studio. . . .'

'Fanny, I'm married now. To Becky.'

Fanny's mouth dropped open in utter disbelief. 'You are . . . *what?*'

'I've married Becky. That's why I'm here now. I want to see Mary Carpenter and have Becky's committal order revoked.'

'Fergus . . . how *could* you? What of your talent? The plans we made for the future? You've thrown them all away!'

Fanny seemed dazed and unable to put her thoughts together.

'No, Fanny, my paintings owe their very existence to Lewin's Mead. And I had Becky to think of. . . .'

'I've always known you felt some absurd responsibility for the girl, but I never dreamed you would go so far as to *marry* her. Why, she's hardly more than a *child*!'

'She's no child, Fanny. Lewin's Mead has never allowed her to be one.'

'But . . . to *marry* her. . . .' Suddenly, Fanny gathered her wits together with a visible effort. 'I wish you well, Fergus, Becky, too.'

'I'll see you again soon. At the ragged school, perhaps?'

'Yes. . . . No! I won't be there. Not for some weeks. I have some work to do for Father. Goodbye, Fergus.' Turning away from him, Fanny hurried off along the street.

Inside the Red Lodge, Fergus was kept waiting for many minutes before being shown into Mary Carpenter's study. The reformatory pioneer was brusque to the point of rudeness.

'I am told your London exhibition was cancelled in most unfortunate circumstances, Mr Vincent. I am very sorry, of course, but I feel unable to make use of your services again for a while. Since the unfortunate incident with the girl who absconded we have revised our thinking on using men tutors. It seems to unsettle the girls. Becky's actions came as a great disappointment to us all.'

'It's Becky I'm here to see you about.' Fergus knew from experience that if he did not break in on Mary Carpenter's flow of words he would be outside the study and on his way again before he had an opportunity to explain the purpose of his visit.

'You know where she is? Have you told the police? Or would you rather I came with you to bring her back? She will not be punished. I accept the fight was the fault of the other girl. Sadly, she has now been committed to prison. I have had few failures here, Mr Vincent, but I regret to admit that Maude Garrett was one. However, she is expecting a child and would have had to go elsewhere anyway. We have no facilities for babies here.'

'Becky is not coming back, Miss Carpenter. I've married her, and so she is now *my* responsibility. I want to rescind the magistrate's order committing her to your care.'

Mary Carpenter looked at Fergus without saying a word for at least ten seconds, then she asked: 'You have proof of this marriage?'

Fergus handed over a marriage certificate without comment.

Mary Carpenter read it carefully before passing it back to him. 'I see. Unfortunately, I can do nothing about the committal order. It was made by a magistrate. Only he can change it.'

'I realise that, but now you know the circumstances I would be grateful if you would inform the police that Becky is no longer wanted by you. I don't want to run the risk of having her locked up and put away while I sort out the whole business.'

Mary Carpenter nodded. 'That makes good sense. I will send word to the police immediately.' She looked accusingly at Fergus. 'I must confess I find your news surprising. I was not aware you had such deep feelings for this girl. *Had* I known, you would not have been allowed to teach here. I trust you did not abuse your privileged position as a member of staff. I would view that as most improper.'

Fergus smiled inwardly at Mary Carpenter's indignation. 'I did nothing you need be concerned about, Miss Carpenter. I conducted myself as one of your tutors should.'

Mary Carpenter gave him a brief nod. 'Then, it only remains for me to offer my sincere best wishes to both of you. Not all the girls who leave here can look forward to marriage with a respectable young man.'

Mary Carpenter stood up and extended her hand.

Fergus was halfway to the door when her voice brought him to a halt. 'Is Miss Tennant aware of your marriage?'

'I told her a short time ago. We met as I was coming here.'

When Fergus left, closing the door behind him, Mary Carpenter sat staring down at the empty desk in front of her for a long time. Then she stood up and, walking to the long window, looked out across the city towards Lewin's Mead.

CHAPTER THIRTY-NINE

FERGUS'S REQUEST to have the magistrate's order set aside was granted with a minimum of fuss, and married life quickly settled down to a pleasant routine for the young couple.

Fergus would paint for most of the day in the attic studio, occasionally sallying forth to make new sketches of life in the Lewin's Mead streets. In the evenings he went to the Hatchet inn, where Charlie Waller had framed a number of Fergus's sketches and put them up around the inn walls. Soon Bristolians were coming to the Hatchet inn especially to have Fergus sketch them.

The money Fergus made at the inn was his sole source of income. It was more than most Lewin's Mead residents earned, but there was little left at the end of each week. There were painting materials to be bought for Fergus, furniture and fittings to turn the attic into a reasonably comfortable home, and clothes for Becky, who had never before possessed more than a single dress at any one time.

Much to Fergus's relief, Becky had learned to cook well during her months at the Red Lodge and there was no repetition of the breakfast she had once made for him.

On Sundays, Fergus and Becky left Lewin's Mead to mingle with families from other parts of the city on their weekly excursions. They never repeated the trip on a steamer, but the city had many other delights on offer. One day they went to Bristol's zoological park where Becky's wonderment at the strange animals on view equalled that of the children about them. She was charmed by a bear cub frolicking in its enclosure, and shivered in fearful excitement as the sensitive tip of an elephant's trunk took a bun from her hand.

That night, lying in bed together, their room lit only by the glow from the fire, Becky declared it had been the most enjoyable day she had ever known.

'Better than our trip on the paddle-steamer?'

'I think so,' Becky admitted, after giving the matter due thought. 'Mind you, I was only a child then.'

Fergus smiled and tightened his arm about her. 'We'll have to go again, one weekend.'

'Why? I've got my *own* shoes now.' Becky giggled mischievously. 'Do you think that girl would recognise me if we met again?'

'No. As you said, you were a child then. You're a woman now.'

Later that night Becky lay cradling her sleeping husband in her arms. She heard Iris return to the house and stand arguing in the hall with a man who objected to paying in advance for what she had to offer. Later still Becky heard the nervous laugh of a young man and Irish Molly's practised reassurance.

Becky hugged Fergus more tightly. Had he not loved her enough, she, too, would have been bringing a stranger back to the house in Back Lane at about this time at night, wondering what demands he would make on her body, hoping he would not turn out to be one of those men who vented his anger on a prostitute in a bid to repay the world for all the wrongs it had done to him.

Becky vowed she would try hard to ensure that Fergus never regretted his decision to marry her.

Fergus was restless. The weather had something to do with the feeling. There was a thunderstorm building up, and the air was heavy and oppressive. From the attic window the edge of a thick black bank of cloud could just be seen edging its way towards the city.

Irritably, Fergus put down his brush. 'I'm going for a walk down by the docks to get some air. You coming with me?'

Becky shook her head. Fergus had recently taught her to

make picture-frames, and she was working on one now. 'I want to finish this. You go; it will do you good to get out for a while. You haven't left the house for three days.'

It was true. After weeks spent making new sketches and painting Becky, Fergus had returned to his earlier works. He had completed about twenty paintings and hoped to have produced enough for a new exhibition by the late autumn.

Most of the doors in the house stood open, and Fergus saw a scantily clad Irish Molly lying on her bed. As he passed the room she called to ask if Becky was in the attic. Fergus grunted that she was.

'Good. I'll take up a cup of tea when I find the energy to make one. I suppose she hasn't got the kettle on?'

Outside in the narrow confined streets it was almost as hot as inside the house. Not until he arrived at the dockside did Fergus feel the first stirring of cool air about him.

Fergus wandered aimlessly about the docks for almost an hour but when the bank of cloud he had seen from the attic obscured the early-evening sun he decided it was time to go home.

Picking his way through the maze of narrow streets that linked Lewin's Mead with the docks, thinking of his work, Fergus was suddenly startled to hear anguished screams coming from a nearby house. Moments later someone began hammering against the street-door from the inside.

A woman squatting on the step of a neighbouring house rose to her feet and called through the door: 'What's the matter? What is it, me darling?'

'Jeannie's on fire! She's all alight!' There was terror in the child's voice.

'The Lord help us! Haven't I said many times that a woman shouldn't go off and leave her children on their own? Five girls in the house and the oldest no more than seven. We'll all be burned out, so we will. . . .'

Fergus tried the latch, but the door was locked. The screams were now continuous, and someone on the other side of the door began sobbing.

'Stand back from the door. I'm going to break it down.' Fergus shouted a warning to the children inside the house, but the deed was more difficult than the intention. He was not a heavily built man, and the door resisted all his attempts to shoulder it open.

By now a crowd had begun to gather, and a man pushed to the front, signalling for Fergus to stand aside. The man wore heavy leather boots, and at his second kick the door crashed open, allowing smoke and three tiny choking figures to spill from the house.

As the heavy accumulation of smoke billowed away flames could be seen along a passageway towards the rear of the house.

'Fetch water – and call out the fire-engine.'

As the man who had kicked open the door shouted his orders Fergus entered the house. The neighbour had said there were five children in the house, but only *three* had come out through the front door.

He found the missing two children close to the door of the blazing kitchen, guided to the spot by the screams of one of the two small girls.

The eldest of the family, she had been trying to drag her badly burned sister to safety when the opening of the front door had caused the flames in the room to reach out and engulf them both.

It took only a moment for Fergus to reach the children, but the older girl's clothing was already well alight. Fergus beat at her with his bare hands, spurred on by the child's agonised screams.

The girl was wearing a surprising amount of clothing, and Fergus beat at it for what seemed many minutes before the flames from the kitchen caught up with them and he was forced to drag her farther along the passageway, away from the heart of the fire. He tried to bring the other child with her, but as he took a grip on her charred dress it disintegrated in his hand. Then the flames reached out towards him, and he was forced to return to the first girl. He dragged her to the door only to be trampled for his pains as firefighters rushed into the house carrying buckets of water.

Then other hands reached out and pulled Fergus and the child out to the street. Someone poured a bucket of water over the blazing clothes of the seven-year-old girl, and her screams died away as she fell into a merciful faint. Not until someone repeated the process with Fergus did he realise that his clothing was also burning.

The cold water brought pain, too – excruciating pain – and Fergus looked down at his blackened hands in disbelief. He, too, was badly burned.

Men and women were clapping Fergus on the back, congratulating him on his bravery, but one man, more observant than the others, suggested he should find a doctor quickly.

'No, I must get home.' Fergus's voice was barely recognisable, his throat dry and painful as a result of the smoke he had encountered inside the burning house.

'Come, I'll help you. . . .' Warding off the hands that reached out to pat Fergus, the man who had suggested Fergus should see a doctor led him out of the crowd. He walked with Fergus to Back Lane, and on the way explained the cause of the fire, as told by one of the three girls who had escaped from the house.

It seemed they had been playing, dressing up in their mother's clothes, when one of the girls tripped on the long dress she wore and fell into the fire. It was the reason why the children had been wearing so much clothing. But when the helpful stranger began airing his views on parents who went out to work all day leaving their children locked in the house Fergus stopped listening. His hands were agonisingly painful by now, and he tucked them beneath his armpits in a bid to protect them in some instinctive way.

When they reached Ida Stokes's house the stranger insisted upon escorting Fergus upstairs to the attic room, and Fergus found events confusing thereafter. As the stranger explained Fergus's injuries, praising him as a hero, Becky was examining the burns to his hands and Irish Molly was insisting that he should receive treatment immediately.

When the stranger left, Irish Molly took a closer look at Fergus's hands and shook her head gravely. 'You'll not be doing any painting for a while, me darling – and you need to be treated right away.'

'Where can we find a doctor?' In common with most of the

residents of Lewin's Mead, Becky regarded the medical profession with awe.

'I'm not thinking of a doctor.' Irish Molly downed the last of a cup of lukewarm tea. 'Don't do a thing to his hands while I dress. I'll take you to someone who knows how to treat burns better than any doctor.'

When Irish Molly had gone to her room, Becky said: 'Do you think we ought to listen to her?'

'I don't care *who* I see, if they can ease this pain. But Molly's right about one thing. I won't be painting for a while. God knows where we'll get money for living.'

'My poor Fergus. I'm a burden to you already. If you didn't have me, you could go to that lady of yours – or to Fanny Tennant. They'd welcome you as a hero and look after you until your hands were well again. You can't do that now because you've got me. But don't worry. I'll get work. I *can*, you know.'

'Time enough to talk about that later. I wish Irish Molly would hurry. These hands are killing me.'

Irish Molly realised more than either of them the seriousness of Fergus's burns. She dressed quickly, forgoing the heavy make-up without which she would not usually leave the house.

The storm that had threatened Bristol had by-passed the city, and Irish Molly led Fergus and Becky northwards away from the Lewin's Mead slum, taking the road that led to Gloucester. For more than two miles they walked, until the houses of the city were behind them and fields stretched ahead for as far as could be seen.

Dazed with the pain of his hands, Fergus was beginning to think he could walk no farther when Irish Molly turned off the road to where a small stream bisected a thinly wooded copse. In the copse was a number of colourful bow-roofed caravans, and the smell of wood-smoke hung heavily on the air. Irish Molly had brought them to a gypsy encampment.

As they entered the camp a man with an outdoor tan stepped into their path.

'Are you wanting something?' His accent was not unlike that of Irish Molly.

'We've come to see Mother Whelan.'

'Who's come to see her?'

'Tell her it's Irish Molly – with a friend who's burned his hands badly.'

'Wait here. I'll find out if she's seeing anyone today.'

When the man walked away towards the caravans, Becky looked questioningly at Irish Molly, as Fergus tried in vain to hold his hands in a position that would ease the pain he felt.

'She'll see him,' declared Irish Molly confidently. 'They're *Irish* gypsies. Mother Whelan knows more about healing than anyone in Ireland – or anywhere else, for that matter.'

'I hope she hurries.' Becky put a comforting arm about Fergus. 'We should have taken him to a doctor right away, in Bristol.'

It was at least ten minutes before the man who had challenged them returned, walking as though there was no sense of urgency.

'Mother Whelan will see you, but try not to tire her too much. There isn't much strength in her these days, and she's a long journey ahead.'

Mother Whelan sat on the steps of a caravan surrounded by men and women of all ages. It was impossible to hazard a guess at her own age, but her wizened face had the appearance of uncared-for leather.

She looked briefly at Becky, nodded to Irish Molly, then turned her full attention on Fergus.

'Show me.'

Her voice was as old as her face, but it carried authority. Fergus held out his hands, and she looked closely at them, supporting his arms with a finger beneath each wrist.

'You're the artist who pulled two children from a fire.'

Fergus was startled. The news had reached the gypsy camp quickly.

'They're both dead. They should have been brought to me. I might have saved one of them, at least.'

'So he burned his hands for nothing.' Becky spoke bitterly.

'If it hadn't been for your man, the other three would have died – and half of Bristol been burned down. Not that anyone would have been any worse for *that*.'

Turning to a woman standing in the doorway of the caravan behind her, Mother Whelan spoke at some length in rapid Romany. When the one-sided conversation ended the younger woman disappeared from view inside the caravan.

'Will Fergus's hands be all right?' Becky blurted out the question when Mother Whelan returned her attention to the visitors.

'If you're asking whether he'll paint again, the answer is yes. You'll carry scars for life, young man, and some days you'll not be able to hold a brush before mid-morning; but if you'd gone to a doctor you'd never have held a brush at all.'

'That's a great relief.' Fergus grimaced with pain. 'I'll make you and your camp the subject of my first painting when my hands are well again.'

'We'll be gone long before then.'

The old woman looked up into Fergus's face. 'I'm being taken back to Ireland to die.'

Mother Whelan cackled her amusement at Fergus's shocked expression. 'I've had a good life, a useful life, and I've outlived all my friends and most of my children. I'm ready to go now.'

Gripping Fergus's forearms, she said: 'Your life is in front of you. Make the most of it. I've heard of your paintings of the cottiers — the homeless Irish you helped down by the river. . . .' She cackled again at Fergus's surprise. 'There's little goes on within fifty miles of Bristol that I *don't* know about. One of my grand-daughters visited your exhibition. She told me it was like watching the cottiers dying before her very eyes. That's *your* path in life, my young artist. To show folks what's going on about them.'

The woman came from the caravan carrying an earthenware jar and a length of clean linen. Mother Whelan took the jar and signalled for the woman to hand the linen to Becky and Irish Molly.

'Tear it into strips about three fingers wide. Use all of it. Now, give me one of your hands, young man. I need to make a good job of this if you're to change the world with your talents.'

Dipping inside the jar, the old gypsy woman scooped out a

handful of a thick green greasy substance.

'This will hurt for a while, but then your hands will feel as cool as a clear Kerry stream. Grit your teeth now.'

Mother Whelan's bony fingers held Fergus's wrist in a strong grip, and she began smearing the thick ointment on his burned and tormented hands. Fergus made no sound as she worked, but occasionally his teeth drew blood from his lip as he bit back the agony he felt.

The old woman worked swiftly and expertly with surprising gentleness, at the same time crooning sympathetically in the strange Romany dialect.

It took a while for the salve to take effect, but by the time the gypsy woman had finished binding his hands, making them immovable, they were more comfortable.

'Didn't I tell you so?' Mother Whelan replied when Fergus told her the pain was easing. 'Have faith in everything else I say and you won't be disappointed.'

To Becky, she said: 'Take the salve with you – but only change the dressings once a week, making quite certain you keep the air out when you bind them.'

'How long will it be before I can stop? When Fergus's hands are well again?'

'Continue with the salve for at least three months. Then use dry dressings for another three. After that he'll need to learn all over again how to hold a paintbrush.'

'Six months!' Fergus was aghast. He had barely enough money to last for two weeks, and without hands he could not paint. Trying to push such thoughts to the back of his mind for the moment, he asked: 'How much do I owe you?'

'More than you can ever repay, my young artist, so we'll not talk of money. Instead, I'll accept your promise to paint the poor and the helpless for as long as there's a need.'

Fergus had looked closely at his hands while the old gypsy woman was working on them with her ointment. If ever they were fully healed, it would be nothing short of a miracle – and no price was too much for a miracle.

'You have my promise.'

'Then, two little girls never died in vain.'

The old gypsy woman struggled to her feet, and one of the men standing nearby came forward to take her arm. Nodding to Fergus, she said: 'Goodbye, Artist. We'll not meet again. Not in this life.'

CHAPTER FORTY

THE NEXT FEW WEEKS were hard ones for Fergus. He watched his money dwindle, knowing there was no way he could earn more. He never explained the full seriousness of their situation to Becky, although he suggested she should cut down on their household expenses as much as possible.

Eventually the day came when Fergus gave Becky the last of his money to go out and buy food. When she had gone he sat in the attic staring at the completed paintings leaning against the wall at the far end of the attic studio.

He looked at the paintings for a long while before choosing two. One was a portrait of Becky, the other a Lewin's Mead street scene. After struggling awkwardly for some time he managed to secure them beneath his arm.

Downstairs he met Irish Molly on the landing. Seeing the paintings, she raised an eyebrow. 'Are things so bad you're on the way to Uncle's now?'

'Uncle's?' Fergus was puzzled.

'The shop with three gold balls hanging over the door. The pawnbroker.'

'Oh. . . . No. I'm taking the paintings off to sell them.'

'I thought you were saving them all for a new exhibition. Does Becky know you've begun selling them?'

'Is there any reason why she should?'

Irish Molly was shrewd enough to guess the reason why Fergus was selling his paintings. She said: 'It's nothing to do with me. I hope you get a good price for them.'

Fergus's intention was to ask Fanny Tennant to show the

paintings to Solomon Stern, in the hope that he might agree to purchase them. Fergus had not seen Fanny since telling her of his wedding to Becky, but he did not doubt she would do such a favour for him.

He enquired for Fanny at the ragged school, only to be informed she was in London. It was a blow to Fergus's plans, but he needed money desperately. The only other person capable of helping him was Lady Hammond. Clutching the paintings tightly beneath his arm, Fergus set off for Clifton.

Lady Hammond's butler was sympathetic about Fergus's burned hands, as were the household staff who gathered about Fergus within minutes of his arrival – but Lady Hammond was not there. She was on a tour of the Continent, and her household did not expect her to return to England for at least another two months.

Making his way homewards, Fergus felt thoroughly despondent. Unable to paint and with no income, the immediate future looked bleak indeed. He wondered how he could break the news to Becky. She seemed to be managing surprisingly well, but she was not a naturally frugal person.

Fergus took a long way home, walking down the steep and fashionable Park Street, heading towards the docks and the heart of the city. He was almost within sight of the docks when he saw three golden balls hanging above the door of one of the shops he was passing and he was reminded of Irish Molly's question. This was a pawnbroker's shop. 'Uncle's.'

Fergus stopped and gazed in at the window for a very long time. There were many varied items offered for sale, each one mute evidence of human failure, carrying price-tags that put a pathetic value on heartbreak and poverty. Wedding rings were here aplenty, with brooches and bangles. Few were of any great value, but most had meant far more than money to their late owners. There were clothes here, too, sharing the window with vases, cutlery, watches – and two small paintings.

When Fergus entered the pawnshop a small, grey-haired, grey-faced man stood up from behind the counter. He had been hunched over a small table cluttered with the workings of a watch, and a magnifying glass held in place by a frown hid one eye. The magnifying glass was removed as Fergus approached, and the liberated eye blinked furiously for a moment or two.

As Fergus clumsily deposited his paintings on the counter, the pawnbroker clucked in sympathy.

'What have you done to your poor hands?'

Fergus thought the man sounded more like a solicitous priest than a pawnbroker, but this impression was swiftly dispelled.

'I trust it's nothing contagious? I'll have only clean goods in my shop.'

'I burned my hands,' Fergus retorted. 'That's why I've brought a couple of paintings to you. I can't work for a while.'

'An artist! Ah, I'm a great admirer of talent. What it is to be gifted. Let me see what you have here.'

The little pawnbroker lifted a painting of Becky. Holding it out at arm's length for a while, he put it down again without comment and picked up the Lewin's Mead street scene.

'This is better – but who would want to buy a painting of such a place? Park Street, perhaps. Clifton, yes. But Lewin's Mead?' The pawnbroker shook his head. 'It's a *business* I'm running here.'

Clumsily, Fergus pulled the paintings towards him, and the pawnbroker looked startled.

'What are you doing? I thought you were here to raise money on your paintings?'

'But you've decided you don't want them.'

'Did I say that? No, my boy, but I want you to have no foolish expectations of them. To me they're worth very little, but I see you as a man of honour. You'll raise the money and get them back some day. In the meantime I'll keep them safe for you, and charge little more than storage. . . .'

'How much will you advance on them?' Fergus broke in on the pawnbroker's insincere patter.

'Three shillings apiece.'

Fergus could not hide his disbelief, and the pawnbroker rapidly made a new offer. 'All right, *six* shillings for the street scene and four for the other one.'

'Both paintings are worth far more. You must know this.'

'So? I am taking them as security for a loan, not buying them. Where will I find a buyer if you don't come back? You want to *sell* them, then take your pictures somewhere else.'

'Ten shillings on each painting. If for any reason I fail to redeem them, you'll get your money back a hundredfold.' Even this was far less than Fergus had hoped for, but his financial state was desperate.

'Your name ... it's Rembrandt, perhaps? Or would it be Constable? Seven and sixpence each.'

Once again Fergus began to struggle to pick up his paintings, and the little pawnbroker sighed. 'All right. All right. *Ten* shillings each – but only because of your poor hands. I can see you have need of the money.'

Unlooping a cord from about his neck, the pawnbroker used a key hanging from it to open a drawer built into his side of the counter. Taking out four five-shilling pieces, he put them in a neat line on the counter. Scribbling a few details on two numbered green tickets, he slid money and receipts across the wooden counter to Fergus.

'There you are, my son. I charge interest of a penny in the shilling per week. Any goods not redeemed within six months are sold.'

Fergus nodded. 'Will you put the money in my coat pocket? I can't pick it up.'

As the pawnbroker reached across the counter to carry out the request, Fergus asked: 'Will you take more paintings if I have a further need of money?'

'Am I to become an art dealer now? All right, but I can't guarantee ten shillings each for all of them.'

When Fergus left the shop the pawnbroker took the paintings and pasted a ticket to the back of each. Then he looked at both paintings again, fingers stroking his chin thoughtfully. Opening a panel door giving access to the shop window, he hung the pictures at the back of the window, then went outside to study them anew.

There were some boys playing in the gutter a little way along the road, racing twig-boats in a stream of evil-smelling water that flowed from a knacker's yard behind the row of shops. Calling one of the boys to him, the pawnbroker produced a penny from a soft leather purse tucked inside his waistband.

Handing the coin to the boy, he said: 'Go across to Phillips the art dealers on the other side of the docks. Ask for Mr Phillips himself. Tell him Isaiah Rodden has something that might be of interest to him. There's no hurry, but tell him it will be worth his while to pay me a visit some time.'

Fergus believed Becky was ignorant of their financial state, but he underestimated her intelligence. Aware there was no money coming in, she saw how carefully he doled out the money he gave her when she needed to go shopping. She also knew the number of paintings in the attic studio was dwindling.

Becky tried to speak to Fergus about the situation but, although he was loving and patient with her in every other respect, he refused to discuss money matters.

Irish Molly had told Becky of seeing Fergus leave the house with paintings tucked beneath his arm, but the Irishwoman did not want to involve herself with their domestic difficulties. She had problems of her own looming on the horizon. The landlord of the White Hart was selling his inn, and the prospective buyer had declared that prostitutes would not be welcome on the premises. His pronouncement caused great concern among Irish Molly's colleagues. The White Hart had been a recognised 'hunting ground' for as long as anyone could remember.

On a day when two more paintings went from the attic, Becky told Fergus she had obtained work to tide them over the next few weeks. She would be washing-up at a good-class inn, the Great Western, not far from the Hatchet. Becky did not add that the work was conditional on her standing in as a serving-maid in the tap-room when the inn was busy. As it was, Fergus declared angrily that it was not necessary for *his* wife to wash dishes in a tavern in order for them to live.

Becky tried to make it clear she did not intend to become the family provider. She was merely helping out until Fergus's hands were healed sufficiently for him to resume painting –

and there were already some signs of improvement. There was movement in two of his fingers, although he needed to be careful with them because the thin skin cracked easily, causing him much pain.

Grudgingly, Fergus came to accept that Becky would be going out to work each day. He could hardly do anything else. His stock of paintings was desperately low, and the day was not far off when he would have none to pledge to the pawnbroker. Besides, he had sensed that Becky was becoming restless with the restrictions his injured hands imposed upon their activities.

The evenings without Becky seemed very long, and by the time she returned to the house in the early hours of the morning she was on the verge of exhaustion. At first, Fergus would wait up for her, but most nights Becky wanted only to go to bed and sleep, so he reverted to his usual bed-time.

Some nights Fergus did not even hear Becky return to the attic room, and more than once he woke in the morning to find her sleeping on the floor, as she had done when she was a homeless street-urchin.

It was not an ideal way of life for a young married couple, but Fergus promised Becky that when his hands were healed he would work hard to make up for all the sacrifices she was making.

During the evenings, after Becky had gone to work, Fergus tried to exercise his hands, willing the burned fingers to move beneath the dressings, feeling a grim exhilaration when pain in the scarred and wasted muscles of his fingers signalled success.

Fergus was assured of a welcome at the Hatchet inn, but he found it difficult to accept drinks from Charlie Waller and Giraldus Reilly, knowing he was unable to return their generosity. Yet Fergus found it difficult to settle in the attic room alone, unable to paint or even to make himself a cup of tea.

He began to spend more and more time wandering the Lewin's Mead streets, observing scenes and incidents that would one day become background scenes for his paintings.

During one of these evening excursions, Fergus heard a

sound as though an illegal prize-fight or dog-fight was being staged. Following the noise, he found himself in a courtyard shared by more than twenty houses, their jumbled outbuildings backing on the rubbish-strewn dirt space.

There must have been at least seventy people crowding the entrance to the courtyard, and at first Fergus had difficulty obtaining a clear view of what was happening. Not until he pushed his way to the front of the crowd could Fergus see it was no form of fight that had drawn such an audience. The attraction was a poor lunatic. Chained to an iron ring set in a great stone, he was being cruelly tormented by two jeering youths who prodded at him with long sticks.

Bearded and ragged, the lunatic sat hunched outside a small shelter constructed from sticks and sacking. When the goading became too insistent the poor lunatic rounded on his tormentors. Bellowing with rage, he scattered them with a rush that ended when the chain snapped taut and he was brought to a halt tearing futilely at the iron collar secured about his neck. His rage and distress brought howls of glee from the onlookers. The more he fought against his iron collar, the greater was their delight.

Ending his bout of tortured frenzy for a moment, the lunatic's eyes suddenly found Fergus. His body became rigid as he stared at him, and then the madman's hands dropped away from his throat and with a shrill scream he sprang at Fergus.

The chain snapped taut and the lunatic dropped to the ground so heavily that for a moment the crowd fell silent, fearing he might have broken his neck. Then, screaming with pain as well as with fury now, his hands went up to the cruel band of iron, and the watchers roared their approval.

Fergus remained silent. He had recognised the lunatic. It was Joe Skewes.

Fergus had more reason than anyone there to hate the violent coal-heaver, but it shocked him to see Joe Skewes in such a state, chained to an iron ring like some captive animal and tormented by those who were sane enough to know better.

'He doesn't seem to like you,' cackled a toothless old hag

gleefully. 'Let him see you again. Go on, we'll have some fun with him.'

Ignoring the woman, Fergus backed away, pausing only to ask a young boy how long Joe Skewes had been chained in the courtyard.

'A fortnight,' came the reply. 'You should have been here last night. We gave him a bath with buckets of water, and he screamed at us the whole time. I don't think water had ever touched his skin before.'

Fergus limped away from the lunatic-baiting crowd as fast as he could go, not slackening his pace until the sound of laughter was far behind him. The scene had brought back disturbing memories of his younger days, and of vigils beside his mother's bed in an asylum ward.

He was still thinking of the scene he had just witnessed when a voice from behind him called: 'Don't you speak to old friends now you're a hero?'

Fergus came to a halt, and Constable Ivor Primrose caught up with him.

'I'm sorry, Ivor, I didn't see you.'

'You weren't seeing anything, Fergus. Are your hands troubling you?'

Fergus lifted up his bandaged hands, then let them drop to his side again. 'No more than usual. I was thinking about Joe Skewes. . . .' He told Ivor Primrose of the scene he had just left.

The constable listened in silence, occasionally nodding his head gravely. When Fergus ended his account of the chained coal-heaver, Ivor Primrose said seriously: 'So Joe Skewes has finally come to the end of the road. It had to come. He's been insane for years.'

'Then, surely he should be locked away somewhere, not chained in a courtyard and treated as a sideshow? God knows, I'd have seen the man *hanged* after what he did to Becky, but this is degrading to everyone concerned.'

'We'd need an army of constables to fetch him out of the rookery – and Joe Skewes wouldn't exactly welcome us with open arms. Forget him, Fergus. Someone must have accepted some responsibility for him or he'd have starved to death by now. Talking of such things, it can't be too easy for you right now.'

Fergus shrugged. 'I manage.'

'Have you seen Fanny Tennant lately? When last I saw her she told me she had some good news for you.'

'Fanny's back in Bristol?'

'Yes, and asking after you. She'd have come to the rookery looking for you, but I warned her against it. She was safe enough a few months ago, when she was teaching regularly at the ragged school, but she's been away for too long. There are villains in the rookery now who've never heard of her. She'd be set upon before she walked fifty yards.'

'Then, I'd better go and find her. Thanks for telling me.'

CHAPTER FORTY-ONE

FERGUS FOUND FANNY at the ragged school where she had just dismissed the evening classes. She was standing in the hallway talking to a tall thin man. When she saw Fergus a guarded expression came to her face. It became concern when she saw his heavily bandaged hands.

'Fergus, how are you?' She lifted one of his hands gingerly and looked with some distress at the bandaging. 'Ivor told me you had burned your hands rescuing some children from a fire. I had no idea you were *still* bandaged. Have you been treated by a doctor?'

'Some old gypsy woman dressed the burns for me. . . .' Fergus intercepted the looks exchanged by Fanny and the tall stranger. 'They're a lot better now. I need to keep a dry bandage on them for another couple of months, that's all.'

Again there was an exchange of glances between Fanny and her companion. Then Fanny said: 'Fergus, this is Dr Pike. He's just been examining some of our pupils. Will you allow him to look at your hands?'

'There's nothing to look at. They're healing, just as Mother Whelan said they would.'

The doctor showed immediate interest. 'Did you say Mother Whelan? I've heard a great deal about her. She has earned a remarkable reputation as a healer. Will you at least allow me to change your bandages? I have some new ones here in my bag.'

Fergus's bandages were still the strips of rags provided by the gypsies. Because Becky was working, they had been overlooked and not changed for more than a week. He nodded agreement.

'Good. Perhaps you have a room somewhere near, Miss Tennant. . . ?'

In the room that served as Fanny's office, the doctor removed the rags from Fergus's left hand, and Fanny gasped in horror when she saw the angry red scarring that disfigured the whole skin area. Fergus's right hand was no better, and when the doctor held them up to examine them together Fanny was brought to the verge of tears.

Not so Dr Pike. Turning them over and peering closer at the skin, he murmured: 'Incredible. Quite incredible.'

'I'm beginning to get some movement back in them. In three months they'll be as good as new.' In an attempt to prove the truth of his words, Fergus managed to twitch one thumb and a couple of fingers.

'I didn't realise you'd been so seriously burned, Fergus. I'm so sorry. . . .' Fanny choked on her words.

'Mr Vincent, you are a very lucky man. Had burns such as these been treated by any doctor I know, you would have lost the use of your hands for ever. As it is . . . Well, they may never be *quite* as good as before, but you'll certainly have enough use in them to lead a normal life.'

The doctor released Fergus's hands reluctantly. Opening his bag, he took out a bandage. 'If I possessed this gypsy woman's skill, I could earn a worldwide reputation.'

Fanny was unimpressed by the doctor's enthusiasm. The sight of Fergus's scarred hands had distressed her, and the shock was slow to wear off.

In a bid to take her mind off his injuries, Fergus said: 'I met Ivor Primrose this evening. He said you've been asking after me.'

'What. . . ? Oh, yes!' His ruse succeeded, and Fanny dragged her gaze away from his hands. 'I have good news for you. Solomon Stern's friend has used some of your sketches in his magazines.'

Fergus looked at Fanny blankly, and she said incredulously: 'Don't you remember? You left some sketches with him.'

Fergus had forgotten. They had not been among his best works, and so much had happened since then.

'It's a good job *someone* has your interests at heart. I have a hundred pounds here for you — and I am assured there will be more when the other sketches are used.'

Fanny nodded towards the now bandaged hands. 'I don't doubt that you have need of the money. Things can't have been easy for you, especially as you are now a married man.'

Fergus scarcely heard her. Fanny had said she had a hundred pounds for him. It was a fortune — and there would be more! His money problems were over. There was no longer any need for Becky to go to work.

'It's *wonderful* news. Yes, things have been hard — but they'll be better now. Bless you, Fanny. You're an angel. Thank you, too, Doctor. The hands feel much more comfortable now.'

He had to find Becky and tell her of the unexpected change in their fortunes. Halfway to the door he stopped and turned back to Fanny. 'I have some paintings Solomon Stern might like to buy. If I bring them to your house, will you give them to him when he next comes to Bristol?'

Fanny nodded. She knew why Fergus was hurrying away.

On his way to the Great Western inn, Fergus passed the pawnbroker's where so many of his paintings were pledged. Half a dozen of them were now exhibited in the window, one being the portrait of Becky. Eager to savour the first fruits of his newly acquired wealth, Fergus entered the pawnbroker's shop to tell the proprietor of his good fortune.

Isaiah Rodden was talking to two young men, but he broke off the conversation and made an expansive gesture of surprise when he saw Fergus.

'Gentlemen! Gentlemen! *This* is who you must speak to if you wish to buy one of the paintings. I am only a poor pawnbroker. I loan money to my fellow-men to help them weather bad times and I take good care of their property until such time as they claim it from me again. If I also sometimes act as an honest broker and both parties are generous — well, that is an unexpected reward. Speak to him, gentlemen. He is a reasonable man. An artist – with a need for money, as you can see by the bandages on his poor hands.'

This last remark was accompanied by a wink, which Fergus was not meant to see, and one of the men said: 'My friend would like to purchase one of your paintings. The portrait of the young dollymop.'

Fergus flushed angrily. The only painting that might be construed as being of a 'dollymop' was the portrait of Becky. It was evident that both young men had been drinking, but this did not render the remark any less offensive.

'The painting's not for sale. I'll be redeeming it in the next few days.'

'Come now, you're an artist. I'll give you a fair price. Five pounds? Six?'

'I'm sorry, it's not for sale.'

'Very well, then . . . ten. Ten guineas. Julian is so smitten with this dollymop I've promised to buy him the damned painting, even if it costs more than *she* did.'

It was a situation Fergus had hoped would never occur. That he would one day come face to face with one of the men who had known Becky when she was taking men home from the White Hart.

'I'll not sell the portrait for a hundred guineas. Good day to you both.'

Fergus turned to the pawnbroker, but one of the young men took Fergus's arm and pulled him back roughly to face him.

'You're being offensive, sir. *Damned* offensive. I've offered you my money and you've refused to take it – and for no good reason that I can see.'

'Oh, come away, Henry. Who wants a picture anyway? We'll go and see the real thing, and I'll let you buy me a drink there. I might even let *you* take her off tonight. Then you'll know what it is I find so special about the girl.'

With a last defiant glare at Fergus, the young man released his arm and walked from the pawnbroker's shop with the stiff-legged gait of a tom-cat who had just asserted his authority over another.

Fergus stared after the two men as they walked off arm-in-arm, their laughter gradually fading in the distance.

'They offered a fair price. Most artists would be delighted to sell a painting for ten guineas.'

'I'm not *most* artists.' Fergus's reply was abrupt. He was puzzling over the conversation between the two young men. They had gone off as though they were expecting to meet up with Becky. But that was not possible.

'I'll tell you what I'll do. I'll take *all* the paintings you've left with me, for seven pounds apiece! It's a fair offer. It should set you up until you're able to paint again.'

Fergus shook his head. Perhaps one of the two young men had seen Becky in the Great Western inn. She might have been sent out to collect his plates or glasses, and he had made up a tale about her when talking to his friend. . . .

'Very well. Seven *guineas*.'

'No.'

Fergus decided he would go to the Great Western inn right away and tell Becky there was no longer any need for her to work. A hundred pounds would tide them over until his hands had healed. Once he began painting again everything would be all right. He would be able to provide Becky with all the things he knew she yearned for, and she would never have to work again. . . .

'All right, I'll give you what the young gent offered you. *Ten guineas a picture* – and I'll take the lot. No argument about whether or not they're worth the money. . . .'

'My paintings are not for sale. I came here to tell you I'd be redeeming them some time during the next day or two.'

Disinclined to discuss the matter any longer, Fergus turned away abruptly and left the pawnbroker's shop. He was anxious to find Becky and take her home.

When Fergus had gone, Isaiah Rodden cursed himself for a fool. He should have offered Fergus his top price of *fifteen* guineas for each painting. His art-dealer friend had seen the first of Fergus's sketches in a London magazine and offered twenty-five. Fergus was arousing considerable interest as an artist. Prices for his paintings could be expected to rise rapidly.

Fergus entered the Great Western inn and stood inside the

door of the tap-room, looking about the crowded interior. There was no sign of either of the men who had been in the pawnbroker's shop. Neither could he see Becky, but he had not expected to find her here.

Suddenly Fergus saw Giraldus Reilly sitting at a table. The big Irishman saw him at the same time and came across the room to greet him with a big grin of welcome.

'It's good to see you, Fergus. I'm enjoying my night off by seeing what the other inns are like. But let me buy you a drink. What is it – a large brandy? I know the cellarman here. He has a nice barrel tucked away specially for his friends. There's no Customs stamp on the barrel, but that adds to the flavour of the brandy.'

'I'm not stopping for a drink, Giraldus. I came to speak to Becky. To tell her she doesn't need to work here any more.'

A puzzled expression came to Giraldus Reilly's face. 'Becky doesn't work here any more. The cellarman told me that Becky was here for only three evenings before she left. I can't say I blame her; it was work for a drudge with no mind for thinking of what she *might* be doing instead. Not for the likes of a young girl married only a few months. But are you telling me you didn't know she'd left?'

Fergus shook his head, thoroughly bewildered. 'She leaves home at the same time each day. I thought she was coming here. Perhaps Irish Molly knows where I can find her.'

'No, she'd have told me – but wait a minute. The cellarman here mentioned seeing her the other day. I'll go and ask him where it was. . . .' The big Irishman hesitated. 'That's if you're really sure you *want* to know where she might be.'

Fergus would dearly have loved to say no, but he could not.

Giraldus Reilly was away for what seemed a long time. When he returned he would not meet Fergus's eyes.

'Where is she?'

'Ah, well. . . . You see, the cellarman wasn't certain at all, you understand. He only thought it *might* have been Becky he saw. I don't suppose it was really her. . . .'

'Where was it he *thought* he saw Becky?'

'Going into the Cabot Arms – but he only saw her from the

back. He was probably mistaken; he admits that himself.'

Now Fergus understood Giraldus Reilly's embarrassment. The Cabot Arms was notorious as an inn frequented by young men of the town. They went there to pick up 'dolly-mops' – servant girls, millinery assistants, nannies and other young girls who sought to supplement the meagre wages they earned in their unexciting occupations.

As Fergus turned to leave the tap-room, Giraldus Reilly said: 'If you're going to the Cabot Arms, you'd best hold your fire for a minute. I'll come with you as soon as I've downed this pint. . . .'

'There's no need.' Fergus held out his bandaged hands. 'I won't be starting any wars.'

Fergus was not clear what his intentions were as he limped through the gas-lit streets, heading for the Cabot Arms. He felt hurt and confused. He had believed Becky's brief foray into the world occupied by Irish Molly and Iris would never be repeated. He *still* believed it. There had to be some other explanation for the circumstantial case building up against her.

As Fergus neared the Cabot Arms he slowed his pace and tried to think things out logically. What would he do if he found Becky inside the tavern? What would he say if she refused to return home with him?

The Cabot Arms was busy. The noise and laughter from inside reached him when he was still fifty yards away. He stopped for a moment in the shadow cast by an overhanging upper storey – then he saw one of the two young men he had last encountered in the pawnbroker's shop. On his arm was a young girl. She was on the side farthest from Fergus, but he did not doubt it was Becky. She was the reason they had come here. . . .

Fergus ran awkwardly along the pavement after the couple. He did not know what he would do when he caught up with them. He did not know what he *could* do, but Fergus would not stand back and watch Becky go off with another man.

'Becky . . .!' Fergus caught up with the couple as they

turned off the thoroughfare into a narrow gas-lit alleyway. Brushing the man aside, Fergus grabbed the girl's arm and turned her towards him – and discovered it was not Becky.

'What do you want? I don't know *you*.'

As the girl drew back from him in alarm her companion recovered from his surprise and pushed Fergus roughly to one side.

'Well I'm damned! It's the artist who won't sell his paintings. The man's mad!'

Shaking a fist at Fergus, he shouted: 'Clear off, or I'll forget you can't defend yourself and give you what you deserve. . . .'

CHAPTER FORTY-TWO

FERGUS KNEW IT WAS BECKY when he heard her footsteps coming up the first flight of stairs from the hallway. She was very late. The last time he had looked at his watch in the dim glow from the fire it had showed ten minutes after two. Now, hunched in a corner of the attic room, he dreaded the confrontation that was only moments away.

There was no way Becky could disguise her progress up the final decrepit flight of stairs to the attic. An inconsequential thought crossed Fergus's mind: Ida Stokes would soon need to do something about the stairs and would no doubt put up the rent to pay for the repairs. . . .

Becky opened the door to the attic studio slowly and quietly, as though trying not to wake him.

She crossed the room towards the fire, but there was insufficient light for him to make out her face.

'You're late.'

His voice, thick and momentarily unfamiliar, startled her.

'Fergus! Where are you? Are you all right?' She sounded alarmed.

'Where have *you* been?'

'I've been working. You know that.' The brief hesitation before she replied was barely discernible, but it was there. 'Have you been drinking?'

'Yes, but I'm not drunk. I've been out looking for you.'

'Oh! Then, you'll know I'm not working at the Great Western inn any more.'

'Giraldus Reilly told me. I'd rather have heard it from you.'

'Would you have approved had I told you I was now working at the Cabot Arms?'

'You know I wouldn't.' Fergus struggled to his feet in the darkness. He had sat hunched up for so long he had cramp in his good leg. 'Why have you gone back to *that* sort of life, Becky? For God's sake, *why*?'

'*What* sort of life? I'm a serving-girl at the Cabot Arms.' The hesitation was there again, but more noticeable this time. 'It's a sight easier than washing-up, and it pays more. I knew you wouldn't like me working *there*. That's the only reason why I've said nothing about it.'

'I met two men today who wanted to buy a portrait of you because one of them had slept with you. When I wouldn't sell they went off to find you – so the second man could share his friend's experience.'

For a long time there was silence in the room. Then the coal on the fire shifted. In the brief light of a short-lived flame, Fergus could see anguish on Becky's face.

'I know the man you're talking about. I only went with him once, Fergus. He came to see me tonight, with his friend. I wouldn't have anything to do with either of them.'

Fergus knew she was lying. 'How many men have there been, Becky? Why have you done this to us?'

'For you, Fergus. For *us*. I've watched you getting more and more worried about money. I know you've been pawning your paintings and they're all you have in the world. It's all so ... *unfair*. I know how much your paintings mean to you. Perhaps you should go back to Clifton, to Lady Hammond – or Fanny Tennant. If you'd done that instead of marrying me, you wouldn't have burned your hands and you wouldn't *need* to sell your paintings.'

'You mean more to me than all my paintings. I married you so you'd never need to do anything like this again – and now you're saying you did it for *me*?'

'It means nothing to me, Fergus. Honest.'

'It means something to me – and to the man I met today, too, otherwise he'd not have wanted to buy your portrait.'

'We needed money. . . .'

'Making money is my responsibility, not yours. That was

why I came to find you. My sketches have been published in a London magazine. I can redeem my paintings and we'll be left with enough to live on until my hands heal.'

Becky was silent for a very long time. Then she said: 'I won't ever do anything like this again, Fergus. Honest, I won't.'

'You promised me the same thing when we were married. What excuse will you find for breaking your promise *next* time?'

'Do you think I *want* other men, Fergus? Is that what you really believe?'

'I don't know *what* to believe any more. I thought that once we were man and wife there would be no one else for either of us.'

Fergus was rubbing salt deep in his own wounds, but he had been nursing the hurt to himself for too many hours. It had to come out.

'Am I asking too much? Perhaps I am. You've grown up accepting prostitution as a way of life. Irish Molly, Iris, Maude Garrett. No doubt it's an easy way to earn money. I don't know.'

'That's right, Fergus. *You don't know.* You paint pictures of life in Lewin's Mead. Life in a slum. But scratch the paint off one of your pictures and what's underneath? I'll tell you. *Canvas.* You're a painter, Fergus, a *fine* painter, but it doesn't mean you understand all there is to know about life. Not my life, or anyone else's in Lewin's Mead. Yes, I've grown up with women like Irish Molly and Iris about me. I've watched them and believed that one day I'd need to do the same. When you came along I thought a miracle had happened. I didn't ask *you* to marry *me*. That was your idea. I'd have cooked for you, worked for you – done *anything* just to be with you, to be *your* woman. If it hadn't been for Rose Cottle, there would never have been any other man. . . . But it's no good talking about what *might* have been.'

'That was in the past, Becky. Before we were married. To do it again now . . .' Fergus choked on his words.

'I told you why I did it. To get money for us. Now I'm asking you to forgive me. Fergus . . . please.'

Fergus made no reply. He had tried to think ahead, to what life would be like when this nightmare was over. But he was afraid. If he closed his eyes when he and Becky were making love, would he see the faces of the young men who had been in the pawnshop? And when Becky went out in the evening would he always be wondering what she was doing?

'Please, Fergus. I beg you.'

'I don't know if I can.'

He wanted to say he would *try* to forgive, *try* to understand. The words would not come – and then it was too late. Becky had gone.

Fergus hardly noticed the dawn arrive, or the grumpy squabbling sound of Ida Stokes's house waking to face another cheerless day. Even when a heavy storm broke over the city it failed to shake Fergus out of his numbed apathy.

There had been other tragedies in Fergus's life. He had survived the loss of his mother, and the injury that had left him a cripple, but this time it seemed fate had dealt him a whole series of shattering blows. First the destruction of his paintings in the London explosion, next the burns to his hands – and now Becky's return to prostitution. For the first time in his life Fergus felt too weary to fight back. He accepted defeat.

It was after noon when Irish Molly and Giraldus Reilly climbed the stairs to the attic studio and found Fergus still huddled in the corner where he had remained since Becky left him.

He might have been dozing, or perhaps his exhausted brain was too tired to function. Whatever the reason, he never heard them arrive and did not turn bleary red-rimmed eyes on them until Giraldus Reilly touched him, concerned at Fergus's stillness.

'What do you think you're doing, sitting there all night and half the day, too?' Irish Molly fussed about Fergus as the big Irishman lifted him to his feet and helped him to the bed.

Fergus made no move to help himself. He felt drained of all energy.

'Becky *was* at the Cabot Arms.' Fergus spoke to Giraldus

Reilly. 'She was one of the dollymops. . . .'

'Was she there because she *enjoyed* what she was doing?'
Irish Molly spoke scornfully. 'Or did she have other reasons
. . . like thinking she was helping a damned fool of a husband
who got his hands burned minding someone else's business?
Oh, yes, I meant to tell you before. One of the three surviving
children you rescued died a couple of days ago. Knocked a
pot of scalding water over herself while her mother was out
at work. *That's* what you damned near lost your hands for.
There are only two sorts of people in Lewin's Mead – fools
and survivors. No heroes. If you live here, you learn to mind
your own business and look after your own. It's something
you can't put down on canvas – but it's what Becky's been
doing. She's looked after *you*, in the only way she knew how.
You ought to be damned grateful to the girl.'

'I can forgive what she did before. Not now. Not having
other men. . . .'

'You're a fool, Fergus Vincent, like all men. So damned
conceited that you believe five minutes in bed with a man
makes him unforgettable. A woman *will* give heart, soul and
mind to a man, but only if she really loves him – and Becky
loves you, I'm sure of it.'

Giraldus Reilly was listening to Irish Molly with great
interest, but she sent him to make some tea in her room. The
fire had gone out in the attic grate.

When her fellow-countryman had gone, Irish Molly said to
Fergus: 'There wouldn't have been any other men for Becky if
she hadn't seen the world falling about your ears. She *had* to
help, but what could she do? All she had to offer was her
body, so she sold it – for *you*. If you think that came easy to
her, then you know nothing about women.'

When Giraldus Reilly returned to the attic Irish Molly
helped Fergus to drink a mug of tea, then she ordered
Giraldus to light a fire in the grate. Meanwhile she began to
clear up grey ash, scattered about the floor by fierce storm
winds blowing down the chimney.

More than once as she worked Irish Molly cast a glance in
Fergus's direction, but when she spoke it was to Giraldus
Reilly.

'Were you very fond of your wife, Giraldus?'

'I was. I couldn't have wished for a finer wife. She was a darling woman.'

Giraldus Reilly's words recalled a memory for Fergus of the big angry Irishman standing off the might of the Bristol police force in defence of his wife and family.

'If she were here now and told you she'd done what Becky's done – and for the same reasons – what would you do?'

Giraldus Reilly was not a fast-thinking man. Squatting on his haunches by the grate, he gave the question his undivided attention. Suddenly his eyes filled with tears. 'Ask any man that question of his wife and he'll tell you straightway that he'd kill her. A year ago I might have said the same myself, but if only I had her and the children back again I'd forgive her *anything*, so help me, I would.'

Irish Molly crossed the room and gave Giraldus Reilly an affectionate hug. 'I believe you, Giraldus. You're a fine man.'

To Fergus, Irish Molly said: 'It'll be too late to have regrets when Becky's gone. You think about what Giraldus said.'

Fergus's mind began to work in a rational manner for the first time in almost twenty-four hours. He thought of Becky, of her past life and of the girl she had become. Then he made an honest appraisal of himself. A crippled, helpless, near-penniless artist. The wonder was that Becky thought enough of him to want to do *anything* for him. Things could never again be quite the same between them, but his life would be empty without Becky.

When Fergus put his feet to the floor both Irish Molly and Giraldus Reilly swung around to look at him.

'And what do you think you're doing?' Irish Molly was the first to speak.

'I'm going to find Becky.'

'Why?'

'To ask her to come back. She's still my wife.'

'You just stay right where you are. Giraldus, go and tell Becky her husband wants to see her. I'll be down as soon as I've swept up and thrown the sweepings out of the window.'

'You know where Becky is?'

'Her sniffling kept me awake for half the night. I'll be pleased to be rid of the girl.'

At the first sound of low voices on the stairs, Irish Molly whispered: 'Remember now, be kind to her. She needs you.' Then the Irish prostitute was gone. Fergus suspected she would pause on the stairs to repeat a similar message to Becky.

Fergus was shocked when Becky walked into the attic room. Her eyelids were heavy and swollen, and her face blotched and streaked as though she had tried to wipe away her tears with a grubby hand.

They both looked at each other uncertainly for a few moments, then Fergus held out his hands.

'Come here, Becky. Come back to me.'

CHAPTER FORTY-THREE

THE NEXT MORNING Fergus removed the bandages from his hands and began exercising his scarred fingers in earnest. At first he despaired of ever bringing life back to them, but by the end of the day he could grip a paintbrush in his fingers for a couple of seconds. The next day he tried again, and the next. He persisted even though each movement brought pain, and the new skin tended to split if he worked too hard.

His painful doggedness was rewarded a week later when he stood at his easel and made his first tentative brush-stroke. He had returned to the world of painting.

It was harder than he had anticipated, and at first he found it frustratingly difficult to control the movement of the brush, but he persevered and three weeks later he walked into the Hatchet inn armed with pad and pencils to spend the evening sketching the patrons.

It was an evening for celebrations. Giraldus Reilly and Charlie Waller kept Fergus liberally supplied with drinks, and at one stage of the proceedings he was called to a back room where a uniformed Ivor Primrose had come in off the streets to raise a glass to his recovery.

At the end of the evening Giraldus Reilly helped Fergus home to Back Lane and up the stairs to the attic. As Becky put him to bed she thought she must be the only wife in Lewin's Mead who was happy to have a drunken husband come home to her.

Fergus worked at his paintings during the days that followed, sketching at the Hatchet inn most nights. He worked as though determined to make up for the time he had lost. He still needed to stop work frequently in order to rest his fingers, as the muscles were not as well developed as before, but his hands had healed astonishingly well.

Fergus had built up an impressive array of paintings by the time Fanny paid a surprise visit to the Back Lane studio when he and Becky were there together. Fergus had not resumed his sketching classes at the ragged school and he had not seen Fanny since receiving the hundred pounds from her in payment for his published sketches.

Fergus told Fanny she was foolhardy to walk through Lewin's Mead on her own, but Fanny brushed his fears aside, saying: 'I was walking through Lewin's Mead before you came here, Fergus Vincent. I doubt if it's any worse now than it was then. Anyway, you should be grateful to me. I've brought you this.'

She pulled something from inside a sleeve and handed it to him. As he took the tightly rolled bundle it sprang open. It was a roll of banknotes.

'You'll find fifty pounds there. Solomon Stern's friend has used more of your sketches. Solomon says he will take any you have left, especially those of Irish vagrants. They are in the news at the moment. He wants you to go to London, so he can discuss them with you.'

As she was talking, Fanny's glance was roving around the attic studio. There was much here that was new: a larger bed, two comfortable chairs, a good table, and curtains at the windows. It was clean, too. Becky had learned a great deal during her stay at the Red Lodge.

Suddenly Fanny saw the paintings leaning against each other in the studio alcove.

'You're painting again!' Fanny's glance dropped to Fergus's hands, and in spite of her resolve she winced involuntarily.

'I've been painting for a couple of weeks.'

'May I look at your work?'

Without waiting for a reply, Fanny dropped to her knees in the alcove and began examining the paintings. She looked at every one, making small sounds of delight and occasionally lifting a painting to examine it in more detail.

Her inspection completed, Fanny remained kneeling on the floor for some while before standing up and turning to Fergus and Becky. Reaching out, she took Fergus's hands in her own. Turning them over, she looked at the extensive scarring and shook her head in disbelief.

'It's nothing short of a miracle. With hands like these the career of most artists would be at an end. Yet you've not only overcome this disaster but *you're actually producing better paintings than before*! You're a genius, Fergus Vincent. I'm proud to know you.'

Fanny's words left Fergus with a warm glow. She would never know how close to despair he had come. No one ever would. It was behind him now.

'Will you go to London, Fergus? Solomon Stern will make all the arrangements. He and his friend would like you there as soon as possible – next week, if you are able to make it.'

'All right.' Fergus made up his mind quickly. He had come so far along the road to recovery, this would be another step forward. 'I'll travel to London on Monday, and take some sketches with me.'

'Good. I'll let him know. I'll tell Lady Hammond of your incredible progress, too. She hasn't been too well lately; this will help to cheer her. You ought to pay her a visit, Fergus. She often talks of you, and always with great affection. Now I must go and write to Solomon Stern immediately.'

'I'll walk as far as the ragged school with you.'

'No, you won't. You'll remain here and continue your painting. Becky can walk with me.'

If Becky was surprised that Fanny should want her company, she said nothing. Throwing a cloak about her shoulders, she followed Fanny down the stairs.

Fergus was busily painting when Becky returned. Hardly looking up, he asked: 'Did you see Fanny safely back to her school?'

'Yes.' Becky waited for Fergus to finish the detail he was

working on and look at her, but he was too engrossed in his work to look away from it.

'It's good news about my sketches. They're proving a life-saver for us. Not that I fancy travelling all the way to London again. . . .'

'Fergus! Fanny's asked me to teach at the ragged school.'

Fergus's astonishment was all that Becky had wished for, and she looked across the room at him smugly.

'That's wonderful,' said Fergus when he found his voice. 'What will you be teaching?'

'Nothing. I told her I didn't want to teach at no ragged school, even if I would be an . . . *inspiration* to the children there.' Becky had made tremendous progress with her vocabulary, but she still had problems with unfamiliar long words.

'Why not? You'd enjoy it.'

'I'm not going there to be bossed about by *her*.'

'That's a pity. Fanny isn't really bossy, and she's right. You'd not only inspire them to work harder, but you'd understand their problems, too. Think about it, Becky.'

At that moment they both heard the sound of someone climbing the stairs to the attic, and Irish Molly entered the room.

'Hello. I hope I'm not interrupting anything between the two of you.'

'No,' said Becky. 'Fergus has work to do because he's going to London again – and I've been asked to teach at the ragged school.'

'Well! You'll be charging folk to talk to you soon. But have you heard the news of Joe Skewes?'

Becky fell silent, but Fergus said: 'The last I saw of him he was chained up in a courtyard and as mad as a weaver.'

'That's where he was until last night, living on scraps that folk threw him when they remembered. But he must have been working away at the ring his chain was fixed to. Last night he pulled it clear and ran off, dragging the chain behind him, and with half the kids and dogs in Lewin's Mead after him.'

'Is he still free?' Becky looked suddenly scared.

'Freer than he's ever been. He got as far as the dock before his chain caught in something or other and he fell back under a loaded dray-cart. It's fast becoming a joke in Lewin's Mead that drink finally killed Joe Skewes.'

'Good!' Becky was fiercely exultant. 'I've wished him dead times enough.'

'Of course you have, and he's no loss to anyone. But I've some more news for you. I'm leaving Lewin's Mead. Going off the game for good.'

'What will you do? Don't tell me you've finally agreed to marry Giraldus?'

'Marry him? No, but we're both going to Ireland together, to the cottage Tomas Casey left to me. When we get there . . . Well, we'll see how things work out. That's partly why I've come to see you, Fergus. I'd like you to write a letter to Tomas Casey's solicitors for me. To tell them I'm coming to claim my property. I *can* read and write a bit, but not well enough to write to a solicitor. Will you do it for me?'

'Gladly, and I hope everything works out for you and Giraldus, even though Becky and I will be sorry to lose two such good friends. When do you expect you'll be leaving?'

'Not for a month or two. There's the business of the cottage to be sorted out first, and Giraldus and I need to see how we'll get along together. Giraldus is moving in here with me. I've been to the White Hart for the last time.'

Irish Molly chuckled happily. 'When I told Ida Stokes she said she hopes Iris doesn't go respectable again, too, or the neighbours around here will refuse to speak to her.'

CHAPTER FORTY-FOUR

ARRANGEMENTS FOR FERGUS to go to London were completed with great speed, but Fergus was unhappy to be travelling alone to the capital.

Becky had at first agreed to come to London with him, but the night before they were due to travel she changed her mind, pleading a mild stomach upset. Fergus believed Becky found the thought of going so far from Bristol frightening. He tried to change her mind, reminding her how much she had enjoyed the paddle-steamer voyage, but Becky was adamant. She would not go to London.

A few weeks before, Fergus might have successfully persuaded Becky to come with him, but the rift brought about by her activities at the Cabot Arms had not fully healed and they were not as close as they had been before. However, Fergus finally wrung a reluctant promise from Becky that she would, after all, help at the ragged school and he left Lewin's Mead happy in the knowledge that Fanny would keep a watchful eye on Becky.

Fergus did not expect to be in London for many days. Nevertheless, he left half of all the money he possessed with Becky. It amounted to twenty-five pounds, so she should not run short of cash.

Fergus was startled to discover he was already something of a celebrity in London. Within hours of his arrival at the offices of the magazine publishing his sketches he was besieged by representatives of London newspapers. Eventually he succeeded in escaping from them and returned to the inn near Regent's Park where he was staying — only to find more of them waiting for him there.

Solomon Stern was already negotiating for the hire of a Bond Street gallery to house Fergus's next exhibition, and Fergus was brought into the negotiations. When he realised he was expected to make suggestions on the décor of the gallery, Fergus wrote to inform Becky that his return to Bristol would be delayed. He was not too concerned. No doubt Becky was being kept busy at the ragged school — and he was finding his new status both flattering and exciting.

Gradually the ranks of waiting reporters dogging Fergus thinned, but now the social reformers moved in on him and Fergus was persuaded to give talks about his experiences in Lewin's Mead. He faced his audiences not in church halls now, but in huge theatres — and he spoke to capacity crowds. His popularity resulted in a second letter to Becky, and the few days he had expected to be away from her soon stretched to twenty.

Fergus realised he had become caught up in a gigantic movement for social reform. He had not *begun* the movement; it had been there all the time. Fergus merely provided its supporters with a tangible *raison d'être*, a standard to which they could flock. Reformers who had never been near a city slum came to his meetings. Waving magazines containing his sketches, they clamoured for something to be done about the city slums.

It mattered not that many of the sketches they waved in the air depicted homeless *Irish* vagrants, victims of an entirely different set of circumstances. The reformers saw what they wanted to see — and would fight harder for the cause because of it. Before long there was not an adult man or woman in London who was not familiar with Fergus Vincent's sketches.

Solomon Stern spoke to Fergus about his popularity and what the future held for him one evening when the two men were having dinner at a restaurant near the gallery, after yet another busy day.

'It's all going very satisfactorily.' The art dealer sat back in his chair and beamed about him. 'Your success so far bodes well for your exhibition, but I am thinking farther ahead now. How many Lewin's Mead sketches do you have?'

'About two hundred. Three hundred if you include the sailors and characters I've met at the Hatchet inn. I can make plenty of sketches, of course; I simply have to walk outside the door of the house in Back Lane.'

'No, you have enough.' It was a surprising reply, but Solomon Stern explained. 'People will eventually become bored if you continue to paint nothing else but slums and slum-dwellers. It's time you moved on to other subjects.'

'But I *want* to paint slums, and those who are forced to live there. That's what I've always intended doing.'

'And you've achieved your objective admirably – but by painting too much of it you'll defeat your own ends. You can best keep interest alive by including other subjects in your exhibitions. Landscapes and scenes of other parts of your city. Portraits, too; the public will always come to look at a good portrait, and I already have an important commission that should satisfy your crusading spirit, yet at the same time take your career a giant step forward.'

'What is this commission?' Fergus had not been convinced by Solomon Stern's argument.

'To paint Lord Carterton, the leader of the campaign seeking to abolish slums like Lewin's Mead. He is also the chief Opposition home affairs spokesman in the House of Lords.'

Fergus grudgingly conceded that if it were *really* necessary to paint a portrait there could hardly be a better subject – but he was unprepared for Solomon Stern's next words.

The art dealer wanted Fergus to begin painting Lord Carterton immediately, first in London then completing the portrait in Oxfordshire. Lord Carterton was preparing to make an extended visit to India and needed to return to his country home to complete his preparations.

Fergus agreed to the arrangements suggested by Solomon Stern, but there were more surprises in store for him. As Fergus painted the reforming peer, he learned that Lord Carterton not only supported Solomon Stern's view on limiting the number of sketches Fergus made of Lewin's Mead but went much further. He suggested that Fergus should move away from the Bristol slum!

'Part of our campaign strategy is to point out how eager these people are to leave such an unhealthy environment,' Lord Carterton explained. 'It has already been pointed out to us by the Government that you live there from *choice*.'

'If I didn't live in Lewin's Mead, there would be no sketches or paintings,' retorted Fergus. 'I went there to record the slums as they really are. It couldn't be done properly unless I actually *lived* there.'

'Quite!' agreed the peer. 'And you have succeeded in everything you set out to do. We have been provided with damning evidence of the state of the poorer areas of our cities. Your sketches have done more to move government and people than fifteen years of campaigning. I don't want to run the risk of losing ground now. Think about it.'

Fergus did think about Lord Carterton's words, both in London and later, when he was staying at the reforming peer's Oxfordshire home, but he had reached no firm decision by the time the portrait was completed.

It was a good portrait, and Lord Carterton was so pleased that he paid Fergus on the spot for his work.

It was a handsome fee, and Fergus rode the coach to Bristol the next day, making plans to buy Becky a present to celebrate his sudden wealth.

CHAPTER FORTY-FIVE

THE JOURNEY from Oxfordshire to Bristol was made on indifferent roads, but the coach maintained good time and rolled into the city shortly before dusk. When they neared St James Square the coach-driver pulled up his horses and allowed Fergus to alight not far from the ragged school.

Evening classes were in progress at the school, and as Fergus passed he could hear singing coming from inside. Acting upon a sudden impulse, Fergus went inside. It was just possible that Becky would be here, taking a class.

Fergus came out of the ragged school a few minutes later frowning deeply. Becky was *not* at the school. What was more, a somewhat diffident tutor had informed Fergus that she had not taught there during his absence from the city.

It seemed that Becky's courage must have failed her without his support and was something Fergus should have anticipated. Suddenly his frown cleared, and Fergus smiled ruefully. He wondered what excuse Becky would give him for the failure to keep her promise.

When Fergus reached Lewin's Mead, a few lamps and candles were already alight inside the houses that hemmed in the narrow alleyways. Everything seemed dirtier than Fergus remembered, and he wrinkled his nose in disgust at the foul stench rising from the River Frome.

The streets of the slum were curiously deserted, yet Fergus could hear a hubbub of sound that grew steadily louder as he neared Back Lane.

Puzzled by the noise, he walked faster. Soon he could hear

shouts of anger and derision. When he came within sight of Back Lane he saw a huge crowd gathered here. They were being held back from the lane by a double line of grim-faced constables.

The policemen were the targets for the crowd's abuse – and an occasional missile. Beyond them, in Back Lane itself, more constables were gathered about Ida Stokes's house.

Thoroughly alarmed, Fergus pushed his way through the close-packed crowd towards the police line, ignoring the angry protests of those he roughly shouldered from his path.

Eventually Fergus reached the double line of policemen, but here his progress was halted. The constables were unable to hear him above the general din when he cried that he *lived* in Back Lane. In desperation he tried to force a way through them, but he was driven back into the angry crowd.

When Fergus saw the tall figure of Ivor Primrose he shouted at the top of his voice. The constable was talking to a white-faced police inspector but he turned and looked towards the crowd. Unfortunately, Fergus's slight figure was lost behind the ranks of tall high-hatted policemen. Then Fergus began jumping up and waving his arms, his antics soundly cursed by those about him as he landed heavily on their toes. But the tactics worked. Leaving the inspector staring after him, Ivor Primrose hurried to where Fergus was wildly waving his arms.

The police lines broke for a moment, and Fergus was hauled through the gap to Back Lane.

'What's happening?' Fergus put the question as soon as he could draw breath.

'It's Alfie Skewes. News of the death of his father was given to him on the prison hulk at Sheerness. Three nights later he killed one of his gaolers and escaped. He was seen today by the docks, but he half-killed a constable who tried to arrest him. Now he's holed up in Ida Stokes's house.'

Fergus felt as though a ton weight was pushing him into the ground. 'Is Becky in there? I'm just returning from London. . . .'

'We don't know who's inside. The door has been locked. We're debating whether or not to break it down and go in.

Alfie Skewes is a desperate and violent man. There's also a possibility that he's armed.'

'You must do *something*. If Becky *is* in there . . . Let *me* go in and talk to him.'

Ivor Primrose shook his head. 'We can't allow that. Alfie Skewes isn't a man to reason with. In his own way he's every bit as mad as his father was.'

'But you can't leave him in the house with Becky. He blames her for everything that's happened to the Skewes family. Let me go in.'

'No.' Ivor Primrose gripped Fergus's arm as he turned towards the house. 'Come and talk to the inspector. . . .'

There was a disturbance at the edge of the crowd and the sound of voices raised in argument. Moments later, scattering constables before him, Giraldus Reilly came towards them, his success in breaking the police cordon cheered by the Lewin's Mead crowd.

A number of constables charged after Giraldus Reilly, but Ivor Primrose waved them back, and he and Fergus hurried to intercept the big Irishman.

'What's going on here?' Giraldus Reilly echoed Fergus's question.

'Alfie Skewes has escaped from a prison hulk. He's in the house. Do you know if Becky's in there?'

'She was a couple of hours ago. I left her with Molly. We've only been waiting to see you before we set off for Ireland. . . .'

The Irishman broke off as an outburst of near-hysterical screaming came from the house. Moments later the door was flung open and Ida Stokes stumbled out through the doorway.

Picking herself up, she waddled towards the policemen who ran to her aid. Fergus and Giraldus Reilly went with them.

As they reached her, Ida Stokes sank to her knees, wheezing noisily.

'What's going on inside?' Ivor Primrose had to put the question three times before Ida Stokes heard and looked up at him with terror in her eyes.

Still wheezing alarmingly, she said: 'He's *killed* her! Stabbed her to death . . . on the first-floor landing. Oh my God! He'd have killed me, too. He's mad . . . as mad as his father.'

Fergus never waited to hear what else Ida Stokes had to say. Running awkwardly, he had almost reached the door of the house before Giraldus Reilly overtook him, with Ivor Primrose no more than a pace behind.

'Go back. We'll deal with him.'

Fergus ignored the constable's order, but the two men beat him to the doorway and were halfway up the first flight of stairs before Fergus reached the hallway.

On the first-floor landing he could just make out the other two men crouching over a still form on the floor.

Ivor Primrose stood up as Fergus reached him. 'She's dead.'

'Becky . . .!'

Fergus's cry died in his throat as Giraldus Reilly turned a tortured face towards him. 'It's not Becky. It's Molly. Why should he want to kill her? Why should *anyone* want to kill her?'

Giraldus Reilly put the unanswerable questions to Fergus as blue-uniformed constables pounded up the stairs from the ground floor, a couple of them carrying lanterns. As they crowded together on the first-floor landing Ivor Primrose sent them to search the rooms off the landing, but it soon became apparent that Alfie Skewes was not on this floor.

Giraldus Reilly stood up from Irish Molly's crumpled body. Without a word, he climbed the stairs to the second floor, with Fergus and a number of policemen close behind him.

Once more the constables spread out to search the rooms, but they found only Mary O'Ryan and some of her young family, for once in their lives too scared to cry.

Giraldus Reilly did not stop here. Checking Fergus who tried to push past him, Giraldus made his way up the final flight of creaking stairs.

There was a sudden noise from the attic room, and Fergus shouted: 'Becky. . . ?'

His words were drowned by the bellow of the Irishman. 'This is Giraldus Reilly, Skewes. I know you're there and I'm coming in for you. It'll not be the hulks this time, nor the rope, neither. I'm going to take that knife from you and slit your throat with it, just as you did to Molly....'

Giraldus Reilly choked on his words. Without pausing to check whether or not the attic door was locked, he put his foot to it and kicked it open.

Alfie Skewes was just disappearing through the attic window to the ledge outside – but he was not quick enough. Giraldus Reilly made it to the window in half a dozen long strides. Reaching out, he secured a grip on the leg of Alfie Skewes's loose canvas trousers.

Alfie Skewes tried to kick himself free, and when this did not succeed he struck back with the sharp carving-knife he carried in his left hand.

It proved to be the escaped prisoner's undoing. The knife-thrust was made at an awkward angle and caused him to overbalance. When he tried to right himself his foot slipped on the pigeon droppings that soiled the stone ledge. For a moment he balanced on the edge of the ledge, staring back at the Irishman, his arms gyrating wildly in an effort to right himself. Giraldus Reilly released his grip, and Alfie Skewes toppled over the edge to crash to the cobblestones of the lane, forty feet below. He landed with a sickening thud that brought a gasp from the crowd, which had fallen silent while the final act of the drama was being played out high above them.

Inside the attic room Fergus was far more concerned about the whereabouts of Becky than in following the final moments of Alfie Skewes.

He was still frantically searching when Ida Stokes was brought back to the house and informed Fergus that Becky had not been in the house when Alfie Skewes had burst in upon the landlady and Irish Molly.

Fergus sank into a chair, suddenly weak with an over-whelming relief, and listened to the landlady's story of her terrifying experience.

Alfie Skewes had entered the house while Irish Molly and Ida Stokes were in the landlady's front room. The two women were having a drink together to celebrate the forthcoming departure to Ireland of Irish Molly and Giraldus Reilly.

The two women were safe enough while Alfie Skewes was drinking the contents of their celebratory bottle of gin, even though it quickly became evident to both of them that he was not sane.

When the drink was gone, the escaped prisoner demanded to know the whereabouts of Becky and Fergus, both of whom he blamed equally for having him committed to a prison hulk, and for bringing about the death of his father.

Whatever retribution Alfie Skewes intended exacting on Becky and Fergus was interrupted by the unexpected arrival of the police outside the house. It took everyone by surprise. Policemen did not enter the Lewin's Mead rookery. It was part of an unwritten understanding between police and the criminal fraternity. The police kept out of Lewin's Mead. In return, the brawling, drunkenness and debauchery of the slum-dwellers was largely contained within its narrow squalid streets.

However, the police viewed the return of Alfie Skewes to Bristol with great alarm. When one of their informants followed the escaped prisoner to Back Lane and disclosed his whereabouts to Ivor Primrose, the police inspector in charge of the area had no hesitation. All available constables, and as many additional men as could be found at short notice, were ordered to enter the slum and arrest the fugitive.

During the initial confusion, Irish Molly and Ida Stokes fled upstairs, but Alfie Skewes came after them brandishing a kitchen-knife. Irish Molly told the landlady to hide while she stayed to reason with him. Irish Molly had known the violent coal-heaver for many years, and he had no quarrel with her.

Unfortunately, the mentally unbalanced man was beyond all reasoning. While they were talking he suddenly attacked Irish Molly without any warning in a sudden irrational outburst of violent temper, and Ida Stokes fled from the house.

While Ida Stokes was still telling her story, Fergus began to worry about Becky again. Leaving the crowded ground-floor room, he went back to the attic studio, hoping to find something that might tell him of Becky's present whereabouts.

In the room he lit the lamp and carried it to the table – and it was then he saw the package. Wrapped in brightly coloured paper, it was on a shelf where Fergus kept his pencils.

Untying the ribbon that bound the package, Fergus unwrapped the paper. Inside was a small leather box. When he opened the lid he found a watch. A *gold* watch.

Filled with trepidation, Fergus lifted the watch from the box and held it in his hand. He thought Becky must have been stealing again – but the watch-case was too highly polished. Too new. He flicked open the case. Inside, the inscription read: *To Fergus from Becky.*

It *was* new. Becky must have bought it for him – but it would have taken all the money he had left with her to buy food. How had she been living during the weeks he had been away?

Slowly, almost with reluctance, Fergus put the expensive watch back inside the box and replaced it on the shelf.

He left the house without a word to anyone and made his way to the Cabot Arms. He hoped his intuition would prove to be wrong. *Prayed* it might be wrong.

The Cabot Arms was busy, the interior heavy with smoke. It was a minute or two before Fergus saw Becky. She was on the far side of the crowded room, sitting at a table between the two young men he had met in Isaiah Rodden's pawn-broker's shop. One of the men had his arm draped about Becky's shoulders. She was laughing. . . .

Fergus was sitting at the table in the attic with the watch in front of him when he heard Ida Stokes wheezing up the stairs. She was the last person he wished to see right now, but he pulled out a chair and invited her to sit down.

'No, thank you, Mr Vincent. I won't be stopping.'

The landlady's unsmiling face and her use of the formal 'Mr Vincent' warned Fergus that this was not a social visit, but he was unprepared for her next words.

'I'm afraid I must ask you to leave my house. As soon as possible, if you don't mind.'

'We're all upset about Irish Molly's death, Ida, but no one

could have anticipated the actions of a madman. . . .'

'It's got nothing to do with Irish Molly, or with Alfie Skewes. We've had murders in Lewin's Mead before – madmen, too – but we've never before had the police come in and take over the place. Lewin's Mead folk don't like it, Mr Vincent. They don't like it at all. They say they won't sleep easy in their beds so long as you're here in case it happens again.'

'While *I'm* here? The police coming in had nothing to do with me. . . .' Fergus's voice faltered. He was too tired, too distracted to argue with anyone.

'That's as may be, but we never had nothing like it before you came.' Ida Stokes glared at him. 'There's another thing, too. It seems there's been a lot about you in the papers lately. Word's going about that you want to have our houses pulled down and put us out on the streets.'

'That's nonsense, Ida. All I've said is that people shouldn't *have* to live in slums like this. My sketches and paintings have been made to show how bad conditions are here.'

Ida Stokes was unimpressed. 'Too much has been said. Lewin's Mead is *our* home. It's where we want to be. I don't expect you to understand; you're not one of us.'

Fergus opened his mouth to counter Ida Stokes's latest statement, when the words that had once been spoken by his friend Henry Gordon came back to him with startling clarity.

'. . . In a slum an artist must observe the rules of the people who live there. *Their* code. Break it and he might as well pack up his things and leave. . . .'

Fergus felt suddenly very, very weary. Bodily and mentally drained of all energy.

'What of . . . Becky?'

Ida Stokes shrugged. 'No one's said anything against her that I've heard. She can go with you, or she can stay. She'll manage without you, the same way as she has while you've been away – and I won't have to put up with all that whispering and giggling on the stairs at all hours of the night. I might be getting old, but I've still got ears – and eyes. No, you don't need to worry about her. She's one of us. . . .'

*　　*　　*

Carrying a bag containing his belongings on his shoulder, and with a slim canvas satchel tucked beneath his arm, Fergus limped along a narrow rubbish-strewn alleyway that led from Lewin's Mead.

Turning to take a last look back, he did not see the urchin lying amidst the rubbish on the ground.

'Here! Mind where you're putting your bleedin' feet. . . .'

The Restless Sea

Man is born with ambition, it is the power source that spurs him on, subjugating adversity and opposition and raising a man above the circumstances to which he was born. Yet neither ambition, determination nor the application of man's labours can avail against the might of the restless sea, that while possessing none of these attributes can put an end to the vain dreams of all men.

Book One

Book One

1

'Kill him, Ned.'

'Take him now . . .'

'Your right, Ned lad. Use your bleedin' right . . . !'

Ignoring the shouts of encouragement hurled at his opponent, Nathan Jago kept his left fist extended well in front of him, not taking his eyes from his adversary's face for even a moment. A quick flick of his right wrist was sufficient to wipe away the perspiration that filtered through his thick, black eyebrows, threatening to blind him with its saltiness.

This was London Fields. Once the waste land beyond the walls of London Town, the fields were now at the heart of London's crowded 'East End' and home ground for Nathan's opponent, Ned Belcher, champion prize-fighter of all England. A Hoxton man, Belcher's home was hardly more than a gargle and a spit away.

Suddenly, Ned Belcher tucked his chin down tight

on his chest. Crouching low, he moved in to the attack, swinging heavy fists that were stained dark brown from hours of soaking in a hardening mixture of vinegar and walnut juice.

One of the champion's punches caught Nathan a glancing blow on the side of his face. Ducking low, Nathan slipped beneath the next punch and brought his own fist across in a short, jarring blow that caught Belcher just below the right ear. Belcher grunted with pain and dropped to one knee on the flattened grass. He kneeled there, shaking his head in the manner of a puzzled dog that had just snapped at a wasp, and the referee declared it to be the end of a round.

Nathan walked gratefully to his corner and slumped down on the stool quickly provided by his seconds. Across the ring, Belcher's seconds ran to help their man back to his own corner before the precious thirty-second interval was over.

Spitting a mixture of wine and water on the muddy turf just outside the ring, Nathan asked, 'How many rounds is that?'

'Twenty-nine.' A man of few words, Sammy Mizler had himself been no mean light-weight fighter, before a broken knuckle put an end to his career. 'The rest of the rounds are yours. Belcher's kissed the gin bottle too often to take a long fight.'

Nathan looked across the ring to where Ned Belcher sat sprawled back in his corner, legs stretched out before him, the loose flesh of his stomach spilling over the leather belt that held up his trousers.

Nathan thought that Sammy Mizler was probably right. Belcher was not the man he had been ten years before, when he fought Hen Pearce to a standstill and took the title from him. Something had gone wrong along the way. Nevertheless, although Nathan was not a small man, Belcher weighed at least three stone more – and he boasted a punch that could stun a bullock. He was an opponent not to be underestimated.

A murmur of concern rose from the vast crowd that stretched back as far as the dingy, grey, gardenless houses fringing the northern edge of London Fields. Looking up, Nathan saw long, sulphurous fingers of mist beginning to reach out into the crowd. The fog had been lurking among the close-packed houses of London's crowded suburbs all day, held at bay only by the weak rays of the autumn sun. Now it was evening, and as the last rays of sunlight left the stinking squalor that was Hoxton the fog emerged to take over England's ancient capital.

Nathan shivered. He knew he would have to chance the power of Ned Belcher's fists in order to bring the fight to a rapid close. As the fog moved closer to the ring, so would the crowd. When the fog became thicker, and the crowd was able to advance no farther for the press of those in front, they would become first restless, then angry, and finally violent. This was a London crowd. An 'East End' London crowd, ever ready to riot.

A disturbance of such a nature would bring the fight to a premature conclusion, the three-hundred-guinea purse being taken home by neither man. And Nathan had plans for the money.

'Time!'

From the side of the ring, the referee called on both men to advance to the centre and assume their stances to his satisfaction.

Ned Belcher's seconds heaved their charge to his feet, and he lurched forward to the centre of the ring, raising his fists when he was two paces away from his opponent.

Nathan's unexpected assault took Belcher by surprise. Until now the challenger had been content to box a mainly defensive fight, allowing the London champion to use up his strength. The two-fisted onslaught brought the crowd to their toes. Partisanship was momentarily forgotten as they revelled in the sight of a skilled and superbly fit prize-fighter moving in for the kill.

As Nathan's punches drove home, Ned Belcher retreated rapidly, his arms raised in ineffectual defence. At one stage his knees buckled beneath him and he almost went down, but Belcher was an experienced and tough fighter. Lungeing forward, he wrapped his arms about Nathan and held on grimly as Nathan pummelled him about the kidneys.

When Nathan attempted to throw Belcher from him, the heavier fighter whispered hoarsely: 'Go easy on me, son. You'll be an old fighter yourself one day.'

So unexpected was the older fighter's plea that Nathan stopped his punishing pummelling. Immediately, Belcher stepped a short pace backward – then brought his balding head forward sharply. The unorthodox blow struck Nathan on the forehead, and a carnival of coloured lights exploded inside his head.

It was only an instinctive sense of self-preservation that kept Nathan's guard up as he was battered backwards across the ring by Ned Belcher. Caught in his own corner, Nathan slipped on the turf, which had become saturated by liberal use of sponge and water-bottle. As he fell, Sammy Mizler protected his boxer from the continuing assault, calling upon the referee to intervene.

The referee had to pull Belcher away from Nathan, so desperate was the ageing champion to ensure that Nathan would not make the mark at the end of the half-minute rest brought about by the fall.

Nathan shook his head in protest as water poured over his head, and Sammy Mizler slapped his cheeks frantically in a bid to bring him back to his senses.

'What d'you think you're doing out there? One minute I'm cheering myself hoarse because you've got him going. A moment later you're standing doing nothing, with Belcher's arms about you. Did you think he was going to kiss you, maybe?'

Nathan grimaced. His head felt as though it had been resting against an exploding cannon. 'He appealed to my better nature. It won't happen again.'

'Better nature, you say? Is it an alms-giver you are now? Or are you fighting for the title of Champion of all England, and a three-hundred-guinea purse? Oi! But the ref's calling "time" now. You'd better make up your mind what it is you want.'

Nathan jumped to his feet and was waiting in the centre of the ring when Ned Belcher came to the mark. Hardly giving him time to raise his guard, Nathan launched an attack that drove the champion before him. It was too much for Belcher. He walked heavily, heels to the turf, the elasticity gone from his legs. Forced to a neutral corner, Ned Belcher lay back against the taut rope, and his hands dropped helplessly to his sides. Blood dribbling from a cut lip, he stood slack-jawed, staring blankly at Nathan.

For one brief moment, Nathan hesitated. Then he remembered Belcher's whispered appeal – and the head butt that had followed. He brought across a straight left that caught Belcher on the side of his jaw. The champion sagged at the knees; but, before he struck the ground, Nathan landed a hard right between Belcher's eyes, and every man in the hushed crowd heard the crack of knuckle upon bone.

Belcher's seconds darted forward to drag their man to his corner as Nathan made his way back to Sammy Mizler.

'You've got him, Nathan. You're the new champion, already.' The phlegmatic Jewish second was more excited than Nathan had ever seen him.

Declining to take the stool for the mandatory thirty-second break, Nathan stood nursing the aching knuckles of his right hand, looking to where Ned Belcher's seconds worked frenziedly on their champion. He, too, doubted whether Belcher would come to the mark for the next round. The punch that had put him down was one of the hardest Nathan had ever thrown.

At a nod from the timekeeper, the referee called upon both fighters to take up their stances in the centre of the ring. Confidently, Nathan made his way to the mark, helped on his way by a resounding slap of encouragement from Sammy Mizler.

Ned Belcher's corner was the scene of utter confusion. The seconds had their champion on his feet, but he seemed not to know what was happening and was shouting in near-hysteria. Nathan could not hear his words because they were drowned by the noise of the crowd, many of whom had bet large sums of money on the locally born champion.

To make matters worse, thick fog was now rolling across the fields. Unable to see what was happening, the spectators at the rear of the huge crowd were pressing forward, clamouring noisily to be told what was going on inside the thirty-foot-square ring.

Ned Belcher was dragged to the centre of the ring by his seconds just in time to beat the referee's deadline. As the seconds scuttled back to their corner, Nathan took his stance. Ned Belcher advanced for only two shuffling paces and then he dropped to his knees, his hands going up to cover his face.

Nathan hesitated, in a quandary. A fighter was not allowed to go down without a punch being thrown but, equally, a man on his knees was deemed to be 'down' and should not be struck.

The crowd entertained no such doubts. Angered at Ned Belcher's unprecedented behaviour, they called to Nathan to 'finish him off'. Their howls of rage mingled with the cries of those frustrated spectators prevented by fog from seeing what was happening inside the ring.

As the fog began swirling across the ring, the noise reached an ugly crescendo. It was now that Nathan saw tears begin to seep between Ned Belcher's fingers.

Convinced at last that this was no trick on the part of the champion, Nathan advanced cautiously towards him and laid a hand upon his head.

Ned Belcher reached up and grasped Nathan's hand in his own. In a hoarse, terror-filled voice, he whispered desperately: 'I can't see! I'm blind, boy. So help me, I'm blind!'

Nathan was still wary of the man kneeling before him. Ned Belcher was an ageing and weary champion, desperate to keep his title.

'It's the fog, Ned. A few more minutes and it will have closed in altogether . . .'

The battle-scarred fingers closed tightly on Nathan's hand. 'It's not fog, boy. I've lost my sight. I'm blind as a maggot. God help me . . .'

The referee was as uncertain as Nathan.

'Get up and fight, Ned. Get to your feet now, or I'll have no option but to give the title and purse to Jago.'

It was doubtful if Ned Belcher heard the words, so loud was the din from the disgruntled spectators. He turned his head this way and that, in total confusion.

Nathan was no longer in doubt. The last blow he had landed had robbed the champion of his sight.

'He says he's blind. I believe him.'

Clods of earth and stones began landing in the ring, hurled by the howling spectators. The situation was rendered more malignant by the foul-smelling fog that now reduced visibility to no more than a few yards. The referee waited no longer.

Raising Nathan's free arm, he declared him the winner of the contest, and the Champion of all England. Thrusting a bag containing the three-hundred-guinea purse at the new champion, the referee scurried away. Ducking beneath the rope, he was quickly swallowed up by the fog and the angry, gesticulating crowd.

Sammy Mizler appeared at Nathan's side, an arm crooked above his head to shield himself from the volley of missiles bombarding the ring from every direction.

'Let's go before half that crowd gets in the ring with us. They're out for blood – yours mainly. But I've no doubt the colour of mine will serve them as well.'

Fighting had already broken out among the crowd at the ringside, and now one of the ropes sagged inwards beneath the weight of struggling bodies.

Snatching his shirt from the worried Sammy Mizler, Nathan turned to where Ned Belcher was being helped to his feet by equally anxious seconds. Thrusting the purse into Belcher's groping hands, Nathan shouted: 'Here . . . It's the purse. Put it to good use. Buy an inn . . .'

The side of the ring collapsed. As the crowd spilled through, Ned Belcher was hustled off; and Nathan Jago, undisputed Champion of all England in the illegal sport of prize-fighting, followed after.

The date was 10 August 1810. At the age of twenty-seven, Nathan had achieved the ambition that had been his since he had left the Navy to become a prize-fighter five years before.

2

The day had not started well for Elinor Hearle, and it became progressively worse as it wore on. It began when her maid failed to awaken her and Elinor overslept. When the maid finally put in an appearance she had such a dreadful chill that Elinor sent her straight back to her bed.

Then, when Elinor reached the stables to take her stallion Napoleon for a morning gallop, the horse had gone. The animal had been taken out by the groom in the belief that Elinor was forgoing her usual morning ride.

The decision to exercise the stallion, although taken in the best interests of the horse, cost the groom his post at Polrudden Manor.

The nagging realisation that the groom had been dismissed unjustly did nothing to improve Elinor's humour as the day wore on. By noon a foul temper possessed her. The few servants in the big house did their best to keep out of her way, but it was not easy. Sir Lewis Hearle, Elinor's father, was returning from London today, and there was much to be done about the house.

Elinor's mother had died when she was a child, and Sir Lewis, Member of Parliament for the nearby port of Fowey, was away in London for most of the year, engaged in parliamentary affairs. He hoped one day to gain high office, and so recoup the dwindling family fortunes. Consequently, the task of running the household staff fell to Elinor.

Elinor was a very capable housekeeper, but the responsibilities thrust upon her so early in life combined with an unusually strong character to produce a wilfulness that had frightened away even the most ardent suitor. Elinor was twenty-five years old now and one of the most attractive girls in the district, but there was no hint of romance in her life. Women in the nearby village of Pentuan shook their heads in disapproval as she galloped through the village on her high-spirited stallion, sitting the horse like a man. They swore that Elinor, heiress to the decrepit manor house and scant fortunes of Polrudden, would end her days an impoverished and eccentric spinster.

If Elinor knew of their disapprobation, she did not allow the knowledge to alter her way of life – and there was not a villager who dared express such views to her face.

Sir Lewis Hearle had written to tell Elinor that he would be travelling from London on the Royal Mail coach, due to reach the Queen's Head inn in St Austell at three o'clock that afternoon. Elinor was to meet him there.

Usually, she would have travelled in a chaise driven by the groom but, smarting under her injustice, the groom had already left Polrudden. Elinor had gone to his house, intending to give the conscientious man another chance. She had been met by his red-eyed wife and three wailing children, and had learned that he had gone to seek the recruiting sergeant in Bodmin Town to take the King's shilling. He had told his wife that he preferred the bayonets of Bonaparte's army to the tongue of the mistress of Polrudden.

Because of this, Elinor was obliged to take the smaller gig and drive the horse herself.

It was a distance of five miles to St Austell, and Elinor set off rather later than she had intended. She drove briskly from the house, situated high on the hill above the busy little fishing village of Pentuan, urging the horse on through the narrow, high-banked lanes.

It was a hot day and, unlike her own riding-horse, the pony pulling the gig had not been exercised daily. Lazy days and lush summer grass had made it fat and out of condition. By the time they had covered less than half the distance to St Austell, the steep hill and Elinor's urging had brought the horse out in an unhealthy sweat.

There was a well-used watering-place nearby and, cursing the delay, Elinor turned aside to give the pony a brief rest and the opportunity to drink.

The watering-place was no more than a shallow pond, fed by a spring, and the ground about it muddy and uneven. Climbing down from the seat of the gig, Elinor led the animal to the water's edge. Suddenly, her foot slipped and she tugged hard at the bridle. Startled, the horse threw back its head and pranced nervously in the shafts of the gig. Elinor's feet went from beneath her, and she fell heavily in the pond, catching her dress on a piece of broken fencing as she went down.

Scrambling out as quickly as she could, Elinor grabbed the horse's trailing reins before the animal could bolt. Backing horse and gig away from the slippery bank of the pond, she secured the reins and then examined the state of her dress.

She was soaked through, and muddied `from shoulder to toe.

The ill-humour that had been simmering inside her since early morning flared up once again. She cursed the horse, the pond, and the groom she had dismissed that morning. Not until it was out of her system did Elinor pause to think of what to do next. She could not continue her journey to St Austell in her present state, and to return to Polrudden Manor to change her clothes was out of the question. She was late already.

About a quarter of a mile away was the cliff-edge farmhouse of Venn. Leading the horse and gig, Elinor made her way there.

A small farm of some fifty acres, Venn had a steep, difficult-to-work patchwork of fields. It belonged to Elinor's father, but was currently rented out to a young yeoman farmer named Tom Quicke. Elinor knew he had married no more than six months before and hoped she might borrow a dress from his young wife.

The first sight of the farmhouse immediately raised her hopes. For many years it had been occupied by a retired sea-captain who had merely played at being a farmer. Widowed for more than thirty years, the sea-captain had allowed the farm and himself to run down towards the end of his ninety-four years. Tom Quicke had changed all that. Gates had been repaired and rehung, and the small farmhouse was bright with new paintwork.

The door of the house stood open and, looping the reins of her horse over a fence-post, Elinor walked inside. She found herself in a low-beamed room with large blue-slate flagstones on the floor and only one small, open window to allow light inside. Full of cool shadow, the room was as clean as the outside of the farmhouse had promised.

Elinor could hear sounds coming from the back of the house and, ducking through a low doorway, entered the farmhouse dairy. A young woman with dark hair tied neatly behind her neck stood at a stone sink. She was busily scrubbing the dismantled workings of a butter-churning machine.

As Elinor entered, the girl looked up, startled at the sudden appearance of this dishevelled, uninvited visitor.

Elinor wasted no time on irrelevant greeting. 'I'm Elinor Hearle and I have had an accident at the watering-place. I need to borrow a dress – and be quick about it. I'm to meet my father in St Austell at three.'

Flustered, the girl stepped back from the sink with soap suds clinging to her bare arms. Dropping Elinor a hurried curtsy, she said: 'I'm Nell, ma'am. Wife of Tom Quicke.'

Elinor thought the girl looked hardly old enough to be a farmer's wife, but she had neither the time nor the inclination to exchange chitchat with the young wife of one of her father's tenants.

'Well, don't stand there gawping. Help me off with these clothes, then run upstairs and bring me some of your dresses to choose from.'

'I . . . I haven't got many, ma'am.' The girl moved towards the door as Elinor began impatiently unfastening those hooks she was able to reach on the back of her dress. 'You'd best come upstairs to the bedroom. Tom will be in from the fields in a minute or two . . .'

'Then Tom will just have to go out again. I'm not staying in this dress for one moment longer. Help me undo these wretched hooks.'

Hastily drying her hands on her apron, Nell Quicke moved behind Elinor and unfastened the metal hooks securing the dress. As she worked she made low sounds of distress.

'You've made a terrible mess of this, ma'am. 'Tis not only muddy, it's torn, too.'

Elinor wriggled the dress down over her hips and it dropped to the floor at her feet. Picking it up, she examined it quickly, then threw it down again petulantly.

'Damn!'

'I can wash and mend it for you, but it won't be ready for you to wear again today.'

'Then take me upstairs and show me what you have. You must have *something*.'

Without waiting for the girl's reply, Elinor strode from the dairy and headed for the staircase in the corner of the living-room. On the way she swept past Tom Quicke, who had just entered the house from the yard. His mouth dropped open at the sight of his titled landlord's daughter advancing upon him dressed only in a wet and bedraggled petticoat. But he hardly had time to snatch the hat from his head before Elinor passed by without a word, Nell in close pursuit.

There were two doors opening off the head of the stairs. One door stood open, displaying a bed, a handmade rag carpet, and marble-topped washstand. This was quite obviously the bedroom in use by the Quicke family, and Elinor swept inside. She looked in vain for a wardrobe.

With a murmured apology, Nell Quicke slipped past her and dropped to her knees beside a leather chest, hidden on the far side of the bed. Of a type used by sea-captains, it had been left behind by the previous occupant of Venn. Raising the lid, Nell Quicke reached inside and carefully lifted out three neatly folded dresses.

Two Elinor rejected immediately. Of gaudy silk, they had evidently been bought for Nell Quicke when she was a much younger girl. The third, made from coarsely woven woollen cloth, was more suitable than either of the others, but it was well worn.

Elinor looked questioningly at the farmer's young wife, and Nell Quicke met her glance with an expression that was a mixture of embarrassment and defiant pride.

'That's all I've got, ma'am. My father's a poor man. I came to Tom with no dowry.'

For a fleeting moment, Elinor felt an unexpected surge of sympathy for this wife who had so little – and was unlikely to gain more while her husband worked Venn Farm as a tenant. But Elinor had a coach to meet. Taking up the woollen dress, she held it against her body. 'Then this will have to do. But first I'll need a wash. I'm covered in mud.'

Nell Quicke hurried from the room. Moments later Elinor heard the sound of urgent whispering from downstairs as pans and kettles clanged upon the kitchen fire.

Elinor's expression softened. There was an intangible, calming quality about Nell Quicke. It was not difficult to understand why Tom Quicke had been ready to take his young wife without a dowry.

Nell Quicke returned with a jug of hot water and convinced Elinor that her petticoat would have to be left behind, too. Not only was it too elaborate to be worn beneath Nell's simple woollen garment, but it was also as wet and mud-stained as Elinor's dress.

After a hurried wash, Elinor put on Nell Quicke's dress. She was not able to confirm Nell Quicke's statement that the dress fitted well. When she asked for a mirror, Nell Quicke produced a small and cheap hand-mirror, proudly declaring it to be a wedding gift. It was the only mirror in the house.

When Elinor went outside, she found Tom Quicke brushing down her pony.

'I gave him a drop of water, Miss Hearle,' he said as he handed her up into the gig. 'He seemed to be thirsty.'

Guiltily, Elinor recalled that she had been so concerned with her own plight that she had not given the horse a drink at the watering-place.

'I'm obliged to you, Quicke.'

To his wife she said: 'Bring my clothes to Polrudden when they're washed and mended. I'll see you're paid for your trouble.'

Flicking the reins over the horse's back, Elinor set the animal off at a smart trot, heading back along the farm track that led to the St Austell road.

When she was out of sight, Tom Quicke scratched his head ruefully and replaced his battered hat. 'That's the first time I've spoken to Sir Lewis's daughter. I can't say I've been missing much. Attractive she may be, but she's no more grateful for anything that's done for her than her father.'

'Oh, she's grateful enough, Tom. I could see that.' Nell Quicke took her husband's hand as they walked inside the house together. 'She's just not used to thanking folks, that's all. Life can't be easy for her up at that big house – alone for most of the time, I shouldn't wonder. I feel sorry for her.'

They had reached the kitchen now, and Tom Quicke looked at the dirty but expensive dress and petticoat lying on the table. Elinor Hearle probably had two or three wardrobes crammed with such clothes. All of Nell's treasured possessions were packed inside a single sea-chest – and yet *she* felt sorry for Elinor Hearle!

Tom Quicke squeezed Nell's hand affectionately. He knew he had married a very special girl and was very much in love with his young wife.

Elinor Hearle arrived at the Queen's Head inn a few minutes after three o'clock. There was no sign of the Royal Mail coach. In answer to her question, a serving-girl informed her that it had not yet arrived.

There was a great deal of noise coming from the Queen's Head and the other inns of the town. Elinor remembered that this was the last Friday of the month, the day when both the weekly paid labourers and the more highly skilled miners received their pay.

St Austell was surrounded by tin and copper mines. In recent years the opening of the china-clay quarries to the north of the town had begun to change the age-old landscape of the Cornish countryside, throwing up tall mounds of china-clay waste, and attracting a great deal of labour to the area. The quarry-owners, members of the local trading fraternity, had learned from their mining associates that a great deal of trading profit could be gained by paying their workers in the St Austell inns. Much of the hard-earned money would return to the businessmen over the tavern bars. More would be spent later in the nearby shops, on gifts for irate wives whose meagre housekeeping money had been further depleted in the convivial atmosphere of a smoke-filled ale-house.

For almost an hour Elinor sat in the gig, growing ever more impatient and annoyed by the remarks and hopeful attentions of passing miners in varying stages of insobriety.

When half-past four came and the mail coach had still not arrived, Elinor tied the pony to a hitching-post outside the Queen's Head and sought the shadows of the archway that led to the yard beside the inn.

Inside the yard was a brewer's wagon. It had arrived earlier in the afternoon, heavily laden with barrels of locally brewed ale. Unloading the barrels and trundling them to the cellars of the Queen's Head inn was hard and thirsty work, calling for constant refreshment for the drayman and his mate. By the time the last full barrel had been replaced on the wagon by an empty one, both brewery employees were red-faced and loud-voiced, their talk liberally laced with oaths.

When the last empty barrels were tied down, the drayman began to turn the wagon around in the narrow yard. It was not an easy manoeuvre. The yard was cluttered with the gigs and light carriages of the inn's wealthier customers.

The brewery horses did not make the drayman's task any easier. They were an ill-matched pair. One horse was aged and experienced, and stood quietly in the shafts, head hanging low. But the other was young and nervous. Ears twitching at every sound, it rolled its eyes fearfully whenever anyone passed by. Had the drayman showed more patience, he might have *coaxed* this horse to do his bidding, but many pints of best brewery ale had drowned all reasonableness. Careless handling soon caused the heavy wagon to jam against the inn wall. In his efforts to work it free, the drayman had the horses moving backwards and forwards time and time again. Thoroughly confused, the inexperienced animal became even more nervous than before and continually tried to back away from the shouting drayman. The wagon jammed tighter against the wall and there came the noise of splintering wood.

Bellowing at the young horse, the drayman picked up a heavy stave that had been used to lever the big barrels from the wagon. Swinging it high in the air, he brought it down upon the horse's flank with a sickening thud. The horse snorted in fear and tried to bolt. The other horse did not budge. With the dray stuck fast, the frightened horse slipped on the cobbles of the yard and crashed heavily to the ground.

The horse's predicament enraged the drayman. He

began raining heavy blows on the animal's side and stomach as it struggled in a vain attempt to rise.

Watching the incident from the very beginning, Elinor had first been faintly amused at the drunken drayman's antics, but when he began beating the horse with the heavy stave she had seen enough. Rushing across the innyard, she pushed herself between the drayman and his horse and called upon him to leave the horse alone.

Elinor was behaving as she would at Polrudden, where she was used to being obeyed. The drayman, who did not know her, saw only a young woman in a cheap and ill-fitting, homespun woollen dress.

He gave her a half-blow, half-push that sent her sprawling to the cobblestones six feet away.

'Mind your own business, girl, or it'll be your arse I'm paddling, not this bloody useless horse.'

There were a few muffled guffaws from behind Elinor, and she realised for the first time that the happenings in the innyard had attracted an audience.

The drayman turned his back on Elinor and resumed his belabouring of the horse as Elinor scrambled to her feet. Glaring angrily at the amused men standing about in the yard, she cried: 'Will you stand here and do nothing while he beats the poor animal to death?'

'I wouldn't take on Bill Coffin for you, my beauty, let alone for some stupid carthorse,' replied one of the bystanders. 'If you've got any sense, you'll be on your way. Bill Coffin's a man of his word.'

'Aw, leave 'er alone, won't 'ee? Let Bill get to work wi' 'is paddling-stick. I'd give a half-pint of brandy for a flash of what she's got under that there dress.'

Incensed by the coarse laughter of the amused bystanders, Elinor pushed her way through them. Running to her waiting gig, she snatched up the short whip from its holder and ran back to the innyard.

Bill Coffin never saw her return. He had dropped the stave and was now standing over the fallen horse, kicking it heavily in the ribs with hard-toed boots while his mate was trying more conventional methods of raising the horse.

Elinor's first blow cut across the side of Bill Coffin's neck and he bellowed in surprised pain. Her second blow caught him across the cheek as he turned. The third never landed. The drayman snatched the whip from her hand and broke it into four leather-linked pieces. Throwing the whip to the ground, he touched a fingertip to his cheek. It came away tinged with blood, and Bill Coffin howled with rage.

'You vicious little cow! I'll give you some of your own medicine . . .'

Before the angry drayman was able to carry out his threat, a young man stepped from the crowd. Almost casually, he pushed Elinor out of Bill Coffin's reach. When the drayman moved after her, the young man stepped into his path.

'Leave her. I didn't agree with what you were doing to that horse, but that's between you and the brewery. This isn't. I won't stand by and watch you beat a woman.'

There was a quiet confidence in the young man that caused Bill Coffin to hesitate – but only for a moment. The drayman stood a head taller than the newcomer, and he knew his mate was behind him.

'Did you hear that, Seth?' Bill Coffin called the

words over his shoulder as he eyed the newcomer's stylish, if somewhat dusty, clothes. 'We've got a young dandy here. Reckons he can tell Bill Coffin what he should or shouldn't be doing.'

'Then ye'd best put him right, Bill. Unless thee'd like me to do it for 'ee?'

'No, I'll do it – and gladly. You see that the maid doesn't run away. I've a score to settle with her.'

Without warning, Bill Coffin rushed at his opponent, arms held wide to secure him in a hug that would squeeze the breath from his body. The sudden move was wasted. With a quick movement, the stranger sidestepped out of reach.

Someone in the crowd let out a muffled titter, and Bill Coffin flushed angrily. He bored in once more, this time with fists flailing. What occurred next happened so quickly that it was the subject of heated argument in the St Austell hostelries for many months to come. A few onlookers would hotly declare that Bill Coffin was hit by a number of blows. Others, also present, swore it was no more than one.

No one cared to ask Bill Coffin. Had they done so, he could have told them he took three of the mightiest punches he had ever experienced in his rough-and-tumble life. The first sank wrist-deep into his ale-inflated stomach. The second took him on the forehead even as his body doubled up in pain. He straightened involuntarily, positioning his chin perfectly for an impeccable straight right.

Arms akimbo, Bill Coffin was knocked back into the crowd, his momentum and unconscious weight carrying upwards of half a dozen men to the ground with him.

The drayman's mate watched the destruction of his colleague in wide-mouthed amazement. A man of great strength but limited discernment, he never paused to ponder upon the character and skills of the man who had so effectively demolished his companion. Placing a heavy hand on the victor's shoulder, he said: 'I'll show 'ee . . .'

The next moment the hand on the stranger's shoulder was clutching air. What happened next, though often talked about in St Austell and the surrounding district, was never a subject of argument. Every man there agreed that the single uppercut travelled no more than six inches to the chin of the drayman's burly mate. Nevertheless, it had sufficient explosive power to stretch the man until his toes barely touched the uneven cobbles. A moment later he crumpled to the ground, no more aware of his surroundings than his horse-beating workmate.

There was a momentary awe-filled hush before the watching crowd roared their loud appreciation of the stranger's skill.

Ignoring their noisy approval, the victorious young man went to where Elinor stood, slightly bemused by the turn events had taken.

'Are you all right, miss?' He nodded towards the inn. 'Would you like to go inside and sit down for a while?'

Elinor shook her head. 'No. No, I'm quite all right.'

The young man grinned suddenly. 'Only a very brave girl, or a stupid one, would take on a drayman for the sake of a horse. You don't look particularly stupid to me, so I compliment you on your courage.'

Elinor was torn between gratitude for this man's

intervention on her behalf and indignation at his words. Then she remembered she was not dressed as the daughter of Sir Lewis Hearle, but was wearing an old woollen dress belonging to Nell Quicke. Realisation came that for possibly the first time in her life someone had helped her simply because she was a woman, and not because she was Elinor Hearle, daughter of Sir Lewis Hearle, local landowner and Member of Parliament for the borough of Fowey. It was an unusual and strangely uncomfortable discovery.

In a bid to cover her confusion, Elinor unfastened the small leather bag she wore dangling from a long thong about her neck. Taking out a sovereign, she proffered it to her rescuer.

'I am grateful for the assistance you rendered me. Please take this.'

It was customary for gentry to reward those who performed outstanding services for them; but the expression on the young man's face told Elinor she had blundered.

Taking her hand in his, he folded her fingers back upon the gold coin.

'Keep your money, young lady.' He fingered the sleeve of her dress where there was a neat but noticeable darn. 'Put it towards the cost of a new dress.'

As he turned away, her rescuer was joined by a thin-faced companion who looked down upon the fallen drayman approvingly before the crowd parted respectfully to allow both men through.

Elinor suddenly realised she had not asked the name of the man who had come to her aid in such

a ready and positive manner. Then she became aware
of the excited talk about her.

'Did you ever see such a punch?'

'Who was he? Does anyone know him?'

'I do.' The speaker was a ferret-faced little miner.
'Recognised him as soon as I set eyes on him. It were
Nathan Jago. Son of the preacher down to Pentuan.'

3

The Royal Mail coach from London rattled into the yard of the Queen's Head inn only minutes after the landlord and his potman had raised the fallen brewery horse. The wagon was sent back to the brewery with two semi-conscious draymen lying between the empty barrels.

Climbing stiffly from the coach, Sir Lewis Hearle gave his daughter a gruff greeting. Then, eyebrows drawn together in a disapproving frown, he demanded to know what she was doing 'dressed like some kitchen drab'.

Elinor offered him no explanation until his luggage had been stowed in the small two-wheeled gig and they were on the road to Polrudden. Only then did she detail the many happenings of the eventful day.

Sir Lewis's reaction was one of amusement when she described her soaking at the watering-place, but his mood changed abruptly when she told him of the incident in the yard of the Queen's Head.

Erupting in a sudden bout of irascibility that did much to explain Elinor's own explosive nature, he shouted: 'Dammit, Elinor! Isn't it enough that you come to meet me dressed like a servant girl? Do you also have to brawl with draymen as though you were some Mevagissey fisherwoman? Such behaviour would be bad enough in a son. In a daughter it's . . . it's *intolerable*. I won't have it, do you hear me?'

Elinor was unperturbed. She knew that the story of how she had horsewhipped a brewer's man for beating a horse would be proudly related in a dozen London gatherings within a week of her father's return to Parliament.

'Who is this fellow who stopped the drayman from giving you the hiding you deserve? Is he a local man?'

'I've never seen him before, but some of the crowd seemed to know him. Nathan Jago was the name I heard mentioned.'

'Nathan Jago? The prize-fighter? What the devil is he doing back in these parts?'

Elinor looked at her father in surprise. 'You know him?'

'I've heard of him. I'm surprised you haven't. He was fishing from Pentuan as a boy, but was too wild to stay in one place. He ran off to join the Navy when he was no more than fourteen or fifteen. He was Admiral Nelson's helmsman, first in *Elephant* at the battle of Copenhagen, and again in *Victory* at Trafalgar. They say Nelson would have no other man at the helm of his ship in battle. Jago was wounded at Trafalgar and discharged from the service. But it couldn't have been a bad wound. Only a year later he fought Ted Laxton, the London prize-fighter, to a standstill over forty rounds.'

Elinor remembered the unmarked features of her rescuer. He certainly did not have the appearance of a prize-fighter. No doubt this was testimony to his skill.

'It seems I could not have chosen a better champion.'

Sir Lewis Hearle snorted. 'He might have saved you a paddled backside, but I'm damned if I'm happy about the Hearle family owing a debt of gratitude to a Jago.'

Before Sir Lewis Hearle could say more, the gig rounded a sharp bend and they found the narrow lane blocked by a pair of yoked oxen. The smocked countryman driving the two beasts gave no indication that he knew the gig was behind him and continued on his way, oblivious of the baronet's mounting anger.

'You there! Get those oxen out of the way. Move them off the road. Damn you, man! Do you hear me?'

The countryman never even turned his head, and Sir Lewis Hearle made a strangled noise in his throat.

Elinor flicked the reins and the pony edged forward uncertainly until it nudged the countryman, causing him to stumble and look behind him.

Muttering beneath his breath, he turned back to his slow beasts and drew them to the side of the road, where they immediately began cropping the grass.

As Elinor and her father drove past, the countryman raised his soft hat of stitched linen, and gave the occupants of the gig an enigmatic smile.

'There! That's the reason I want nothing to do with the Jagos. You saw that man's insolence? A peasant thinking he's being clever by holding up his betters.'

Elinor smiled tolerantly at her father. 'I don't think he was being insolent. It is far more likely that he is deaf. He never realised we were behind him until the pony nudged him.'

'Nonsense! The man's been listening to the teachings of your young hero's father. He's a dangerous bigot. He and his kind are stirring up the scum of the earth, seeking to destroy all that's good in this land of ours. Unless he and those like him are checked, England will go the same way as France. Preacher Jago is a rabble-rouser. A sower of sedition. A Wesleyan Methodist.'

At dusk that day, Nathan Jago and Sammy Mizler paused at the top of Pentuan Hill. A few hundred yards to their left, hidden behind a copse of tall trees, was Polrudden Manor. Below them, a quarter-mile break in the cliffs was filled by a wide scimitar of smooth, golden sand, unevenly bisected by a narrow, fast-flowing river. Huddled on the near bank of the river was the small fishing village of Pentuan.

Nathan filled his lungs with air, expelling it again noisily.

'Breathe in that air, Sammy. Go on, you can *taste* it. You won't find air like it within a hundred miles of London Town.'

Sammy Mizler sniffed more cautiously. 'It smells like Billingsgate to me.'

Nathan grinned. 'The wind must be blowing from Mevagissey. All the offal from the fish-cellars goes into the harbour there. It's a smell you'll need to get used to, Sammy. This is Cornwall, and we're here to go into the fishing business.'

Sammy Mizler grimaced. 'So you've been telling me for more than two hundred and fifty miles. The idea would have more appeal had we come by mail coach and not walked every step of the way.'

'You'll feel different about it when we come to buy a boat and nets. We'll need every penny we've saved. Had we come by coach and then found we were a few guineas short, you'd have begrudged every bone-jarring mile we'd travelled.'

Sammy Mizler shrugged. 'You're the fisherman, not me. I just want to be around when you come to your senses and return to your prize-fighting – and to London. Why, you could be undisputed *world* champion within twelve months! Just think of it, Nathan. The world would be yours! To give all that up for' – he sniffed disdainfully – '*this*. It's madness!'

Sammy Mizler spread his hands in a gesture of helpless frustration. 'It's not too late. Go and visit your ma. Stay for a week – a month. You've earned yourself a rest. But don't throw away the very real gift that God has given to you. There's magic in your fists. It showed itself back there, in St Austell, when you downed the two draymen. It was beautiful to watch. Beautiful . . .'

Sammy Mizler stopped talking and hurried to catch up with Nathan, who, his face devoid of expression, had begun to walk down the steep hill to Pentuan village.

'All right, so Ned Belcher was blinded. It was unfortunate – a tragedy, even – but nobody blames you. His own seconds told me his sight had been going for years. He'd been in the prize-fighting game for too long and was never very clever at dodging a punch. Nathan boy! To give up now is nothing short of . . . felonious! If you take the world title, you'll be able to come home in a year or two and buy a whole armada of fishing-boats. Yes, and a house like that, too.'

Sammy Mizler pointed to where the roof and high chimneys of Polrudden Manor rose through the trees far to the left of them.

Nathan checked his stride and looked towards the great house. 'When I was a boy I used to hide on the hill behind Polrudden for hours, wondering what it would be like to live there. But it was just a boy's dream. Save your tongue for tasting my ma's cooking. You'll find it a sight more satisfying, I promise you.'

Sammy Mizler shook his head in despair. But he found consolation in remembering the manner in which Nathan had disposed of the two draymen. Nathan might *think* he was through with prize-fighting, but a man who possessed such devastating power in his two fists would be a fool not to put them to good use. And Nathan Jago was no fool.

Annie Jago bustled about her kitchen-cum-living-room. As she lifted a heavy iron skillet from the fire and raked hot ashes from the cloam oven, she could scarcely contain her happiness. It was a rare occasion for her to have her only son in the house. Indeed, this was only the third time he had been home since coming ashore after Nelson's great, yet tragic, victory at Trafalgar. Over the mantelshelf were proudly displayed the medals presented to Nathan for his part in this battle and in the earlier victory at Copenhagen.

'Why didn't you let me know you were coming?'

asked the hot and beaming Annie Jago. 'I'd have got in something special for you. I might even have persuaded your father to stay home to greet you – though I doubt if I'd have succeeded in that, even for you. The Lord's been calling loudly of late, and your father has never been a man to allow His voice to go unheeded. No, not even if his only son were to be here for no more than five minutes.'

Nathan grinned. 'It's good to know some things in life never change. But where's our Nell? Working in the fish-cellars?'

'Working in the cellars? Lord bless you, no. I'm forgetting how long it's been since you were last home. Your sister's been married for six months. She's not Nell Jago any longer, but Nell Quicke. The wife of young Tom Quicke from over by St Ewe. You'll remember him when you meet him. He's a fine man. It was a good marriage for her, Nathan.' Annie Jago could not keep the pride from her voice as she added: 'Tom's a farmer – a *yeoman* farmer. He rents Venn Farm from Sir Lewis Hearle.'

It mattered not to Annie Jago that her daughter probably had less money to spend on herself than a miner's wife, or the lowest-paid worker in a fish-cellar. She was married to a *farmer*, a man making his own way in life. Nell had married well.

She turned to Nathan, holding a kettle of boiling water, her apron wrapped about its handle. 'You haven't said how long you'll be staying?'

Nathan hesitated. He had told Sammy Mizler that his prize-fighting days were over. He had told himself the same thing. Yet now he was at home in the house he had known from childhood, the house in which he had been born, he was suddenly unsure. Everything was somehow smaller than he remembered: the house, the village, the fields – even his mother. He had grown both mentally and physically since leaving Pentuan. He wondered whether he might have grown too big to be part of this tiny community ever again. Aware of Sammy Mizler's quizzical gaze, Nathan did his best to ignore the unwanted doubts.

'I'll likely be around for a long time, Ma. I've come back to buy a boat – perhaps my own cellar, too. I'm going to do a spot of fishing once more.'

An expression of incredulous joy spread over Annie Jago's face, and Nathan leaped to his feet to relieve her of the kettle of steaming water which, unnoticed, had begun to tilt alarmingly in his mother's hands. Placing the kettle on the granite stone of the hearth, he shook his hands in pain. The kettle was very, very hot.

'Do you mean that, Nathan? But what about the money? Boats are not cheap, you know. Colin Arthur's been saving for years to buy his own boat. Even with a couple of good fishing seasons behind him he still hasn't got enough. And to be talking about a fish-cellar, too . . .'

'I've got the money, Ma. At least, me and Sammy together have. Not only that; Sammy has the keenest business brain outside of Threadneedle Street. We'll stay here and grow rich. All of us.'

Annie Jago's pleasure at Nathan's announcement that he was home to stay was diluted by doubts. The Jagos were a poor family, and Josiah Jago's dedication to evangelism would ensure that he and his wife remained poor to the end of their days. It did not matter overmuch. Their friends were poor, too, and the county in which they lived was a poor one. Even Nell, who had made such a good marriage, had gained nothing but pride in her change of status. Now here was her son talking of *owning* a fishing-boat.

Annie Jago knew nothing of the rewards to be gained in the prize-fighting ring and she was concerned that Nathan might have come by his money dishonestly.

'You'll need more than a business brain to grow rich from pilchards,' she said eventually. 'Last year there were no more than two shoals came close enough to shore to be taken – and there's been but one this year so far. We have four fish-cellars in Pentuan, yet not enough fish is being caught to keep one of them going. If you've got money to spare, you'd do better looking for something else on which to spend it.'

Sammy Mizler looked at Nathan triumphantly. 'Isn't this what I've been telling you every step of the way from London Town? Come back there, Nathan. If you've a mind to put your money into a business, let me find something that will make money for you while you carry on with the thing you do best – prize-fighting.'

Ignoring his friend's plea, Nathan leaned forward in his chair, addressing his mother: 'You're talking of *seine*-fishing, Ma. I'm not. Any fisherman who sits around on the shore waiting for the fish to come to him deserves to go hungry. The boat I'm going to buy will be a deep-water drifter. I intend going out *looking* for the fish.'

Once again Annie Jago came close to dropping a kettle, but this time there was no joy in her expression.

She was genuinely horrified. 'Drift-fishing? You can't do that. We have no drift-fishermen in Pentuan. Never have had. We've always been seiners here.'

'Not any more.' Nathan stood up and walked to the window of the small, warm, comfortable kitchen. 'Look out there. What do you see? A fishing village that's dying through poverty, ignorance and an unwillingness to change. If they'll listen to me and follow my example, the village will come to life again. Children won't need to move away to make a living; they'll have a future here.'

Such talk was beyond Annie Jago's understanding. She shook her head unhappily. 'It will take more than fine words to persuade Pentuan fishermen to take up drifting.'

Sammy Mizler had been looking from Nathan to Annie Jago as the two talked, his dark eyebrows drawn together in a puzzled frown. Now he spoke to Nathan.

'You didn't tell me you were setting out on a fishing crusade when you persuaded me to come to Cornwall as your partner. What's all this talk of drift-fishing and seine-fishing? I've always thought one fisherman was the same as another.'

'So he is – but Cornish fishermen are too stubborn to admit it. Drifting and seining are two different ways to catch fish, that's all. About this time of year the pilchards suddenly appear close inshore in their millions. Every available boat puts to sea, and the pilchards are encircled in long nets – seine-nets – and hauled as close inshore as possible. Then the fish are "tucked in" and taken ashore to the salting-cellars. Tucking might last a week. Salting, bulking, pressing and packing might provide work for the village for another two months. If it's a good season, there might be another run of pilchards before the season's out. On the other hand, if luck's running against the seiners, a storm might blow up while the fish are held in the nets. Then they'll lose fish and nets as well. When this happens the whole community comes close to starving for the remainder of the year. *That's* seine-fishing.'

'What's so different about drift-fishing?'

'Drifting's the only sensible way to fish. You go out to where the fish are and put out a net that stretches like a barrier for perhaps half a mile. When you hoist the net back on board you empty out your fish and bring them ashore. It's a year-round business – and the only way to fish, to my mind.'

'There are many men in these parts who'd argue against you – and that includes the whole of Pentuan. They say it's a selfish way to fish. By laying those nets across the bay you stop the pilchards from coming close inshore and deprive everyone else of a living.'

'That's a load of nonsense, Ma, as every thinking fisherman knows very well. Over the years all sorts of laws have been passed in a bid to control drifters and make fishing more difficult for them. It's made no difference at all. The pilchards still come inshore some years and stay away for others.'

'I'd rather you kept such views to yourself, especially when your father's around. He's as strong against drifting as anyone else when he thinks of *anything* other than doing the Lord's bidding.'

'When do you think Pa will be home?'

Nathan deliberately changed the subject. There had

always been a deep and unreasonable division between deep-sea drift-fishermen and those who pursued the more traditional fishing methods. Cornish fishermen had always resisted change, whatever form it took, and Annie Jago came from a long line of seine-fishers. Nathan would keep his thoughts to himself until he had both a boat and a cellar. There would be time enough then to tackle opposition.

'Your father won't be home until he's saved enough new souls to satisfy him, or until he falls off his donkey with sheer exhaustion because he's forgotten to eat or sleep.'

4

Preacher Josiah Jago had still not returned home two days later, when Nathan set out early to visit his sister and her husband at Venn Farm.

Sammy Mizler remained behind at Pentuan. Later in the day he would hobble to the nearby harbour wall, there to bask in the warm autumn sunshine, but he had done enough walking in recent weeks.

Instead of taking the road direct to Venn Farm, Nathan set off along the cliff path that passed behind Polrudden Manor. He paused along the way to gaze down into the deep, overgrown cleft in the cliff face from which great blocks of Pentuan stone had once been quarried. He remembered, as a boy, watching the huge blocks of stone being winched into the dark holds of blunt-bowed, dust-coated merchantmen. Pentuan stone was a distinctive buff colour, and Nathan had recognised it in many of the fine London buildings.

Not far from the disused sea-edge quarry, Nathan passed within a few hundred yards of Polrudden. He was close enough to view with sadness the air of neglect that the old house wore like a shabby cloak.

Nathan had business to discuss with Sir Lewis Hearle, but it would have to wait for another day.

Nell Quicke was sweeping the flagstones immediately in front of the small farmhouse door when Nathan came into view. She saw him when he was still some distance from the house. With a hand shielding her eyes from the slanting sun, she squinted uncertainly until he came closer. Then, dropping the broom, she ran to greet him.

'Nathan! It *is* you, isn't it? How wonderful.'

Nell Quicke flung herself at her brother, and Nathan hugged her to him, swinging her clear of the ground as her arms tightened about his neck.

'How long have you been home? Why didn't you let us know you were coming?'

'I'm no letter-writer, Nell, as well you know. But you're a fine one to talk. I come home expecting to be cared for by my loving young sister, only to find she's up and married some rich young farmer!'

Nell laughed happily. Releasing her grip on Nathan, she took him by the hand and led him towards the house. 'Hardly rich, Nathan. There are so many things we need. A good milking-cow, for one thing. But we'll get one sometime. Tom says so.'

'Where is this husband of yours?' Nathan looked about the empty yard. He had seen no one working in the fields on his way to the farm.

'Tom's taken a litter of pigs to St Austell market. It's

the first litter we've raised at Venn,' Nell added proudly.

Nathan ducked his head to enter the house through the low doorway. It was warm in here and smelled of wood smoke.

'I'll get you a drink. One of Tom's friends gave us a barrel of cider as a wedding present.'

Nathan nodded. Glancing around the room while Nell was fetching the drink, he observed the lack of luxury. Yet there was an air of serenity, almost well-being, that put him immediately at ease.

Nell returned to the room and placed a cider-filled jug on the white-scrubbed table in the centre of the room before reaching down a mug from a shelf.

'Are you enjoying married life, Nell? You're happy with your Tom Quicke?'

The answer was in Nell's eyes when she looked up at her brother. 'I'm *very* happy, Nathan. Tom's a wonderful man. He's good to me.'

'I'm glad. I've often worried about the sort of man Pa might have found for you. I felt sure he would be some ageing, lonely circuit preacher.'

Nell and Nathan were very close to each other, even though they had seen little of one another in recent years and there was ten years between the two. Nell idolised Nathan. He, in his turn, felt very protective towards her.

'You can stop worrying about me now. You'll like Tom. He's . . . Oh, he's just a *wonderful* man. He makes me feel really good.'

Sheer happiness threatened to choke Nell, and Nathan held out his arms and hugged her to him.

At that moment a long shadow reached into the

room. Still holding Nell, Nathan turned and saw Elinor Hearle.

The mistress of Polrudden had Nell's woollen dress in her hands, and her eyes opened wide in astonishment as she recognised Nathan. Recovering her composure, her manner became icily cold. Ignoring Nathan, she threw the woollen dress on the table and spoke to Nell Quicke.

'I came to return this. I had expected you to bring my clothes to Polrudden before this.'

Flustered, Nell Quicke said: 'I . . . I had to borrow some cotton of the right colour. I had none at the farm. I was going to bring them to Polrudden this afternoon. I'll fetch them; they're upstairs.'

Nell Quicke hurried from the room. She had made no introductions, but they were not necessary as far as Nathan was concerned. Polrudden Manor had been mentioned. There would not be two girls like this one at the old manor-house.

'Well . . . So you are Elinor Hearle. I had no idea I was rescuing the squire's daughter from a beating.' He lifted the woollen dress from the table, then allowed it to fall back again. 'This fooled me. Do you often visit the town in borrowed clothes?'

Elinor's head went up haughtily. 'I had an accident and fell in the watering-place pond. I borrowed this dress because I had no time to go home and change.' Elinor owed this man no explanations and she could not understand why she was giving him one. 'If it makes a difference to you that I have no need to buy more clothes, I still have the sovereign I offered to you. I believe you *usually* fight for money?'

There was an edge to her voice that caused Nathan to respond in a similar vein.

'My fights are arranged in advance – and for considerably more than a guinea.'

'Oh? And are your assignations arranged for you, too? Or do all young married women fall into your arms when they learn they are in the presence of Nathan Jago, champion prize-fighter of all England?'

The scorn in her voice came as more of a surprise to Elinor Hearle than to Nathan. She had no reason to be concerned with the liaisons of a *prize-fighter* – and she certainly cared nothing for the young wife of a farmer, even if he *were* one of her father's tenants.

To add to her chagrin, Elinor saw that Nathan was grinning broadly. 'I don't confine my embraces to married women. Single girls are high on my list, too.'

At that moment Nell Quicke returned to the room, unaware of the strained atmosphere. Over her arm lay Elinor's dress and petticoat, both neatly pressed and folded. Placing them on the table, she carefully opened out the dress to show the neatly repaired tear. 'I mended this. It hardly shows at all. You'll be able to wear it again.'

'I have no doubt you have repaired it adequately.' Throwing a coin on the table, Elinor snapped: 'Here's a shilling for your work.'

Keenly aware of the amused expression upon Nathan's face, Elinor refused to meet his eyes. 'I'm sorry if I've interrupted anything.' With this remark, she turned about abruptly and strode from the house.

Behind her, Elinor's barbed words were lost on the young wife. Nell Quicke's mind was filled with thoughts of how she would spend the welcome shilling.

Elinor's horse was grazing on the lush grass just beyond the farmyard. Placing her left foot in the stirrup, she grasped the pommel of the saddle and was about to swing herself on to the horse when she heard a step behind her.

It was Nathan. Still grinning, he said: 'I'd better set matters straight before you go – about Nell and me.'

'Why?' Elinor shrugged. 'The morals of our tenants, or of their wives, are no concern of mine.'

'All the same, I think you should know that Nell is my sister.'

Elinor felt the colour rise to her face. She had made a fool of herself in front of this exasperatingly self-assured man. It was not a comfortable feeling. She swung her leg across the saddle in a masculine fashion and found the second stirrup.

Nathan felt he had goaded Sir Lewis Hearle's very attractive daughter enough for one day. Resting a hand upon the horse's neck, he looked up at her and smiled. 'I would like to discuss a business matter with your father sometime. When would be a good time to call at Polrudden?'

Elinor wondered what business Nathan Jago could possibly have with her father. She did not ask. Instead, she said: 'He's a busy man. Is it urgent?'

Nathan wanted to speak to Sir Lewis Hearle about the fishing tithes payable to the manor of Polrudden by all boats fishing out of Pentuan. He said: 'It will keep for a day or two. It's a matter that I'd like to discuss with my father first.'

Nathan's reply touched a sudden chord in Elinor's memory. Her father had told her that Nathan was the son of a Methodist preacher, and now she remembered the St Austell court messenger who had come to Polrudden seeking her father late the previous evening.

'Your father . . . where is he now?'

The question took Nathan by surprise. 'Out riding his circuit. He's a Methodist preacher.'

'Does he ride the Mevagissey and Tregony circuits?'

'Yes. Why?'

Elinor remembered the exact words of the messenger to her father: 'The Methodist minister who rides the Mevagissey and Tregony circuits has been arrested. The other magistrates feel the case is important enough for a full bench to meet to hear his case.' She told Nathan.

Absent from home not on the Lord's business, but held in St Austell lock-up in the name of His insane Majesty, King George III, Preacher Josiah Jago was a bewildered and unhappy man. He had been arrested, quietly and discreetly, whilst homeward bound from Fowey. The constables making the arrest told him only that he was being arrested as a result of a complaint lodged by the Reverend Nicholas Kent, rector of the busy south Cornish port of Fowey.

Taken in custody to St Austell, Josiah Jago was charged with being an itinerant preacher, contrary to the Toleration Act of 1689. This ancient Act of Parliament, enacted in the year that William of Orange and Mary took the throne vacated by the Catholic King James II, decreed that a dissenting preacher had to be settled in the parish in which he preached. The Act had been intended to give dissenters a greater degree of freedom than they had hitherto enjoyed. Now, more than a century later, it was being resurrected as a weapon to curtail the activities of the most popular religious movement England had known since Christianity ousted paganism.

Such popularity was spreading alarm and hypocrisy among the leadership of the Established Church and its political counterparts.

For very many years the Church had neglected the people it claimed to serve. Parish clergymen who should have been protecting the interests of miner, fisherman and farmworker had long ceased to see the Church as a heavenly-inspired vocation. It had become a business – a very lucrative business for many – and an ambitious curate had more prospect of furthering his career by riding with the local hunt and dining frequently at the manor. Ambition apart, it was a far more *comfortable* way of life than sharing the many insurmountable problems of the poor.

But the Church was not yet ready to relinquish its age-old hold on the poor and allow them to seek their God outside the high grey-stone walls of the churches of the established faith. Nonconformists had always aroused the fury of the church of the land. *Successful* nonconformists, especially those with the fervour of the Methodist movement, did far more. They posed a long-term threat to the wealthy and powerful bishops who ruled profitable sees from feudal palaces.

Acting as the spokesman for the bishops, the Archbishop of Canterbury drew the attention of Spencer Perceval's government to the dangers that were posed by the followers of Wesley. The Wesleyan Methodist movement was a church of the common people. Most of their preachers were themselves *of* the people. Yet the disciplines they imposed upon themselves and their followers would have done credit to the army of Viscount Wellington, Britain's popular new hero.

The Archbishop reminded Prime Minister Perceval that the flood of war currently engulfing Europe had sprung from just such a deep well in eighteenth-century France. He convinced Britain's traditionalist Prime Minister that untutored preachers with the ability to rouse the masses to such heights of fervour were dangerous men.

To add weight to his arguments, the Archbishop was able to point to the industrial discontent that had recently erupted in the Midlands and the North of England. Much of the discontent was mistakenly – or perhaps maliciously – blamed upon the Methodists.

Spencer Perceval, himself destined to die a violent death only two years later, needed no further persuasion. Word went out from London that the preaching of Methodism was to be 'discouraged'.

This was all that was needed by the Cornish gentry – as represented by the county's magistrates. Seriously alarmed already by rioting miners protesting against the high price of corn, they were eager to deflect blame from the landowners. Methodist preachers would make excellent scapegoats.

Josiah Jago spent most of his day and night in St Austell lock-up asking the Lord for strength to face whatever might be in store for him. The Wesleyan preacher knew the Reverend Nicholas Kent. The Anglican rector was an unremitting opponent of Methodism. Nevertheless, he would not have laid his complaint without the full backing of his own Church Authority.

It was this that worried Josiah Jago more than
anything else. In common with most Methodists, he
felt an affection, a family bond, with the mother
church. Wesley himself had been ordained in the
Church of England and had urged his followers to
pursue his particular brand of evangelism within the
established faith. It was impossible, of course. Such a
vital and energetic movement soon left the conserva-
tive Established Church far, far behind. Yet the older
members of the Methodist Church were still keenly
aware that they had sprung from the church founded
by Henry VIII. An organised campaign against them
by the mother church would cause such men great
distress.

The magistrates' court was due to sit at eleven in the
morning. Long before this time, Josiah Jago became
aware of a gradually swelling hubbub beyond the
walls of the lock-up. At first, he dismissed the sound
as being that of the Cornish market-town awakening
and gathering pace as the morning wore on; but there
was no levelling-off in the unseen noise, and it
puzzled the imprisoned preacher. Josiah Jago wished
he could see outside, but there was only a tiny, barred
aperture, far up in one corner of his cell, higher than
he could reach.

Then, when the blue-faced clock in St Austell
church tower chimed the hour for ten o'clock, a single
voice beyond the barred window began to sing one of
John Wesley's hymns. As Josiah Jago thrilled to the
sound, the words were taken up by more voices, until
all the noises of the busy market-town were lost in the
defiant words pouring from the throats of a thousand
men and women.

Joyful though the sound was, Josiah Jago found himself at a loss to think of the reason for such a religious gathering. It was not a feast day. Even if it had been, he had never known a holy day to be celebrated with such a rousing display of religious fervour.

When the hymn ended it was followed by another. Then, in a brief pause before another hymn was called for, the powerful voice of a speaker rang out, drawing prolonged cheering from the unseen crowd. Josiah Jago could not hear what was being said, but he caught three words. Those words were 'Preacher Josiah Jago'!

Enlightenment filled him with a sense of emotional awe. The crowd gathered outside the lock-up were there to show support for him – Josiah Jago.

The preacher was a simple man, a truly humble servant of the Lord. Men listened to him, but only because he was guiding them to God. As a man he had never claimed to amount to much. The thought of all those people gathered outside to protest at his arrest and to offer him encouragement in his time of need overwhelmed him. Sinking to his knees, his voice choked with emotion, Josiah Jago begged the Lord not to make a martyr of him. He asked only that he be released and allowed to serve Him in a comfortable, familiar way.

At ten-thirty, the church bells began to ring, the bell-ringers hurriedly summoned by the vicar of St Austell in an angry bid to drown the voices of the Methodist hymn-singers. The battle between bells and hymn-singers was still going on when a nervous Town Constable arrived at the lock-up to take

Josiah Jago up the stone stairs to the magistrates' court.

Sir Lewis Hearle, MP and Justice of the Peace, entered St Austell while the Methodists and the church bells were vying with each other for supremacy. He frowned angrily at the size of the crowd in front of the court-room. It extended the whole length of the road, making entry to the magistrates' court impossible.

But Sir Lewis Hearle was not going to the courtroom immediately. A second messenger had intercepted him while he was on the road to St Austell.

The Sheriff of Cornwall, Richard Oxnam, had also been told of Josiah Jago's arrest and had immediately hurried to St Austell. He sent a message to Sir Lewis, suggesting that the baronet meet him before taking his place on the bench at the magistrates' court.

Sir Lewis Hearle found Richard Oxnam lounging in the best room of the White Hart inn. The Sheriff had a scowl on his face, and a jug of best claret on the table at his elbow. Waving Sir Lewis to a seat, he poured him a glass from the jug.

Richard Oxnam took the opportunity to top up his own glass, and promptly poured half the contents down his throat.

'Those blasted bells! At least the singing was *half*-musical. I trust it will remain so. I would hate to see such a crowd turn ugly. How many would you say were there, Sir Lewis? A thousand? Two?'

Sir Lewis Hearle merely nodded. He would have placed the total closer to two thousand than to one.

The Sheriff of Cornwall pursed his lips, and Sir

Lewis was undecided whether the Sheriff was savouring his drink or was lost in thought. His next words proved that Richard Oxnam was deeply concerned about the situation that had brought about the scene in the streets outside.

'You've been called in to hear the case against the Wesley preacher, Jago, I believe?'

'That's right. It's high time action was taken against these Methodist rabble-rousers. They are driving the country to the brink of revolution. You have only to look at the mob outside. If the Constable hasn't dispersed them by the time the court sits, I'll have the Riot Act read out to them.'

Richard Oxnam's eyebrows had risen just sufficiently to cause Sir Lewis Hearle to pause in his tirade.

'Because they are singing hymns? I trust you'll take the same line with those wretched bell-ringers. They're causing a breach of the peace, if ever I heard one.'

The baronet could not disguise his surprise.

'You're not telling me you approve of the Wesleyans? Why, the Prime Minister himself is anxious to curb their activities.'

Richard Oxnam snorted derisively. 'Spencer Perceval was incapable of forming an opinion of his own during the years we spent at school together. I doubt he's changed. Perceval's views on the Methodist Church are those of my Lord Archbishop of Canterbury – and he can hardly be said to be impartial! The Wesleyan movement has gained more converts in the last thirty years than the Church of England during the whole of its existence. Whether or not I approve of Methodism doesn't matter. I'm a realist.'

The Sheriff of Cornwall topped up his glass again before fixing a shrewd look upon Sir Lewis Hearle. 'I'm going to do you a favour, Sir Lewis. Don't sit on the bench for this case against the preacher. Not only that; do your best to see he's given a sentence that will enable him to walk free from the court-room, in full view of his fellow-Methodists.'

Sir Lewis Hearle opened his mouth to register a protest, but Richard Oxnam raised a hand to silence him.

'Hear me out before you say anything. That crowd is going to double, perhaps even treble, by midday. Send Jago to prison and you'll have a riot on your hands, whether you've read the Act to them or not. What's more, you'll have given them a leader – a martyr to the Methodist cause. He will become an inspiration to every malcontent Methodist in the county – and, just in case you don't already know, *one in three of Cornwall's population is a Methodist*. It means that the county you represent in Parliament is a *Methodist* county. I know . . . I know, you're about to tell me that these people are miners, fishermen and farm labourers – non-voting peasants, whose views don't matter a damn.'

Richard Oxnam leaned forward in his chair and emphasised his next words with an admonishing finger. 'You're wrong, Sir Lewis. Dangerously wrong. Oh, I don't doubt that in London and these new industrial towns of the north, the Wesleyans are attracting riff-raff. The Methodists are organised. They have discipline and communications, and are reaching the people. No agitator worthy of the name will miss the opportunity to join such an organisation and use it for his own ends. But things are different here in Cornwall. Our people don't follow like sheep just because someone happens to bleat louder than his fellows. Methodism is becoming respectable here. One day it will be the same elsewhere. It's showing men the way to God. Before you know it, Methodism will be attracting respectable men of substance to its ranks – your artisan, yeoman farmer and merchant. Householders, Sir Lewis. *Voters*. Men who put you into Parliament at the last election – and who'll damn soon vote you out again if they don't like what they see.'

Richard Oxnam sank back in his chair once more. 'Be very careful, Sir Lewis, very careful indeed – whatever your personal feelings about Methodism. No doubt you'll have many opportunities to make life difficult for them but, for now, be circumspect, I beg you.'

Satisfied that he had put his message across to the baronet, Richard Oxnam picked up his glass and sat looking at his visitor across the rim of it.

Sir Lewis Hearle viewed Cornwall's sheriff with suspicion. 'If I were the Prime Minister, I would go much farther than Perceval in putting down dissident religious groups, such as the Wesleyans. They are spawning-beds for disaffection and revolution. However, I am grateful to you for expressing concern about my future. Perhaps you will tell me why you have this sudden interest? As far as I am aware, we have never met socially. Are you one of Wesley's converts?'

'I find you offensive, Sir Lewis, and I don't give a damn about your future. But, if the Methodists are pushed too hard, they – and other dissenters – are likely to follow the example of the Luddite reformers and other malcontents. Such unrest will bring about the downfall of your party. This would not please me at all just now; the Whig opposition is far too committed to reform. It might also light the fires of a popular revolution, enthusiastically aided by France, of course. If you and your government wish to curb the power of the Methodists, I suggest you resort to more subtle means than you appear to favour at the moment. Make the practice of their religion difficult for them. They have few enough places of worship at the moment – be sure you keep it that way. God's bounty is less apparent when a man's family stands in the open for two hours every Sunday, with rain trickling down their necks. Make them discontented with their church, and with one another. It should not be impossible for a determined man. Without Wesley, Methodism is a church without a leader. The movement is already falling apart in other parts of the country. There is a breakaway group calling itself "The New Connection", or some such. Before long there will be another, the "Primitive" Methodists. Your Preacher Jago will become one of these. As the groups become smaller and more introspective, their following will fall away and members will return to the Established Church. But use a sledgehammer to crack them and they will band together so tightly they will break the Government.'

The Sheriff gave Sir Lewis Hearle a disarming smile. 'Even if the consequences for the remainder of the country are far less serious than I have painted them, there will be a major disturbance here if Jago is convicted. Couple this with the demonstrations staged by the miners against rising food-prices and it might be sufficient to deny my son the baronetcy I am determined he will one day inherit from me. Do you understand my concern now, Sir Lewis?'

Sir Lewis Hearle rose to his feet and extended his hand. 'I owe you an apology, Mr Oxnam. I assure you I will do nothing to put your baronetcy in jeopardy.'

Nothing Richard Oxnam had said had changed Sir Lewis Hearle's opinion of Methodism. He detested their pious dedication and narrow-minded views on religion. He saw them as a threat to the rural way of life he and his ancestors had enjoyed for centuries and which was beginning to crumble away throughout the land. But Sir Lewis was no fool. Richard Oxnam had offered him sound advice. He would act upon that part of it which affected him.

Josiah Jago might be convicted in the St Austell magistrates' court, but Sir Lewis Hearle would not be sitting on the bench.

5

As Preacher Josiah Jago emerged from the St Austell court-room, the cheers of the huge crowd greeted a thoroughly bewildered man.

Even as he waited on the stairs that led from the dark and dank cells to the magistrates' court above, a gloating gaoler had informed him that he was likely to meet many of his fellow-preachers in prison. The gaoler had added darkly that in other parts of the country Methodist preachers were being referred to higher courts, with recommendations for transportation to the Australian penal colonies.

Josiah Jago knew he had done nothing to bring such a dreadful sentence upon himself, but, then, he *had* been arrested without reason. Anything was likely.

Then Josiah Jago's name was called, and suddenly everything became confused. Following a heated exchange between magistrate, constables and the rector who had laid the charges, it appeared there had been an error in the wording of the charge for which he had been arrested.

The matter was discussed in a three-cornered, shouted argument that was more often than not drowned in the din made by the church bells. A constable had been despatched to order the bell-ringers to cease their vigorous enterprise for the duration of the court hearing, but he returned to shout an explanation for his lack of success. The bell-ringers had locked themselves inside the tower and would not open the door to anyone.

Upon receipt of this information, the magistrate made a ruling that left the rector of Fowey angry and red-faced. The charge against Josiah Jago was reduced to that of causing an unlawful obstruction in the streets of Fowey whilst holding a prayer-meeting.

The case was swiftly proved and he was fined ten shillings, or fourteen days in prison in default. Josiah Jago declared himself unable to pay the fine when, much to his surprise, the voice of his son called from the back of the crowded court-room, offering to pay the fine into court immediately.

Passing the money to a court official, Nathan grasped his father's arm and bustled him from the court, half-afraid that the determined preacher would take a stubborn stand on the sheer injustice of his arrest and conviction.

Fortunately, Josiah Jago was much too confused to invoke his principles. The events of the morning had proved too much. The unexpected appearance of his son came as a great relief.

Josiah Jago's confused state of mind was not helped when he saw the huge crowd waiting beyond the doors of the magistrates' court. As their cheers momentarily rose above the bell-ringers' determined cacophony, Nathan felt his father's fingers tighten their grip upon his arm.

There followed a wild scene on the steps of the magistrates' court, as joyful Methodist well-wishers surged forward to shake the hand of the circuit preacher and slap him on the back in boisterous greeting.

A cry went up calling for a prayer of thanksgiving to the Lord for His servant's release, and Josiah Jago sank to his knees, grateful for the opportunity to perform such a familiar act.

Preacher Josiah Jago had been found guilty of obstructing a little-used footpath on the outskirts of Fowey village. Here, in busy St Austell Town, with more and more Methodists pouring in from the surrounding countryside, three thousand men, women and children sank to their knees in prayer in the main thoroughfares, bringing the whole town to a standstill. It made a mockery of the preacher's conviction. None was more aware of the irony of the situation than the Reverend Nicholas Kent. Unable to pick his way through the kneeling throng, he was forced to stand in silent fury and observe the paean of an alien congregation, one larger than any he had ever seen before.

The prayers over, father and son made slow progress through the ecstatic crowd until they arrived at the stable where the St Austell Constable had boarded the preacher's donkey.

The preacher led the animal through the waiting masses until Nathan insisted that he ride the beast, and eventually they left the people and the deafening noise of the bells behind them.

For the first mile, Josiah Jago rode in a deeply troubled silence, reliving the events of the last couple of days, his mind trying to grasp the implications of his arrest.

Glancing frequently at his father, Nathan saw a thin, ageing man, dressed soberly in a black serge suit, his low-crowned hat pulled down over his forehead, the wide brim misshapen by many inclement seasons. Josiah rode the donkey with only a threadbare blanket for a saddle, and rope harness with which to guide the beast. It was a small donkey, and more than once the preacher's feet touched the ground as he swayed on his thoughtful way.

In a bid to break into his father's morose mood, Nathan said: 'I would have thought a pony better for your work. You'd find it quicker, surely?'

With a visible effort, Josiah Jago brought his thoughts back to the present. 'Speed isn't essential to an itinerant preacher. I've composed many a fine sermon sitting on the back of old Barnabas here. Besides, he's not such a fussy feeder as a horse.'

Suddenly, Josiah Jago smiled wanly. 'I'm sorry, son. I haven't yet told you how pleased I am to see you. But, then, I doubt if you expected to arrive home to find your pa in prison! It's a strange homecoming. How did your mother take the news?'

'I don't know. I was at Venn Farm when I learned of your arrest. I sent Nell to Pentuan and arrived at St Austell just in time to pay your fine. What's it all about? You must have upset someone very important to have them turn the full force of the law upon you. If the magistrate hadn't reduced the charges, you'd be on your way to Bodmin Gaol to await sentencing at the Quarter Sessions, with the certainty of transportation ahead of you.'

'I know . . . I know,' Josiah Jago nodded grimly. 'But I am guilty only of bringing the message of the Lord to His people, and of leading them to Him. I've caused hurt to no man, though I may have pricked the pride of a few Church of England clergy.'

There was a pained expression upon Josiah Jago's face. 'That's the truth, Nathan. It was the Church who brought the prosecution. It was aimed, not at me, but at the Methodist movement as a whole. The gaoler told me preachers are being arrested throughout the land.'

'Something must have happened to upset the government,' mused Nathan. 'They'll be behind the Church, you can be certain. You'd best remain at home in Pentuan for a week or two. The situation will be clearer by then. We'll know what's happening.'

As Nathan had expected, his father shook his head vigorously. 'I won't be turned from my duty. I'll go about the Lord's business as usual – and so will every Methodist preacher in the land. This is a time for determination. We need to show both the Government and our friends that the Methodist Society is here to stay. Perhaps I'll be arrested again, but there will be another preacher eager to take my place. You saw that gathering in St Austell today. They came to show the world we are no "hole-in-a-corner" society. We are a church, Nathan. One day the Government will have to recognise us. When that glorious day arrives I want to be able to thank the Lord for allowing me to be a party to His will. But enough of my chatter. There will be much thinking and even more praying before such hopes are realised. Tell me about yourself. How are you keeping? Are you home for long? And this . . . this "prize-fighting" – are you still earning your living in a manner that's shameful to the Lord?'

Nathan knew the futility of attempting to persuade his father to change his mind. Josiah Jago was a stubborn man. Once he had come to a decision about something, he closed his mind to all argument. It had happened many years before in respect of Nathan's prize-fighting. John Wesley was known to have been opposed to wrestling, Cornish hurling, and all other aggressive forms of sport and recreation. Therefore, Josiah Jago had never approved of his son's career as a prize-fighter, even when success and fame came Nathan's way.

Nathan told his father he had retired from the ring. He had, he said, returned home to Cornwall to resume fishing for a living.

Josiah Jago was overjoyed to know his son had forsaken the temptations of the great cities to take up the way of life followed by generations of Cornish Jagos. Then Nathan informed his father that he intended to break from Jago tradition in favour of drift-fishing.

Josiah Jago's dismay caused him temporarily to forget his own problems. As Annie Jago had predicted, her husband echoed the argument of the majority of Cornish fishermen, declaring that drift-fishing deprived inshore seine-fishermen of a living and ought to be banned.

Nathan could be almost as stubborn as his father when he chose to be, and he had been prepared for such opposition. He pointed out that the laws of the land provided more than ample protection to the seiner, and were as outdated as the law that had resulted in Josiah Jago's arrest. In support of drift-fishing, Nathan repeated the argument he had given to his mother and to Sammy Mizler. A drift-fisherman could operate all year round. He used a large boat that would give work to a fair-sized crew and employment for many women in the fish-cellars.

Josiah Jago would not allow himself to be convinced, and Nathan thought the argument was closed when he remarked that, as everyone felt the same about drifting, it was doubtful if he would ever be able to purchase a cellar.

For some minutes the preacher struggled with his conscience as he weighed the evils of drift-fishing against those of prize-fighting. Eventually, he said quietly: 'I don't agree with drift-fishing. I never will. But John Wesley pointed out the evil in prize-fighting. He said nothing against drift-fishing. I know of a fish-cellar for sale. It's in Pentuan – or as near as makes no difference.'

Reaching out excitedly, Nathan brought his father's donkey to a not altogether unwilling halt in order to hear more.

'You know of a *Pentuan* fish-cellar for sale? Who's selling?'

There were only four fish-cellars in Pentuan, each owned by a number of shareholders. Shares were occasionally offered for sale, but unless a concern had suffered a particularly disastrous season it was rare for a whole cellar – which included boats, nets and equipment – to come on to the market.

'Two weeks ago I buried Ned Hoblyn. You've heard of him?'

Nathan nodded silently.

'He moved to Portgiskey Cove a few years back and went into business with a few partners – most of them as dubious a set of characters as Hoblyn was himself. Over the years he bought them all out. Now there's just a widow and a daughter left behind. No doubt they'll be pleased to sell to the first customer who comes along. Try them. Perhaps when you start thinking like a fisherman again you'll come back to seining.'

Nathan's interest had been whetted far more than his father knew. Ned Hoblyn had once been the south coast's most notorious smuggler. That was when he lived farther west, in Prussia Cove. Nathan had once known him *very* well, but he could not tell his father that *he* had once worked for the well-known smuggler.

Nathan also knew Portgiskey Cove. Situated just off the end of Pentuan's half-mile strip of sandy beach, it would have suited Hoblyn's clandestine purposes admirably. Hidden from the view of the fishing village by a protruding fold of the cliff, Hoblyn could have carried out his chosen trade in absolute secrecy. Access to Portgiskey was easy enough from the beach at low tide, but when the water rose it could only be reached via a tortuous path from the adjoining cliffs, or by a long and steep-sided, wooded valley that stretched inland from the late smuggler's cottage.

In addition to the house and fish-cellar, Portgiskey

also boasted a tiny deep-water berth. It was an ideal spot for a smuggler – or a fisherman who intended earning his living with an unpopular drifter.

Once he had obtained a cellar, Nathan knew his biggest problem would be over. He had already placed a provisional order for a boat. It was a Brixham-built lugger, one of the best small sea-boats in the world, built in the large Devon fishing village sixty miles away along the English Channel.

Nathan was impatient to hurry to Portgiskey and make an offer to the widow of Ned Hoblyn, but there was no hurrying either Josiah Jago or his donkey.

When father and son reached Pentuan they found that news of the popular preacher's release had gone ahead of them. The whole village, together with Methodists from surrounding communities, waited to give Josiah Jago a triumphant homecoming.

Not until dusk did Nathan manage to slip away from the celebrations, taking Sammy Mizler with him. The tide was on its way in, but they were able to walk to Portgiskey along the firm sand of Pentuan Beach and into the shadow of the cliff separating the beach from Portgiskey Cove.

When they came within sight of the cottage and fish-cellar, Nathan stopped and looked at them with a professional eye. They were in shadow, but he could see enough to fuel his enthusiasm. The incoming tide lapped against black, barnacled rocks lining both sides of the cove and pressed close to the tiny quay wall that rose to twice a man's height. The boat Nathan had ordered would berth here comfortably.

Behind the quay was a tiny cottage. It was surrounded by a low wall that served little purpose, but would prove useful as a seat for men repairing nets. The 'cellar' was attached to the side of the cottage. With an adjacent store and a loft for fishing-tackle, it was larger than the cottage itself.

There was a low, uncertain light burning inside the cottage, but Nathan knocked for many minutes before there was any movement within.

Through the lightly curtained window he saw a shadow cross the room, then the flickering lamp was turned down so low that everything inside became indistinct. A few minutes later there was a sound from behind the door and a woman's voice called in a hoarse whisper.

'Who's there? What do you want at this time of night?'

Nathan and Sammy Mizler looked at each other quizzically. Although it was quite dark in the shadowed cove, it was hardly more than six o'clock.

'It's Nathan Jago. Preacher Jago's son. I'd like to talk to you – about the fish-cellar.'

'I've not met any son of Preacher Jago. Away with you and come back at a decent hour, when I can see your face in the light of day.'

A quickly stifled giggle escaped from Sammy Mizler. In London the working day would just be drawing to a close. Men and women would be looking forward to the delights of the evening. Yet here was a woman complaining that it was too late to receive callers.

Nathan frowned in annoyance. His was the impatience of a man anxious to secure his chosen future.

'I'd like to talk to you about your fish-cellar, Mrs

Hoblyn. I'm prepared to make an offer to buy it from you.'

After a long pause, the unseen woman replied: 'You'll need to talk about that to my daughter, Amy. I don't have nothing to do with the business.'

'Fine. Ask Amy to come to the door. I'll talk to *her*.'

'You can't. She's not at home.'

Exasperated by the futile conversation, Nathan asked: 'Where is she? I'll go and find her.'

'Amy's out . . . She's fishing,' came the reply.

'Fishing? At this time of night?' Nathan was momentarily puzzled. She would not be seine-fishing in the darkness, and Nathan knew his father would have told him had the Hoblyns been engaged in drifting. Then a thought occurred to him. After all, Amy *was* a Hoblyn.

'Who's with your daughter? Can I wait to meet her when she comes back?'

'She's on her own – line-fishing. Now, go away – right away. Don't think that because I'm a widow-woman you can do as you like. I've got a blunderbuss here. It's loaded and it's pointing straight at the door.'

Sammy Mizler scrambled away from the thin wooden door, and Nathan hastily moved to one side of the doorway.

'All right, Mrs Hoblyn. I'm going. I'll be back to see you and your daughter tomorrow.'

Calling an unanswered 'Good night', Nathan walked away. He headed to where the low waves broke against the shore, the sea-water swirling across the gently sloping beach until, all momentum spent, it percolated through the sand.

'The sooner we're away from here the better,' said

Sammy Mizler, looking anxiously over his shoulder at the shadowy outline of the dimly lit cottage. 'Guns make me nervous at the best of times. Put one in the hands of a woman who thinks we're going to break into her home and attack her and I become terrified!'

'We're not leaving,' said Nathan unexpectedly. 'We'll go as far as the rocks and wait there for Amy Hoblyn.'

'I don't understand. The woman in the house said her daughter was off somewhere, fishing. Our business will wait until morning.'

'I don't believe she *is* fishing,' explained Nathan. 'Ned Hoblyn was once the most notorious smuggler along this coast. I doubt if he gave it up when he moved here. It's my belief that his daughter is carrying on the family business. It's something I'll need to know about before I make an offer for the fish-cellar. If the Hoblyn women are out to make as much money as possible before selling up, they'll take chances. If word gets about that Portgiskey is being used for smuggling, we'll never be free of the Revenue men. They'll stop and search our boats most nights, raid the fish-cellar and generally do their best to ruin us.'

'But what if this girl and her friends find us here and mistakes *us* for Revenue men?'

Nathan smiled in the darkness at Sammy Mizler's fears. 'Then we'll have a fight on our hands. It will be just like old times. Remember the prize-fight you arranged for me in Whitechapel – when the referee gave me the verdict and the crowd disagreed? Now, that was a fight to remember.'

'I didn't have a blunderbuss pointing in my direction then.'

'Don't worry, Sammy. She'll probably miss,' said Nathan unsympathetically. 'We'll settle down on these rocks. But keep quiet. Sound travels for miles across the water on a still night like this.'

Sammy Mizler pulled his coat collar high about his ears and wedged himself between two damp rocks. He thought longingly of the familiar narrow streets of London. There would be a hint of fog there on such a night as this, and the sounds and smells of a busy city all about: the clip-clop of horses' hooves on cobbled streets; the rattle of carriage wheels; hoarse voices of hawkers advertising their wares; and the all-pervading smell of pitch hanging on the air from the flaming torches borne by carriage-boys. But, most of all, Sammy missed the people who filled the litter-strewn streets – busy, lounging, chattering, drunken, happy, belligerent people.

An hour after the two men had settled themselves among the rocks, the lamp in the little Hoblyn cottage was turned up and placed in a window, its arc of light falling just short of the spot where they sat. It was quite obviously a signal to a boat, but nothing occurred immediately. After remaining in their positions for another half-hour, Nathan and Sammy Mizler were obliged to move to higher ground as the tide came in farther.

Another hour went by before Nathan suddenly reached across and touched Sammy Mizler's arm.

'Listen,' he whispered. 'Can you hear anything?'

Sammy Mizler had heard the sound at the same moment as Nathan. It was the squeak of a small pulley, as a boat's sail was lowered. It was some little distance out, probably at the entrance to the small cove. Moments later there came the sound of muffled oars, straining against cloth-bound rowlocks.

Easing himself from his uncomfortable position, Nathan moved stiffly and cautiously in the direction of the cottage. Sammy Mizler, heart beating rapidly in nervous anticipation, followed. The two men skirted the cottage and moved into the shadow of the fish-cellar. A few minutes later a boat bumped against the quay steps. A small figure jumped from the boat into the dim light, rope in hand, and secured the vessel.

Nathan waited to see how many others had taken part in Amy Hoblyn's nocturnal 'fishing' trip. To his surprise, Peggy Hoblyn had been telling the truth. The girl had been out alone.

As he watched, Amy Hoblyn went to the door of the cottage and knocked softly, calling: 'It's me, Ma. Let me in.'

There was the loud sound of bolts being drawn, the door opened and the girl slipped inside, the door being quickly closed and bolted after her.

'Now's our chance. I want to look at that boat.'

Crouching low, Nathan ran across the space between fish-cellar and quay, scrambling down the steps to the boat riding easily below. Sammy Mizler followed, but hesitated at the bottom of the steps.

'What are we looking for?' Sammy Mizler could just make out Nathan's shadowy figure at the stern of the small boat.

Nathan's reply took the form of a grunt of satisfaction as he located a thin rope leading out over the stern of the fishing-vessel. He began to haul on the rope. It was hard work, and he knew that the other end had been weighted with a heavy rock. It took fully five minutes of determined heaving and straining before something hard bumped against the wooden stern of the boat.

Reaching over the side with both hands, Nathan lifted a small barrel into the boat. He did not need to trace the chiselled words on the side of the barrel to know it contained French cognac. The taut rope extending from the barrel out towards the bay was a clear indication that there were more out there.

Suddenly there came the rasp of flint upon steel above them, and a crude pitch-coated brand spluttered into life on the quay. In the inconstant light, Nathan and Sammy Mizler saw two women looking down at them. The one who held the torch was a scrawny, wild-eyed woman of middle-age. The other was young, with short, dark hair. In her hands she held a brass-barrelled blunderbuss, its bell-shaped mouth yawning in their direction.

'That's them,' screeched the older woman. 'That's them, I tell you. I'd know Revenue men anywhere. Knew it as soon as I saw them from the window. Preacher's son, indeed! Shoot them now, Amy.'

Sammy Mizler moaned in fear and crouched at the bottom of the steps as the young woman raised the gun menacingly.

'I *am* Preacher Jago's son,' declared Nathan firmly. He was as aware as Sammy Mizler of the danger they were in.

'Oh? Then what are you doing in my boat, preacher's son?'

Amy Hoblyn's voice was steady, but the tone was no more friendly than her mother's had been.

'I was wondering what fishing you'd been doing in

the darkness. Before making an offer for your fish-cellar I wanted to satisfy myself that I'm not likely to have Revenue men tramping through the place at all hours of the day and night.'

'Don't listen to his crafty talk, Amy. If we don't kill them, we'll end our days rotting in the straw of a gaol cell.'

'Hush, Ma.' To the relief of both men, Amy Hoblyn lowered the barrel of the blunderbuss slightly. To Nathan she said: 'The cellar's not for sale. Who told you it was?'

'My father. He told me he'd buried Ned Hoblyn two weeks ago. I was sorry to hear the news. Your pa was a good fisherman, as well as being one of the best sailors I've ever met.'

'You knew Pa? How? When? I've never seen you before.' Amy made her mother hold the spluttering torch out over the edge of the quay in a bid to see Nathan more clearly.

All the time they had been talking, Nathan had been holding the keg of brandy in front of him. Now he lowered it slowly to the bottom of the boat. Straightening up, he said: 'When I was fifteen. I was finding it difficult to live up to my father's standards. I ran away to sea, and made my way to Falmouth. Getting a berth in a ship wasn't as easy as I thought it would be. Then I met up with your pa. He gave me work. You and I *have* met, but you were hardly more than a babe then – and Ned Hoblyn liked to keep his family and his work separate.'

Amy Hoblyn was still undecided whether or not to believe Nathan, although she knew that what he had said was true. When they were living farther west, her father *had* tried to keep work and home life apart.

Her mother was less easily won over. 'Take no notice of him, girl. He's said no more than any Revenue officer would know about your pa. It's a trick.'

'No, Mrs Hoblyn,' Nathan said evenly. Ned Hoblyn's widow was evidently not in her right mind. He did his best to humour her. 'I knew your husband. I knew Beville, too. He and I were impressed into service with the Royal Navy together.'

The effect of Nathan's words upon Peggy Hoblyn was astounding. Her attitude changed immediately. After twice trying unsuccessfully to mouth the words, she whispered: 'You knew Beville? You knew my boy?'

'I was with him when he died in *Victory*. Some of the grapeshot that killed him is still lodged in my leg.'

Sammy Mizler breathed a sigh of relief at the sudden raising of tension. He was interested, too. He knew little of Nathan's life before he had taken up prize-fighting.

The brand in Peggy Hoblyn's hand was spluttering in its death throes, and Amy said: 'You'd better both come inside the house where we can see you better – but don't come empty-handed. Bring two of those kegs with you and haul the others close to the boat. There are eight altogether. Ma and I will bring them in later.'

She paused, then added: 'Just in case you aren't all you claim to be, remember I'll have this blunderbuss with me.'

Sammy Mizler helped Nathan to haul in the remainder of the brandy-kegs, then they each brought one up the steps and carried them to the empty fish-cellar. Here they were hidden in a tomblike hole beneath one of the flagstones.

There were already more than a dozen kegs inside the stone-lined hole. It was clear that this was not the first occasion on which Amy had been 'night fishing'.

Peggy Hoblyn led the way inside the house, with Amy bringing up the rear. The lamp was turned up and, in its steadier light, Nathan saw that Amy was no more than seventeen years of age – the same age as Nell, Nathan's sister. Her next words confirmed that Amy, in fact, knew her.

'If you're telling me the truth about being Preacher Jago's son, you'll have no difficulty in naming your sister.'

'Nell? She's married to Tom Quicke now, living up at Venn Farm. You know her?'

'Yes. Pa might have been a smuggler, but he came from a Methodist family. He wanted me to learn to read and write a little. He sent me to classes in Pentuan chapel. Nell was there, too.'

The conversation was interrupted by a pitiful plea from Amy's mother: 'Tell me about Beville. I never saw him from the time he was taken. He was my only son . . .'

Peggy Hoblyn screwed up her eyes in an unsuccessful bid to dam the tears that trembled there.

Nathan looked questioningly at Amy, and she nodded her head. Then, in the little room, lit by a single pilchard-oil lamp, Nathan told his story, the noise of the sea lapping against the quay outside providing a background to his words.

He told how he and Beville, with two other men,

kept a rendezvous with a French merchantman on behalf of Ned Hoblyn. They were transferring an undutied cargo to their boat when they were surprised by a frigate of the Royal Navy, on her way to join Nelson's fleet in Mediterranean waters. The frigate captain put a prize-crew on the French ship, hanged the two experienced smugglers for trading with the enemy, and pressed the two fifteen-year-old boys into service with the Navy.

Once in the Mediterranean, Nathan and Beville were transferred to *Vanguard*, Admiral Nelson's flagship. They were just in time to take part in the battle of the Nile.

For two years the boys gained experience of shipboard warfare in the service of King George III's most famous admiral. Then, in 1800, Nelson resigned his command to travel overland to England from Naples with Lady Hamilton and her ageing ambassador husband.

Soon afterwards, Nathan and Beville were chosen to help sail a captured French man-of-war to England, where they transferred to *Elephant*, another English man-of-war.

In 1801, called back to the service he loved, Vice-Admiral Lord Nelson hoisted his flag in *Elephant*. On two foggy March nights, Nathan and Beville crewed an open boat from which Nelson himself took vital soundings in the treacherous waters of Copenhagen. They were to enable him to take his ships within cannon range of the Danish capital.

Nathan was at the helm of *Elephant* when the three ships in line ahead of the flagship ran aground on their way to do battle with the enemy. With the assistance of Beville, Nathan put the helm over and led the remainder of the fleet past the stranded men-of-war. The result was another glorious victory for the brilliant British admiral.

In 1803, when Nelson raised his flag in HMS *Victory*, he scoured the fleet to locate his Cornish helmsman and transferred him to the flagship. Yet again, Beville Hoblyn went with Nathan. Together they pursued the fleet of the French Admiral Pierre de Villeneuve from the Mediterranean to the West Indies, and back again to the waters of Europe.

On Monday, 21 October 1805, within sight of Cape Trafalgar, Nelson's fleet and the combined fleets of the French and Spanish navies met in battle. At one o'clock in the afternoon a shot shattered the wheel of HMS *Victory*, fatally wounding Beville and driving splinters of wood and metal deep into Nathan's legs. Beville died that same evening, within minutes of England's adored admiral. Nathan was with him.

When Nathan ended his narrative, husky-voiced with emotion, Peggy Hoblyn, eyes red from prolonged weeping, clasped his hands in hers and drew them to her face.

'God bless you, boy. When my time comes I'll rest easier for knowing what happened to my Beville.'

Dropping his hands, the weeping woman drew her apron to her face and scuttled from the room, and Amy hurried after her.

'Was that really how it happened?' Sammy Mizler put the question.

Nathan nodded, not trusting himself to speak again just yet. He felt emotionally drained after reliving the dramatic events of five years before. It was the first time he had related the story of Trafalgar to anyone.

When Amy returned to the room, she looked at Nathan with new respect. 'Thank you for telling Ma about Beville. The news of my brother's death affected her very deeply at the time. Not long after that the Revenue men raided our house down the coast, while Pa was away. Ma fought them off as best she could, but one of them hit her on the head with his musket. She was unconscious for days and was never the same again. Since then, the only things in life that have had any meaning for her have been the memories of Beville – and a deep hatred of Revenue men.'

Nathan nodded sympathetically. 'She'll have had as much excitement as she can take for one night. We'll leave you now. Before we go, Sammy and me will bring the rest of the brandy to the cellar. Your ma will be in no state to help you tonight, and by dawn they'll be high and dry. A Revenue man will be able to see them from a mile away.'

Nathan turned to leave the cottage, but Amy Hoblyn put out a hand to stop him. 'I thought you came here because you wanted a fish-cellar?'

Nathan looked puzzled. 'But you said your cellar isn't for sale.'

'It isn't. But I can't run a fishing business by myself. If I could, I wouldn't need to spend the night hours in an open boat, waiting for a French night-runner who might keep the rendezvous or might not. If he does come, I'll have to spend at least half an hour convincing the captain and his crew that my body isn't part payment for their brandy. I may even have to draw the pistol I carry before they believe me. One day I'll need to use it. I don't want that.'

For a moment, Amy Hoblyn looked very young and vulnerable. 'I'm not going to part with the cellar, but I *could* do with a partner. I'll put up the cellar and pay a fair amount towards nets and any other equipment we'll need. The profits can be shared equally.'

Nathan's interest quickened. It was a generous offer. In the few minutes they had spent in the cellar he had seen that it was fully fitted out for fish-curing. But there was another matter to be settled.

'I've already got a partner – Sammy. I also have firm ideas about the kind of fishing enterprise I want to run. Sammy is the man who'll organise the sale of all the fish I catch, and he's ready to risk his own money on his ability to sell.'

Amy looked from Nathan to Sammy, and back again. After some hesitation, she said: 'I'll not allow others to have a bigger share of the business, but I'm willing to make it a four-way partnership. You and Sammy . . . me and Ma. You'd run the fishing side of the business and I'd organise the cellar with Ma. She may not be able to think as straight as she once did, but she knows as much about curing, packing and salting as anyone in Cornwall.'

'Right! We'll need to employ two crews and keep them busy night and day if we're to fish my way – and they won't have to mind being unpopular. I'll be bringing a deep-water boat here, for year-round fishing. For drifting.'

Amy's expressive eyes widened. Drift-fishermen were as welcome as lepers in this part of Cornwall. She lapsed into deep thought. When the seconds had become minutes, Nathan said: 'You've had a busy evening, and I've given you much to think about. Discuss what I've said with someone whose opinion you value. Let me know your decision when you make up your mind. I'm staying with my family in Pentuan village. You know the house.'

Amy looked directly at Nathan for the first time in many minutes and met his gaze. To Sammy Mizler it seemed they had forgotten that he was in the room with them.

'I've thought about it as much as I'll ever need to. What name are we going to give our boat?'

6

Nathan realised that in the small, gossip-hungry community of Pentuan his new fishing venture would not remain a secret for very long. Before it became general knowledge, he wanted to have a word with Sir Lewis Hearle. As squire of the manor of Polrudden, he claimed the tithe rights of the fishing village.

Every fisherman in the village paid tithe money to Sir Lewis Hearle on the amount of fish he landed. The origins of such payments had been lost along the tortuous path of history. It was believed tithes at one time provided an income for the Church. In return, the Church fulfilled the spiritual needs of the community. The money would also have subsidised the lord of the manor, who was responsible for the defence of surrounding villages and contributed heavily towards poor relief, asylums and law and order.

Many of the responsibilities of both Church and

landowner had fallen away over the centuries, but the tithe payments remained, a source of irritation to those forced to pay them.

Nathan had only ever seen Polrudden Manor from a distance. As a village lad he had fallen in love with the beautiful old house, but had never dared to come close. To have approached the manor-house along the curving tree-fringed driveway as he was doing now would have been quite unthinkable. The driveway had been reserved for the gentry of the county and their families. In all probability it still was, but Nathan was no longer a young village boy wearing a threadbare jersey and clumsy boots roughly put together from leather remnants. He had travelled the world, earning the respect of great men such as Admiral Lord Nelson. He was also a prize-fighting champion, and had been entertained in fashionable London clubs by aristocratic supporters of the prize-ring.

As he approached the manor-house that had over-awed him only a few years before, Nathan observed that the magnificently proportioned house had an unmistakable air of genteel neglect. Nathan was re-minded of an aged member of the Naples royal family he had seen in a welcoming party assembled to greet Nelson after his great victory of the Nile. She had been an elegant but infirm old lady, her clothes faded tokens of an earlier, splendid age.

The first person Nathan saw in the grounds of the house was Elinor Hearle. Bloodied from fingertips to elbow, she had just acted as midwife to one of her father's prized mares. Coming round the side of the house from the stables, she was on her way to tell Sir

Lewis that the mare had produced a splendid black filly, sired by her own stallion, Napoleon.

Recovering from her surprise at seeing Nathan, she exclaimed: 'Are you looking for me?' She was in a rare good mood. Holding both hands out in front of her, she added: 'I've just delivered a foal. It was a messy business.'

Seeing Elinor Hearle like this, her hair hanging untidily about her face, he was reminded of the first occasion on which they had met, when he had mistaken her for a town girl. He preferred this image to the haughty, autocratic girl who had come to Venn Farm.

'I'm here to see Sir Lewis, but I *have* been hoping I would see you again. I want to thank you for telling me of the arrest of my father. I was able to get to St Austell in time to pay his fine and save him from prison.'

Elinor shrugged. 'It cost me nothing – but don't mention the matter to my father. He'd not thank me for keeping a dissenter from prison – especially a Methodist preacher. I hope you're not here because of that incident?'

'No, I'm here to discuss business with Sir Lewis.'

Elinor's face suggested disbelief, but they had arrived at the front door now and she said: 'Wait here. I'll find him and see if he wants to speak to you.'

Elinor Hearle was gone for twenty minutes. When she returned she had washed her arms and brushed and drawn back her long, dark hair.

'My father is in his study. I'll take you to him.'

She did not mention that Sir Lewis Hearle had watched Nathan's arrival from the window of his

study and angrily declared that he should have come
to the back door of Polrudden. The very fact that she
kept his words to herself surprised Elinor. She attributed her unaccustomed tact to the manner in which she
and Nathan Jago had first met.

Sir Lewis Hearle was seated at a large rosewood
desk, close to the study window. Panelled from floor
to ceiling in the same wood, the room contained an
impressive carved marble fireplace. Around the walls,
the portraits of successive Hearles cast stern-faced
disapproval upon the visitor. It had once been a truly
magnificent room but, in keeping with the remainder
of the house, the wooden panels were dulled by years
of neglect and the room smelled damp and musty.

On the desk were a number of letters to which Sir
Lewis Hearle appeared to be writing replies. The
baronet did not look up immediately, neither did
he acknowledge Nathan's presence. For some minutes
his quill pen continued to scratch across the page,
occasionally replenished from a squat, silver-capped
inkpot.

Elinor stood silently beside Nathan for a couple of
long minutes. Then she strode to the door, opened it
and slammed it noisily before returning to the centre
of the room.

Sir Lewis Hearle looked up and frowned at his
daughter.

'I thought you probably had not heard us arrive,'
she said defiantly.

Ignoring her outburst, the baronet MP turned his
unsmiling attention to Nathan.

'So you're Nathan Jago, the prize-fighter. Champion of all England, I believe? Well, what business do

you have with me? If you're looking for a sponsor for one of your prize-fights, you can forget it. Prize-fighting is outside the law. As far as I'm concerned, that is where it will stay.'

'It's a matter on which you and my father seem to be in full agreement,' said Nathan easily. He did not miss the sudden tightening of the baronet's expression at mention of Josiah Jago. It came as no surprise; Sir Lewis Hearle's opposition to Methodism was no secret. 'But I'm not here to discuss prize-fighting. I'm setting up a fishing venture, buying into the Hoblyn cellar and drift-fishing the year round.'

'Hoblyn a fisherman? Why, the man's a scoundrel. A notorious smuggler. Are you telling me he's had a change of heart and intends earning an honest living? If drift-fishing can be called "honest".'

'Ned Hoblyn is dead and buried, but many so-called "honest" men acquired a rich source of income because of him,' retorted Nathan, stung by Sir Lewis Hearle's attitude. He brought himself under control quickly. He would gain nothing by antagonising the bigoted landowner. 'I'm going into partnership with Ned Hoblyn's widow and daughter. As for drift-fishing, it will bring more work and prosperity to Pentuan than seine-fishing ever has.'

Sir Lewis Hearle glared at Nathan. In truth, he knew little about either drifting or seining, and he cared less. He kept the tithes as high as he dared. Just so long as they were paid on time, he was happy for the fishermen to stay with the smells of their work at the bottom of Pentuan Hill.

'You know the arrangement I have with the seine-fishers, Jago? I take eight pence for each hogshead of fish that leaves the cellar. If sold fresh, it's a twelfth of the value. In addition, owners of boats pay me six guineas a year for each seaworthy boat they own.'

Nathan hid the anger he felt at the sums mentioned by Sir Lewis Hearle. They were exceedingly high. The huge shoals of pilchards might come close inshore once or twice a year – three times in an exceptional year, none at all during a bad one. In these brief and uncertain periods, the fisherman had to catch enough fish to support his family and the families of the cellar workers for a whole year. In an age when a man considered himself fortunate if he averaged a weekly wage of ten shillings throughout the year, Sir Lewis was taking most of the profit and ensuring that the fishermen of Pentuan remained poor. He possessed this right because of an ancient custom that had little or no relevance in early nineteenth-century life.

Sir Lewis Hearle leaned back in his chair and looked up at Nathan arrogantly. 'Of course, if you intend fishing the whole year round, you'll be using your boat more than a seiner, so you'll pay me more boat money. Shall we say twenty guineas a year?'

It was a disgracefully high sum, and Nathan heard Elinor suck in her breath in a gasp of surprise.

Nathan struggled to keep his temper, but only partially succeeded. 'You could as easily say *two hundred* guineas, Sir Lewis, but I'll pay none of the sums you've mentioned. I'll not run the risk of bankruptcy for you. I intend eventually owning a whole fleet of drifters, and there are many tithe-owners along the coast who'll be glad to welcome my business in their ports. I apologise for taking up your time and bid you "Good day".'

'Not so fast.'

Now it was Sir Lewis Hearle's turn to hide both pride and anger. Nathan Jago's name was mentioned with a proprietary approbation by both squire and hired man throughout Cornwall. There was no doubt that he would be welcomed in any fishing community – Fowey, for instance, the town represented by Sir Lewis in Parliament. Sir Lewis's re-election was by no means assured. He needed to woo every voter. If Nathan Jago set up business there, his assets would be sufficient to make *him* a voter. Such a man would also make many friends among the voting community.

'If it's your intention to work a number of boats, you'll naturally employ many local men. I have no wish to do anything that might take work away from them. I'll make it twelve guineas a boat.'

'You'll make it six guineas, the same as a seiner – and *five* pence per hogshead, or a twentieth for fresh fish,' declared Nathan defiantly. He was not certain why Sir Lewis Hearle had not allowed him to walk from the room and seek a cellar outside Pentuan, although he knew it had nothing to do with the well-being of Pentuan fishermen. He thought the answer might lie in the neglected state of Polrudden Manor. The baronet was in sore need of money.

Sir Lewis Hearle shifted his gaze to the desk in front of him, not trusting himself to look at the man who stood before him. It was bad enough that he should have a Methodist preacher's son here in his own house. To listen to him dictating his own terms on a business matter was more than any man of his breeding should have to bear.

However, Sir Lewis Hearle realised that more than money and political security might be gained by having Nathan drift-fishing from Pentuan. He had no doubt that the prize-fighting champion of all England would be able to ride the anger of the Pentuan fishermen, but some of their anger might be directed against Nathan's father. The fact that Nathan was going into business with the family of Ned Hoblyn would also excite comment. Smugglers were known to have been anathema to John Wesley. If it were hinted that Nathan Jago had taken on the mantle of the late Ned Hoblyn under the cover of his drift-fishing business . . .

The Member of Parliament for Fowey looked up from his desk and smiled at Nathan. 'I admire enterprise, Jago – especially when it's likely to improve the lot of Cornishmen. All right, I'll have an agreement drawn up along the lines you suggest. It will be ready for your signature before I return to London.'

Turning to his astonished daughter, Sir Lewis Hearle said, 'Perhaps you will be kind enough to show Mr Jago out, my dear.'

Without another glance at his visitor, Sir Lewis picked up his quill and the sharpened point of the long goose feather began once more to hurry across the surface of the paper on the desk before him.

Outside the house, Elinor looked at Nathan with new, if slightly bemused, respect. 'I never thought I would ever hear anyone dictate to Father as you did without provoking a reply that would have been clearly heard in Pentuan village.'

'It couldn't have been my tactful manner,' Nathan admitted truthfully. 'When I *demanded* tithe reductions I thought I'd gone much too far.'

'So did I!' Elinor laughed and, in a warm, impulsive gesture, laid a hand upon Nathan's arm. 'I held my breath then, hoping you wouldn't mention your father again. That would have been more than he could have accepted – even from *me*.'

'You *hoped* I wouldn't mention my father?' asked Nathan softly. 'Are you telling me you were on my side in there?'

Colour rushed to Elinor's cheeks, and she took her hand from Nathan's arm. 'My father is not the only one who admires enterprise.'

She gave Nathan a look that, had it come from anyone else, he would have regarded as coy. But coyness had no place in Elinor Hearle's character. 'You are a rather remarkable man, Nathan Jago. War hero, champion prize-fighter . . . And now you are turning your talents to fishing. Drift-fishing at that. Had my father been more business-minded, he would have offered to finance your new venture. I am quite certain it will prove highly successful.'

'I'll do my best to justify your faith in me,' mocked Nathan. 'But thank you for your help – and for your support.'

He had taken no more than a dozen paces when Elinor called to him.

'Nathan Jago . . . do you ride?'

'No, I've had very little opportunity to learn.'

Elinor was disappointed, but she did her best to give her shrug the appearance of nonchalance. 'I thought you might be interested in the new filly, but it doesn't matter.'

Turning away, she hurried off round the side of the house. After a moment's hesitation, Nathan walked from Polrudden Manor, heading for Pentuan village.

In his study, Sir Lewis Hearle was watching Nathan's departure. The baronet's expression combined anger and parental concern. He had witnessed Elinor's spontaneous gesture when she rested her hand on Nathan's arm. He had also been watching her face when she called to Jago to ask if he rode. Sir Lewis Hearle knew his daughter well enough to recognise that Nathan Jago's reply *had* mattered to her.

With an oath, the baronet brought his clenched fist down hard upon the wooden windowsill. It was the first time, to his knowledge, that Elinor had shown any interest in a man – and it had to be a man with Nathan Jago's background.

Sir Lewis, in common with his daughter, recognised the exceptional qualities possessed by the prize-fighting champion; but Jago was a villager, a man from common fishing stock. It was unthinkable that Elinor should ever cast more than a glance in his direction. He, Sir Lewis Hearle, third baronet, Member of Parliament for Fowey, and Senior Magistrate of the St Austell Bench, would have to ensure there never was more than a *look* between them.

7

Now the matter of tithe money had been settled, Nathan was ready to collect his new fishing-boat from the Brixham boatyard. At a meeting held that evening at the Hoblyn cottage, Nathan told Sammy Mizler and Amy of his intention.

'How will you travel?' asked Sammy.

'By carriage from St Austell to Plymouth, then either by carriage or on foot from there. It's little more than thirty miles to Brixham from Plymouth. It would be quicker by fishing-boat from Mevagissey, but I want to put off any questions from the Mevagissey men until we have the boat here.'

'I'll travel with you as far as Plymouth,' declared Sammy Mizler. 'I have a feeling we'll be able to market most of our fish there. I would like to go and have a look around.'

'I was hoping you'd come on to Brixham with me. It will need two of us to sail the boat back to Portgiskey.'

'You thought *I* would help you to sail a *boat?*' Sammy Mizler looked at Nathan incredulously. 'Oh, no! I've put money into this dream of yours, I'll direct all my efforts into ensuring its success – but I stay on dry land. Why, I feel ill if an innkeeper rocks my soup when he puts it on the table before me.'

'I'll come with you.' The offer came from Amy, and both men looked at her in surprise.

'Can you think of anyone better to crew the boat? I'm a partner in the business, and I can handle a boat as well as any man.'

Nathan thought of Amy's activities the night before. Few men would have relished the thought of bringing a small boat into Portgiskey Cove on a dark night, as she had done. He shrugged. 'I agree. But who'll look after your ma?'

'She'll be all right for a few days. She can cook and do things that are familiar to her.'

Suddenly the air of mature capability dropped away from Amy as she allowed the eager excitement of a seventeen-year-old girl to come to the fore.

'I've never travelled by coach. How long will it take to get to Plymouth? Will we travel inside or outside?'

Sammy Mizler watched Amy's enthusiasm directed towards Nathan and there was an aching emptiness within him. He looked at Nathan questioningly, wondering if he knew how Amy felt about him. Sammy doubted whether he did. Nathan accepted the admiration of others as a matter of course. Very often he did not even notice. It was most unfair on those like Sammy Mizler who could only stand back and watch the world fall at Nathan's feet.

Nathan thought about Amy's question. The fare to

Plymouth was a guinea for an inside passenger, but only half this amount for a seat outside. He was about to declare that they would travel outside, when he looked up and saw her eager anticipation.

'We'll travel inside, in a style befitting partners in a great new fishing venture.'

Amy squealed with delight. Stretching up on her toes, she reached up and kissed Nathan quickly on the cheek. 'Thank you, Nathan. When do we go?'

'Tomorrow morning. There's no sense wasting time. With any luck there will still be some pilchards about when we get back to Portgiskey. I'd like to have a share in them. Does this suit you, Sammy?'

Sammy Mizler shrugged. 'Who wants my advice? I'll be with you in the morning.'

With this enigmatic remark, he walked out of the cottage, leaving Nathan and Amy gazing after him, wondering what had happened to upset him.

Sammy was not certain himself. Less than a year older than Nathan, his acquaintance with women had been confined to those he had met in London's inns. Many of these had possessed Amy's self-assurance and determination, but not one of them had ever known her natural innocence. Amy was unique in Sammy Mizler's limited experience. He was jealous of Nathan's easy relationship with her – and of the affectionate kiss she had just given him.

In truth, Sammy Mizler was himself something of an innocent, certainly as far as women were concerned. Brought up in London's 'East End', one of a Jewish tailor's over-large family, he had quite literally to fight for recognition, if not his very existence, from an early age. From fighting his brothers and the brutal

Jew-baiting youths of Shoreditch, it was a small step to the prize-ring. Here Sammy Mizler fought brilliantly and with great success for many years. Unfortunately, Sammy was not a big man. In an age when prize-fighting had no weight division he was frequently matched with larger opponents and forced to absorb an increasing amount of punishment. When Sammy met Nathan he left the ring and became advisor and matchmaker to the man who, even then, was tipped as a future champion of all England.

In this world of men, Sammy Mizler felt at home, confident of his own ability. With women he was shy and reserved, unable to express his thoughts. This was how he felt with Amy Hoblyn. After only two meetings with her, Sammy Mizler found himself floundering well out of his emotional depth.

The journey to Plymouth took eight hours and the trio shared the coach with two clergymen from Truro and a very large farmer from Falmouth, who sat in a corner sneezing and snuffling the whole way. The presence of the farmer caused Sammy Mizler great concern. Sammy had an unreasonable fear of colds and illness. It was as much as Nathan could do to prevent his friend from leaving the carriage and travelling outside.

The last part of the journey involved a crossing of the River Tamar at Saltash Passage. At the water's edge the horses were unhitched and the carriage manhandled on to the flat-bottomed ferry-boat. A fresh south-easterly wind was blowing and Sammy Mizler spent the journey huddled dejectedly in a corner of the carriage as the ferry bobbed on the water.

Sammy found some consolation in Amy's very real concern for his well-being, but he breathed a sigh of relief when the ungainly craft was driven ashore on the soft mud of the Devon river bank. The passengers climbed inside the carriage beside Sammy Mizler, four reluctant horses were backed into their traces and, with a jolt, the coach was driven off the ferry, lurching dangerously as it dropped into the mud at an acute angle.

The road from the ferry was both narrow and steep and the coach passengers were tumbled against each other frequently as the coachman whipped up his horses around every sharp bend.

It was not long before the brow of the hill was reached and the coach began the long, gradual descent into Plymouth Town. Soon the high-hedged country road gave the passengers glimpses of muddy creeks and tide-grounded cargo-ships, their masts leaning at a hundred different angles. Around the merchantmen were clustered groups of sailors. Knee-deep, occasionally waist-deep, in black, foul-smelling mud, they scraped and painted, caulked and tarred keels that had gathered barnacles from every ocean of the world.

Then all talking ceased inside the coach as it rattled over the cobbles of Devon's great port. The cobbles soon gave way to stone blocks, and now there were houses on either hand, crowding in upon the coach as it travelled the narrow streets of Plymouth Town. Here Sammy Mizler suddenly blossomed into life, his temporary indisposition cured by the street cries and the bustle of a busy seaport town.

Watching his friend's rapid recovery, Nathan

grinned wryly. Sammy Mizler was an irredeemable city-dweller. A man of his word, Sammy would remain with Nathan and find markets for all the fish that were caught, but his heart would always be in the city. Nathan knew that one day he would return to London.

There was an unmistakable smell of fish in the air as the coach rolled to a halt at the heart of the Barbican. This was the harbourside area of Plymouth, a tangle of inns, narrow streets and alleyways.

This was where Sammy Mizler would find the fish-dock, the market and the merchants. He was to make his own way back to Pentuan – and he had already determined he would find an alternative route to the Saltash passenger-ferry.

Nathan and Amy were fortunate enough to catch a coach from the Barbican inn within minutes of their arrival. It would take them to Dartmouth, from where they would catch a ferry across the river that gave its name to the town, and walk the final two or three miles to Brixham.

There was hardly time for last-minute instructions from Nathan to Sammy Mizler and a breathless 'Goodbye' from Amy as they clambered inside the waiting coach. Then, with horn sounding stridently to clear their path, the coachman slapped the reins over the backs of his horses and the coach moved off on slim, well-greased wheels.

The roads were much better on this side of the River Tamar. As a result, the coaches in use were built for speed, and not for rugged endurance. The coach and horses clattered through tiny villages of thatched houses, covering the miles to Dartmouth in under three hours, Amy enjoying every moment of the speedy journey.

In Dartmouth there was an hour of daylight remaining, and Nathan booked rooms for them in the coaching inn, close to Dartmouth's busy harbour. He told Amy they had travelled far enough for one day. They would make an early start the next morning.

That evening, Nathan and Amy sat down to a meal in the dining-room of the inn, grateful for the fire which crackled cheerfully in the great stone hearth, keeping the chills of the autumn night from the room. The inn was busy, and the talk and laughter from the tap-room beyond the dining-room provided a comforting background for an excellent meal.

Nathan was beginning to feel at peace with the world, warmed by the fire, good ale and Amy's happy chatter, when the sounds coming from the tap-room underwent a dramatic change. Men's voices rose in shouted warning, and the sudden uproar was accompanied by the noise of crashing glasses and splintering wood.

As diners ceased their conversations and serving-girls stopped their work in consternation, the door from the tap-room crashed open and three men hurtled into the dining-room. The door swung shut behind them, and two of the men ran between the tables, fleeing through the door that led to the kitchen. The third man, in search of a way out of the inn, chose the door to the cellar. He disappeared down the steep stone steps with a shout that ceased abruptly as he cannoned off the wall somewhere in the region of the tenth step and fell into the darkness below.

Moments later four blue-jacketed sailors, armed

with cudgels, crowded inside the dining-room. Behind them Nathan could see two more sailors carrying a wildly struggling form between them from the now deserted tap-room. It was a naval press-gang.

A scowling man wearing the uniform and insignia of a boatswain entered the dining-room and glared about him, apparently looking for the three men who had made their escape.

'I'm looking for deserters from one of His Majesty's ships. Where did they go?'

Not a person in the room said a word, and the boatswain's scowl deepened. To his men he said: 'Question every man in the room. If they don't satisfy you as to their identities, take 'em aboard. The Cap'n says he wants ten men. These will do as well as any – and they'll be better fed than most we're likely to gather.'

When the three fugitives had fled from the tap-room, Amy had started up in alarm. Now Nathan stood up slowly, putting himself between her and the men of the press-gang.

'You won't find your deserters in here, bos'n. They'll be long gone by now. I suggest you and your men go off and search elsewhere, leaving us to finish our dinner in peace.'

'You suggest . . . ?' The boatswain glared across the room, head thrust forward aggressively. 'I've seen you somewhere before, mister. Why, you might be a deserter yourself. What's your name?'

'Nathan Jago – and my discharge papers are in order, but they're staying where they belong, in my pocket.'

It was by no means unusual for an able-bodied

sailor's discharge papers to be 'lost' by a press-gang desperate to gather crewmen for one of His Majesty's men-of-war.

'Call off your men, or your captain will find himself short of another five members of his crew.'

Nathan's warning was unnecessary. At the mention of his name, the closest member of the press-gang took a hasty step backwards and the boatswain's expression underwent a sudden change.

'Nathan Jago of *Elephant* and *Victory*? The prize-fighting champion of all England?'

Nathan ignored the question, wary of those members of the press-gang close enough to jump him if the boatswain gave them the order. But the leader of the press-gang had lost all interest in securing Nathan for the Royal Navy.

'That's where I've seen you before – in *Elephant*. I was a gun-layer then.'

Nathan nodded his head in acknowledgement. There was a proud sense of comradeship between men who had served in any ship which Admiral Lord Nelson had commanded, but he had a message for the press-gang boatswain.

'I was in *Elephant* because I'd been pressed into service. These days I get nervous when a press-gang begins to crowd me.'

The boatswain signalled for his men to fall back. At that moment the cellar door crashed open. The man who had fallen down the cellar steps staggered into the dining-room, blood pouring from his nose.

'That's one of them.' A member of the press-gang pointed to the unfortunate and confused deserter. Nathan was temporarily forgotten as the sailors of the press-gang pounced upon their colleague, a dining-table crashing over in their eagerness.

'Take him outside.' The boatswain saw his order carried out, then returned his attention to Nathan. 'I'm proud to renew your acquaintance, Mr Jago. You and your good lady enjoy your dinner, sir. We won't be bothering you again.'

As Nathan pulled out the chair for Amy, the boatswain backed to the door. Pausing there, he called: 'Are you here for a prize-fight, sir? If you are, I'd like to see it.' Giving Nathan a jovial wink, he added: 'I've got a few guineas put aside that I'll wager on your winning.'

'I'm here to buy a fishing-boat and sail it home to Pentuan.'

'Oh!' The boatswain sounded disappointed. He was about to leave when the full significance of what Nathan had said sank into his none-too-agile brain.

'Taking a boat to Pentuan, you say. Then I'll give you a word of caution, Mr Jago. The French are busy about that way. That's why we're here trying to pick up men. We fought a French privateer off Mevagissey only yesterday morning. *Montendre* was her name. She put up a stiff fight. Before we sent her to the bottom with all hands more than ten of our own men were wounded. The Cap'n sent them ashore today. That's when the three men deserted. We're only a frigate, and with ten crew short we need to impress more.' He looked apologetically at Nathan. '*You* know how it is, sir.'

Nathan said nothing and, looking about the dining-room for a last time, the boatswain left, closing the door behind him. Immediately, a buzz of excited conversation rose from the diners and more than one grateful look was cast in Nathan's direction. Had it not been for him, there would have been a number of empty seats in the dining-room by now. A press-gang was supposed to impress only seamen, but when desperately short of sailors they would carry off any able-bodied man, enquiring as to his calling after-wards.

At a nearby table were a number of men dressed in the style popularised by the future King George IV, and later to be termed the 'Regency' style. Their noisy hilarity was proof that they had not feared the press-gang. Now one of their number stood up and came to Nathan's table.

Bowing first to Amy, and then to Nathan, the stranger asked: 'Were you telling the truth about not being here for a prize-fight?'

'I was.'

The stranger's shrug expressed disappointment. 'A pity. I've seen you in action twice, Nathan Jago. I'd put up an uncommon purse to watch you fight again.'

He dropped a card casually on the table beside Nathan's plate. 'When you decide to fight again, make no arrangements before you've spoken to me. I'll put up a stake that will make you the envy of every prize-fighter in England. I won't discuss it now. I can see the events of the evening have distressed your lady. Sir . . . Miss . . .'

Inclining his head at Nathan and Amy in turn, the man returned to his own table.

Turning to Amy, Nathan saw tears in her eyes.

'Nathan, take me out of here, please.' Her voice was a distressed whisper.

Hurriedly, Nathan pushed back his chair and helped Amy to her feet. Aware of the stares of their fellow-diners, he led her from the room. He would have taken her upstairs, but at the doorway she said: 'I . . . I would like to walk for a while.'

'Of course.'

Nathan led her outside, and she clung to his arm as they walked along the uneven pavement, sheltered beneath the upper storeys of houses propped up by granite pillars. Whenever they passed by a lighted window he could see she was still distressed.

'You mustn't upset yourself because of what happened at the inn. The press-gang isn't something of which I approve, but the Navy isn't a bad life for a man.'

Amy shook her head vigorously. 'It's not that. It's what he said about *Montendre*.'

For a moment Nathan was baffled, then he remembered the boatswain's story of the sea-battle.

'*Montendre*? You mean the French ship sunk off Mevagissey? Why should that upset you? We're at war with the French.'

'The crew of *Montendre* weren't at war with anyone. Only the other night you hid the brandy they'd carried to England.'

Now Nathan understood. *Montendre* had been a smuggler's vessel.

'But you said you'd be happy if you never had to deal with them again. That they'd made . . . "suggestions" to you.'

'Did they deserve to die because of that?' Amy rounded on Nathan. 'They were . . . they were just *men*. Like you and Sammy. Oh, this war!' she wailed. 'It's so senseless.'

They walked on in silence for a while. Then, as they turned a corner, they came within sight of the river and could see the lights of the British frigate anchored offshore.

'Yes,' Nathan said unexpectedly. 'It *is* a senseless war. It would have ended years ago had it not been for one man's selfish ambition. Because of it the country has lost some of its greatest men. Lord Nelson . . . Sir John Moore . . . Aye, and a good, honest man like your brother – and a dozen more I was proud to call my friends.'

Immediately, Amy's own sorrow was forgotten in her concern for Nathan. Gripping his arm in her two small hands, she pulled him to a halt. 'Nathan, I'm so sorry. I must have stirred up so many unhappy memories for you – memories you would rather forget.'

'Some I wish I *could* forget. Others I am proud to remember.'

Amy looked up at Nathan's face as they stood at the water's edge. 'Are all your unhappy memories to do with war, Nathan?' she asked quietly.

'No. But the things that have happened during this war are the only ones that ever bother me now.'

Back in his room later that evening, something dropped to the floor from Nathan's pocket when he hung his clothes over the back of a chair. It was the card given to him by the man in the dining-room.

Picking up the card, Nathan carried it to the light. With considerable astonishment, he learned that the man who had offered to finance his next fight was none other than William, Duke of Clarence. Third son of the reigning monarch, George III, the Duke was a renowned patron of the prize-ring. The area about his estate at Bushy Park had been the venue for more than one great championship bout.

Nathan was glad that Sammy Mizler had not witnessed the offer made by the sporting royal duke. He would never have been satisfied until he had persuaded Nathan to take part in the richest fight ever staged in Great Britain.

8

The next morning Nathan and Amy crossed the River Dart estuary in a small, one-oarsman ferry and walked the remaining three miles to Brixham.

Nathan had recognised the qualities of the Brixham-designed boats many years before and, once he had made up his mind to use his prize-ring winnings to become a fisherman on his own account, he had ordered a lugger from a small Brixham yard. It was an astute move. Many other fishermen were learning to appreciate the exceptional qualities of Brixham-built fishing-craft. Demand for them now far out-stripped production.

Amy and Nathan arrived at the fishing village at low tide and found the lugger they were to purchase standing proudly on the mud beside the quay. It was a much larger craft than Amy had been expecting. With its deep-water keel, half-deck and tadpole-shaped belly, it should prove to be a good sea-boat and one with an incredible carrying capacity.

The boat-builder was proud of his vessel and explained its construction, inside and out, in great detail. For full-time fishing the boat would require a crew of at least five men. The boat-builder looked horrified when told that Nathan and Amy alone would be crewing the boat on its maiden voyage to Mevagissey. When he was able, he took Nathan to one side and suggested that one man and a young girl could not hope to handle a forty-two-foot fishing-boat without help. Nathan merely smiled, saved from making a reply by the return of Amy.

That afternoon, when the tide had risen sufficiently to float the fishing-boat, Nathan, Amy and the boat-builder took the new craft to sea. The vessel handled beautifully, delighting its new owners. By the time the trip ended, the boat-builder no longer entertained doubts about Amy's ability to crew a fishing-boat. He confessed that she could handle a boat more skilfully than he could himself.

Nathan and Amy remained at Brixham for three days, staying with the boat-builder and his family. During this time Nathan purchased the drift-nets and other fishing equipment he would need at Portgiskey. He knew that none would be made available to him in Pentuan, Mevagissey or any of the other fishing villages on Cornwall's south coast.

Nathan also had the opportunity during these few days to observe Amy in the kind of family surroundings to which he had been accustomed as a young boy. The boat-builder had a young wife and three active young children. The children took to Amy immediately, and it was evident to everyone that she thoroughly enjoyed their attentions. The three days spent in Brixham re-awoke in Nathan some almost-forgotten memories of the more pleasant days he had spent in Pentuan before constant arguments with his father had driven him from home.

The youngest of the boat-builder's children, taking Nathan's hand when they went walking, reminded him of how his young sister Nell's hand would seek his on the frequent occasions when their preacher father thundered his wrath at Nathan's 'evil ways', swearing that his only son was destined for damnation.

It was the first time Nathan had experienced any form of family life since then, and he was glad that Amy was part of this experience. It showed her in an entirely new light and gave an added depth to their unusual partnership.

Nathan and Amy set off on the sixty-mile sea-voyage to Portgiskey on an overcast morning. There was a fresh south-easterly wind that hinted at an autumn storm to come. However, Nathan thought that if the wind held from the south-east they would be safely moored in Portgiskey Cove long before the storm broke.

It was not to be. By the time they stood off Plymouth the wind had veered to the south-west and was already blowing a gale. It was now that the Brixham-built boat proved her seaworthiness. Tacking into the wind involved a number of changes to the sail arrangement, and Nathan found it comparatively easy to slacken off a halyard here and tighten somewhere else, while the wind whistled exhilaratingly through the rigging.

The strength of the wind and the acute angle of their tacking meant that they alternated between steering dangerously close to the rocky shore and heading far out into the grey rain-mist of the English Channel, with the land out of sight, far astern.

On one of these outward tacks, when the boat rose from a deep trough and lurched drunkenly up the uneven slope of a high-sided wave, Nathan spotted the outline of another vessel, indistinct in the damp, grey mist.

Fighting the heavy wheel as wind and tide vied with each other for control of the boat, Nathan shouted to Amy as she crouched close to his feet, sheltering from the wind and spray behind heaped nets and baskets.

'There's a ship out there.'

Amy rose unsteadily to her feet and ducked hurriedly again as the lively craft shipped a wave. Rising for a second time, she peered into the grey gloom.

'There it is.' Nathan pointed as the lugger rose on a wave and the ship came into view once more. Broadside on, it was about half a mile away.

'What is it?' Looking up at him, Amy retied her short hair behind her neck. 'Do you think it's French?'

Nathan shook his head. He did not want to alarm her unnecessarily, but the unusual lines of the ship, coupled with an absence of any form of national flag, told their own story. The ship was undoubtedly a corsair from the Barbary Coast of north Africa. Corsairs were the scourge of the high seas, ranging far and wide in search of slaves and booty to carry back to their Mediterranean kingdom. Knowing full well that the British navy was engaged elsewhere with the

French, the corsairs had recently become very active around the coasts of Ireland and south-western England, claiming more victims than the rich annual harvest reaped by the sea.

Nathan hoped the corsair would pass down-Channel without seeing them. His hopes were dashed when the lugger rode the next wave. The masts of the corsair tilted towards the sea as the foreign craft executed a tight turn. When the ship righted itself, more sails snaked up the masts as the Mediterranean pirates prepared for a chase.

Amy had witnessed the other vessel's change of direction and she, too, now realised what type of vessel they had encountered.

'Quick, turn about and make for Plymouth.'

'No.' Nathan put the wheel over and called for Amy to hoist more sail. 'Give me as much sail as she'll take,' he called as Amy made her way forward. 'If we try to run before them, they'll overhaul us in no time. Our only chance is to outmanoeuvre them.'

Guessing his intention, the master of the corsair sailed across their stern in an attempt to bring his guns to bear on the fishing-vessel.

Nathan saw small clouds of black smoke erupt from two cannon on the corsair's deck, but wind blew the sound away, while the condition of the sea made accurate shooting an impossibility. Bringing the lugger over to the opposite tack, Nathan waited only until the corsair followed suit before swinging back to resume his original course, heading for the grey and indistinct shoreline.

Nathan had made up his mind to wreck the new vessel rather than allow Amy and himself to fall into the hands of the corsairs. After the battle of the Nile, *Elephant* had rescued some American seamen taken prisoner by a corsair ship. Every one of them had been crudely emasculated in readiness for their duties as harem guards. Nathan did not dwell on the thought of what such men would do to Amy.

Through the mist he could now see the outline of Cornish cliffs, and he strained his eyes for a break in the cliffs that would indicate a beach or cove. Meanwhile, the corsair ship gained rapidly on the lugger.

Suddenly, Amy climbed up beside him. 'Quick, give me the wheel.' Seeing his uncertainty, she added: 'I know this part of the coast well. Go forward and be ready to do as I say.'

There was little alternative. The sound of the corsair's bow gun was close enough to carry to them now, and a plume of water rose in the air not twelve feet from the lugger.

Amy took the wheel and pursued a zig-zag course towards the shore. They gained no advantage on the other craft, but the irregular course spoiled the aim of the north African gunners.

When the shore was no more than a couple of hundred yards away, Amy suddenly spun the wheel desperately. As the lugger leaned away from the wind Nathan gasped with alarm. The boat was sliding past a cluster of foam-encircled rocks protruding from the sea only yards away.

Amy spun the wheel back again, and Nathan was given a similar view on the other side of the boat.

'Drop the sail – quickly!'

Spurred on by the urgency in Amy's voice, Nathan untied the halyards holding up the sails and allowed them to drop in a most unseamanlike manner. Moments later the fishing-boat slid into smooth, deep water, the wind cut off by a wall of glistening black rock.

Leaving the wheel, Amy scrambled over the tangle of sail and rigging to heave the anchor over the side. The lugger was left riding comfortably, a hundred yards of rock-encrusted water between boat and shore.

Looking out to sea, Nathan was in time to witness the confusion on board the corsair ship. Already aware of the proximity of the shore, they had been waiting confidently for the lugger to come about and fall into their hands. Expecting this to happen, they had taken in much of their sail – and it was this that saved them from total destruction.

The corsair's master saw the partially submerged rocks only seconds before Nathan. He screamed out his orders, and the highly manoeuvrable pirate-ship slewed around in little more than its own length. Frenzied activity was needed to raise every square inch of sail, and when it seemed that disaster was imminent the Mediterranean craft began slowly to edge its way to safety, grazing the farthermost rocks on the way. It was enough to deter the corsair master from pursuing the English fishing-lugger any further. One small boat was not worth the risk posed to his own vessel.

As the corsair sailed away into the mist, Nathan hugged Amy to him, filled with exhilarated relief. 'Amy, you were wonderful. I know of no man or woman who could have done better. The way you put the boat between those rocks was nothing short of brilliant . . . Amy, what's the matter? It's all over now.'

Amy had begun to shake in his arms. Now she turned a white face up to him. 'I didn't even see the rocks until we were almost on them . . .'

As the full implication of Amy's words sank in, Nathan went cold with horror. They had been within seconds of wrecking the lugger – and of almost certain death. Then he remembered how quickly she had changed the boat's direction in order to avoid the second group of rocks, and how she had dashed forward to drop the anchor. Amy might have been taken by surprise, but her actions proved she lacked neither courage nor resourcefulness.

'Amy, you saved both our lives – and almost wrecked a Barbary pirate. You're the finest sailor I've ever put to sea with – and I've sailed with the very best.'

Giving her a hard but brief kiss on the lips, Nathan released Amy with an affectionate hug, then began gathering in the sail that hung flapping over the side of the boat.

Had Nathan turned round, he would have seen Amy standing watching him, a strange expression on her pale face, her fingers touching the lips he had just bruised.

The blustery, grey October day had brought more than Barbary pirates to the coast of Cornwall. Three hours after the encounter with the corsairs, Nathan and Amy sailed the lugger into Portgiskey Cove and saw that Pentuan beach was the scene of fevered activity. Boats were offshore shooting nets, encircling shoals containing millions of pilchards. So vast were the shoals, it seemed the whole sea was a heaving silver mass. It was the harvest for which Cornish fishermen had been waiting and praying for almost a year.

Proud as he was of his new vessel, this was not the moment for Nathan to show it off to the seine-fishermen of Pentuan. Leaving Amy to take her mother on board, Nathan hurried along the beach and here met up with Sammy Mizler. The one-time London prize-fighter had good news. The fishmarkets in Plymouth would take all the fish Nathan could land – fresh or salted. There were also rumours that buyers in Bristol were outbidding all their competitors and buying all the heavily salted fish they could lay hands on. From Bristol it was being shipped to West Indies sugar plantations to feed the many thousands of negro slaves employed there.

It was the news for which Nathan had been hoping. Not only did they now have a well-proven boat, but the partners also had assured markets should the hostility of local men towards the drift-fishermen prove too great for them to make local sales.

Yet, even while Sammy Mizler was giving him the good news, Nathan found himself caught up in the age-old excitement that swept over a fishing community when the pilchards were 'running'.

This was a huge shoal, the largest seen in the vicinity for very many years. Every boat and every net was being pressed into service as still more fish came shorewards. Those villagers who were not at sea crowded the sands of the beach, screeching encouragement and advice to those who were. Others – men, women and children – heaved on long, stout ropes, to which were attached great nets drawn about a writhing mass of fish.

The aim was to draw the net to shallower water. Once here, the ropes were secured on land and the fish left trapped inside a circular mesh wall until the hard-pressed fishermen could scoop them out and carry them away to the fish-cellars.

A boat scraped ashore on the sand not ten feet from Nathan and Sammy Mizler. Yelling almost unintelligibly for assistance, a fisherman leaped ashore, one end of a long rope held in his hand. Instantly, Nathan sprang to his aid. Not certain what it was all about, Sammy Mizler followed his example and they were joined by some girls and a few old men. Most were related to the man in the boat and they had deserted other seine-nets to secure their own harvest from the sea.

Those holding the rope heaved with every ounce of muscle they possessed, yet it was thirty minutes before the fish were close enough inshore to be secured. Immediately, the happy Pentuan villagers hurried away to join another tug-of-war.

Offering a reluctant 'Thank you' to Nathan, the fisherman who had brought the rope ashore said: 'I'm obliged to you, Nathan, but I saw your new boat come in. We'll be working against each other from now on.'

'Nonsense, Dan. We've known each other since we could first walk. I'll not work against you – or any other Pentuan man. We're all fishermen here.'

'You'll find few to agree with you hereabouts, not if you intend shooting a mile or two of net every night to keep the fish away from us. No, Nathan,' – the fisherman waved away Nathan's protest – 'don't try me with any of your arguments. I've heard them all before, I dare say. You're Pentuan-born. Because of that you'll have no trouble here – just as long as we continue to make a living. But you'll not find the Mevagissey men of the same mind. They boast of having forced two drifters out of business in their own village. A third disappeared at sea with all hands on a flat-calm night. No, you'll not find them as kind to you as we. They'll give you plenty of trouble, you mind my words.'

'Thanks for the warning, Dan. But there's fish enough for all of us out there. You'll learn that soon enough.' Nathan hesitated. 'I don't suppose you know any good fishermen who are looking for work?'

While Nathan and the Pentuan fisherman had been talking, a thin-faced man had been loitering close enough to overhear their conversation, although he seemed to be interested in nothing more than the sand he was aimlessly kicking at his feet. Now he straightened up and spoke eagerly.

'I'll crew for you, Mr Jago. I can fish and handle a boat as well as anyone.'

Nathan could scarcely hide his delight. Then the fisherman to whom he had been talking let out a snort of derisive laughter. 'Before you take him on you'd better ask him to shake hands on the agreement.'

The man who had offered his services to Nathan had been standing sideways-on to him. Now, with a despairing look at the fisherman who had spoken, he turned to face Nathan.

His right arm was missing, cut off at the shoulder.

'Having only one arm has never stopped me from doing things that other men do, Mr Jago – except find work. You come to my house and you'll find it as clean and up together as any other, and my garden grows more than Dan Clymo's. *Please*, Mr Jago. I've got five little 'uns to feed.'

'How did you lose your arm? In the King's service?'

'Calvin Dickin in the King's service?' Dan Clymo's derisive laughter contained no humour. 'Not unless King George is in the habit of drinking smuggled brandy. You don't like folk talking about such things, do you, Calvin? But I reckon Nathan has a right to know, seeing as how you've asked him for work. Shall *I* tell him how you came to lose your arm, Calvin?'

'I doubt if I'll be able to stop you, Dan Clymo.'

The one-armed Calvin Dickin spoke with an air of defeat that was ignored by the seine-fisherman.

'Where shall I begin? With the years you worked for Ned Hoblyn – when ships were lured on to rocks with no survivors around to say why? Somehow you were always there on such occasions, Calvin, I remember. Or shall I simply tell him about the night the Revenue men were waiting above Portgiskey and surprised some night-runners? They weren't part-time smugglers like the rest of us, content with a keg or two of Spanish brandy. Oh, no, they were Ned Hoblyn's men, carrying guns and only too ready to use 'em.'

Dan Clymo glared malevolently at Calvin Dickin. 'Two Revenue men died that night – but that wasn't all. Ezra Partridge and his Revenue men caught a fifteen-year-old Pentuan lad. They wouldn't believe him when he said he'd been excited by the noise of the fighting and had just gone out to see what was happening. The Revenue men had him transported – for life. There wasn't one of Ned Hoblyn's men with the courage to step forward and say the boy had nothing to do with night-running. Not one. Yet they were quick enough to help one of their own who'd been sabre-slashed to the bone. Took you to an inland doctor, didn't they, Calvin? Kept you out of the way until you were fit to return to the village – leaving your arm behind you.'

'Who was the boy, Dan?' Nathan asked the question, aware that the fisherman's bitterness went far deeper than a sense of community injustice. 'Couldn't Ned Hoblyn have been asked to sign a sworn statement before he died?'

'He might, but it would have come two years too late. The fifteen-year-old was my brother. You'll remember him as a lively two-year-old. You and I took him to chapel with us more than once when we were boys.'

The fisherman paused to gain control of his emotions. 'He died on the transport, before it reached Australia.'

Dan Clymo turned away abruptly and walked off, up the gently sloping beach.

'Is his story true, Calvin? You worked for Ned Hoblyn?'

Calvin Dickin nodded defiantly. 'Yes. But I knew nothing about Dan Clymo's brother being caught. After the loss of my arm I fought for my life for weeks. By the time I was well enough to return to Pentuan he'd been sentenced and transported.'

Nathan inclined his head. 'It's a sad tale, but it was the Revenue men who were responsible for his sentence, not you. Can you really do a man's job with only the one arm?'

Calvin Dickin's face lost its expression of despair. 'Try me, Mr Jago! Try me.'

'All right. My boat is at Portgiskey. Go there and help get it ready for fishing. We put to sea on tomorrow night's tide.'

9

When Nathan's 'crew' gathered at Portgiskey to prepare both boat and equipment for their first fishing trip, the men wanted to give the boat a name, as tradition demanded. Nathan refused to be drawn on the subject. He would name the vessel, he said, when circumstances suggested a suitable name.

Looking at the men about him as he helped to secure corks to almost a mile of nets, Sammy Mizler wondered, as he had many times before, why he had risked so much of his hard-earned capital on such a venture. Only Nathan would have satisfied the minimum requirements of an underwriter from Lloyd's, London's shipping insurers. His crew would have brought on hysterics.

In truth, there were only three. First was the one-armed ex-smuggler, Calvin Dickin. Next, Nathan had found Ahab Arthur, an aged fisherman who had been the owner of the two drifters put out of action by

Mevagissey seiners. The last member of the crew was Amy Hoblyn.

Because of Nathan's difficulty in obtaining more men, Amy had insisted upon becoming a crew member. Nathan had refused at first, but he had experienced the standard of her seamanship and the situation *was* desperate. Even with four of them it would be a herculean task to haul in almost four hundred fathoms of net at the end of a night's drift-fishing – especially if they had a good catch.

Sammy Mizler had listened to the argument between Amy and Nathan, and at first it had amused him to hear the young girl argue with the prize-fighting champion of all England to such effect. Then he saw her expression when Nathan turned away after a curt refusal, early in the argument. Sammy realised that Nathan had the power to hurt Amy deeply. It was a responsibility of which Nathan was unaware, and one he certainly did not want, yet it *was* there. In that moment of realisation, Sammy Mizler's heart went out to Amy. Sammy too knew what it meant to have one's future hinge upon Nathan's arbitrary decisions.

At mid-morning, a horse and rider came round the headland into Portgiskey Cove from Pentuan beach, splashing through the shallow waters of a receding tide. It was Elinor Hearle. Casting a quick glance at the busy group, her eyes lingered on Amy for a few moments. Then she gave her full attention to Nathan.

'My father returned to London yesterday. Before he left he had an agreement drawn up, setting out the tithes you are to pay him. I have it at Polrudden. It requires your signature.'

Nathan wanted to have the matter of tithe payments settled beyond all dispute before he began fishing. Strong hostility to him from local fishermen might induce Sir Lewis Hearle to change his mind.

'When can I come to Polrudden?'

Elinor shrugged in exaggerated indifference, 'Whenever you please.'

'Today?'

Elinor nodded. 'I'll be riding for another hour, but I'll be home for the remainder of the day.'

'I'll come to Polrudden early this afternoon.'

With no acknowledgment that she had heard him, Elinor Hearle pulled on the rein and turned the horse, cantering away in the direction from which she had come.

Watching her leave, Amy felt all the pleasure she had derived from becoming a member of Nathan's crew drain away.

Nathan said: 'With luck we should have these corks tied on and the nets stowed on board before I go to Polrudden.'

'Don't let us hold you up,' snapped Amy irritably. 'Her ladyship might get the impression she's less important than your livelihood. *That* wouldn't suit her at all. If the agreement is so important, why didn't she bring it *here* for you to sign?'

Nathan grinned at her indignation. 'Perhaps I should have told her that. It's of importance to us at Portgiskey, not to Elinor Hearle.'

Amy snorted, only slightly mollified. 'Nobody *tells* Elinor Hearle to do anything – not even her father. She does only what *she* wants to do, and no more. I can't understand why she bothered to come here to pass on her father's message.'

'She owes me a favour. Sammy will tell you all about it sometime.'

'Elinor Hearle accepts favours as her due. I saw Nell just before we set off for Brixham. She told me how Elinor came to the farm *demanding* Nell's best dress.'

Fiercely, Amy jerked the thin rope she was holding and pulled it into an unwanted knot. 'I don't *like* Elinor Hearle.'

She said it emphatically and with such determined unreasonableness that Nathan smiled to himself.

By the time Nathan set out for Polrudden the sky had become dark and overcast. A storm was building up over the sea. If it was accompanied by a fierce wind, it would delay the maiden fishing voyage of the Brixham-built boat. However, the storm was still holding off when Nathan arrived at Polrudden.

Elinor Hearle met him before he reached the house. She had been occupying herself within sight of the entrance to the driveway for some time. The excuse she gave to herself was that she was inspecting the newly cut and layered blackthorn hedge. The labour had been carried out by a team of out-of-work labourers from the inland farms who were now begging for more to do. Desperate for any form of employment, the whole team had contracted to work for less money than one man would have received in better times.

When Elinor saw Nathan, she told the delighted men to trim all the remaining hedges on the Polrudden estate, then hurried away to meet him.

By the time Nathan saw Elinor coming towards him she was no longer hurrying, although inside she had the same eager feeling she had experienced only once before. When visiting friends on Exmoor she had been taken stag hunting. The same tight thrill of anticipation had come to her when she sighted a superb stag bounding up a steep hill, closely pursued by a pack of excited, baying hounds.

'You are prompt, Nathan Jago. I thought you might have been so busy you would put off coming to Polrudden until another day.'

'I'll be even busier soon. Tonight, weather permitting, we begin fishing.'

'I'm impressed. I admire a man who knows what he wants and who wastes no time in going out after it. I'm surprised you have been able to find a crew so quickly. Are they local men?'

Nathan gave an amused chuckle. 'You saw my crew when you came to Portgiskey – and you can leave out Sammy Mizler. He wouldn't make a fishing trip if it meant the difference between life and death to him.'

Elinor Hearle knew immediately which man was Sammy Mizler; his clothes had set him apart as a city man. Her mind ranged over the others who had been at Portgiskey Cove that morning and she looked at Nathan in disbelief. 'You're going deep-sea fishing with a one-armed smuggler and an old man who should be at home in a rocking-chair?'

'There's a girl, too. Amy came with me to pick up the boat. She's probably a better sailor than any of us.'

Elinor Hearle frowned. 'You're talking of Amy Hoblyn, the smuggler's daughter?'

'Yes. You know her?'

Elinor Hearle sniffed disparagingly. 'There can be few people in Cornwall who don't know *of* Amy Hoblyn. I have heard it rumoured she has taken over her father's activities. Why should she work for you?'

'We're partners. I've provided the boat, she's put up the fish-cellar.'

'Oh, yes, I forgot. You told my father.' Elinor Hearle was silent for some moments. She looked at Nathan's face as though expecting to learn more there. Then she shrugged. 'Who you work with is your business. The agreement is in my father's study. I'll take you there and you can sign it.'

It was dark and gloomy in the house, the windows reflecting the overcast sky outside.

Halfway up the stairs Elinor placed a warning hand upon Nathan's arm. 'Be careful. There's a broken stair here. I must get someone in to fix it soon.'

Nathan negotiated the broken stair with no trouble, but Elinor Hearle kept her hand on his arm and Nathan was acutely aware of her closeness, experiencing a sense of disappointment when she released his arm to open the door of the study.

Inside the study Elinor moved to her father's desk, beside an open window. 'Here is the agreement. You'd better read it through. You *can* read?'

Nathan nodded and bent over the document. It was written in bold, lawyer's writing on a large sheet of stiff paper. Beside him, Elinor leaned close, reading over his shoulder. He found his concentration wandering, distracted by the headiness of the perfume she wore. It was a perfume that was out of place here in Cornwall. It belonged beneath the chandeliers of the fine salons of London. No doubt her father had bought it for her – or was it a present from someone else?

There had been few girls in Nathan's life. He had been brought up by his father to believe that involvement with a nice girl led inexorably to marriage – and marriage for a prize-fighter was the first step to disaster. Consequently, Nathan had kept well clear of marriageable girls. There had been others, of course, girls of whom his father had said nothing – probably because Josiah Jago *knew* nothing of them. Then there were the girls who could be found in the hostelries frequented by prize-fighters. Girls eager to please, who asked for little but who, more often than not, passed on a debilitating disease to ruin the career of more than one promising champion.

Nathan brought his straying thoughts back to the present. He was no longer a champion prize-fighter, idol of the London 'Fancy'. He was a Cornish fisherman – and Elinor Hearle was the haughty daughter of a man who was a landowner, Member of Parliament and baronet. Nevertheless, try as he might to be rational, the stirrings within his body mocked at common sense.

In order to put an end to such disturbing fantasies, Nathan took up the goose-quill pen, dipped it in the ink and scratched his signature at the foot of the page. Suddenly he stopped, quill in hand. He could smell something more than Elinor Hearle's perfume. It was smoke. It appeared to be drifting in through the open window.

'Do you have a garden fire going?'

The question startled Elinor, but she shook her head. 'No, the gardener is cleaning out the well.'

Nathan flung the window open wider, and immediately they both heard an ominous crackling sound.

'It sounds like thatch . . .'

Elinor paled. 'The stables!' Turning, she ran from the room and down the stairs. Nathan followed her.

In the darkness of the downstairs hall, Nathan almost bowled over a startled maidservant. Steadying her, Nathan said urgently: 'Fetch all the servants you can find – and the men cutting the hedge by the lane. There's a fire in the stables. Quickly now!'

Running from the house after Elinor, he rounded the corner just as a section of the stable roof ignited with a frightening roar.

'There are horses inside,' Elinor cried above the din of flames devouring the dry straw roof.

'Get some water organised. I'll release as many as I can.'

Without waiting for a reply, Nathan ran to the stable-door. The door was closed, but not secured. Flinging it open, Nathan put up an arm in an instinctive, if useless, gesture, warding off the thick black smoke that billowed out, engulfing him.

As the smoke thinned temporarily, Nathan moved cautiously into the stables. He could hear horses snorting in terror as they crashed about inside their loose-boxes. Reaching the first of them, he slipped the bolt and threw back the gate, jumping clear as the horse bolted for the exit.

He started coughing as he reached the second loose-box, and for a moment he thought he might have to abandon his rescue attempt. Then he remembered how, in the thick of battle on the gun-deck of a man-of-war, the gunners would crouch low beside the guns to escape the acrid smoke that collected in dense clouds about the low deckheads.

Dropping to all fours, Nathan found he could breathe a little easier. Occasionally, he could even see a few feet ahead as a breeze from outside cut a thin path through the smoke. One by one he slipped the bolts, flinging himself to one side as the panic-stricken horses slipped and slid on the cobbled floor in their haste to reach safety.

The smoke was thickening now, catching at his throat as the dirty straw in the boxes, and the boxes themselves, began to burn. In the last loose-box he found a terrified mare and a near-helpless foal. The mare bolted the moment Nathan opened the gate of the loose-box, but the foal was confused and had to be manhandled to the stable-door.

Outside, Nathan sat on the ground, sucking in clean air, ignoring the sparks that showered about him. Wiping his streaming eyes on the back of a sleeve, he saw Elinor and Will Hodge, her new groom, catching the horses and turning them out in a nearby paddock.

At that moment a young woman came running up, looking about her in wide-eyed horror. To the groom she screamed: 'Sarah? Where's Sarah?'

Will Hodge stared at her, not understanding. 'Why, when last I saw her she was at home with you.'

'No!' The young woman's fingers clutched at her face. 'She came to the stables to find you!'

Will Hodge stared stupidly from his wife to the

burning stables. 'Then it must have been her. She must have knocked the lamp over. I set it on a box, up by the tackle-room. It was dark, you see . . .' The groom was too stunned to think rationally.

'Perhaps she ran out again, frightened at what she'd done.' Nathan spoke to the groom's distraught wife.

Ann Hodge shook her head, her face twisting and distorting in anguish. 'She'd have come home if she were frightened. She's only four. She must be in there.'

She started towards the stables just as a section of the roof collapsed with a snapping of blazing beams and a roar that blew sparks and fragments of burning straw as high as the roof of the manor-house.

Grabbing the wife of the groom as she began screaming, Nathan thrust her at Elinor. 'Hold her here – and get some water on the fire. *Now!*'

He dived towards the open stable-door. Pausing to take a deep breath before plunging inside, he thought he heard Elinor shout, telling him not to be a fool, but the sound was quickly lost in the noise of the conflagration about him.

Nathan knew exactly where he was going. Alongside the loose-box which had housed the foal he had seen a closed door. It had to be the tackle-room. If young Sarah had fled inside and closed the door when the lamp fell to the floor and started the blaze, she might still be alive.

The woodwork inside the stables was well ablaze now. As Nathan sidestepped a burning loose-box, the heat reached out and struck him in the face with the strength of a prize-fighter. Putting both arms over his head, Nathan stumbled on to the far end of the building.

He cannoned into the closed door of the tackle-room and blindly fumbled for the latch. When he found it he realised it was too high for a child to reach. Either the door had been open when Sarah reached here, or she was not inside.

As he pushed open the door, smoke billowed out to meet him and a bundle of burning thatch dropped to the floor at his feet. Kicking it to one side, Nathan tripped over another obstacle and fell to his knees. He was choking for breath now. Above him there was an angry hiss of steam. Someone outside, with a knowledge of the building, was trying to damp down the roof of the tackle-room. It was too late to have any lasting effect. The fire had far too strong a hold on the whole building.

Nathan crawled across the floor, his arms moving ahead of him with the action of a breast-stroke swimmer in his search for the missing girl. Twice he was fooled by tumbled horse-blankets. Then, when he knew his lungs could take no more of the heat and smoke, he touched something soft. It was a small arm. He had found the missing child.

Sarah was lying in a tangle of harness, and Nathan hurriedly extricated her. She was a small four-year-old and weighed very little. Nathan held her close to him with one arm as he crawled from the tackle-room. The fire in the main stable was fearsome now. For a moment Nathan hesitated, but he could afford to waste no more time. He was having great difficulty in breathing, and his senses were beginning to fail him.

Rising to his feet, Nathan put his head down and ran, a large hand protecting Sarah's head. As he plunged through the flames he heard a deafening roar in his ears, but he felt no pain. Once he stumbled and almost fell. Then, staggering helplessly, his shoulder bouncing off the cob wall at every other step, his shoulder suddenly missed the wall and he fell sideways – out through the open doorway.

A moment later the child was snatched from him and Nathan was dragged away from the almost-gutted stables.

As Nathan lay coughing up smoke, tears streaming from his eyes, he heard the crying of the child's mother and thought his rescue bid must have been in vain. But when he was able to sit up and wipe his eyes sufficiently to see what was going on about him, he saw the daughter of the groom in her mother's arms, retching as healthily as Nathan himself. Her mother was crying from sheer relief.

The employees of the estate had now been joined by fishermen from Pentuan who had seen the plume of black smoke rising high in the sky above their village. Although they would be unable to save the stables, there was now little danger that the fire might spread to the house.

'And how is the hero of the day?'

The mocking words were belied by the expression of concern on Elinor Hearle's face as she looked down at him. Putting out a hand, she touched his shoulder where a piece of burning thatch had landed on him. It hurt.

'You've burned yourself. You had better come inside to clean up and have something put on that shoulder.' She smiled at him. 'I'm afraid you've lost most of your eyebrows, too.'

There were no servants inside the house. The few

who remained in the service of Sir Lewis Hearle were outside, helping to fight the blaze. Elinor took Nathan upstairs to a bedroom heavy with the perfume she herself wore. Off the bedroom was another, smaller room. Here Elinor poured water from a jug into a bowl and put soap and a large towel on the marble-topped table beside it.

'That shirt is ruined. Take if off and wash yourself. I'll go and find some balm and an old shirt of my father's. It will be too small for you, I've no doubt, but it will serve.'

When Elinor had gone, Nathan stripped off his shirt. It had been badly holed by flying sparks and was so charred in parts that it fell to pieces beneath his touch.

Elinor returned to the room carrying a small earthenware jar in her hands. Nathan was drying himself and she made disapproving noises. 'There's a whole area of your back that hasn't been touched. It looks as though you have another burn there, too.'

Taking the sponge from the bowl, she rubbed it gently over his back, dabbing the area dry with the towel afterwards. When she had finished, she began applying the ointment to his burns. She rubbed it over most of his back before turning her attention to his shoulders, and finally smearing it carefully over his chest, on which numerous red scorch-marks showed now the grime of the fire had been removed.

As she worked, Elinor murmured reassuringly that, although Nathan was burned here and there, he was not seriously hurt.

Elinor Hearle was a tall girl, but the top of her head came no higher than Nathan's chin and she was standing so close to him that he could smell the fire smoke, lingering in her hair.

Suddenly, with both hands resting on his chest, her voice took on a new, strangely fierce note. 'God! Nathan Jago, you have a magnificent body . . . A Greek god . . .'

When Nathan looked down at her face he saw the same hunger he had witnessed on the faces of men when they first saw a woman after spending months at sea. He had never before known such a need in a woman.

She was looking up at him. Waiting . . . Willing him to make the first move. He told himself it would be madness. It *was* madness, but he reached for her and she came to him, mouth on his, with a ferocity that was unlike anything he had ever experienced. His whole body became aware of her as she strained to him, hands at first kneading his scorched back before her nails dug into his flesh.

Her mouth moved fiercely beneath his, and suddenly her teeth sank into his lower lip and he tasted his own blood.

With a stifled oath, Nathan jerked his head back. Elinor was looking up at him, and in her eyes was an animal hunger that called up an equally primitive need deep within him. Picking her up, Nathan carried Elinor to the bed.

Nathan awoke, aware that he had been disturbed by an alien sound. Raising his head from the soft pillow, he was momentarily confused by his surroundings. There was a drowsy protest from the pillow beside him – and he remembered.

Elinor's leg was trapped beneath his. As she pulled it free, a rumble of thunder rolled across the sea beyond the window. A gust of wind brought a rattle of heavy raindrops against the diamond-paned windows.

'What are you doing?'

Elinor spoke without moving her head from the pillow as she freed an arm from a tangle of bedclothes and slipped it about Nathan's neck.

'I must go. We both should. You to see what's happening at the stables, me to my boat. I have to get it ready for a night's fishing.'

'Damn the fire. If the servants haven't put it out yet, the rain will do the job for them. As for your boat, it will wait. I won't.'

Propping himself up on one elbow, Nathan looked down at Elinor, and she squirmed the smooth roundness of her body beneath his before pulling him down to her.

'Love me again, Nathan. Love me again . . .'

Her voice was hoarse with desire. Moments later the storm, the fire and Nathan's boat were all forgotten as he was swallowed up by the passion of the woman whose bed he shared.

10

By the time Nathan returned to Portgiskey the storm had blown inland, washing the pale sky clean and leaving the world to await the arrival of night.

As he approached it was apparent from the manner of the men that there had been much speculation about the reason for his long absence. Nathan tried to put some spring into his step. It was not easy. His feet felt as though they were encased in lead.

When he reached the small group waiting on the quayside, the men would not meet his eyes. It was left to Amy to voice their thoughts.

'No doubt Elinor Hearle had more to offer you than a wet afternoon spent preparing a fishing-boat for sea?'

Nathan was too honest not to feel a sense of guilt at the sarcastic question. But on the walk from Polrudden he had anticipated the resentment of Amy and the others. He had convinced himself that whatever he did was none of their business. Nevertheless, he felt the need to defend himself to Amy.

'I would have been here sooner had I not needed to go home first to change my clothes.'

Amy gave a derisive snort. 'If you intend taking up fishing seriously, you'll need to get used to getting wet. You can't run home to change every time it rains.'

'I said nothing about rain. There was a fire at Polrudden. My shirt was scorched. I left the manor wearing one of Sir Lewis Hearle's shirts. I didn't think he would approve if I wore it for fishing.'

'A fire? Was it a bad one?'

The question came from Ahab Arthur, the oldest man there. He hurried to explain his concern. 'My daughter's living up by the house. She's married to Will Hodge, Sir Lewis Hearle's groom. He's been there only a week.'

'The stables caught fire. They were gutted. Will Hodge left a lamp alight inside while he went off and did something else. Your grand-daughter came in looking for her father and knocked the lamp to the ground, starting the fire.'

Ahab Arthur's face paled. 'Was young Sarah harmed?'

'No, but she had a very narrow escape. The blaze terrified her and she ran into the tackle-room. Fortunately the door slammed shut behind her and held the flames back. When I found her she'd been overcome by smoke, but hadn't a burn on her.'

'You brought her out? But there's no way into the tackle-room except through the stables. If they were burning . . . ?'

Nathan shrugged, wishing he had not gone into such detail. 'As I said, she had a very lucky escape.'

'And all the time I thought . . .' Amy choked on her words. 'Was that how your shirt was burned? Bringing out Ahab's grand-daughter?'

'Yes.'

Nathan was embarrassed by the hero-worship he saw in Amy's eyes. His bid to keep the real reason for his absence from her and the others had worked too well. Gruffly, he said: 'We've wasted enough time in talk. Come on, into the boat. Pilchards will be at a premium. The seiners at Pentuan lost all their fish and most of their nets in this afternoon's storm.'

The Portgiskey drifter arrived at Nathan's chosen fishing-ground a few minutes after nightfall. Some four miles from the coast, it was close enough to the land to enjoy shelter from a westerly swell, yet far enough out to avoid any risk of drifting ashore during the night.

Amy took the helm while the three men shot half a mile of nets in a line across the wide mouth of St Austell Bay. Once this task had been completed and a sail set to hold the boat steady, Calvin Dickin and Ahab Arthur enjoyed a late-night smoke before settling down on hard canvas-sail beds to await Nathan's call to stand watch in his stead.

In a talkative mood, Amy stayed up for a while, declaring she was not tired. Nathan would have welcomed an opportunity to think about what had happened between Elinor Hearle and himself at Polrudden Manor. Instead, he was obliged both to listen and to reply to an inexplicably happy Amy.

'I love being out here at night. Don't you, Nathan? You and I could be the only people in the whole world. Even the lights of Pentuan and Mevagissey could be so many fallen stars scattered on the ground.'

The residents of the two fishing villages did not keep late hours, and there were no more than two dozen lighted windows to be seen.

'I feel so contented. More than I have for years. Pa was ill for a very long time and I've missed the nights he and I would spend out here together, waiting for a French smuggler. We'd just sit here like this, talking together for hours.'

Nathan struck a light for his pipe and saw her sitting hugging her knees, one cheek resting lightly against one arm.

'We talked lots, Pa and me. He missed Beville. I suppose that's why I always tried to do everything Beville would have done with him. I was very young when he was taken off to sea. I hardly remember him, really. What kind of man was he?'

'He was a good man, Amy. A great sailor and a wonderful friend. I miss him, too.'

Nathan could not see Amy's face, but he sensed that he had made the reply she wanted to hear.

'That's what I've always believed, but I've never before met anyone who *really* knew him – not in the way you did. It's strange really, the way things have worked out. You and Beville being such good friends, and now the Jagos and Hoblyns being partners. It's unexpected, too, I suppose, after what happened between your pa and mine.'

Nathan's brow creased in a puzzled frown, and he

took the pipe from his mouth. 'What *did* happen between them?'

'You don't know? But of course you wouldn't. They had an awful row. When we lived farther west Pa always went to church every Sunday, without fail. He was a Methodist for years, ever since he met John Wesley himself. Pa went to the Sunday meetings here, too, until your father criticised him in front of the whole congregation for night-running. Preacher Jago said John Wesley had called smuggling "the work of the Devil". Pa stood up and told your father he reckoned he'd known Wesley a sight better than anyone in Pentuan. Everyone took sides, the meeting became a bit heated – and then fighting started. It almost wrecked the inside of the chapel, and Pa was thrown out of the Methodist Society. We had nothing more to do with Methodism until Preacher Jago came along and offered to say the prayers when we buried Pa. It made Ma very happy.'

Nathan shook his head. 'That was my father's way of saying he was sorry. He's never found it easy to forgive anyone who disagrees with him – and I should know. I wondered why he told me about your fish-cellar when he is so opposed to drift-fishing. It was his way of making amends for the way he'd behaved towards your pa. He thought you and your mother might need money.'

'I'm glad he did tell you. I . . . I like working with you, Nathan.'

Nathan broke the embarrassed silence that followed Amy's simple admission. 'I hope it will prove to be a profitable partnership for all of us. But having you crew the boat with us is only a temporary arrangement. When we can find enough men you'll remain ashore, supervising the cellar.'

Amy opened her mouth to argue, then snapped it shut again. She had plans of her own, but it would not do to bring them all into the open just yet. Rising to her feet, she hesitated for a moment, then she leaned forward and kissed Nathan on the cheek.

'Good night, Nathan. Thank you for listening to me.'

As she went forward to find a place to sleep, Nathan compared Amy's kiss with the kisses of Elinor Hearle. Remembering the hours he had spent in the bedroom at Polrudden Manor, all thoughts of Amy Hoblyn slipped away.

Nathan and his crew began hauling in their nets before dawn. They soon learned they had spent a very successful night at sea. It had been light for two hours before all the nets were inboard. By then the boat was heavily laden and everyone was in a jubilant mood.

Ahab Arthur was standing in the bow of the boat as they sailed into Portgiskey Cove on a light breeze and he called back: 'It looks as though Sammy has gathered a welcoming party to cheer us in.'

Nathan leaned over the side of the boat. There was a large black-and-white-painted cutter drawn up on the tiny beach beside the waterside cottage and a dozen or more men stood flanking Sammy Mizler on the small quay.

Nathan frowned. 'That's no welcoming party. Unless I'm very much mistaken, the Revenue men are waiting for us.'

Amy appeared at his side. 'You're right, The fat one in the middle is Ezra Partridge, Chief Revenue Officer of the Mevagissey preventive men. He's the most hated man in Cornwall. He was responsible for having a Polperro man hanged for smuggling last year. I wonder what he's doing at Portgiskey.'

'We'll soon find out,' replied Nathan grimly. He had remembered the casks of brandy he and Sammy Mizler had carried ashore for Amy's boat and hidden beneath the fish-cellar. If Chief Revenue Officer Partridge had found them, they would all be in serious trouble.

The next few moments were too busy to speculate on the presence of the Revenue men at Portgiskey, as sails were lowered and the boat brought alongside the quay. When the boat was secured, Chief Revenue Officer Partridge stepped aboard with two armed Revenue men in close attendance. The remainder formed an armed line on the quayside.

Without offering to identify himself, Ezra Partridge asked: 'Your name is Jago?'

Nathan nodded.

'I have reason to believe you have contraband spirits on board this boat. My men are here to carry out a search.'

'You'll find no spirits on this boat, Chief Officer Partridge – and I'll have no clumsy-footed Revenue men trampling on good fish. Your men can search my boat when the catch has been landed. That's unless you want to be taken to court for the value of the catch?'

The Chief Revenue Officer hesitated, speculating whether Nathan was trying to bluff him. Finally deciding that Nathan meant every word, Partridge scowled angrily. He knew that a Cornish magistrate would delight in convicting him and awarding Nathan whatever damages he claimed. Speaking to the Revenue men who had boarded the boat with him, he ordered: 'You men remain here. Check everything that's taken ashore. The others on the quay can come with me and search the house and fish-cellar.'

Nathan's heart sank. He had been hoping to take the pilchards ashore and begin stacking them over the flagstone that concealed the smuggler's hiding-place. He tried to catch Amy's eye, but she would not look at him.

Nathan hurriedly filled a large basket with pilchards and carried it himself to the fish-cellar. He was too late. Ezra Partridge had already located the underfloor hiding-place. As Nathan dumped his fish on the stone floor, the Revenue men were prising up the huge flagstone, using iron bars they had brought with them in their boat.

The Chief Revenue Officer turned to Nathan triumphantly. 'Is this why you were so confident I'd find no contraband on your boat, Jago? Because you'd brought it ashore earlier?'

Nathan shrugged; it would be no use denying all knowledge of the brandy. It was his cellar. His and Amy Hoblyn's. She was standing impassively nearby and still would not look at him.

Nathan wondered what would happen to her. He had never heard of a woman being convicted of involvement in smuggling, but there was always a first time.

With cries of triumph, the Revenue men raised the

flagstone – and the shouts died on their lips. Ezra Partridge looked from the hiding-place to Nathan. 'What's this?'

Nathan crossed the floor of the fish-cellar as casually as he could. Looking down into the hole he saw it was filled with a white substance that resembled hard-packed snow.

'It's salt.' The unexpected explanation came from Amy.

'Salt? Salt? What's it doing here?'

'Keeping dry.' Amy looked at Ezra Partridge scornfully. 'How long have you been stationed in fishing villages? You should know that damp salt loses its strength, and there's no way salt can be kept dry at Portgiskey if it's exposed to the air. It needs to be kept in a dry, sealed place. That's a specially made salt-store.'

Ezra Partridge looked from Amy to Nathan suspiciously. 'I don't believe you.'

Amy shrugged. 'Please yourself. You asked why there's salt here. I've told you.' With that she turned her back on the Chief Revenue Officer and walked from the fish-cellar.

'You men. Find something to probe into this . . . salt. I want to know if there's anything hidden beneath it.'

There was nothing. But not until the Revenue men could see the bare boards of the fishing-boat beneath the small amount of fish remaining in the hold did they accept that their early-morning raid had been a waste of time.

Standing beside Amy on the small quay as the Revenue men rowed Chief Revenue Officer Ezra

Partridge away from Portgiskey Cove, Nathan said quietly: 'You had me scared for a while, Amy. When did the brandy go?'

'It was collected the very next night after you and Sammy brought it ashore for me.'

'And the salt?'

'Delivered while we were in Brixham picking up the boat.'

'Amy, you're a truly remarkable girl. I'll never doubt you again, I promise.'

Amy grinned delightedly. 'Good. But I must admit I was worried for a while. I thought Ezra Partridge was going to ask me some awkward questions about the salt. It's best Brittany salt, delivered from France – duty unpaid.'

In London, Sir Lewis Hearle was both surprised and excited to receive an invitation to have lunch with Spencer Perceval, the Tory Prime Minister, at 10 Downing Street. Such invitations were issued to back-benchers when they were being considered for promotion to Cabinet rank.

The Cornish baronet was not disappointed. After an exchange of pleasantries, and some meaningless chit-chat about the progress of the war, the state of the rural economy, and the disarray of the Whig opposition, the two men sat down to eat and to discuss the purpose behind the invitation.

'I thank you for your report on the growing strength of Methodist dissidents, Sir Lewis. A very well-written and detailed communication. Indeed, I confess to finding much of your information quite startling. It has given my colleagues and myself food for thought. To have such a popular dissident movement in the land in time of war is causing us all much concern. We have little control over their actions, and there's not a damned fellow of note among the lot of them! You've produced a first-class report, Sir Lewis; but can you put forward any ideas on how we might bring these Wesleyans to heel?'

Sir Lewis Hearle took a swig of burgundy, still readily available in London, even after many weary years of war with France. Leaning back in his chair he gazed speculatively at his Prime Minister. He had submitted the report on the dangers of Methodism, uncertain of its reception. Perceval had made public utterances against 'Methodist rabble', but such words may have been intended merely to appease the Archbishop of Canterbury, who had powerful support in the House of Lords. Now Sir Lewis felt that perhaps the Prime Minister's stated dislike of Methodism was genuine. He determined to speak his mind.

'I have given this matter a great deal of thought, Prime Minister. As you know, these Wesleyans have taken a firm hold in my own county. Nevertheless, serious cracks are developing in their organisation, and I feel we should take full advantage of such a situation. Divide and rule would appear to be the order of the day. Part of the Wesleyan movement is calling for more militant evangelism. They point to the example set by their founder, who took the Methodist message to the masses. Others favour consolidation, and wish to gather the trappings of respectability about themselves. Yet another group resents the central ruling body of the Wesleyan movement and is calling for more power to be given to local Methodist societies. Such dissension comes as no surprise to me – certainly not where Cornish Methodists are concerned. Rebellion against all forms of authority is part of the Cornishman's nature. Yet my information is that this state of affairs exists throughout the whole Methodist movement. It had to happen, of course. Since John Wesley died his followers have had no leader. They are reliant upon a "Council". I suggest, Prime Minister, that the time is ripe to remove the threat posed to this country by these dissidents – once and for all.'

'And how do you suggest we pursue such a policy?' Spencer Perceval leaned forward eagerly to hear what Sir Lewis Hearle had to say. The Cornish baronet had been recommended to him as a capable man whose hatred of Methodism matched the Prime Minister's own mistrust of their aims.

'There are a number of courses open to us. At a local level we must prevent Methodists from building new churches and, wherever possible, close down those already in existence. Force the Wesleyans to hold their meetings in the open air. Not only shall we be able to see and hear what is happening, but it will be a simple matter to introduce agitators, should we find it necessary. The expectation of violence will deter decent, law-abiding people from attending such meetings and attract riff-raff. Consequently, it will come as no surprise to anyone when magistrates appear among them to read the Riot Act and arrest their ringleaders – the so-called "preachers". Indeed, before long the whole country will no doubt be clamouring for legislation to put an end to such disturbances.'

Spencer Perceval looked at Sir Lewis Hearle speculatively. 'You have some interesting ideas, Sir Lewis,
but to implement them on a national scale would
involve my government. The risk is considerable.'

'Not necessarily, Prime Minister. Any government
in time of war would be lacking in its duty if it did not
examine very closely the activities of a dissident
group established in its midst, even though such a
group were operating under the cloak of religion. But
I realise that it would be necessary to proceed with a
great deal of discretion.'

'Of course, and it would be embarrassing if no
substantial evidence of subversion were to be proven
against these Methodists. Very well, Sir Lewis. I intend giving you the opportunity to put your beliefs to
the test. I am offering you the post of Under-Secretary
at the Home Office. You will have special responsibility for investigating the affairs of dissident groups
in His Majesty's Kingdom.'

Sir Lewis Hearle rode home from Downing Street in
a mood of great self-satisfaction. He had worked
tirelessly for years to achieve Cabinet rank. Now at
last he had a foot on the ladder to his goal, together
with a mandate to destroy a dissident organisation he
loathed with an intensity that had become obsessional
over the years.

There was only one matter that cast a shadow over
the baronet's happiness. Money. If he were going to
attain and hold Cabinet rank, the Tory baronet knew
he would need to win over a great many influential
men. His bills for entertaining would soar to frightening heights. Somehow he had to raise more money.
Lack of money was an embarrassment that had been

with him for many years. But now there was an end in sight. A Cabinet Minister could amass a fortune securing posts for the sons of grateful acquaintances, accepting directorships on the boards of suitable companies, and generally performing favours for men of means.

In the meantime, Sir Lewis Hearle decided he must sell off a number of his less profitable Cornish farms for which the rents were negligible – Venn, for instance.

Thinking of Cornwall set Sir Lewis to think of Elinor. She would be pleased at the news of his appointment. He would write and tell her when time permitted. She might be more inclined to come to London when he began entertaining. She might even find herself a husband here. Yes, he would have to persuade her to join him in the capital. Elinor had spent far too long going her own way in a remote corner of Cornwall. He sometimes thought she had forgotten her station in life. He had observed the casual and informal manner in which she had touched the arm of the Jago upstart. A prize-fighting fisherman was no fit company for the daughter of a baronet.

Sir Lewis Hearle would have to run Nathan Jago out of Cornwall at the time had he not believed that the new fishing venture would add a considerable sum to the income of Polrudden Manor. Once Sir Lewis was established in the Government the need would not be so pressing. Then Nathan Jago would go the way of his Wesley-preaching father.

11

Fishing from Portgiskey continued to prove highly profitable for Nathan and his partners, but it was not without incident. One morning, as Nathan and his crew were hauling in their nets, they were surprised by a daring French man-of-war. Cutting free the two nets still in the water, Nathan put on every inch of sail the lugger possessed and made the safety of Mevagissey harbour just ahead of the French warship.

The incident was watched by dozens of astonished fishermen and a few early-rising villagers who quickly roused the Revenue men from their beds. Led by Chief Officer Partridge, the Revenue men turned the small coastguard signalling-cannon on the daring raider from across the English Channel.

The shots from the ineffectual weapon drew a broadside from the French vessel, and the cannon-balls fell close enough to Ezra Partridge's men to send them scurrying for cover. After firing another scornful broadside, the man-of-war put about and headed out to sea.

It was a lucky escape for the crew of the Portgiskey drifter. Only a few miles along the coast the crews of two Looe drifters were less fortunate. Scooped up by the same man-of-war, they were taken captive to Verdun. Here they joined Captain Nicholas Lelean and the crew of *The Seven Brothers*, a Mevagissey vessel taken outside its home port seven years before.

Serious though this incident might have been, it caused Nathan less concern than an occurrence a few nights later. Under cover of darkness, a number of fishermen in small seine-boats slipped out of Mevagissey harbour and cut away Nathan's nets as his craft drifted across the entrance of St Austell Bay.

Nathan feared it might herald the beginning of a war between the Portgiskey boat and the seine-fishermen of Mevagissey. To his great relief, it proved to be an isolated incident – little more than a savage expression of disapproval.

Paradoxically, the night attack actually worked to Nathan's advantage. Because the action had been taken by Mevagissey men, it angered some of the Pentuan fishermen. The result was that Nathan was able to make up a full crew of Pentuan men who would otherwise have remained unemployed until the next pilchard season came around.

It was now November, and winter was close. Sometimes the weather proved too rough for the Portgiskey boat to put to sea. Nathan spent these nights at Polrudden Manor, with Elinor Hearle.

Nathan thought his bedroom romance with Sir Lewis Hearle's daughter was a well-kept secret, until one stormy evening his mother tackled him as he prepared to leave the house.

'Where are you off to tonight?'

Nathan did his best to appear nonchalant. 'I'm a fisherman, Ma. A drift-fisherman. Where do I usually go when I leave home at this time of night?'

'Is that supposed to be an answer? You're squirming like a Mevagissey eel, my son. No, don't say any more. I'd rather you didn't tell me a lie. Rumour has it that you've taken up with Sir Lewis Hearle's daughter. I've scoffed at such silly talk. Elinor Hearle is far too high and mighty for the likes of us. Am I right or wrong?'

'I see her sometimes. We enjoy each other's company. Is there anything wrong with that?'

Nathan's very defensiveness told Annie Jago that the incredible half-rumours were true. She was aghast. Annie Jago had not always been married to a preacher. She knew what went on in the soft thyme of the Winnick, the rough pastureland behind Pentuan Beach. But that was between the girls and boys of the village, sons and daughters of fishermen.

There were also a number of bastards dwelling in the surrounding countryside who bore a remarkable resemblance to generations of Hearles. Indeed, bastards sired by men of good family were in great demand as husbands and wives. The paternal consciences of those who dwelled at Polrudden meant that *their* families would never go hungry in hard times.

All such relationships were accepted as part of the pattern of rural life. But for a village *man* to form such a relationship with the daughter of a great house was unheard of!

'There's everything wrong with it, as well you know. The Lord only knows what Sir Lewis Hearle will say when he hears what's going on behind his back – and he *will* find out, you can be sure of that. Oh, heaven help us! This could kill your father.'

Nathan was white-faced but unrepentant. 'Would you rather I moved out of the house, and found somewhere else to live?'

'And cause tongues to wag all the more? No, you're a grown man now, but you're still my son. Your road may not be my road – and it's certainly not your father's – but you'll never be turned out of this house while I'm alive.'

Annie Jago's words troubled Nathan greatly, but they did not prevent him from making the walk to Polrudden Manor that same night.

Between dusk and dawn, in Elinor Hearle's bed, Nathan entered a world far removed from the lot of a Pentuan fisherman. Not for him the cold comfort of a dingy, rough-blanketed room and a wife smelling of sweat and fish, her hands calloused and red-raw from constant immersion in rough preserving salt. Nathan lay with Elinor in a spacious bed, with clean linen covering their newly bathed bodies, and the fresh woman-smell of her in his nostrils as they made love in the darkness.

Nevertheless, after his mother's talk of rumour, Nathan was even more cautious than before. Labouring up the hill on his way to Polrudden Manor, he kept to the shadows, moving back out of sight if he heard anyone approaching along the pathway. In the mornings he always left the house before dawn, making his way direct to Portgiskey, where he would be hard at work on the boat by the time the others arrived.

One rough night the wind was gusting a gale from the south, driving heavy belts of rain inland off the sea. In the small cottage at Portgiskey, Amy lay awake listening to the thunder of the sea on the nearby rocks. Above her the beams creaked and groaned as the wind roared from clifftop to clifftop on either side of the house. Occasionally, lightning illuminated the room, but none of these noises was responsible for her wakefulness. They had all been part of life at Portgiskey Cove for as long as she had lived there. The cause of her sleeplessness was far more difficult to define.

Since Sammy Mizler and Nathan had gone into partnership with Amy and her mother, the days had been more fully occupied than any since the death of her father. Sammy had found a ready market for all the fish they could catch. All day long Portgiskey Cove rang to the voices of the fishermen and their wives, elbow-deep in fish and brine in the busy cellar. Yet deep inside Amy there was a dull emptiness that had not been there in the long, lonely days following her father's death. The pleasure and anticipation of working with Nathan had ebbed away. Nathan no longer talked of the plans he had for the future of the drift-fishing partnership. There were no longer exciting days when he carried everyone along with his enthusiasm. True, Nathan still worked harder than anyone when the weather permitted fishing, but his mind was elsewhere. His heart and soul had gone from his work.

Amy was certain she knew where the responsibility for the change lay, but she did not know what *she* could do to make everything right once more.

As Amy lay in her bed, she thought she heard a stone turn on the path outside. It was followed by what might have been a man's voice, uttering a muffled curse. Throwing back the blankets, Amy took two swift paces to the rattling window overlooking the path outside. As she opened the window the wind rushed in, billowing out the curtains. Carried on the wind was the sound of running footsteps, receding along the path that led inland from the cove.

Pulling a coat over her nightdress, Amy made her way to the living-room. Here she took down a pistol from a peg on the wall. Checking its loading and priming, she slipped the gun inside her coat and let herself out through the cottage door.

The wind out here was so strong that there was no way she could have kept a lamp alight; but she had sensibly placed a lamp in the window before leaving the house, and the light reached far enough to show Amy that the door of the fish-cellar was closed and did not appear to have been tampered with. Puzzled, Amy turned back to the darkened quay.

The boat was gone! Horrified, Amy ran to the edge of the quay. Kneeling in the rain and spray, she saw that the ropes used to secure the boat had been cut through.

The loss of their boat would be disastrous for the enterprise. Looking out into the darkness, Amy called upon all her years of experience of Portgiskey tides and topography in an effort to guess where the boat might now be.

It was three hours after high tide. Amy estimated that, if the boat had been cut adrift shortly before she had heard the footsteps, it would now be somewhere close to the rocks dividing the cove from Pentuan Beach. Once past the rocks the boat would be fully exposed to the wind and running sea. As the tide came in it would be swept on to the shore and quickly battered to pieces by the ferocious waves.

Without pausing to think of the dangers involved, Amy ran from the jetty to the pebble beach where her own small boat was drawn up beyond the reach of the swirling waters. There were several inches of rain-water in the bottom of the boat, making it heavier than usual; but, exerting all her strength, Amy heaved and slid the small boat down the beach until an incoming wave lifted the bow. It took only a moment for Amy to scramble on board and, unshipping the oars, she rowed the boat into the darkness of the cove.

Amy's one chance of saving the fishing-boat lay in locating it before it drifted clear of the cove. The bay beyond the cove was much too rough for her small craft, and it would be suicidal for her to attempt to go any farther.

Amy searched close to the rocks, gauging her distance from them by the white froth bubbling about their dark outlines. She found no trace of the large fishing-boat, Soaked by heavy rain and spray she twice searched the perimeter of the cove before accepting that the fishing-boat must already have been swept out into the heaving waters of St Austell Bay.

She had begun the hard pull back towards the light in the cottage window, when a dark shape suddenly loomed up ahead of her. Although Amy desperately tried to hold off the small rowing-boat, the two vessels collided with a thump that brought a screech of protest from the smaller vessel's timbers, and pitched Amy from the thwart. She had located the missing drifter.

Amy regained her feet as the two craft collided for a second time. For the next fifteen minutes, unable to climb on board the fishing-boat, she worked hard to secure a line from the rowing-boat to the larger fishing-craft. By the time she succeeded, the movement of the two vessels told her that she was passing from the comparative shelter of the cove into the bay.

Then began the most exhausting half-hour of Amy's young life. With her sodden clothes clinging to her body, and battered by wind and sea, she struggled to tow the fishing-boat to safety. Inch by hard-fought inch she pulled the dinghy towards the light, but it never seemed to get any closer. Finally, Amy knew she could go on no longer. She was weakening so much that, before long, the sea must win and carry both boats out to sea.

But she had gained the few yards that might make all the difference between saving or losing the drifter. It would have to suffice; she had no more strength in her.

There was an anchor in the rowing-boat. Too small to hold the drifter for long, it would have to do. Untying the rope that joined the two craft, Amy secured the anchor to the free end, trusting the other end would not break free from the drifter. It was a dreadful moment when she tossed the anchor out into the water. She felt as though she had deserted the fishing-boat, but she could do no more out here, alone.

At Polrudden, the ferocity of the storm had penetrated the self-induced exhaustion cocooning the two lovers. Nathan lay awake listening to the wind howling about the tall chimneys of the manor-house as lightning cast dancing shadows about the bedroom. He fancied the wind was shifting round to the east. An easterly gale brought the worst possible weather conditions to this part of the coast. It was the only gale that could seriously threaten the otherwise sheltered cove at Portgiskey.

He shifted an arm that was trapped beneath the naked body of Elinor. She lay with her back towards him, curled into the contours of his body. Untroubled by anything that might be happening beyond the bedroom walls, she slept easily, her breath a feline purr in her throat.

Nathan had been lying awake listening to the storm for about half an hour, when he heard another sound. It brought him to a sitting position in the bed, and Elinor stirred sleepily, protesting at the sudden movement.

'Sh! Can't you hear? There's someone at the door, downstairs.'

'In this weather? You're imagining things, Nathan. Something's broken loose in the wind, that's all.'

'There it is again! You must be able to hear it . . .'

The sound was unmistakable now. The heavy iron knocker on the front door of the house was being wielded determinedly by the late-night caller.

'Who on earth . . . ? Where are the servants? They can't *all* be deaf . . .'

'Hadn't you better go down and see who it is? What if it's someone with an urgent message and the servant brings him up here? It might even be your father!'

'He has more sense than to be out on a night like this. But you are right.' Elinor swung herself reluctantly out of bed. 'I had better go downstairs. Where's that blasted tinder-box . . . ?'

A moment later there was the repeated sound of steel on flintstone, and a flicker of flame as Elinor lit a candle.

A white silk dressing-gown lay on the floor at the foot of the bed. Picking it up, Elinor slipped it on to cover her nakedness. Then, with candle held aloft, she opened the door and went out, leaving the bedroom in darkness.

A few minutes later Nathan heard voices in the passageway outside the room and he had a brief moment of panic. What if it were Sir Lewis Hearle and he was insisting upon coming upstairs to his daughter's room? Then Nathan heard Elinor speak – and the answering voice was that of another woman. It was probably one of the servants. Nathan relaxed. They must have got rid of the visitor and were both returning to their beds.

But when the door opened Nathan could see in the candlelight that the other woman was still with Elinor, although only her dripping cloak was visible as she stood behind the baronet's daughter.

With malicious amusement, Elinor said: 'You have a visitor, Nathan. I told her you weren't dressed for company, but she insists that she must speak to you.'

Moving to one side, Elinor allowed the light from

the candle to fall upon the wet and dishevelled figure of Amy.

Nathan would have given much to have been able to pass responsibility for Amy's expression of deep hurt to someone else; but, even as he cringed in remorse, Amy's chin came up defiantly.

'Someone's been to Portgiskey and cut the boat adrift. I managed to get out to her and put an anchor down, but it's too small. It won't hold in this wind. I've sent Mother to rouse the others, but they'll not risk their lives for someone else's boat.'

There had been no hint of a tremor in Amy's voice while she passed on the dramatic information. Now her resolution faltered and she looked away from Nathan unhappily. 'I . . . I thought you ought to know.'

Nathan's embarrassment vanished. Much to Elinor's chagrin, his immediate concern was for his fishing-boat – and for Amy.

'You put to sea in this storm? To save the boat . . . ?'

'You weren't there to do it. What else could I do . . . ?' The words died in Amy's throat.

'Would you two mind if I return to my bed while you continue this conversation? Your little friend has brought the cold in with her, Nathan.'

Quite unashamedly, fully aware of the effect it had, Elinor Hearle undid the cord at the neck of her dressing-gown and allowed it to slide to the floor at her feet. Quite naked, she stepped clear of the tumbled heap of silk and climbed into bed beside Nathan.

Unable to control the tears that had threatened to shatter her outward composure from the moment of her arrival, Amy turned and fled from the room.

Nathan caught up with her halfway down the muddy track that led down the hill to Pentuan.

'Amy . . . I'm sorry that happened. Very sorry.'

'Sorry? Why, because I disturbed your love-making? Shouldn't *I* be the one apologising for that?'

Amy spoke fiercely, grateful that Nathan could not see her eyes in the storm-black night.

'That isn't what I meant. I'm sorry I caused you the humiliation of having to come and find me at Polrudden.'

Nathan reached out for her arm as she slipped on the mud of the track and fell against him. She shook his hand away angrily.

'Why should *I* feel humiliated? I wasn't the one in someone else's bed – and *she* certainly didn't feel humiliated. I got the impression she was actually enjoying it. Besides, how you live your life doesn't matter to me. We're partners, not husband and wife. Ma and me have put up the fish-cellar and you've provided the boat. The arrangement works very well – although I'll no doubt be looking for another partner when Sir Lewis Hearle learns what's going on. Now, save your breath – and mine. We'll both need it if we're to save the boat.'

With this final remark, Amy surged ahead at a furious pace that did not slacken until they were at Portgiskey.

Amy's mother had roused Calvin Dickin, Ahab Arthur and one of the new young members of the fishing crew. When Nathan and Amy arrived they were all standing in the shelter of the fish-cellar doorway. Peering out into the darkness, they were nervously debating their first move. If they wondered why it had taken Amy so long to find Nathan, no one voiced his thoughts aloud.

'It doesn't seem right that someone should cut another man's boat adrift in this weather,' said Ahab Arthur. 'Not that it surprises me. They did some terrible things before they managed to put me out of business. D'you have any idea who did it, Nathan?'

'Never mind that now. We need to get out to the boat. Amy's been out to her and put an anchor down, but it's too small. It won't hold in an easterly gale. We'll need to get on board, take her out to sea and ride out this storm well clear of land.'

Three faces turned to him, yellow-white in the lamplight. 'Put to sea – in this? 'Tis madness, Nathan, and no mistake.'

The young fisherman spoke for them all.

'Damn you! While we're here saying what we *can't* do, my boat is probably dragging anchor and heading for the rocks. I'll not ask any one of you to go farther than the mouth of the cove. Take me there and I'll go on board and take the boat to sea myself.'

Nathan ran from the cellar doorway to Amy's boat, riding in the shallow surf at the edge of the beach. With considerable trepidation, the three men followed. Amy went with them.

Nathan stood in the bows, scanning the darkness to catch a first glimpse of the drifter as the men pulled away from the shore. Amy called directions from the stern. She guided them to where she thought the fishing-boat should be, but it was not there. When Amy's small boat nosed from the cove into the agitated waters of the bay, it began pitching alarmingly. Without waiting for an order, the three crewmen hastily back-oared the boat to the shelter of the cove once more.

They made another search, this time closer to the rocks – and here they found the drifter. It had dragged its ineffectual anchor, and was pitching and bucking close to the black, sea-washed rocks, only a matter of yards from the cove entrance.

With the changing direction of the wind, it could only be a matter of minutes before the drifter dragged anchor once more and was dashed to pieces on the rocks.

'Go alongside – on the lee side,' Nathan called. 'I'm going on board.'

'It's madness,' Calvin Dickin shouted as he leaned on his oar, holding it firm between his body and his one good arm. 'Leave her be. Better to lose a boat than your life.'

'We've lost neither yet – and we're not going to. Get me to the other side of her. *Pull!*'

The fishermen brought the small boat to the far side of the wildly bucking drifter. In the scant shelter offered by the larger craft, they eased Amy's boat in towards it, stern first.

'Take it steady now.' Nathan had made his way to the stern and now he crouched beside Amy, his face protected from the driving rain by an upflung arm.

The dark bulk of the drifter loomed above the small boat now, but neither vessel was still. At one moment the two boats were almost touching, the next they were many feet apart.

'Hold it now . . . *Hold it!*' Nathan was reaching out but could not quite touch the other vessel. The men behind him heard his cry and strained on their oars to hold the small boat in position. The drifter rose above Nathan; then, as it dropped away, Nathan leaped into the darkness.

For one frightening moment Nathan thought he had misjudged the distance. Then the drifter rose hard to meet him and he tumbled on the half-deck.

'Nathan, *help me! help . . .!*' Amy's cry came from nearby as Nathan scrambled to his knees.

'Where are you? Keep shouting!'

'Here, close to the backstay. Help me – quickly!'

Nathan scrambled across the deck to where the taut rope-stay securing the mast was attached to the side of the boat. He found Amy hanging over the side, her arm hooked about the water-tautened rope. Her body, from the waist downwards, was being dipped in the sea every few moments as the drifter rocked violently from side to side.

Putting an arm down, Nathan secured a grip on the sodden dress Amy wore beneath her waterproof coat. Waiting until the roll of the drifter was to his advantage, Nathan heaved Amy inboard and dropped her ignominiously to the bottom of the boat.

'That was a damned foolish trick! What were you doing?'

'C-coming on board w-with you. You can't manage the sails and steer the boat in this w-weather.'

Amy's teeth were chattering as much from fright as from the repeated ducking she had received in the cold water. She had leaped from the smaller boat only seconds after Nathan, but the leap had been badly mistimed. While she was in mid-air the drifter had reared from the water and passed her by. She only just managed to grip the gunwale and hook an arm about the backstay. There she clung like a limpet while the movements of boat and sea combined in a wild attempt to fling her off.

Nathan realised how close Amy had come to death, and the knowledge frightened him as much as it did her. But Amy was right. It would take two of them if they were to have a real chance of saving the drifter. The weather was far more severe than he had realised.

'Help me to shorten the anchor rope.' He shouted the words, his lips close to her ear. 'We've got to get away from the rocks before we risk raising any sail.'

They both made it safely to the bow of the drifter, and then began the gruelling task of hauling the rope in, and so pulling the boat away from the rocks. They had to be very careful. If they brought the boat too close to the anchor, the force of the swell would combine with the movement of the drifter to dislodge the anchor from the bed of the cove.

They worked for twenty minutes before Nathan called a halt.

'That's it. You take the wheel while I hoist a sail. Steer across the cove. When I feel the wind begin to take us I'll cut through the anchor rope.'

Amy crawled away towards the wheel. Giving her time to unlash the rope that held the wheel, Nathan close-hoisted the foresail. He dared not hoist the larger lugsail in this wind; it was strong enough to overturn a larger boat than the drifter. As it was, the wind threatened to sweep them inside the cove, complete with dragging anchor.

When the boat started straining into the wind, Nathan cut through the anchor rope with a couple of slashes from the sharp knife he wore at his belt – and the drifter was free.

Amy held her course for no more than a minute before bringing the boat about and sailing on the opposite tack. Meanwhile, Nathan worked frantically to adjust the sail and so gain maximum controlled propulsion from the wind.

They tacked twice more before Nathan estimated they must now be well clear of the tiny cove. The violent movement of the boat tended to confirm his view. On the last occasion Amy brought the boat about it seemed they would capsize, and Nathan had to scramble aft to help her hold the wheel as the rudder was caught between the will of man and the incredible power of the sea.

'We're clear of the point now.' Amy echoed Nathan's thoughts.

He nodded. 'We'll make for clear water, then put out a sea-anchor and ride this out.'

With the initial excitement over, Amy once more had great difficulty in stopping her teeth from chattering noisily. She had been thoroughly soaked by sea and rain, and the chill of the November night was biting deep into her bones.

By the time Nathan felt they were far enough out from shore to put out a sea-anchor, Amy could no longer hide the effect the cold was having on her. Teeth chattering, she shook uncontrollably. When Nathan came to lash the wheel he was thoroughly alarmed. Then he remembered the dripping figure standing outside the bedroom at Polrudden, and later clinging to the side of the boat. It had been a long, cold and exhausting night for Amy.

'Come on, you need to get out of those clothes and into something dry.'

As he put an arm about her shoulders to help her inside the shelter of the small and shallow hold, Amy tried to protest that she could manage by herself, but she was unable to stop her teeth from chattering for long enough to put the words together.

Sheltered from the wind, Nathan rummaged through a locker and found the spare shirt and trousers he always kept there.

'Get your things off and put these on.' Nathan thrust the dry clothing into her hands, and she promptly dropped them again.

Picking them up, Nathan said: 'You'd best let me do it for you.'

Amy jerkily voiced her protest, but by the time it was out Nathan had unfastened her soaking 'waterproof' coat and eased it over her shoulders. He unfastened the buttons on the top of her dress, too, but as he tried to slip it down over her shoulders she stopped him. 'I c-c-can do it.'

She was wrong. Amy was so cold that her hands would no longer function. After she had fumbled at the dress for more than five minutes, Nathan completed the task for her.

'Come on now. Everything off – and no arguments.'

In the darkness, Nathan stripped the clothes from Amy's shivering figure, pausing only when lightning beyond the open hatchway bared her body to him and she vainly attempted to shield her nakedness with her arms.

He slipped the rough flannel shirt over her head and then gave her the trousers to pull on, tying the waist with a piece of cord and rolling up the bottoms of the oversized trousers. Finally he took off his waterproof coat and, pulling off his heavy, fisherman's jersey, handed it to her.

Forestalling her objections, he said: 'Keep it on until you're warmer. There isn't another waterproof, so you'd best stay down here for a while.'

He helped to pull the neck of the jersey over her head and could not prevent a grin as another flash of lightning showed him the small, tired and cold figure in the oversized clothes.

'That was a foolish thing you did back there in the cove. You could have got yourself killed. But it's something I'll never forget. Without you we'd have lost the boat.'

He put an arm about her shoulders in an affectionate gesture, but she shrugged it away, determined not to let him know how much pleasure his words gave her. 'Save your embraces for Mistress Hearle. You and I are business partners, that's all. Without the boat we'd both have suffered. I did what needed to be done. I went to Polrudden for the same reason.'

Nathan suddenly realised that he had not thought of Elinor Hearle once since setting out from Polrudden, and he doubted whether he had occupied her thoughts for a moment more. She would be lying in her bed, safe and warm, the storm no more than a rattle of wind against the window.

Nathan wondered how Elinor would have behaved in circumstances such as those he and Amy had encountered tonight. Elinor was a strong-minded girl – a *wilful* girl – but would she have risked her life to save his boat?

Nathan checked his thoughts. He was making unfair comparisons. Elinor was risking much – not least, her reputation – because of their relationship. She, too, was a remarkable girl – and he had fallen in love for the first time in his life.

The dawn brought a welcome improvement in the weather. Thunder still occasionally grumbled far out in the English Channel, but the rain had stopped, and the wind was now no more than a stiff breeze.

Nathan and Amy sailed the drifter to Portgiskey Cove and a welcome from the whole of the crew, Peggy Hoblyn and Sammy Mizler. The relief of everyone was evident, although it was noticeable to Nathan that most of Sammy Mizler's concern was for Amy. She, in her turn, was embarrassed as much by the fishermen's expressed admiration for her heroism as by her unusual garb.

When the boat was safely moored alongside the quay, the events of the night caught up with Nathan and he suddenly felt very, very tired. Picking up his waterproof coat, he announced brusquely that he was going home to Pentuan to sleep, and told Sammy Mizler to ensure that Amy did the same.

'When you've done that I've another job for you. You can paint a name on the boat.'

The fishermen beamed their delight. Putting to sea in an unnamed vessel had troubled them. It was a break with tradition. Such things were likely to bring ill-luck. They would have pointed to the events of the previous night as an example, had not the cut mooring-ropes pointed to the more positive influence of a Mevagissey or Pentuan seiner.

'What's the name to be?'

The question came from Calvin Dickin. 'After last night it should be something like *Storm Queen*, I'm thinking.'

'I've a better name than that, Calvin. She'll be called *The Brave Amy H*, and there'll be no fishing-boat with a prouder name.'

12

It seemed that the wild weather of 1810 had spent itself in the storm which almost wrecked the newly named fishing-boat. From that night the weather steadily improved, and December brought crisp, clear days and skies unscarred by a single cloud.

The first week of December also saw the return of Sir Lewis Hearle to Polrudden. With him came some of the glory the ancient Cornish manor had enjoyed in former days. It seemed that the whole of the county's gentry wished to call upon Sir Lewis in order to offer him their congratulations on his Home Office appointment. There were so many visitors that was obliged to take on more staff to work in the house, and Elinor assumed the unaccustomed role of hostess to her father's guests.

Suddenly, Polrudden was no place for a lovelorn fisherman.

But not all of Sir Lewis Hearle's visitors came to

Polrudden to murmur insincere good wishes and drink his rather less than excellent sherry. There were those who came on more serious business. Among these was the Reverend Nicholas Kent, the Methodist-hating rector of Fowey.

The Reverend Kent was closeted with Sir Lewis for two hours and left the house a happy man. He believed that at last there was a man in government office who *really* understood the threat posed to the country by the followers of Wesley.

Others spent less time in Sir Lewis Hearle's study – and left Polrudden deeply unhappy. Some even had tears streaming down their sunburned cheeks. These were the tenant farmers who rented their farms from the baronet MP. Many had worked their rented lands for a lifetime, as had their fathers and grandfathers before them. Now Sir Lewis had told them they must prepare to leave. The farms were being sold to raise badly needed money for the newly promoted Member of Parliament.

One of the farmers so affected was Tom Quicke, husband of Nathan's sister. The young farming couple came to Pentuan to break the news to the Jago family when Nathan, Amy, and Sammy Mizler were there. Nell was in a particularly distressed state. She sat in a high-backed chair in the kitchen of the tiny cottage, wringing her hands, the tears that filled her eyes threatening to overflow at any moment.

Nell's undisguised misery surprised Nathan. He was aware that she loved the farm where she and Tom lived, but Nell had always been such a selfless girl. It would have been more in keeping with her nature had she tried to shrug off the grim news in a bid to lessen the blow for her husband.

It was not long before the reason for her deep distress became known, eased on its way by a sudden flood of tears. Nell imparted the news that she was expecting a baby. It would arrive in May 1811. She and Tom had delayed telling anyone until they were absolutely certain.

The news brought delighted congratulations from both Annie and Josiah Jago.

'It's wonderful news . . . just wonderful.' Annie Jago hugged her daughter, then looked pointedly at Nathan. 'I was beginning to wonder whether your father and I would live long enough to see grand-children in our home.'

'But it's *not* wonderful.' The flow of Nell's tears increased. 'That's what makes Sir Lewis Hearle's decision so heartbreaking. We've nowhere to live, and Tom will have no work. You know what things are like for men who work on the land. More than half are in the country's poor-houses . . .'

Tom Quicke put an arm about his young wife's shoulders, murmuring that they would manage some-how.

Josiah Jago was embarrassed by his daughter's anguish. An unemotional man himself, he found his aloofness an asset when dealing with those who looked to him for comfort in times of grief, even though it set him apart from the members of his own family. But he cared for his children and ago-nised because he expressed less feeling for them than he had for others.

'Did you tell Sir Lewis Hearle about the baby?'

Tom Quicke nodded ruefully. 'I did. He was quick to tell me that the decision to have a child was mine and not his. He said its future was my concern.'

Josiah Jago shook his head sadly. 'Sir Lewis is an uncharitable man for one in his position. Now, if he only came to listen to my preaching. I would give him a sermon taken straight from the New Testament. Jesus himself once said—'

'What price does Sir Lewis Hearle put on your farm?' Nathan interrupted his father's homily brusquely. The sermon had always been Josiah Jago's answer to the many problems of life. It was one of the reasons why Nathan had run away from home at the age of fifteen.

Tom Quicke was less accustomed to the ways of father and son. He felt uncomfortable at Nathan's abrupt interruption.

'What difference does it make? Be it a thousand guineas, or a hundred, I can raise neither. We've been scratching a living at Venn, no more. The land's improving, but it will – it would have been a while before we made any money. Now, if only I'd had a milking-cow, we'd have brought money in, make no mistake . . .'

He caught Nathan's eye and blushed.

'I'm sorry; I'm day-dreaming. Even with the best milking-cow in the land I'd never be able to raise enough money to buy Venn. It's beyond the likes of me, as Sir Lewis Hearle knows full well.' For the first time since coming to the cottage, Tom Quicke allowed some of the bitterness he felt to show. 'He's asking a thousand guineas.'

Nathan looked across the room at Sammy Mizler.

Correctly interpreting the unasked question, Sammy shook his head. There was not nearly enough money in the partnership to buy a farm, even had the other two partners agreed to the suggestion. There had been a lot of nets to replace, in addition to the everyday expenses associated with fishing.

'Don't give up all hope yet, Tom. Or you, Nell. I'll see if I can think of something.'

'Do you think because there's something between you and Elinor Hearle her father will change his mind? Huh! You don't know Sir Lewis – or his daughter.'

In her anger, Amy had spoken without thinking of who was in the room. Now she caught her breath in dismay when Preacher Josiah Jago pounced on her words.

'What kind of talk is this? What can there possibly be between Nathan and the Hearle girl?'

Annie Jago provided the answer that neither Nathan nor Amy could find: 'Amy means that Nathan earned the gratitude of Sir Lewis Hearle by saving his daughter from a beating at the hands of a drunken drayman when she tried to prevent a horse from being mistreated.'

Josiah Jago looked from mother to son suspiciously. 'Why haven't I heard anything about this before?'

'It happened in St Austell when Nathan was on his way home from London. You were too busy getting yourself arrested to know about anything else that was going on. Now, you can all sit down at the table while I serve something up for you. Then we'll talk of babies and the like – not of Sir Lewis Hearle and his doings.'

It was an order that Annie Jago would allow no one to disobey for the remainder of the evening.

Later, Nathan and Sammy Mizler walked Amy to the small cottage at Portgiskey. Since the night the mooring-ropes on *The Brave Amy H* had been cut, one of the men always slept at Portgiskey Cove, in the fishing-store beside the cellar.

Tonight was Sammy Mizler's turn. Sammy would have preferred to walk with Amy without any other company, but Nathan had something to say to his friend.

The opportunity to speak to Sammy alone did not come until the night was well advanced. The three partners sat on the quayside talking until then and, for the first time, Nathan became aware of the easy relationship that now existed between Sammy Mizler and Amy. Indeed, Amy seemed intent upon provoking Nathan into commenting upon their close friendship, but Nathan refused to be drawn and eventually Amy announced that she was going to bed.

When the two men reached the fishing-store, Sammy Mizler said: 'All right, what's on your mind? You've been simmering like a tripe stew all evening. What is it?'

Instead of replying, Nathan took a card from his pocket and handed it to his companion.

Sammy Mizler read the name printed upon the card and looked at Nathan in bewilderment. 'The Duke of Clarence? Where did you get this?'

Nathan told him of the evening he and Amy had spent at the Dartmouth inn.

Weighing the card in his hand as though it were a nugget of pure gold, Sammy Mizler whistled softly.

'Oi! What an opportunity! What a wonderful opportunity. When I was finding fights for you I'd have given my right arm for such a chance . . . But why are you showing this to me now?'

The look he saw on Nathan's face caused Sammy to leap to his feet in excitement. 'You've come to your senses at last? Nathan, tell me you're giving up this idea of chasing small fishes for a living. You're going back to the prize-ring?'

'Not quite. But I'll fight again if the purse is right.'

'With the Duke of Clarence as your backer? You'll be able to name your own purse. Five hundred. Six . . . *seven* hundred guineas, even.'

To Sammy's astonishment, Nathan shook his head. 'It needs to be more than that, Sammy. I want you to take that card to the Duke of Clarence in London. Tell him I'm ready to defend my championship against any fighter of his choice – but only if he's prepared to put up a thousand guineas.'

'A thousand!' Sammy Mizler gasped. 'You'll never get it, Nathan. Who has ever heard of a thousand-guinea purse for a prize-fight?'

'Hen Pearce. He defended the title I hold for a thousand guineas in 1805. And who do you think put up the money?'

Sammy Mizler nodded his head vigorously, acknowledging Nathan's prize-fighting knowledge. 'It was the Duke of Clarence. So what do you want me to do?'

'I want you to take a fast coach to London. See the Duke, and tell him my terms. If he agrees, have him use the thousand guineas to buy Venn Farm and make it over to Tom and Nell. Sir Lewis will sell Venn to the

Duke of Clarence without asking questions. If *I* try to buy the farm, he'll probably refuse to sell it to me.'

Sammy Mizler had already guessed the reason behind Nathan's return to the ring, but he could not hide his astonishment that Nathan should fight for such a colossal sum – and then give it all away.

'If the Duke of Clarence agrees to put up the purse, I'll leave it to you to arrange everything. Try to get the fight staged close to Cornwall, if you can. I can't spare too much time away from my boat.'

'*Our* boat,' corrected Sammy softly. 'And what about my share of the purse? Or are you going to give all this money away without consulting me, just as you did with the purse you won from Ned Belcher?'

Nathan was unsure whether Sammy Mizler was joking or serious. They *did* have a longstanding arrangement that Sammy should take a percentage of the purse, and he was quite within his rights to demand that Nathan should honour the agreement.

'You'll get your share, but it will have to come from the profits I get from fishing. Nell and Tom need that money desperately.'

'All right! All right!' Sammy Mizler threw up his hands. 'Forget my share. With you in this mood I can guarantee to win twice as much on bets. I just wanted to remind you that I'm doing you a favour, that's all. Besides, what do I want with money – unless I need to get married, maybe?'

Nathan frowned, remembering how Amy and Sammy had behaved together that evening. He wondered if Sammy was trying to tell him something, but the Jewish ex-fighter was already talking about another matter.

'When do you want me to leave? I haven't a lot on just now.'

'Good, then go tomorrow. Return to the house and pack your things now. There's a coach from St Austell in the morning that will have you in London in forty hours. I'll stay here tonight.'

Sammy Mizler was taken aback by such haste, but he knew Nathan too well to argue. Besides, this was an opportunity that was too good to pass up. For a while Sammy would be back enjoying the camaraderie of the prize-ring, the fluctuating fortunes of the fighters, and the hurly-burly and feverish excitement of a championship fight.

After Sammy Mizler had gone, Nathan extinguished the fish-oil lamp and lay on the makeshift bed in the fishing-store. No more than a couple of blankets laid upon a pile of new fishing-nets, it was more comfortable than many beds he had known, but sleep was slow in coming. He was not surprised. The prospect of fighting again was both exciting and daunting. In common with Sammy, Nathan shared a love of the atmosphere of a prize-fight: the noisy crowd; the well-dressed men of the 'Fancy' – the gentlemen who followed the sport: and the awareness that prize-fighting was still illegal. At any moment the local magistrate might appear on the scene with his constables or the militia, bringing a fight to an end amid scenes of wild pandemonium.

Yet, in spite of the thrill of ducking beneath the rope of a ring to the accompaniment of a mighty roar from the crowd, every champion prize-fighter always knew that the man standing in the far corner of the ring at the start of a fight might be the one to best him and take away his title.

No champion had yet come back from defeat to regain a title. For this reason many tried to enjoy the glory of their title for as long as possible without fighting in its defence. Others – and Nathan had hoped to be one of them – simply faded from the prize-fighting scene. Investing his hard-earned purses in a small business, more often than not an inn, the ex-champion would content himself with rapidly fading local fame, enjoying a way of life he might otherwise never have known.

All these thoughts came to Nathan as he lay on his fishing-net mattress. He had many other thoughts, too, not all connected with the prize-ring.

There was a strong wind outside, and breakers crashed heavily against the rocks beneath the cliff-base. But it was not raining, and after lying awake for more than an hour Nathan decided to take a walk.

The lights were off in the Hoblyn cottage; Amy and her mother had gone to bed. In the sky above, scattered cloud fled before the wind, intermittently covering the moon.

Turning his jacket collar high about his neck, Nathan walked along the sand before turning inland, returning to Portgiskey after about an hour, approaching the cove along the narrow valley from the Mevagissey road.

He was close to the house, all sound of his approach muffled by the booming surf, when he saw a flicker of light in the vicinity of the quayside, where *The Brave Amy H* was moored. Seconds later the light became a flame that leaped into the air, fanned by the wind.

Nathan began to run. The moon was temporarily hidden behind a cloud, but he was guided by the flickering yellow flames that grew with every second. Nathan's running footsteps on the soft grass of the little-used pathway made no sound – and suddenly the figure of a man loomed up before him.

The other man uttered an exclamation of surprise, but even as the sound left his lips Nathan's fist moved to shut it off.

Nathan knew his blow was a good one, but he did not stop to make certain. He could see now that the fire was inside *The Brave Amy H.* It needed to be extinguished quickly.

There was a second man running along the path from the quay, but he saw Nathan and turned to flee back the way he had come. Nathan was close on his heels by the time he reached the cottage. Unable to escape any other way, the unknown arsonist jumped from the quay. Unfortunately for him, he chose the end of the quay where a huge flat rock was embedded in the sand. Landing awkwardly, he gave a scream of pain that quickly gave way to agonised howling.

Nathan ignored the man's cries. The fire was burning in the nets stowed on board *The Brave Amy H.* Someone had emptied a couple of bags of wood shavings inside the boat and struck a flint to them. Loaded ready to put to sea the moment the wind dropped, there was almost a mile of nets on board. They were valuable – and highly inflammable.

Nathan began pulling the nets from the boat, concentrating on those that were already well alight. He had not been working long when he heard a shout from the quay above him. Looking up, he saw Amy and her mother holding a large wooden tub between them. He just had time to leap out of the way before they tipped the contents of the tub over the edge of the quay.

A cascade of water descended upon the blaze inside the boat. It hissed loudly and raised a cloud of steam, but seconds later the flames were regaining lost ground.

However, with Nathan pulling nets from the boat as fast as the flames would allow, and Amy and her mother attacking the blaze from above, it was possible to prevent any permanent damage being caused to the boat. By the time the last net was pulled clear, the fire had been extinguished, charring no more than a thwart and scorching the boat's paintwork.

As the remains of the nets smouldered on the quay steps, or trailed on the damp sand beside the boat, Nathan strode to where the unknown arsonist had dragged himself to a sitting position, his back propped against a rock. He was groaning less noisily now, but both his hands clutched his right leg, just beneath the knee. The moonlight showed the lower section of the leg extending sideways at an unnatural angle, indicating a serious fracture.

'It's broken . . . My leg's broken.' The man gasped the words painfully.

'You'll wish it was your neck by the time I'm finished with you,' growled Nathan angrily. 'Likely it will be. Setting fire to a man's property is a hanging offence. Why did you do it? I've never seen you before.'

It was the truth, although there was something about the man that was vaguely familiar.

Nathan received no reply and he called for Amy to bring a lantern. In the meantime, he ran back along the path to where he had knocked the second arsonist to the ground. The man had gone.

Returning to the quayside, Nathan found Amy bending over the injured man. She had slit his trousers to the knee and was examining the area about the break. Looking up at Nathan, she said: 'This leg will need to be set. Mother can do it, but she'll need your help.'

'There will be no help from me. He'll hang as well with one leg as with two. What I want to know is, why did he set fire to our boat?'

'He's a seiner. I suppose that was reason enough for him.'

'Perhaps, but it's not for me. You know him?'

'Yes, it's Dick Coffin, from Mevagissey.'

'Coffin?' Nathan looked at the man more closely. Now he thought he knew why he looked so familiar. 'Is he a brother to the Coffin who's a drayman in St Austell?'

'He was a drayman until you cost him his job.' The man on the ground spoke through his pain.

'Is that the man you knocked unconscious in St Austell?' Amy asked the question.

'And again tonight, unless I'm mistaken. You pick up the lantern. I'll drag this one to the storeroom. He can wait for the constable in there.'

'Nathan . . .' Amy touched his arm as he leaned over the injured man. Leading him some paces away, she said softly: 'Don't inform the constable

. . . please. I know Dick Coffin's family. His wife and children – all six of them. The youngest is blind, and Dick is her whole life. He's wonderful with her, he really is.'

'He should have thought of her before coming here and trying to destroy our boat. It isn't the first time, you know that?'

Amy nodded. 'You have every right to have him arrested. But please don't, I beg you.'

Nathan thought he knew why Amy and his sister Nell were such good friends. They both cared too much about other people.

'Dick Coffin and his brother have cost us a lot of money tonight, Amy – and they damn near cost you your life, too, the last time they came calling. I can't think of one good reason why he shouldn't hang.'

'I can. A little blind girl named Sophie Coffin.'

Nathan looked seriously at Amy for a long while, and she thought he was going to insist on informing the magistrate. Instead, he shrugged. 'Very well. But we're not standing the loss we've suffered tonight. Dick Coffin and his brother will pay for those nets. I don't care how they raise the money, but they *will* pay.'

Amy's whole body sagged in sudden relief. Few people would have criticised Nathan had he insisted upon handing Dick Coffin over to the constable. Not even the Mevagissey fishermen themselves.

'Thank you, Nathan.'

'Go and fetch your mother,' said Nathan gruffly. 'I'll carry Coffin to the store. She can set his leg there. I'll find his brother tomorrow.'

*   *   *

Nathan did not find Bill Coffin the next day, or any other day. Returning home during the night, Bill Coffin made up a bundle of his clothing and left hurriedly, never to be seen in his native Cornwall again.

13

Up at the first hint of dawn, Sammy Mizler walked to St Austell, arriving in good time for the mail coach. As on the much shorter journey to Plymouth a few weeks before, Sammy travelled inside the coach. He was on his way to call on the Duke of Clarence, son of the reigning monarch. He could not arrive in clothes that had been subjected to rain and spattered by mud thrown up from country roads.

It was the boast of the coach operators that their forty-hour service to London was the fastest the West Country had ever known. It undoubtedly was, but in order to achieve such a time all else had been sacrificed to speed. The journey was a nightmare of jolting and jarring on indifferent roads, and was accompanied by constant noise. There were squealing coach springs, complaining passengers, drumming hooves, the shouts of the driver, and the long, drawn-out note of the coach horn warning tollmen of their rapid approach.

For Sammy Mizler, all discomfort became worth-while when potholed, rutted roads gave way to the cobbled streets of London. Life inside the coach became more bearable as the volume of traffic and the hazards of London at dusk forced the coach driver to slacken his pace.

That night, with the sounds of London in his ears, and its sulphurous night odour in his nostrils, Sammy slept more soundly than he had for many months.

The next morning he rose late and dressed slowly and carefully. At noon he summoned a hackney carriage, taking snobbish delight in instructing the cabbie to take him to Almack's Club, the most fashionable establishment in London's St James's. Sammy had been told by reliable friends that it was here he was most likely to find the sporting Duke of Clarence.

Sammy Mizler's pride suffered a blow at Almack's, when an immaculately liveried doorman blocked his path and directed him to the back door before Sammy had uttered a single word. His reply was to grasp the haughty doorman about the waist, lift him with deceptive ease to one side, and stride in through the open doorway. Immediately, he was surrounded by a whole host of club employees and bustled hurriedly to a large office. Sammy could have taken them all on and beaten them without too much difficulty, but he had come here to arrange a fight, not to become involved in one himself.

In the office a man jumped to his feet and one of the men surrounding Sammy explained quickly what had happened.

'This man was stopped at the entrance, Mr McAlmack, but he forced his way in.'

'I was told to go to the back door before I had time to state my business,' Sammy Mizler interrupted the speaker. 'I objected – peaceably.'

The club employee began speaking again, but McAlmack cut him short with an impatient wave of his hand. Speaking in a clipped Scots accent, he asked Sammy: 'And just what *is* your business?'

'I'm here to see the Duke of Clarence.'

McAlmack's eyebrows rose so high they merged with the grey hair that hung down over his forehead. 'Indeed? And who shall I tell his Grace is here to speak to him?'

'My name is Sammy Mizler, but I'm here on behalf of Nathan Jago.' Sammy reached inside his pocket and drew out the card the Duke had presented to Nathan. 'The Duke gave him this, some time ago.'

McAlmack glanced at the card and waved his staff from the room, brushing them before him with his hands. When they had all gone, he said to Sammy: 'You'll stay here while I speak to his Grace. But I give you due warning, Mizler. If he doesn't wish to talk to you, I'll call the constables and have you charged with forcing your way in here.'

'He'll see me,' replied Sammy, with more confidence than he felt. Without even putting his mind to the matter, he could think of many reasons why the Duke of Clarence might not wish to speak to him. Prize-fighting *was* an illegal sport, and even dukes of royal blood were not above the law.

Sammy Mizler need not have worried. A few minutes later McAlmack hurried to the office and held the door open for him.

'If you'll come this way, Mr Mizler, his Grace will be pleased to receive you.'

Sammy Sammy's relief was tinged with nervousness. He was over the first hurdle, but now he had to persuade the Duke of Clarence to back Nathan on terms that Sammy himself believed to be unrealistic.

McAlmack knocked at a door and waited with his ear pressed against it until he heard a muffled 'Come in!' Opening the door, he pushed Sammy inside and bowed low.

'Your Grace, my Lords. Mr Mizler.'

There were four men seated about a table on which were strewn cards, money, and a number of glasses and bottles. At the far end of the room a fire burned cheerfully. The heat inside the room was such that Sammy wished he had removed his heavy worsted overcoat before stepping inside.

As McAlmack backed from the room, Sammy Mizler bowed to each of the men about the table in turn. He had seen them all before – at prize-fights. In addition to the Duke of Clarence, there was the Marquess of Queensberry, Lord Pomfret and Sir Francis Boynton. Each was an enthusiastic follower of prize-fighting.

'I believe you've come here on behalf of Nathan Jago? What does he want, sponsorship for a fight, I suppose, eh?' The Duke of Clarence's manner was as bluff as his appearance, but he was smiling and Sammy Mizler was given new hope.

'Yes, your Grace. He says he'll fight anyone of your choosing – but he wants a purse of a thousand guineas.'

'A thousand guineas?' The Duke of Clarence's astonishment was echoed in the gasps of his companions. 'I could be tempted to step inside a ring myself for a thousand guineas. What does Jago want with such a sum? Is he in trouble?'

Sammy realised that his only hope of persuading William, Duke of Clarence to put up a purse for Nathan's fight lay in telling him the truth.

The four men listened in silence until Sammy Mizler had finished talking, then they exchanged glances among themselves.

'So this is to be Jago's last fight,' mused the Duke of Clarence.

'Jago's always drawn a good crowd,' declared the Marquess of Queensberry. 'I'm willing to put up two hundred and fifty guineas of the purse.' He looked at his companions. Both Lord Pomfret and Sir Francis Boynton nodded.

'Then I'll gladly put up the other two hundred and fifty.' The Duke of Clarence looked thoughtfully at Sammy Mizler. 'Jago has his thousand guineas. But I'm damned if I'll get involved in any village politics – and I'll act as no estate agent for a prize-fighter. I'll arrange for the purchase of this farm to be made through my brother's Duchy of Cornwall office. They are buying and selling land all the time, as far as I can make out. What they do will excite no curiosity. Now, about the fight itself. I'm not going to be made to look a fool by having Jago fall to the ground at the first punch and walk off with a thousand guineas in his pocket. Jago gets his money, but only if he wins, or is still on his feet after, say, *twenty* rounds? Is this understood?'

Sammy Mizler nodded. He was confident that Nathan could beat any fighter in the British Isles.

'I've not finished yet. There is one more condition. If Jago wins this fight, he'll defend his title again – at Bushy Park. But this time for a nominal purse.'

Bushy Park was where the Duke of Clarence lived. It had been the venue for many famous prize-fights in recent years.

Sammy hesitated, reluctant to commit Nathan to two fights.

'Those are my conditions, Mizler. You can accept them or refuse. Just as you wish.'

'I accept them, your Grace.' Sammy Mizler fervently hoped that Nathan thought his sister Nell's future was worth *two* fights.

'Good. Pull up a chair and have a drink while we discuss a suitable opponent for Jago. It will need to be someone very good if we're to draw a crowd large enough to cover a thousand-guinea purse.'

Sammy Mizler did not return to Pentuan until seventeen days after his departure, with Christmas only a week away. His return journey had not been without incident. First, the coach had been held up by a highwayman when no more than ten miles out of London. The would-be thief had been shot dead by one of the passengers, a wounded artillery officer returning from the Peninsular Wars. Then, crossing the high expanse of Dartmoor, the coach was caught in a blizzard. For a whole night passengers and coachman huddled together inside the coach to keep warm while the driver floundered through deep snow with the unhitched horses, in a desperate bid to find help. The shivering passengers were dug out the following day by French prisoners-of-war from Dartmoor prison. Afterwards, the same prisoners dragged the carriage through the snow until they reached a more sheltered spot, where fresh horses were hitched up to take the coach on its way.

But the story of Sammy Mizler's adventures would have to await a quiet evening beside the fire in Amy Hoblyn's Portgiskey home. Nathan was eager to know the result of Sammy's mission to the Duke of Clarence.

As Sammy had anticipated, Nathan was not pleased with the condition that meant he would have to fight again at Bushy Park. It would mean a long spell away from fishing. However, that was in the future. The main consideration was that he had saved Venn Farm for Nell and Tom – providing, of course, he did not lose the first fight. But Nathan entertained no thought of losing. Sammy Mizler had done well. Nathan told him so and asked who he would be fighting.

Some of Sammy Mizler's pleasure at Nathan's praise faded a little.

'You're to fight Abraham Dellow, an American sailor. His ship is expected in Bristol from Africa, bound for America, some time in January. A horseman will be sent to tell us of its arrival. He'll also carry a letter with full details of where the fight is to be held, but I've been assured it will be in the Bristol area. I spoke to the London agents of the ship and I've been able to make a good deal for our fish with them. They'll take all the pilchards we can let them have in Bristol. But they want them double-cured. They'll be going to the West Indies. They also insist on thirty-two-gallon hogsheads, but they're willing to pay fifty shillings per hogshead.'

Nathan made some rapid mental calculations. 'That's half as much again as normal rates!'

Sammy Mizler nodded. But Nathan was already thinking of something else.

'What ships would ask for double-salted pilchards on the West Indies run . . . ?' Sudden enlightenment came to Nathan. 'Slavers! We'll be selling to slave-ships.'

'So? We'll be doing the slaves a service. From us they'll get good fish. Many others aren't so fussy about what they sell.'

'I thought the slave trade had been abolished. I seem to remember Methodists throughout the world holding a day of prayer and thanksgiving.'

Sammy snorted. 'Slavery has been abandoned *here*, and British ships aren't supposed to carry slaves anywhere in the world, but hang an American flag on the yardarm and the business becomes legal. Anyway, such matters are best left to the reformers. We're running a business – and we give good value for money. Leave me to attend to the sales. You catch the fish – and train for your fight.'

14

The messenger from Bristol reached Pentuan at the end of January 1811, on a day when breath hung on the air like a formless spectre. Arriving at the house when Preacher Josiah Jago was at home putting the finishing touches to a new series of sermons for the coming year, the startled messenger scarcely had time to catch his breath before he was hustled from the house. Nathan sent him on his way with half a guinea for board and lodging in St Austell.

Nathan had managed to keep the forthcoming fight a secret from his family. Indeed, Sammy was the only other man in Cornwall who knew that the prize-fighting champion of all England would soon be defending his title.

Prior to the arrival of the messenger, Nathan and Sammy Mizler spent at least an hour each day in sparring practice on the lonely cliff-edge above Portgiskey Cove. But Nathan continued to fish, taking *The

Brave Amy H out on the unseasonably calm waters of St Austell Bay, adding to the large amount of fish being double-salted in the Portgiskey fish-cellar.

Nathan had tried on more than one occasion in recent weeks to speak to Elinor Hearle, but Polrudden remained a very busy manor-house. Coaches and riders arrived and left at all hours of the day and night, and Nathan could never get close to her. He did see Elinor once from a distance as she rode in the company of a man of considerable elegance. Nathan thought she looked in his direction, but she showed no recognition and he consoled himself with the belief that she probably had not recognised him.

The journey to Bristol was to be made in *The Brave Amy H*, and the boat would be heavily laden with salted pilchards for the West Indian trade. Sammy was unhappy about making a sea-voyage around the toe of England, but he would not allow Nathan out of his sight with such a short time to go before the fight.

Calvin Dickin and Ahab Arthur were to crew the heavily laden fishing-boat to Bristol. Neither had been told of the forthcoming fight. Such secrecy was necessary in order to keep Preacher Josiah Jago from learning the truth. Nathan knew his father would not hesitate to send word to his fellow-Methodists in Bristol. They would inform the authorities and have the fight stopped.

Because of the need for secrecy, it came as a shock to Nathan when he arrived at Portgiskey on the day of departure to find Amy waiting in the boat with Calvin Dickin and Ahab Arthur.

Bubbling with excitement, she answered Nathan's sharp question happily. 'I'm coming with you to

Bristol. I'm looking forward to it very much. My pa used to tell me that Bristol is the finest sea-port in the land. He went there many times. Now I'll be able to see it for myself.'

'This isn't a holiday trip. Who said you could come?'

Nathan's tone of voice was sharply disapproving. Amy's elation vanished with the realisation that Nathan did not want her on board *The Brave Amy H* for the voyage to Bristol.

'Sammy told me I could come – and you don't have to worry yourself about carrying a passenger. I'll do my share of the work, and I won't get in your way.'

With this remark, Amy turned away from Nathan and went forward, out of sight behind the hogsheads of pilchards piled dangerously high in the boat. Nathan realised that he had robbed Amy of much of the thrill she had felt at going to Bristol. The knowledge did nothing to improve his temper when he tackled Sammy a few minutes later.

'Why did you tell Amy she could come to Bristol with us? It's a damned foolish idea.'

Sammy Mizler's eyebrows rose only very slightly. 'I thought we were all partners? I mean, if she wants to come to Bristol in *our* boat, who has the right to say "No"? Not me. Not even you.'

'That has nothing to do with anything, and you know it.'

'I know only that you're angry with Amy for no good reason. I was speaking to her about Bristol, telling her what a wonderful city it is. She hung on every word, as though I were talking of Paradise, maybe. When she says how much she would like to go there, I ask: "Then why not come with us?" You don't have to worry about her, Nathan. You should know that already. She's a sensible girl – and I'll look after her.'

'Your job is to look after *me*,' Nathan snapped, but at that moment the two members of the crew who were to remain behind put in an appearance and he did not pursue the matter further. During the absence of *The Brave Amy H* the crew would be kept busy repairing nets and overhauling fishing-tackle.

Sammy Mizler knew from past experience that much of the all-England champion's edginess was due to thought of the forthcoming fight. Nathan was always this way for days before a contest. It was as though he needed to build up a deep reserve of aggression that would spill out when he entered the ring with his opponent.

But Amy knew nothing of this. She believed Nathan was in a bad mood simply because he did not want her to go to Bristol with him.

The voyage turned out to be far smoother than Nathan and Sammy had dared hope. Rounding Land's End on the afternoon of the first day, they picked up a useful westerly breeze. Anxious to make the most of such favourable conditions, Nathan decided they would sail all night instead of putting into shelter. Taking the boat out a couple of miles from shore, a course was set for Bristol.

In spite of such good weather conditions, Sammy Mizler was extremely sea-sick, but he received no sympathy from anyone but Amy. Ignoring the grins and jibes of Calvin Dickin and Ahab Arthur, she crouched on the deck beside Sammy and held his head in her lap, talking to him as though he were an invalid child.

During the night Sammy Mizler's stomach seemed to accept the unaccustomed, gently rocking environment in which it found itself, and by morning he was able to make his groggy way aft to where Nathan stood at the wheel. Well wrapped up against the cold, Sammy settled himself in the stern – upwind of Nathan's pipe.

'Feeling better now, Sammy?'

Sammy Mizler nodded unhappily. 'This morning I'm satisfied I'll live. Last night I didn't *want* to. You don't understand such a feeling, Nathan?'

Nathan took the pipe from his mouth. 'If you're asking if I've ever been sea-sick, the answer is "No". But I can think of at least two great sailors who were always sick for the first day or two of every voyage. One was an admiral, the other a commodore.' Nathan gave Sammy the first grin he had seen from him in thirty-six hours. 'But neither of them ever had such a comfortable pillow as you.'

'Amy's a good girl, Nathan. A very special girl. I . . . I'm very fond of her.'

Something in Sammy Mizler's voice stopped Nathan from making a flippant reply.

'You're not thinking of taking things any farther, Sammy?'

'Why not? Because I'm Jewish?'

It was the first time Sammy had ever mentioned his Jewish origins to Nathan, and it came as a shock to realise that Sammy thought of himself as 'different' from his fellow-men. It had never mattered to Nathan. Yet this was an age when Jews were still barred from governmental posts, foreign-born Jews were not allowed to take out British citizenship, and there was much prejudice levelled against them. It would be another fifty years before Great Britain afforded them the full benefit of its laws.

'You know better than that, Sammy. I'm concerned only because you're city born and bred. Amy is part of Cornwall. She would never settle to city life – any more than you'll ever be able to make the country your permanent home.'

'I'll stay in Cornwall, if that's what Amy wants,' retorted Sammy Mizler. 'If she would agree to marry me, I'd even become a fisherman . . .'

Nathan turned away from Sammy and studied the sea ahead of the drifter. He knew he should be wishing Sammy well, telling him he hoped he would win the girl he loved, but the words would not come. He told himself it was because he cared for both Amy and Sammy; because they were totally unsuited for each other. A marriage between them would prove disastrous.

At that moment a heavily laden merchantman, outward bound from Bristol, and only a few hundred yards from *The Brave Amy H*, changed course. Tacking close to the wind, the vessel bore down upon the Cornish drifter. Nathan had to put the wheel hard over very quickly to avoid being run down. The movement brought Calvin Dickin hurrying to the stern of the boat.

After cursing the helmsman on the merchantman for a fool, Calvin Dickin settled down to tell his companions of his escapades when he had last visited the port of Bristol.

Nathan found he was not in the mood to listen to sailors' tales. Handing over the helm to Calvin Dickin, he found a space between the barrels shielded from the wind. Wrapping a couple of blankets about him, he went to sleep.

When Nathan awoke, *The Brave Amy H* was in the Bristol Channel. The rugged cliffs of Devon, backed by the green heights of Exmoor, were to the south. Farther away, on the port side, were the dark hills of Wales, with the tall, foul-smoking chimneys of the Swansea smelting-houses in the foreground.

There was much more shipping about now, boats of every description: wide, flat-bottomed estuary barges; fishing-boats; merchantmen from all the continents of the world. Among them was a sleek, Baltimore-built schooner. With its raked masts and combined fore-and-aft and square rig, such a vessel could outsail any ship afloat. The Baltimore schooner overtook *The Brave Amy H* rapidly, its sharp bow slicing through the water like a knife, leaving a single, narrow wake to mark its passing.

The Brave Amy H reached the entrance to the Avon river soon after noon, then waited for two hours until the tide was sufficiently high for the waiting vessels to enter the river safely. The port of Bristol was some six miles up-river. Ships making their way there had to negotiate a series of narrow bends and high-walled gorges along the way.

A pilot vessel was the first to enter the river, followed closely by the first of the merchantmen. A small vessel, her captain took advantage of his ship's shallow draught to gain an early berth. *The Brave Amy*

H entered the river sixth in line, passing many larger vessels still awaiting deeper water.

Reaching the Bristol Docks, Nathan haggled with the Bristol Docks boatmen before *The Brave Amy H* was taken in tow by an eight-oared longboat and taken to a pre-arranged berth at Welsh Back, close to the Llandoger Trow, an old and noisy tavern.

Darkness was falling, but in spite of the late hour a lighter was brought alongside *The Brave Amy H* and the unloading of the hogsheads of salted pilchards went on until the drifter had been emptied of its cargo. But the day's work was not over yet. The boat reeked of fish and fish-oil that had leaked from the hogsheads. The small crew set to, cleaning the boat from stem to stern, until Amy declared she was satisfied.

By now it was almost midnight, but the noise from the Llandoger Trow had not diminished and Nathan suggested they should take advantage of the tavern's facilities. Not wishing Amy to be subjected to the attentions of the tavern's noisy customers, Calvin Dickin and Ahab Arthur were sent to fetch brandy with which to celebrate the sale of their cargo.

Although she was tired, Amy was too full of excitement to contemplate sleep. She chattered about the places she intended visiting while she was in the great port. However, when she found her companions would not tell her of their own plans, she lapsed into a hurt silence.

Neither Sammy Mizler nor Nathan could say anything about their plans until they had visited Clifton Down, the venue for the prize-fight, on the following day. Whilst there Sammy would satisfy himself about the arrangements for seconds, time-keeper, referee and all the other officials, in discussion with the men responsible for staging the championship fight.

The two men left *The Brave Amy H* together the next morning. After inspecting the natural amphitheatre where the fight was to be staged, they walked back to the heart of Bristol for an early lunch with the Duke of Clarence's men. Afterwards, Nathan left Sammy to complete the final arrangements for the fight and returned to *The Brave Amy H*.

He found Calvin Dickin and Ahab Arthur splicing new stays on the drifter's mainmast. They were in good humour, having spent an hour at the Llandoger Trow enjoying good Bristol ale.

In sharp contrast to the two fishermen, Amy sat on the jetty dejectedly lobbing pebbles at the still waters of the harbour. Her expression lightened momentarily when she saw Nathan, but then she resumed her desultory pastime with increased vigour.

Nathan hesitated for only a moment. He knew she was unhappy because he and Sammy had not taken her with them when they set off that morning, and had not told her where they were going. It had been Nathan's hope to keep the fight forever a secret from his father, but he had already accepted that it was a forlorn hope. When Nathan secured Venn Farm for Nell and her husband, Josiah Jago would have to know from whence the money had come. He spared little thought for anything other than his religion, but he would know that such money could not be earned from a few months' fishing. But Josiah Jago would not learn of the fight in time to have it stopped now, so there was no reason why Amy and the two crewmen should not know the real reason for the voyage to Bristol.

Nathan sat down beside Amy, but she chose to pay no attention to him and viciously aimed pebbles at a worm-eaten piece of wood floating six feet from the side of the quay.

'I'm sorry Sammy and I couldn't take you with us this morning. There was something we had to do.'

'I'm *sure* there was!' Amy's stone splashed a full ten feet away from the inoffensive target.

The two fishermen had stopped their work to listen, and Nathan addressed his next words to them.

'Sammy and I couldn't tell you before we left Pentuan why we were coming to Bristol. Had word got back to my father, he would have found a way to stop us.'

Nathan had Amy's full attention now. 'The *real* reason . . . ? We came to sell fish.'

'No – although bringing the hogsheads here provided us with a very profitable excuse. I'm here for a prize-fight. The Championship of all England will be at stake tomorrow afternoon on Clifton Down, above the gorge. There's room for the whole of Bristol there, should they choose to come along. Sammy and I have been to inspect the place this morning.'

Calvin Dickin gave an evil chuckle. When Nathan looked at him quizzically, the fisherman glanced mischievously at Amy.

'That isn't where Amy thought you were. She was certain you was spending your time with some of they women Ahab and I saw cavorting in the Llandoger Trow last night.'

Looking at Amy, Nathan saw her cheeks had

turned a fiery scarlet. But her eyes met his boldly, and he knew she was thinking of the stormy night when she had called him from the bed of Elinor Hearle.

Her expression dared him to comment on Calvin Dickin's observation as she said briefly: 'We all make mistakes.'

Nathan felt happier now there were no secrets between them. When the many questions about the fight had been answered, he said to Amy: 'Put your things in a bag. We have rooms at an inn for a couple of nights. We'll go there now and you can change into that pretty dress I'm sure you've packed. You and I are going to see something of Bristol. You haven't come all this way to spend your days throwing stones in the dock.'

Some of the excitement that Amy had shown before leaving Pentuan returned to her. She leaped from the edge of the quay to the drifter and disappeared inside the hold.

Ahab Arthur watched her go and shook his head wistfully. Turning to Nathan, he said quietly: 'It doesn't take more than a kind word from you to make that maid happy, Nathan. Take care; it's a heavy responsibility. You can break her heart just as easily.'

Thinking of what Sammy Mizler had said to him on the voyage, Nathan made no reply. Instead, he flipped two golden guineas to the two fishermen. 'Here, finish your work, then go off and enjoy yourselves. We have rooms at the Golden Fleece, hard by the bridge. We'll all meet up there later.'

Amy came from the hold carrying a bulging leathern bag over her shoulder. She reached a hand up to Nathan and, taking it, he lifted her easily to the jetty and relieved her of the bag.

Walking beside Nathan, Amy took three happy steps to two of his, occasionally skipping to keep up when she fell half a pace behind.

'Am I going too fast for you?' Nathan had been walking along lost in his own thoughts about the fight that was to take place the next day.

Amy shook her head and took his arm happily. 'No. If I had to walk any slower, I'd bust.' She gave him a coy, sidelong glance. 'I thought this was going to be the most miserable birthday I'd ever spent.'

'Your birthday? Amy, why didn't you tell me before?'

He gave her a hug. 'Does Sammy know?'

When Amy shook her head, Nathan said: 'He should be at the inn by now. We'll meet him there and go out for a special celebration.'

Sammy Mizler was not at the Golden Fleece inn. After waiting for half an hour, Nathan declared they could waste no more of the day, or Bristol would be in darkness before they had seen any of its sights.

The innkeeper provided them with a small open carriage and a driver. Leaving a message for Sammy, Nathan and Amy set off from the inn.

Bristol was a large and ancient city, but for Amy much of the thrill came from riding in the open carriage, a warm blanket over her knees, tucked about her by the carriage driver.

After they had marvelled at the lofty magnificence of St Mary Redcliffe Church, once described by Queen Elizabeth as 'the fairest, the goodliest, and the most famous church in England', the driver took them to Clifton Downs. Here they stood on the very edge of the deep, tree-lined gorge of the River Avon. The knowledge that they stood just a single pace from eternity was an exciting, yet frightening, experience.

Next, Amy asked Nathan to show her the spot where the prize-fight was to take place.

Viewing the site from the carriage, Amy asked Nathan a number of questions about prize-fighting, then she fell silent for some minutes. Nathan was about to order the driver to move on, when Amy suddenly looked up at him.

'Why have you decided to fight again, Nathan? I thought you had given up the prize-ring.'

'So did I.'

'Then . . . *why*?'

Nathan found himself tongue-tied, and Amy took his silence as an indication that he did not want to tell her.

'Do you look upon fishing as something you can give up when the prize-ring calls to you, Nathan? Is it just something to keep you amused? It's more than that to me. I look upon fishing as a way of life – a *respectable* way of life. Can you understand what that means to the daughter of a smuggler? Do you know what it's like to spend the whole of your life frightened of everything and everyone? At sea you're suspicious of every boat that draws near. On land you hide whenever a stranger approaches the cottage. I don't want that sort of life any more.'

'I understand, Amy. Fishing isn't just a game for me. It means more to me than any other way of life – more than prize-fighting.'

'Then this will be your last prize-fight?'

Nathan thought of the conditions the Duke of

Clarence had attached to his thousand-guinea purse. 'No . . . I'll be fighting again.'

Amy bit off the angry retort that came to her lips and turned her head away. 'Then there's no more to be said.'

'Not at the moment,' Nathan agreed. 'But there *is* a reason for what I'm doing. Trust me, Amy.'

She turned to look at him, and for the second time that day he had an uncomfortable feeling that she was thinking of Elinor Hearle. Unconvinced, she said stiffly: 'I'll try.'

Back at the Golden Fleece they found Sammy Mizler waiting for them. He looked hurt that they had been out without him until Nathan explained.

Sammy Mizler was as indignant as Nathan had been that Amy had not mentioned her birthday earlier. Kissing Amy warmly, he hooked his arm through hers. 'Well, now it's my turn to give you a treat. Tonight you'll enjoy the best meal that Bristol can provide.'

Sammy was as good as his word. The landlord of the Golden Fleece provided his guests with a meal that had Amy gasping with delight.

During the meal Sammy Mizler was at his amusing best, and Amy's happy laughter brought smiles to the faces of even the most dour diners at the inn. So happy was she with Sammy that Nathan, by nature more serious than his light-hearted partners, felt himself an interloper. But when he found an excuse to go to his room and leave them together Amy protested that there were still a couple of hours of her birthday remaining. She demanded that her two escorts take her for a walk through the streets of the great sea-port.

She would probably never visit Bristol again, she said, and wanted to take away enough memories to last her a lifetime.

Outside the inn they were pounced upon by torch boys carrying pitch torches. For a sum that began at a shilling, and eventually dropped to twopence, they were offered a light to guide them about the city. Amy refused all their offers. It was a bright, moonlit night and she wanted to savour the atmosphere of the city without the distraction of a flickering, spitting torch held in the hands of a mercenary and garrulous torch boy.

'Where shall we go?' Nathan asked, as they walked three abreast along the rough cobbled road.

'Let's just go where the whim takes us,' Amy replied. 'But first let's make certain all is well with our boat.'

The boat was as securely moored as when they had left her, and they resumed their walk past the Llandoger Trow. The lights of the waterside tavern shone out like a beacon, attracting many sailors. Ahab Arthur and Calvin Dickin were probably among their number; they had not yet found their way to the Golden Fleece. The din from inside was considerable. Fiddlers were ensconced in every bar room, each playing a different tune, accompanied by an enthusiastic but less-than-tuneful choir. Outside the inn were a number of drabs, either too drunk or too well known to be welcome inside the seamen's tavern.

As the trio passed by the door it opened and two women fell shrieking and clawing into the street. An excited crowd of onlookers swiftly gathered about them, shouting words of encouragement to the combatants.

Soon Amy, Nathan and Sammy Mizler left the sounds of the Llandoger Trow behind and walked beside the docks, the moon reflected dully in the dark, dirty water.

'I have an idea,' said Sammy Mizler suddenly. 'Let's go and have a look at the ship in which Nathan's challenger arrived. She's the *Seneca*, lying at Redcliffe Wharf. We might even see Abraham Dellow training on the deck.'

'At this time of night?' snorted Nathan. 'If he's got any sense at all, he'll be below decks, sleeping in a warm bunk.'

'Is he a good prize-fighter?' Amy asked anxiously. 'I mean, do you think you'll beat him, Nathan?'

'He's good enough to claim he's the "world" champion,' Sammy Mizler replied seriously. 'But Nathan's better. Of that I'm certain. Abraham Dellow has fought no one I've met – and I know all the best prize-fighters.'

Amy shuddered. 'I think it's dreadful that two men should fight each other for money. It's even worse that other men pay money to watch them.'

'If it weren't for prize-fighting, we wouldn't all be partners, with a fine boat and a thriving business,' Nathan pointed out.

'No, and if it hadn't been for prize-fighting I'd as likely as not be skulking in a dark London alley, waiting to relieve some unsuspecting gent of his watch and purse. There were a dozen boys of my age in the street where I was brought up. So far, two have been hanged as footpads and five transported for petty thieving. Thank God for prize-fighting, I say.'

Sammy spoke with great feeling, and Amy hugged his arm sympathetically. 'I'm sorry, Sammy. I was talking without thinking.'

'You were merely expressing your opinion – and why shouldn't you?' Sammy Mizler patted her hand affectionately. 'Would you rather return to the inn?'

'No, let's go and see this ship.'

There were surprisingly few vessels moored in this part of the port. Judging from the accumulation of rubbish, and the derelict warehouses visible in the moonlight, it seemed that this corner of Bristol's sprawling docks was little used. Nathan wondered why *Seneca* was moored here. The answer was soon provided for him.

They saw the ill-lit ship at the far end of a long quay. As they drew closer, Amy wrinkled her nose. 'Ugh! What's that smell? It's foul.'

Sammy Mizler shook his head, but Nathan knew. He had experienced such a smell before. When he was in the Navy his ship had come downwind of a slaver that was sailing with its hatches open. It was the smell from hundreds of captive bodies, shackled together and imprisoned in cramped quarters, with insufficient air and no sanitation.

'*Seneca*'s a slave-ship,' he said. Pulling Amy and Sammy to a halt, he added: 'I don't think we should go any closer. Do you hear that?'

From somewhere ahead of them they could hear the sound of clanking chains. There were other sounds, too. The regular 'crack' of what might have been musket shots – and a low, continuous moaning that set the hairs on the back of Amy's neck tingling. The sound was an expression of human helplessness and despair.

'This is no place for a young girl on her birthday. We'll get you back to the inn.'

'No!' Amy hissed her refusal. 'I want to get closer, to see what's going on.' Snatching her arm from Nathan's grip, she ran towards the sounds.

Taken by surprise, Nathan and Sammy both ran after her.

They caught up with Amy as she rounded the hulk of a rotting brigantine, drawn up on the quayside. The sight that met their eyes brought all three to a sudden halt and Amy gasped incredulously.

In the light of no more than three torches held by seamen, a long line of wretched humanity – men, women and small children – stretched from the ship to a man-made cave set high in the cliff beyond the quay. Shackled at wrist and ankle, they were linked to each other by heavy chains that passed through iron belts fastened about their waists. The African slaves moved slowly and painfully, driven on by two men wielding whips.

One of these men, a heavily built white man, wielded his whip enthusiastically, and the bodies of those selected as his targets jerked in pain as the leather lash curled about them. They were unable to escape. All movement was restricted by the slaves in front and behind. It was the sound of this whip that Nathan had mistaken for musket shots.

The second man wielded his whip with rather less enthusiasm. A giant African, his whip cracked for much of the time on empty air, but he shouted all the while, calling to the slow-moving slaves in a language that was unintelligible to Nathan and his two companions.

'Get moving! Jesus, I've never carried a lazier cargo of niggers. You'll need to move faster when you reach America. If you don't, you'll taste more whip than water.'

The whip-wielding white man had the accent of America's deep south.

'Johanson . . .' he called to one of the torch-bearing sailors. 'Get on board and make sure they've made a start washing out the holds. I want this lot back on board before morning.'

One of the female slaves tripped and fell. As she struggled to rise, the movement of the long line of slaves dragged her along with them across the cobbled quayside. The white man used his whip on her brutally, until she finally ceased her efforts to rise and was bumped, a limp, unconscious figure, across the rough stone quayside.

'Check this one when you've got them inside,' the man called to another torch-bearer. 'If she's dead, throw her down with the others. If not, give her a beating she'll remember.'

For the first time, Nathan noticed a heap of some twelve or fourteen bodies lying on the quayside beside the ship. No doubt they would be carried on board before morning, to lie in a corner of the hold with their live fellows. Once at sea they would be thrown overboard and lost for ever, or perhaps washed up on the shore somewhere, to be buried without ceremony below the high-tide line.

Amy watched the whip-wielding seamen in horror.

As the woman, inexorably linked to the other slaves, bumped away like a rag puppet, she cried: 'Nathan . . . *do* something. Stop them . . . !'

'Sh! There's nothing that can be done. Let's get out of here. Now!'

During his naval days, Nathan had experienced more than one encounter with slavers. They were a thoroughly ruthless lot, the very nature of their chosen trade rendering human life cheap. The British government had made slaving in British ships illegal, but slaves were still employed on British plantations in the West Indies and they still occasionally entered British ports when carried in foreign ships. However, William Wilberforce was pursuing a vigorous anti-slavery campaign in Parliament and his cause had many supporters throughout the land, notably among the country's Methodists. This was why *Seneca* had been given a berth as far from inquisitive eyes as possible. It was also the reason why the ship's slave-holds were being cleaned during the hours of darkness.

Nathan had called for the horrified Amy to be quiet, but it was already too late. Her cry had been heard. Peering into the darkness, the big, whip-wielding white man called for a torch. As one of the seamen ran after him, he advanced towards Nathan, Amy and Sammy Mizler.

'What are you doing here? Who are you?'

'We're three people who were enjoying a pleasant moonlit walk until we came across you.'

'Ah! So you've got delicate innards, have you? I don't suppose it'll put you off enjoying a spoonful or two of sugar in your toddy when you get home. And you' – the slaver reached across and fingered the cloth of Amy's coat – 'who do you think picked the cotton for this? I'll tell you. It was slaves.'

He jerked his head derisively in the direction of the slaves who were now disappearing into the cavern opening. 'They're like animals. Show 'em who's boss and you'll have no trouble. Treat 'em like humans and they'll turn on you. This is what they understand.' He cracked the whip in his hand expertly.

Unexpectedly, Sammy Mizler reached out and casually took the whip from the seaman's hand. Before anyone could make a move to stop him, he snapped it in two across his knee and tossed it far out into the waters of the harbour.

'What the hell?'

The American took an angry step forward. Sammy Mizler held his ground and, putting his face close to the seaman's, said: 'I once heard a man say similar words about my people. I'm a Jew.'

Sammy made the flat statement softly and proudly, but it brought a sneer to the slaver's face. 'I don't know who that man was, but I reckon I wouldn't argue with him. There ain't much to choose between niggers, Indians and Jews when you get right down to it. They all need to be taught their place.'

The seaman made a grab at Sammy Mizler – but he grabbed air. Sammy ducked quickly and poked out two swift left jabs. As the American seaman staggered back, Sammy went after him. Seizing the dazed man by the shoulder, he turned him around. With his other hand gripping the back of the seaman's belt, Sammy propelled him to the edge of the quay and hurled him into the dock.

The American's cry of protest ended abruptly as the water closed over his head. Behind him on the quayside the seaman holding the blazing torch shouted. Answering cries came from the ship, demanding to know what was happening.

'Good work, Sammy.' Nathan took Amy's hand. 'Now it's time we got far away from this place – and I'll have no arguing from you, young lady.'

With Sammy holding Amy's other hand, they ran back the way they had come, until the cries behind them were lost in the familiar sounds coming from the waterside taverns.

When they eventually stopped running, Amy was so breathless it was difficult to know whether she was laughing or crying.

'Sammy, you were wonderful! But those people. That poor woman . . .'

Used to standing in the shadow of Nathan's prize-fighting achievements, Sammy Mizler was unaccustomed to taking on the role of a hero. He held Amy self-consciously as she clung to him. 'There's nothing we can do tonight, but I don't doubt we've saved more than one slave from a whipping.'

'We might have done much more than that,' said Nathan thoughtfully. 'The man you threw into the dock had the build of a prize-fighter. You might have just thrashed the so-called "world champion".'

15

Nathan was wrong. Emile Levinsky, boatswain of the Baltimore-built clipper *Seneca*, was in the ring opposite Nathan the following day, but he was acting as a second. The man Nathan would fight was the huge African who had been wielding the second whip on Redcliffe Wharf.

Levinsky recognised his assailant and glared angrily across the ring at Sammy from his one good eye. The other was tightly closed and impressively discoloured. Sammy did his best to ignore the American seaman, but as he went about his business in the corner he gave Nathan a whispered warning.

'Watch Dellow for dirty tricks, Nathan. His corner will desperately want to win the fight now, and we already know what manner of men they are.'

Nathan nodded, eyeing his opponent across the ring. The African was huge, being at least four inches taller than Nathan, and more than forty pounds heavier. But it was also apparent that the cold weather was not to his liking. He had a heavy blanket thrown about his shoulders, yet still shivered uncontrollably.

Sammy had also seen the challenger's discomfort. 'Make the fight last, Nathan. The longer it goes, the better it will be. And make the rounds short. The more time Dellow spends sitting in his corner, the colder he's going to be. If a round looks as though it's lasting too long, take a drop. None of the spectators will complain about a long fight. The only one who won't enjoy it is Abraham Dellow.'

Nathan nodded once more, only half-listening. He was busy watching the other corner. *Seneca*'s boatswain was instructing his fighter in very much the same way as Sammy Mizler – but Abraham Dellow was listening as though his very life depended upon remembering every word.

With Nathan and Sammy Mizler in the ring was Calvin Dickin. He was to act as Nathan's 'knee man'. His job was to provide Nathan with a knee to sit on in the intervals between rounds. In London, the knee had been replaced by a stool for a while, but there had recently been an unfortunate incident when an irate second, incensed at a referee's decision, had cracked the misguided adjudicator's skull with the stool. Referees were now insisting that fighters should revert to the more traditional knee man.

Calvin Dickin's secondary role would be to help Sammy Mizler get Nathan to the mark in the centre of the ring at the end of each thirty-second break. This was a most important task. If a boxer failed to come up to the mark and stand there unaided, the fight was given to his opponent.

Amy was also watching the fight, but from the outer ring. The only woman to been seen anywhere near the prize-ring, she had been taken into the Duke of Clarence's party and they had taken up a position close to Nathan's corner.

The Duke of Clarence was accompanied by two other dukes, three marquesses, and a large number of earls and barons. Looking at them, Sammy Mizler commented drily that one could be forgiven for thinking it was Agincourt, and not Clifton Down.

The Duke of Clarence brought Amy to Nathan's corner shortly before the fight began, to wish him well. After a lengthy conversation with Sammy Mizler, carried on in low tones that did not carry to Nathan, the Duke made Amy take his arm. He then escorted her back to his party with great dignity.

'The Duke wanted to know what I thought of your chances,' said Sammy casually, when the Duke of Clarence had gone. 'I told him you were a sure winner, so he's gone to lay a few wagers. He'll cover your purse *and* make himself a handsome profit, too, I don't wonder.'

'I hope you're right,' grunted Nathan. Abraham Dellow was a big man. No doubt he also possessed a big punch. Nathan would need all his skills to avoid walking into one of them.

The referee for the fight was a serving cavalry officer, approved by both sides. Now he stepped inside the single-rope ring, inspected the mark, then called both fighters to the centre of the ring to ask if they both understood the rules of prize-fighting. Still wrapped in his blanket, Abraham Dellow stared at Nathan and appeared to be paying scant attention to

what the referee was saying, but he nodded vigorously enough when pressed for an answer.

Both fighters returned to their corners for last-
minute instructions while the referee spoke to the
two timekeepers. Suddenly, Amy was at Nathan's
corner, just outside the ropes. Unfastening a blue silk
scarf, a very recent purchase, from about her neck, she
tied it to the rope beside Nathan. The act brought a
chorus of howls and catcalls from the huge crowd that
had gathered to view the prize-fight.

Her face scarlet, Amy said breathlessly: 'The other
man has a scarf in his corner. The Duke of Clarence
says most prize-fighters show them, but you never
have. I thought it was time you did.'

She hesitated, very much aware that the eyes of
every man in the vast crowd were upon her. 'The
Duke also told me why you're fighting – for Nell and
Tom. I'm proud of you, Nathan. Very proud. I wanted
you to know that before you started fighting.'

Leaning over the rope, she kissed Nathan quickly,
then fled back to the Duke of Clarence as the whole
crowd erupted in a tumult of cheers and whistles.

Displaying no outward signs of jealousy, Sammy
Mizler said dourly: 'Well, Amy might have swung the
crowd over to your side, but don't expect Abraham
Dellow to kiss your cheek. His corner is warming him
up for action.'

In the far corner, Boatswain Levinsky had his man
running hard on the spot in an effort to warm up his
muscles. Moments later the referee ducked out of the
ring and called on the fighters to take up their stances
at the mark.

Nathan was wearing a heavy jersey and he slipped

it over his head. Stripped to the waist, he took up a position in the centre of the ring. At the same time, Abraham Dellow let the blanket fall from his shoulders. A gasp went up from the crowd. Dellow was magnificently muscled, but his back was criss-crossed with the scars of a lashing such as few men might have been expected to survive.

Abraham Dellow took up a stance facing Nathan. At another signal from the referee, both men began to circle cautiously about each other. Their seconds shouted encouragement from inside the ring, where they would remain for the whole of the fight.

Nathan struck the first blow after half a minute of wary circling. It was a good punch, landing high on Dellow's cheek, and brought a faint show of blood from the broken skin. Dellow brushed at it as he might a fly that had settled on him and immediately countered with a right that sang past Nathan's ear. There followed a flurry of blows before Nathan was tripped and knocked to the ground. It was a perfectly legitimate move, and the end of the first round was called.

In his corner, the fighter from the slave-ship was fed brandy and water in an attempt to put more warmth in his body. Boatswain Levinsky was also drinking heavily from the same flagon, possibly for the same reason.

The second round got off to a brisker start than the first, Dellow coming off the mark full of aggression. As Nathan had already realised, the huge African had little prize-fighting skill, but he carried a devastating punch in each of his fists. This round lasted for eight minutes before one of Dellow's mighty blows exploded against the side of Nathan's head and he fell to the ground, stunned.

Dragged to his corner by Sammy Mizler and Calvin Dickin, Nathan received their anxious attentions for the full thirty seconds in a desperate and successful bid to get him to the mark. He then avoided Dellow's punches as best he could for another minute before allowing his opponent to hurl him to the ground with a cross-buttock throw, rolling away quickly as the heavy African attempted to drop on him.

'You're doing all right,' said Sammy encouragingly. 'Dellow isn't enjoying these breaks. It's giving him time to remember just how cold it is. Keep away from him and take a drop whenever you get the opportunity.'

Nathan looked to where a jubilant Boatswain Levinsky towelled his man down enthusiastically, convinced it was only a matter of time before he scored a knockout punch. If the fight continued as it was going, Levinsky might well prove to be right. Nathan came to a sudden decision.

'I'm changing my tactics, Sammy. By letting him set the pace I'm laying myself open to a lucky punch – and he's a mighty hard hitter. I'm going to take charge now. Abraham Dellow will know he's in a fight.'

Sammy Mizler began to argue, but moments later the referee called for the two men to recommence fighting. As Nathan and Abraham Dellow came from their respective corners the spectators were strangely hushed. Nathan realised they were expecting to see him lose his title to the African. Dellow was equally confident that the undisputed championship of the world would be his before the afternoon was over. He was taken completely by surprise when Nathan switched from dogged defence and launched a two-fisted attack that drove Dellow all the way back to his corner.

The negro fighter recovered quickly, however, and for the remainder of the twelve-minute round the two prize-fighters had the great crowd roaring approval. The round ended when Nathan caught Dellow off guard. A punch to the stomach sent Dellow to his knees on the turf, gasping for air.

This round set the pattern for a fierce fight that kept the huge crowd on its toes, and men shouted themselves hoarse at the skill of Nathan and the courage of his opponent. Twelve gruelling rounds lasted an exhausting hour and forty minutes, and for nine of them Abraham Dellow was on the ground when the referee called a break.

In Dellow's corner, Boatswain Levinsky leaned over his battered fighter, gesticulating angrily. The African's eyes rolled in fright as he listened to a tight-lipped summary of his fate, should he lose the fight. Sammy Mizler did not miss the drama being enacted across the ring and he was quick to warn Nathan.

'Be on your guard now, Nathan. Dellow knows he's a loser and he's been ordered to win *at all costs*. It looks to me as though his life may depend upon winning.'

Nathan nodded. He had kept his eyes on his opponent during every break. He, too, realised that *Seneca*'s boatswain was putting Dellow under tremendous pressure.

Called to the centre of the ring for the thirteenth round, Nathan looked at his opponent's bloody face with some pity. It was short-lived. Lowering his head, Abraham Dellow charged at Nathan as though he were an angry bull. The unorthodox attack ended in disaster for the challenger. Sidestepping, Nathan brought his fist down hard behind the negro's ear. Dellow crashed to the ground and lay still on his face.

Boatswain Emile Levinsky and his fellow-second worked hard on their prize-fighter, pouring a bucket of water over his head, and spilling a generous measure of brandy down his throat. When the end of the break was called, the two men dragged Abraham Dellow to the mark in the centre of the ring, supporting him for as long as they dared. When Sammy Mizler protested in a loud voice, the referee ordered Levinsky and his companion to their corner. They went reluctantly, and behind them Abraham Dellow sank heavily to his knees, supporting himself shakily with both knuckles resting on the turf.

Crossing the ring to the challenger, the referee bent low to look into his eyes. Straightening up, he declared Dellow unable to defend himself.

Nathan had won!

As the crowd erupted in roars of jubilation, Nathan stood looking down at Abraham Dellow's brutally scarred back. While members of the Duke of Clarence's party, and others, crowded inside the ring to offer him their congratulations, Nathan squatted beside the African as he attempted to rise upon legs that refused to support him.

'It's all right; the fight's over. Just stay down for a while.'

Abraham Dellow looked up at him, and Nathan had never seen such fear on a man's face.

'He'll kill me for this, boss. That Bos'n Levinsky's going to kill me for sure.'

Across the ring, Boatswain Levinsky was watching

his defeated fighter, his face distorted with rage. Nathan did not doubt Abraham Dellow's words.

'You don't have to go back to *Seneca*. Come with me. I'll see that you're looked after.'

Instead of providing the defeated boxer with hope, Nathan's words seemed to add to his terror. 'You don't understand. I can't do that. I'm not a free man. I *belong* to Bos'n Levinsky.'

Now Nathan understood Abraham Dellow's fears. As a slave on an American slave-ship he had no rights at all. He belonged to Emile Levinsky. The boatswain could do with him whatever he wished. Having seen Levinsky's love of the whip, and Abraham Dellow's scarred back, Nathan had no doubts about the fate in store for the negro prize-fighter.

'Forget Levinsky. You're not in *Seneca* now. This is England. We no longer recognise slavery. Come with me.'

Helping Dellow to his feet, Nathan forced a way through the throng to the corner where Sammy Mizler was surrounded by many of his prize-fighting friends and a few members of the Duke of Clarence's party.

Brushing aside their jubilant congratulations, Nathan said: 'Sammy, we need to get Dellow back to the inn. Don't let him out of your sight for one minute.'

Startled, Sammy Mizler began to protest that Nathan had just won a fight. The Duke of Clarence wanted to speak to him to offer his own congratulations.

'The Duke of Clarence knows where we're staying – and it will be better if he leaves here right now. Abraham Dellow's a slave. He's owned by Boatswain

Levinsky – the man who's so handy with a whip. I've told Dellow he's not going back to the ship. There are a number of *Seneca*'s crew here. That means there's going to be trouble. Get Dellow away – and make certain Amy goes with you, too.'

A North Country peer who had been listening to Nathan's story immediately set off to warn William, Duke of Clarence. The Duke would not wish to become involved in a brawl at an illegal prize-fight where one of the participants was a slave!

On his way, the peer intercepted Amy as she tried to reach Nathan's side. Ignoring her protests, he forced her to return with him to the Duke of Clarence.

He was none too soon. As Nathan had feared, crewmen from *Seneca* were gathering about their boatswain – but formidable support was also rallying to Nathan's side.

Before and during a long prize-fight, the outer ring – the area immediately adjacent to the prize-ring itself – was reserved for those gentlemen of the 'Fancy', who paid considerable sums of money in order to watch the fight with a degree of comfort, without being jostled by the noisy, unwashed and frequently unruly crowd. In order to keep the mob beyond the limits of this outer ring, a number of 'would-be' and 'has-been' pugilists were employed. Now, with the fight over, the pugilists' task was to fall back upon the prize-fighting ring to escort Nathan away.

They reached him in ones and twos, until there were a dozen of them, keeping a breathing-space for the man who was being hailed as the champion of the world. Among the prize-fighters was Jem Belcher, cousin of Nathan's unfortunate last opponent and himself once Champion of all England. Among the others were men with whom Nathan had sparred on more than one occasion.

Above the din of the excited crowd, Nathan managed to convey to his prize-fighting bodyguard what was happening. Some of the spectators also heard Nathan's words and they began howling for the blood of Boatswain Emile Levinsky and his slaver colleagues. Minutes later, Levinsky abandoned all thought of repossessing his frightened slave as he and his fellow-Americans were set upon by the crowd.

Abraham Dellow had won the respect of the Bristol men for the courageous fight he had put up against Nathan. Many of those close to the ring had seen the ugly scarring on his back and rightly attributed it to the big American boatswain.

'You'll have little trouble with the American now, I'm thinking,' said Jem Belcher. 'You put up a good fight, Nathan Jago. I couldn't have done much better myself.'

Nathan grinned. Jem Belcher had been a good champion, but had never been strong on modesty. 'Thanks. How's that cousin of yours?'

'Ned? He's dead. Died three months since. Drank himself to death, didn't you know?'

Much of Nathan's exhilaration left him, and Jem Belcher said hurriedly: 'It was none of your fault, Nathan. Don't you think it was. He'd been slowly killing himself with drink for years, ever since he reached the top in the prize-ring. Blind or sighted, he wouldn't have lasted no longer than he did. It was a happy release really, you might say.' Jem Belcher handed Nathan a blue silk scarf. 'Here, don't leave your lady's favour tied to the rope. She'd never forgive you – and pretty young things like her are hard to come by for scarred old veterans like you and me.'

Nathan was about to protest that there was a tremendous age difference between himself and the former champion, but he stopped himself quickly. Jem Belcher, himself blind in one eye, had fought his last two prize-fights with a broken hand. Consequently, his battered features had taken far more punches than was good for them. Belcher also had the sickly pallor of ill-health, and would be dead within six months. Yet Bristol-born Belcher was only twenty-nine years of age – barely two years older than Nathan.

That night the private room of the Golden Fleece witnessed a party such as the inn had not known in all the years of its existence.

The Duke of Clarence was in a jovial mood and provided the highlight of the evening with his rendering of between-deck naval songs. He had good reason to be well pleased. The prize-fight on Clifton Down had netted him a great deal of money – though he admitted to suffering 'palpitations' during the early rounds of the fight.

The Duke and his companions also had lengthy discussions during the course of the evening with Abraham Dellow – the name had been given to him by Emile Levinsky, when Dellow had been purchased as an oversized boy of fourteen.

Subjected to all forms of humiliation on board *Seneca*, Dellow had been thrashed many times by his owner, the worst beating being the one that had left him scarred for life.

The cause had been a young slave girl. Selected by Emile Levinsky to provide the boatswain with some of the pleasures of life during the long voyage from Africa to America, she had preferred the charms of Abraham Dellow. The two Africans were surprised by the boatswain when they were making love in Levinsky's own cabin.

The boatswain had gone berserk. The screaming girl was taken to the side of the ship in mid-Atlantic and thrown overboard. Abraham Dellow, pinned to the deck by a dozen seamen, had been given a choice. Castration, or a beating that would last until Emile Levinsky was too exhausted to wield a whip.

Abraham Dellow chose the beating. It lasted for two hours, by which time even the crew of *Seneca*, hardened by years of slave-trading, were sickened.

All night long Abraham Dellow lay twitching and groaning on the deck of the ship in a pool of his own blood, the flesh on his back in ribbons. The boatswain had forbidden anyone to go to his aid.

Dellow lived, but the boatswain boasted that he had broken his slave as he might have broken a horse and would have no more trouble from him. To prove his words, Emile Levinsky took every opportunity to demonstrate Dellow's incredible servility, degrading the slave in every possible way before the European crew and the African slave cargo. With the memory of his cruel beating in his mind, Abraham Dellow was careful to ensure that only the slaves ever saw the looks of hate he occasionally cast in the direction of his brutal owner.

To the Europeans, Abraham Dellow became all that a 'good' negro should be: trustworthy and servile, a model for his fellows. Because of this he was given the post of slavemaster on board *Seneca*.

When Nathan asked him why he had never tried to escape, Abraham Dellow shrugged his shoulders. 'Where would I have gone?' He went on to explain that he came from a tribe of Africa's interior. Had he tried to escape when *Seneca* called at an African port, the tribesmen of the coast would have taken great delight in handing him back to Boatswain Levinsky. After explaining all this, Dellow added: 'Before this trip the only ports we called at were either in Africa, the West Indies or America. They are not healthy places for a runaway slave.'

Abraham Dellow had drunk heavily at the Golden Fleece and he now added something that made Nathan wonder whether they had heard the whole truth of Dellow's experiences on board *Seneca*.

'Besides, it wasn't such a bad life when Bos'n Levinsky was in a good mood. I could have as many of the slave women as I wanted – except those chosen by white men. I took them whether they wanted me or not. When they were put up for auction, Boatswain Levinsky would have me stand on the platform with them, then he'd tell the buyers that most of the women were probably in child by me.'

The huge African smiled proudly. 'It sure did put up the price of them slave girls.'

'Ahem!' William, Duke of Clarence looked at Dellow with faintly raised eyebrows. 'I doubt if we can provide you with pleasures on the same scale as those you enjoyed on board *Seneca*, but if you wish to stay in

England as a free man I can place you with someone who'll improve your prize-fighting technique. I, and the gentlemen with me today, will sponsor you. I think we can promise you a satisfactory life.'

There were murmurs of agreement from the men of the 'Fancy' gathered about the Duke. Abraham Dellow had the strength and courage required of a prize-fighter. Once he had acquired some of the art of a boxer he would be a tremendous crowd-pleaser.

'Now that's settled, I propose a toast to Nathan Jago, prize-fighting champion of the world. He gave us all a wonderful display of skill today.'

While the party in the private room of the Golden Fleece was at its height, the slave-ship *Seneca* was passing from the River Avon into the wider waters of the Bristol Channel. It marked the premature end of the vessel's first and last visit to an English port.

The reason for *Seneca*'s deviation from her usual run between Africa and America had been twofold: she had come to load preserved fish, provided by Nathan and his fellow-fishermen – and also so that her master and crew might make a fortune in wagers when Abraham Dellow beat the all-England prize-fighting champion.

Instead, *Seneca* left Bristol with a furious boatswain and a disgruntled crew. Their champion had been beaten and was now lost to them. In addition, the ship had been driven from the port of Bristol by angry anti-slave demonstrators before it had taken on a full load of provisions.

Much worse was to come. Caught in a howling snowstorm when no more than twenty-four hours outward bound from Bristol, *Seneca* blundered blindly on her way for the whole of one terrifying night. Then, on Sunday, 17 February 1811, hopelessly off course, *Seneca* drove on to the infamous Gilstone Reef, on the fringe of the Scilly Isles. While the snow held back the dawn, two hundred and seventy slaves entered eternity chained together. With them went the captain of *Seneca* and all forty men of his crew, swallowed up by the cold, grey, undiscriminating sea.

16

The February blizzard raged for four days and nights, before ceasing as suddenly as it had begun, leaving the land hushed and white. For these four days, Nathan, Amy, Sammy Mizler and the two fishermen shared the warm intimacy of the Bristol inn. The Duke of Clarence and his entourage had left for Gloucestershire in the early hours of the morning after the fight, taking Abraham Dellow with them.

Amy was pleased to see the former-slave go. She, too, felt they had not heard the truth of Abraham Dellow's role in the slave-ship *Seneca* and she hoped Nathan would never regret his part in rescuing the slave.

Nathan welcomed the delay caused by the snow. He had absorbed a certain amount of punishment from the prize-fighting slave, and his face was bruised and grazed. The few days spent in Bristol would allow the wounds to heal and perhaps excite less anger from Josiah Jago.

But Preacher Jago was concerned with far more serious problems than his son's prize-fighting activities.

South Cornwall had escaped the blizzards that swept the remainder of the country. A little snow fell during the course of a single night, but by noon it had melted, leaving only tiny pockets of snow in creases of the hills and beneath sheltered hedgerows. It meant that Preacher Jago, well wrapped up against the wind, was able to go about the Lord's business as usual.

On the Sunday following the fight, Josiah Jago preached in four of the tiny fishing hamlets to the west of Mevagissey. Each of the congregations was given the benefit of one of his newest sermons, entitled 'I look upon all the world as my parish', based on the stirring evangelical words of John Wesley.

Warmed by the belief that his message had entered the hearts and minds of his flock, Preacher Jago continued on his circuit on Monday morning, well pleased with life. At noon he stopped to share a meal with two elderly spinsters who worked a corn-grinding mill in a lonely valley, two miles inland from the coast. It was here that he was finally traced by the young son of one of his Pentuan lay preachers. Chosen for his fitness, the youth had run nine miles to find the Methodist preacher.

The news he carried hit Josiah Jago with more force than any blow landed on his son by Abraham Dellow.

Sir Lewis Hearle had sent men to Pentuan to demolish the Methodist chapel. The young runner reported that by the time he had left the village the roof had already been stripped of slates, and the men were putting axes to the rafters.

Filled with shock and disbelief, Josiah Jago tried to conjure up coherent speech. 'But . . . but Sir Lewis Hearle has no right . . . ! The land on which the chapel is built was given to us by old Captain Dunne before he died.'

'Ah, so 'twas,' agreed the exhausted youngster. 'But it seems it weren't his to give away. That piece of land and a whole lot more was sold to Polrudden by Captain Dunne's father, many years ago. The Dunnes were allowed to carry on using it, but 'tis part of Lower Polrudden Farm. Sir Lewis only found out about it when he put the farm up for sale. He says the chapel's got to come down.'

Still trying to grasp the situation, Preacher Jago could only keep repeating: 'I can't believe it . . . I just can't believe it.'

'It's right enough, Preacher Jago. Sir Lewis has brought in St Austell men to do the job – and you know what they're like. They'll hang their grand-mothers for the price of a pint of ale – ay, and draw and quarter 'em afterwards for an extra shilling. Folks in Pentuan have begged 'em to stop knocking the chapel down, but they won't listen. *You'll* need to persuade Sir Lewis to leave chapel be, I reckon . . . But you'd best hurry, or there won't be much of 'en left standing.'

Josiah Jago had his thoughts under control now, disbelief giving way to anger. Leaving the two agitated spinsters to tend to the blistered feet of the young Pentuan youth, Josiah Jago mounted his old donkey and set off homeward, urging the startled animal to a faster gait than it had ever before achieved.

News of the destruction of the Pentuan chapel had

spread to the surrounding countryside by the time Josiah Jago rode into Pentuan that afternoon. The tiny village was thronged with angry Methodists.

His arrival prompted an outbreak of cheering, and cries of 'Here comes the preacher,' and 'Make way for Preacher Jago. He'll soon put a stop to it.'

Preacher Josiah Jago was aware of the hopes of his Methodist parishioners, but he looked in horror at the destruction already achieved by the St Austell men. The roof of the chapel had been totally demolished, and an end wall was reduced to little more than a heap of rubble. Inside the half-destroyed chapel, the pulpit rose above the rows of wooden benches, the whole being covered in dust and debris.

The sight of such desecration brought Josiah Jago close to tears. He had collected the money for this building himself, much of it in pennies and two-pences, the most the donors could afford. He had gone without many meals during his circuit-riding in order to put a few extra pence in the chapel fund. Much of the actual building work had also been carried out by his own hands, and all had been done for love of the Lord.

In this emotional mood, he appealed to the St Austell men to cease work. He *begged* them to destroy no more of the Lord's house.

The St Austell men's refusal brought an angry swelling of sound from the listening crowd. Finally, Josiah Jago pleaded with the demolishers to cease their work at least until he had spoken with Sir Lewis Hearle, and they grudgingly agreed, moved more by the ugly mood of the Wesleyan crowd than by the preacher's arguments.

Still stiff from his long ride, Josiah Jago remounted his donkey and kicked his heels into the animal's flanks. Old Barnabas had just carried his agitated rider for nine miles at an unaccustomed speed. The ageing donkey was tired, thirsty and exceedingly stubborn. It refused to move. Bystanders came to the aid of their preacher, and the donkey was poked and prodded, his tail twisted, and his ears tugged until he threw back his woolly head and kicked out at his tormentors in protest. But he took not a single pace forward. When some of the younger members of the crowd began to laugh, Preacher Jago dismounted. He would need to walk to see Sir Lewis Hearle.

This was to be the only moment of humour in a day of disaster for the Methodist community.

Preacher Josiah Jago toiled up the hill to Polrudden Manor, accompanied by a number of his friends. Along the way all offered their breathless, disjointed advice. At the entrance to the manor driveway, he asked his companions to wait and leave him to carry out his mission alone.

Not knowing that the preacher was absent from Pentuan, Sir Lewis Hearle had been expecting Josiah Jago much earlier in the day. In fact, he had become more and more anxious as the hours passed and he did not arrive. Watching the ageing figure in a shabby serge suit making his way wearily along the driveway to Polrudden Manor, Sir Lewis was filled with a sense of relief. It was late, but there was still time to effect the main object of his carefully prepared plan.

Preacher Josiah Jago received short shrift at the hands of Spencer Perceval's Under-Secretary for

Home Affairs. Tongue in cheek, Sir Lewis Hearle expressed sympathy with the preacher at the loss of his chapel, but Josiah Jago had to understand the baronet's own position. He had put Lower Polrudden Farm on the market. Indeed, he felt the Duchy of Cornwall was prepared to purchase it from him, just as they had bought another of his farms. But the Duchy was the property of the future King of England. It could not be expected to buy land upon which there was a dissenting place of worship.

Sir Lewis reminded Josiah Jago that the chapel had been illegally built on Polrudden land and he would be within his rights to sue the Methodists for the costs incurred in having the chapel knocked down. He would not do this, of course, but he wanted the preacher to understand the legalities of the situation.

Preacher Jago was a simple man. He had been brought up to believe that the lord of the manor – any manor – was a man of honour. It was certainly not for men like himself to question either his rights or the manner in which he exercised them. He accepted the cruel setback to his life's work.

Murmuring incoherently that Sir Lewis could have given him due warning of his intentions, in order that the chapel records and some of the fittings might have been carried to safety, he bowed to the baronet's authority.

'Oh! Weren't you given notice? I feel certain I asked one of my servants to tell you – last week some time, I believe,' Sir Lewis lied jubilantly as he rang for a servant to show the preacher out of the study.

The friends waiting outside the manor gates

listened to the story of their preacher's failure in dismayed silence. Each knew how much the loss of the chapel meant to him personally. They took little notice of the groom who kneed his horse between them, a sealed note from Sir Lewis Hearle tucked inside a pouch at his waist.

The crowds at Pentuan were less restrained. They maintained their silence only long enough to catch the gist of what Josiah Jago had to say and then they let out loud howls of anger.

The St Austell men had been listening, too, and now they resumed knocking down the Wesleyan place of worship. Immediately, the workmen became the focus for the crowd's frustration and anger. At first it involved no more than shouted abuse. It might have become nothing more, had one of the workmen not made a ribald comment about the barrackers. It was made in a moment of bravado, but when the other workmen laughed at his words the mood of the Methodist crowd became ugly.

A clod of grass and earth hurtled through the air, landing close to one of the workmen. There was a brief hesitation before another missile, this time a stone, was hurled with more accuracy. It struck one of the workmen on the leg.

Even now all might not have been lost had the workman chosen to ignore the provocation. Instead, he picked up a piece of masonry and hurled it back into the crowd. It was not large, but it struck a young girl on the face. Her cry was more of fright than of pain, but it became a scream when she put a hand to her face and it came away streaked with her blood.

Given an example of how best to vent their feelings,

the crowd erupted in violent anger. Stones, earth and even wooden fence-staves flew through the air towards the St Austell workmen. One was struck on the head by a stone and fell off the half-demolished wall, to lie sprawled in a grotesque heap on the rubble below.

Greatly alarmed at the sudden turn events had taken, Preacher Josiah Jago climbed on a mounting-block outside the Jolly Sailor tavern and called upon the crowd to show restraint. His words were lost in the uproar, as missiles continued to fly through the air in the direction of the St Austell workmen.

This was the moment chosen by a magistrate from St Austell to arrive upon the scene accompanied by forty mounted men of the North Cornwall Yeomanry, mustered at Bodmin.

The fact that the yeomanry arrived so swiftly was certain evidence that the authorities had anticipated trouble. In fact, they had been waiting since dawn at Nansladron, no more than a mile along the valley. The messenger sent to summon them urgently to Pentuan had left Polrudden Manor while Preacher Jago was admitting the failure of his mission to his friends, outside the manor.

The magistrate's words, calling on the angry mob to disperse, were lost in the general din. Only one or two people standing nearby guessed that the Riot Act had been read.

One of these few was Preacher Jago. He shouted himself hoarse in a bid to bring the people in the packed village square to their senses, but missiles continued to rain down on the workmen, who now cowered in the ruins of the Methodist chapel.

The magistrate gave the crowd no further warning. At a word of command, the yeomanry drove their horses into the surprised and angry crowd, using the butt ends of their muskets to clear a path. The bulk of the crowd scattered before the determined drive of the part-time soldiers, but not before seven of their number had been arrested, on orders from the magistrate. One of the seven was Preacher Josiah Jago.

Across the square, Annie Jago had been watching events from her kitchen window, determined not to leave the house while the noisy, unruly crowd remained. Then she saw her husband summarily and roughly arrested. Running from the house, she tried to force a way through the fleeing crowds to reach him. As frightened Methodists fled past her, Annie Jago inched her way forward until she reached those who were hardest pressed by the horses and flailing muskets of the mounted yeomanry.

Unable to make further headway, Annie Jago found herself being carried backwards by the terrified crowd. Caught up in their mood, she began pummelling those about her in a bid to break through to reach her husband. Suddenly her ankle turned on a rock dropped to the ground by one of the protesters and she stumbled to her knees. As she tried to rise someone fell over her and bore her to the ground. Within moments there were a dozen men and women lying in a heap, among them a member of the yeomanry whose horse had been downed.

When the last of the fleeing Methodists finally cleared the square, four men and a woman still lay on the ground. The four men moaned in agony, but Annie Jago lay quite still.

Josiah Jago recognised the still figure of his wife as one of the part-time soldiers was in the process of shackling his wrists with heavy iron bands joined together by a chain.

Pushing the surprised man to one side, Josiah Jago ran towards his wife, forgetting the chains that already secured his ankles.

The soldier of the yeomanry called that the preacher was trying to escape. One of his companions, crossing the square on his horse, ran the preacher down. As Josiah Jago shouted and tried to explain his actions, he was beaten into insensibility by the butt end of a musket wielded by another soldier.

Two of the arrested men helped to lift the unconscious form of the preacher inside an enclosed prison-wagon, thoughtfully provided by the magistrate for the occasion. The injured St Austell workman, nursing a broken arm, rode with the driver of the wagon, escorted by the magistrate and thirty members of the yeomanry.

Not until the wagon and horses had clattered from Pentuan Square did the stunned residents of the fishing village leave their houses to tend to those who still lay where they had fallen, watched by ten men of the yeomanry. Left behind to protect the workmen who were completing their task in silent haste, the part-time soldiers fingered their muskets nervously.

They had nothing to fear. The violent scenes had shocked the Methodist villagers and they went about their ministrations in silent grief.

Two of the injured villagers had broken limbs. A third suffered internal injuries.

Annie Jago was dead.

17

Nathan was told of the death of his mother and the arrest of his father when *The Brave Amy H* tied up alongside the quay at Portgiskey.

Amy watched helplessly as he struggled to control his anguish and bewilderment, and she was filled with an urge to hold him to her. She knew he needed someone to comfort him. Nathan Jago, prize-fighting champion of the world, needed someone to help him bridge this terrible chasm that had suddenly appeared before him.

Amy could have provided the bridge. She desperately wanted to help – but she hesitated too long. The moment came – and as quickly went.

Drawing a deep breath, as though sucking new life into his body, Nathan questioned his fisherman informant. 'Does my father know that Ma is dead?'

'Yes. Your sister Nell went to see him in Bodmin Gaol. Word is that he's taken the news badly. He feels that he's responsible.'

It was on Nathan's tongue to retort that his father's narrow interpretation of his religion could be blamed for most of the misfortunes that had befallen the Jago family, but he bit back the words. This was not the time to air such thoughts, and they were probably not true. He realised his father must have been desperately unhappy to have made such an admission.

Then Nathan seized upon something else the fisherman had said.

'Why is he in Bodmin Gaol, and not in St Austell lock-up?'

'He's been charged with inciting the riot in Pentuan. It's an offence that needs to be tried at Bodmin Assizes. He's also been charged with repeatedly preaching in the open air. But, whatever the charges, we all know he's been arrested simply because he preaches Methodism.'

'I'll go and see him straight away.'

To Amy and Sammy, Nathan said: 'I might be away for a day or two. There's Pa to see . . . and a funeral to arrange. Can you keep things going here?'

'Of course.' Amy and Sammy spoke in unison, and Amy added: 'We'll keep things going. But hurry back. We need you here with us.'

The fisherman who had given Nathan news of the happenings at Pentuan said quickly: 'About the funeral . . . It might not be so easy to arrange. You see . . . she's been refused burial by the Church.'

It was a strange anomaly of the country's religious laws that the Methodists, young and dynamic as they were, and so often in conflict with the Church of England, were reliant upon the Established Church for the sacraments. Indeed, John Wesley, founder of the Methodist Church, was himself ordained in the Church of England and had never originally intended that his great revivalist movement should advance outside the Church of England.

'I don't believe it!' Nathan stared at the fisherman in disbelief. He had heard of dissenters being refused burial elsewhere in the country, but never here in Cornwall. The vicar of St Austell was responsible for the spiritual needs of Pentuan. He disapproved of the Methodist separation, but had never before refused them any of the benefits of his church.

'The vicar of St Austell's been taken ill. He'll likely not live long. Until a new vicar is appointed, the Reverend Kent, rector of Fowey, has taken over from him.'

Now Nathan understood. The Reverend Nicholas Kent was as notoriously opposed to Methodism as Sir Lewis Hearle – and he had a particular dislike for Josiah Jago.

Turning away, Nathan strode off without another word. Behind him, Sammy Mizler was watching the expression upon Amy's face and he reached for her hand. When Nathan rounded the rocks separating Portgiskey Cove from Pentuan Beach, he looked back briefly and saw his two partners standing hand in hand. He felt very much alone. He did not see Amy dissolve in tears as he passed out of sight.

Nathan called first at Venn Farm. He found Nell and Tom Quicke deeply unhappy. Married life had begun for them with such high hopes for the future. Now, it seemed, their whole world was crumbling about them. Tearfully Nell began to tell Nathan about the death of their mother. He told her he already knew and led her to a seat close to the wood fire that defied the despondent gloom in the room with its crackling cheerfulness.

'It's a sad business, right enough,' echoed Tom Quicke, Nell's serious and steady husband. 'First the farm's taken away, then your father's arrested and your poor ma killed in Pentuan square. They called an inquest on her, but they held it in St Austell. "Fear of inflaming local opinion" was the reason they gave for not having it here. We knew better. They knew full well that if they held it far enough away from Pentuan no one from here would go and tell the truth of what happened. "Misadventure" was the verdict they recorded. "Murder" would have been a more honest finding. I've spoken to some who said one of the soldiers rode his horse right over your poor mother while she lay helpless on the ground.'

'Then it's a pity they didn't have the courage to go to St Austell and say so,' said Nathan bitterly. 'Tell me about Kent's refusal to bury Ma.'

'What is there to say?' asked Nell. 'Tom and I went to see the Reverend Kent, on our way back from Bodmin, after visiting Pa. He said that by supporting Pa in his ways she'd forfeited the right to a decent Christian burial. He swore she'd not have a single inch of Church ground.'

Tom Quicke put an arm about his wife. 'Kent said a whole lot more, but what Nell's told you is about the strength of it.'

'Where is Ma now?'

'Upstairs. We didn't like to leave her down at the village – alone. But she'll need to be buried soon, Nathan. We've got to get out of the farm, Nell and me.

We had official notice yesterday from Sir Lewis Hearle. Venn's been sold already.'

'Did Sir Lewis mention the name of the buyer?'

'He didn't, but his solicitor did. I've been to see him this morning. It's been bought through the Duchy of Cornwall Land Agent – for the Duke of Clarence. Why he should want a farm like Venn beats me . . .'

Nathan's shoulders sagged with relief. There and then, he told Nell and Tom Quicke about the arrangement he had made with the Duke of Clarence.

If Nathan had ever entertained any doubts about his decision to fight again in order to give Nell and her husband Venn Farm, one look at their faces now would have dispelled them for ever.

Tom Quicke was utterly dazed at the sudden change in his fortunes.

'You . . . you fought to give us the farm? Why, Nathan? Why should you do so much . . . ?'

'I can give you two reasons,' replied Nathan slowly. 'I've gained a lot from prize-fighting. I have a good boat, and a fishing business. It's always been my wish to help Ma and Pa, but Pa has strong feelings about prize-fighting. He'd never accept anything from me. If he ever did, he'd give it away again – to his church.'

Nathan managed a wan smile. 'That left you, Nell. You and Tom wanted Venn Farm. Well, thanks to prize-fighting, you've got it.'

Tom Quicke, still in a daze, seized Nathan's hand in a fierce grip. 'I just don't know what to say, Nathan. "Thank you" don't hardly seem enough. I'm sorry . . . I'm lost for words. Me and Nell want to keep Venn Farm, more than anything in the world. I . . . I wish your ma could have known about this . . .'

Tom Quicke choked on his words as Nell rose and flung her arms about her brother's neck. Her own emotions were such a tangled mixture of grief, relief and happiness that she dared say nothing at all.

Nathan remained at the farm that night, going on to Bodmin at dawn the following day. He travelled on foot. Tom and Nell Quicke had Josiah Jago's donkey at the farm, but the animal was a one-man mount. He allowed Nathan to sit upon his back, but when Nathan tried to persuade him to move forward he was unceremoniously dumped to the ground.

Nathan knew there was little he would be able to do to help his father. Before leaving Bristol he had heard disquieting rumours that Methodist preachers were being arrested throughout the land. There seemed to be a determined plan afoot to destroy Methodism, once and for all.

Before Nathan left Venn Farm, Tom Quicke said something to him that appeared to indicate that the plan was succeeding.

'Your father's arrest has taken the heart from Methodism in this area,' said the slow-thinking farmer. 'We've suffered a blow that has put Methodism back fifty years. With your pa's support we might have survived the loss of the chapel. Without him . . .?' Tom Quicke shrugged. 'Do what you can for him and for *us*, Nathan.'

When the heavy cell door swung open with a loud squeal of protest, Josiah Jago did not even look up to see who was there. He sat hunched on the straw-strewn floor. It was a very small cell, the focal point and only form of furnishing being an iron-bound wooden slop-bucket.

'Pa? It's me, Nathan.'

Josiah Jago turned pain-filled eyes up to his son, and Nathan was deeply shocked at what he saw. One of the preacher's eyes was blackened and the side of his stubble-cheeked face discoloured by an ugly dark bruise.

Nothing Nell or Tom had told him had prepared Nathan for this.

Rounding on the gaoler angrily, he demanded: 'Who did this? Who gave my father a beating?'

The gaoler was an aged, limping ex-soldier and he cowered before Nathan's anger.

'No one in here's touched him, Mr Jago. I'll swear to that. I've never struck a prisoner in my life – though I've had many as I'd like to have looked at along the barrel of a Baker rifle, I don't mind telling thee. No, sir. Your father was struck by a musket at the time of his arrest. He was out for nigh on three hours, so the St Austell turnkey told me.'

'All right. Leave us for a while.'

It had cost Nathan a golden half-guinea to grease the gaoler's key in the rusty locks of Bodmin's decaying and stinking old gaol. Nathan had not paid the money to have a gossiping old turnkey listen to all that was said.

The gaoler touched a finger to his hat respectfully. 'That's all right, Mr Jago, sir. If there's anything you want afore you go, just you let me know. I'll be pleased to oblige.'

The gaoler went out, shutting the rusty-hinged door behind him.

'He's right,' mumbled Josiah Jago suddenly, painfully fingering the bruised side of his face. His bottom lip trembled in the manner of a hurt child. 'I was only trying to reach your mother. She was running to me – concerned for me, as she always was. She didn't deserve to die, Nathan. She'd done nothing wrong. I don't think she ever did a wrong thing in the whole of her life. She was a good woman, such a good woman.'

Preacher Josiah Jago's chin sank to his chest, his eyes closed. His whole body shook in spasm after spasm, as the painful memory of that dreadful afternoon returned to him.

Nathan dropped to his knees beside his father and put an arm about his shoulders. It was the first physical demonstration of affection he could ever remember between them.

Josiah Jago leaned against his son for about two minutes. Then he pulled away and struggled stiffly to his feet. Putting a hand against the crumbling stone wall, he stood looking up at the small, barred window, his back to Nathan.

'I'm finished, son. My life's work is in ruins, the Methodist cause in disarray. I've failed myself, I've failed your mother – God rest her soul – and I've failed the Lord.'

Nathan had never heard his father accept defeat before. He said so.

'Perhaps I've never been honest with myself before. I am now – and I'm deeply troubled. I'm beginning to question all that I've ever done in my lifetime. Was I right to sacrifice the affection of you and Nell – yes, and of your mother, too – for my own beliefs?'

Preacher Josiah Jago turned an agonised glance upon his startled son. 'Did you think I didn't know what was happening? I knew, Nathan. I took *pride* in the sacrifices I made for Him. *Pride* in building His Church. *Pride* in being looked up to by other men and called "Preacher". *Pride*. That's what's brought me down. I, who dedicated my life to spreading the Lord's Word, forgot what it says in Proverbs 16, verse 18: "Pride goeth before destruction, and an haughty spirit before a fall." Well, now the Lord and the whole world bear witness to my downfall. I spend my days sitting in the corner of a cell measuring three paces by two. Surrounded by my own filth. A pig in his pen.'

Josiah Jago's bitter laugh became a cough that hunched his body and alarmed Nathan. The robust preacher who would ride miles in all weathers, defying rain and storm with a hymn on his lips, had become a frail old man.

Nathan looked about the gloomy cell. The walls were scratched with names, dates and primitive calendars.

'I'll speak to the gaoler on my way out. I'll have you moved to a better cell. That will be a start. Then we'll see about having these ridiculous charges dropped, and get you out of here.'

'Don't waste your time, Nathan. The authorities are out to destroy Methodism. I don't really matter to them – or to anyone else, for that matter. But they'll convict me. It's all part of their scheming. Go back to your fishing, my son. Live your own life. I've given you little enough happiness in the past. Don't allow an old fool to ruin your *future*, too.'

'Pa . . .' Nathan took hold of his father's stooped

shoulders and turned him round to face him. 'You just quoted the Bible at me. Now I'm doing the same to you. It's something you made me learn when I was a small boy. I've never forgotten it and I refuse to believe you have. It's from the New Testament. St Matthew, chapter 17, verse 20.'

Josiah Jago's face became animated for the first time since Nathan had entered the gloomy, depressing cell. 'You remember it? After all this time?'

'Every word. But I want *you* to quote it to me.'

Josiah Jago licked his dry lips. Looking up at his son, he said in a hoarse, emotional whisper: ' "If ye have faith as a grain of mustard seed, ye shall say unto this mountain, Remove hence to yonder place; and it shall remove; and nothing shall be impossible unto you".'

Nathan nodded. 'You've lived your life by those words, Pa – and you've proved them true. I've always admired you for that. Are you going to cast them aside now?'

For a few moments the old religious fervour shone from Josiah Jago's eyes. Then the fire died and his shoulders shrugged helplessly beneath Nathan's hands. 'Will faith bring your ma back to life? Or raise my chapel again?'

'You and I will always look at our Nell and see Ma in the way she walks, and talks, and smiles. Ma will never be dead for us. And, yes, faith *will* raise your chapel. What's more, it will have its own burial-ground – and Ma is going to be the first Methodist buried there.'

Nathan was trying desperately hard to rekindle the fires of faith burning so low in the heart of his father.

He was also expressing the ideas that had occupied his thoughts on the long walk from Pentuan. The things he had promised Josiah Jago would not be easy, but the promises *would* be fulfilled.

Josiah Jago shook his head. 'There will never be another chapel in Pentuan. Sir Lewis Hearle will see to that. He and his friends own every inch of land about Pentuan.'

'Not any more. Listen to me, Pa. Tom and Nell own Venn Farm now. True, it's not right in Pentuan, but it's close enough to serve well enough. They'll give you a plot of land for a chapel and burial-ground. There's an ideal piece of rough ground close to the road that will suit you perfectly.'

'They *own* Venn Farm? What nonsense is this? They can't afford to buy a cow, let alone a farm . . .'

'I've bought it for them.'

'You? Where did you get the money?'

'I had another prize-fight. It was a big purse. Big enough to buy Venn Farm.'

Nathan expected his father to be angry. He *hoped* he would be angry. Any positive state of mind would be better than the present mood of depression. But Josiah Jago was in no mood to quarrel with his son.

'I don't hold with prize-fighting, Nathan. You know that. I've told you so many times. But if you've used money from it to buy Nell and Tom their farm, then I'm proud of you. It's more than I've been able to do.'

'And the chapel?' Nathan prompted his father.

Josiah Jago shook his head. 'Where would the money come from? It took me almost three years to raise enough for the chapel Sir Lewis Hearle destroyed. Now there isn't even a preacher for my circuit. People are frightened to stand up and address an open-air congregation for fear of being arrested. Three of my lay preachers are in St Austell lock-up now, awaiting trial before a magistrate on charges of preaching in the open air.'

'That's one of the charges levelled against *you*. How long has it been an offence to preach to people in places where there is no church – of any denomination?'

'Since the St Austell magistrate decided it should be. We won't be the first Methodists to be convicted for nothing more than preaching the Word of the Lord – and convicted we shall be. I'm convinced Sir Lewis Hearle planned my arrest, and I believe the Prime Minister is behind him.'

Nathan was sceptical, but he said nothing. Josiah Jago was talking rationally now.

'I've had time to think since I've been in here. Sir Lewis Hearle is now an under-secretary at the Home Office, appointed by the Prime Minister. He is responsible for various aspects of law and order. I believe he must have sent out orders telling magistrates to make things harder for us Methodists. One thing is certain: since he took office there have been more preachers arrested than ever before. It's happening all over the country. When I was arrested, the magistrate and the yeomanry couldn't have been more than a few minutes away. Sir Lewis knew I would be in Pentuan when they arrived because I had only just left him at Polrudden. I seem to remember, too, that a rider came from the house while I was outside talking. He went as though the Devil were after him. I suspect he'd been sent to inform the magistrate and his men that I was on my way to Pentuan.'

Nathan was still sceptical, but what his father had said made too much sense to ignore.

'This rider, did you recognise him?'

'Yes, I know him well. It was Will Hodge, Sir Lewis Hearle's groom. He's married to the daughter of Ahab Arthur, one of your fishermen.'

'Then I'll see him and ask the truth of what happened.'

'What difference does it make now? What can you do if I'm proved right?'

Nathan countered with a question of his own. 'How would you set about building a chapel at Pentuan?'

'Why, I'd call for special collections at my open-air services. Not that I could expect to take much money. My open-air services are so popular because those who attend are usually too poor to afford clothes decent enough to wear to church or chapel.'

'We might not need as much as you think. Can any of your Methodists build?'

'Most of them – and there's no shortage of fishermen with time on their hands in winter. Yes, if you're serious about it there are many who'd be only too pleased to help build a new chapel.'

Nathan was satisfied that his father was at last taking a real interest in what was being planned. 'I'll have pen and paper brought to you in your new cell. Draw me a rough sketch of how you want the chapel built. I'll do the rest.'

'How will you get word to all my congregation of what is happening?'

'I'll call them to services throughout your circuit – and take the services myself.'

'But you'll need a preaching licence. There isn't a magistrate in St Austell will give one to you.'

'You have a licence. Did it prevent you from being arrested? I'll preach without one. Let them arrest me, if they dare. I'm going now. I have much to do. But I'll be back to see you again soon.'

Nathan called through the grille in the door. A few minutes later he heard the sound of keys jangling as the gaoler hobbled his way along the gloomy corridor.

As Nathan left the cell, his father called quietly to him: 'Nathan? Are you doing all this for the Lord – or for me?'

Nathan knew what his father wanted to hear, but he could not be hypocritical, even when the answer meant so much.

'I'm doing it for you. *You* can further the Lord's cause yourself when you get out of here. I'll do my best to ensure that it's soon.'

18

Nathan headed for Polrudden Manor when he left Bodmin Gaol. Although tired after his long walk and the anguish of finding his father in such a poor condition, he would not rest until he had confronted Sir Lewis Hearle. He wanted to learn the truth of the baronet's part in the arrest and imprisonment of his father.

It was a dismal grey day that had deteriorated into light drizzle by the time he neared the manor-house. When he was almost within sight of Polrudden he saw two riders on Hearle land, riding a parallel course with him. It was a moment or two before he recognised the smaller of the riders as Elinor Hearle.

Nathan's heart began to beat faster at the sight of her, and he had to remind himself of the part Elinor's father had probably played in the events of the past week. Even so, Nathan's mouth became dry with subdued excitement when Elinor turned her head in his direction and he realised she had recognised him, too.

The two horses slowed to a halt, and for some minutes the riders were engaged in earnest discussion. Eventually, and with obvious reluctance, one of the horses moved away. The rider looked back twice before digging heels into the horse's flanks, to be quickly swallowed up in the mist that hid Polrudden Manor from view.

Elinor Hearle waited until the other rider was out of sight before she turned her horse from the bridle path and let it pick a way across the rough grassland to the road where Nathan waited.

Before Nathan had left for Bristol, he had decided that Elinor was deliberately avoiding him, for reasons best known to herself. If this were true, it would seem that something had happened to change her mind. Her smile of welcome began when her horse was still some lengths away. Reaching him, she pulled the animal to a halt, leaped from the saddle, and hurled herself at Nathan, kissing him as though they were in the privacy of her bedroom.

'Nathan, I've missed you. Where have you been? No, there's no need to explain. I've heard all about your prize-fight in Bristol. Everyone in Cornwall is talking about *our* champion. 'Tis said you are now undisputed champion of *the world*. I am so proud of you.'

Standing close and looking up at him, she put a hand to the extensive bruising about his right cheekbone. 'Your poor face. Does it still hurt?' Without waiting for a reply, she went on: 'Never mind, it's over now. You won. Where have you been today, to see that sister of yours?'

Nathan stiffened. 'No, to Bodmin. My father is in the gaol there.'

'Oh, yes. He was arrested in Pentuan, where all those foolish people threw stones at my father's workmen and then fought the North Cornwall Yeomanry.'

Elinor Hearle spoke so unconcernedly that they might have been discussing happenings in far-off India.

'My mother neither threw stones nor fought the soldiers, yet she died in Pentuan square.'

Elinor Hearle's eyes widened in shocked horror. 'Oh! My poor, poor Nathan. I didn't know. I am sorry . . . so very, very sorry.'

It was very difficult not to believe her. He *did* believe her. After all, she could have had nothing to do with what had occurred. Elinor could not be blamed for Sir Lewis Hearle's complicity.

'My father wasn't involved, either. He was trying to *stop* the stone-throwing. That's why I'm on my way to Polrudden now. I want to speak to Sir Lewis and ask him to use his influence to have my father released.'

It was only a small lie, Nathan told himself. Even so, it was wasted.

'You won't find my father at home. He's in London. He is a very busy man these days.'

Nathan was not sure whether he was disappointed or relieved at the news. He did not know what he would have done had he been able to prove that Sir Lewis Hearle *had* played a part in his father's arrest. He shrugged. 'Then there's no reason for me to go to Polrudden.' He rubbed a hand wearily over his face. 'I might as well go to Venn.'

'Are you *really* going to walk out on me so soon,

Nathan?' Elinor began picking imaginary threads from Nathan's shirt front. 'It's been such a long time since you came to visit me.'

Nathan was weary. It had been a long day, and he had much to do – and even more to think about. But this girl plucking at his shirt front was able to stir him in spite of all the physical odds against her.

He grabbed Elinor roughly and kissed her – hard. Immediately, her arms went about his neck and she pressed herself to him. His hands began to move over her body until, gasping, she pulled away from him.

'No, Nathan. Not here . . .'

Without releasing her, he whispered: 'All right, I'll come to Polrudden tonight. As soon as it's dark.'

'That's impossible.' She slipped away from him. 'We have house guests. It's a damned nuisance, but I have to play at being a hostess for my father in his absence.'

The light drizzle was more persistent now, falling as fine rain. Elinor looked about her. Two fields away the outline of a building stood out from the gathering gloom. It was the shell of what had once been the farmhouse of Polrudden's home farm. Now it was used to store hay.

Nodding towards the building, Elinor said: 'We're getting soaked here. Let's go there and talk.'

Catching the bridle of her horse, Elinor pulled the animal towards her and turned to Nathan. 'Show me how fit your fight has left you. I'll race you to the hay-store.'

After his long walk, the last thing Nathan wanted was a race. But once in the saddle Elinor hung back, taunting him. When they came to a narrow gap in the hedge, between two elm-trees, Nathan squeezed through and began running, leaving Elinor to ride to a gate at the far end of the field. Even so, Elinor won the race and entered the old house ahead of him, laughing and out of breath.

It was dark inside, the grey evening light seeping weakly through a small and dirty window. The whole building carried the scent of hay. It was a good, clean smell. So, too, was the smell of Elinor's hair, damp from the rain, as she took off her hat and shook her hair down about her shoulders.

Without a word, she took his hand and led him to a mound of hay, put out for distribution to the cattle in the morning. When she released his hand she fumbled with the laces at her throat. Moments later she shrugged her shoulders out of the dress. It fell about her feet, and in the dim light Nathan could see the whiteness of her.

'Nathan . . . I'm cold,' she whispered, her mouth close to his. 'Make love to me. Warm me . . .' Her fingers fumbled at the buttons of his coat. 'It's been so long, Nathan. *Too* long . . .'

They made love in the grey twilight, and again in the full darkness, then Elinor murmured that she must return to Polrudden before they sent out a party to search for her.

Putting on his wet cold clothing in the darkness was a sobering, romance-chilling experience. It did not help when Nathan's many problems returned to his mind to remind him that Elinor's father was undoubtedly responsible for most of them.

The knowledge did not prevent him from taking her arm and pulling her towards him as she was about to pass out of the doorway ahead of him. But when he tried to kiss her once more she moved her face away irritably. 'No, Nathan. I'm wet and I'm cold. I *must* get home.'

He released her reluctantly. 'Will I be seeing you again?'

Untying her horse, she said, 'You want to?'

'Of course.'

'Then you'll think of a way.'

She swung up to the saddle, turned the animal's head and rode away.

Hurt by her manner, Nathan struggled to think of a word to describe his feelings. Her abrupt departure had amounted to a virtual dismissal. The word he finally settled on was . . . 'used'.

Nathan did not go to see Will Hodge, Sir Lewis Hearle's groom, immediately. First he went home, to Pentuan, to clean up and change his clothes. The house was cold and comfortless. Nathan had hoped that Sammy would be at home, but he was probably at Portgiskey Cove. Nathan envied him the warmth and companionship he would undoubtedly be enjoying. There was none of either in the Jago cottage at the moment. Even when he lit a fire it failed to chase away the gloom.

Nathan left the house and was relieved to find it had stopped raining. As he passed the heap of rubble that had once been Pentuan's chapel, the moon slid briefly from behind the clouds. It gave him a ghostly reminder of the events that had so changed the lives of the people of Pentuan.

When Nathan stepped over the threshold of Will

Hodge's cottage, he found all the warmth that had been lacking in his own home. Seated beside a blazing fire, he was treated as a hero. Ann Hodge insisted upon cooking a large meal for him, and young Sarah was brought from her bedroom to say a sleepy 'hello' to the man who had saved her from the stable fire.

Sarah stayed up until a steaming meal was placed in front of Nathan. Not until then did he realise how hungry he was. Over the meal he asked the question he had carried with him from Bodmin Gaol. Where had Will Hodge gone on the afternoon of the 'riot' at Pentuan?

'Why, to Nansladron Farm.' Nansladron was about a mile along the valley from Pentuan. 'That's where the magistrate was waiting with the yeomanry. I'd say they'd probably been in camp there, although the horses were all saddled up and ready when I arrived.'

'Did you carry a message from Sir Lewis?'

'Not a message. It was a sealed letter. Not that it would have made any difference, sealed or not. I don't read. Mind you, now I come to think about it, Sir Lewis did tell me to impress the need for great haste upon the magistrate. I didn't know what he was talking about at the time. I reckon I do now.'

'You believe he knew there would be trouble in Pentuan?'

'He *must* have known. What I don't understand is why he didn't have the yeomanry in Pentuan before the work started, so as to *prevent* trouble.'

'I can answer that,' said Ann Hodge. She had put Sarah to bed and entered the room in time to hear her husband's last statement. 'You haven't lived in Pentuan all your life. You don't know Sir Lewis Hearle as

I do. He hates Methodists – Methodist preachers in particular. He didn't want the soldiers in Pentuan until there *was* trouble, with Preacher Jago caught in the middle of it. You said yourself you'd seen the preacher leave Polrudden not half an hour before he was arrested. Sir Lewis knew exactly where he'd be.'

Tears welled up in Ann Hodge's eyes. 'I cried myself to sleep that night, just thinking about your father, poor man. Him in prison, your mother dead, and you away. It was enough to turn his brain. I was so sorry to hear about your mother, Nathan. She was a good woman. I knew her well and never heard her say an unkind word about anyone.'

'Thank you.'

There was no need to say more. Nathan had learned what he wanted to know. Sir Lewis Hearle *had* brought in the magistrate and the yeomanry *before* trouble had started – but not until he knew Josiah Jago was there. Nathan did not believe the stone-throwing had been started by Pentuan men, either. There were probably men in the crowd who had been hired to ensure there *would* be trouble when the military arrived. Nathan knew he would never learn the whole truth of the matter. Sir Lewis was far too clever to have hired the men himself, but Nathan had no doubt that his suspicion was well founded.

Although reluctant to return to an empty house, Nathan did not remain late at the Hodge cottage. Tomorrow was going to be another busy day.

Will Hodge insisted on accompanying Nathan to Pentuan, saying he would show him a short cut through the gardens of Polrudden Manor.

As they approached the manor-house they could see a great many lights burning in the downstairs rooms, and a number of well-dressed people milling about inside. On the driveway leading to the house, half a dozen carriages were lined up, the horses munching contentedly on the contents of straw nose-bags.

Nathan commented that it looked as though there was a party going on inside the house. Will Hodge snorted derisively.

'You'd think Sir Lewis had been crowned King of England, the way things have changed here. I hope he's being paid well in his new government post. He'll need to be. He might have sold some of his farms, but he's spending twice as much as he's getting in. He and Miss Elinor have had to take on more servants to cope with all the folks who want to see them now. They have house guests most of the time – especially the Rodds. They're here at the moment.'

'Rodds? I don't think I've heard of them. Are they a local family?'

Will Hodge chuckled. 'I'm glad old Lady Rodd wasn't around to hear you say you haven't heard of her family. They're very important. They have an estate at Trebartha, on the edge of Bodmin Moor. I think one of the family sits in the House of Commons with Sir Lewis, but they never took much notice of him until he was made an under-secretary. Now they seem to spend more time here than at Trebartha.'

Will Hodge gossiped on happily, pleased to air his knowledge of the family for whom he worked, and of those who came to stay at Polrudden Manor. 'If you ask me, there's a wedding in the offing between young Francis Rodd and Miss Elinor. He dotes on her. Mind you, he'd be a handsome catch. He's heir to all the Trebartha lands, with enough money to solve all Sir Lewis's problems.'

Nathan listened to Will Hodge's prattling with dismay. The talkative groom was mistaken, of course. He had to be. Had he known what had occurred at the old home farm that very afternoon, he would have realised that Elinor could not possibly be contemplating marriage with anyone.

But fate decreed that it was to be *Nathan* who would suffer disillusionment.

Will Hodge suddenly gripped his arm. 'There's someone coming. Quick, hide here. In the bushes.'

He drew Nathan to the deep shadows of a nearby shrubbery and here they waited as footsteps crunched along the driveway, heading in their direction.

There was a faint breeze blowing, and suddenly Nathan caught the fragrance of a perfume he knew well. It conjured up memories of a darkened bedroom, and naked bodies tangled beneath silken sheets. But there were two sets of footsteps – and it was a man's voice he heard first, raised in mild complaint.

'. . . been trying to speak to you for days now. I came riding with you today thinking you'd give me an opportunity to speak my mind. Dammit, Elinor! You *must* know how I feel about you. But what do you do? You take off on that stallion of yours and it's as much as I can do to keep you in view! Then when you did finally slow down, and I was trying to gather enough breath and courage to talk seriously, you packed me off like some disobedient child.'

'Did I, Francis? I'm sorry. But I saw someone with

whom I needed to speak. What was it you wanted to say to me?'

There was a coyness in Elinor's voice that Nathan had never heard before.

'You know full well. You *must* know. I love you, Elinor. I want you to marry me.'

'Francis! This is neither the time nor the place to be saying such a thing!'

Elinor sounded primly shocked. Nathan struggled to keep his own emotions in check, remembering her as he had seen her only a few hours before. Naked in the home farm hay-store.

'I realise it's something that should be discussed with your father first, but dammit, Elinor, we're not children. We don't have to rely upon others to make up our minds for us. I'll speak to your father, certainly. But first I must know how *you* feel. And I want to know *now*.'

There was a long silence during which Nathan realised his fists were clenched so tightly his fingers were hurting.

'Francis, is this a proposal – or an ultimatum?'

Nathan recognised the teasing tone of Elinor's voice. Francis Rodd did not.

'It is not an ultimatum, Elinor. *Desperation*, yes. I'll tell you once more. *I love you*. I want you to marry me. Please say "yes".'

Beside Nathan, Will Hodge began to fidget uncomfortably. He and Nathan were eavesdropping on a very intimate scene. His movements almost caused Nathan to miss Elinor's reply, so softly was it given.

'Yes. Yes, Francis, I'll marry you – if you are quite certain it's what you want.'

Nathan's involuntary sharp intake of breath almost betrayed the two eavesdroppers. Elinor heard and said sharply: 'What was that sound?'

'I heard nothing.' Francis Rodd was determined to allow nothing to detract from this moment. 'I-I'm quite s-sure you are teasing me again. B-but it doesn't matter any more. You've said y-you'll marry me. I feel like sh-shouting the news to the whole world.' In moments of stress, Francis Rodd suffered from a stutter.

Briefly, the two shadowy figures standing on the driveway merged and became one.

'Francis!'

Elinor sounded shocked. Nathan's thoughts were in a turmoil, but he could not help admiring Elinor's prowess as an actress.

'I'm s-sorry. That was presumptuous of me. But you've made me s-so happy. May I tell Mother to-night?'

'No.' Elinor was in full command of the situation. 'Keeping our love a secret from your mother will be your way of proving you really love me. You'll tell no one until you've spoken to my father.'

'Dammit, Elinor. I shouldn't have to prove any-thing. I've told you I love you. Isn't that enough?' Francis Rodd spoke sulkily, but when Elinor gave him no answer he said: 'Oh, very well. But I'm not waiting until your father returns home. I'm going to London to speak to him there.'

'That would make me very happy.'

Elinor could hardly hide the jubilation in her voice. Francis Rodd was probably the most eligible man in the county, and once he had spoken to her father he would have committed himself to marriage without giving his formidable mother the opportunity to raise any objections. Once married, Elinor knew she could persuade the heir to the Rodd fortunes to do whatever she wanted.

Elinor gave Francis Rodd a brief kiss. 'You must go to London and hurry back to me as quickly as you can.' Grasping his arm, Elinor leaned against her intended husband in a display of affection that caused him to puff up with proprietary pride. 'We must return to the house now. If we've been missed for too long, there will be such a scandal that your mother will refuse to allow you to marry me.'

'Sh-she'll never do that, Elinor. Mother doesn't like upsetting me.'

The unofficially betrothed couple walked away along the driveway, returning to the company of family and friends who lived by the strict rules of social etiquette demanded by their society.

Behind her, unseen, and probably already forgotten, Nathan was left to nurse his own foolish, broken dreams.

19

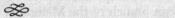

When Tom and Nell Quicke received the deeds of Venn Farm, they immediately ceded a piece of land to the Methodist Society, for a church and a burial-ground. They agreed with Nathan that it would prove to Josiah Jago that his work for the Methodist cause was not at an end.

Preacher Jago was sorely in need of heartening words and deeds. Nathan and Sammy Mizler had been to St Austell in a futile bid to have the preacher released on bail to attend Annie Jago's funeral. They had offered to provide substantial bail money, but the magistrate declared that the crime for which Josiah Jago had been arraigned was of too serious a nature for bail to be granted. He also pointed out somewhat maliciously that Methodist preachers were classed as 'itinerants', travelling from place to place to carry out their religious vocation. Such a way of life could hardly be regarded as settled enough for bail to be seriously considered.

Angry and frustrated with St Austell's custodians of the law, Nathan returned to Pentuan to find a stranger waiting for him. Very tall and vigorous, with a shock of unruly white hair, the stranger spoke with a pronounced American accent. He gave his name as Uriah Kemp – the *Reverend* Uriah Kemp, of the American branch of the Methodist Church.

Kemp explained that he had been on his way from a camp meeting in the North of England, heading for Falmouth to take a return passage to America, when he had heard of the plight of Josiah Jago.

Observing Nathan's bewilderment, Uriah Kemp asked: 'Have you ever attended a camp meeting?'

When Nathan shook his head, the American preacher said enthusiastically: 'Then you've missed one of life's truly great experiences – one that fires the souls of even the most determined unbelievers. Thousands of people on their knees, each promising himself to the Lord, the "Hallelujahs" reaching to the very sky.'

'But why are you here, in Pentuan?'

'I've been guided here by the Lord . . . You doubt me?'

Nathan thought it would take a very brave man to confess to Uriah Kemp that anything he said was doubted. He shook his head.

'Let me explain, brother. Many years ago, soon after my ordination into the Anglican Church, I was caught up in my country's war of independence. I fought against the British. But something happened to me during those unhappy years. I was converted to

Methodism. I ended the war preaching to British prisoners. It's a habit I have never lost. Whenever my footsteps guide me to a town, I head for the nearest prison. There I find souls ripe for the Lord's harvesting. Usually I am given a free night's lodging at the gaol, too. That's what happened when I entered Bodmin Town. I preached mightily for the good of both gaolers and prisoners. My reward was to share your father's cell for the night. He told me of his troubles and I knew the Good Lord had taken me to him because He had work for me again. So here I am. Tell me, what have you done so far?'

Nathan told Uriah Kemp of his plans for the chapel site and the burial-ground alongside, where his mother would be laid to rest. He also told Kemp of the unsuccessful attempt to have his father released on bail.

The Reverend Uriah Kemp nodded sympathetically. 'Bigotry is an enemy we Methodists know well. The best way to help your father is to prove to the authorities – and to him – that his absence affects his circuit not one whit. Let them see that the Methodist Church hereabouts will not collapse with the loss of one preacher. Do this and the reason for holding him has gone. There's little sense in making an example of a man if it doesn't damage his cause in any way. But we'll take things in order of importance. You say your dear mother is to be laid to rest in your new burial-ground? Who is going to take the funeral service?'

'I was hoping one of my father's lay preachers would conduct it, but those I've approached so far are reluctant to commit themselves. One is a good evangelist, but he doesn't read a word and so feels incapable of conducting a burial service. Another is employed renovating the parish church in St Austell, and he fears for his livelihood if he takes the service. The third man I approached simply refused. He says it's a sin to bury my mother with Christian ceremony in unconsecrated ground.'

'Then *I'll* conduct the service. I'll send your mother to the Lord with a reference that will be the envy of every Christian who hears it. As for unconsecrated ground, I'll consecrate it for you. Personally, I don't think it matters a green fig whether the ground is consecrated or not. I've seen men buried where they died, on muddy, unholy battlefields. Many were brave and honest men. I've never doubted that they went straight to the waiting arms of the Lord. I've seen others laid to rest in cathedral aisles, wearing fine clothes inside their satin-lined coffins. I don't doubt they're some of the best-dressed men sitting around the fires of hell. If you're good enough, the Lord will make you welcome. If you're not, no amount of consecrating's going to save your damned soul.'

The Reverend Uriah Kemp glared at Nathan, as though daring him to argue. Once again, Nathan said nothing.

'Now, what arrangements have you made to ensure that regular services are held for Methodist ticket-holders on your father's circuit?'

'None yet.' Nathan spoke hesitantly. 'I think I ought to tell you . . . I'm not a preacher. Not even a lay preacher.'

'I don't give a muleskinner's cuss about that, brother. There are a great many folk who say I don't behave like a preacher, either. But I've given some powerful sermons in my time and shown the road to heaven to a great many sinners. Your pa told me with some pride that you were going to put some backbone into his flock – turn doves into hawks, and make eagles of the chicken-hearted.'

Uriah Kemp was pacing the room on long legs. Round-shouldered and possessing a noble nose, he made a fine caricature of a hawk himself.

'You won't rally your father's flock behind you by pointing out the differences between you and them. You need to show them they can do everything you're doing – and much more. "Look at *me*," you must say to them. "I was born right here, the same as you. I fish for a living, the same as you. Yet the Lord has made me the greatest prize-fighter in the whole world. What are you going to let Him do for *you*?" Rouse them. Let them see that every mother's son and daughter can be a world-beater. You want to build a church? Let *them* do it for you. Persuade a thousand people each to put a stone into the building of a church wall and you have a thousand defenders if the enemies of the Lord try to pull it down again.'

The American preacher stopped in front of Nathan and jabbed a talon-like finger at his chest. 'You want your father out of prison? Right, then let the Methodists of Cornwall show the authorities their strength, not their weakness. Move in on the towns – Bodmin, St Austell, Truro, Launceston. Go there in your thousands – to pray. No marching, no banner-waving – and no leaders. Simply pass the word throughout the county that on a certain Sunday prayers will be said in Bodmin. The week after in St Austell. Let everyone gather in the streets and, at an agreed time, fall to their knees and pray. Set an example for the whole country to follow. Show your government the strength of Methodist support. Make them realise that they'll never stamp out Methodism – unless they are prepared to arrest so many people that there won't be prisons enough to hold them all.'

The hawk-like appearance was accentuated when Uriah Kemp tilted his head to one side. 'You doubt whether it will work, brother? I remember seeing the same doubt on the faces of your generals and colonial officials when told there was a danger of us Americans rebelling and taking the country from you.'

Uriah Kemp laid a long-fingered hand upon Nathan's shoulder. 'All it takes is *faith*, brother. *Faith*. The word has the same number of letters as "sword" and "rifle" – yes, and "Devil", too. But when a man has faith he can take a stand and defeat all three.'

The next week was a busy one for Nathan. It began with the funeral of Annie Jago. She was laid to rest on 3 March 1811, in a coarse-grassed burial-ground, fenced off by a rope that separated burial-ground from unworked pasture. A few yards away, also within the rope fence, the turf had been cut to mark out the shape of the new chapel.

More than a thousand mourners came to pay their last respects to the wife of their preacher – and also to see the American preacher, about whom many rumours were already circulating.

Uriah Kemp did not disappoint them. Both mourners and the curious returned home with their faith revitalised, convinced that Methodism was in the vanguard of the fight against evil and that Uriah

Kemp could lead them through fire and brimstone to safety on the other side.

This success was followed by outdoor prayer-meetings in several nearby villages, all of which were on Preacher Josiah Jago's circuit. Advance warning went out that the prayer-meeting would be held, with the result that large, if apprehensive, crowds gathered to hear Nathan and Uriah Kemp conduct their joint services.

Despite Nathan's earlier fears that he lacked the faith and dedication of his listeners, he was able to impress them by his very simplicity, and by his determination to keep his father's circuit active until Preacher Josiah Jago was free to resume his calling.

There was nothing simple about Uriah Kemp's message. He bullied and cajoled, berated and praised his congregation until it had been moulded into a receptacle, perfectly shaped to receive the message he brought to the followers of Wesley.

The fears of the local Methodists were soon conquered. Neither magistrate, nor constable, nor militiaman attempted to break up the meetings, or arrest the unlicensed preachers. It seemed the authorities were aware of the storm that would break if they arrested the nationally famed prize-fighter – one, moreover, who was rumoured to be sponsored by a royal duke.

At only one meeting did the two men encounter any hostility. This was the gathering on the quayside in Mevagissey. Hecklers moved to the front of the crowd when Nathan was talking about the new chapel. They began shouting remarks back and forth among themselves, declaring they did not want drift-fishermen in their village telling them what they should do.

Nathan knew from their flushed faces that the fishermen had been drinking. He braced himself for the fight he felt certain would ensue when they had worked up sufficient courage. Then Uriah Kemp silenced the fishermen in a manner that proved he was used to keeping order at much tougher meetings than this.

The tall American strode forward and seized the two nearest hecklers by the hair. Before they guessed his intention, he brought their heads together with a crack that was heard all around the quayside. One of the fishermen dropped to the ground, unconscious; the other staggered dangerously close to the edge of the quay, holding his head between both hands, dazed to the point of idiocy.

But the Reverend Uriah Kemp was not through yet. Marching up to another of the Mevagissey ringleaders, he tangled his long fingers in the fisherman's thick, black, curly beard – and twisted. The fisherman, his head at a painful angle, was unceremoniously dragged before the crowd. Here he was asked by Uriah Kemp whether he had something to say that was of more importance than the message of the Lord.

The unfortunate fisherman tried to shake his head, but Uriah Kemp was already doing it for him and the man cried out in pain.

'That's the first sensible sound I've heard from you since you arrived,' roared Uriah Kemp. Twisting the man's head still more, he brought him to his knees.

'That's better. This is a prayer-meeting. Now you're on your knees you can beg for the Lord's forgiveness – and you, too!'

His bellowed command and pointing finger took in

all the uncomfortable fisherman's companions. One by one, they sheepishly obeyed.

The Reverend Uriah Kemp made the kneeling fishermen repeat a humiliating plea for forgiveness. This was followed by a rendering of the Lord's Prayer, during the course of which he continually called upon the men to raise their voices. Finally, the American preacher led them in a spirited rendering of a well-known Wesley hymn.

Then, with a strength that belied his age, Uriah Kemp threw the bearded fisherman from him. As the unfortunate sinner sprawled on the ground ten feet away, the American preacher dusted loosened hairs from his fingers.

Rising to his feet, the fisherman twisted his head first one way and then the other in a bid to loosen his abused neck muscles, all the while glaring wild-eyed at the tall preacher. When much of the pain had gone, the fisherman took a pace towards Kemp. Nathan was ready and blocked his path.

Although incensed by the treatment meted out to him by Uriah Kemp, the fisherman was not willing to take on Nathan. With an oath that brought shocked gasps from some of the inland women, he turned and strode away. Most of the Mevagissey fishermen followed him, but Nathan was surprised to see that a few remained to join in the service.

The remainder of the prayer-meeting was uninterrupted, and it ended with a thousand Methodists promising to put in as much time as could be spared to help rebuild Pentuan's chapel.

Later the same evening, a number of lay preachers, shamefaced at their earlier lack of courage, promised that when the call came they would ensure a maximum attendance for the street prayer-meetings in Cornwall's towns.

The lay preachers kept their word. On the following Sunday, Bodmin townfolk were startled and alarmed when more than eight thousand Methodists from outlying villages and hamlets converged on the mid-Cornwall town. Twenty-five militiamen on standby duty were called out. They took one look at the mass of men, women and children advancing towards them and promptly retreated to the safety of their assembly-hall.

The residents of the town watched from behind closed doors and windows in growing apprehension as the Methodists gathered in an uncanny silence, quickly filling the streets about the prison. Then a voice that carried a distinctive American accent began to recite a prayer in a sonorous voice, and the vast congregation sank to its knees and joined in.

Two more prayers followed on behalf of the man incarcerated in the town's gaol for his beliefs before the Methodists rose to their feet and sang a dozen hymns, their voices filling the air to the exclusion of all other sounds. One more prayer, then the vast host turned about and departed as silently and orderly as it had come.

Behind them the stunned townsfolk unbolted their doors to discuss with neighbours the significance of such an assembly. Most knew of Josiah Jago's imprisonment in the town's gaol and all agreed it must have been a declaration of support for the imprisoned preacher. All were deeply impressed by the discipline and peaceableness of the demonstrators. The unusual prayer-meeting had achieved what Uriah Kemp had said it would. It had called the attention of the authorities to Methodist numbers, and showed their determination to uphold a right of assembly.

When the others had left the town, Nathan and Uriah Kemp paid a visit to Josiah Jago. They found him greatly heartened by the hymns and prayers that had been clearly audible inside the grim, grey-walled prison.

Josiah Jago's faith was further strengthened when Nathan informed his father that the walls of the new chapel had reached roof height, and the new burial-ground was already enclosed within four stout walls, and planted with trees and bushes.

The Pentuan preacher was much more comfortable in his surroundings now. The transfer of three golden guineas from Nathan to the gaoler had brought the change about. Josiah Jago now shared a large, dry cell with a cheerful young man of about Nathan's age. The young man's 'crime' was no more than an accusation that he had fathered the child of an unmarried village girl and was refusing to contribute to its upkeep. As he had explained to Nathan on an earlier visit, he would have been most willing to pay maintenance for the child had he honestly believed it to be his. However, he could have named half a dozen men with stronger claims to paternity than his own. The baby's mother had chosen Preacher Jago's cell-mate for the very simple reason that he alone of her lovers could afford to support her misbegotten child. She had already spent a year in prison herself for refusing to give the magistrate the name of her child's father and, for his display of stubbornness, the young man had been resident in Bodmin Gaol for almost two – sent there by St Austell's senior magistrate, Sir Lewis Hearle.

So far, the cheery young man had resisted Preacher Jago's pleas for him to make amends for his profligate ways, but his lighthearted presence had lifted the preacher out of his trough of self-reproach. Preacher Jago was now ready to stand his trial, when the spring Assizes commenced in a few weeks' time.

On the way back to Pentuan, Uriah Kemp expressed satisfaction at the manner in which their campaign was progressing. He also told Nathan something more of his earlier life in America. So interesting did Nathan find it that the miles passed by almost unnoticed.

Orphaned as a young child, Uriah Kemp had been brought up by an aged Quaker couple of pioneer stock. They provided him with a strict upbringing, substituting religion for affection. They, too, died in a smallpox epidemic when he was only thirteen years old. Uriah Kemp quickly broke his ties with the Quaker background, preferring the less exacting demands of the Anglican Church. He spent three winter seasons trapping the rivers of North America, ranging far ahead of the narrow borders of civilisation. When he had earned enough money to continue his learning, he went back to the East and was eventually ordained in the Anglican Church.

However, Uriah Kemp was by nature a missionary. He had explained earlier to Nathan how he had become a Methodist during the War of Independence, while preaching to British prisoners-of-war. When the war ended, Uriah moved westwards again, preaching to isolated pioneer families, and to the Indians of the Sioux nations who roamed the lands on both sides of the Canadian border. Privation and hardship became a way of life for this remarkable preacher.

It was late afternoon when they returned to Pentuan, and Nathan suffered a sense of guilt when he saw the sea spread out before them, smooth and inviting. There were no fishing-boats out today. Fisherman did not put to sea on a Sunday, but it had been many weeks since Nathan had been to sea with *The Brave Amy H.*

Nathan knew the boat was going out regularly, manned by Ahab Arthur, Calvin Dickin and the others, but he had little idea of how much fish they were catching. Sammy Mizler was rarely at home when Nathan returned to Pentuan, and on the occasions when he came to the house Nathan was usually deep in discussion with Uriah Kemp about the new chapel or other Methodist affairs. Neither had Nathan seen Amy since the fateful return of the fishing-boat from Bristol. He determined he would find time in the next few days to pay a visit to Portgiskey. He might even spend a day fishing with the crew of *The Brave Amy H.*

With these thoughts uppermost in his mind, it came as a pleasant surprise when he reached the Jago cottage to find both Amy and Sammy Mizler waiting there.

Kissing Amy affectionately, Nathan beamed his pleasure. 'I was just thinking it was time I faced up to my responsibilities and took *The Brave Amy H* to sea again, but I've been kept so busy. No, that excuse is not good enough. I *will* take the boat out – tomorrow!

Why don't you come out with me, Amy? Then you can tell me all that's been happening at Portgiskey...'

Nathan's delight at seeing Amy again had made him unusually talkative and it was some minutes before he realised he was receiving no replies. Both Amy and Sammy Mizler were looking at him with embarrassed expressions upon their faces.

'Is everything all right? Has something happened to *The Brave Amy H*?'

Sammy Mizler smiled suddenly. 'Yes . . . but I'm not talking about the boat, but the *real* Amy H.' Reaching out, he took Amy's hand. 'Congratulations are in order, Nathan. Amy has agreed to marry me.'

20

When he thought about the progress of their relationship, Sammy Mizler told himself he had been in love with Amy since the night she had surprised himself and Nathan in her boat. Even with a loaded blunderbuss in her hands, Sammy had forgotten his fear for long enough to admit that he had never seen a more beautiful girl. With her short black hair and sunburned skin, she might have been a young sabra girl from ancient Israel.

For many months Sammy Mizler kept his infatuation from Amy. More difficult to hide was his deeply felt jealousy when he saw the way she occasionally looked at Nathan. But Sammy was a philosophical man and for a long while he resigned himself to enjoying Amy's friendship, and an occasional shared confidence.

Amy and Nathan struck sparks from each other when they were together. Sammy Mizler, accepting

the role of interested spectator, waited for the sparks
to ignite an emotional fire between the two partners. It
never came. Why, Sammy did not know. He thought
perhaps Elinor Hearle was the biggest stumbling-
block between the two – and Sammy was constantly
reminding Amy of the association between Nathan
and the mistress of Polrudden.

Sammy Mizler believed he had lost Amy when he
saw how she had shared Nathan's grief at the death of
Annie Jago, but her unhappiness passed unnoticed by
Nathan himself.

Then, the evening following their return from Bristol,
Amy had left Portgiskey to meet Nathan, due back
from a visit to his father in Bodmin Gaol. Later that
same night, Sammy Mizler had gone to Portgiskey after
dark and found Amy crouched in the stern of *The Brave
Amy H*, crying as though her heart was breaking.

She never explained what had happened to upset
her so, but from that night she began to lean more
heavily on Sammy and the name of Nathan was
dropped from their conversations.

One fine day, Amy persuaded Sammy to go fishing
with her in her own small boat. He agreed with great
reluctance but, much to his surprise, he was not sea-
sick. In fact he almost *enjoyed* the experience. So, too,
did Amy, and Sammy saw her laugh for the first time
in many days.

A week later, Sammy proposed to Amy. It was not
easy. Sammy was a careful man, and he had a little
money put by in addition to his investment in the
Portgiskey fishing venture, but he had little else to
recommend him to Amy. He was used to a rootless
mode of life – and he was a Jew.

Sammy Mizler had never practised the religious ritual of his ancestors, but the fact remained that he belonged to a race that was persecuted in every country of the world, and treated with contempt and prejudice everywhere. It was not a tempting future to put to a prospective wife, but it was all Sammy had, as he told Amy.

Amy put an end to Sammy's dogged self-deprecation with a single word. The word was 'Yes'.

Sammy had stared at her in disbelief. 'What . . . ? What did you say?'

'I said "Yes". There, now I've said it again.'

'You mean . . . ?'

'I mean, yes, I'll marry you. That is, if it's what you really want. Although no one hearing you now could be sure.'

'Even after all I've just told you? Are you quite certain?'

'Sammy Mizler, do you *want* me to marry you, or not?' Amy said in amused exasperation.

'I want it . . . It's just . . .'

'Just nothing. You've been very kind to me, Sammy. I'm a lucky girl.'

'When, Amy? When will you marry me?'

Amy frowned. 'Not too soon, Sammy. I'd like a while to get used to the idea of becoming a wife.'

Sammy wondered whether this was the reply she might have made to Nathan, had he asked Amy to marry him. But he said: 'Of course. Of course, my dear.' Not certain what was expected of him now, he wrung his hands in acute nervousness.

'Where will you want us to live when we're married, Sammy?'

'Live? Oh . . . I'm not sure.' Sammy Mizler was unable to think straight. 'Here, I suppose.'

Amy smiled at his confusion. 'Will you really be able to settle at Portgiskey for ever, Sammy? You're a Londoner through and through. You've told me so yourself, many times. Perhaps we could visit London before we marry. I might want to live *there*.'

Sammy was unable to hide his delight. 'Let's do that, Amy. I will enjoy showing you London.'

'Then that's what we'll do.'

Amy suddenly became matter-of-fact. She kissed her future husband in the same manner, but Sammy hardly noticed. He had achieved the impossible. Amy had agreed to marry *him*. Sammy Mizler's cup of happiness was filled to the brim. He would not look upon the dregs for a long time to come.

Nathan's enthusiasm for the proposed wedding did not match that of his friends. He offered Sammy and Amy his congratulations, but they went no farther than a handshake for Sammy and a kiss on the cheek for Amy.

His lack of enthusiasm might have put a blight on the apparent happiness of his partners had Uriah Kemp not been at hand to extol light-heartedly the virtues of married life to the pledged couple.

Nathan listened politely for a few minutes, then abruptly announced that he was going to visit the boat at Portgiskey. Aware of Amy's hurt expression and the questioning frown on the face of Sammy Mizler, Nathan made a hasty exit. He had been travelling the lanes of Cornwall, talking to so many Methodists, that he was beginning to feel more like a preacher than a fisherman. But Uriah Kemp was a real preacher and, as a couple about to embark upon matrimony, Amy and Sammy would doubtless want to speak to him without Nathan's presence.

Before Nathan left the kitchen of the Jago cottage he caught Uriah Kemp's glance, filled with concern. But Nathan ignored a gesture that was meant to detain him. He did not want to explain his unforgivable and hasty retreat to anyone. Not even to himself.

His departure left an embarrassed silence behind him in the small Jago cottage, but Uriah Kemp was adept at handling such situations. He told them that Nathan had been very busy working to keep his father's preaching circuit together and was distressed because of his visit that day to Bodmin Gaol.

Nathan walked from the house to the Pentuan foreshore, trying to subdue an unreasonable resentment that was smouldering inside him. He had an absurd feeling that he had been betrayed and was irritated that he should be entertaining such thoughts. When he arrived at the low barrier of scattered rocks that partitioned Portgiskey Cove from Pentuan Beach, he sat on a rock and tried to analyse his feelings.

Moodily tossing pebbles towards the sea, he felt he needed time to think. He would not be happy until he was able to take up the reins of his life and guide his own destiny once more. As things were at the moment, he felt he was being pushed along an unfamiliar path by the events about him: his mother's tragic death; Josiah Jago's imprisonment; the arrival of the mercurial Reverend Uriah Kemp; Elinor's forthcoming marriage . . . And now Sammy and Amy's marriage, too.

For some reason, this last announcement had disturbed him far more than it should. He thought that his mood was due to the fact that the future had suddenly become as uncertain as the present, with the fishing partnership under threat.

Nathan looked at the sea. There was only a slight swell with a light breeze blowing from the land. Of a sudden he felt the need to be out there, away from the cares that were on the land. Rising from his rock-seat, Nathan clambered over the rocks to Portgiskey.

From the window of the cottage, Peggy Hoblyn saw him and scuttled to meet him, complaining that she had been left alone all day with neither food nor heat in the cottage. She whined that her daughter did not care for her any more. Nobody cared.

Nathan offered to come to the cottage to light a fire and find some food for her, but Peggy immediately went on the defensive. She declared that no stranger was coming inside her house to report to the villagers of Pentuan how shabbily she was being treated by Amy.

Backing away from Nathan as though he had threatened her life, Peggy Hoblyn turned and ran to the cottage with short, quick steps. She turned for a moment at the doorway, and Nathan called to tell her he was borrowing Amy's small boat. Before the words were out she had slammed the door shut. Moments later he saw the white blur of her face at the window.

The poor woman's condition was much worse than when Nathan had last seen her. Her eccentricity now verged on madness. Nathan felt suddenly sorry for Amy and Sammy Mizler. It would be their joint responsibility to care for Peggy Hoblyn in her old age.

Nathan pulled the boat down to the sea until he was standing calf-deep in water and the boat was afloat. Pushing the boat farther out into deeper water, Nathan lay bellydown on the gunwale before swinging himself on board. Rowing clear of the headland, he hoisted the sail and headed out to sea. He had gone about a mile when he passed an empty keg bobbing in the water. Something about its movement made him put the boat about and investigate.

Dropping the sail, he reached over the side and brought the keg inboard. There were two ropes attached to it. One seemed to have an anchor on the other end. The other felt heavy, too, but it moved through the water as Nathan tugged upon it. A fathom's length away from the first keg Nathan found another, but this one was full. The rope led on again, and Nathan brought three kegs to the surface before he gave up. There were probably a dozen kegs attached to the rope. Throwing them all back into the sea, he raised his sail and left the area.

Smiling, Nathan thought it was good to know there were some things that never changed. Smugglers were still active along this part of the coast, even though Amy was no longer among their number. As he remembered Amy, Nathan's smile left him. He wondered how many times he thought of her in a normal day.

He sailed on for another half-hour, towing a fishing-line baited with feathers behind the boat, before he lowered the sail once more and pulled in his catch. He had caught enough fish to bait a long-line. Dropping it in the water, he lit his pipe and sat back to savour the sense of being alone that comes only in a small boat, far from shore.

Inevitably, his thoughts turned once more to Sammy and Amy and it brought an empty feeling to the pit of his stomach. He told himself yet again that it was fear of the marriage bringing the fishing partnership to an end. Perhaps he should have seen it coming, but he was honest enough to admit that since his return to Pentuan his thoughts had been elsewhere for much of the time.

Dusk was approaching when Nathan began bringing in his line. He had caught more than three dozen fine mackerel.

In the distance he had seen a boat leaving Mevagissey harbour a short time before. As it drew closer he saw it was the Revenue cutter. Nathan looked about him uneasily, hoping he had not drifted too close to the anchored line of brandy-kegs. He was relieved that they were nowhere in sight.

The cutter came steadily towards him, and when it was almost alongside the crewmen rested on their oars and a man rose to his feet in the stern. It was Ezra Partridge.

'Well, well, Jago. All on our own out here, are we, sir? What are you carrying?'

Ezra Partridge's manner was more polite than it had been at their earlier meeting, and Nathan looked at the Chief Revenue Officer suspiciously.

'Three dozen mackerel. I wouldn't swear to it, but I doubt if they're from France.' Nathan began carefully coiling his hooked line.

'What are you doing out here?'

Nathan bridled. 'Fishing. That's how I earn my living. I also came out here to get away from people for an hour or two.'

Much to Nathan's surprise, Ezra Partridge nodded, apparently accepting the irritable reply.

'Ay, I've no doubt you'll have plenty to think about. You've not had it easy since you returned from your prize-fight in Bristol.'

Nathan said nothing, but it seemed Ezra Partridge was not expecting a reply. The two boats touched and Ezra Partridge braced his legs to steady himself against the movement of the Revenue cutter. Leaning over the side towards Nathan, he said conspiratorially: 'We're men of the world, you and I, Mr Jago.' He cast a contemptuous look at the crew of the Revenue cutter as they leaned on their oars, chatting among themselves. Reaching out, he grasped the gunwale of Amy Hoblyn's little boat and leaned still closer. In a low voice he said: 'You can do yourself a favour, Mr Jago. With your father a Wesleyan preacher you'll no doubt be against smuggling.'

Nathan stifled a grin. This was a very different man to the one who had led the raid on the Hoblyn fish-cellar a few months earlier. He wondered what the Chief Revenue Officer would have done had he known that Nathan had once worked for Ned Hoblyn, when that prince of smugglers had been at the height of his nefarious career.

'Help me put a stop to smuggling and you could make yourself a lot of money. I'm authorised to pay a reward of twice the market value for any contraband recovered as a result of information given to me.'

'Thank you. I'll remember,' said Nathan, doing his best to appear suitably impressed.

'Do that,' said Ezra Partridge. 'It's been a pleasure meeting you again, Mr Jago.'

He pushed off the smaller boat, then called upon his crew to pull away across the bay.

It was quite cold now, and Nathan decided it was time to return to Portgiskey. The wind had strengthened off the shore with approaching darkness, and Nathan was obliged to make a long tack to reach the small harbour against the wind.

He was at the far end of one of his tacks, not far from the entrance to Pentuan harbour, when he thought he heard a sound from nearby. It was dark now and, turning the boat into the wind until it was hardly moving, he listened carefully. For a while there was no sound but the wind and the sea, then he heard the splash of a carelessly handled oar in a leather-muffled rowlock.

'Ahoy there! Can you hear me?'

Three times Nathan called, softly at first. After the third and loudest call, the sounds of rowing ceased and a hoarse whisper came back to him across the water.

'Who's there?'

'Nathan Jago. Is that you, Dan?'

Nathan had recognised the voice of Dan Clymo, his childhood friend.

'Yes. What are you doing out here?'

'That doesn't matter.' Nathan had no need to ask Dan Clymo the same question. Seine-fishermen did not pursue fish at night. Dan Clymo was on his way to pick up the anchored brandy-kegs. 'Turn about and go back to Pentuan. Ezra Partridge and his Revenue men are at sea.'

The anxious muttering of the men in the other boat carried clearly across the water to Nathan.

'How do you know?'

'He stopped me less than an hour ago. Thought I might be interested in helping him capture undutied goods.'

More muttering followed, louder this time. Twice Nathan heard the words 'go back'.

The two boats were drifting apart now as a slight shifting of the wind caught the sail of Amy Hoblyn's boat.

'Head back to Pentuan.' Dan Clymo's voice was barely audible above the slap of the water against the bow of Amy's boat. 'We owe you, Nathan. I'll remember.'

Nathan was battling with the wind now. The tide was on its way in, and the small boat had drifted closer to the shore than he would have liked. However, he cleared the rocks at the entrance to Portgiskey with ample room to spare. Moments later the boat ran ashore on the sand beside the small quay. Someone moved from the shadows and held the bow as Nathan leaped ashore. It was Amy.

'Ma said someone had taken the boat. Her mind is so bad she couldn't tell me who, but I guessed it would be you.'

'I'm sorry if I've kept you up. I just felt like going out for an hour's fishing.' His words sounded stilted, as though he were talking to a stranger. Nathan heard it himself and tried to correct it.

'Where's Sammy?'

'I left him entertaining Uriah Kemp in Pentuan.'

After a moment's hesitation, Amy asked softly: 'What's the matter, Nathan? Don't you want me to marry Sammy?'

'It's none of my business. You won't find a better man.'

'I know. But that wasn't what I asked you. Never mind. As you say, it's my business, no one else's. How about you, Nathan? Have you decided to make your future with Elinor Hearle? Tell me "yes" and I'll believe you. I think you're a man who gets whatever he goes after. Is she what you want?'

Nathan was on the point of telling Amy about Elinor's new love. Instead he said gruffly: 'I'll take care of my own future.'

'Yes . . . I'm sorry.'

'Amy . . . ?' Nathan caught her arm as she went to move away. 'I didn't mean it to sound that way. It's just that I have a lot to think about just now. You and Sammy getting married gives me even more . . .'

'Oh! I thought you might . . . Never mind what I thought.' She shook her arm free. 'I realise it's going to be *inconvenient* for you, but your gallivanting about the countryside hasn't exactly made things any easier for the rest of us. If you'd been here, there would probably have been no talk of marriage between Sammy and me . . .'

Something in Amy's voice sounded to Nathan like a desperate cry for help. He called to her, but she had gone and the door of the cottage slammed shut behind her. Nathan cursed himself for being an unthinking fool. Scooping up the mackerel he had caught, he set off for home more unsettled than ever.

From inside the cottage, Amy heard his footsteps crunching away as she leaned with her back against the door. She was having difficulty holding back tears. Why did she and Nathan quarrel so much – and why did it matter to her? Sammy Mizler was her man now. Her thoughts should be of him – and they ought to be happy thoughts. She was to be married.

'Amy? Is that you, girl?' Her mother's complaining voice called from a darkened bedroom. 'Are you leaving me to starve to death? I haven't had a bite to eat . . .'

'All right, Ma. I'll get you something. But there's nothing to stop you doing your own cooking, you know.'

Amy sighed. Physically, her mother was as fit as any other woman of her age, but her mind was making an invalid of her. Peggy Hoblyn's welfare would have to be taken into consideration when she and Sammy discussed their marriage in more detail.

21

In order to satisfy the many lay preachers who were unhappy at having an unlicensed preacher responsible for the circuit, Uriah Kemp took out a preacher's licence. As an ordained minister of the Anglican Church, he had no difficulty in obtaining such a licence, but the magistrate who issued it warned the American preacher of the consequences of open-air preaching. It was a warning Uriah Kemp had no intention of heeding.

The unorthodox American Methodist was at his evangelical best when preaching in the open air, with no pulpit to enclose him, and no walls to limit the enthusiasm of his congregation. His open-air services became famous throughout the length and breadth of the county. Men and women flocked from miles around to listen to him preach.

The Methodist chapel at Pentuan had been completed within a month of the foundations being dug, but Uriah Kemp declared that Preacher Josiah Jago must be the first man to preach inside its cob walls. Those who came to attend the Sunday services stood in the green burial-ground, beside the chapel, where Annie Jago had now been joined by the late Hannah Hunkin, who died a week after Annie's funeral. Aged ninety-eight years at the time of her death, Hannah Hunkin had been able to remember John Wesley's first and last visits to Cornwall, as well as most of those in between. She had been one of the most respected Methodists in Cornwall. Only days before her death she had declared that she would die happy in the knowledge that she would lie in a Methodist grave in her native Pentuan, and not in St Austell among strangers.

Now that the lay preachers had resumed their duties with renewed enthusiasm, Nathan was content to leave the affairs of the local Methodist church in their hands, with Uriah Kemp supervising their duties. He resumed full-time fishing, but it was not a good time to return. The fish were in short supply.

Nathan took the boat farther west, fishing the dangerous waters around the Scilly Isles, where 'wrecking' was as much a part of everyday life to the islanders as smuggling was to the Cornish. Sometimes the boat would be away for three or four nights, but by taking his catch direct to Falmouth a good price was obtained from the merchants who supplied the packet vessels plying from the busy port.

Whilst in Falmouth, Nathan received another substantial order for salted fish for the West Indies. For a whole week he ferried hogsheads from Portgiskey, emptying the cellar of their entire stock of preserved fish. Meanwhile, Sammy Mizler was travelling the south-west, securing markets for the coming season's catch, each order marginally more profitable than the last. Amy was usually in evidence at Portgiskey, but no date had yet been set for her wedding to Sammy Mizler.

In early May, Nathan took *The Brave Amy H* just two miles out from Pentuan and located one of the largest shoals of mackerel that he, or any of his fishermen, had ever found. They were present in millions. Almost as fast as the nets were shot, they could be hauled in again, heavy with fish. *The Brave Amy H* returned to Portgiskey carrying more fish than ever before. When they had been hurriedly unloaded, Nathan took the boat out again. Finding the shoal once more, he reaped another incredible harvest.

For three days and nights Nathan and his crew worked the same shoal without making any noticeable difference to its numbers. Then, as suddenly as the fish had appeared, the shoal vanished. Ahab Arthur suggested that the mackerel had been moving with a warm current that had brought them close to the surface. Once the current cooled, they dived well below the depth of a drift-net. Whatever the explanation, the mackerel had certainly gone, but enough had already been caught to keep the Portgiskey cellar busy for many weeks.

Mackerel had always been caught along the Cornish coast, but rarely in such quantities that curing them became accepted custom. However, with so many mackerel at Portgiskey, the only way to avoid wasting them was to cure in some way. The fish were laid in man-high walls in the cellar, each layer separated by a generous layer of salt. Nathan also had a smoke-house hastily constructed. Here he produced 'fumados', the smoked fish so beloved by Spanish seamen.

Both these processes provided welcome work for the wives of the Pentuan fishermen. The women worked swiftly, though noisily, their shouted conversations and screeches of ribald laughter carrying far across the still waters of the bay.

Outside the fish-cellar, their husbands came to inspect the size of the catches and stayed to view the industry in silent envy, squatting on the quay in small groups, mouthing their comments past the short, stained stumps of their four-a-penny clay pipes. They were happy to have their women working, even though it was for a drift-fisherman. The work brought much-needed money to households that would have little until the pilchard shoals put in their uncertain annual appearance in the bay.

Sammy found markets for the cured mackerel in Plymouth. Some would be sold to the crews of men-of-war, anchored in the Sound. The remainder were to go up-river, destined for French captives, imprisoned behind the high, grim walls of the prison they had built for themselves on Dartmoor.

Nathan brought his almost exhausted crew back to Portgiskey after the disappearance of the mackerel; to find Amy waiting for him in a state of great excitement. She had received a message from Tom Quicke. Nell's time had come. The baby would be born before the day was out.

Leaving the others to secure the boat before they went home for a well-deserved rest, Nathan set off for

Venn Farm. Amy went with him, hoping she could be of some assistance to her friend.

It was the first time Amy and Nathan had held any conversation since that night on the quay at Portgiskey, and Nathan opened the conversation with an observation on Sammy Mizler.

'We're having a good year, Amy. It's thanks in no small measure to Sammy's good work in finding profitable markets for us.'

Amy nodded. 'He works hard. He's a good man.'

Nathan looked sideways at her. 'Have you fixed a date for the wedding yet?'

Amy shook her head. 'We're in no hurry.'

'Are you still quite certain it's what you want?'

Amy rounded on him angrily. 'I'm *quite* certain, thank you.'

They walked on in silence for some minutes before Nathan said apologetically: 'I didn't mean to upset you, Amy.' He shrugged helplessly. 'Somehow, I don't seem to be able to avoid it.'

Amy noticed how tired he looked and she felt sudden remorse for having rounded on him so swiftly. With a warm gesture, she reached for his hand. 'I should be apologising, Nathan, not you. But we're still friends?'

He squeezed her hand gratefully. 'Yes, still . . . friends.'

They continued to Venn, walking hand in hand, and in spite of his tiredness Nathan felt more content than he had for a very long time.

A round, motherly woman from a nearby farm was already at Venn Farm with her daughter, and it was clear that further help was not really needed. But Amy was given a number of tasks in the kitchen and was soon as busy as the other two women.

Nathan found Tom Quicke in the outbuildings that opened on to the farmyard. He had cleared out all the animals' sheds and pens, and was now working vigorously moving straw from one place to another. When Nathan taxed him with making unnecessary work for himself, while his wife was in the house giving birth, Tom Quicke readily admitted the charge.

'If I don't keep myself busy out here, I'll be up those stairs to see Nell every few minutes – and the house is no place for a man today.'

Nathan grinned. Taking a pitchfork from a rack on the wall, he set to and helped Tom Quicke to throw straw from the ground floor to a loft.

They were still working here when Sir Lewis Hearle rode into the farmyard. His arrival came as a surprise to both men, neither of whom had known of Sir Lewis's return to Polrudden.

One look at the baronet was enough to see that he was in a foul mood. Tugging on a rein, he caused his horse to turn a complete, head-jerking circle.

'Quicke, what's the meaning of allowing a Methodist church to be built on Venn land?'

Tom Quicke, overawed by the presence of the angry landowner, looked to Nathan for support.

'I built the chapel, Sir Lewis. It's to replace the one you had pulled down.'

Sir Lewis Hearle turned a malevolent glance upon Nathan. 'I don't recall addressing you, Jago. Quicke should know better than to associate himself with the son of a discredited preacher. I'll see you lose your tenancy for this, Quicke. I don't know what arrangement you've come to with the Duke of Clarence, but he won't tolerate a dissenting church on his land.'

'I doubt whether the Duke of Clarence cares a fig what happens on Venn Farm,' said Nathan as evenly as he could. He knew that the facts would have far more impact upon Sir Lewis Hearle than anger. It was not easy. This man was responsible for the imprisonment of his father. 'The farm belongs to Tom Quicke and his wife, who also happens to be my sister.'

For a few moments Sir Lewis was speechless as he stared from Nathan to Tom Quicke in disbelief. 'I don't believe you. When Quicke took on a tenancy from me he could hardly raise the rent money. Where has he found the money to buy Venn?'

'That's his business, and his alone. But the chapel is on Methodist land, properly signed over to them by Tom Quicke . . .'

Suddenly from the house there came a sound that momentarily halted all conversation. It was the first, long-drawn-out protest of a newborn baby, and Amy's voice was calling: 'Tom, come quickly. It's a boy. A wonderful son.'

In the magic of the moment, Tom Quicke forgot his fear of the baronet Member of Parliament and turned to Nathan with an expression of sheer joy upon his face.

'Go to Nell, Tom,' Nathan said gently. 'She'll be wanting you now.'

Tom Quicke threw down his pitchfork and ran to the farm without another look at Sir Lewis Hearle.

When he had gone, Nathan spoke to the baronet as softly as he had spoken to Tom Quicke. 'You're on another man's land here, Sir Lewis, and that man's wife has just given birth to their first son. It's a happy time – and you have no place in their happiness.'

Sir Lewis bristled with suppressed rage, and Nathan braced himself for a blow from the riding-crop the baronet was holding.

Instead, Sir Lewis said: 'I don't know how you managed to get Venn Farm for Tom Quicke, but I'm quite certain it's your doing. You'll regret it one day, very soon. I'll put my mind to the matter once I've seen your father put away.'

He jerked his horse's head around cruelly and took the animal out of the farmyard at a canter.

Nathan watched thoughtfully until Sir Lewis Hearle passed from view at the end of the farm track. Then he went inside the farmhouse to share Tom and Nell's joy in their son.

Sir Lewis Hearle's return to Cornwall had a twofold purpose. The first concerned his daughter's marriage, and the restoration of Polrudden's fortunes. Francis Rodd had visited Sir Lewis in London, and Elinor's father had bestowed his parental blessing on the union of the two ancient Cornish families.

Since that day, the baronet had heard nothing from his daughter. He had despaired of marrying her off many years before, and did not intend losing this unexpected opportunity to have the heir to Trebartha's considerable estates as his son-in-law.

Sir Lewis was once again hard pressed for money. The cost of maintaining the standard of hospitality expected of even such a junior government official was much higher than he had anticipated.

Furthermore, there had so far been few requests made to him for highly paid favours. He was relying heavily upon the forthcoming marriage of Elinor to save him from further financial embarrassment – but the marriage needed to be soon.

Sir Lewis Hearle also intended combining his paternal duties with a determination to be present at the trial of Preacher Josiah Jago. The Judge of Assize at the spring sitting in Bodmin was to be Mr Justice Vincent, one of the country's most senior judges.

In the past, Judge Vincent had shown himself less than ready to bow to government pressure when giving a judgement on matters of national importance. Sir Lewis's presence was intended to impress upon the learned judge the need to award Josiah Jago a salutary sentence. The power of dissident preachers and their 'churches' needed to be broken before the seeds of sedition took firm root and a bloody harvest of rebellion was forced upon the country. The memory of events in France and the wholesale slaughter of aristocrats and public officials that followed the act of revolution was still fresh in the minds of King George's ministers.

Where the marriage was concerned, Sir Lewis found his daughter equally frustrated in her own efforts to bring Francis Rodd to the altar quickly. The husband-to-be insisted he was as eager as Elinor herself for the marriage. Unfortunately, neither of the young people had been able to induce a similar enthusiasm in the daunting bulk of Admonition, Lady Rodd, the widow of Sir Philip Rodd, KCB.

Named by her naval admiral father after the flagship in which he was serving at the time of her birth,

Admonition Rodd was a forceful, domineering woman. She had given her blessing to a marriage between her only son and Elinor Hearle, but she saw no reason why they should rush into the married state.

Indeed, Lady Rodd would have preferred to defer the wedding for a year or two. She wished to be quite certain that Sir Lewis Hearle would prove more durable than many other under-secretaries, and would one day achieve even higher office in Spencer Perceval's Tory government. Her son was too great an asset to waste on the daughter of a junior Minister.

There was another reason for her reluctance to hasten the wedding. Sir Philip Rodd had died when his son, Francis, was a small child. Aware that death was imminent, the Lord of Trebartha had drawn up a tightly detailed will, with the aid of the family solicitors.

Rather than allow the young child to inherit all, and risk manipulation and exploitation by the many influential members of the Rodd family, Sir Philip had left everything to his wife, Admonition. It would remain hers until the day Francis Rodd married. When such an event occurred, Trebartha, its lands and its fortunes would become his. It was not surprising, therefore, that Lady Rodd was in no hurry for her son to take himself a wife.

Elinor, unaware of the terms of Sir Philip's will, tried very hard to apply pressure to Francis Rodd. Unfortunately, the heir to Trebartha was not a strong character. When he was with Elinor he made solemn promises and left her side filled with a determination to be master of his own destiny. But after only a few minutes with his mother all his bold resolution ebbed away.

Plagued with his own monetary problems, Sir Lewis berated Elinor unfairly, accusing her of doing little to restore the fortunes of Polrudden. He hardly knew that Elinor, too, had pressing reasons for wanting to become Francis Rodd's wife as quickly as possible.

No more than a week after his confrontation with Sir Lewis Hearle, Nathan was walking to Venn Farm in the late evening. The next day would see Josiah Jago brought to trial at Bodmin Assizes. Nathan wanted a final chat with Nell, to assure her he would be in the court-room throughout the proceedings.

He had reached a quiet spot on the footpath that skirted Pentuan village, when he saw someone seated on the grass verge farther along the path. As he drew closer he was surprised to see it was Elinor Hearle. Grazing some yards away was her stallion, Napoleon.

It all looked very casual, but Elinor had been watching from the top of the hill when *The Brave Amy H* returned to Portgiskey. She waited impatiently for the fishermen to unload the vessel. Then, when Nathan left the boat and made for Venn Farm, she rode to head him off.

Seeing her sprawled carelessly on the grass bank, Nathan felt the familiar excitement for her surging through his veins. A great deal had happened to sour their relationship, but she was still the loveliest girl he had ever known.

Looking up suddenly, Elinor smiled. 'Hello, Nathan. You haven't been to see me for such a long time I thought I must come and find you. It wasn't easy. You're a very elusive man.'

'I'm a *working* man,' said Nathan ungraciously, doing his utmost to dismiss the pleasure her words gave him. 'Besides, I doubted whether you'd want to see me again.'

Elinor smiled mockingly. 'After our last meeting at Home Farm?'

'That was before Francis Rodd asked you to marry him – and you accepted him.'

Nathan had not intended saying anything about the scene he and Will Hodge had witnessed, but he could not hold back the words.

Elinor paled. 'That is a secret between the Rodd and Hearle families. Nothing was to be announced until a wedding date is decided. Who told you? I *demand* to know.'

'It doesn't matter.'

'Damn you, Nathan. It *does* matter. I'll not have my servants carrying gossip to the village.' Elinor stood with clenched fists on her hips, her nostrils flared with anger.

'You didn't come to find me just to get angry about gossip?'

Nathan would have liked to take Elinor and crush the anger and arrogance out of her but, much to his amazement, his words had the same effect. Her arrogance vanished. Suddenly she looked very tired and vulnerable.

'No, I did not come seeking a quarrel with you – and, unless I can find someone to help me very soon, the villagers will have something more than *idle* gossip to talk about. I'm carrying your child, Nathan.'

'*My* child? You're certain?'

'Am I certain it's yours?' Elinor's ready temper

flared again and fury accentuated the pallor of her skin. 'Do you think I am one of your village trollops? I should whip you for such a remark, Nathan Jago.'

'That isn't what was meant.' Nathan felt the stirrings of a ridiculous thrill deep inside him. 'There can be no doubt . . . you *are* with child?'

'No doubt at all! That's why I am here to see you. You put it there. Now you can tell me how to get rid of it – and quickly.'

'How long have you known?'

'What does it matter? I suspected I was pregnant about two months ago. I've been quite certain these last few weeks.'

'Why haven't you tried to see me before? Surely you wouldn't have married Francis Rodd knowing you were carrying my child inside you?'

Elinor's chin came up in a defiant manner that Nathan remembered well. 'Would it have been *so* terrible? To give your child an inheritance that included Trebartha and Polrudden?'

Understanding had been slow in coming to Nathan, but it was with him now. 'You haven't been able to arrange the marriage in time, have you? Now you need to rid yourself of the baby before it becomes an embarrassment.'

'I *must*. Another month or so and there can be no question of marriage with Francis Rodd. What can I do, Nathan? Is there a herb or potion I can take? What do the village girls do?'

'Perhaps you should ask the man who shares a cell with my father. Sir Lewis sent him to prison two years ago because of a disputed bastardy order. The unfortunate mother had been in gaol for a year before that, for refusing to name the father of her child. Don't you think she would have got rid of the baby had it been possible?'

Elinor looked at Nathan suspiciously, but suspicion gave way to dismay when she saw no guile in his expression. 'What are you telling me – that nothing can be done?'

'Very little – although I do have one possible solution.'

'Thank God! What is it?'

'Marry *me*, Elinor.'

Her relief turned to anger; then, when she saw Nathan was quite serious, to incredulity. 'Marry you? Marry . . . !'

For some moments Elinor spluttered incoherently. When she regained control of herself, she said in an icy voice: 'What would you have me do, as your wife? Stand in a stinking fish-cellar working my hands raw until the day I give birth to *your* baby? Would you have me become a "good" wife, too? Spending half of each day elbow-deep in salt and fish, the other half caring for a brood of brats that would increase with every year that passed? Is this how you see *me*, Nathan Jago?'

'No,' replied Nathan patiently. 'I won't always be a working fisherman. I own a good boat now and have earned enough money to buy a second. Next year I'll probably buy two more. Before long I'll own the largest fleet of boats on the Cornish coast. You won't have to do anything but remain at home, caring for the child you have inside you now, and thinking of ways to spend the money I'm going to make. You'll be better off than you are now, Elinor.'

Elinor's scornful look cut into him with the keenness of a boning-knife. 'Better off as a fisherman's wife than as Mistress of Polrudden? You're a fool, Nathan Jago. I am the daughter of a baronet – one who might one day become Prime Minister of Great Britain. I am going to marry Francis Rodd. You and I have had . . . fun, together. Because of this I am carrying your child. I thought you might help me. I never realised you entertained such foolish dreams. Never mind. I'll get rid of your bastard in my own way.'

Elinor ran for her horse. Snatching up the reins of the startled animal, she sprang to the saddle. Wheeling the horse to face Nathan, she cried: 'This is one form of abortion your fisher-girls can't try; but it will work, I promise you.'

She brought her riding-crop down hard upon Napoleon's flank and the horse leaped forward, almost bowling Nathan over. Clearing a ditch beside the path in a mighty bound, it then jumped the low hedge beyond. Twenty paces more and the horse was stretching out in a long-striding, reckless gallop down the slope of a field.

Nathan opened his mouth to call to Elinor not to be so foolish, but the sound died in his throat. She was riding like a maniac. Any distraction could be calamitous. Elinor was a superb horsewoman; Nathan hoped she would be able to keep full control of the powerful horse and come to her senses before she had an accident.

But Elinor was courting disaster, and it came to her very quickly. At the bottom of the small field was an untrimmed hedge of briar and bramble. Elinor put the horse to it at full gallop. At the last moment the animal baulked, but it was going much too fast to stop and so made a belated attempt to clear the high hedge. The horse's front legs tangled in the briars, and sheer momentum caused the animal to somersault.

Elinor's scream came back to Nathan, before being cut off as horse and rider crashed to the ground, out of sight beyond the hedge.

Nathan ran to a nearby gate and vaulted over. Running down the slope of the field, he followed the path taken by Elinor. Forcing a way through the tall hedge, he ignored the briars that tore at his clothes and hands.

The stallion was lying dead, its neck broken by the terrible fall. Elinor lay clear of the animal, her right foot still caught in the stirrup. She was dazed, but conscious, and there was no blood to be seen on her.

She appeared to have had an amazing escape, but as Nathan stooped and attempted to free her foot from the stirrup Elinor began screaming.

At first Nathan was unable to get any sense from her. Then she sobbed that the pain was in her back, and when Nathan freed her foot he discovered she could not move her legs.

Nathan was thoroughly alarmed. He had experienced a similar injury on board a man-of-war, when a sailor had fallen from the rigging. His back broken, the sailor had died a pain-filled death two days later.

'I'll need to get help, Elinor.' Taking off his jacket and placing it over her, he repeated his message. It was doubtful whether she heard him, so great was the pain of her injury.

Running to Venn Farm, Nathan found the house filled with neighbouring farmers. With their wives, they had come to see the Quickes' new son. One of the farmers had ridden to Venn, and Nathan despatched him to Mevagissey to find the physician. Then, with Tom Quicke and the other men, he returned to the scene of Elinor's accident, carrying a sheep-hurdle.

As a group of the farmers marvelled at the height of the hedge Elinor and her horse had almost cleared, Nathan, Tom Quicke and two of his neighbours lifted Elinor between them and carefully laid her upon the hurdle. Fortunately, perhaps, she fainted as the men set out with her, bound for Polrudden.

Sir Lewis Hearle was at home and he showed great concern for his unconscious daughter. As the men carrying her began to ascend the wide staircase, the physician arrived.

Dr Ellerman Scott was red-faced and puffing heavily. He had been attending a patient in a cottage on Portgiskey Hill, high above the cove, when the farmer found him. A newcomer to Mevagissey, it was the first time he had been called to the house of one of the area's leading citizens. He set out to create an impression of efficiency and thoroughness.

Supervising the placing of Elinor upon her own bed, he allowed only her maid to stay in the room. The remainder of the men, including her father, were sent out.

Downstairs, Sir Lewis Hearle served brandy to the farmers, who stood around red-faced and embarrassed as the baronet thanked them for their assistance. Nathan was served with a drink, too, but the baronet avoided looking at his face and said nothing to him.

After a single, large drink, the farmers began to

mumble about having work to do and edged self-consciously from the room, Nathan with them.

In the hall outside, Nathan saw the grave-faced physician coming down the stairs. He hung back, in the hope of overhearing what was said.

Meeting Sir Lewis Hearle in the hall, the physician said 'I have grave news, Sir Lewis. Your daughter's back is broken. I think she will live . . . but she will never walk again.'

The baronet took the news in stunned horror. 'You are certain? There can't possibly be some mistake . . . ?'

The physician shook his head sorrowfully. 'No doubt you will want to call in a surgeon . . . perhaps one of your London acquaintances. But I am afraid he will only confirm my diagnosis. I spent many years treating miners in the St Agnes district, Sir Lewis. I have see many men – *too* many men – with such injuries. By the way, is your daughter's husband in the house?'

'Her husband . . . ?' Sir Lewis looked puzzled.

'Yes.' The doctor had totally misinterpreted Sir Lewis Hearle's response. 'Fortunately – or unfortunately, as it may well turn out – your daughter has not lost the baby she has been carrying for the last three months.'

Flabbergasted, Elinor's father opened his mouth to tell the doctor he had made a mistake. Then he saw Nathan standing a few paces away. Suddenly Sir Lewis recalled the look Elinor had given Nathan when he came to Polrudden to negotiate the tithe payments for his drift-fishing venture. He had memories of his own misgivings at the time.

The physician had made no mistake – and Sir Lewis Hearle knew he needed to look no farther than the hall of Polrudden Manor for the father of Elinor's unborn child. He could also hazard a guess why the 'accident' had occurred – and why Nathan Jago had been on the spot.

With a great effort, Sir Lewis kept his feelings under control. If he allowed them to show now, the news of his shame would be carried to every household in the county within days. The farmers were too far away to have heard the doctor's words, but they had not yet left the house.

He cursed the fates that had allowed the accident to happen without bringing about the miscarriage he believed Elinor had wanted so desperately. He also prayed that Elinor had allowed Francis Rodd to enjoy the liberties she had allowed this . . . this . . . *fisherman*! If she had, it should still be possible to arrange a marriage, quickly and discreetly. If she had not . . . Sir Lewis did not dare contemplate the possible consequences. The county would be scandalised. When the news reached London it could also cost him his future in government.

'Jago. Stay here. I want to see you after the physician has gone.'

Nathan felt a thrill of apprehension run through him. He had been watching Sir Lewis after the physician had made his unwitting remarks. He knew why the baronet wanted to talk to him.

The physician left after receiving a sherry and the thanks of the Squire of Polrudden. When he had closed the door behind him, Sir Lewis Hearle walked back to the hall, with its magnificent, curving staircase, panelled walls, portraits and faded tapestries. Stopping before Nathan, the landowner made no attempt to disguise the hatred that trembled in his voice as he spoke.

'Jago, you heard what the physician said. I'm not going to give you an opportunity to lie and tell me you're not responsible for the child Elinor is carrying. Everything fits together far too neatly. Elinor has paid the price for her stupidity. God, but she's been punished! Yet, if things do not work out, it might have been better had she been left to die! You may think you've got away scot free, Jago. You haven't. If it weren't for the scandal it would cause, I would horsewhip you here and now. I *will* if I ever see you near this house again. Do you understand?'

'I'm not an innocent preacher who'll turn the other cheek when violence is offered, Sir Lewis. I hit back. What's more, I love Elinor. Yes, it *is* my child she's carrying, and I'll be back to see how she is . . . when my father's trial is over.'

22

The trial of Preacher Josiah Jago at Bodmin Assizes lasted little longer than the pomp and ceremony that accompanied the opening of the half-yearly court of law.

Mr Justice Vincent arrived at the Assize Court in an impressive carriage, escorted by a troop of Essex Yeomanry, currently performing garrison duties in Cornwall. Behind him came the coaches bearing the Sheriff and lesser dignitaries. All were met at the entrance to the court by the mayors of Cornwall's towns, together with the senior magistrates and court officials.

There were a number of judges on the western circuit. Most enjoyed the ritual pageantry that accompanied the opening of the Assizes, and the subsequent functions and social gatherings that helped to make this one of the highlights of the county year. Some would sometimes spend as long as half an hour at the court entrance, greeting friends and acquaintances, meeting new dignitaries and accepting – or declining – invitations calculated to while away the long rural evenings.

Mr Justice Vincent was not one of these.

Devoid of humour and unsmiling, Judge Vincent regarded himself not as a leading figure in West Country society, but as a servant of England's legal system, chosen to be a judge because of his great knowledge of the law. Scrupulously impartial, Mr Justice Vincent was a forerunner of the incorruptible judges who would one day make Great Britain's judiciary a pattern for the courts of the world.

Nodding his head to acknowledge the obeisance of the gathered officials, the Judge of Assize swept past them all and made his way to the judges' rooms. Ten minutes later, as the occupants of the sombre courtroom rose to their feet, the stentorian tones of a court usher announced the approach of the man who would grant life or death, freedom or hell, to the thirty-seven men and women shivering with apprehension in the damp cells beneath the Assize building.

Judge Vincent cut short the many messages of welcome directed at him by court officials. Curtly, he demanded that a roll be called of all those mayors and chief magistrates who were required to attend a Court of Assize. Many were missing, although a few had sent men to make apologies on their behalf. Mr Justice Vincent brushed aside all such apologies, fining the absent mayors forty shillings on the spot. Those mayors and magistrates who had not bothered to send anyone to explain their absence were to receive an even greater shock. The unsmiling judge directed the court to have them arrested and brought before him. His ruling produced a gasp of shock from those dignitaries who were present, but there were carefully concealed smiles of delight from the less respectful junior court officials.

Preacher Jago's case was fourth on the court list. When his name was called, the preacher climbed to the dock looking frail and apprehensive. His arrival prompted a brief burst of hand-clapping from a number of Methodists who had journeyed from the Pentuan area to witness the trial of their minister. Mr Justice Vincent brought the applause to an abrupt end by threatening to clear the court and arrest the offenders.

The prosecution outlined its case and called four witnesses. Two were men who had been demolishing the Pentuan chapel, and another a soldier of the North Cornish Yeomanry.

All three gave evidence that Preacher Jago was present when the Pentuan crowd got out of hand and began stoning the workmen. All agreed that Josiah Jago had been addressing the crowd, but increasingly impatient questioning by Judge Vincent established that not one of the three had heard the preacher's words.

The fourth and last prosecution witness was the landlord of Pentuan's Jolly Sailor tavern. Red-faced and ill-at-ease, Silas Caldicutt spoke of the alarm he had felt when the 'Methodees' gathered outside his premises.

'They was fair angry with they St Austell men,' he added. 'I wasn't at all surprised when they turned nasty on 'en.'

'You saw Josiah Jago addressing the crowd at the time they turned nasty?' The question came from the prosecuting counsel.

'That I did. Standing on the mounting-block outside my tavern, he was. Right outside my window and shouting at they Methodees fit to bust a gut.'

'And they responded by hurling stones at Sir Lewis Hearle's workmen, and generally behaving in a riotous manner?'

'They did. They was riotous, right enough. Throwing everything they could lay their hands on. Tore up part of the square. I had to pay my own hard-earned money to make it fit to walk on again.'

'Would you say it was Josiah Jago's presence that incited the men and women in the square to violence?'

'No doubt about it. It were his words that set 'em off, and no mistake.'

Smirking, the prosecuting counsel sat down, satisfied he had at last produced a witness to clinch the case against Josiah Jago.

He had not reckoned with Mr Justice Vincent's obsession with justice. Leaning on his bench and fixing his stern gaze upon the tavernkeeper, the judge said: 'You have said that Mr Jago's words were responsible for the riots. Will you tell this court exactly what those words were?'

'Ah . . . ! Ah, well, me Lord. I'm not saying I can remember his *exact* words. I do know they made everyone some angry.'

Judge Vincent looked at the tavernkeeper fiercely: 'The people gathered in the square were men and women of deep religious conviction. Their church was being demolished. I assume they were "some angry" long before Josiah Jago addressed them. You were closer to him than any other witness. You *must* have heard his words. What were they? And I would like to remind you at this stage of the solemn oath you have taken to tell this court the truth.'

The tavernkeeper opened and closed his mouth twice without a sound emerging. He looked at the prosecuting counsel for help, but the barrister was staring at the floor at his feet. He knew better than to break in upon Mr Justice Vincent's questioning. Next, the unhappy tavernkeeper cast a significant glance at Sir Lewis Hearle, seated with his fellow senior magistrates. The Lord of Polrudden Manor was also studiously avoiding the tavernkeeper's glance, leaving him to his own inadequate resources.

'Mr Caldicutt, I am waiting.'

'Preacher Jago told them Methodees he'd been to see Squire Hearle, to ask him not to pull down their chapel. He said Sir Lewis told him it had to come down. Then the crowd started throwing stones.'

Mr Justice Vincent waited for Silas Caldicutt to continue. When nothing was forthcoming, he leaned far over the bench. 'Is this all you can tell me? What did Josiah Jago say when the people began throwing stones – and I'll have the truth, if you please, Mr Caldicutt.'

Running a finger around the neckband of his shirt, suddenly uncomfortably tight, the landlord of the Jolly Sailor tavern croaked: 'He . . . he called on them to stop throwing stones, me Lord.'

'Louder, if you please. I want the jury to hear your every word.'

'He told the crowd to stop throwing stones. Said it would do no good and only lead to trouble.'

Mr Justice Vincent leaned back in his hard, high-backed chair and drummed his fingers angrily on the polished bench in front of him.

'So at last we have the truth of this sordid matter. Far from inciting a riot, it would appear that Josiah Jago was attempting to *end* one. Is there something you haven't told us, Mr Caldicutt? Did the prisoner perhaps behave violently himself?'

'Only when his wife was killed. He pushed one of the soldiers. I . . . I think he wanted to reach his wife.'

The judge sat bolt upright. 'His wife was killed? Was she one of the rioters?'

Silas Caldicutt was about to lie, when he remembered the judge's stern warning. 'No . . . Annie Jago were no rioter. She were looking from her window and had seen Preacher Jago arrested, I reckon. She were on the way from the house to him.'

Mr Justice Vincent was angry. Very angry. Turning to Richard Oxnam, Sheriff of Cornwall, seated beside him, he said: 'Mr Oxnam, certain matters have been disclosed about this case that I find particularly disturbing. The true nature of this witness's evidence should have been ascertained at the magistrates' hearing. Had that been done, this matter would never have come to court, and the defendant would not have spent months wrongfully imprisoned. I am going to direct the jury to dismiss this case and I want you to instigate an enquiry into the manner in which the hearing at the magistrates' court was conducted.'

The judge looked along the line of senior magistrates, and his glance fell upon Sir Lewis Hearle. 'Such an enquiry would normally be the duty of the senior magistrate for the area. However, it would appear that Sir Lewis Hearle has a strong personal interest in this matter. For him to conduct such an enquiry would be quite improper.'

Amidst scenes of uproar in the public gallery, the prosecuting barrister rose to his feet to remind the judge that Josiah Jago still faced charges of 'preaching in the open air'.

Before proceeding farther, Judge Vincent dealt with the uproar in his court-room. When the last of the spectators had been cleared, the judge suggested pointedly that in view of the length of time Josiah Jago had already been held in prison, and the personal grief he had suffered, the prosecution might be well advised to drop all further charges against the Methodist preacher.

Such a 'suggestion' coming from Mr Justice Vincent was tantamount to a directive. The prosecuting counsel promptly announced that no evidence would be offered on the remaining charges.

The decision greatly angered Sir Lewis Hearle. Later, in the judge's private rooms, he had a heated argument with the Assize Court Judge. He pointed out the dangers of allowing ministers of dissident churches to preach against the Establishment and added that the Prime Minister himself had approved a campaign to limit the powers of such men. The Home Office Under-Secretary also hinted that the acquittal of Preacher Josiah Jago would be viewed with great displeasure by the country's first minister.

Mr Justice Vincent gave Sir Lewis Hearle a cold, hard look, his eyes as expressionless as those of a fish. 'I am sixty-seven years of age, Sir Lewis, and have a delightful estate in Hampshire awaiting my retirement. I have no ambition to become Lord Chief Justice, or even a Judge of the Court of Appeal. However, should Perceval wish to dismiss me as an expression of his displeasure, he will need to take his case to both Houses of Parliament. I doubt whether even a man possessed of Spencer Perceval's lack of discretion will embark upon such a course of action merely because an innocent man has been acquitted. Furthermore, I have no intention of distorting the image of justice in order to appease a man who has a personal – and, if I may say so, totally unreasonable – hatred of a nonconformist religious movement. I will, of course, repeat this conversation to the Lord Chief Justice. You may leave now, Sir Lewis – and you have my permission to excuse yourself from attending the remainder of the spring Assize.'

Having dismissed Sir Lewis Hearle, baronet, Under-Secretary at the Home Office, Member of Parliament, Justice of the Peace, and landowner, as though he were a recalcitrant schoolboy, Mr Justice Vincent returned to the court-room to dispense honest law to the people of Cornwall.

When Preacher Josiah Jago walked from the Bodmin Assize a free man, he looked up to the blue sky, opened his arms wide and allowed the warmth of the late spring sunshine to flow over him. This was something he had missed dreadfully. The opportunity to stand in the open, with the sky above him, and the ability to roam freely and admire God's handiwork about him.

Josiah Jago embraced Nathan and then the

American preacher who had served the Methodist cause so well, before setting off on a homeward journey that soon became a triumphant procession. Josiah Jago had become a living martyr to the cause he had always served so loyally.

By the time he arrived in Pentuan, the village street was packed with jubilant well-wishers, and tears of humility glistened on Preacher Jago's face as he looked at his friends and parishioners.

But before he returned to the quiet of his own house Josiah Jago climbed the hill to visit the grave of his wife. When the widowed preacher kneeled by the graveside to offer up a private prayer, everyone who had turned out to celebrate his homecoming kneeled, too. In the surrounding lanes, in the burial-ground itself, and in the green fields of the steep hillside, a prayer went up for the soul of Annie Jago. Nathan thought that he had never before experienced such a moving moment.

Afterwards, Josiah Jago inspected his new church in silence. Nathan, who had been responsible for the construction of the building, waited with some apprehension for his father to approve the work.

It was not forthcoming until Josiah Jago had inspected every aspect of the workmanship and had stood for some silent minutes in the lovingly carved pulpit, gazing out over an imaginary congregation.

Then, looking at Nathan, he nodded his head three or four times, and said softly: 'Your mother would have been proud of you for this, Nathan. It's a pride I happily share. Thank you, son.'

Nathan was reminded of the infrequent occasions when, as a boy, his father would give him a passing pat on the head. It had given a warm glow to the coldest morning. In those days, Nathan would have built ten chapels to receive praise such as his father had just bestowed upon him.

That evening a constant flow of visitors passed through the Jagos' Pentuan cottage, and Nathan was forced to call a halt to them shortly before midnight. It had been a gruelling day, both physically and mentally, for Josiah Jago. He was unused to such activity. He had exercised neither body nor mind during his long imprisonment.

When the exhausted preacher had been persuaded to retire to his bedroom, Nathan and Uriah Kemp sat for a while before the kitchen fire, discussing the events of the day.

'Your father will go to sleep a happy man,' declared Uriah Kemp. 'He's proved that justice can be obtained by a Methodist in your English courts.'

'He was lucky. There aren't too many judges like Judge Vincent.'

'Perhaps not, yet many oppressed preachers will take heart from this verdict.' Uriah Kemp looked at Nathan shrewdly. 'But there is still something troubling you, Nathan. Can I help?'

'No, it's something I must work out for myself.' Nathan stood up and reached for his coat. 'I'm going for a walk before I turn in. Don't wait up for me.'

It was a fine night, with a three-quarter moon and a sky full of stars. Nathan went first to the sands that extended from the tiny Pentuan harbour to Portgiskey Cove and he paced the sands for a full hour. At the end of this time he was close to Portgiskey and he sat down, hunched on the rocks at the entrance to the cove.

Deep inside the shadows of the cove was the cottage where Amy slept. Nathan felt he had somehow let Amy down. She had expected more from him than he had been prepared to give to her. Perhaps it would have been different had he never met Elinor Hearle. But the love he felt for Elinor was stronger than anything he had ever known.

Nathan wished he could convince himself that marriage with Sammy Mizler would bring Amy the happiness she deserved. Sammy was a good man. Nathan believed he was also a kind man, but he really only came fully to life in London. Amy's heart and soul were here, on the Cornish coast. If Sammy Mizler took her to London after they were married, she would wilt and die, as so many country girls had before her. But nothing Nathan could say would change their minds – and he had his own problems to resolve.

Before returning home, Nathan climbed the hill behind Pentuan and stood looking at Polrudden Manor, proud and solid in the moonlight, its crumbling stonework hidden in shadow. There was one tiny light showing from a window. Beyond that window lay Elinor – and his unborn child.

Standing in the shadow of the trees, Nathan remembered how much he had admired this house as a boy. It had always drawn him, although he had never dared to approach as close as this in those days. As he looked, he felt that his destiny lay here; but it was not a comforting feeling. Of a sudden, he shivered violently and shrugged the collar of his coat higher.

Dawn was only an hour or so away. He would go home and sleep for a while. Then he would return here, to Polrudden, and face Sir Lewis Hearle once more.

Nathan's meeting with Sir Lewis Hearle was postponed in a violent and dramatic manner.

The residents of Mevagissey and Pentuan were awakened soon after dawn by the sound of heavy cannon-fire from close at hand. Men, women and children spilled from the houses, latecomers pulling jerseys over their heads as they ran to vantage-points. A sea-battle was taking place offshore between two British sixth-rate frigates, carrying only sixty cannon between them, and four French seventy-four-gun ships-of-the-line.

Heading up-Channel, the heavier French vessels had surprised the British ships at dawn and engaged them immediately. The first broadside from the leading French vessel had brought down the mainmast of one of the frigates, preventing the British vessel from making use of her superior speed.

The second frigate might have escaped at this time; instead, her captain chose to engage the French men-of-war in a bid to enable the damaged British ship to escape inshore. It was a brave but futile attempt, and the one-sided engagement could have only one ending.

At one stage both frigates tried to escape by making for Mevagissey's small harbour. Guessing their intentions, the Frenchmen manoeuvred between the shore and the frigates. Refusing to strike their ensigns, the battle became a 'shoot-and-dodge' engagement for the frigates, while the French battleships lumbered in like a pack of great mastiffs worrying two crippled terriers.

As the fishermen on shore watched, the foremast of the already crippled frigate crashed to the deck, a mass of splintered wood, torn sail and tangled rigging. A few minutes later, a heated cannon-ball from a French man-of-war found the frigate's powder-store.

The explosion tore the yellow and black hull apart, sending men and timbers hurtling through the air into the sea.

As the spectators on shore gasped in horror, Nathan called: 'Those are British sailors out there – Cornishmen among them, I don't doubt. They need rescuing. Who's with me?'

There was no shortage of volunteers, and Nathan sprinted to Portgiskey, a long line of fishermen of all ages strung out along the sand behind him. He took the first half-dozen to arrive. The remainder, helped by his boat's namesake, heaved *The Brave Amy H* into deep water.

With her sister ship a shattered wreck, the second British frigate crowded on full sail in an attempt to outstrip the enemy. But by now the French men-of-war were ranged on either side of the frigate and were able to concentrate all their considerable fire-power upon her. Soon, two masts crashed to the deck of the frigate and, hanging over the side, they dragged the single-decker around in a tight circle to face yet another broadside.

It was nothing short of slaughter. With the second frigate wallowing helplessly in the water, in imminent danger of sinking, the French admiral called off his vessels. Putting out into the Channel, the four French vessels headed for deeper waters in which to celebrate their victory.

Other fishing-boats had put off from Mevagissey, and all were needed. Dozens of men from the first frigate were in the water, all with wounds and many of them serious. *The Brave Amy H* picked up eight survivors before going alongside the second frigate, which was now on fire, flames licking at the rigging on the remaining mast.

Nathan did not leave the frigate until he had taken twenty-two survivors on board *The Brave Amy H* and could carry no more in safety.

Leaving others to save the remaining seamen, Nathan set a course for Plymouth. There would be Fleet surgeons there, and a hospital where they had experience in treating seamen with battle wounds. Neither Mevagissey nor Pentuan would be able to cope with a hundred and fifty wounded men, many of whom would need to have limbs amputated.

Under normal conditions, the sailing-time to Plymouth from the scene of the battle might have been no more than four hours. Today it was to be much longer. Emboldened by his success, the French admiral unexpectedly returned two of his men-of-war to the English coastline.

They chanced upon a luckless, unarmed merchantman, loaded with tin ore, and a French prize-crew was sent on board. Then the French warships met up with the flotilla of fishing-boats, heading for Plymouth with the survivors from the frigates. In the ensuing chase, two of the Mevagissey fishing-boats were sunk and three taken.

The largest of the fishing-boats was *The Brave Amy H* and one of the French captains tried very hard to capture her. However, emulating Amy on the occasion when she had saved the boat from corsairs, Nathan took his vessel close inshore, braving the many rocks that frothed in the sea only feet away.

The Frenchman's answer to this strategy was to cannonade *The Brave Amy H* in a bid to force Nathan out to sea. But Nathan remained close inshore and eventually found the shelter of the tiny fishing village of Polperro. Here he remained until the French men-of-war set off in pursuit of a promising new conquest, hull down on the horizon.

Plymouth was reached at noon. After putting the wounded sailors ashore, close to the naval hospital, Nathan was asked to go to the Admiral's office, on a hill above the naval dockyard. Here he gave the Admiral a first-hand report on the battle between English and French ships, and the subsequent activities of the French men-of-war.

It transpired that there were only two British warships of comparable size at the Admiral's disposal. The remainder had been sent to join two fleets that were at sea hoping to engage much larger French formations.

The survivors of the attack on the rescue fleet were still limping into Plymouth Sound and the Admiral suggested that all the fishing-boats should remain at Plymouth, under his protection, until he had assembled sufficient vessels to escort them safely home to their villages.

Three days later a large British fleet of men-of-war, under the flag of Rear-Admiral Keats, entered Plymouth Sound. They had been in action off Cadiz and, on their way homeward, had fallen in with the French admiral and his marauding squadron. One had been sunk, another captured and the remainder put to flight. On board the captured French ship, the British sailors had released many prisoners, among them a number of Mevagissey fishermen. It was now safe for Nathan to return home with *The Brave Amy H*.

Nathan and his crew arrived at Portgiskey Cove to learn that rumours had been rife during their absence. One of the fishing-boats carrying wounded British sailors had turned back to Mevagissey when the French men-of-war attacked. The crew of this boat had seen a French warship in close pursuit of *The Brave Amy H* and had assumed that the Portgiskey drifter had been either sunk or captured. As the days went by without any news, it seemed their assumption was correct. There was even talk of a memorial service being held for the missing men in the new Pentuan chapel!

The Brave Amy H and her crew returned cheerfully unaware of the rumours, and Nathan was startled when Amy hurtled from the cottage and threw herself at him. The other crew members had little time to enjoy Nathan's embarrassment. Cornish wives and daughters, traditionally undemonstrative, deserted their salting duties and ran from the fish-cellars of Pentuan and Portgiskey to greet their men.

During the days and nights in Plymouth, with little to do, Nathan had found plenty of time to think upon his future, and he had settled on a course of action; but, looking down at Amy as she clung to him, he felt his resolve weaken alarmingly. He put up a hand to stroke her hair and assure her that he was well – and then he saw Sammy Mizler watching them from the doorway of the Hoblyn cottage.

Gently, Nathan put Amy from him and smiled at her before waving cheerfully to Sammy.

'I hardly expected such a warm welcome, after idling in Plymouth for three days and nights,' he said, taking Amy's hand and leading her to where Sammy Mizler waited. 'But the holiday's over now. As soon as the women have satisfied themselves that their men are alive and well, I want the boat made ready for fishing. There's a fine shoal of mackerel not two miles off Gribbin Head. Ahab can take _The Brave Amy H_ out. It's at times like this I wish we had another boat. But no doubt one will bring in enough fish to keep the cellar busy for another week or two.'

'And you? What will you be doing while the men are out fishing?'

The relief at seeing Nathan alive and well had threatened to overwhelm Amy a short while earlier, but as she stood at Sammy Mizler's side it was difficult to read her expression.

'I'm going to Polrudden. To keep a promise I made to Sir Lewis Hearle – and Elinor.'

23

At Polrudden Manor, Nathan knocked heavily on the stout wooden door and stood waiting for it to be opened. He displayed far more confidence than he felt. At last the heavy door creaked open and a maid stood in the doorway. Nathan had not seen her before.

'I've come to visit Miss Elinor,' Nathan announced briefly.

'Yes, sir. Will you come inside, please?'

Nathan stepped into the great hall. After taking his name, the maid hurried away in the direction of Sir Lewis Hearle's study.

She returned quickly. 'Will you come this way, Mr Jago? Sir Lewis would like to see you in his study before you visit Miss Elinor.'

If the baronet's reaction to Nathan's arrival had been violent, there was no hint of it in the maid's manner. She chattered on, telling Nathan how pleased the servants were to see Miss Elinor growing stronger with each passing day. Nathan was deeply puzzled.

At the study door the maid knocked, opened the door and announced Nathan. She flashed him a quick smile as he stepped inside the study, and the door closed quietly behind him.

Sir Lewis Hearle was seated close to the window on a captain's swivelling chair. He had his back to Nathan and was looking out of the window, a glass of brandy at his elbow. He must have seen Nathan approaching the house from the lane. In view of the threat he had made when the two men last met, it was more than surprising that Nathan had been allowed to enter the house.

'I'm here to see Elinor.'

'There was talk in the village that the French had either taken or killed you, Jago. You've disappointed me.' Sir Lewis Hearle spoke without turning around.

'As you can see, I'm alive. And I intend to see Elinor.'

'All in good time.' The baronet swivelled the seat about to face Nathan. He looked at him as though seeing him for the first time, and Nathan could see neither cordiality nor yet dislike in his expression. 'What do you hope to gain from seeing my daughter?'

'I intend repeating an offer I made to her just before she had the accident.'

'You are talking of your offer of marriage, of course.'

Nathan was taken aback. He had not expected Elinor to repeat any part of that conversation to her father. But Sir Lewis Hearle had more to say. 'I must add, of course, that she told me the story to amuse me.

What could you possibly offer Elinor – although a girl who will never walk again can have few expectations from life?'

'I would look after her. Give her *loving* care – more than she will ever have at Polrudden. Besides, I feel that I'm responsible for what happened. If she hadn't been expecting my child, there would have been no accident.'

'Is that so?' The look Elinor's father gave Nathan was coldly calculating. 'This "loving care" of yours . . . Does it go beyond having Methodist prayers said for her by your father, and receiving second-rate attention when the brat is due?'

'My father says prayers for every sick person in the area; that's his way. But there would be no interference with me, or Elinor. As for the baby, Elinor would have the best attention that money could buy.'

Sir Lewis Hearle rose to his feet abruptly and turned his back on Nathan, looking out through the window once more. Nathan was puzzled. He was also very excited. Sir Lewis had not erupted with either anger or mirth – and he had not ordered Nathan from Polrudden. Could it possibly be that he was seriously considering a marriage between Nathan and Elinor?

This was exactly what Sir Lewis was considering, but his motives had nothing to do with the well-being of his daughter.

Within hours of the accident, Sir Lewis had sent a rider galloping to inform Francis Rodd, at Trebartha. When Sir Lewis returned from the humiliating Assizes, after Josiah Jago's acquittal, he found Francis Rodd waiting at Polrudden. With him was the

formidable Lady Admonition Rodd – and a surgeon
from London. When news of the accident reached
Trebartha, the surgeon had been at the house, brought
from the capital to treat her ladyship's troublesome
varicose veins.

The surgeon had examined Elinor before Sir Lewis's
arrival, and his prognosis was gloomier than that of
the Mevagissey physician. Elinor's spine was fractured low down on her back. It would cause her
periods of acute pain throughout her life – and he
confirmed that she would never walk again. Needless
to say, the surgeon had also discovered that Elinor
was pregnant, although he was of the opinion that the
child would be stillborn, as a result of the accident.

He suggested the Mevagissey physician should
keep Elinor well supplied with an opium-based pain-
killer, and trusted that the Lord would grant her a
quick release from her sufferings.

Sending the surgeon from the room, Lady Rodd
was characteristically blunt with Sir Lewis Hearle.
Elinor, she said, should have known better than to
put a spirited horse at a high fence at full gallop. Then
she added pointedly: 'Although it might have been
better had she jumped the horse over a cliff. She's
wild, Sir Lewis. Wilder than any girl should be. Why
my son ever considered marrying her I'll never know.'

'Are you forgetting the child . . . ?'

'I'm forgetting nothing.' Lady Rodd's mouth
snapped shut in the manner of a steel gin-trap. 'Least
of all *that!* You'd have had Francis marry a girl who
carried another man's bastard in her belly.'

She glared at Sir Lewis contemptuously. 'No doubt
you were hoping to pass it off as a premature child of

the marriage, had I given my permission for an early wedding?'

'I knew nothing of Elinor's regrettable condition before the accident. It *must* be your son's.'

'*It most certainly is not!* I have already asked him. Francis does not lie to me.'

'Others might not agree with you.'

Lady Rodd thrust her aristocratically beaked nose close to Sir Lewis Hearle's face and gave him a look such as a perching buzzard bestows upon a young rabbit.

'I don't give *that* for the opinion of others.' She snapped her fingers loudly – a trick she had learned years before from her sailor father.

Straightening up, she looked disdainfully at him. 'Fortunately for you, Sir Lewis, I am prepared to accept your word that you knew nothing of Elinor's condition before the accident. Any scandal there may be will not originate with me. If Trebartha is to remain in Rodd hands, Francis will need to select a bride elsewhere – and there will be those ready to think the worst of him. I suggest you find some fool to marry your daughter quickly. Now, have my carriage brought round to the door and I will bid you "Good-bye", Sir Lewis. I doubt if you and I shall meet again.'

Sir Lewis Hearle burned with humiliation when he remembered the conversation with Lady Rodd, but he had thought much about it since.

'If Elinor married me, she would want for nothing . . .' Sir Lewis had been silent for too long. Nathan was eager to impress him that such a marriage *could* work. 'I have ambitions . . .'

'Your ambition led you to my daughter's bedroom. Shut up and listen to me.'

Sir Lewis Hearle turned to face Nathan once again. 'All right. You and Elinor may marry – but I'm having no elaborate service. The marriage will take place in Elinor's room, and there will be no guests. If witnesses are needed, I'll find a couple of servants with enough schooling to write their names. After the wedding you will live here, at Polrudden. But I don't want to see you in the main part of the house when I am home. You can have the east wing. It will require a great deal of work carried out before it's habitable. That will be your responsibility.'

Elinor's father felt the bile rising in his throat as Nathan's incredulity gave way to delight. He silently cursed Elinor for allowing this oaf to make love to her, thus forcing him to take such a humiliating course of action. He despised himself, too, for not carrying out his original threat to horsewhip Nathan from the house.

But there was far too much at stake.

Quite apart from the scandal of Elinor's pregnancy, there was Sir Lewis's quarrel with Mr Justice Vincent. The judge's report on Josiah Jago's acquittal would doubtless accuse the Home Office Under-Secretary of being dangerously biased against Methodists. Mr Justice Vincent was a highly respected judge, and as the report was being submitted through official channels the Prime Minister would be forced to act upon it – unless Sir Lewis could prove beyond all doubt that such an accusation was groundless. What better proof could he give than to show that his only daughter was married to the son of a Methodist preacher – the very preacher he was accused of wrongfully trying to convict?

But Sir Lewis Hearle was equally determined that

Preacher Josiah Jago's son would not profit from the union at his expense.

'I have other conditions to impose on you. The first is that, while I continue to enjoy all income from Polrudden lands, you will be responsible for the upkeep of the *whole* of this house.'

This was a harsh imposition. The manor-house needed some urgent repairs. Then there were servants' wages to be paid, food bills . . . It was a high price to pay for a bride. All the same, when Nathan bought his second boat . . . He nodded his agreement to Sir Lewis Hearle's terms.

'There is more. Whatever happens to Elinor, *you* will not inherit Polrudden. If her child is delivered safely, and is a boy, my title, together with Polrudden and its lands, will pass to him in the event of my death. You will have nothing.'

Sir Lewis paused and glared at Nathan. 'Finally, your father is never to set foot in Polrudden, not even for the wedding. I'll not have a Methodist preacher in this house. Do you understand?'

It was a humiliating condition – to decree that a man's father could not visit him or the grandchild he would one day have. Nathan hesitated . . . then he nodded once more.

'In that case the marriage will take place just as soon as it can be arranged. *Now* you may visit Elinor.'

Leaving Sir Lewis Hearle's study, Nathan was in a daze. At the top of the magnificent staircase, he paused to look down upon the glistening chandelier, the dark wood panelling and the portraits of former squires of Polrudden. If he had a son, all this would be his inheritance.

Nathan was under no illusions about his own life, here in Sir Lewis Hearle's house. The baronet had imposed many harsh conditions, and he would continue to make things as difficult as he could. But Sir Lewis would not be able to still the tongues of Cornish villagers.

From the day of his marriage, Nathan would no longer be Nathan Jago, fisherman of Pentuan. Not even Nathan Jago, champion prize-fighter of the world.

To Cornishmen, Nathan would be something that meant far more to them in this corner of the country. He would be Nathan Jago *of Polrudden*. And he would have Elinor.

Book Two

Book Two

1

The marriage of Nathan Jago and Elinor Hearle took place in Elinor's bedroom at Polrudden, on Friday, the last day of May, in the year 1811. The ceremony was conducted by the tight-lipped Reverend Nicholas Kent, rector of Fowey. It was not the happiest of occasions.

Prior to her 'accident', Elinor had been expecting to become the Mistress of Trebartha. Instead, she was marrying a fisherman whose boat had been bought with money earned in a prize-ring. She felt the humiliation keenly.

When Sir Lewis had first told his daughter about the proposed marriage, Elinor had not believed him. Then, when she realised he was telling the truth, she had declared she would not go through with the ceremony. Sir Lewis told his daughter bluntly that she had lost the freedom to choose her own destiny by allowing Nathan to share her bed and becoming pregnant by him. Now he, her father, was making the decisions. Elinor would either marry her fisherman or she would be sent away to spend the remainder of her life in a hospital run by nuns for incurables, not far from London Town. If she chose the latter course, her baby would be taken away from her at birth and placed immediately in an orphanage, with only a faint chance of survival.

Elinor wept and pleaded, but Sir Lewis Hearle remained unmoved. The scandal of an illegitimate child would bring his already uncertain career to an abrupt end.

Given the dark hours of a single night to make her choice, Elinor had accepted the inevitable.

It was not an auspicious beginning to a wedded life already beset by more than its fair share of difficulties. But this was no ordinary marriage.

Sammy Mizler, chosen by Nathan to be the best man, was convinced that Nathan was mad to marry Elinor Hearle, however pressing his reasons. He even tried to talk Nathan out of the marriage, but Nathan was as obdurate as Sir Lewis Hearle. The wedding would take place.

Nathan's family and friends were upset at the haste and secrecy of the marriage – and none more so than Amy. It did not help to tell herself that she did not *want* to witness Nathan tying himself to Sir Lewis Hearle's crippled daughter.

Sir Lewis had been drinking heavily before the ceremony and commented rudely upon the incongruity of a Jew being the 'best man' at a Christian ceremony. Only Nathan's restraining hand on his arm stopped Sammy Mizler from giving the baronet a suitable reply.

The bizarre ceremony was witnessed by Elinor's personal maid and a new footman, and was followed by no traditional celebrations. Later, Nathan spent his wedding night futilely trying to convince his bride that there *could* be a happy future ahead of them.

Nathan was determined to make a success of his marriage. Helped by many of the craftsmen who had built the new Methodist church for Josiah Jago, he quickly had the east wing of Polrudden Manor habitable and moved in with his crippled bride.

The move was an uncomfortable one for Elinor. She screamed her agony as she was carried to her new quarters on a litter. Her physician had assured Nathan that she would one day be able to move about the house in a wheelchair, but that day seemed far away.

Nathan had hoped that Elinor would show some improvement once they were established in their own wing of the house, but she refused to listen to his words of encouragement. Indeed, his very presence seemed to upset her for much of the time. It became clear that Elinor blamed Nathan for everything that had happened to her.

Then Sir Lewis was summoned to London to answer the charges brought against him by Mr Justice Vincent. The Tory Prime Minister had attempted to keep the report quiet, but it was receiving much publicity in the capital and looked set to become an embarrassment to Spencer Perceval.

With the departure of Sir Lewis, a new atmosphere began to show itself at Polrudden. Elinor was occasionally seen to smile, and the physician, a frequent visitor, reported that the child inside her was growing normally, despite Elinor's accident.

Elinor had declared frequently that she cared nothing for the unborn baby, but she often found herself thinking about the child and the servants reported to Nathan that she was asking them many questions about feeding and caring for new-born babies.

Then, in mid-July, Nathan went to Portgiskey Cove to take *The Brave Amy H* out for a night's fishing and found Amy and Sammy waiting for him. Inside the small Portgiskey cottage, they broke their news to him. Amy and Sammy had decided to marry at the end of July – little more than two weeks away. But this was not all. After the wedding, Sammy and his bride intended leaving Portgiskey and moving to London.

The wedding was not entirely unexpected, but the decision to move to London came as a surprise to Nathan. He believed Amy would bitterly regret leaving her native Cornwall.

'Who will you put in to run the fish-cellar for you?' he asked Amy.

The answer came from Sammy Mizler. 'That will be for you to decide, Nathan. You and your new partners. Amy and I have decided to put our share of the business up for sale. It makes sense. If we keep it, we'll need to employ people to take our places here. That will cut profits for everyone.'

Sammy spread his arms expressively. 'Today we can afford to do this, but one month of bad weather would result in the business making a loss.'

Amy looked at Nathan apologetically. 'Sammy's right, Nathan. You know that. We realise that new partners might have ideas you can't agree with; that's why we're telling you before we try to sell. We want to give *you* the chance to buy our half of the business.'

'With what?' Nathan stood up and strode to the window. From here he could see the activity in the fish-cellar. Bitterly, he added: 'I haven't got enough to buy out either of you.'

After a few moments of embarrassed silence, Sammy Mizler said: 'All right, so you can't raise all the money by yourself, Nathan. But Sir Lewis Hearle is your father-in-law now . . .'

Nathan's laugh was short and devoid of humour. 'Sir Lewis Hearle is so pleased to have me as his son-in-law that he's given me responsibility for running Polrudden. I also have to meet all the bills.'

'Oh! We didn't know,' said Amy unhappily.

'It isn't our intention to *ruin* you.' Sammy was at his businesslike best. 'But we're starting married life, too. We'll need some capital if we're to find ourselves a place in London. However . . .'

As he was talking, Sammy Mizler's sharp business brain was making rapid mental calculations. 'Can you afford to pay Amy and me a quarter of the value of our share of the business?'

After only a moment's hesitation, Nathan nodded. 'I think so.'

'Then, if Amy agrees, we'll take that. You can repay the remainder over a two-year period. You should be able to manage that.'

Sammy Mizler glanced at Amy, and she nodded her assent.

'Done!'

Nathan clasped an arm about each of his friends. He felt weak-kneed with relief. For a while he had stood eye to eye with total ruin. Now he held a majority holding in the Portgiskey fishing venture. With a great deal of hard work, and a lot of luck, he should be able to make a success of the business.

'Now I suppose I must congratulate you both on your forthcoming marriage. Although why you should want to leave Cornwall I just don't know . . .'

Amy said nothing. She could not tell Nathan that Cornwall had not been the same for her since the day he had gone to live at Polrudden with his new wife.

Sammy Mizler knew. He had always known of Amy's feelings towards Nathan. He was more aware of them than Amy herself, but he had become adept at hiding his own emotions. To Nathan he replied: 'As you've often said yourself, I'm a Londoner. Nowhere else has the same appeal for me. Cornwall is nice, yes. Beautiful, even. But it's not for me. Besides, there are a few promising prize-fighters about now. I've had some good offers to go to London and train them.'

'But what about Amy?' Nathan looked down at the girl crooked in his left arm. 'How do you feel about leaving Portgiskey?'

Amy shrugged, not meeting his eyes. 'I've spent a lifetime in Cornwall. It's time I saw more of the world. I'll go wherever Sammy goes.'

The wedding of Sammy Mizler and Amy Hoblyn took place in Josiah Jago's Methodist chapel. It had everything that Nathan and Elinor's wedding had lacked. There was warmth and happiness, and the whole of the tiny Pentuan community was involved.

Sammy Mizler was a stranger in the village – a 'foreigner' from across Cornwall's natural border, the River Tamar. He would never be anything else if he remained at Portgiskey and lived to be a hundred. But his cheery ways and business acumen had gained a firm place for him in the hearts of the Cornish villagers. Amy, too, had moved to Portgiskey from another area of Cornwall, but many village women worked in the Portgiskey fish-cellar and all were fond of her. They gave her a wedding that any Cornish girl would remember all the days of her life.

After the ceremony, a party went on at Portgiskey until early in the evening. Only one person there did not enjoy herself. In truth, Peggy Hoblyn appeared confused by all that was going on. She did not know whether to smile or to cringe from the people who spoke to her.

Concern for her mother was all that marred an otherwise happy day for Amy. Peggy Hoblyn's mental state had deteriorated rapidly in recent months. Amy knew she could not be taken away from familiar surroundings. If she were moved, Peggy's sanity would disappear altogether. She was to remain at Portgiskey, the only other shareholder in Nathan's fishing business. The anticipated income should ensure that she wanted for nothing. A distant cousin, Lizzie Barron, at present living in Mevagissey, had moved into the cottage at Portgiskey to take care of her, and Nathan would ensure that Peggy Hoblyn was looked after.

The party broke up when a hay-wagon arrived to take the bride and bridegroom to St Austell, accompanied by all those wedding guests able to find a few square inches of space on the overcrowded wagon.

In St Austell a patient coachman was holding the London-bound coach for the newly-weds. As their travelling-chests were being lashed down on the coach roof, Nathan said a sad goodbye to his late partners. He and Sammy Mizler had been together for a great many years. Had it not been for Sammy's skills and managerial ability, Nathan would not have gained the success in the prize-fighting ring that had made his present mode of life possible.

The farewell between the two friends was almost wordless, so deep was their emotion. Yet the sense of loss felt greater when Nathan embraced Amy.

Amy clung to him unexpectedly fiercely, and Nathan whispered: 'Goodbye, Amy. I shall miss you. Be happy.'

Pulling away from him reluctantly, Amy did her best to blink back foolish tears. 'If I don't find happiness with Sammy, it will be my fault, not his.'

Looking up at him, Amy added: 'I wish I felt the future had as much to offer you, Nathan.'

Warmed by her concern, he said: 'Don't worry about me. I'll be all right.'

Observing the determined lines of his face, Amy replied quietly: 'Yes, Nathan. I expect you will.'

To the accompaniment of rowdy cheers, Amy was handed inside the mail coach and Sammy Mizler climbed in beside her. Moments later, the coach rattled out of the cobbled innyard, its departure signalled by the strident notes of the coachman's long, highly polished post-horn.

The guests who were still in a mood for celebrating hurried inside the inn. They would be thoroughly drunk before they set off for Pentuan in the haywagon.

Nathan did not go with them, nor did anyone try to persuade him to remain. He would walk home on his own. Born in Pentuan, Nathan could never be totally excluded from the tight little community, but by marrying into the Hearle family and moving to Polrudden he had set himself apart from them as surely as though he, too, had moved to London.

2

Putting a deposit on Sammy and Amy's shares of the business had left Nathan desperately short of money. In order to earn more he needed to keep *The Brave Amy H* at sea for every hour of the day and night. He took on an extra crew, putting Calvin Dickin in charge of the day crew and going out with the night men himself.

Nathan was a hard taskmaster, but he had no shortage of crewmen. The pilchards were late coming inshore this year, and fishermen were eager to make what money they could.

Owners of the idle seine-boats blamed Nathan for the absence of the pilchards. They repeated the arguments of generations of seine-fishermen, that the long drift-nets stretched across the mouth of the bay broke up the massive shoals on their way inshore. It was doubtful whether there was any substance in their accusations. In later years, even though existing laws were amended to drive the drifters farther and farther from the coast, and to limit their hours of fishing, the seine-fishermen still enjoyed good years and bad years, as they always had. Some seasons, the pilchards came close inshore in their tens of millions. Other years, they did not arrive at all.

There was no shortage of fish in the deeper waters off the Cornish coast. Night and day *The Brave Amy H* returned to Portgiskey laden with as many pilchards as she could safely carry. Nathan took on additional cellar-women, but they still worked so hard they swore their arms were salt-preserved for ever.

Less than a month after Sammy and Amy had left for London, Nathan decided to take a bold gamble. He used all the money he had made to purchase a second drifter. By naming her *Annie Jago*, Nathan helped to heal the breach with his father, brought about by Nathan's unusual wedding at Polrudden.

Annie Jago was not a new boat. She had been put up for sale by a fishing syndicate in nearby Fowey, whose luck did not match Nathan's own.

For a couple of weeks it seemed that Nathan's gamble was going to pay him handsomely. Both vessels worked together, and the catch doubled. Then a south-easterly storm blew up and raged the length of the English Channel for a whole week. During this time not a boat put to sea from the south Cornish ports.

At Polrudden, Nathan paced the floor of his bedroom night after night, as the storm raged outside. He listened in vain for some change in the tone of the wind howling off the sea, and there was no slackening in the rhythm of the rain beating against the diamond-paned windows of the old manor.

Occasionally Elinor would call querulously from the adjacent bedroom, wanting something that lay just out of reach, or simply demanding that he keep her company and read to her. She could be safely propped up in her bed now, but she preferred to lie down, complaining that unless she did so the child kicking inside her made life unbearable.

It was not a happy time for Nathan. Worried about his fishing business, he found neither sympathy nor affection at home.

Then, one stormy night when the wind was rattling the windows in their frames and swooping down wide-built chimneys to scatter the ashes of dead fires around cooling fireplaces, Nathan was awakened by strangled screaming. The sound came from Elinor's room.

Fearing that the baby was coming early, or that Elinor might have somehow fallen out of bed, he threw back the bedclothes and hurried to her.

Elinor lay with her eyes closed, twitching as though she were having a fit, the skin of her face glistening with perspiration.

Alarmed, Nathan leaned over her. 'Elinor . . . what's the matter? Wake up . . .'

She continued twitching and a low, long-drawn-out animal noise rattled in her throat.

'Elinor. Wake up.' Nathan shook her by the shoulder.

Suddenly, Elinor's eyes opened, filled with fear. A moment later they filled with tears and she reached up for him. Incredibly relieved, Nathan held her to him as she began to sob as though her heart were breaking.

'Hush! It's all right, Elinor. Everything is all right.'

Gradually the sobs subsided, but still she clung to him. Looking down at her pale, dark-eyed face, Nathan brushed back a long strand of dark hair. 'You must have been having a bad dream.'

She nodded. 'It . . . it was horrible.' Her fingers dug into him as details of the dream returned. 'Nathan, put out the candle and lie with me for a while.' She whispered the words.

Reaching across her to the bedside table, Nathan snuffed out the ragged yellow flame and slipped into bed beside her. It was the first time he had shared her bed since their marriage and he put his arms about her, careful not to twist her body.

'Nathan?' Elinor's hoarse whisper cut across his thoughts. 'I haven't been very kind to you, have I?'

'You've been in a lot of pain. With that and the baby, I haven't exactly been the best thing to come into your life.'

'I've thought about that, too – a lot. After the accident my father told me I had chosen my own destiny when I let you make love to me. It's quite true, Nathan. You neither ravished nor seduced me. *I* wanted *you*.'

In making her admission to Nathan, Elinor said more to him than at any time since their improbable marriage, and Nathan had never known her in such a self-critical mood as this.

'I wanted you, too. I loved you very much, Elinor.'

'Do you still love me, Nathan?'

'Yes. Nothing has happened to change that.'

'Thank you.' Elinor pulled Nathan to her fiercely, kissing him with all the exciting ardour he remembered from nights when he had entered this same house secretly. Resting her cheek against his, she said: 'I dreamed you had stopped loving me and told me you were going away. I . . . I didn't like it very much. It mattered to me.'

'People who put great store by such things say you should always reverse your dreams. So you see, your dream was really telling you that I'll never leave you.'

Elinor would not tell him about the remainder of her dream, of watching him walk into terrible danger, a small child clutching his hand. The child looked like Nathan, and she knew it was *their* child. She called, but neither of them heard. She tried to run to them, to warn of the danger, but she was crippled. She could not move. Then they turned, and she held out her arms, begging them to come back to her. They did not see. Turning away, they walked on. There was nothing more she could do to save them. That was when she began to scream, and scream . . .

In the darkness of her room that night, as Nathan held his wife close, he felt their child stir inside her crippled body. Elinor smiled at the wonder in his voice. Nathan had discovered the miracle of life, but she, too, had made a wonderful discovery. On this wild and stormy night, as the result of a terrifying nightmare, Elinor had discovered that she loved her husband.

When Nathan awoke the next morning, he was immediately aware of something different. For a few minutes he lay still, telling himself it was no more than the unfamiliar shape of his wife's room. Then he realised there was no wind rattling the windows. No rain beating against the panes.

Easing himself gently from the bed, so as not to wake Elinor, Nathan went to the window and looked outside. The sky was a miscellany of rain-washed pastel shades. Blues and pinks and yellows, and a delicate mauve, with not a hint of grey. The storm had finally blown itself out.

Back in his own room, Nathan dressed hurriedly in his fisherman's clothes, anxious to take advantage of the change in the weather.

'Nathan? Where are you?'

'In here. The storm is over. I'll be able to take the boats out again.'

Nathan entered her bedroom in time to catch the pout she tried to hide. 'Must you go? I don't *want* to be left.'

'I must. We've already lost a week. We need the money.'

Elinor said no more until he came into the room again to kiss her farewell. Hugging him to her, she whispered: 'Hurry back. I shall miss you . . . husband.'

That morning Nathan arrived at Portgiskey as happy as any fisherman has a right to be. Unfortunately, the feeling did not survive the day. *The Brave Amy H* and *Annie Jago* put to sea together, both crews eager to bring in good catches after a week of enforced idleness, but the fish were not to be found. Handlining, in an attempt to locate them, the boats beat up and down the Channel across the wide mouth of St Austell Bay before being forced to accept the truth. The fish had gone.

Bringing both boats to Portgiskey that evening, Nathan was filled with gloom. The women in the fish-cellar were still noisily salting fish caught before the storm, but unless more were brought in before the end of the week the number of women would have to be reduced. The uncertainty of the remainder would cast a pall over Portgiskey.

Day and night the two Portgiskey drifters took it in turn to go to sea. Each time they returned with no more than a basket of fish to show for their efforts. Convinced the fish *must* be out there somewhere, Nathan took his boats farther and farther from Portgiskey. Still they returned empty. It was as though the fish had deserted the coasts of Cornwall for ever.

The situation rapidly became serious. Nathan had bought *Annie Jago* in anticipation of at least a normal fishing season. Now he had no fish, and an extra crew to pay.

Nathan brought *The Brave Amy H* home to Portgiskey after yet another fruitless search, to find the one-armed Calvin Dickin waiting for him on the quay. Skipper of *Annie Jago*, Dickin was a good fisherman but he was having no more success than Nathan.

'No luck?' The question was unnecessary. Calvin Dickin could see for himself the empty baskets piled high in the boat.

'If I didn't know better, I'd swear the storm scared every last fish from around the coast.'

Nathan looked tired, and Calvin Dickin knew that worry was beginning to take its toll on him.

'Things are going hard just now.'

'If they don't soon improve, I'm going to have to put one of the boats up for sale and take a loss on it.'

'So it's as bad as that?' Calvin Dickin began skilfully packing a pipe with his one hand and as dexterously brought it to life with the aid of a tinder-box. Tucking the box away inside a pouch suspended from a cord about his neck, Calvin Dickin removed the pipe from his mouth. Breathing smoke, he said quietly: 'I can offer you a way out of your troubles – if you're the man I believe you to be.'

Nathan looked at Calvin Dickin sharply. The one-armed man had worked for Ned Hoblyn as a full-time smuggler. 'You're suggesting I become a "night trader"?'

'There's harder ways of earning a living. Less certain ones, too.'

'The days of making easy money from smuggling are long gone, Calvin. There are too many men like Chief Revenue Officer Ezra Partridge around today.'

Calvin Dickin spat expertly over the edge of the quay into the water below. 'Ezra Partridge is blinded by your prize-fighting title. He'll not bother *you*. You've got the perfect smuggling arrangement here. Ned Hoblyn earned a good living for many years . . .'

Calvin Dickin looked about him quickly, to ensure he was not being overheard. 'I've been approached by a customer who wants brandy in larger quantities than most boats can carry. I also know a French captain who is sitting out there in the Channel at this very moment, hoping someone is coming to relieve him of a prime cargo. All I need is a boat, and space to store it for a night or two.'

'So you thought of me . . . and Portgiskey?'

'Would you rather I approached someone else? This is a chance for you to make money, Nathan. Perhaps your only chance. Not only that, if the Revenue men ever look like getting close to Portgiskey you've got room at Polrudden to hide cargoes from a whole fleet of night traders.'

Nathan wondered how Sir Lewis Hearle would feel if he knew Polrudden was being considered as a hiding-place for undutied goods. But Nathan took Calvin Dickin's proposal seriously. He did not *want* to use his two boats for smuggling, but if he did not earn some money very soon he would have no boats.

'Where is this French ship?'

'She'll come in to anchor off Deadman's Point to-night, and the next two nights.'

'All right, I'll do it. Get *The Brave Amy H* ready. She'll outsail anything we're likely to meet, if the need arises.'

Nathan glanced to where his crew were spreading the nets from *The Brave Amy H* on the quayside. Some were men he did not know well.

'I'll leave you to choose a crew – and choose carefully. Take no one you can't trust. I'm going to Polrudden now. I'll see you here at sunset.'

Nathan arrived at Polrudden to find that Elinor had prepared a surprise for him. A table was laid in her room and, carefully dressed to hide her pitifully wasted legs, Elinor sat in a chair, cushions piled about her to prevent her from falling. Her face was freshly powdered and her long black hair had been washed and brushed until it shone.

Nathan's astonishment at finding her out of bed delighted Elinor, but she was to surprise him even more. Holding out her hands for him to take, she squeezed his fingers and declared: 'Nathan, I am going to walk again.'

He looked at her in alarm, afraid that the strain of

leaving her bed had been too much. As gently as he could, he said: 'We'll talk about that when you're stronger. Both the physician and the surgeon said—'

'Damn the physician! And damn the surgeon, too!'

Elinor used the mode of speech that had disappeared with her accident. Nathan kissed her and hugged her to him happily. 'When you use that "Hearle" tone of voice to tell me you're going to walk I *have* to believe you. Why, the Lord himself would give way to such arrogance!'

The determined line of Elinor's chin softened and she smiled. 'Perhaps He already has.' Her excitement bubbled over again. 'I'm getting feeling back in my feet. I am quite certain of it. Watch my big toe. I'll make it move for you. No, the *right* foot. Hurry now, before I exhaust myself *talking* about it.'

Nathan removed her slipper carefully and looked at the thin, white foot. After a couple of minutes' silence during which Elinor watched his face eagerly, she exclaimed: 'There! Did you see it move then?'

'You could be right . . .' Nathan did his best to sound convincing.

'You *didn't* see anything.'

Nathan feared Elinor would burst into tears.

'I'm not saying it *didn't* move,' he lied. 'I think it *did*. But I don't want you building your hopes too high, that's all.'

To Nathan's great relief, her chin rose in an expression of renewed determination. 'It doesn't matter. I *know* my toe moved – and it's only a beginning.'

She smiled at him, and he saw that her disappointment had not entirely disappeared. 'One day I'm going to ride to Portgiskey to meet your boat when it comes in. I'll put on my best clothes and have every fisherman's wife in Pentuan hate me for my airs and graces.'

Nathan grinned. 'They can hate you as much as they like. The day you are well enough to sit a horse I won't care if you ride stark naked through Pentuan and Mevagissey. I'll cheer you every inch of the way.'

Elinor smiled with him. 'Such a ride has already been made, my love, by a certain Lady Godiva. But I promise I won't even think of such a thing until I've got rid of this.'

She patted her swollen belly, and the baby obligingly writhed beneath her hand.

'He has too much room to move about in there. A belly full of food will put a stop to his nonsense. We'll eat, then you can carry me to the window so I can watch the sunset while you read to me. After that you can take me to bed and hold me all night to keep my bad dreams away.'

Nathan remembered the plans he had agreed with Calvin Dickin for the night. 'I'm sorry, Elinor. I have to take the boat out again at sunset.'

Elinor's dismay almost persuaded Nathan to change his mind, but he desperately needed money. He could not pass up such an opportunity.

He kept silent when Elinor argued that, with no fish being caught, there was no need to put to sea. 'Even if they were, you employ enough men to take out the boats without you,' she added.

Nathan still said nothing, and Elinor studied his face as he began the meal brought in by a maid.

'This is not a fishing trip, is it? You are going smuggling.'

'We need money, Elinor. I must make it any way I can.'

Elinor was aware of Nathan's problems. She also knew that Polrudden was an additional burden he had taken on for her sake. Reaching across the table for his hand, she said: 'Please be careful, Nathan. It has taken me so long to realise that I need you.'

Later that evening, when Nathan had left the house, Elinor lay in her darkened room with the curtains drawn, gazing out at a full moon – a smuggler's moon. She was reluctant to sleep. Sleep brought too many nightmares. They were haunting her all too frequently lately, and every one had the same theme. The loss of Nathan.

There had been a time, even after her accident, when Elinor would have scorned a suggestion that she would one day become dependent upon a man – any man. That had now changed dramatically. For the first time in her life Elinor was in love, deeply in love. The knowledge that Nathan loved her, too, gave her great happiness. There was also a thrill in the thought that his baby lived inside her body. All she needed now was to regain the use of her limbs – and she *would* walk again. Determinedly, she gritted her teeth and *willed* life into her foot. The toe *had* moved. She was quite certain of it . . .

Nathan was watching the same moon with something less than enthusiasm. Ezra Partridge and his Revenue men could sit on the cliffs at Chapel Point, south of Mevagissey, and see everything that went on for miles around. With the aid of a good telescope they might read the name of every vessel in St Austell Bay.

Not until *The Brave Amy H* was more than a mile offshore, hidden from Chapel Point by the tall and dangerous rock island known as The Gwineas, did Nathan relax a little.

He kept *The Brave Amy H* close to The Gwineas until past midnight, and the crew talked in whispers as they strained their eyes across the calm, moonlit waters. Suddenly, Calvin Dickin gripped Nathan's arm excitedly. 'Look! There on the starboard bow. It's a ship.'

'About time, too. I'll signal to him. The sooner we load up and get on our way the better I'll like it.'

The speaker, one of the seamen, was about to strike life from a tinder-box when Nathan knocked it from his hands.

'That's no French ship. It's far too small. Quick, start shooting the nets.'

Startled into action, the fishermen began throwing nets over the bow while Nathan raised the drift-sail. As the nets splashed into the water, a line of cork floats began to drift away from *The Brave Amy H*.

The other vessel turned towards them, and the fishermen could now see it was a large cutter, propelled through the water by an impressive number of oars.

As it drew closer, pitch torches spluttered into life and Nathan called: 'Stay clear, whoever you are. We've a line of nets upwind.'

The cutter changed direction and came alongside *The Brave Amy H*.

'Is that you, Mr Jago?' It was Chief Revenue Officer Ezra Partridge. He sounded both disappointed and suspicious. 'I haven't seen you fishing over this way before.'

'With the luck I've been having lately I need to fish new waters.'

'Ay, I've heard things aren't going too well for you.'

The Revenue cutter was close enough now for Ezra Partridge to peer inside *The Brave Amy H* as the flickering pitch torches held aloft by his men threw dancing shadows into the recesses of the fishing-boat.

When he had satisfied himself that *The Brave Amy H* carried no contraband, Ezra Partridge ordered his men to extinguish their torches – a feat that was accomplished by plunging them in the sea.

'I wish you luck, Mr Jago.'

'May none come your way – or the way of any King's man,' muttered Calvin Dickin under his breath.

When the Revenue cutter was well out of hearing, Calvin Dickin asked Nathan: 'What do we do now? We'd be foolish to wait for the Frenchie with Ezra Partridge out of harbour.'

'We'll put in an honest night's fishing,' declared Nathan. 'If we haul in the nets and go home now, Ezra Partridge will know exactly what we are doing out here. If we continue to fish, he'll never be certain.'

It was a profitable decision. When the nets were hauled inboard at dawn, they held a good catch. Nathan went home to Elinor a happier man.

3

The weather was more to Nathan's liking when he made his next attempt to rendezvous with the French smuggler, on the following night. The sky had been overcast since early afternoon. By the time night fell the moon was sandwiched between thick banks of dull, grey cloud, emerging for only brief periods.

Nathan took both boats out with him on this occasion, but left *Annie Jago* fishing off The Gwineas, where the previous night's catch had been made. He then took *The Brave Amy H* out into the deeper waters of the English Channel, hoping to meet the French ship on her way in.

Everything worked out exactly to plan. Three miles from The Gwineas, Nathan saw the brief winking of a candle-lantern and a reply flickered out from the fishing-boat. Fifteen minutes later *The Brave Amy H* bumped gently against the side of a dark-sailed

French schooner of rakish lines, with three open gunports on either side.

Nathan went on board the French vessel with Calvin Dickin and was introduced to the French captain. The introductions over, Calvin Dickin pointed to the captain's leg which ended at the knee and was supplanted by a wooden stump. 'Between us, Cap'n Pierre and I just about make one good man.'

To the Frenchman, Calvin Dickin said: 'This is my captain – Captain Nathan. He was at Trafalgar, too.'

'Ah! So we are both sailors of war, eh? Which ship, monsieur – at Trafalgar?'

'*Victory*.'

'Indeed! Admiral Nelson's own ship. I am honoured. I was the First Lieutenant in *Bucentaure*.'

'Then you, too, served with a great gentleman,' acknowledged Nathan.

Bucentaure had been the flagship of the gallant French Admiral, Pierre Charles Jean de Villeneuve. During the battle of Trafalgar, *Bucentaure* lost all her masts, and the Admiral had been forced to strike his colours. The following year, after Villeneuve had been repatriated to France, he was threatened with a court-martial for his conduct in the fierce battle. Broken-hearted at the unjust criticism levelled at him by his countrymen, Villeneuve committed suicide by thrusting a long pin through his heart.

Memories of their respective admirals kept the hands of the two men clasped in a mutual regard that only men who had fought each other well and honourably would understand. It mattered not that it was *Victory*'s guns that had shot off Captain Pierre's leg and killed a hundred of his shipmates.

For twenty minutes Nathan remained with the French captain, drinking his best brandy and exchanging reminiscences of the great sea-battle. During this time the crew of the French smuggler were passing cask after cask of brandy down to *The Brave Amy H.*

Their business completed, the two vessels parted company. Agreement had been reached for a fortnightly rendezvous, and the crew of *The Brave Amy H* were happy at the success of their midnight business. The mood held until the moon appeared momentarily, and Calvin Dickin called that he could see a vessel making for them in the darkness.

The moon disappeared before Nathan could glimpse the other boat, but Calvin Dickin was certain it had been the Mevagissey Revenue cutter.

'What will we do?' One of the men asked the question apprehensively. It was his first smuggling trip.

'Crowd on every inch of sail,' was Nathan's crisp reply. 'With this breeze behind us there's nothing afloat in these waters can catch us. It could have been especially ordered for *The Brave Amy H.*'

'If Ezra Partridge saw us, he'll head straight for Portgiskey and be there before we've unloaded half our cargo.' The comment came from Calvin Dickin.

'Possibly,' agreed Nathan. 'But we won't be unloading at Portgiskey. Do you know the old quarry dug into the cliff below Polrudden?'

Calvin Dickin did. Stone from the quarry had been used to build many churches and fine mansions in the area. Idle for many years, the quarry was now overgrown by bushes and coarse grass. A boat could drive to within feet of the workings at high tide. It would make an ideal hiding-place for contraband.

By the time the moon appeared once more there was no sign of the Revenue cutter, but, as Calvin had predicted, Ezra Partridge *had* thought he recognised *The Brave Amy H* and he was on his way to Portgiskey.

The Chief Revenue Officer and his crew waited impatiently at Portgiskey before accepting that their quarry was not on the way home to the little cove. Putting to sea again, they searched until the grey light of dawn showed *The Brave Amy H* hauling nets off The Gwineas, not half a mile from *Annie Jago*.

Unwilling to accept that he might have been mistaken, Ezra Partridge went alongside Nathan's boat and carried out a thorough search. All he found on board was a good haul of pilchards that increased with every net that came inboard. To all intents, it seemed the two Portgiskey vessels had been fishing all night.

For Nathan, it was a highly successful night's work. The fish had returned, and he had a substantial amount of contraband stored in the disused quarry.

Nathan's career as a smuggler suffered a setback the following evening. When he set off from Polrudden, Calvin Dickin was waiting for him outside the manor entrance. One look at Dickin's face was enough to tell Nathan that the one-armed fisherman was the bearer of bad news.

'It's our buyer . . . for the brandy,' said Dickin in answer to Nathan's question. 'He's gone. Fled the country one step ahead of the Revenue men. If the reports are to be believed, he's taken a ship for America.'

'Can you find another buyer?'

Calvin Dickin shrugged miserably. 'Probably, but it

will take time – and Cap'n Pierre will be back again in two weeks. We've got too much money tied up in that brandy to allow it to lie in the quarry doing nothing. What's to be done, Nathan?'

The two men walked on in silence for some time. Then Nathan stopped and snapped his fingers in sudden jubilation. 'What price were we expecting for our brandy?'

'At least twenty-four shillings a gallon.'

'What if I told you I could get *forty-eight*?'

'That's madness! Good brandy is hard enough to come by these days, but no one is fool enough to pay that much for it.'

'You're wrong, Calvin – and our fool is none other than Ezra Partridge himself.'

Quickly, Nathan told the fisherman of the offer the Chief Revenue Officer had made to him some months before, to pay double the market price for any contraband he found and handed in.

'How many kegs do we have?'

'Fifty.'

Calvin Dickin tried to work out their worth at the Chief Revenue Officer's unrealistic price. He gave up, leaving Nathan to arrive at a figure.

'I make that close to nine hundred pounds. It will leave us with a handsome profit.'

Calvin Dickin nodded his head in stunned agreement. They stood to make a colossal sum.

That night the crew of *The Brave Amy H* reloaded the kegs from the Polrudden quarry and sank them close to Deadman's Point, with a small marker buoy to mark their position.

The next morning Nathan went to Mevagissey and

sought out Ezra Partridge. The Revenue man was delighted with Nathan's information about a cache of spirits discovered off Deadman's Point. He confirmed that the reward would be twice the value of the contraband goods and insisted that Nathan immediately show him where the cache was located.

Declaring that he could not risk being seen putting to sea with a Revenue man, Nathan met the Chief Revenue Officer outside the fishing village and together they walked the four miles to Deadman's Point.

After showing the marker buoy to the eager Revenue officer, Nathan walked him the four miles back again. By the time he reached Mevagissey, Ezra Partridge was perspiring like a blown horse and staggering from sheer exhaustion. But he would not rest. Before Nathan was halfway home to Polrudden, Ezra Partridge had set off for Deadman's Point in his Revenue cutter.

A fortnight later, Nathan made another 'find', this time of sixty kegs. He had decided upon the greater number because Ezra Partridge had paid out on only forty-five kegs on the previous occasion, assuring Nathan with a great show of sincerity that only forty-five had been found.

When the second consignment of brandy was taken to the Revenue Collector's warehouse in Fowey, the Area Revenue Officer complained that if many more such rewards were paid out the Revenue Service would have to accept a cut in salary to afford them.

By now word of what was happening had leaked out, in spite of all Nathan's precautions. The fishing community of Mevagissey cast glances of contemptuous amusement at Ezra Partridge whenever he passed by.

Nathan realised that such a lucrative source of income would not continue for much longer, and when he next made a rendezvous with the French smuggler he took a hundred kegs of brandy from the French captain, and a large quantity of tobacco, sealed inside a barrel.

On this occasion Nathan carried the whole cargo direct to Mevagissey and handed it over to the Chief Revenue Officer in the presence of his officers. Ezra Partridge had been greedier than before with the last haul, rewarding Nathan for only fifty kegs instead of sixty.

As Nathan had expected, Ezra Partridge's gratitude on this occasion was tempered with more than a little suspicion. It was heightened by the presence of a number of grinning fishermen, standing on the quayside nearby.

Nathan was grudgingly paid his reward, but Ezra Partridge informed him that if he 'found' any more contraband the circumstances surrounding the discovery would be thoroughly investigated.

The story of how the Chief Revenue Officer had been tricked spread through Mevagissey like a thatch fire. Women grinned saucily as he passed, and cheeky children called after him to ask if he had 'found' any brandy lately. Soon Ezra Partridge had only to see two men in conversation to imagine they were talking about him. He decided to do something quickly to put a stop to the malicious amusement.

* * *

By October the pilchard shoals had still not moved inshore, although Nathan was catching them regularly further out to sea. Along the coast more fishermen were following his example. Those who could afford to do so were selling their seines and buying larger boats in order to take up drifting.

One evening, Nathan's two boats put to sea as usual, shortly before dusk. Calvin Dickin took *Annie Jago* to the area beyond The Gwineas, while Nathan and *The Brave Amy H* worked the deeper waters out beyond the Fowey Estuary.

At dawn Nathan and his men hauled in their nets and returned to Portgiskey laden with a very satisfactory catch. *Annie Jago* was nowhere in sight, neither was she alongside the quay in Portgiskey, but there was nothing in this to alarm Nathan. *Annie Jago* might have drifted a mile or two out to sea and, consequently, was taking longer to return to the cove.

However, when *Annie Jago* had not returned by the time *The Brave Amy H* was unloaded, Nathan sent a young member of his crew to the top of the cliffs above Portgiskey, to see if he could sight the missing fishing-boat.

When the young fisherman returned to say he could see nothing of *Annie Jago* anywhere, Nathan felt uneasy for the first time. Calvin Dickin would have begun hauling in his nets at dawn. Whether or not he had made a good catch, he should have been back by now.

There was no need for Nathan to communicate his concern to his crew. They, too, knew that Calvin Dickin and *Annie Jago* should have returned before this. They quickly made *The Brave Amy H* ready for sea again. Minutes later the fishing-boat was heading for The Gwineas.

Nathan scoured the sea for miles about The Gwineas without making a sighting of *Annie Jago*. In spite of this, he still expected to see his second fishing-boat unloading at the quay when he returned to Portgiskey. After all, it had been a calm night, and Calvin Dickin and his crew were all experienced fishermen.

Annie Jago was not at Portgiskey, but when *The Brave Amy H* berthed all the women from the fish-cellar crowded round to tell Nathan what they had learned. At first, Nathan received an excited and garbled account of what had happened, but gradually a story began to emerge. Calvin Dickin and his crew had been arrested on a smuggling charge. Ezra Partridge had taken them to Fowey during the night. Once ashore, the fishermen had been taken to the lock-up in St Austell, while *Annie Jago* remained at Fowey, confiscated by the port Revenue authorities.

Nathan was dumbfounded. Captain Pierre and his ship were not due for another week. Calvin Dickin must have been engaged in an illicit deal about which he had told Nathan nothing.

Cursing Calvin Dickin for putting *Annie Jago* at risk without telling him, Nathan hurried home to Polrudden. After telling Elinor what had taken place, he saddled a horse and set off for St Austell. He was not a good rider, disliking riding, but he was tired and there were many miles to be covered before dusk.

Nathan went first to St Austell. There he found his despondent crew crowded inside the tiny lock-up. Allowed to speak to them, Nathan demanded to know what Calvin Dickin had been doing to get himself and his crew arrested.

'That's the damnable part of this whole business, Nathan. We weren't doing anything except fishing.'

'But the gaoler has just told me that four kegs of brandy were found in *Annie Jago* by Ezra Partridge.'

'It's easy enough to find something when you've put it there yourself,' said Calvin Dickin bitterly. About him, the nodding heads of the other fishermen provided confirmation that the one-armed man spoke the truth.

'Ezra Partridge deliberately put kegs of brandy in *Annie Jago* and then arrested you for smuggling them? Did any one of you see him do this?'

This time the heads were equally unanimous that no one had seen anything.

'Ezra Partridge brought the Revenue cutter alongside before dawn,' explained Calvin Dickin. 'He stayed with us until we began hauling in the nets. That's when he found the brandy, sitting among the fish-baskets. They were there, right enough, but they certainly *weren't* on board when we shot the nets last night.'

'But why *Annie Jago*? Had he put the kegs in *The Brave Amy H* when I was on board it would have made some sense. But to do this to you . . .'

In truth, Nathan was shocked that Ezra Partridge should have fabricated evidence in such a manner. Smuggler and Revenue man bitterly opposed each other's stand on the issue of smuggling. They fought on many occasions, and blood was frequently spilled. But there had always been a grudging mutual respect between the two sides. Lying in order to secure a conviction was a despicable act that would be neither forgiven nor forgotten among the fishing communities of Cornwall. Ezra Partridge had broken the unwritten laws of the game, and all Revenue men would be subjected to some rough handling as a result.

'I fancy Ezra Partridge was disappointed that it wasn't *The Brave Amy H* he'd found,' said Calvin Dickin. 'But no doubt he thought we'd do instead.'

The one-armed fisherman tried to appear nonchalant, but he failed miserably. 'It's me for transportation this time, Nathan. I was convicted of smuggling ten years ago and spent six months on the treadmill for my sins. The judge won't treat me so leniently this time.'

'That was ten years ago. You've lost an arm since then. He'll treat you as a new offender. He's bound to.'

Nathan's optimism was ill-founded. Calvin Dickin's fellow-fishermen were each sentenced to six months on Bodmin Gaol's treadmill, with instructions to use the time so employed to contemplate the error of their ways.

Calvin Dickin was labelled a 'hardened criminal' and sent to the Assizes for sentence. Two weeks later, heavily chained and fettered, the one-armed fisherman left Bodmin Gaol to begin a seven-year sentence in the penal colony of Botany Bay. The judge felt obliged to explain the 'leniency' of his sentence. He had, he said, taken into account Calvin Dickin's disability. Having only one arm, the prisoner would have to work harder than his fellow-convicts at the business of survival. Such moments of 'benevolence' earned for the judges of His insane Majesty King George's courts the right to have the word 'merciful' included in their funeral eulogies.

Nathan had already learned that the law was less benevolent in the matter of his boat, *Annie Jago*. The magistrates ordered its confiscation after Ezra Partridge had insinuated that Nathan was fully aware the boat was being used for the purpose of smuggling. Nathan was at the hearing and leaped to his feet demanding that the Chief Revenue Officer substantiate his accusation, only to be ordered from the courtroom until the trial was over.

It was a disastrous setback for Nathan. He now had little hope of surviving the stormy days of winter, when fishing would be impossible for weeks at a time. His only hope lay in stepping up his smuggling activities. But he would first need to do something about Ezra Partridge.

Nathan's opportunity came in early November, at a time when his own participation in fishing was restricted to daylight hours. Elinor was suffering great discomfort, and there were signs that the baby might come earlier than expected.

Nevertheless, when the time came round for another rendezvous with Captain Pierre and his smuggling vessel, Nathan knew he must take a chance and sail *The Brave Amy H* to meet him. He would have liked to leave the task to Ahab Arthur, his new lieutenant; but, although the old fisherman had willingly taken on the night-fishing trips, he had none of Calvin Dickin's knowledge of smuggling.

Elinor worked herself into a state of near-hysteria

about Nathan's night trip. She still suffered the recurring dream about reaching out and not being able to touch him, and many nights she sobbed herself back to sleep in his arms.

Had there been any other way, Nathan would have forgone the night rendezvous, but with only one drifter working the bills were piling up.

Nathan set off from Polrudden, leaving Elinor weeping behind him in the care of a maid who would stay with her throughout the night. It was a crisp November evening. A new, early-rising moon hung over the sea, and there was just a hint of early frost in the air.

The crew of *The Brave Amy H* stowed a minimum of fishing-gear on board. They needed to satisfy the passing glance of a Revenue man with a telescope, looking down at them from a clifftop hideout above Portgiskey Cove.

The Revenue man had been seen on the cliff-top for some nights now. It made the fishermen nervous. The fate of Calvin Dickin and the crew of *Annie Jago* was still fresh in their minds. They left Portgiskey that night wondering whether they would be returning to their families in the morning.

Nathan headed *The Brave Amy H* towards The Gwineas. Hidden from the view of much of the mainland, it had become customary to wait here for full darkness before heading out to meet the Frenchman.

Their course took them past the entrance to Mevagissey harbour and they were not far past it when Ahab Arthur said quietly to Nathan: 'There's a boat coming out of Mevagissey. It looks mighty like Ezra Partridge and his Revenue cutter to me.'

Quiet though Ahab Arthur's words were, they were overheard by two of the fishermen, and they waited anxiously for Nathan to give the order to return to Portgiskey. There were not enough nets on board to remain at sea and make a pretence of fishing. But, instead of giving the order, Nathan nodded his head in acknowledgement of Ahab Arthur's words and said brusquely: 'I saw the boat. It *is* the Revenue cutter.'

'It's turning our way,' exclaimed one of the anxious fishermen. 'We'd best be putting back to Portgiskey. The amount of fishing-gear we've got on board won't fool anybody. Not Ezra Partridge . . . nor a magistrate.'

'Ezra Partridge won't be coming close enough to see what fishing-gear we're carrying,' said Nathan. '*The Brave Amy H* can outsail any cutter built for a Revenue man. But I don't think we'll need to put it to the test just yet. My guess is that someone's been talking. Probably a relative of one of our men in Bodmin Gaol. It means Ezra Partridge will know there's a rendezvous due. But he won't make a move until he's certain we've got dutiable goods on board – not a second time.'

'You'll not go ahead with the rendezvous? Not now you know Ezra Partridge is out?'

'There are Revenue boats out all along the Channel coast tonight. Do you think they'll keep every night trader from putting to sea?' Nathan scoffed at the man's alarm. 'You don't need to worry yourself. I'm no more anxious to see the inside of Bodmin Gaol than you.'

The suggestion that they should return to Portgiskey was not repeated, but the fishermen were unhappy. The men spoke to each other in low tones, and more than one baleful glance was cast in Nathan's direction.

The Brave Amy H remained close to The Gwineas until an hour after dusk. Then Nathan set sail and headed out into the Channel. The moment they got underway the crew of the fishing-boat were hanging over the side, peering anxiously to see whether the Revenue cutter was following.

It was. Only minutes after they had left the shelter of the rocky island, one of the fishermen called to Nathan in a hoarse whisper: 'They've spotted us. Ezra Partridge is following!'

'Good.' Nathan's reaction was not what the crew were expecting, but he gave them no opportunity to debate the matter. 'Instead of wasting all your time trying to fall overboard, clear some space for the brandy. I'm taking a double cargo on board tonight. Keep a look out for the Revenue cutter. I want to be sure we don't lose it. Jump to it, now.'

Nathan's tone allowed for no argument. Although deeply concerned about their fate, the fishermen did as they were told. For half an hour Nathan maintained the same course and speed. Suddenly he said: 'Right, now we'll crowd on every bit of sail we have. You've wanted to lose Ezra Partridge; this is your chance.'

The men did not need to be told twice. The farther they were from Partridge, the happier they would all be. Soon *The Brave Amy H* was surging through the water, hitting every low wave with a thump that jarred the bones of each man on board. Now that Nathan had drawn the Revenue cutter out to sea, the fishermen believed he would put about and return to Portgiskey, outstripping Ezra Partridge.

Much to their surprise, Nathan maintained the same course. Surprise turned to alarm when a light winked at them from the darkness and Nathan told Ahab Arthur to signal a reply.

Even Ahab Arthur could not believe that Nathan was going to keep the rendezvous and take brandy on board with a Revenue cutter in such close attendance.

'How far behind do you think Ezra Partridge will be when we reach the Frenchman?' Nathan asked his lieutenant.

'Not much more than twenty minutes.'

'That's all the time I need. Hurry and reply to that signal. I want Cap'n Pierre to heave-to out there. The farther he is from the coast, the better it will be for the plan I have in mind.'

Fifteen minutes later *The Brave Amy H* bumped alongside the French vessel and Nathan scrambled on board the larger craft. To the men in the fishing-boat he called: 'Get the brandy on board as though the Devil were nipping at your heels – and if you're not quick enough he might be.'

Captain Pierre was on deck and greeted Nathan warmly. 'I have been worried about you, my friend. I thought something might have happened to you. But where is Calvin? He is not with you tonight?'

'Calvin's been taken by Revenue men and sentenced to transportation. The same Revenue men followed me out here tonight. We have less than twenty minutes. Tell your men to place as much brandy in my boat as she'll carry. In the meantime

I want to talk to you – in your cabin. There's something I want you to do for me – and for Calvin.'

The French smugglers and Nathan's crew had *The Brave Amy H* fully laden in fifteen minutes. As Nathan swung over the side of the French vessel, he called back: 'Goodbye, Cap'n Pierre. I won't see you for a month. You'd best avoid this part of the coast until then. Good hunting!'

Once in *The Brave Amy H*, Nathan gave the order to cast off. But then, instead of turning back to Portgiskey, he headed out into the Channel. Behind them the voice of the French captain called soft orders to his crew and Nathan heard the once-familiar rumble of cannon being run out through open ports.

On board the Revenue cutter, Ezra Partridge peered out across the choppy waters, the darkness of the night relieved by the soft light from the stars and a thin crescent moon.

He cursed his tired crew for not keeping up with *The Brave Amy H* when Nathan had crowded on sail. The Revenue cutter was large, and with her twelve oarsmen was capable of a fair speed, but oars were no match for a sailing vessel in a good breeze.

'There's something up ahead.' The coxswain of the boat pointed to where a tell-tale bow wave reflected pale green luminescence against the darker green of the sea.

'It must be Jago on his way back.'

'No, it's too large.' Suddenly the coxswain put the tiller hard over. 'It's a ship – probably the French smuggler!' To the listening oarsmen he called: 'Pull hard. The Frenchman's trying to run us down!'

But Captain Pierre had no wish to sink the Revenue cutter. Nathan's plan was far more subtle than sending a boat and her crew to the bottom of the English Channel. At the last minute the French sailing ship heeled over and turned into the wind.

'Ahoy there! Come alongside. I wish you to come on board my ship.'

The English words, spoken with a strong French accent, rang over the water.

'Pull away from here quickly,' Ezra Partridge hissed at his men.

The cutter turned, but she had gained no more than ten lengths when a cannon was fired from one of the open ports along the French ship's side. So close was it that the flash and roar threw the oarsmen into utter confusion as acrid smoke drifted about the cutter.

'The next shot will sink you. You will do well to obey my order.'

Captain Pierre's amused voice called across the water once more. He had seen the effect of his first shot.

When the cutter bumped against the side of the French ship, Captain Pierre ordered her occupants to come on board.

The huge bulk of Ezra Partridge had to be helped up the side of the French smuggling-ship. When he eventually stood on the deck, trembling with a mixture of fear and anger, he blustered: 'You'll regret this. I am a Chief Revenue Officer in His Majesty's service . . .'

'And your country is at war with mine, monsieur. Very soon you will be a prisoner of France. Until then I am happy to offer you my hospitality.'

*   *   *

The disappearance of Mevagissey's Chief Revenue Officer, together with his cutter and crew, created a furore. Revenue boats from Falmouth and Fowey, and a frigate from the naval dockyard at Plymouth scoured the seas about the coast for three days. On shore the militia was called out to search the rocky coastline for signs of wreckage.

Nothing was discovered, of course; and when word was received six weeks later that the Chief Revenue Officer and his crew were prisoners the mystery deepened. The information said that they and their coastguard cutter, still flying the British flag, had been captured by the French navy in the Gironde, the forty-five-mile-long river estuary that brought the world to Bordeaux, and provided access to the vineyards of Cognac. The Gironde was more than three hundred miles from Mevagissey!

4

Nathan kept *The Brave Amy H* heading away from the shore until he heard the report of the French smuggler's cannon in the distance. Not until then did he turn his boat round and head for the disused quarry below Polrudden Manor.

The nervous fishermen wanted to know what had happened to Ezra Partridge and his crew, believing that the French vessel had sunk the cutter. Nathan would say only that the less the fishermen knew about the incident, the better it would be for everyone. They would learn the truth in due course, but the thought that the Chief Revenue Officer might have been killed would keep them tight-lipped when the Revenue authorities began their enquiries. Telling them now would give them a story that not one of the fishermen was capable of keeping to himself.

When the brandy was safely hidden, Nathan took *The Brave Amy H* back to Portgiskey. It was still a couple of hours short of dawn, but there was no sense in going out again. Ezra Partridge was out of the way and there was no one to question the reason they had returned without fish.

It had been a night to remember. Nathan looked forward to sharing the story of the night's adventure with Elinor. Letting himself quietly into the east wing of Polrudden Manor, he made his way quietly upstairs.

He frowned when he saw no light shining beneath the door of Elinor's room. The maid staying with Elinor must have fallen asleep and allowed the candle to burn out. Opening the bedroom door quietly, Nathan immediately became aware of a low moaning, as though someone was in deep pain.

Thoroughly alarmed, he made his way to the bed. He was still a pace away from it when his foot touched something on the floor. Bending down he ran his hands over the cold form of Elinor, lying on her side.

Elinor's stomach muscles contracted beneath his hand, and she moaned again. Hurriedly, Nathan lifted her bodily from the floor and placed her on the bed. Then he searched at the bedside for a light. He found the burned-out stub of a candle in the holder with another lying on the table beside it. Striking a light, Nathan set the candle in a small spot of hot candle-wax on the cabinet top before turning his full attention to Elinor.

She opened her eyes as he leaned over her, but she was delirious with pain and showed no recognition. She was also in labour – but there was no sign of the maid who should have been in the room.

'Elinor, can you hear me?'

Nathan bent low over his wife, but she gave him no sign that she could hear him.

Distracted with concern for Elinor, Nathan was momentarily at a loss. There were no servants in this wing of the house. Those who did not live out were accommodated in the attic of the main house. Then suddenly Nathan knew where he would find the maid who should have been with Elinor. She and a new stable-boy had been seen walking hand in hand in recent weeks, and the stable-boy lived in a partitioned-off corner of the hay-loft.

Nathan was halfway to the door when Elinor moaned again. Hurrying back to the bed, he was beside her when she opened her eyes; but this time there was recognition in them.

'Nathan . . .' Her hand reached up to him, and he took it in his. 'Where have you been? The baby is coming . . .'

A pain racked her body, and she gripped Nathan's hand hard. When the pain eased she gasped: 'I was frightened. It was dark . . . I remembered my dream.' Her hand gripped his once again, and he knew it was almost time for the baby to come. 'I tried to reach for a new candle. I must have leaned too far. I fell . . .'

'It's all over now. I'm back. Everything will be all right. Lie still and conserve your strength.'

Nathan thought of Elinor lying alone in the darkness of the room, aware that the baby was coming and having no one at hand. Beneath his breath he cursed the maid who had left her alone. But he needed help.

'Elinor, I must leave you for a few minutes and send someone for the physician.'

The fear returned to Elinor's eyes, but she was able

to control it better with Nathan standing beside her. She nodded. 'Be quick, Nathan. The baby won't be long now.'

The pain returned yet again, and Nathan waited it out before he slipped from the room.

Dawn was showing in the east as he ran to the barn. A lamp was burning low in the stable-boy's makeshift room – and the maid was coming down the ladder from the hay-loft. Hair tangled and dishevelled, it was clear she had dressed in a great hurry.

When she saw Nathan, the maid's eyes opened wide in fear – and with just cause. He had actually drawn back his hand to strike her when reason returned to him.

'Wake someone to help you, then go to Mistress Elinor's room – *now!*'

He shouted the word, and the maid fled from the barn. A tousled head appeared at the hay-loft trap-door, and Nathan called: 'Get down here quickly. Take a horse and ride to Mevagissey to fetch the physician. Tell him it's Mrs Jago. The baby's almost here.'

Nathan returned to Elinor's bedroom. A few minutes later an elderly woman, Sarah Davey, a part-time kitchen help and wife of the Polrudden gardener, hurried to the room. Dropping Nathan the briefest of curtsies, she came to the bedside and looked down at Elinor with motherly concern.

'Hello, me dear. 'Tis your time, then. Never you mind, my love. We'll soon have you to rights.'

'Where's the maid? I told her to come here.' Nathan's anger with the girl flared once more.

'And I told her to go to the kitchen to light fires, boil

water and get things cleaned up down there.' Sarah Davey sniffed expressively. 'She's no good for anything else. She's shaking like a leaf – and with good reason, I've no doubt. Now, I'll thank you to find something to do elsewhere for a while, Mr Jago. There's chores to be done here that no husband should see. There's no need for you to fret. She's in good hands. I've had nine children of my own and delivered fifteen grand-children without losing a single one. Off you go, now.'

Nathan looked uncertainly at Elinor, and she attempted a tired smile. 'Don't go too far. I want to see your face when I give you a son.'

Leaving the room, Nathan felt guiltily relieved at handing responsibility for Elinor to someone else.

He had washed, shaved and changed by the time the physician arrived, full of brisk *bonhomie*. 'Don't you worry yourself,' he told Nathan, patting his shoulder reassuringly. 'Go away and find a close friend. Share a celebratory bottle of something with him. Childbirth is no time for a man to be alone with his thoughts.'

Dr Ellerman Scott was less cheerful when he came to find Nathan four hours later. 'I've sent your groom to fetch Surgeon Isaacs from Bodmin. He has had much experience in cases of childbirth. The fact is, when a baby is due to be born, the bones of the pelvic region become more pliable, to allow the baby to pass through. This has not happened to your wife. It probably has something to do with her accident. The bones are rigid and we're getting no help from her muscles, I'm afraid.'

'What does it mean? What's going to happen?'

'I don't know.' Dr Ellerman Scott spoke with alarming candour. 'I wish I did. However, Surgeon Isaacs will know what to do. He is excellent in cases like this. I knew his name long before I ever came to Cornwall.'

'This Surgeon Isaacs is not likely to be here for hours. Can I go in to see Elinor?'

'Yes, but don't tire her with too much talking. We need to conserve her strength as much as we can.'

When Nathan entered the bedroom he was shocked by Elinor's appearance. Tired and drawn, she looked at him with eyes that expressed weary resignation. Nathan was alarmed; Elinor was a fighter. She had always been a fighter. That she should give up now was quite unthinkable.

Taking her hand in both his, he forced a smile for her. 'It won't be much longer now. The physician has sent for a childbirth expert, one who's famous all over the country. When he gets here the baby won't dare cause any more trouble.'

Elinor licked dry lips before speaking. 'Your son is making his mark on the world early. You'll be proud of him, Nathan. I know you will.'

A labour pain gripped Elinor, and Nathan saw how very tired she was. The spasm drained all life from her for many minutes.

'We're *both* going to be proud of our son,' declared Nathan in desperation. 'I . . . I think you should rest now. I won't be far away . . .'

'No! Don't leave me.' Elinor's fingers tightened on his.

'All right, I'll stay. But only if you promise to sleep.' Elinor nodded wearily and closed her eyes.

The next few hours were long ones for Nathan. Twice when he thought Elinor was sleeping he tried to leave the bedroom. Each time she opened her eyes, and he had to remain.

Late in the afternoon, Dr Ellerman Scott came to the room. He had been in and out for most of the day, and Nathan took little notice until the doctor placed a hand on his shoulder. When Nathan looked up, the physician motioned for him to accompany him from the room.

Elinor's eyes were closed, and on this occasion Nathan was able to take his hand from hers without disturbing her. Outside the room, Dr Ellerman Scott's manner was grave as he told Nathan that the messenger had returned from Bodmin – alone.

'Surgeon Isaacs is in London. He will not be returning for two weeks. We can't wait even two days, Mr Jago. I very much doubt whether we can really afford to wait for another two *hours*.'

'I don't understand. Wait for what? If you can hurry the birth along, why haven't you done so before?'

'I can't hurry the birth along any faster than the Lord himself is doing. The baby wants to come. It's trying hard to be born; but you can't push a cow through a sheep's gate, Mr Jago – and that's the fact of it. The baby is large, and the gap in your wife's pelvis is small. What's more, because of her accident she has no pushing power.'

'Then what do you mean by saying you'll have to act before another two hours have passed? What more can you do?'

The physician looked ill-at-ease. 'If we allow things to go on as they are, both mother and child will die. If I operate to remove the baby, there is a chance that I can save the child.'

'And Elinor . . . my wife?'

The doctor's silence provided its own dramatic answer, and Nathan recoiled in horror. 'You're suggesting I allow you to . . . to *kill* Elinor in order to save the baby? Is this what you're saying?'

'I am merely suggesting a way to save one life. The alternative is to lose two. I realise it is not an easy decision to make . . .'

'Decision? Decision, you say? You're asking my permission to murder my wife! *That's* a decision?'

Dr Ellerman Scott's shrug was a combination of embarrassment and resignation. 'I understand how you must feel, Mr Jago. It is a decision I trust I will never be called upon to make for myself; but for some families an heir is all-important. When there is a title in the family – a baronetcy, for instance, or even higher rank now Sir Lewis has government office . . .'

'Damn Sir Lewis, and his titles.' Nathan paced up and down the corridor outside Elinor's bedroom, his thoughts in a turmoil. 'I'll send a messenger on the next mail coach to this Surgeon Isaacs. I'll ask him to return immediately.'

Dr Ellerman Scott shook his head sadly. 'If I thought it would save your wife's life, I would ride to London myself. Sadly, things have already gone too far. Go in and remain with her, Mr Jago. I'll be there soon. If you change your mind— No, of course you won't.'

Without another word, Nathan went in to Elinor. He thought she was asleep, but as he sat down wearily by her side she opened her eyes.

'I am a worry to you, my husband.'

Her voice was so weak he had to put his head close to hers to catch the words.

'Of course you're a worry to me. Childbirth is a worrying time. Why, I can remember how Tom Quicke was when my sister Nell was having their child . . .'

Nathan was trying desperately to give Elinor hope and strength, but she shook her head and relieved him of the need to lie.

'This is not the same. I know. It doesn't matter for me . . . not now. But your son . . . I want him to live, Nathan. For you. For me, too . . .'

Elinor's eyes closed and her mouth dropped open as another pain came. When it passed away she lay on the bed breathing shallowly. Nathan thought she had sunk into unconsciousness, but then her lips moved again.

'Tell the physician . . . to do what must be done. Save the baby. Please, save the baby.'

'No, Elinor. No!'

Nathan's cry brought Dr Ellerman Scott to the bedside.

'What is it? What happened?'

Nathan shook his head, unable to speak, and the physician took Elinor's wrist.

'She's very, very weak.'

Nathan knew the physician was waiting to hear him say he had changed his mind, but he shook his head. Nathan was aware that nothing short of a miracle could save Elinor now, but he could not bring himself to give the doctor the role of executioner.

Seated by Elinor's bedside, Nathan *willed* her to live.

For a few unbelievable hours soon after dusk it appeared that a miracle might occur. At least, Elinor grew no weaker. Then, when the moon rose faint beyond the curtains, her strength ebbed away and she slipped into unconsciousness.

Shortly before midnight, Elinor opened her eyes and looked directly at Nathan. Her lips moved, and he put his ear to her mouth. He could never be certain, but afterwards he swore that the two words she spoke were 'Our son'. Immediately afterwards her eyes closed as though she would sleep – but Nathan knew she was dead.

'Doctor . . . Doctor!'

The shout came from the gardener's wife, who had not left the room all day. It brought Dr Ellerman Scott bounding up the stairs, two at a time. He looked down at Elinor for a few moments, then slid a small hand-mirror from his waistcoat pocket and held it in front of her mouth. Removing it, he turned it towards Nathan. There was not even a hint of the mist of life upon the glass.

Next the physician picked up a small instrument shaped like a funnel from the table beside the bed. Putting the small end to his ear, he drew back the sheets and placed the other end upon Elinor's swollen belly.

His eyes opened wide in disbelief and he beckoned to Nathan. 'Quickly, listen to this.'

Nathan put his ear to the funnel-like instrument, and heard something that sounded like the heartbeat a man hears in his ears when he wakes in fright in the darkness of night.

'It lives! We might save it yet. For God's sake, man. Let me try!'

Fighting back his tears, Nathan nodded his head blindly; then nodded again so there could be no mistake. Rising to his feet, he stumbled from the bedroom. He was unaware that, even as he was leaving the room, Dr Ellerman Scott had made his first incision in Elinor's body.

Such was the speed of the Mevagissey surgeon that Nathan was still at the head of the stairs, composing himself before breaking the news to the servants, when he heard the baby's first cry.

He turned in disbelief – and met Dr Ellerman Scott in the doorway of Elinor's room. Jubilantly, the physician placed a bloody bundle of humanity into Nathan's arms. Half-choked with unaccustomed emotion, he said: 'Here . . . It's your wife's last gift to you. The son you damned near refused.'

Looking down at the screwed-up face, fighting to close its tiny lips about a bloody fist, Nathan sank to his knees in the doorway and wept. He wept for his dead wife, and for the future of the child in his arms, and his tears washed Elinor's blood from the tiny, naked body of their son.

It was 6 November 1811. A day Nathan would never forget.

5

News of the birth and death at Polrudden was carried to the village by the servants within minutes. Half an hour later Josiah Jago was knocking at the door of the manor, hat in hand. Roused from his bed, he had hurried to offer comfort to his son. At his own request, the preacher was taken to see Elinor. Kneeling by the bedside, he said a prayer for her.

Rising to his feet again, he looked down at the bloodless face. 'I find it sad to be gazing in death at the face of a daughter-in-law I never knew in life.'

'I was only just beginning to know her myself,' replied Nathan, his voice unsteady.

'Then your loss will be all the sadder for that,' said Josiah Jago. Taking Nathan's arm, he led him from the room and together they walked to the nursery where Nathan's son lay sleeping, wrapped in a white sheet. A maid, her eyes red from weeping, sat in the room nearby.

Preacher Jago reached out a gentle hand and caressed the baby's cheek with a finger, stopping when the child stirred.

'If only your mother could have seen him,' the preacher said gruffly. 'It's been a sad year for us, Nathan. Will you be burying Elinor in our little burial-ground?'

'No. I'll not let Elinor's death be the cause of a quarrel between Sir Lewis Hearle and myself. She'll be buried with the other Hearles, in St Austell.'

Josiah Jago nodded his understanding. 'She'll have our prayers from Pentuan. No doubt you'll be bringing my grandson to live in the village?'

Nathan shook his head vigorously. 'This is where he was born. This is where he'll stay. Polrudden is his heritage. I'll give Sir Lewis no excuse to keep it from him.'

'But who will feed the poor mite?'

'I've sent for our Nell. Baby Tom gets all the sustenance he needs from that new cow of theirs, and he's already taking solid food. Nell was complaining the other day that her own milk is showing no sign of drying up. The doctor says there's another woman heavy with milk in Mevagissey, but she's just lost her own baby through some mystery illness. I'd rather not put Elinor's – *my* son at risk.'

'Our Nell will welcome the opportunity to pay you back for giving her and Tom their farm. That was a very generous and brotherly thing to do, Nathan. It makes me very proud of you whenever I think about it.'

Looking down at the sleeping child, Preacher Josiah Jago swallowed the lump that rose in his throat. 'You deserve better fortune. Life hasn't always been kind to you.' Shaking his head, Josiah Jago added: 'The Lord works in mysterious ways, Nathan. My Annie, and now your Elinor . . .'

Abruptly, the preacher turned away and walked from the room. At the doorway, he paused. 'You are right not to allow your wife's death to cause argument. Lay her to rest where her family have always been buried. But there will be a service for her in the church you built for me. I would like to see you there, my son.'

Sir Lewis Hearle reached Polrudden Manor four days after Elinor's death. Nathan met him on the east-wing staircase. The baronet looked very tired after his journey from London and he wasted no time on either pleasantries or commiserations.

'Where is she?'

'In her own room. I'll—'

Sir Lewis Hearle brushed Nathan to one side and hurried up the stairs.

Nathan was in the baby's room when the baronet left the bedside of his dead daughter and came looking for his grandson. Nell was in the room feeding the baby, but when Sir Lewis entered the room she pulled her teat from the baby's mouth and slid her breast inside the bodice of her dress. Robbed of its feast so unexpectedly, the baby continued sucking, not understanding what was happening, or why.

It was impossible to know what Sir Lewis Hearle was thinking as he stared at his hungry grandson. When he did speak it was to jab a forefinger in Nell's direction.

'Who is this?'

'My sister Nell. Tom Quicke's wife.'

'Wife to the man who had a chapel built upon his land? I'll have no *Methodist* wet-nurse in this house.'

Nathan's eyes glittered angrily. The baronet had made no mention of Elinor's death.

'Wrap the baby up well and take him to Venn Farm, Nell. I'll come later.'

Nathan's words took Sir Lewis Hearle by surprise. 'What? Where do you think you're taking him?'

'My son is going where he'll be warm and well fed. Where he'll continue the progress he's made since he was born.'

'It's a pity you didn't show such concern for your offspring before. You came within an ace of having him branded a bastard, and crippled his mother . . . my own daughter . . .' Sir Lewis Hearle's hate and grief spilled out in the open, but with a visible effort he regained control of himself again. 'Find another woman for him.'

'The only other woman available is in Mevagissey. There's an epidemic of stomach sickness there – her own child died from it. I'll take my son from this house rather than expose him to such a risk.'

Sir Lewis fought a fierce mental battle between his hatred of anything that smacked of Wesleyism, and common sense.

'All right, the wet-nurse can stay. Just keep her out of my sight.'

The baronet took another look at the baby. 'Have you given the brat a name?'

'Yes. Beville Hearle Jago. It's the name Elinor and I decided upon many months ago.'

'H'm!' Sir Lewis directed another expressionless look at the baby, then left the room without another word.

'We've a bad-tempered old boar at Venn with better manners.' The vehemence of Nell Quicke's words startled the baby, and he began to cry in a high, thin voice. Nell quickly silenced him by putting him to her breast once more.

'Sir Lewis finds it difficult to show any emotion except anger,' explained Nathan. 'But he'll cause no trouble for you. He couldn't take his eyes from his grandson.'

Nathan rested his hand lightly on his son's head. 'Beville Hearle Jago has just won the first and most important round of the fight for his heritage.'

Baby Beville might have won over his maternal grandfather, but Nathan was no more acceptable to the baronet than before. Sir Lewis even suggested that Nathan should stay away from Elinor's funeral, hinting that his attendance would be an embarrassment.

Nathan countered by pointing out that *he* could insist on the funeral taking place at Pentuan's chapel, where Sir Lewis would be received with courteous respect, and where there would be no such embarrassment.

Nathan's presence did cause a stir at the funeral service held in St Austell parish church, but the mourners were sharply divided in their attitude towards him. Most ignored Nathan, offering their condolences only to Sir Lewis Hearle. Others went out of their way to express sympathy to Nathan. The latter were, for the most part, people who had known Elinor personally, and had heard the story of her first meeting with Nathan. Marrying the prize-fighting champion of the world was in keeping with Elinor's wild nature and undisciplined upbringing. These mourners believed Sir Lewis Hearle's daughter might just as readily have eloped with a stable-lad or a wandering gipsy.

After the day of the funeral, the two men saw little of each other. Nathan had expected Sir Lewis to tell him to leave Polrudden Manor. The order did not come, but Nathan knew his presence was tolerated only for the sake of Beville and because of the bills Nathan paid for the upkeep of the house.

The baronet never came near the baby when Nathan was at home, but Nell and the maids said Sir Lewis spent much time with his grandson. He had even been heard talking to him in a language strangely akin to 'baby talk'.

Any thoughts that Sir Lewis Hearle might be softening his attitude to the world in general were quickly dispelled on his return to London in mid-December.

The baronet arrived to find that anti-Methodist feeling had now reached an unexpectedly high level among those in the capital who were responsible for running the affairs of the country.

In Nottingham and other centres throughout the newly industrialised Midlands, workers were clamouring for higher wages to meet the soaring cost of buying food to feed their large and undernourished families. They were also calling for the removal of the machines that were taking the places of men in the factories. When their demands were not met, angry voices were raised against the employers and a number of the more impetuous workers called for universal action.

Older men were reluctant to take the law into their own hands against the men who paid their wages, however meagre the sum might be, but hot-headed younger men were not. A number of weaving-frames were deliberately smashed by the discontented labourers, and the Midlands drew in its breath and awaited retribution.

None came. Mill-owners were playing the affair down, hoping the very act of destruction was enough to shock the workforce into the realisation of their responsibilities. Unfortunately, the millowners had miscalculated the mood of the workers. The more militant weavers took the lack of action to be a sign of weakness. The discontented workers set out on an orgy of wrecking. In two months more than nine hundred frames were smashed. The militia were mustered and troops despatched hurriedly to the area. Hundreds of workmen were arrested and some were killed or wounded.

The actions of the weavers brought rumblings of sympathetic discontent from the colliers, who had themselves been seeking higher wages for many years. For a while it seemed that the workers of the Midlands would unite in common cause.

Because of this hitherto unknown display of co-ordination between all sections of the working population, the authorities, in desperation, sought a scapegoat for the troubles they were experiencing.

Quick to seize upon such an opportunity, Church leaders pointed to the Methodist Church, whose rate of recruitment appeared to be advancing in proportion to the growth of industrial unrest. Here, they said, was a dissenting church whose name invoked discipline and 'method', who drew its recruits from those very people who were terrorising the countryside, destroying machinery and the means by which law-abiding people earned a living.

These critics ignored the fact that Methodist preachers

were standing up and pleading with their congregations *not* to join the lawless bands who roamed the countryside smashing machinery, and that unrepentant agitators suffered dismissal from the Methodist Society.

Spencer Perceval saw no reason to question the accusations made by his leading churchmen. Methodism would serve well as a scapegoat for the shortcomings of his own administration.

When three rioters were arrested after a number of weaving machines were smashed in Manchester, the Home Office reported that the three had demanded the services of a Methodist minister. It was conveniently ignored that their request was refused because all three men had been expelled from the Methodist Society some months before.

In Parliament, Sir Lewis Hearle listened with great satisfaction as the anti-Methodist storm gathered momentum. Talkers began to compare Methodists with the Puritans of the seventeenth century – agitators who had overthrown the King and plunged the country into bloody civil war.

In the House of Lords ecclesiastical dignitaries angrily decried their nonconformist brethren. The Bishop of Gloucester called them 'malignant' and 'subtle adversaries', accusing them of concerting measures to undermine the country's civil and religious constitution.

Once again Methodist preachers were arrested on the most ridiculous charges, and convicted on the flimsiest of evidence. In Cornwall the magistrates were wary of arresting Preacher Josiah Jago yet again. Instead, Sir Lewis Hearle found another way to hit hard at the Cornish Methodists. He had Uriah Kemp taken into custody.

Immensely popular with the Methodist community, the American had fallen in love with Cornwall. He tramped the length and breadth of the county, drawing huge crowds to his meetings. By ordering his arrest, Sir Lewis Hearle made a very shrewd move. Government officials were becoming increasingly aware that war with America was inevitable. In accusing Kemp of stirring up disaffection, Sir Lewis Hearle added further fuel to the rumour of Methodist disloyalty. One great advantage to the Government was that it was not even necessary to bring the American to trial in a court-room, where his oratory might prove an embarrassment. After a two-minute appearance in St Austell's magistrates' court, Uriah Kemp was ordered to be deported from the country. Immediately after the order had been made, the American preacher was bundled into a prison van to begin a long and uncomfortable journey to London.

But, as on so many previous occasions, the well-thought-out ministerial ploy foundered on human frailty. As the journey to London progressed, the distance between stops at the numerous inns along the way grew shorter. One week after setting out, the prison van stood outside a Wiltshire inn for three long hours. When the driver and guard finally lurched back to their vehicle, Uriah Kemp demanded to be taken inside to a privy.

After a drunken discussion about which of the two escorts should take their prisoner inside the inn, both men went inside with him. Whilst there, each in turn returned to the bar for yet another drink to see him along the road.

The inn was crowded, and both escorts had made

the acquaintance of a number of fellow-tipplers. When they finally staggered separately from the inn, each thought the other had locked the prisoner inside the van. Not until they arrived at Salisbury Town lock-up, where the prisoner was to spend the night, did they discover their drunken error.

The chief magistrate of the area was informed and immediately ordered out a troop of Dragoon Guards stationed in the town. The soldiers galloped back to the inn, but Uriah Kemp had disappeared.

A futile search was carried out among the lanes and highways for miles around, but no trace was found of the American preacher.

The escape was well publicised in newspapers throughout the country and provoked considerable admiration for Uriah Kemp's resourcefulness. War with America had still not been declared, and it was even hinted that *if* war came it would be the fault of the British navy. Stories were circulating of American ships stopped on the high seas and their crewmen ordered to prove American citizenship. Those who failed, for whatever reason, were accused of desertion from the British navy and impressed into service in His Majesty's men-of-war.

Sea-port towns and coastal villages of Great Britain had long and bitter experience of the activities of the naval press-gangs. Until war came and British lives were lost, there would be much sympathy for the American cause in Britain. Consequently, there was no pressure on the Methodists to return Uriah Kemp to the authorities and thus demonstrate their loyalty to the Crown.

6

In February 1812, seven months after the wedding of her daughter to Sammy Mizler, Peggy Hoblyn's finely poised mental balance dropped violently on the side of insanity. She murdered Lizzie Barron, her house-keeping cousin.

Had there been anyone at Portgiskey who cared sufficiently for the ageing fisherwoman, the grisly tragedy might have been averted. As it was, much of the story had to be pieced together by a coroner's court.

Lizzie Barron had been steadily increasing the pressure on her simple-minded cousin. She was far more interested in enjoying her own life than in caring for Peggy. When Lizzie went out for an evening with her friends, Peggy Hoblyn was locked in her own bedroom. Nathan remonstrated with the cousin on two occasions, but Lizzie merely bided her time, ensuring that Nathan was out of the way before she went out.

Peggy Hoblyn hated being locked away in such a manner. The women in the nearby fish-cellar would frequently hear her hammering on the door to be let out, when she felt she had been in the room for long enough.

The breaking-point came when Peggy's cousin went to St Austell market early one morning and stayed on to enjoy a drink with some friends. The women in the fish-cellar had heard Peggy banging on the door of the bedroom for most of the day, alternately demanding to be released and pleading for someone to come to her assistance. One of the fisherwomen *did* try to go to her, but the outside doors of the cottage were also locked. No one thought of contacting Nathan, who had been night-fishing and was sleeping at Polrudden.

By the time Nathan reached Portgiskey for his night's fishing, the women from the cellar had gone home and all was quiet inside the Hoblyn cottage. Nathan was a little later than usual and, after checking his boat, he put to sea without going to the cottage.

What happened that night would never be known. Peggy Hoblyn's cousin was known to have been drinking heavily before she left the St Austell inn to return to Portgiskey, and this was the last occasion on which she was seen alive.

The following morning, Nathan brought *The Brave Amy H* back to Portgiskey Cove to find the women from the fish-cellar crowded about the door of the cottage. When Nathan leaped to the quay, the women rushed to tell him what was happening.

'Something terrible's happened inside the cottage,' explained one of them. 'No doubt about it.' After telling Nathan of Peggy Hoblyn's cries the previous day, the woman added: 'I went to the cottage this morning to see if Peggy was all right – and she jumped out on me like some wild beast, screaming fit to frighten the Devil.'

All about Nathan the women were nodding their agreement, and Nathan's informant went on: 'I don't mind telling you, I feared for my life. There's no sign of that cousin of hers; but the door's unlocked, so she must have come home.'

'All right, come away from the door. I'll go inside and find out what's been going on.'

Pushing his way through the women who were reluctant to give up their individual vantage-points, Nathan reached the door. Once inside, he closed the door behind him, much to the chagrin of those waiting outside.

Nathan searched the downstairs rooms and ascertained no one was there before mounting the creaking stairs. He was about a third of the way up when Peggy Hoblyn appeared at the top and began screaming incoherently at him.

'It's all right, Mrs Hoblyn. It's me . . . Nathan Jago. I'm a friend of your Amy, remember?'

At first his words made no difference, but very gradually Peggy became calmer. The physical signs of her madness were clearly in evidence this morning. Wild-eyed and tangle-haired, she crouched with fingers extended like the claws of a defensive wild cat.

Talking all the while, Nathan gradually edged his way upstairs, pausing whenever Peggy appeared to be particularly agitated. When he was almost within touching distance of her, she retreated backwards inside the bedroom. Slowly and cautiously, Nathan followed.

He was inside the room before he saw Lizzie Barron. She lay sprawled untidily on the bedroom floor. It was clear to Nathan before he leaned over her that Lizzie was dead, and her face told its own story. Nathan had seen more than one unfortunate sailor hanged from the yardarm of a ship. The dead woman's face had the same purplish hue, her eyes starting from her head, an expression of terror glazed permanently upon them.

Nathan did not need to see the dark bruises on Lizzie Barron's neck to know she had been strangled.

On a table in the corner of the room was a pile of stale crusts, and an overturned water-jug lay beside a cracked and stained mug. The room stank of continuous occupation, and the stout bolt on the outside of the bedroom door completed the wordless story for Nathan. Peggy Hoblyn had been kept prisoner in this bedroom for long periods. Her gaoler had paid a grim price for the lack of concern for her deranged cousin.

There was no way in which the death could be kept a secret. A runner was sent to inform the St Austell coroner, while a couple of nervous fisherwomen cooked a meal for the insane murderess. Peggy Hoblyn was ravenously hungry, and the fear of the fisherwomen turned to pity as they watched her wolf down plate after plate of cooked fish. It was apparent that she had been kept hungry as well as a prisoner in her room.

The coroner arrived at Portgiskey accompanied by a magistrate and two constables, and Peggy Hoblyn was taken in custody to St Austell. Two days later, after the coroner had recorded a verdict of 'murder' on the dead woman, Peggy Hoblyn was brought before the magistrate. Nathan was present to hear her found not guilty of Lizzie Barron's murder by reason of her insanity and he visited her in the cells beneath the court. Then she was transferred to the old lunatic asylum in the nearby village of Lostwithiel.

Had Amy been at home, Peggy Hoblyn might have been discharged into the custody of her daughter, but Nathan had no London address for her and was unable to prevent Peggy from being sent to the asylum.

Two days later Nathan travelled to Lostwithiel to see how the Portgiskey woman was settling in at her new 'home'. He was deeply shocked by what he saw. The unfortunate woman was lodged in a large, stone-walled room that was reminiscent of a medieval dungeon. She shared this accommodation with a number of other inmates, all with a history of violence. Each occupant had a stinking straw pallet for a bed, a canvas bag in which to keep her meagre possessions, and two wooden buckets, one to hold water, the other slops. Each woman wore an iron belt about her waist from which a chain led to a stout ring set in the wall behind her pallet. The chains were positioned to give each woman a degree of free movement, whilst keeping her at least an arm's length from her neighbour.

The smell in this part of the asylum was appalling, and twice one of the chained women rushed at Nathan in a vain attempt to claw his face, screaming abuse when the chain brought her to a halt.

Peggy Hoblyn would not speak to him and started nervously at each sudden movement made by her fellow-inmates. There was just cause for such nervousness. The seven women chained in the room had been responsible for thirteen deaths. One woman had killed her husband, mother and two children.

These details were given to Nathan when he gave the Superintendent of the asylum money with which to buy Amy's mother a few luxuries. Nathan was aware that most of the money would go straight into the Superintendent's own pocket, but the knowledge that someone cared for Peggy Hoblyn would at least ensure that she received her full dues. Many others in the asylum were less fortunate.

When the heavy, iron-studded doors slammed shut behind him, Nathan breathed unfouled air deep into his lungs and looked back at the dirty, grey stone asylum building. He knew he had to get word of Peggy Hoblyn's plight to Amy.

It was a quiet time of the year at Venn Farm. Nathan had little difficulty in persuading his sister to come to Polrudden to look after Beville while Nathan was in London finding Amy. Beville Jago was now three months old and Nell's own son six months older, and Nell enjoyed caring for both children together.

It was eighteen months since Nathan had last seen London. In that short time the great, greedy city had gobbled up vast tracts of the surrounding countryside. From the coach Nathan was astonished to see that houses now reached almost to Kensington and Paddington villages. But his business did not lie here, among the houses being built by merchants and

traders. He was heading for the narrow streets of
London's 'East End'. Here were tens of thousands
of dingy houses. They owed their origins to medieval
peasants who built their hovels against the stout walls
of the Tower, in the vain hope that its garrison would
afford them protection.

Since those earlier years, this fringe of London had
developed a unique character of its own. It was a
maze of alleyways and crooked streets, the dark
windows of its houses patched with rags and scraps
of stained paper. In the shadow of the houses, shoe-
less, undernourished children played in stinking
pools, surrounded by piles of rotting rubbish. The
residents here were a breed of Londoner noted for
their guile and sharp wit, with a slang language that
had no meaning for anyone who lived outside the
area. In addition, the 'East End' Londoner possessed a
will to survive unmatched by any of his countrymen.

Sammy Mizler had been born here. In common
with the vast majority of his fellow 'East Enders',
he was truly happy living nowhere else. It was here
that Nathan would find Amy.

Nathan entered this cockney kingdom on foot. No
hackney-carriage driver would risk his purse, or his
horse and vehicle, in the lawless streets and alleyways
beyond the ancient east wall of England's capital.

Nathan visited two inns he had once frequented
with Sammy Mizler, only to learn that the landlords
had changed. His questions brought only hostile
glances from both owners and customers alike.

He was more fortunate in the third tavern only
because a customer recognised him. But the presence
of the prize-fighting champion caused such a commo-

tion that it was some time before he was able to put his question.

'Sammy Mizler?' The landlord worked a finger in his ear as he nodded slowly. 'Yus, I knows him. Leastways, I know *of* 'im. Good little fighter in his day, 'e was. Come up in the world since then, I do 'ear. Some of the boys 'ave see 'im up west, running wiv the Duke of Clarence's crowd and spending 'is young wife's money.'

'Do you know where his wife is?' asked Nathan eagerly.

The landlord shook his head. 'No, but Charlie Harrup might.' Raising his voice, he called across the crowded tap-room. 'Charlie? You know where Nathan Jago can find Sammy Mizler's missus?'

Charlie Harrup turned a pock-marked face towards the speaker and wiped a watery eye with the back of a dirty hand.

'Dunno for sure.' Charlie Harrup sniffed, wiped his hand with a greasy sleeve, then with a hopeful grin held up an empty pewter pot. 'Perhaps anuvver drop o' 'Ollands might 'elp me mem'ry.'

The landlord looked enquiringly at Nathan. After a moment's hesitation, Nathan nodded. He watched as the mug of gin passed from hand to hand until it reached the widely grinning Charlie Harrup.

Taking a long swig, the cockney pulled a face, then smacked his lips noisily. 'Ah! That's better. Wonderful wot a drink does for a geezer's memory. Sammy Mizler's missus . . . Nah, is she a dark-'aired little piece? Got bags of go in 'er?'

Nathan smiled at the description. 'That's her. You know where she's living?'

Much to Nathan's annoyance, Charlie Harrup shook his head. 'Nah, dunno that . . . But I've seen 'er a few times in 'Aggerston market. You go there and ask Tillie Carver. She runs the fish-stall. Tillie's Cornish 'erself. She'll be able to tell yer.'

Leaving the landlord with a shilling to keep Charlie Harrup in cheap gin for the remainder of the afternoon, Nathan set off for Haggerston market.

Half an hour later he was knocking on the door of a poky little house, built in the space between a tallow works and a brewer's stable.

Nathan waited with a sense of apprehensive excitement for the door to open. The Cornish stallholder, rendered garrulous by the appearance of a fellow-Cornishman, had told the same story as had the tavernkeeper. Sammy Mizler was not likely to be at home, preferring the company of his London friends to that of his bride of only seven months.

Then the door opened – and Amy stood before him. Her face registered a mixture of joy and disbelief. Then she was in his arms, hugging him.

'Nathan! Is it really you? What are you doing here? Why haven't you written?'

Suddenly, Amy held him off, her face registering alarm. 'Is something wrong? Yes, I can see by your face it is. It's Ma, isn't it? Is she . . . dead?'

As she spoke, Nathan was looking more closely at her. This was not the carefree, healthy girl he had known in Cornwall. Amy was thinner, pinch-faced and pale. Dreadfully pale.

'No, Amy, she's not dead. But . . . can we talk about it inside?' Nathan had fought and trained in this area. Ostlers from the brewery stables had recognised him and were crowding from their building on to the street.

Amy drew him quickly inside the house. When the door closed behind them, Nathan told Amy details of the tragedy that had occurred at Portgiskey.

Amy was shocked, horrified and deeply distressed. 'Poor Ma . . . Oh, poor Ma! I should never have left her on her own. I should have realised she wouldn't be able to cope without me to look after her. Where is she now, Nathan?'

'The lunatic asylum in Lostwithiel. I went to see her there. It . . . it's not a good place to be, Amy. But they won't allow *me* to take her away.'

'Then *I* must go to her. When is the next mail coach?'

'Tomorrow morning at eight o'clock from the Bell inn at St Paul's.'

'I'll need to leave early. It's two miles to St Paul's. But how long has she been as bad as this? Why didn't you write and tell me?'

'I had no address for you. I've spent most of today making enquiries. It was Tillie Carver who finally told me where you and Sammy lived.'

'But my letters . . . didn't you get them?'

'You disappeared from my life when I waved good-bye to you and Sammy on the London-bound coach from St Austell. There has been no word from you since.'

'I wrote *three* letters . . .' Amy closed her eyes for some moments, as though she were in pain. 'Sammy . . . It *has* to be Sammy. I gave the letters to him to send off for me.'

'Where is he? What time will he be home?'

'I don't know. It's been three days since I last saw him. He . . . he doesn't come home very often.' She finished lamely, as though the words constituted an explanation. 'But you must be famished. There's plenty of time before I need to pack for the journey. I'll give you some food.'

Nathan followed Amy to the kitchen, and as she busied herself preparing a meal for him he sat at the table asking endless questions about her life in London. It was a form of self-defence. He had no wish to answer any of Amy's questions about the happenings in Cornwall.

He learned that Sammy had been a warm and attentive husband for only a very short time before he gravitated to the growing circle of followers about the Duke of Clarence. The Duke's brother, George, had recently been appointed Regent, to rule in the place of their insane father, King George III. With the advent of the Regency, the Duke of Clarence had advanced a number of rungs up the ladder of nineteenth-century society. He was now the brother of the man who effectively ruled the country and no longer a rather happy-go-lucky younger royal son.

Nathan also learned that Sammy Mizler had founded a club in Shepherd's Market, under the sponsorship of the Duke of Clarence. The object of the club was to advance the cause of prize-fighting. Here Sammy encouraged promising young pugilists and taught the art of 'fisticuffs' to blue-blooded gentlemen of the 'Fancy'.

While Sammy was enjoying the company of his aristocratic friends, Amy kept herself occupied helping the local Methodist Society to feed near-starving children in the worst slums of nearby Hoxton. Many were the sons and daughters of soldiers serving in the ranks of Wellington's victorious army. In varying stages of malnutrition, they suffered the ills and diseases that attacked many children who lived in the overcrowded slums of the largest city in the world. For some, the only way of life they knew was picking over the accumulated filth in narrow streets as foul-smelling as the sluggish, contaminated waters of the River Thames.

Then Amy put the first of the questions Nathan had been dreading.

'We've done nothing but talk of me since you arrived. What's been happening at Portgiskey? Is Calvin still with you?'

'No. He was transported – for smuggling.' As Amy temporarily abandoned her cooking, Nathan told her of his second boat and the events surrounding Calvin Dickin's arrest and sentence.

'So Portgiskey is once more a haven for smugglers,' commented Amy quietly. 'It's a foolish way of life, Nathan. My pa got away with it, and so did many other men of his time, but times are changing. There are far more Revenue men now. How long do you think it will be before you are arrested, too?'

When Nathan did not reply, Amy asked: 'Does Elinor . . . your wife, know what you are doing?'

At last the name of Elinor had entered the conversation. It hurt, as Nathan had known it would. He had realised he would have to talk about Elinor, but he found it necessary to compose himself before replying.

'Elinor's dead. She died in childbirth.'

Amy had been watching Nathan closely and had anticipated his reply. Tears filled her eyes, and now it was her turn to struggle for the words she wanted to say.

'Oh, Nathan, I'm *so* sorry. I know how much she meant to you. What . . . what happened to the baby?'

Nathan's taut expression softened immediately. 'Beville? He's a grand boy. Nell is at Polrudden looking after him while I'm away.'

Tears were still lurking in Amy's eyes when she asked: 'Beville? Does the name have anything to do with my brother?'

'Yes.'

'Thank you, Nathan. I'm so glad your son lived. If only . . .'

The hoarse-voiced Amy never completed the sentence. Clouds of dark smoke rose from the fish cooking in the frying-pan on the fire behind her. Snatching up the pan, Amy hurried it to the back door. As the door opened, Nathan caught a glimpse of a tiny, flagstoned yard behind the house. It was dark and damp, tall buildings on either side blocking out the sun. At Portgiskey, the Hoblyns had enjoyed a large, shrub-filled garden, with the sea and distant cliffs on one side, and a green, steep valley extending behind the house to woodland at the top of a hill.

When Amy returned, Nathan had opened the kitchen window, allowing the smoke to billow out.

'I'm sorry, Nathan,' Amy said despondently. 'I so rarely have an opportunity to cook for anyone. Then, when a chance arises, I make a mess of everything.'

She looked so crestfallen that Nathan said: 'Never mind about cooking a meal. I'll take you out to eat. I remember one or two good taverns from my prize-fighting days.'

Amy's face lit up instantly. 'I would like that. I haven't been out very often since Sammy and I came to London.' She gave Nathan a doleful half-smile. 'It's strange, isn't it, to feel lonely surrounded by thousands of people? Yet I'm lonelier here than ever I was at Portgiskey.'

Amy gave a rueful shrug. 'But my troubles are nothing when compared with yours. I'll go and fetch a shawl.'

The tavern Nathan chose was no more than half a mile from Amy's little house and they walked there arm in arm. It was a cold, raw London evening, but the tavern was warm and cheerful. The landlord had once been a prize-fighting champion himself and he greeted Nathan effusively. When Nathan introduced Amy as the wife of Sammy Mizler, only the very best would do for the tavern's two guests.

Shifting the tables about, some already occupied by early diners, the landlord secured Amy and Nathan a place beside the cheerful fire. At the same time, he confided to Amy: 'Your husband was the first man ever to beat me in the prize-ring. Nathan here is a good champion, I'm not denying that. But that fight 'twixt me and Sammy was one of the best ever seen in London. Sixty-four rounds, with not a man willing to risk his money on which of us would win. Then Sammy brings up a punch that felt as though it had travelled all the way from Billingsgate – and gaining speed every inch of the way.'

The cheerful landlord rubbed his jaw in rueful memory. 'They told me I was out cold for an hour and a half. I was in no state to argue for days afterwards.'

Winking at Amy, the landlord added: 'Taught me the most important lesson of my life, did Sammy. Until that fight, I thought I was unbeatable. But while I was nursing my jaw I got to thinking. What Sammy Mizler had done, another fighter might do, too. I started choosing my fights a bit more carefully, and putting away the money I earned. The result was that when I was beaten again – by Nathan this time – I had enough money put by to buy this tavern. Now I can entertain those friends who helped me along the way. Now, what's your pleasure? Tonight, everything is on the house – and I'll take it as an insult if you don't order the very best.'

For almost three hours, Nathan and Amy were able to push to the back of their minds all the problems that awaited them in Cornwall, and to enjoy the conviviality of the tavern, its landlord and customers. It was Amy's first opportunity to observe at first hand the all-embracing warmth of the cockney out to enjoy himself. Tapping her foot in time to the fiddler, or clapping her hands in time to the bawdy singing, Amy became more like the young girl Nathan had known in Cornwall.

Regretfully, when the party was still in full swing, Nathan decided to bring the evening to a close. Amy would have things to do to prepare for her trip to Cornwall in the morning. Nathan himself had to get back to his room at the Bell inn, from whence the mail coach would leave. Before then he wanted to go to the boxing club in Shepherd's Market, to tell Sammy Mizler of his wife's impending departure for Cornwall.

Outside the tavern, Amy's hand found Nathan's for a moment. 'Thank you, Nathan. This was the nicest evening I've spent since leaving Portgiskey.'

'I find that very sad, Amy. I felt sure you and Sammy would have a good life here together.'

'So did I.' She turned her face towards him as they walked along. 'But you mustn't blame everything on Sammy. When we first came here I missed Cornwall so much I cried myself to sleep most nights. I couldn't have been much fun to live with. In fact, had my letters reached you, and you replied, I would probably have packed up and come home. It's not really surprising that Sammy began to find things to do that would take him out of the house.'

'There are many places he could have taken you,' said Nathan. 'The tavern where we've spent this evening, for instance.'

They walked together in silence until they turned a corner and came within sight of the little house that was Amy's London home.

'There's a light showing. Sammy must be home.'

Nathan was unable to tell from the tone of Amy's voice whether she was pleased or apprehensive. Her steps quickened and she hurried Nathan to the door. Pushing it open, she called: 'Sammy? Sammy, look who's here.'

Sammy Mizler appeared at the door of an upstairs room, the sleeves of an expensive, lace-trimmed shirt flapping loose. When he first saw Nathan, Sammy's face lit up with uninhibited delight, but as he took the first step down the stairs the pleasure was chased away by a frown.

'Where have *you* been,' he growled at Amy. 'I've been home for almost two hours.'

'You've *not* been home for three days,' corrected Amy. She gave Nathan an embarrassed look before returning her attention to her husband. 'Nathan has come from Cornwall to tell me Ma's in serious trouble. I'll need to go home to her for a while.'

Sammy had reached the bottom of the stairs. Adjusting the lace cuffs of the shirt he wore, he looked at Nathan almost casually and, without proffering his hand, passed on to the tiny parlour.

'When did you reach London?'

'This morning. I spent half the day asking for you. It seems most of the landlords we once knew have moved on. Your address was eventually given to me by the Cornish fish-seller in Haggerston market.'

Sammy Mizler eyed Nathan for a few minutes. When he finally accepted that Nathan was telling the truth, Sammy relaxed. His suspicions could hardly have been clearer had he spoken them. Sammy had believed that his old friend had been staying at the house for a day or two.

'There should have been no need for Nathan to seek us over half of London,' said Amy to her husband. 'I've written three letters since we came here. You took them to a post office for me, Sammy. What happened to them?'

Sammy shrugged. 'Who knows? The mail has never been reliable since all the best men went off to war. Probably some drunken mail-coach guard lost them along the way.'

Amy opened her mouth to pursue the matter, but Sammy had turned back to Nathan. 'I'm going out for a drink and something to eat. You'll come with me?'

'I'll need to get back to the Bell inn, at St Paul's. I'm catching the morning mail coach back to Cornwall.'

'Leaving London so soon? Well, if you must, I suppose there's nothing I can do about it. But you'll stay here tonight. We've a spare room, and you and I have a lot to talk about. I want to tell you about my club. I've got some fine fighters training there. Abraham Dellow is one of them. Remember him – the negro slave you fought in Bristol? He's good, Nathan. You'd be hard put to beat him now. He's the Regent's favourite. I spoke to the Regent only the other day and he said to me—'

'Sammy . . . Sammy!' Amy had been vainly attempting to gain her husband's attention while he was talking. When he turned to look at her, she said: 'Can you talk about nothing but prize-fighting? I'm leaving London in the morning, too. Ma needs me.'

Sammy Mizler's suspicions returned. 'What's wrong with her? Is she dying or something?'

'She's been committed to a lunatic asylum. Chained to a wall there like an animal. She'll not survive long if I don't get her out quickly.'

Amy did not tell Sammy the full story, and Nathan did not feel like amplifying her brief outline of the situation. Instead, he said: 'Why don't you come with us, Sammy? There are many old friends who will be happy to see you again. Not as many as there were, but enough to give you a real Cornish welcome.'

'I've got too much to do. The Duke of Clarence has

plans . . . But come out with me. I'll tell you about them over a drink.'

At the doorway, Nathan cast an apologetic look back at Amy and saw her standing forlornly in the centre of the room. He wished he could have invited her, too, but Sammy had joined the ranks of those husbands who did not take their wives out with them. Nathan also suspected that the couple found much to quarrel about. He had no wish to add something more.

Sammy Mizler was full of the plans he and the Duke of Clarence had for Sammy's prize-fighting club, and the 'nobs' to whom Sammy was teaching the rudiments of a prize-fighter's art. On the infrequent occasions when Amy's name entered the conversation, Sammy dismissed her with a derisory remark that jarred upon Nathan. He also drank far more than in the past. It was not the comfortable evening between old friends that it might have been, and Nathan brought it to an end as quickly as he was able.

That night, Nathan lay in bed in the Mizlers' tiny house and could hear the sound of low voices in the adjacent bedroom. Later, in the early hours of the morning, when sleep still eluded him, Nathan was certain he could hear the sound of Amy weeping.

7

Sammy Mizler did not accompany his wife to the Bell inn, but put in a brief, bleary-eyed appearance at the top of the stairs as she and Nathan set off to begin the long journey to Cornwall. Sammy reminded Nathan that a payment was almost due in respect of the dissolved Portgiskey fishing partnership.

Shouldering the bundle that held all the possessions Amy was taking with her, Nathan set off from the tiny house in the dingy back street with a feeling of relief. Beside him, Amy walked along in silence. She had lightly powdered her face in an attempt to hide the puffiness about her eyes, but Nathan suspected she had shed a great many tears in the darkness of the bedroom she shared with her husband.

Misreading the cause of her unhappiness, Nathan said gently: 'Perhaps Sammy will change his mind and come to Portgiskey after all.'

'He'll have to if he wants to see me again,' declared

Amy fiercely. 'I'll not return to London. I hate everything about it, and what it's done to Sammy – to us.'

Nathan remembered the warning he had given to Sammy Mizler about marrying Amy and taking her from Cornwall. He said nothing. Sammy and Amy had learned the hard lesson for themselves. Amy belonged to London no more than did Sammy to Portgiskey.

They reached the Bell inn with only minutes to spare. Two other passengers were on board, both elderly gentlemen who spent the first hour of the journey complaining about the hardness of the coach seat. They consoled each other with copious draughts of brandy, contained in the numerous flasks both had concealed about their persons. The brandy proved an acceptable substitute for the upholsterer's failings. By the time the houses gave way to fields and trees, the two men were slumped against each other, snoring noisily.

The first glimpse of the countryside after so long in the crowded alleyways of London's East End put new life into Amy. She smiled for the first time that morning and nodded in the direction of their two fellow-passengers. 'Do you think all the grumbling was part of their regular travelling ritual, or merely an excuse to bring out their brandy-flasks? Look at them; they're sleeping like babies now.'

Nathan smiled. 'I think it must have been a bachelor who first thought of the expression, "sleeping like a baby". It certainly doesn't apply to Beville. He thinks the night hours are for playing.'

'You have him in the room with you?'

'When I'm not fishing. I see too little of him otherwise.'

'You're very proud of your son, Nathan.'

'Yes. He'll be a fine man one day.'

The offside coach wheels dropped into a deep pothole, but a quick glance at their fellow-passengers assured Amy that they were still sleeping. 'What will Beville think when he learns his father is a smuggler?'

'What did you think when you discovered *your* father was a smuggler? Beville will understand that I have no choice. It's the only way I can keep Polrudden.'

'Is Polrudden so important to you.'

'More than ever before. It's my son's heritage. I'll ensure that it isn't lost to him.'

The mail coach was fast. At dusk the following day it pulled on to the yard of the Talbot inn in Lostwithiel, to the accompaniment of long and noisy blasts on the coachman's horn. Here, Nathan and Amy climbed stiffly from the vehicle, grateful that the long journey was over. Their two sleeping companions had left the coach at Salisbury, but others had joined at stops along the route and the passengers squeezed uncomfortably close together inside the coach. A few rowdier travellers clung tenaciously to the outside, hurling abuse and an occasional bottle at the inhabitants of villages along the route.

The lunatic asylum looked even more forbidding in the half-light. Inside its dark and draughty corridors, candles flickered in smoke-darkened recesses. As they walked behind the Superintendent, shadows from the swinging lamp he carried reached into cells where the minds of chained and manacled lunatics gave them grotesque substance in the tragic world of the insane.

Walking beside Nathan, Amy jumped nervously at each new cackle of mad laughter that reached out at her.

'Take no notice,' said the Superintendent reassuringly, as he led the way along the dark, evil-smelling corridors. 'They're always worse at this time of day. If there's going to be trouble, this is when it usually happens. We say it's the Lord of Darkness taking the roll call of his servants – begging your pardon, Miss. Meaning no offence, of course. Here we are. This is the room where you'll find your mother. Stand back a minute now, while I check they're all fit to be seen.'

Taking a heavy ring of keys from his belt, the Superintendent selected one and inserted it in the lock. Turning the key, he swung the door open and held the lamp up to see inside the large room. Immediately, a screaming form hurtled from the darkness and flung itself upon the Superintendent, knocking him to the ground.

For a moment there was pandemonium in the corridor, the mad woman's screams taken up by her companions and the occupants of nearby cells. Then Nathan got a grip on the struggling woman and hauled her off the asylum official. He was amazed by the strength in her puny body, but he held her in the air as she kicked and fought in his arms.

Struggling to his feet, the Superintendent cursed the woman as she hurled vile abuse at him. He drew back his fist to strike her, then remembered that Nathan and Amy were visitors and not asylum staff. Picking up his lantern, he relit the extinguished candle from one burning in the corridor and held it to the woman's face.

'Oh, it's *you*. Bring her over here.' Reaching down a chain and manacles from the wall, the Superintendent fastened the woman's wrists and ankles swiftly, then linked a chain to them and secured it to a ring in the corridor wall.

'She's lost weight and slipped the band about her waist. It sometimes happens, especially with the women.'

'Is it *really* necessary to chain her like this?' Amy asked indignantly as the Superintendent bent the woman double and added another, smaller chain, linking her ankles to her wrists.

'Necessary?' echoed the Superintendent. 'I'll say it's necessary. This woman has already killed four people. She'll kill more given half a chance.'

'And she's been sharing a room with my ma?' Amy was horrified.

'Your mother is in here because she, too, killed someone,' retorted the Superintendent brutally. To Nathan he said: 'Keep the young woman here, sir. I'd like to look inside that cell before I allow you in.'

'But my ma . . . ?'

'Do as he says.' Nathan took a firm grip of Amy's arm.

The noise of the struggle had aroused the inmates of cells leading off the corridor in which they waited. The din was terrifying. Screams, shouts, curses and other sounds that Nathan found difficult to believe originated in human throats were hurled at them from all sides.

Then the Superintendent backed out of the cell, but as Amy started forward he slammed the door shut behind him.

His face pale in the lantern light, the Superintendent said to Nathan: 'That mad bitch has raised her score to six! There's two women in there strangled with their own chains. Two others badly hurt. I need to fetch a surgeon. I must ask you both to leave for now.'

'But what about my ma?' cried Amy. 'Is she all right?'

'Mrs Hoblyn is one of those who's been hurt,' replied the Superintendent. 'I can't tell how bad she is at this stage . . . She's unconscious.'

'Oh, my God! I want to see her. She's my mother . . .'

'I'm sorry – but the sooner I can bring a surgeon here the better it will be for her.'

'He's right.' Nathan put his arm about Amy, who was still inclined to protest, and led her away. Over his shoulder he called to the Superintendent: 'We'll be staying at the Talbot inn tonight. Should there be any cause for concern about her you'll let us know?'

The Superintendent nodded. Then, roaring at the shrieking inmates of his institution, he hurried past Amy and Nathan and unlocked the door for them.

At the Talbot inn, Nathan was able to book two rooms for himself and Amy. Then he called for a bottle of the landlord's best brandy and forced Amy to drink down a large tumblerful. The brief glimpse of the inside of the lunatic asylum had badly shaken her. Concern for her mother was now coupled with a renewed determination to have her released as soon as was possible.

Nathan talked to Amy for a long time that evening, and he insisted that she try to eat a meal. She was in no mood for eating but obligingly pushed the food about her plate with her knife, occasionally picking at it with a fork.

When the desultory meal was almost at an end, the door opened and a man stepped into the room, blowing warm air into cupped hands. Nathan recognised him as the magistrate who had dismissed the case against Preacher Josiah Jago eighteen months before. He must have been brought from St Austell to deal with the incident at the Lostwithiel lunatic asylum.

Telling Amy he would be back in a few minutes, Nathan went to the table close to the hearth, where the magistrate had settled himself. Amy saw a frown appear on the man's face as Nathan began talking. Then both men looked across the room towards her. The stranger nodded to Nathan and, after a few more words, rose to his feet and accompanied him to where Amy was sitting.

'Amy, this is Mr Carlyon. He's the magistrate who was asked to come here by the Superintendent.'

Amy started up, all her earlier fears returning. 'What's happening? Is Ma going to be all right?'

'Your mother was still alive when I left the lunatic asylum, only a few minutes ago.' The magistrate's expression became grim. 'In that she is fortunate. A third victim died shortly before my arrival. However, I don't want to build your hopes too high. The surgeon who examined your mother could find no indication that her skull was broken, but he feels it is probably cracked. She received a violent blow to the side of the head, most probably with a heavy wooden stool that was normally kept by the door, out of reach of the inmates. I discovered blood and hair adhering to it . . .' Observing the stricken look on Amy's face, the magistrate coughed noisily to cover his embarrassment. 'The surgeon fears she may be unconscious for many days. It is even possible she may never regain consciousness. I am sorry to be the one to give you this news, but I feel you have a right to the truth.'

Amy gave Nathan a grief-stricken look, and he wished there was something he could do for her. When she spoke, it was to the magistrate. 'Must she stay in that place as she is so ill?'

The magistrate looked thoughtful. 'Your mother was committed to the lunatic asylum because there was no relative willing to accept responsibility for her. I understand you were living in London at the time. Have your circumstances changed?'

Amy hesitated for only a moment. 'Yes, I've returned home now.'

'And are you willing to accept full responsibility for her?'

'Yes . . . Oh, yes!'

'Very well. Come to my office tomorrow – or whenever the surgeon says she may be moved. I will give you the necessary authority to remove her from the lunatic asylum. But I suggest you consult the surgeon on the best mode of transportation for her. Now, if you will excuse me, I see the landlord's wife with the meal I ordered. Good evening to you both.'

Amy was greatly cheered by the magistrate's decision, and Nathan had to remind her that Peggy Hoblyn was still unconscious and the future uncertain for her.

'I know,' replied Amy. 'But when she's home where she belongs, where she's loved, she'll improve. I'm quite sure of it. Thinking about her being in that *horrible* place all this time, with no one to care for her, makes me want to weep.'

She shuddered, then looked at Nathan gratefully. 'Thank you for coming to London to fetch me, and for bringing the magistrate to speak to me just now.'

'I wish I could have done more, and sooner. I've always felt guilty that I didn't know what was going on at Portgiskey, and wasn't there when I was most needed.'

Amy reached across the table and squeezed his hand. 'None of it was your fault. You've had problems enough of your own.'

'Did you mean what you told Mr Carlyon – about returning to Cornwall for good?'

Amy withdrew her hand from his and looked down at her plate. 'Yes.'

'What about Sammy?'

Amy looked at Nathan defiantly. 'I went to London expecting to be an important part of Sammy's life. I knew I wouldn't enjoy living in a city, but I was willing to try for Sammy's sake. He didn't give me a chance. From the moment we arrived he busied himself seeking out old friends from the prize-fighting world. I might not have existed for him.'

'The prize-ring has always been the most important thing in Sammy's life, Amy. I thought you understood that?'

'I do, and I don't mind – but I wanted to be *part* of that life. Instead, Sammy cut me off from it completely. I was "the little woman" or "the old lady", as I heard myself called by one of his London friends. I was expected to wait patiently at home, ready to do the bidding of my lord and master, on the rare occasions when he returned home – usually just to get a change of clothing.'

Amy's chin came up in a way Nathan remembered well. 'I'm not a "little woman". Neither am I an "old lady". I was fishing and smuggling with my own boat for too long to allow all my independence to be suddenly taken away – by anyone. I went to London with Sammy because I knew that was what *he* wanted, and because I felt he needed me. I was right about him wanting London, but wrong about him needing me. He only needed me while he was *here*, because Sammy was a stranger in Cornwall. In London, Sammy has prize-fighting – and he needs nothing more. After he met up with the Duke of Clarence I was lucky if I saw him twice a week. I'm not prepared to live that way. I told Sammy so.'

'What was Sammy's reply to that?' Nathan prompted, when Amy fell silent.

'He said I'd feel different when I had a brood of "kids" to look after. He made having children sound like taking a dose of physic. I told him I didn't want the children of a man who felt like that about them.'

'Was that why you were crying, that last night in London?'

'You heard? I'm sorry. Yes, he tried . . .' Abruptly, Amy stood up. 'I . . . I'm going to my room now, Nathan. It's been a long day. I'm very tired.'

'Of course. Don't worry about your ma. We'll go and see her first thing in the morning. Then we'll get her home to Portgiskey. Everything will come right for you, you'll see.'

Amy leaned over and kissed Nathan on the cheek.

'Thank you for listening to my problems, Nathan. And thank you especially for caring.'

Peggy Hoblyn went home to Portgiskey two days later. Still unconscious, she travelled on a bed of hay in Tom Quicke's high-sided wagon. Nathan drove, with Amy in the back of the wagon, at the side of her mother.

Nathan allowed the horses to rest for a while at the watering-place, before going on to tackle the long and steep hill that dropped down past Polrudden to Pentuan. It was here that Nell Quicke found them. A servant from Polrudden accompanied her, and with them Nell's young son, Tom, and baby Beville.

When Amy jumped down from the wagon and took the baby from the servant, Beville, always ready to please an audience, obligingly gurgled and cooed. Clinging to her finger, he gave Amy a lop-sided, gummy smile. Amy was completely captivated. For many minutes she was so engrossed with Nathan's son that she forgot the others who stood and watched her.

When Amy finally raised her head from the baby and saw she had everyone's attention, she was only mildly embarrassed. 'He's *lovely*, Nathan. Such a happy baby. Poor Elinor.'

Amy hugged Beville to her again, then reluctantly handed him back to his nurse.

After seeing Nell Quicke, the servant and two babies on their way to Venn Farm, Nathan guided the horses slowly along the lane, and down the steep hill to Pentuan village.

As was so often the way in Cornwall, news of

Peggy Hoblyn's return to Portgiskey travelled ahead of the wagon. It might have been an unguarded remark made by Tom or Nell Quicke, or a piece of gossip passed on by one of the Polrudden servants.

What was more certain was that not all the villagers were well disposed towards Peggy's homecoming. As the wagon creaked through the village women stood around in small, disapproving groups and not a welcoming smile was to be seen. Nathan sensed the hostility, but he knew better than to say anything. If he could get Peggy Hoblyn to her home without incident, the village would soon forget about her – as it always had in the past.

It was not to be. A group of seine-fishermen, some holding pewter tankards half-filled with ale, stood in a loose-knit group outside the Ship inn, which, with the Happy Sailor, catered for the drinking needs of Pentuan's fishermen.

The group of men extended halfway across the narrow village street. As Nathan approached, they gathered together in a tight bunch, blocking the way. Nathan considered whipping up the horses and driving them straight through the fishermen's ranks, but common sense prevailed. Nathan's livelihood and the future of his son depended very largely upon this community. If something needed to be said, it was better to have it out in the open here and now.

Nathan hauled on the reins and the two horses leaned back in their leather harnesses, bringing the wagon to a halt.

A babble of sound immediately rose from the assembled fishermen.

'You shouldn't have brought her home.'

'We don't want Peggy Hoblyn close to our village. There are children here to be considered.'

'Nothing personal to you, Nathan.'

'Just a minute.' Nathan held up his hand for silence. When it came, he said: 'I'm not going to attempt to speak to everyone at once. Is there anyone who would like to speak for the rest?'

A number of the fishermen looked at Dan Clymo, Nathan's boyhood friend.

'You've got something to say to me, Dan?' Nathan sat easily on the wagon seat as the fisherman was pushed somewhat reluctantly to the front of the group.

'Nothing aimed at you personally, Nathan,' said Dan Clymo eventually. 'But we heard you were bringing Peggy back to Portgiskey.'

Nathan jerked his head to indicate the back of the high-sided wagon. 'You heard right. She's in the back, with Amy.'

The crowd about the wagon began to talk and gesticulate excitedly, but it seemed to Nathan that no more than half were perturbed about Peggy Hoblyn's return. The remainder were expressing more interest in the presence of Amy, whom they had last seen setting off as Sammy Mizler's bride.

'It's said she killed someone else in the lunatic asylum in Lostwithiel. We don't want her back here. No mother will feel safe letting her child out to play . . .'

The hay behind Nathan erupted, and Amy's angry face came into view.

'There's not a child in Pentuan has ever had to fear my ma – and they never will. She's looked after your children often enough, Dan Clymo. Or have you forgotten? When your wife was off helping to bring in the harvest on some farm while you sat in the Jolly Sailor for month after month, waiting for the pilchards to come in and give themselves up, remember? Yes, and she looked after your wife more than once, too, when she returned from the farm so drunk on harvest cider she couldn't carry her own child without falling over.'

As men about him sniggered, Dan Clymo's face became as red as Amy's own. 'That was before your ma went mad,' he retorted. 'She hadn't killed anyone then.'

'My ma killed a grown-up woman who was keeping her a prisoner for no good reason she could see,' said Amy. 'There was no one about her she knew, and her mind snapped. I'm not excusing murder; I'm just explaining what happened. Ma is no child-killer, as well you know.'

'Then what about the business at the lunatic asylum? I've heard—'

'Whatever you've heard is wrong, Dan Clymo. You should take no more notice of such rumours than I or my ma ever did about rumours of your wife's carryings on with other men. I'll *tell* you what happened in Lostwithiel. Someone who'd killed four times before broke free in the asylum. She killed three times again – and badly injured my ma. Here, all of you. Come to the back of the wagon and you'll see the woman you're so frightened of. She's been unconscious for two days and two nights, and she may never regain consciousness again . . .'

Here, Amy's voice broke with emotion and one or

two of the fishermen crowding about the wagon looked embarrassed.

'That's all very well,' Dan Clymo persisted doggedly, 'but suppose she *does* come round. What'll happen to her when you go back to London to your husband?'

'You don't have to lose any sleep over that. I'm not going back.'

Dan Clymo shuffled his feet uncertainly for a minute or two, then he turned away without another word. He had not succeeded in preventing Peggy Hoblyn's return, but seeing her unconscious in the back of the hay-wagon he doubted whether she would ever pose a threat to anyone. Moreover, Amy had provided Pentuan with a piece of gossip that would last longer than the return home of an unconscious lunatic. Amy Mizler had left her husband after only a few months of marriage. What was more, she had returned home in the company of Nathan Jago!

A few of the men in the crowd outside the Ship inn were interested in neither Nathan Jago nor the Hoblyn family. They had been drinking for many hours prior to the gathering of the fishermen in the street outside the tavern. They had anticipated some excitement and were disappointed because nothing had transpired.

Now they stood their ground in front of the wagon, and Nathan was forced to make a quick decision. Amy had succeeded in winning the Pentuan crowd to her side but, if the handful of drunken men caused trouble, opinion was likely to swing against her and Nathan once more.

Nathan climbed down from the wagon seat and

walked to the head of one of his horses. Taking hold of the bridle, he clicked his tongue against the roof of his mouth and the horses moved forward. They took a couple of paces before stopping, heads tossing uncertainly. Four drunken men barred the way. Nathan realised that time had run out for diplomacy.

Before any of the drinkers guessed his intention, Nathan released his hold on the horse and stepped forward quickly. Grabbing two of the men by the hair, he crashed their heads together, as he had once seen Uriah Kemp deal with Mevagissey hecklers.

One man collapsed to the ground immediately. His harder-headed companion dropped his tankard and staggered away, too dazed and drink-sodden to realise who was responsible for what had happened. One of the two remaining men opened his mouth to protest, but the words had not left his mouth when his head came into violent collision with that of his remaining companion.

Both men would have dropped to the ground instantly had Nathan not kept his grasp on them and laid them to one side.

So swift had the action been that not more than two or three fishermen standing to one side of the wagon saw what had occurred. Nathan gave them a brief grin, then took the bridle of his horse once more and led animals and wagon past the men on the ground. Serious violence had been averted, and Peggy Hoblyn was almost home.

But the day had not yet given up all its surprises. When Nathan eased the wagon down the steep hillside behind the Hoblyn cottage at Portgiskey Cove, he found his father waiting by the door of the fish-cellar.

Calling a delighted greeting, Nathan said: 'Hello, Pa. It's nice of you to come and meet us. I'm glad you weren't one of the "welcoming" party who tried to turn us back outside the Ship inn.'

'I see they didn't succeed,' commented Josiah Jago. 'But my presence here has nothing to do with Peggy Hoblyn. I've just received news that Uriah Kemp has been recaptured in Plymouth. He was arrested near the naval dockyard in Devonport – and has been charged with spying.'

'That's absurd!' Nathan cried incredulously. 'Uriah is a preacher, not a spy. Who is he supposed to have been spying for?'

'For his own country, America. There's been a sea-battle off the coast of Cornwall. A British man-o'-war tried to board an armed American merchantman, to impress seamen. The American ship opened fire and dismasted the British man-o'-war, which then ran aground and sank. To make matters worse, Napoleon has declared his support for America. It seems that a declaration of war between America and Great Britain is likely any day now.'

Nathan was stunned. Uriah Kemp was in serious trouble, but Nathan would never believe that he was a spy. He was a fine preacher and a good man.

'There's more yet.' Preacher Josiah Jago was grim-faced. 'When your father-in-law announced Uriah's arrest in Parliament, he claimed that the Methodist Society was behind his activities. He's proposing a Bill to have us outlawed.'

8

The Reverend Uriah Kemp refused to take seriously the charges brought against him, at first. Having escaped from the prison van and eluded the Dragoons sent out after him, he had been making his way towards Falmouth in an almost leisurely fashion. Once there, he intended taking a ship for America. On the way he decided to call at Plymouth, to visit the spot from which the members of an earlier persecuted sect of dissenters had sailed to colonise America, almost two hundred years before.

It was ill-fortune that one of the St Austell constables should have been in Plymouth that day. Recognising the fugitive preacher, he arrested him and took him before a Plymouth magistrate. News of the action between the British and American ships had been received in Plymouth only an hour before, and the American preacher was closely questioned about his reason for being in Plymouth Town.

Not satisfied with the replies he was given, the magistrate ordered Kemp to be held in custody in Plymouth's Citadel, and sent a report of the matter to London. Here it passed through the hands of a number of Home Office clerks until one noticed that the report was about a Methodist minister. He promptly passed it on to Sir Lewis Hearle.

Sir Lewis seized the opportunity afforded by Uriah Kemp's arrest eagerly and sent for the Plymouth magistrate to come to London immediately.

In London the magistrate had numerous meetings at the Home Office with the Under-Secretary. Later, at Sir Lewis Hearle's club, he was introduced to members of London Society whose views on Methodism coincided with the baronet's own. All were prepared to go to great lengths to suppress the thriving religion.

The Plymouth magistrate returned to his home town armed with Sir Lewis Hearle's assurance that, if he were able to produce sufficient evidence to send Uriah Kemp for trial, the country would be eternally grateful.

Within a week of the magistrate's return, Kemp was sent to London to face trial as a spy and on this occasion was given no opportunity to escape. Chained and manacled, he was conveyed in a frigate of the British navy to the Pool of London. Here he was taken through the busy streets of the capital to Newgate Prison.

Even now all might have gone well for Uriah Kemp had not a tall, pale-faced man with the gleam of insanity in his eyes stepped from the shadows in the lobby of the House of Commons with a pistol in his hands to change the course of Great Britain's political history.

Spencer Perceval, the Tory Prime Minister, was shot through the heart at point-blank range by the deranged Liverpool businessman John Bellingham in the early evening of Monday, 11 May. Uriah Kemp's trial was to be held in the same week.

A few days after the shooting, Uriah Kemp and John Bellingham shared a cell beneath the Old Bailey Hall. Both were waiting to face trial before London's Recorder, in the presence of the Lord Chief Justice of England.

John Bellingham's trial was biased to the point of vindictiveness. His counsel entered a plea of 'Not guilty, by reason of insanity', and produced evidence that Bellingham had a history of insanity. Indeed, his father had died insane before him.

In spite of this, the defence plea was rejected. Then judge and jury listened impatiently for eight hours to the story of Bellingham's life of failure before pronouncing his guilt to a waiting nation. He was sentenced to be hanged at eight o'clock on the morning of Monday, 18 May, barely a week after committing the murder for which he was to die.

With the formality of Bellingham's trial over, rumour spread through the corridors of the Old Bailey Hall that Bellingham had merely been the tool of a sinister society. Its aim was the overthrow of responsible government in Great Britain. A dozen countries and organisations were named as being behind the society. Among these were France, America, the Midland industrial agitators – and the Methodist Church.

Such totally unfounded rumours were denied by all

those named. Before he died on the gallows, Bellingham himself declared that the assassination had been the result of a personal grudge he held against the unfortunate Spencer Perceval.

The denials came too late to save Uriah Kemp. In an atmosphere of near-hysterical suspicion, it was disclosed to a beetle-browed Recorder and the jury of upright citizens that Kemp had been a chaplain to the American rebels during the War of Independence. Returning British prisoners-of-war had spoken of his frequent visits to their camps.

Since the end of that war, the American had been a regular visitor to Great Britain. His travels in the British Isles were related to the court, together with details of the 'happenings' that followed his progress.

Uriah Kemp had preached many times in the Midlands, where public unrest had become the cause of great concern. From here he had made his way to Cornwall, whereupon that most loyal of counties had experienced its first serious riot for many years. The American Methodist minister had in fact been arrested in Cornwall, but had proved his remarkable resourcefulness by escaping in a 'daring' fashion when being conveyed to London. After his escape, Kemp had made his way to Plymouth, evading all efforts to recapture him. He was arrested in the vicinity of the naval dockyard only hours after a ship from the port had been sunk by an American vessel off the Cornish coast. Finally, whilst awaiting his trial in the cells beneath this very court-room, Kemp was seen to be uncommonly friendly with the man who had been convicted of murdering the Prime Minister of Great Britain.

There was much more so-called 'evidence' against Uriah Kemp. All of it was circumstantial, some was hearsay, some mere speculation. Unfortunately for the American, the trial of John Bellingham had been so brief it had not satisfied the populace of the capital. Vengeance, wearing the guise of 'justice', demanded more.

A judiciary reeling under the assassination of the country's leader dared not oppose such strong popular feeling – certainly not for the sake of an eccentric American Methodist preacher.

Uriah Kemp had ministered to a wide spectrum of humanity for many years. He recognised the feeling that gripped the people of London as being akin to mass hysteria. He also understood the workings of government, and the principles they would sacrifice in order to remain in office.

The preacher realised he was to be the Tory government's sacrifice. The Lord he served had been offered to the multitude for similar reasons, eighteen hundred years before.

Standing in the dock of the Old Bailey Hall, Uriah Kemp expressed his feelings succinctly and forcefully, but wholly unsuccessfully. Looking at the set faces of the Recorder and the jurors, he knew his words fell on deaf ears. He had been pre-judged, not on the facts of his own case, but as a result of the trial that had gone before.

His speech serving no useful purpose, Uriah Kemp brought it to a dignified close. Standing tall and proud before his accusers, he concluded: 'Gentlemen, I stand innocent of all the charges levelled against me in this court-room. Whilst in your country I have served no master but the Lord. I wish I might have served Him better. However, if I am to be convicted, however unjustly, of serving any country, I could not wish to suffer on behalf of a finer or more honourable land than my own.' With a stiff bow to the jury, Uriah Kemp added: 'May the Lord guide your deliberations.'

'So be it,' snapped the Recorder brusquely. 'But first the jury will need to listen to what *I* have to say.'

With that the Recorder began a summing-up that in less emotionally charged surroundings would have been scurrilous. His words left no room for an acquittal and so it came as no surprise when, after only the briefest of discussions among themselves, the jury returned a verdict of 'guilty' against the Reverend Uriah Kemp.

'Uriah Kemp' – the Recorder deliberately spurned the use of the epithet 'Reverend' – 'Uriah Kemp, you have been justly convicted of a dastardly crime against a country whose hospitality you have grossly abused. I am in no doubt that your conduct has deliberately provoked much of the industrial troubles we have experienced in recent years. It matters not which country you serve, be it France or America. Both were spawned in violence and insurrection, subjects in which you are apparently well versed. It is my solemn duty to pass upon you a sentence to deter others, and to remind them that Great Britain will not tolerate treasonable acts committed in this realm. You will be taken from here to a place of execution. There you will be hanged by the neck, taken down while you yet live, and suffer execution on the block. May the Lord have mercy on your soul.'

The sentence, traditional for acts of treason, brought a gasp from many of those in the hushed court-room. Decapitation was no longer a fashionable mode of execution. The excesses of those who had employed 'Madame Guillotine' during the recent revolution in France had caused Englishmen to lose all taste for the executioner's axe.

Uriah Kemp paled and momentarily swayed in the dock, but he angrily shook off the steadying hand of the gaoler.

'I fancy *you* will have more need of the Lord's mercy than I, when the time comes for you to meet Him. I trust you will not then be judged in the manner you judge others.'

With these words Uriah Kemp turned and left the dock, his heavy ankle-chains rattling noisily as he shuffled awkwardly down the stairs to the cells beneath the Old Bailey Hall.

Preacher Josiah Jago stepped off the coach in the Bell innyard the day after Uriah Kemp's trial and stared upwards in wonder at the great dome of St Paul's Cathedral. It was the Methodist preacher's first visit to London and he was already overawed by its size and bustling activity.

Josiah Jago had travelled alone to the capital to see his friend, Uriah Kemp. Nathan had originally intended travelling with his father, but two days before the proposed journey *The Brave Amy H* had been rammed and holed by a Mevagissey seiner as the night crew brought her in after a successful fishing trip. It was not certain whether the incident had been an attempt to put Nathan out of business, or merely a careless accident, but Nathan could take no chances with his only boat. He remained at Portgiskey to see the repairs carried out, and to ensure there was no repetition of the incident.

Neither Nathan nor his father had fully realised the seriousness of the charges against Uriah Kemp. Consequently, it came as a great shock to Josiah Jago when he overheard excited servants at the Bell inn talking of the American preacher's conviction and sentence.

Filled with horror at the thought of his friend's plight, Josiah Jago did not delay even to change his clothes. Dressed in his dusty, ill-cut serge suit, the Cornish preacher hurried to the house in City Road where John Wesley had once lived. It was currently the headquarters of the Methodist Society.

Josiah Jago hoped to learn what was being done by Britain's Methodists to overturn the verdict on Uriah Kemp. Instead, after he had given his name to a rather bored clerk, he found himself warmly received by the senior officials of his church, fêted as a hero. It was many minutes before Josiah Jago was able to explain his reason for coming to London.

Immediately, the joyous reception he was being given lapsed into embarrassed silence.

'Ah, yes . . . The American evangelist. Most distressing. *Most* distressing.' The awkward silence was broken by a Methodist preacher who had achieved senior status for no other reason than that he had accompanied John Wesley on one of his innumerable provincial tours. He had never been invited on another, but to those who came after Wesley's death it was enough merely to have spoken to the founder of the Methodist Church.

Josiah Jago waited for the doyen of the Methodist Church to add something to his murmur of polite sympathy. He waited until it became clear that the other man had no more to say.

Preacher Jago stared about him in disbelief. 'Is *nothing* being done to save Uriah Kemp? In God's name . . . His only offence is to preach the word of Our Lord in the manner taught to us by John Wesley himself. Should he be condemned to die for this? If so, not one of us here is safe.'

None of the men about him would meet his eyes, and Josiah Jago asked: 'Well, how is Uriah bearing up? You *have* sent someone to console him in prison?'

'You don't understand, Josiah. These are difficult times for us. Uriah Kemp's name has been linked with that of John Bellingham, the assassin who murdered Spencer Perceval. There are many men in government and the Church of England who would dearly love to involve the Methodists in such matters.'

'I don't doubt you. But Uriah is one of *us*. He and my son kept the Methodist Church alive in Cornwall when I was in prison. It's for this he's been convicted, not for anything else. He's as innocent of all other charges as you and I.'

'Josiah, these are difficult times for our church.' Laying a hand upon Josiah Jago's shoulder, the senior preacher spoke to him as he might a young child having difficulty learning the lesson set by a Sunday-school teacher. 'We are being accused of all manner of crimes against government and public order. Sir Lewis Hearle has asked Parliament to ban the Methodist Society and he has powerful support in the House of

Lords. We must be careful to give him no more fuel for his sacrificial fire.'

'Even if it means Uriah Kemp must die abandoned by those to whom he has given his faith and friendship?'

'Even so. If he is as true a Christian as you believe him to be, he will understand and find comfort in the Lord.'

Josiah Jago looked about him at the nodding heads of his fellow-preachers. Suddenly he realised he was a stranger among them. Here at the heart of Methodism, in the home of its founder, he felt the cause to which he had dedicated his whole life crumbling about him.

'Uriah has always found comfort with the Lord. The years he spent in the American wilderness brought him closer to Him than we, who find ourselves distracted by the material things of the world about us.'

Overcome by tired emotion, Josiah Jago's Cornish accent was so heavy that some of the London preachers had difficulty understanding his words. But there could be no mistaking the depth of his feelings.

'Uriah Kemp has always preached that faith will reap its own reward. *I* believe the Methodist Church will survive all the trials it's suffering today. The Lord will see to this. But Uriah Kemp has always maintained faith not only in the Lord, but also in his fellow-men. I intend showing him that this faith is not unfounded. I am going to visit him in prison, gentlemen. I would welcome your company, for Uriah's sake. I also intend asking permission to accompany him to the scaffold. I crave your indulgence if I appear to be going against the wishes of the Society. My conscience will not allow me to do otherwise. It's the same conscience that prompted me to do the things for which you called me a hero when I walked into this house – the house that was once John Wesley's. I bid you good day. I doubt if we shall meet again.'

Preacher Josiah Jago was not a big man but, as he walked away from the policy-makers of his church, dignity gave him a stature that dwarfed every man there.

Getting permission to see Uriah Kemp proved to be very difficult. For two days Josiah Jago was told that the American preacher could have no visitors. Apparently it was a government directive. Not until the execution was only eighteen hours away did the Governor of Newgate Prison take it upon himself to allow Josiah Jago to enter and see his friend.

Uriah Kemp had accepted his fate with a calmness typical of the man, but he was touchingly grateful to the Cornish preacher for travelling so far to see him. He enquired after the journey and hoped that Josiah was not tired. Had it not been for the grim surroundings, it might have been the meeting of two old friends at a wayside inn.

Not until Josiah Jago repeated his conversation with the Methodist preachers at City Road did the American show any emotion.

'If they believe the way for our church to survive is by not offending those who seek to destroy us, they are sadly mistaken. We must assert the right to worship in our own way. If the arrest and, yes, *execution* of one man will stop Methodists from standing up and *shouting* our beliefs for the whole world to hear, then we have no right to claim recognition as an independent church. As a person I am of no more importance than that fly climbing up the wall. Neither are you, Josiah, my good friend. Yet you and I, and all those who believe as we do, represent a revived faith. The Methodist Church has been responsible for showing thousands – no, *tens of thousands* – of sinners the way to God. It is *this* which is important. Our work must pause for *no* man, whether he be a friend or against us.'

His oratory was interrupted by the arrival of the Governor, accompanied by two turnkeys. In his hand, the Governor carried a document written in careful script. At the foot of the paper was a large and impressive seal.

Addressing Uriah Kemp, the Governor said: 'Reverend Kemp, as you know a plea was sent to the Regent on your behalf, begging him to exercise mercy towards you. I regret that he feels unable to overturn the findings of the court. However, I am pleased to inform you that instead of being hanged and then beheaded, you are now to suffer hanging only.'

Josiah Jago's hopes, which had soared when the Governor entered the cell, now plummeted. He had imagined the Governor had come bearing a pardon for his friend.

If Uriah Kemp had held out the same hope, he concealed it well, even managing a quip for the Governor. 'Does this mean I'll be any *less* dead when the hangman's through with me?'

Unsmiling, the Governor said: 'There are many ways for a man to die, Reverend Kemp. Death by the axe is not one of the more pleasant forms of execution, either for the victim or for those of us forced to watch. I have never met a sober executioner. While I appreciate his need for alcohol, it adds nothing to such meagre skill as he might possess. However, such talk is out of place here and now. Your friend may remain with you until dusk, but I regret he will not be allowed to accompany you to the scaffold in the morning. I can flout orders within the walls of Newgate Prison, but I must needs be more circumspect with half of London's populace gathered to bear witness of my deeds.'

Josiah Jago stayed with the American preacher until two gaolers entered the cell, bearing lamps to keep at bay darkness and the thoughts it afforded a condemned man. The gaolers would remain with Uriah Kemp until the macabre procession comprising Governor, doctor, padre and hangman arrived to escort the condemned man to the plank-wood platform where the grim reaper had his throne.

After sharing a prayer, kneeling on the cold flagstones of the American preacher's cell, the two friends embraced. Then, blinded with tears, Josiah Jago was escorted away through the dark prison corridors.

When the heavy gates slammed shut behind him, Josiah Jago found himself standing on the pavement outside the high-walled prison. Not far away was the scaffold where the insane John Bellingham had died at the end of the hangman's rope and where Uriah Kemp would hang in a few hours' time.

In the dim light from nearby windows, and lanterns hung high on the prison walls, Josiah Jago could see that the street was littered with all manner of debris.

Left behind by the great crowd that had assembled to witness Bellingham's execution, the rubbish was being methodically turned over and examined by two old crones who placed useful and edible items in the folds of tattered and grubby skirts.

In the shadow of the scaffold, Josiah Jago sank to his knees. With his chin sunk upon his chest he began a night of prayer for the soul of Uriah Kemp. As the night wore on he was joined by others. Most were there to ensure they had a good view of the morning's execution, but a few joined Josiah in prayer.

By the time dawn arrived, a thousand or more people were already gathered about the scaffold. Soon afterwards there was a sudden movement in the noisy throng and two of the Methodist ministers to whom Josiah Jago had spoken at City Road sank to their knees beside him.

Too weary to express surprise, Josiah Jago turned a haggard, unshaven face towards them.

'You have been here all night, Josiah?'

He nodded without speaking, and one of the Ministers laid a hand on his arm. 'We should have been here to share your vigil, but we were busy. Our efforts have not been in vain. When Uriah Kemp walks out to the scaffold, almost every Methodist in London will be here to send his soul soaring straight to heaven.'

Josiah Jago was so tired that his face registered blankness rather than surprise. The hand on his arm tightened sympathetically. 'You shamed us with your words, Josiah, and you were right. John Wesley would be ashamed of us were he alive today. He was a man like yourself – one who went out and followed the dictates of his heart. He would not have cowered in a corner, keeping quiet and hoping to escape the notice of those who sought to kick him. But enough of words. Will you lead us in a prayer, Josiah?'

By the time the prison bell began to toll, announcing to the waiting crowd that the condemned man and his escort had begun the walk to the scaffold, there was no room for a child as far as the eye could see. Josiah Jago could not believe that the vast majority of such a huge crowd were Methodists, until Uriah Kemp, his hands pinioned behind his back, appeared on the platform above them.

Instead of a roar from a spectacle-seeking crowd, there was a sudden silence. It was broken by a single tremulous voice singing the first line of Charles Wesley's hymn, 'Jesu, lover of my soul'. As the singer progressed to the second line, 'Let me to thy bosom fly', thousands of voices joined in.

The sound swelled impressively, and Josiah Jago raised his eyes to the scaffold. Uriah Kemp smiled down at him as he, too, joined in the hymn, joyously aware of the composition of the great crowd. Those on the scaffold about the condemned man were aware of it, too, and the hangman was ordered to carry out his task as quickly as he could.

Uriah Kemp tried to shake off the hood as the hangman put it over his head, but even as his lips framed the 'No!' the black mask was pulled down, hiding his face.

As the voices of the crowd faltered and came to a ragged halt, the hangman took a step backwards. Grasping the lever that released the trapdoor beneath Uriah Kemp's feet, he gave it a sharp tug. The condemned man dropped almost from view. Only the shrouded head remained above the level of the scaffold floor, jerking grotesquely.

In most executions, this was the signal for the crowd to roar its approval. Today, it brought only an involuntary gasp. Then, as the prison bell ceased to toll, an uncanny silence fell upon the vast crowd. It was more impressive than any uproar.

Moments later the vast concourse dropped to its knees and the leaders of the Methodist Church led their followers in a prayer for the soul of the Reverend Uriah Kemp.

It was a convincing demonstration that the death of Uriah Kemp had not succeeded in crushing Methodism. The message was not lost upon the Earl of Liverpool, the new Tory Prime Minister. He had watched the proceedings from the upper window of a building opposite the prison, the guest of Sir Lewis Hearle.

9

Peggy Hoblyn lay unconscious at Portgiskey for a full week, and Amy despaired that she would ever recover. Then one morning Amy looked in the small bedroom at Portgiskey cottage and saw her mother lying still in her bed, her eyes fixed upon the curtains flapping at the open window. Overjoyed, Amy hugged her mother, certain that everything was going to be all right again. Holding the frail, thin body in her arms, Amy promised she would never go away again; that mother and daughter would live happily at Portgiskey once more.

Peggy Hoblyn said nothing at all. Neither words, nor tears, nor affection produced any response from her. The long period of unconsciousness had wiped her memory as clean as a rain-washed slate. She remembered nothing, and no one. Even speech came to her with great difficulty.

When Peggy was strong enough to walk, she

wandered about the cottage, running exploratory fingers over once-familiar furniture, and gaping open-mouthed through the windows at the work being carried on in the fish-cellar and on the quay at the water's edge.

When she could venture outside, the fisherwomen in the fish-cellar were at first apprehensive. After all, they had seen the strangled body of Lizzie Barron, the woman Peggy Hoblyn had murdered. But, as it became increasingly evident that she was no longer to be feared, the fisherwomen began to poke cruel fun at her. So innocent and childlike was she now, that Peggy would do everything she was told. She ate the raw fish given to her by the fisherwomen, and retreated in distressed bewilderment at their laughter. She raised her skirts to the fishermen when so ordered by the other women, and obediently repeated dictated obscenities when told to do so.

Amy remonstrated angrily with the fisherwomen when she caught them playing tricks on her mother, and Nathan dismissed one of them as a warning, but the unkind tormenting continued.

Then, only a week after Preacher Josiah Jago returned from London, cholera reached Mevagissey. For many months the disease had been sweeping through the towns and cities of Europe, claiming tens of thousands of victims. Around the coast of Great Britain, the authorities in every sea-port had taken stringent precautions to prevent the killer disease from spreading to these islands. Any ship with sickness on board was held in an anchorage well clear of the port until doctors were satisfied that the malady was not cholera.

The precautions worked well until a Sicilian vessel, bound for Sweden, made an unscheduled stop at Mevagissey. It had been a bad voyage for the crew of the Mediterranean ship from the moment she sailed from Gibraltar into the deeper waters of the Atlantic. One after another the members of the crew fell ill. Two died and were buried at sea. Then, becalmed off the Scilly Isles, the ship's captain collapsed and was carried to his cabin, protesting vainly that he was not seriously ill. The wind picked up from the south-west, and the vessel was off Mevagissey before the captain died. With the mate too ill to assume command, the crew voted unanimously to make for the nearest landfall.

The Sicilian ship rode the tide into Mevagissey's small fishing-harbour just as dawn broke. When the village awoke, half the crew were ashore, collecting fresh water, searching for fresh provisions, and seeking the services of a doctor.

Dr Ellerman Scott was called to the ship just as he was about to sit down to his breakfast. Listening to the symptoms, explained partly in halting English and completed in mime, he hurried from the house, leaving his untouched meal on the table.

His diagnosis was immediate and unequivocal. There was cholera on board.

Those members of the crew still ashore were quickly rounded up and returned on board. The contaminated vessel was then towed clear of the harbour by Mevagissey's new Revenue cutter, and the unfortunate Sicilians abandoned to their fate on the high seas.

It was too late. During the short time they had spent

ashore, the effusive Sicilians had shaken hands with half the men in Mevagissey, and patted the heads of countless black-haired children. In addition, two of the crew, with an instinct inherent in professional seamen of the time, had found their way to a decrepit cottage, standing no more than a hurried prayer from the vicarage. Here a sleepy but accommodating troll tested their Sicilian gold coins between bad teeth and, in an equally businesslike manner, relieved them of the pent-up passions accumulated in the course of their long sea-voyage.

One week later, four fishermen, two wives and three children were dead. A hundred more lay sick in their beds.

In a village where each household could claim a blood relationship with at least ten others, doors were locked against neighbours for the first time in living memory, and friends crossed to the other side of narrow streets to avoid each other.

In this atmosphere of fear and death, Dr Ellerman Scott toiled day and night in a vain bid to contain the epidemic. His only helper was the troll of Vicarage Hill. For the first time in her lurid life, the doors of respectable homes were opened to her. Her tireless and selfless efforts encompassed men, women and children; churchman and sinner alike. The Sicilian gold she had earned was spent on herbs to ease the pain of her patients, and much more of her money went the same way.

Pentuan closed its doors to fisherfolk from Mevagissey, but a young Pentuan fisherman was courting a Mevagissey girl and the two met unobserved in the woods on the hill between the two villages. Three days after the girl's brother died in Mevagissey, the illness struck down its first Pentuan victim.

Cholera swept through Pentuan with alarming rapidity, and when the disease was confirmed in three Polrudden servants Nathan sent Beville to Venn Farm. He believed the isolated farmhouse to be probably the safest place in the whole of the area. Tom and Nell Quicke had no need to leave the farm for anything. Their cow gave them milk from which they made butter and cheese, and they had all the produce and meat they required.

There was no doctor in Pentuan and, because villagers were frightened to enter a house where sickness was present, much of the work of caring for cholera victims fell to Josiah Jago, as the village preacher.

When two of the women working at Portgiskey contracted the sickness, Nathan closed down the fish-cellar and helped his overworked father to tend to his patients.

For weeks there was no fishing anywhere along the length of the Cornish coast. Cholera had now spread to most of the fishing communities, and a rumour began that the disease was in fact contracted by eating fish. There was no truth in such an absurd assertion, of course, but the ignorant and frightened populace was ready to listen to any advice in a bid to end the present epidemic. The housewives of Cornwall stopped buying fish.

The day after Nathan closed down the fish-cellar, Peggy Hoblyn was struck down with cholera. The illness was the final blow to a constitution weakened by weeks in prison cell and asylum. Forty-eight hours after the first symptoms showed themselves, Peggy was dead.

Nathan and Josiah Jago were with her when the end came. Both sought to comfort Amy, but she remained remarkably calm. Amy declared it was enough for her that her mother had died in her own home and not in a lunatic asylum, surrounded by uncaring strangers.

However, when a summer storm threatened later that night and Nathan returned to Portgiskey to check that *The Brave Amy H* was properly secured, he found Amy huddled beside a huge pile of fish-baskets on the small quay, crying as though her heart would break.

When he lifted her to her feet she clung to him desperately and he held her until her sobbing subsided. When she eventually spoke, her words were punctuated by long-drawn-out sobs that shook her body.

'Wh-what do I do, Nathan? I've lost Sammy . . . and now Ma. What will I do?'

Drying her eyes gently, Nathan said: 'This doesn't sound like the girl who put to sea with me in a storm and saved a fishing-boat from being wrecked. The first thing you'll do is to stop trying to work out your future all alone in the dark with your ma lying dead in the house. There will be time enough for that in the morning, when you're rested and with friends.'

'I think you . . . must be the only friend I have left.'

Nathan smiled, but was glad that the darkness hid it from her. Amy was not yet nineteen years of age, but in that moment she sounded far younger and terribly vulnerable.

Acting upon affectionate impulse, Nathan cupped

her face in his hands and kissed her. He knew immediately that it had been a mistake. After the first moment of surprise she stiffened. When he dropped his hands from her, she took a backward pace away.

He tried to think of the right words for an apology, but Amy spoke first.

'You shouldn't have done that, Nathan. You shouldn't have kissed me.'

'I know. I'm sorry.' He felt embarrassed and awkward. 'You're a married woman now, not a young girl . . .'

'That isn't what I meant.' She spoke fiercely. Then suddenly she was kissing him with an ardour that took him by surprise. His arms went about her and he pulled her to him. With body pressed hard against his, Amy felt his need for her – but then she twisted away.

'Nathan, why couldn't you have wanted me like this before?'

After flinging the unexpected question at him, Amy turned and fled to the cottage and Nathan heard the thud of the heavy wooden bolt slamming into position.

Peggy Hoblyn was buried the next day in Josiah Jago's Methodist burial-ground, her body carried to the village on board *The Brave Amy H* and from there in a Polrudden wagon. It was a brief, simple ceremony. In these times people did not gather together for funerals, especially when the burial was for a cholera victim. Only the gravedigger remained as a disinterested bystander. Too old to fear death, he was too drunk to care.

As Josiah Jago closed his book Amy turned to him, dry-eyed. 'How many villagers are ill with cholera now?'

'Twenty-four . . . although I've just been told that young Dolly Kittow and her brother are sick, too.'

'Can you do with some help?'

'Can I . . . ? My prayers are a constant cry for help. But are you ready to take on such a burden, so soon after the funeral?'

'It can't be soon enough. I'm in sore need of something to occupy my mind until I've decided where my future lies.'

As she spoke, Amy glanced swiftly at Nathan, who was listening nearby. Josiah Jago missed neither the glance nor the significance of her words.

'Your future lies with your husband, my dear,' he said quickly. 'But you can't risk carrying cholera to London Town. It would spread through those crowded streets like the wrath of God. In the meantime I'll find plenty to keep you busy.'

When Nathan returned to Polrudden to change his clothes after the funeral, he found Sir Lewis Hearle in the house, newly arrived from London. The baronet was in his study, tugging futilely at a bell-pull. He was in a furious mood.

'What the devil is going on here, Jago? Where are the servants? Where's my grandson? Dammit, I leave the place for a month or two and everything stops. Well, don't stand there like some stupid village oaf. Tell me. Are things so bad that you can't afford to keep the servants on?'

'Not yet. But if this cholera epidemic doesn't soon end they will be.'

'Cholera epidemic? Here?' Sir Lewis looked startled.

'Surely the news has reached London? Cornwall is very badly hit.'

'I had heard it was at Falmouth, and an unconfirmed report of a case at Plymouth. I never dreamed it would be here, in Pentuan. Is it bad?'

'I've just come from the funeral of Peggy Hoblyn. She's the fourth to die in Pentuan. Things are much worse in Mevagissey. Three of our servants here at Polrudden have the sickness. I've told the remainder to stay away, as a precaution. For the same reason I've sent Beville to stay with my sister and her husband at Venn Farm. He should be safe there.'

Sir Lewis Hearle raised a half-filled brandy-glass to his lips with a shaking hand. He had turned suddenly pale. 'This is dreadful. I must return to London at once.'

'Is death by cholera so much worse than death at the end of a rope, Sir Lewis? Or do you consider your life of more value than an American preacher whose only crime was to love God and his fellow-men?'

Colour returned to Sir Lewis Hearle's face in a sudden rush of blood. 'Uriah Kemp was convicted in an English court of law. The man was an agitator and a convicted spy.'

'He was a Methodist,' retorted Nathan. 'Nothing more. But no doubt it was sufficient cause for you and your friends to have him put to death.'

'If I consider Methodism to be contrary to the interests of my country, I will not shirk my duty,' declared Sir Lewis pompously. 'As for Uriah Kemp, before you say something you will regret, I think I should tell you his country has just declared war on Great Britain. No doubt Kemp's information was intended to give America the numbers of the warships still in harbour and not fully engaged against Napoleon's navy. If so, it was a fruitless exercise. This country has enough men-of-war available to tackle any American threat to our shipping.'

Sir Lewis poured himself another brandy and looked across the room waspishly at Nathan. 'Pass my information on to your father. It should interest him to know the company he and his Methodist friends have been keeping. Oh, and you can give your fishermen friends some news, too. These are hard times. I'll be increasing tithes for the coming pilchard season. Tell them not to spend their money unwisely until I have discussed a new rate with my solicitors.'

Nathan looked at him in disbelief. Then he startled the baronet by laughing. The moment of apparent merriment was brief. When his eyes met Sir Lewis Hearle's a moment later there was no mirth in them.

'I have news for *you*, Sir Lewis. Go to Pentuan and check on the boats and the fish-cellars. You'll find neither working. Half the boats, including mine, are rotting away for lack of work. Nobody has brought in fish for weeks, because no one is buying. Raise the tithes as much as you like. A sixth of nothing is no more than a twentieth – and that's exactly what you'll be getting. Nothing!'

10

The American declaration of war gave renewed strength to Sir Lewis Hearle's anti-Methodist campaign. He had taken a gamble in having the American Methodist preacher indicted for spying. Now he had been vindicated by the action of that country. It also threw further suspicion on the loyalty of the whole Methodist movement. It was well known that Uriah Kemp had been preaching to open-air Methodist meetings throughout the land. Sir Lewis ensured that the arrest of Methodist preachers for breaches of laws and by-laws received maximum publicity. When three Midlands 'Methodists' were convicted on charges of inciting riots and smashing valuable weaving machinery, anti-Methodist feeling was already running high.

In the House of Lords, bishop after bishop rose to his feet to launch scathing attacks on the Methodist Church, calling upon Great Britain's new Prime

Minister to declare the Methodist movement unlawful.

Paradoxically, Methodists were also coming under attack in the Midlands from those newspapers who supported the activities of the discontented workers. They denounced Methodists as 'enemies of the people', because of their alleged support *for* the Government!

The stage was set for a final assault on Methodism. The Home Secretary introduced a Bill that would effectively curb all those in the Methodist Society who declared themselves to be 'preachers'. The Home Secretary claimed derisively that among their ranks were cobblers, tailors, pig-drovers and chimney sweeps. He proposed that every so-called 'preacher' should have to prove his qualifications to a local magistrate before being issued with a licence allowing him to preach. It was also proposed that the two-hundred-year-old Toleration Act should in future be rigidly enforced. This Act stipulated that even a licensed preacher must preach only in the town or village where he resided.

By these two moves the Home Secretary would give local magistrates absolute jurisdiction over the granting of licences to dissenting preachers. He would also wipe out the very cornerstone upon which Methodism had been founded: the circuit preacher.

Throughout the country, Methodists realised their church was facing extinction. But now, when it was most needed, they received unexpected support. Other dissenters realised that the Methodist fight was theirs, too. Any new laws or restrictions would affect them just as much as their Methodist brethren.

Their leaders met with Methodist preachers, and all across the land lamps burned in chapel meeting-houses until their meagre glow was lost in the greater light of dawn. Meanwhile, Methodist worshippers approached every reasonable man of influence with whom they could claim acquaintance, begging for help to keep Wesley's church alive. It became apparent to all at Westminster that this was to be a hard-fought battle.

Only in Cornwall did this bitter war for religious survival pass almost without notice. Preachers like Josiah Jago were busy fighting a battle of a different kind, this one for the lives of their congregations, struck down by cholera. They had little time to spare for involvement in something that was little understood and quite remote from life here, in the extended toe of England.

Gradually, the two villages of Mevagissey and Pentuan began to win their fight against the cholera epidemic.

In Mevagissey, the troll of Vicarage Hill had nursed the sick of the fishing village through three dread months of epidemic. By this time there were thirty-seven bodies in the roped-off corner of the church-yard, and the gaunt and exhausted village physician declared that the cholera had finally run its course.

The troll returned to her decrepit cottage, and not for ten days did anyone give her a thought. When the physician entered her house, he found that she had probably been dead for at least half that time. Alone and untended, she was the last victim of the disease she had worked so hard to contain.

Only now was it realised that no one knew the

troll's full name. To the doctor she had been 'Nan', but she was also known by at least five other forenames. Her surname had never been mentioned in the village. She was buried in an unmarked corner of the mass cholera grave, among those she had tended so diligently. In a few weeks it was as though she had never been.

In Pentuan, as walls and houses were whitewashed and cleaned, the village slowly came to life again. Neighbours no longer avoided one another. Instead, somewhat shamefaced, they stopped and enquired after families and friends, exchanging harrowing details of the ordeals each had survived.

During these difficult weeks, Nathan saw little of either his father or Amy. With no servants at Polrudden, he did all the work of feeding animals and tending crops.

Both Amy and Preacher Jago also worked hard, tending the sick day and night. For a while they were helped by a mission doctor, newly returned from India. It was hoped that his experience of cholera would prove invaluable. Unfortunately, all his experience had not given the doctor immunity from the sickness. After only a week he contracted cholera himself and died three days later.

Then, late one evening, Nathan went to the village and discovered Amy and his father sitting in the kitchen of the Jago cottage, enjoying a cup of tea together. Both looked weary. Amy, in particular, looked as though she should sleep for a week. But Josiah Jago looked up at his son and smiled happily.

'We've finally won through, Nathan. There has been no fresh case of cholera for three days, and I believe all those patients we already have will recover.'

Nathan pulled a chair out from the table and sat down. 'Good. It means I'll be able to bring Beville home. I miss him.'

Josiah Jago shook his head. 'I'd leave the little chap with our Nell for another day or two yet – perhaps another week. By then we'll know for certain that the epidemic's over.'

'We've come out of it better than some villages,' said Nathan grimly. 'In Mevagissey they've lost whole families. But the sooner things are back to normal, the better it will be for everyone. I need to find a market for the fish I have in the cellar at Portgiskey soon. I've no ready money left.'

'It will feel strange to be sleeping at Portgiskey again,' commented Amy. 'What little sleep I've had since Ma died has been here, in this house.'

'I gave Amy the use of your room,' explained Josiah Jago to Nathan. 'She would never sleep until she reached the verge of collapse and wouldn't have made it to Portgiskey.'

'I won't make it tonight unless I leave now,' said Amy, rising to her feet. 'I've been putting off returning to Portgiskey, but I'll have to go back some time.'

'Leave it until tomorrow,' urged Josiah Jago. 'Stay here for tonight.'

'It's time I went home. There are lots of things to be done there.'

'I'll walk to Portgiskey with you.' Nathan pushed back his chair and stood up.

'No!'

Amy knew immediately that she had answered too

quickly, in too positive a manner. Josiah Jago had been startled. Now he looked from Amy to Nathan suspiciously.

'I don't mind walking there on my own,' explained Amy, doing her best to make the words casual. 'It will be nice to breathe in good, sweet air and think about something more than the next case of cholera.'

'You'll have all the time you need to be alone and think. I doubt if the Portgiskey fish-cellar will be working for another week or two. Besides, I'm not offering to walk with you just to be chivalrous. I go to Portgiskey every night to check my boat.'

Watching Nathan and Amy leaving the house together, Preacher Jago thought they would have made a splendid couple. He had always thought so; but now Amy was another man's wife, and her husband was many miles away. He should have said something to keep Nathan at the house while Amy went home alone. But he was too tired for guile. Shaking his head, Josiah Jago closed the door of his cottage and made his way wearily up the stairs to his bedroom.

He had always known that Nathan and Amy had made a great mistake in not marrying each other. He sincerely hoped they would never reach the same conclusion.

Crossing the narrow Pentuan bridge, Amy turned towards the beach, but Nathan stopped her with a touch on her arm. 'The tide's in too far. We'll need to follow the road and double back through the valley.'

These were the first words either of them had spoken since leaving the Jago house and they effectively broke the silence that had sat awkwardly on both of them. Each was thinking of the last occasion on which they had been alone.

'You've worked hard these past few weeks. My father couldn't have carried on without you.'

'*He's* the one who's been working too hard. But for him, Pentuan and most of the people in it would have died.'

A silence descended upon them again for some minutes before Nathan asked: 'What are you going to do, Amy? Will you go back to London? To Sammy?'

'Your pa thinks I should. He says that's where my duty lies.'

'He would. He's always taken "duty" seriously. If he hadn't, I would never have run away from home – and perhaps my mother would have been alive today. Think very carefully before you make up your mind, Amy. You have a right to be happy – and you're not happy with Sammy. I know it, and so do you.'

'At the moment I'm not sure about anything.' Amy stopped and turned towards him. 'But thank you for caring, Nathan.' She was silent for a few moments, before adding quietly: 'I would like you to leave now.'

The feeling that had come to both of them on the night he had kissed her had inexplicably returned. Nathan wondered what would happen if he kissed her again now.

'Good night, Nathan.' Amy turned and hurried away into the darkness – and Nathan hurried away after her.

It was some moments before Amy realised he was behind her. When she did, she whirled to face him.

'Nathan, I don't *want* you to come to Portgiskey with me . . . please!'

'All right, walk ahead of me, if you wish, but I have business to attend to at the cove.'

'Checking your boat? I'll do that for you.'

'I *do* check my boat regularly, but I have other things planned for tonight. I have a rendezvous to keep.'

'Oh, of course. You need to bring in smuggled goods if you're to keep Polrudden.'

'That's right. I've lost weeks of fishing. I must make money somehow.'

Amy suddenly became thoughtful. 'How will you manage *The Brave Amy H* without a crew?'

'I can't. I shall do what I did for the last rendezvous – take your small boat and bring back what I can.'

There was a strong breeze blowing at their backs as they made their way along the descending valley towards Portgiskey. The cliffs and surrounding hills meant that Portgiskey Cove was well protected, but beyond the bay it would be rough.

'This is no night to take a small boat out as far as you'll need to go. Do you have such need of money that you must risk your life to get it?'

'Yes. One day I intend buying another boat. With only one I can barely pay my debts, even in a good year. When Sir Lewis raises his tithes, I'll be hard pressed to do even that.'

'You can forget everything you owe to me, Nathan. Ma left more money than I knew she had. It must have come from Pa. I don't need more from you.'

'That's very generous of you, Amy, but I can't accept such an offer. You'll be paid, you and Sammy, but more of the money will come from smuggling than from fishing.'

'Then you'd better make as much as you can – before the Revenue men put an end to smuggling, once and for all. You can only do that with the drifter. Take her; I'll crew for you.'

'You? You'd fall asleep if I left you alone for a moment. No, I'll take the small boat. Besides, there's a new Chief Revenue Officer in Mevagissey. He'll no doubt be eager to make a name for himself. I won't risk having you caught.'

'There's not a Revenue boat built that can catch *The Brave Amy H*; you've said so yourself, many times. Remember how we gave the slip to those Moorish pirates when we brought her from the boatbuilder's yard?' Amy's eyes sparkled with an infectious enthusiasm.

Nathan grinned at the thought of that exciting chase. It seemed to have happened a lifetime ago, yet it was hardly two years.

'Do you *really* feel up to making a trip?'

Nathan knew he should not be asking her, but Amy was right. *The Brave Amy H* could bring back ten times the amount of contraband that her own little boat could carry – and Nathan was desperately in need of money.

'Of course I do. I can't think of anything I'd rather be doing. It will be marvellous to breathe fresh sea-air and get the smell of sickness and unwashed bodies out of my nostrils. Come on, hurry yourself. The thought of going to sea again has given me new energy. It's been months and months . . .'

Half an hour later, with the moonlight giving the

water the appearance of beaten pewter, *The Brave Amy H* slipped her moorings at Portgiskey. Catching the wind almost immediately, she heeled over and headed out towards the deep water of the English Channel.

The wind was almost dead astern, and *The Brave Amy H* was soon away from the shelter of the coastal headlands.

It must have been close to midnight when Amy called: 'There's a sail coming up from the south, no more than a mile away. It looks like Captain Pierre's ship.'

'That's the one I'm looking for. Haul in the sea-anchor. I'll show him a light before he goes away again.'

There was a brief flicker of answering light from the dark-sailed ship approaching from the Channel and the two vessels closed each other rapidly. Minutes later, Nathan brought *The Brave Amy H* alongside the smuggler as French seamen lowered plaited rope fenders over the side. There was a heavy swell, and damage might easily have been caused to the smaller fishing-boat.

From the deck of the French vessel, Captain Pierre looked down into Nathan's boat. 'Welcome, Captain Nathan – but please do not come aboard. The cholera, you understand?'

'Of course.' Nathan understood the sailor's fear of cholera. Once on board a ship it would almost certainly affect every member of the crew. 'But with any luck the epidemic is over in this part of the country – as my crew can tell you. She's nursed the victims in Pentuan back to health.'

The captain stared down at Amy, standing in the bow of *The Brave Amy H*, shadowed by the bulk of the French vessel. 'Who is that? Can it be my beautiful Amy? It is? Ah, *ma chérie!*' He gave a loud groan of Gallic despair. 'To meet you again after so long and not be able to kiss you. This is torture, indeed!'

To Nathan he said: 'Captain Nathan, you will kiss her for me. A Frenchman's kiss, if you please. Not like one of your English chickens. You understand me?'

'I do – but you'll need to persuade Amy.'

The banter continued, with Amy occasionally contributing a remark of her own, while the French crew lowered small kegs of brandy and waterproof packs of tobacco to the deck of *The Brave Amy H*.

Nathan had told the French captain he would take every keg of brandy and packet of tobacco that could comfortably be carried. But the fishing-boat was no more than half-loaded when there was a cry from the look-out that caused alarm among the Frenchmen.

Captain Pierre had disappeared from the side of the ship at the first shout. Now he reappeared.

'It is a ship, Captain Nathan. Coming from the direction of your English coast. I think it may be a warship. Cut your ropes quickly.'

Already the French vessel was under way, crowding on sail and dragging *The Brave Amy H* through the water with her.

Nathan was attacking one of the mooring-ropes with his knife, when something struck the side of the ship not four feet away from his head and splinters of wood flew about him. He felt a searing pain in his arm, and as he tumbled to the bottom of *The Brave Amy H* he heard the familiar rumble of a cannonade.

'That was British shooting . . .'

As the thought was passing through Nathan's mind he heard Amy's cry. Suddenly he realised that the peculiar angle at which he was lying had nothing to do with his fall. The rope he had been cutting was still holding. *The Brave Amy H* was being towed through the water by the rear mooring-rope and bouncing awkwardly over the waves. Amy was sawing away at the rope, but it was eventually severed by an axe-wielding French seaman on board the boat towering above them.

Scrambling to his feet in the wildly rocking boat, Nathan helped Amy to hoist the sails. As he did so, he saw that the man-of-war with the outline of a British frigate had altered course to pursue the French vessel. The new course did not prevent a gunner from firing off a smaller cannon at *The Brave Amy H*. Fortunately, the shot fell well short, and Nathan was able to alter course and pass well astern of the pursuing naval vessel.

As he brought *The Brave Amy H* round in a wide circle to take the craft shorewards, Nathan felt another sharp pain in his arm. Reaching up to explore his upper arm, he discovered a deep groove carved in the flesh, and his finger came away sticky with blood.

'Are you all right?' The moonlight was bright enough for Amy to be able to see Nathan exploring his arm with his fingertips.

'It's nothing. A splinter of wood must have caught me when the man-o'-war opened fire.'

'Let me have a look.' Amy clambered aft to stand beside him. His shirt sleeve was already torn, and now she ripped it still more in order to examine the wound better.

'It's not pretty, but fortunately it's not *too* serious. I'll bind it up for you.'

Amy had a kerchief about her neck. Taking it off, she folded it into a long, narrow strip and bound it about the wounded arm. 'That will do until we get ashore and I can bind it properly.'

The bandaging over, Amy remained beside Nathan, looking out across the water to where both the French vessel and the British frigate had vanished into the gloom of the distance.

'Do you think Captain Pierre will be all right?' Amy asked anxiously.

'Sure to be,' replied Nathan confidently. 'He has a good ship. It will outrun a man-o'-war.'

'Where did the frigate come from? Was it on patrol, do you think?'

'I doubt it. I'd say it was outward bound from Fowey. It was probably sheer bad luck for us that the captain was keeping such a good look-out. He wasted no time running out his guns, either. Nelson would have been proud of him.'

Nathan shook his head ruefully at Amy. 'Things have a nasty habit of happening to us when you and I are at sea together.'

'Yes.'

Amy did not pursue the conversation. When she had seen Nathan take a bloody hand away from his arm she had felt a moment of panic. Not until she had learned for herself that it was not too serious had the panic subsided. She had been so relieved she could have hugged him. The urge to do so was still there.

Leaving Nathan's side, Amy stepped into the well-deck, just aft of the wheel. She took only one step before turning hurriedly back to Nathan.

'There's water in the boat! It must be a foot deep.'

'Damn! I thought she wasn't handling as she should. Take the wheel for me while I have a look.'

Handing the wheel over to Amy, Nathan dropped into the well-deck and took up the bottom boards. Amy was right. There was at least a foot of water in the bottom of the boat. If any more came in, the drifter's handling would be seriously affected. Nathan worked his way forward, trying to locate the damage, but he was unable to find the spot where the water was entering the boat.

'Some of the planks must have sprung when we were being battered against Cap'n Pierre's ship,' he called to Amy. 'Head straight for Portgiskey. We'll have to risk the man-o'-war coming back to find us. I'll crowd on all the sail we've got and then start pumping. We should make it all right.'

They almost did. With sails close-hauled, Amy kept the boat's bow pointed towards Portgiskey, while Nathan worked the bilge pump as hard as he could.

It soon became apparent that the water was gaining, but Nathan continued to pump until his muscles were numb and the blood from his wound ran down his arm, making the pump-handle slippery. Then, with the cliffs about Portgiskey no more than a mile away, the bilge pump became blocked. Water had seeped inside some of the packets of tobacco and split them open. Their contents completely clogged the pump.

Nathan worked furiously to clear the tobacco, but soon realised it was an impossible task. The water was rising too fast. *The Brave Amy H* was now so low in the water that small waves were breaking over the side.

Making his way to Amy, Nathan said: 'The pump's blocked. The boat will go under at any moment. We'll need to swim home. I'll take the wheel and keep her on course for as long as I can. You strip off. You can't swim in those clothes.'

As he was talking, Nathan grasped the wheel. Holding it firmly with one hand, he bent down and unlaced his heavy boots, kicking them off into the bottom of the boat.

Looking up again, he saw that Amy, too, had removed her shoes, but she was standing with her hand poised uncertainly on the unlaced cord at the neck of her grey linen dress.

'For God's sake, Amy! This is no time for modesty. You'll need to swim close on a mile . . . !'

Amy tugged the cord free and dropped the dress from her shoulders, then down over her breasts. As it fell to the wet deck at her feet, she wriggled out of her cotton petticoat. At that moment, *The Brave Amy H* shipped a wave that surged over the bow and swept the length of the boat. Nathan had to hold the wheel with all his strength to prevent the boat being swept broadside on to the sea and swamped.

The Brave Amy H was still making headway, but she handled heavily and sluggishly. Nevertheless, Nathan was determined to bring his boat as close inshore as was possible before abandoning her.

Another wave rose over the bow into the half-filled boat, but still the sturdy drifter ploughed on towards the cleft in the cliffs that was Portgiskey Cove. They were less than half a mile from shore now and the wind coming off the high land was beginning to play tricks on them, yet still *The Brave Amy H* ploughed shoreward.

Amy was kneeling in the bow of the boat now. Looking at her, bare-breasted in the moonlight, Nathan was reminded of a beautifully carved figurehead he had once admired on the prow of a French merchantman, captured in the Mediterranean.

Amy looked back at him and called excitedly: 'We're going to make it, Nathan. *The Brave Amy H* will get us home.'

The words had hardly been spoken when the wind dropped away suddenly, leaving the boat wallowing heavily in the lee of the cliff. Seconds later a low wave, hardly more than two feet high, broke against the side of *The Brave Amy H* and hundreds of gallons of seawater poured inside the foundering fishing-boat. It was the end. Slowly, the boat tilted and began to slide beneath the water.

'Jump!'

Nathan matched word with deed and leaped over the side himself. As he struck out for the shore, he called to Amy. To his relief, she answered him from near at hand as they both swam into the long shadows cast by the cliffs.

'Keep going. I'm right behind you,' he called. He knew that Amy was a strong swimmer and he began heading towards Portgiskey Cove, grateful for the fact that the tide was in their favour.

The salt water was stinging his wounded arm, and Nathan stopped swimming for a few minutes to remove the neckerchief that was beginning to chafe the wound.

Looking back, Nathan saw that *The Brave Amy H* had somehow righted herself. Although filled almost to the gunwales with water, she still refused to sink.

The Brave Amy H represented Nathan's sole means of earning an independent livelihood. Treading water and looking at the vessel, Nathan knew he could not allow her to sink without some attempt to salvage her.

Making a sudden decision, Nathan struck out for the boat. Minutes later he dragged himself back on board. He swiftly located a length of rope long enough for his purpose. Knowing just how deep the water was along this part of the coast, he paid out enough to mark the drifter's position when she finally went under. On most trips he and his crew were in the habit of putting out a few lobster-pots, with wooden keg marker-buoys. Pulling one of the small buoys from a water-filled locker, Nathan secured it to one end of the rope. The other end was secured to a brass ring screwed into the gunwale.

The work was completed just in time. As he slipped back into the sea and struck out for the shore once more, *The Brave Amy H* dipped her bow into a wave and failed to rise again. Slowly, the two masts slid beneath the water until only the keg buoy and a few loose packs of contraband tobacco were floating on the surface of the water to mark her position.

With a heavy heart, Nathan turned his back on the spot and struck out strongly for Portgiskey Cove.

When he reached the shallows, Nathan found Amy in a desperate panic. As he pulled himself to his feet and staggered ashore, he saw Amy frantically dragging her own small boat to the water's edge.

'What are you doing?'

At the sound of his voice, Amy spun round to face him.

'Nathan . . . Oh! Thank God!' She rushed at him with such eagerness that she almost knocked him back into the water. As he held her, he felt her naked body tremble uncontrollably in his arms.

'What happened? I thought you were right behind me, but when I came ashore you were nowhere to be seen. I called and called. When you didn't answer I thought something must have happened to you. Your arm . . . I didn't know what to think.'

'I didn't hear you. There's so much noise out there – the wind, and the sea crashing against the rocks. I saw *The Brave Amy H* was still afloat. I went back to fix a marker to her.'

'You fool! You frightened the life out of me.' Amy clung to him as though he might rush back into the sea again. 'When I thought you were lost I didn't know what to do. I . . . I've never been so panic-stricken in all my life.'

Nathan tried to push her gently away, in order to look down at her face, but she clung to him tenaciously.

'No. Just hold me. Please, just hold me.'

It was not a difficult duty to perform. Her wet body was smooth beneath his hands as he stroked it in what began as a bid to calm her nerves. Nathan never knew at what moment his compassion became desire – but Amy knew. She knew, too, that she should have slipped from his arms and hurried inside the Portgiskey cottage. She did neither. The events of this night had badly shaken her resolution. She raised her head as his lips came down upon her mouth and the next moment she was meeting his ardour with a passion that took his breath away. His hands grew bolder, and for long, gasping moments Amy writhed to their touch. Not until now did she break away from him.

As Nathan tried to take hold of her again, she took his hand and held it up to her cheek. 'Not here, Nathan. Let's go inside.' Her voice was husky with the same desire that held Nathan in its grip, and hand in hand they went to the cottage together.

Nathan was awakened in the morning by the raucous crying of gulls outside the window. It was a moment or two before he realised where he was. Then he sank back on the feather-filled pillow and thought of what had happened only a few hours before.

'You'll never raise *The Brave Amy H* by lying abed all day.' Amy came into the room. Much to Nathan's disappointment, she was fully dressed.

'The sun is hardly up yet. Come back to bed.'

'No, Nathan.' She leaned over the bed and kissed him lightly on the forehead, eluding his hands.

He smiled up at her, but saw no answering smile on her face. Raising himself on one elbow, he said: 'What do we do now, Amy?'

Amy went to the window. Drawing back the curtain, she looked out across St Austell Bay before answering.

'Unless we want to change everything – to lose everything that we both enjoy here – we do nothing. We must go on as though last night never happened.'

'We can't do that! Not after . . . everything. Amy, you know I love you?'

'Things would have been very different had you

discovered that before I went away, Nathan.' She spoke with her hands clenched tightly at her sides. 'I'd have done anything – gone *anywhere* – with you.'

'What are you saying, Amy?'

She turned to face him. 'I'm saying that I'm no longer Amy Hoblyn, a little girl in love with a man who's blinded by the daughter of the manor. I'm Amy *Mizler* now – the wife of another man.'

'But you don't love him.'

'No, and I don't think I ever have. Poor Sammy was a means of escape. I used him. I couldn't stay here to be constantly reminded that *you* belonged to someone else. I was ashamed of my reason for marrying Sammy at first. Then I learned that he hadn't really married *me* for love, either.'

'I'm sorry, Amy. I don't understand.'

'No, I don't suppose you do. It's probably never occurred to you that Sammy was jealous of you from the first moment you met. You were on the way up then, a future prize-fighting champion. Sammy was on the way down. He'd never *quite* managed to be the best, and now he never would, because you would always be ahead of him. You became "friends"; but at any gathering, at any prize-fight, it was always *you* people wanted to see, to talk to. He was just Sammy Mizler, the man who arranged *your* fights. The little man who looked after *you*.'

Nathan listened to Amy in astonishment. 'I don't believe it. I don't believe Sammy ever felt that way.'

'It's true enough, Nathan. When I was in London it came out every time Sammy had too much to drink – which was most nights he was home.'

'But what has this to do with him marrying you?'

'Ah! That's where Sammy thought he was being clever. He convinced himself a long time ago that it was *me* you really loved, not Elinor. Even after you'd married her he believed that one day you'd realise your mistake and want me. But it would have been too late then. I would be his. Whatever happened, he would have had me first. He had beaten you for the very first time.'

Nathan was deeply shaken. 'I'm sorry, Amy. I never realised Sammy hated me so much. I always thought we were good friends.'

'He doesn't hate you. He *envies* you. He envies you so much it's become an obsession with him. He *has* to prove he can beat you.'

'But, if this is true, why do we have to forget last night? I can make you happy, Amy. I know I can.'

'Yes, Nathan. You could make me happy. But . . . Oh, I'm so confused at the moment. I only know that I'm still married to Sammy. Try as I might, I can't just put it behind me as though it never happened. I told you once that Pa brought me up as a Methodist. Perhaps that's got something to do with it.'

'You managed to forget it last night,' Nathan reminded her.

'Yes . . . and I'm not going to say I'm sorry about it. But it mustn't happen again, Nathan. I want you to promise me it won't happen again.'

Nathan shook his head.

'Please, Nathan. Unless you promise, I must leave here – probably go back to London. Yes, I know it's foolish, but I *can't* let you make love to me while I'm another man's wife. Try to understand.'

Nathan knew he would never understand, but Amy

had worked herself up to such a highly emotional state he believed she really would go away if he did not give her the promise she demanded.

'All right, Amy. I promise to try.' It was a promise that would be almost impossible to keep, but it had to be given.

Amy sagged with relief. 'Thank you. If you hadn't agreed, I would have gone away. Then I would have had nothing left at all. Now I have Portgiskey – and I have you, too, don't I, Nathan? I've taken over Ma's share of the business, so we're partners again.'

Nathan wondered which of them would weaken first but, throwing back the bedclothes, he swung his feet to the floor.

'Yes, Amy. We're partners.'

11

Nathan and Amy were working on the beach at Portgiskey Cove when Sammy Mizler arrived.

Riding a horse he had hired in St Austell, his approach along the sands from Pentuan had gone unnoticed by the busy couple.

The Brave Amy H had drifted inshore, as Nathan had anticipated, and was lying on her side in no more than a fathom of water. Amy had rowed Nathan out to the boat, where he dived to attach a very long rope to the sunken drifter. He had already salvaged everything movable – together with a dozen kegs of good French brandy that were now safely stowed beneath the fish-cellar.

Amy saw her husband first. She and Nathan were kneeling together in the sand, their heads close as they spliced a rope to extend the length attached to *The Brave Amy H*.

Nathan heard Amy's gasp of disbelief and looked

up to see the blood rush from her face. She swayed as though she might faint. He reached a hand out
hastily to steady her, but she scrambled to her feet
after giving him a dismayed glance. Then Nathan,
too, saw his one-time partner and prize-fighting
companion.

'Well, now, here's a fine scene of domestic industry,' said Sammy Mizler mockingly. 'But you've made
a mistake, Amy. *I'm* your husband, remember?'

'I remember it every waking hour,' replied Amy,
gathering her wits together.

'What do you want, Sammy?' Nathan put down the
half-joined ropes and stood up to face the other man.

'Is that the way to greet an old friend? "What do
you want, Sammy?" How about, "Hello, Sammy. It's
nice to see you, Sammy," or "Hello, Sammy, I'm
pleased to see you because I owe you some money
for the partnership I bought out"?'

Nathan pointed to where the long rope disappeared
beneath the sea. 'There's your money, Sammy. Sunk
in a fathom of water, but with the help of your horse
we may be able to haul *The Brave Amy H* clear.'

Sammy Mizler shook his head. 'No, my friend. You
are wrong. That's *your* money beneath the water. I'll
thank you to pay mine in golden guineas. As for this
horse . . .' Sammy cuffed an ear of the sway-backed
animal upon which he sat. 'I've paid good money for
its hire – as a *riding*-horse. You'll need to find yourself
a cart-horse if you want your boat pulled from the
water. You don't seem to have had much luck with
your boats, Nathan. First *Annie Jago*, and now this
one.'

Sammy leaned forward in the saddle. 'Could it be

that your thoughts are too occupied with other things?'

Angrily, Nathan took a pace towards Sammy Mizler; then he remembered what had happened between himself and Amy the previous night, and he stopped. Anger left him and a sense of shame took its place. Sammy Mizler had been his friend for many years. Together they had climbed the ladder of success in the prize-fighting world and reached the top.

'You didn't come all this way just to be insulting, or to collect a few guineas. Why are you here, Sammy?'

'A few guineas, Nathan? I'm due a hundred now, I believe. Then there's what you owe my wife . . .'

'I'll manage my own business affairs, thank you, Sammy. And I'm just as curious as Nathan to know why you're here.'

'I don't doubt it, my dear wife. Would you believe me if I were to say I've come all this way to enjoy your charms once more? No, I can see you wouldn't. But suppose you and I go inside the house while Nathan plays with his boat. You can talk to me while I change my travelling-clothes, then I'll let you cook me a meal. Is your mother in the house? Or did you decide it would be more "convenient" to leave her in the lunatic asylum?'

Mention of her mother struck Amy like a blow. During the weeks of epidemic she had worked hard, pushing thoughts of her mother to the back of her mind. Now Sammy had brought her cruelly and abruptly face to face with the reality of her death. Amy was not yet prepared for it. Turning away, she ran to the house, leaving Sammy staring open-mouthed after her.

'Peggy Hoblyn's dead. She died of cholera, here at Portgiskey.'

'Cholera?' Sammy Mizler's sallow London complexion paled even more. It was a typical reaction when the disease was mentioned. 'You've had cholera here?'

'We still have. My father said last night there were more than twenty villagers ill in Pentuan, and the burial-ground has been the busiest place in the village these last few weeks. I believe Mevagissey is faring even worse.'

Watching Sammy Mizler's expression come close to sheer terror, Nathan was reminded of the obsession Sammy had always had with his health. Nathan had known him leave a room or a tavern bar because someone had sneezed.

'Ask Amy for the details when you go inside. She's been nursing the worst cholera cases throughout the whole epidemic.'

'Amy has . . . !' Sammy sounded as though he was being strangled.

'Yes. She's been staying in the village with them. Last night was the first she'd spent at Portgiskey for five weeks.'

Sammy Mizler might have an obsession with his health, but he was no fool. He knew that Nathan was quite capable of using this knowledge to drive him away from Cornwall – and from Amy.

'I don't believe you.'

Nathan shrugged. 'Please yourself, Sammy. Go to Pentuan and ask my father. If he's not there, go up to the burial-ground and count the number of graves. Better still, go to Mevagissey and check there. I hear they've fenced off a whole area of the churchyard for those who die of cholera. You won't be able to ask the preacher; he was one of the first to die. Now, I'm sure you'll forgive me, but I've got a boat to salvage. If you want your money, come to my father's house tonight. I'm owed money in the village. I'll collect from those well enough to pay and give you whatever I raise.'

Nathan turned away, but Sammy called after him. 'I'll have no money that's passed through the hands of anyone with cholera. You can bring it to London when you come.'

Sammy Mizler's words brought Nathan to a halt.

'That's right. You've business in London. Pressing business. I'm here to tell you that the Duke of Clarence thinks it's time you honoured the agreement you made with him. He's arranged a prize-fight for you. On 6 November, at Bushy Park, close to his estate. He expects to attract the largest crowd ever seen at a prize-fight. It's mooted that the Prince Regent himself will be there.'

Nathan had almost forgotten that he had agreed to a second fight for the purse the Duke of Clarence had put up early the previous year. Now he was being called upon to fulfil that promise, and on his son's first birthday.

Sammy Mizler was watching Nathan closely. 'Can I tell the Duke you'll be there? Or shall I tell him you honour *your* word in the same manner as some women honour their marriage vows?'

Nathan flushed, but controlled his anger. Sammy had every right to make such a jibe.

'I seem to recall that the marriage service also demands that a man should "love and cherish" his wife, Sammy. You can tell the Duke of Clarence that I'll be there. Who will I be fighting?'

Sammy Mizler smiled triumphantly. With more than a touch of malice in his expression, he replied: 'Abraham Dellow. Remember him? The negro slave you fought in Bristol. He's much improved now, Nathan. Greatly improved. I've trained him for many months and he's the best prize-fighter I've ever seen in action. Even better than you were in your prime. I've told the Duke it will be a one-sided fight – that he ought to match my man against a good, strong, young fighter, not a has-been – but the Duke wants you. He wants Abraham to become the undisputed champion of the world.'

Still smiling, Sammy flicked the reins of his horse and brought the animal round in a half-circle. 'Tell Amy I'll not bother to claim my rights as a husband on this visit, but she'll do well not to forget she's married to *me*. I'll be back for her some day. Good-bye, Nathan. I'll see you in London in November. You'll need to provide your own men in your corner; I'll be with Abraham Dellow. But for old time's sake I'll use my skills to bring you round when the fight's over.'

With this parting jibe, Sammy dug his heels into the flanks of his ribby nag. The animal set off along the seashore with a resigned gait, heading for the St Austell road.

From the window of the cottage, Amy saw her husband leaving and hurried out to Nathan's side.

'What's happening? Where's Sammy going?'

'Home. Back to London.'

Amy looked at Nathan in disbelief. 'But why? I

thought . . .' Sudden relief overcame her and she took Nathan's arm. 'When he spoke of coming back to me I . . . felt sick. I couldn't live with Sammy again.'

Gripping Nathan's arm with both her hands, she said fiercely: 'I'd kill myself before I let him touch me again. I *swear* I would . . .'

'Hush!' Nathan watched Sammy Mizler until he rode from view beyond the rocks separating Portgiskey Cove from the Pentuan sands. 'We won't have to think about that for a very long time. I told Sammy there was cholera in Pentuan, that you'd been nursing the victims. You know what he's like about coming into contact with illness. The thought of cholera terrified him. Had he been riding any other horse, he'd have galloped all the way back to St Austell.'

'But why did he come all this way, Nathan? It wasn't just to collect the money you owe him, surely? Sammy can live very comfortably on what the gentlemen of the "Fancy" pay him to teach them prize-fighting.'

Nathan became suddenly thoughtful, and Amy said: 'There is something else . . . Tell me, Nathan.'

'The Duke of Clarence wants me to defend my title against Abraham Dellow again. This time near London.'

'The slave you fought in Bristol? Nathan, you *can't*. You've been away from the prize-ring for too long. You told Sammy so, of course?'

'When the Duke of Clarence gave me a purse large enough to buy Venn Farm, he made it clear it was for *two* fights. I must honour the promise I made then.'

'But . . . does it have to be Abraham Dellow? Sammy has been training him hard. He's been prize-fighting ever since he went to London from Bristol.'

Nathan nodded ruefully. 'Sammy says he's the best – and no one is a better judge. The most damnable part is that I doubt if I'll make a penny from the fight.'

Nathan shrugged. 'But I've got two months to worry about the fight, and only about four hours in which to haul *The Brave Amy H* to safety before the tide comes in. When I've finished that splice, I'd like you to bring the rope up the beach as far as you can and secure it to a rock or a stake – anything. I'm going to Venn. Tom hired a team of oxen to plough his steepest fields. If he's still got them, I'll bring them down here.'

'And if he hasn't? There's a storm blowing up—' Amy stopped. There was no need to say more.

'If he hasn't, I lose my boat.'

Fortunately, Tom Quicke still had the oxen and he brought them to Portgiskey as fast as the steady, slow-plodding animals would travel. All Nathan's crew turned out to add their strength to the combined weight of the oxen. Slowly but surely, *The Brave Amy H* was tugged from the water. A great cheer went up from the men and a few watchers as the drifter cleared the water and slid on her side across the sand to a patch of sloping shingle beside the Portgis-key quay. Here *The Brave Amy H* would remain until she was made seaworthy once more.

Nathan's speed in salvaging his boat saved her from becoming a total wreck. That night a fierce storm broke along the length of the south Cornish coast. Boats were torn from their moorings, waterside houses flooded and deep-sea vessels scurried to mid-Channel, there to ride out the storm, well clear of dangerous Cornish rocks. The storm raged for two days and two nights before moving on, leaving the sea exhausted and the land washed clean.

Things quickly returned to normal at Polrudden. There had been no more cases of cholera in Pentuan village, and the servants had returned to their duties. But now they were working they would expect to be paid – and Nathan's boat lay on her side at Portgiskey.

On his way to Portgiskey on the first morning after the storm, Nathan called at Venn Farm and he arrived at the cove shouldering the ten-month-old Beville.

Ahab Arthur and two of Nathan's fishermen were already at Portgiskey, shaking their heads pessimistically as they examined *The Brave Amy H*. Amy had seen Nathan approaching and she ran from the cottage to take Beville from his father. The expression on her face as she took the baby from him caused the fishermen to nudge each other knowingly.

'Have you got the timber we're going to need?' Nathan asked Ahab Arthur sharply. He had seen the men's knowing glances, and they annoyed him.

'I've got it, but there's no certainty we'll be able to make *The Brave Amy H* seaworthy again. As well as the sprung planks there's a broken stem and a couple of broken ribs. I don't know what you hit, Nathan, but whatever it was you hit it damned hard.'

He looked at Nathan slyly. 'By the way, there was a man-o'-war left Fowey the night you had your accident. She returned only yesterday evening. It seems the crew had a rough time in the storm. 'Tis said they surprised a French smuggler not a mile or two off

Fowey and chased her halfway to the French coast. The Frenchie got clean away. I thought you'd likely want to know.'

Nathan had not told his crew how *The Brave Amy H* had been damaged – and he would not. Such a yarn would be repeated, and the fewer men who knew of his smuggling activities the safer he would be. But he could not prevent men from arriving at their own conclusions.

It took the men five days of frustrating work before *The Brave Amy H* was righted and floated on the waters of Portgiskey Cove to check on her seaworthiness. Much to everyone's delight, the boat rode the water perfectly, none entering between the newly caulked planking. Two hours later *The Brave Amy H* was heading out to sea, with Nathan at the helm, to lay her nets.

The fish ran well for Nathan. He found an abundance of pilchards well off shore, and the Pentuan women were able to return to full-time working in the fish-cellar at Portgiskey once more. The market had revived, too. The foolish rumours that fish had been responsible for spreading cholera had been discounted by learned medical men in London. In fact, the physicians declared that fish was actually *beneficial* in warding off the much feared sickness.

This conclusion was, in all probability, no more sound than the rumour it was intended to discredit, but it had the effect of creating a sudden demand for fish that Cornish fishermen were unable to meet. There was still cholera in one or two fishing villages, and no more than half the county's boats were at sea.

The clamour for fish coincided with a disastrous

harvest throughout the land. Only a fraction of the corn needed to meet the needs of Britain's growing population had been harvested. With grain from the Continent denied them by Napoleon, a crisis was at hand. Already prices had soared beyond the reach of ordinary working people, and discontent was spreading rapidly. All over the country militiamen were being urgently called up for service and sent to towns far from their own homes. By detailing the militia for garrison duties in other counties, it was hoped their sympathies would not be so easily aroused as they might in their own towns and villages.

When bad weather finally brought fishing to a temporary halt, Nathan spent some hours in the Portgiskey cottage, working on his accounts. Beville was playing on the floor with Amy, and every so often Nathan would pause in his work and watch them for a while.

Glancing up from the simple game she was playing with the child, Amy caught Nathan in one of these moments. 'Are we disturbing you, Nathan? Would you rather I took Beville to the kitchen to play?'

Nathan smiled. 'No, I enjoy listening to Beville chuckling – and to you too, Amy. There's been little to make you smile for a very long time.'

'I'm happier now than I can ever remember. I know there's so much more that I want – that we both want – but it's wonderful to have Beville here.'

Beville crawled to Amy and tried to pull himself to a standing position, using her dress. Losing his grip, he fell backwards, landing heavily on his bottom. Before he had made up his mind whether to laugh or cry, Amy picked him up and whirled him high in the air.

As Beville chuckled, Amy hugged him to her. 'Ooh! You young rapscallion. I wish you were all mine . . .'

Her words caused Nathan to recall Elinor and the night almost a year ago when she had died without ever seeing the child she had carried inside her body for so long.

Amy saw Nathan's change of expression and guessed at the cause. She could have bitten off her tongue. To give him something else to think about, she asked: 'How have you done during the past few weeks? Has *The Brave Amy H* made a huge profit?'

'H'm? Oh, yes, she's made money. But not as much as I need. The tithes are due this month. Then there's Sammy's money, your money – and Polrudden. *The Brave Amy H* just can't catch enough fish to pay all the bills.'

'Then let's buy another boat.'

'It's just not possible,' replied Nathan patiently. 'Every penny I earn is taken up in one way or another. I simply can't afford to buy another boat.'

Amy stooped down to move a tempting, charred piece of wood out of Beville's reach before answering. 'I can.'

'You buy me a boat? No, it's out of the question.'

'It's nothing of the sort,' Amy retorted. 'And I wouldn't be buying it for you. Not entirely, that is. I've inherited my ma's share in the business, right?'

Nathan nodded.

'That gives me a quarter interest, so it means I have *some* say in what goes on at Portgiskey. Ma also left me some money – rather a lot of money. If I use some of it to buy another boat, and we agree to forget the money you owe me, would you accept me as a full partner?'

'Would I . . . ?' Amy's generous offer made sound business sense and it had been put in a way that Amy hoped would be acceptable to Nathan.

Nathan could hardly hide his elation. Another boat would pull him clear of the near-poverty in which he now found himself. But he had to be certain Amy was not doing this merely because of her feelings for him.

'You'll be risking a lot of money, Amy.'

Amy snorted loudly. 'I'll be risking nothing. You're the best drift-fisherman on this coast. You've made money when others were being forced to sell off their nets and boats. Most of the money I have now was earned by my pa. You knew him. What would he have wanted me to do with it? I'll tell you: he would have wanted me to have a good boat and a share in Portgiskey. If it also happened to help a little boy, named "Beville", after his own son, that would clinch it.'

Hugging Beville to her, she smiled at Nathan. 'Besides, we'll still be carrying on Pa's own trade. He'd have to approve of that.'

12

Nathan bought his new boat in a Falmouth auction. A fine French-built lugger, she had been taken as a prize by an English man-of-war in a daring raid on a French harbour. Nathan was well pleased with his purchase and proudly showed off her paces to Amy when he brought the boat back to Portgiskey.

As they scudded across St Austell Bay, running before a stiff breeze, Amy agreed it was a fine craft.

'But she'll never mean quite as much to us as *The Brave Amy H*,' she added nostalgically. 'You and I were the first to sail in her, and she was our very first boat. There will never be another like her. What will you call this one?'

'Well, we've had an *Annie Jago*. How about *Peggy Hoblyn*?'

'Yes, I'd like that very much.'

Amy's hand found Nathan's, on the wheel. If any of the crew noticed, not one of them made any comment.

Nathan still did his share of fishing during the day, but he would not be taking a boat out at night until after the fight. Instead, he spent his evenings training. Common sense told him that he had little chance of retaining his title, but he was determined that the giant ex-slave would leave the prize-ring well aware he had been in a fight.

There were more drifters working the coast now. Many of the older seine-fishermen still harboured a deep-rooted resentment against the drifter, but more and more fishermen were coming to realise that drifting offered them an opportunity for a year-round living. Because of this, Nathan had no difficulty finding crews to keep his two boats at sea day and night, and the Portgiskey fish-cellar was busier than ever before.

With the arrival of the second lugger, Nathan hoped his money troubles were over for a while. He thought he might even be able to purchase a third boat once Sammy Mizler had been paid off. But this would mean buying another fish-cellar . . .

Meanwhile, events were taking place in London that would ultimately concern Nathan deeply.

Sir Lewis Hearle's well-planned final assault on the Methodist Church had foundered.

The combined might of the Established Church and many of the country's great landowners had failed to push Sir Lewis's Bill through Parliament. Indeed, the dissenting churches were united as never before, and as they never would be again. In unity, they learned they were not without influence themselves. The Earl of Stanhope, acting as their champion, utterly demolished the arguments of Sir Lewis Hearle and his friends.

Visiting Lord Liverpool, the country's new Prime Minister, at his Downing Street home, the Earl of Stanhope pointed out that the Methodist religion was now beginning to attract solid citizens to its ranks – men with votes. He provided the Prime Minister with a wealth of impressive statistics, clinching the argument with the result of a recent survey. This showed that in the area covered by the survey the Established Church possessed 2533 places of worship, most of them no more than a third full for each Sunday service. By contrast, the dissident churches had 3454 churches and chapels, all of them packed to capacity for every service, be it Sunday or weekday.

Lord Liverpool and his government, later to be known as the best-hated cabinet England had ever known, had no wish to earn the enmity of such a vast percentage of the populace at this early stage of Lord Liverpool's reign as First Minister. There was serious trouble in the Midlands with disgruntled weavers, and farmworkers and miners were on the verge of riot because of low wages and the high price of corn. Meanwhile, the Irish, taking full advantage of the absence of the army who were fighting Napoleon in the Peninsula, seemed poised for open rebellion. Lord Liverpool could not risk trouble from yet another section of the populace, especially one with such deeply held beliefs.

Summoning Sir Lewis Hearle to his office, Great Britain's Prime Minister berated the Home Office Under-Secretary for bungling the brief given to him by Spencer Perceval. If the Government followed Sir

Lewis Hearle's advice, it would bring the Tory administration down and provoke rioting on a scale that would overwhelm the overburdened forces of law and order. The stage would then be set for a popular uprising such as that which had choked the gutters of Paris with the blood of France's aristocracy.

In a remarkable political *volte-face*, the Tory Prime Minister made an astounding announcement.

'After giving this matter a great deal of thought, Sir Lewis, I have reached a conclusion. I prefer to have the bulk of the Methodist Church on my side and not against me. I therefore propose to give them full religious freedom: the right to practise their religion as they see fit, without let or hindrance.'

Standing before the leader of the party he had supported for all his political life, his face pale and strained, Sir Lewis Hearle fought to maintain control of himself.

'Will you allow me to resign my office? Or do you intend dismissing me?'

'Dismiss you? My dear sir, of course not. Submit your resignation couched in the usual terms. Pressure of private business commitments . . . something like that. I will accept it with regret, and publicly thank you for your hard work whilst in office. You already have a baronetcy or my gratitude would take a more tangible form. Perhaps I could persuade his Royal Highness, the Prince Regent, to make some additional gesture . . .'

'That will not be necessary, my Lord. I have no son to inherit my titles. I have *no* children . . . now.'

'Very sad, Sir Lewis. Now, if you will excuse me? I have much work to do. My secretary will show you out. Thank you for coming to see me.'

Outside, in the streets of London, it was drizzling. Apart from shrugging his cloak higher about his shoulders, Sir Lewis hardly seemed to notice. He walked slowly in the direction of his club, thinking of the bleak future that lay before him. The post of Under-Secretary was to have been merely a beginning – the first step on the ladder that might have taken him to the highest office in the land. He snorted angrily, frightening a passing governess carrying a small child. What was left to him now?

The tide of the Napoleonic war was beginning to turn in Great Britain's favour in Europe. It was being said that the mercurial little French General had over-extended his army in Russia and would soon begin a disastrous retreat from that vast, unconquerable country. If peace came, Lord Liverpool would no doubt call an election. After gaining and losing a ministerial post during his present term of office, it was doubtful whether Sir Lewis would be chosen by Fowey's fickle voters to represent them again, so strongly were they influenced by the county's gentry.

Sir Lewis knew he would have little difficulty obtaining a nomination to another seat, but it would need to be closer to London. Such a move would break all his ties with Cornwall. His wife was dead. Elinor was dead. He had only Polrudden there – and Beville.

The baby was Elinor's son, of course. His only grandson. But he had been cut from Elinor's dead body. The brat bore as much responsibility for her death as did its father. The child was not even a Hearle, but a Jago. Sired by a prize-fighter – a fisherman – and the son of a Methodist minister. Sir Lewis could not prevent his grandson from inheriting his title, but should he have Polrudden, too?

The baronet stopped in his tracks. Behind him, a fat washerwoman bearing a heavy basket on her shoulder was forced to step from the footway into the filth of the gutter, grumbling at the inconsiderate ways of the class of person for whom she was forced to work.

'Dammit! I've had this millstone about my neck for years and for what? So it can be enjoyed by a *fisherman*? Or in order that a brat steeped in Methodism may claim it for his inheritance? No, by God! I'll sell it first! That's what I'll do. I'll sell Polrudden.'

Sir Lewis Hearle banged fist into palm, and passers-by ushered their children from the footpath, giving a wide berth to this wet, wild-eyed man who stood muttering angrily to himself.

The decision made, Sir Lewis felt marginally better. He was a ruined man, of course. He had overcommitted himself in a gamble on his political future. But selling Polrudden would keep him going until he had established himself in a new constituency. He contemplated changing his allegiance and joining the Whigs, but dismissed the idea immediately. His well-known anti-Methodist views were not popular with them. He could expect little advancement in their ranks, should they come to power in the foreseeable future – and that in itself was highly unlikely.

Sir Lewis had been walking as he was thinking and now found himself in St James's Street, where his club was situated. A respectable club was essential to any man with political aspirations – but they had more to offer than respectability. The son of more than one great house had gambled away his inheritance here, on a session of hazard that might have lasted for two days and nights.

There was excitement in the air when Sir Lewis Hearle entered the club. He thought it probable there was a 'hot' game underway, but when he sat down and called for a drink he quickly learned the truth. One of his fellow-MPs came across the room and spoke to him – a certain indication that news of his removal from office had not yet reached the House. Once it was common knowledge, Sir Lewis knew he would be avoided as though he had the plague.

'I would have expected you to be in the thick of the argument about the outcome of the prize-fight, Sir Lewis. After all, the champion *is* a fellow-Cornishman, though I fear he'll not be champion for very much longer.'

'Nathan Jago is fighting?'

'Yes, it surprises me, too. He's been a good champion and I would have thought he'd have the sense to rest on past glories. But it seems he's indebted to the Duke of Clarence and has to fight Clarence's man. Poor fellow, I wouldn't take his place if they offered me the Regency. I've been over to Mizler's club and watched Clarence's man sparring. Huge black chap named Dellow. Freed from slavery by Jago himself, they say. If it's true, there's damned little gratitude in him. He's boasting that Jago will fail to make the mark before the fifth round. I, for one, don't doubt it. Dellow's a *giant* of a man. I saw him knock out three sparring partners in one evening, one after the other. Clarence says he's the best prize-fighter he's ever sponsored. The clubs certainly believe him. They're offering five to one against Jago everywhere in St James's.'

Looking about him quickly, the informative MP bent low over Sir Lewis Hearle. 'Mind you, I know an old Jew who's willing to offer evens on Dellow. That's a sight better than you'll get here. You'll be lucky if you can persuade anyone to take your money.'

The baronet was not a gambling man. On any other occasion he would have dismissed his fellow-MP's offer without another thought. But money matters were foremost in his mind today. He thought he saw a desperate way out of his immediate problems. Yet, even now, he was reluctant to commit himself.

'You say you've actually seen this ex-slave prize-fighting?'

'He gives an exhibition in Mizler's club every evening. I'm on my way there now. Come with me.'

The uninformed Member of Parliament was delighted at an opportunity to advance his acquaintanceship with an under-secretary.

Sir Lewis arrived at a sudden decision. 'Dammit, I *will* come! What's more, if he's as good as you say, then I'll place a handsome wager on him, too.'

Abraham Dellow did not disappoint his spectators, each of whom had paid five guineas for admission to the prize-fighting club. To a chorus of admiring gasps and appreciative applause, the big ex-slave quickly disposed of a burly stevedore, and two bulging-muscled coal-heavers with dust-stained bodies. His fist was a devastating weapon, and the three unfortunate sparring partners were helped from the ring glassy-eyed. If anyone noticed that the three men reeked of cheap gin, nobody blamed them. Few men would be fool enough to provide a target for Dellow's iron-hard fists when sober.

Watching the superb fighter in action, Sir Lewis Hearle remembered Nathan as he had seen him some mornings. Grey-faced and round-shouldered with exhaustion, Nathan looked anything but a champion prize-fighter. In Cornwall, the problems of earning a living from the sea constantly with him, Nathan would have little chance to train himself for a championship fight. Dellow, on the other hand, had every opportunity. Furthermore, with royal patronage and the hero-worship of the public to spur him on, he had all the incentive any man could ask for to become the next world champion.

'Well?' Sir Lewis Hearle's companion posed the half-question as they left Sammy Mizler's club.

'I think you'd better take me to your Jewish friend before he shortens the odds on Dellow.'

Sir Lewis had no money, but such was the standing of a parliamentary baronet that he could lay a bet and pick up his winnings without having to find a single guinea. A signature from a gentleman on a simple IOU was sufficient, even for the five thousand guineas he wagered on the outcome of the prize-fight.

Sir Lewis Hearle returned to Polrudden in mid-October. There were many reasons for his departure from London. The first was to escape the snubs of his colleagues and the speculation that followed upon his removal from office. His letter of resignation had been made public, as was the Prime Minister's politely worded letter accepting the 'resignation' of the Under-Secretary, but few people had been fooled. Lord Liverpool had not yet announced his intention to free the Methodist Church from petty restrictions, so rumour was rife about the real reason for Sir Lewis's sudden downfall.

Sir Lewis Hearle also wanted to see how fit Nathan was. There was no possibility he could reach Abraham Dellow's high standard, but the baronet had a great deal of money riding on the outcome of the fight. He felt the need to reassure himself. No doubt the news he bore would help his cause, by giving Nathan Jago something else to worry about.

Nathan learned of Sir Lewis's return when he came home from a day's fishing, running up the steep hill from Pentuan as part of his preparation for the fight. As he approached the door of the east wing, the window of the study opened and the baronet's head appeared there.

'Jago, come up here. I want to speak to you.'

Nathan stopped beneath the window and looked up. 'If it's about the tithes, I'll bring the money to you tomorrow.'

'Bring them tonight. I have something to tell you, but I have no intention of shouting for the whole of Cornwall to hear.'

Half an hour later Nathan entered Sir Lewis Hearle's study and placed a heavy leather pouch on the desk in front of the baronet. 'There's your tithe money. I'll have a receipt before I go.'

'You'll have a receipt when I've counted the money.'

Sir Lewis scrutinised Nathan anxiously. Nathan

was fit, very fit. But in attaining such fitness Nathan had sacrificed more weight than a champion prize-fighter would care to lose. He was a big man, yet he must have weighed at least three stones less than Abraham Dellow, and he lacked Dellow's recent experience in the prize-ring. Sir Lewis relaxed in his chair, satisfied that his stake in the fight was secure.

'I hear you're defending your prize-fighting championship soon? I watched your opponent the other night. He's good, Jago. *Very* good indeed. So good that a gambling man can get odds of five to one against you winning.'

'He was good when I beat him in Bristol,' said Nathan, with more confidence than he felt about the outcome of the fight, but he was gratified at the effect his remark had upon Sir Lewis.

'You've fought him before . . . and beaten him?'

'That's right. He was wielding a whip on an American slave-ship in those days.'

Sir Lewis Hearle felt suddenly uneasy. No one had told him the two men had already met in the prize-ring. But the Negro must have improved a great deal since then. No one in London had any doubts about the outcome this time.

'He's been well trained since then by an old friend of yours. Mizler . . .? Is that his name? You won't beat Dellow this time, Jago. I've bet money on the outcome, and I don't back losers.'

'I've heard those same words spoken by many a gambler who has followed the fortunes of the prize-ring. Most ended their days in Newgate's debtors' gaol, wondering what went wrong. Is that your reason for calling me up here? If so, I hope you've enjoyed our little chat. I'll have my receipt and bid you good evening. I have other things to do.'

'Don't be in such a hurry, Jago. When you've gone from Polrudden you'll probably wish you'd made more use of your time here.'

'When I've gone from Polrudden? Are you telling me I have to leave?'

'I'm telling you that I'm selling the manor. Lock, stock and barrel.'

'You can't! It's Beville's inheritance. That's why I've kept things running here . . .'

'You're the one who has had the pleasure of living here. As for your son, you'll need to make your own arrangements for him. I'm selling up and concentrating my interests in London.'

Sir Lewis smiled maliciously at Nathan's dismay. 'Of course, if you can raise six thousand guineas, you're quite welcome to remain at Polrudden Manor – as the new owner.'

'You know very well I can't raise a tenth of that – hardly a hundredth, thanks to your tithes and the money I've already spent keeping Polrudden running.'

Nathan spoke with great bitterness. 'It's as well Elinor isn't here to see how little you think of your grandchild. Her son.'

Sir Lewis Hearle's good humour vanished abruptly. 'If it had not been for your brat, and your attentions, Elinor would still be a lively, healthy girl with a wonderful future ahead of her. Now leave me, Jago. Get out. I want you and your brat clear of Polrudden by the end of this month. Prospective buyers will be coming around after that. I don't want them wondering what a fisherman is doing behaving as though he belongs here.'

Nathan spoke to his father the next morning, asking whether he and Beville could come and share the little Pentuan cottage with him. The Methodist preacher agreed immediately, but he listened to details of Sir Lewis Hearle's intended sale of Polrudden Manor with scarcely concealed impatience. He had news of his own. News of *truly* great importance. Rumours had reached the Methodist Executive Committee in London of Lord Liverpool's intentions. As with most rumours, this one had lost nothing in the retelling.

Excitedly, Josiah Jago told his son that the Methodist Church was to be given full parity with the Church of England. Its ministers would be recognised – even by the gatekeepers on the country's turnpikes, who had instructions to allow ministers of the church free passage on the toll roads, but who delighted in taking money from the 'Methodees'. Methodist ministers were also to be authorised to administer the sacraments and to perform weddings. In short, the Methodist Church was to be allowed to go forward proudly, and not forced to fight for its very existence.

With such a heady prospect in view, it was hardly surprising that his son's more material problems hardly registered with Josiah Jago. He was eager to fetch out his old donkey and spread the glorious news among his far-flung flock.

Amy was much more sympathetic, and genuinely distressed at Sir Lewis Hearle's actions. She said: 'But Polrudden is your home – yours and Beville's. He can't just sell it and throw you both out. He has a duty towards Beville, at least.'

Nathan shook his head: 'He can do just as he likes – and he's selling Polrudden.'

Amy knew how hard Nathan had worked to keep Polrudden, and she was distressed to see him so unhappy. For the first time since she had known him, Nathan Jago looked a defeated man.

'What will you do with Beville?'

'He'll live with me in Pentuan eventually. But while I'm in London for the prize-fight he'll go to Nell at Venn Farm.'

'No, he won't,' said Amy firmly. 'Beville will stay with me. He's happy here, and he knows you always come back to Portgiskey. He can wave to the fishermen, and I'll let the fisherwomen spoil him, just as they always do. It will be much better for him, especially as Nell's expecting another.'

Nathan knew Amy's idea was sensible. Nell was six months pregnant again; she would not want another child thrust upon her. He nodded. 'All right. If you're quite certain you want him.'

'I want him. God, but I want your child, Nathan Jago! If only he were mine, too . . .'

The words were not spoken aloud, and Amy closed her eyes for a long moment before she trusted herself to speak.

'You mustn't worry, Nathan. It won't matter to Beville whether he's brought up in a cottage or in a manor. He'll be happy, you'll see.'

Nathan looked at Amy, but the faraway expression on his face told her that he was not thinking of her. 'Polrudden is Beville's birthright, Amy. Sir Lewis is doing this quite deliberately. He knows he can't prevent Beville from inheriting his baronetcy, but he's determined his grandson will have nothing else belonging to the Hearles.'

'Beville will inherit the baronetcy? You mean he'll become *Sir* Beville when Sir Lewis Hearle dies?'

'That's right.' Nathan's face relaxed for a moment as he witnessed her astonishment. '*Sir Beville*. But who has ever heard of a baronet living in a cottage belonging to a penniless Methodist preacher?'

'Is *this* the reason Polrudden means so much to you?'

'Of course. What other reason would I have?'

Amy did not reply. She was not certain what she had thought, but she had believed that Nathan's reason for wanting Polrudden so much had something to do with his memories of Elinor.

'Nathan, you told me that Sir Lewis Hearle mentioned your prize-fight – that he had wagered money on the outcome?'

'Yes, he's wagered that I will lose the fight. It seems most of London is behind Dellow. They are offering odds of five to one against me.'

'You don't think this talk of selling Polrudden is a ploy to worry you – to affect your preparation for the fight?'

'I don't doubt that Sir Lewis hopes it *will* upset my training, but I believe he's telling the truth about putting Polrudden on the market.'

'Are you going to allow him to succeed in everything, Nathan – to sell Polrudden *and* make certain you lose the fight?'

'There's nothing I can do about Polrudden . . .

unless I can find six thousand guineas quickly. As for the prize-fight, they say Dellow is one of the best fighters ever seen in this country.'

'You beat him in Bristol. You can do it again. I *know* you can.'

'Amy, I love you.'

They were standing on the quay, looking out across the cove. When Nathan put an arm about Amy's shoulders and gave her a kiss, there were catcalls from the women working in the fish-cellar, who had been watching Amy and Nathan's earnest conversation with a great deal of speculative interest.

Nathan ignored them. 'Amy, you've solved my problem of what to do with Beville while I'm in London, and done your best to assure me that I'm not an absolute failure. Perhaps you'd like to try to persuade Sir Lewis Hearle that he doesn't need to sell Polrudden? Although I doubt if even the Devil's own persuasion could change his mind about that.'

13

Nathan left for London at the end of October. He intended having a week there before the date of the fight. He was as fit as he had ever been, even at the peak of his prize-fighting career, but he needed to spend the final week sparring with some of the prize-fighting friends he had made in the past. By the time a week was over he would have a better idea of his chances against Dellow.

At the last moment, Amy tried to persuade Nathan to let Beville go to Venn Farm after all, and to take her with him to London. Nathan refused, even when Amy became surprisingly persistent. He needed to concentrate on his preparations for the fight. He did not want the additional worry of having Amy in London, within reach of Sammy Mizler.

On the journey to London, Nathan startled the other passengers by leaping from the coach at the first steep hill and running to the top beside the labouring horses. However, when the reason for this unusual behaviour was explained to the passengers and coach driver they became excited about having the prize-fighting champion of the world on their coach. Whenever Nathan alighted from the coach at the bottom of a hill the driver obligingly adjusted the pace of his horses to suit Nathan, while the passengers shouted encouragement to him from the windows.

When the coach stopped at an inn for the passengers to dine, a word from the driver was enough to ensure that sufficient food was set before Nathan to satisfy a farmer's whole family.

In London, Nathan put up at the Plough inn, in Carey Street. The landlord was John Gully, himself a former great prize-fighting champion. Not only did Gully promise to supply Nathan with all the tough sparring partners he required, but he also declared his willingness to become one of their number.

That very first evening, after a full hour's training in the innyard, the heavily perspiring Gully declared it was time for a respite. Clapping a 'muffler'-encased hand upon Nathan's shoulder, he boomed: 'You're good, boy – damned good – but you'll need to be even better if you're to keep your title against Abraham Dellow.'

Inside the inn, Gully called for the tapster to bring two tankards of best ale.

'You'll have one?' he asked Nathan.

'No. I'll take porter with my meals, but nothing in between.'

John Gully nodded his approval. 'There have been more prize-fights lost in a tavern than in a ring. This fight of yours could prove to be one of them. Dellow's taken a great liking to strong drink, so I've heard. He even calls for it between rounds. He hasn't enough years of drinking behind him to have developed the belly to hold it. He would have tasted little beer on a slaver.'

The wily former prize-fighter winked at Nathan. 'Watch him carefully, boy. If you see him drinking between rounds, you'll know you have the beating of him in a long fight – say, over twenty or thirty rounds. After that you'll only need to sink a good solid right hand in his belly and you'll tap him like a good barrel of the Plough inn's best. Remember that, Nathan; it's good advice. Now, if you're not drinking you'll want to be fighting, and I can see just the man for you coming through the door at this very minute. Ned . . . Ned Panter! Over here. You've told me often enough you're going to be a champion one day. Here's your chance to show us just how good you are.'

After Nathan had gone, Amy remained at Portgiskey with Beville for twenty-four hours before taking the small boy to Venn Farm.

Young Tom was out in the cart with his father, and Nell Quicke was alone in the house. Heavily pregnant, Nell looked a picture of health. Amy thought, with a tinge of envy, that Nell and Tom Quicke would probably have a happy, healthy family of ten or twelve children, bringing the old farmhouse well and truly to life.

'Hello, Amy . . . and young Beville, too! Well, what a lovely surprise.' Nell Quicke held out her arms, and Beville went to her eagerly for a warm hug.

Smiling at Amy, Nell Quicke said: 'Nathan told me

you'd be looking after Beville. I'm pleased. He's a little boy who brings his own love with him. You'll both be good for each other.' She drew Beville to her. 'Dear little mite, I love him as though he were my own.'

'I know. That's why I'm here to ask if you'll look after him for a few days.'

Nell Quicke said nothing, but her eyebrows posed a question.

'I want to go to London. I think Nathan may need me – and there's a chance I may be able to save Polrudden for him. Nathan said something before he left that gave me an idea.'

Amy was talking in riddles, and Nell Quicke understood none of it, except that Amy intended going to London to see Nathan.

'But your Sammy? He's in London.'

Amy smiled. Nell Quicke had travelled no farther from her home than to St Austell. She had no conception of London's size.

'London's a big place, Nell. I'll be able to keep out of Sammy's way. But it might be better if you said nothing of my whereabouts to your father. He wouldn't approve.'

Nell's snort made Beville jump. 'Right now you could tell Pa the world had come to an end and he wouldn't hear a word. News has come from the Methodist Conference that Lord Liverpool has announced the changes in the law that Pa's been expecting. There are to be no more arrests of Methodist preachers. They can go their way without hindrance, and we are free to worship in the way John Wesley taught us. Methodists are now respectable people, Amy. Pa is riding his circuit on that old donkey of his, passing on the glad news to anyone who isn't sick to death of hearing about it. He says these are the greatest days of his life. Poor Pa, but he *has* suffered more than most for his beliefs.'

Nell Quicke was a simple, emotional girl. Moved by her own thoughts, she smiled tearfully at Amy. 'If only you hadn't married Sammy Mizler. You and Nathan always did make a lovely couple.'

'But I *did* marry Sammy – and Nathan married Elinor Hearle.'

Amy spoke more sharply than she intended. She had too much on her mind to indulge in thoughts of what might have been.

'Will you look after Beville for a few days?'

'Of course I will, won't I, me darling?' Nell kissed Beville, then over his head said: 'I don't know what you have in mind, but I'll help you do anything for our Nathan. He gave Venn Farm to Tom and me, and we'll neither of us ever be able to repay him for that. He deserves more happiness than he's found in life so far. You give him that, Amy, and you'll always be in *my* prayers, whatever Pa or anyone else says about it.'

Amy caught the mail coach from St Austell the next morning. She endured a cold and bumpy ride to London in the company of a clergyman, his wife and four daughters. They complained bitterly about everything, from the lack of comfort in the coach to the poor standard of food and accommodation along the way. The reverend gentleman was constantly putting his head out of the coach window, demanding that the coachman drive more carefully. Instead, the horses were urged to even greater speeds and, as the coach bounced over the potholes, the passengers were tumbled in a shrieking heap upon the coach floor.

Once in London, Amy quickly found a room in a quiet and respectable inn, only a short distance from the coaching tavern. Then she set about locating the Duke of Clarence. It was not easy. First, Amy tried the clubs in the vicinity of St James's. As they were all male haunts, and there was a very real likelihood of Sammy being in one of them, she hired a hackney carriage. While she waited in the carriage, the somewhat reluctant driver was sent to make enquiries for her.

By the end of the day it became apparent that the Duke of Clarence was not in London, but was at his Bushy Park home, some miles outside the city. Amy decided she would go there the next morning.

It was a pleasant ride. Crossing the bridge at Westminster, the carriage followed the river for a couple of miles before turning south, through the pretty villages that would one day be swallowed up by the ever-expanding capital.

After skirting the royal park of Richmond, the hackney carriage turned through a pair of impressive but unpainted gates and followed a driveway that led eventually to a mansion set among trees, lawns and tangled gardens.

Here Amy's self-confidence temporarily deserted her. She had come to London with a simple plan in mind, a plan that she hoped would enable Nathan to keep Polrudden. Now, seeing this great house, realisation came to her that she, Amy Mizler, of Portgiskey Cove in Cornwall, daughter of a Cornish smuggler, was calling upon the Duke of Clarence, son of King George III, to ask a favour.

In a moment of panic Amy leaned out of the carriage window to tell the driver to turn the carriage about and return to London. The coach had cleared the trees, but as she put her head out of the window a young girl darted from some bushes, into the path of the horse.

The driver hauled back on the reins, at the same time stamping on the brake, causing horse and carriage to skid to an untidy halt on the gravel of the driveway.

The child escaped without injury, but Amy's cheek came into sharp contact with the window-frame. The blow stunned her for a few minutes. When she raised a hand to her face, it came away stained with blood.

It was no more than a scratch, but it looked far worse. When a matronly, blowzy woman appeared on the scene, surrounded by children of various sizes, her hand flew to her mouth in a dramatic gesture.

'Oh, my dear child! Your poor, poor face. It was that naughty Sophie. You must come inside and allow me to clean that wound for you. Driver, don't sit up there on your seat gawping. Help the young lady out. Quickly now!'

The driver leaped from his seat and, despite her protests, Amy was handed from the carriage and hurried inside the house by the woman who had come to her aid.

Amy was taken to a small, untidy sitting-room. Procuring a bowl of water, her rescuer began bathing Amy's face. As she worked, she chattered incessantly, and in a relieved tone declared that the wound was not as serious as she had at first feared, although Amy was told she would have a bruised cheek for a week or two.

From outside the sounds of children engaged in rough play drifted in through a window. Believing the woman to be a housekeeper, or perhaps a children's maid, Amy said: 'I didn't expect to find so many young people here.'

'Nobody ever does, my dear. Most of them are the Duke's, although I believe they have some friends in today. Sophie – the girl who ran in front of your carriage – is one of the Duke's favourites. She is also the wildest . . . Ah! Here she is now. Sophie, come here at once and apologise to this lady. You caused her to injure her poor face. Come now, apologise immediately.'

For a moment it seemed as though the young, tomboyish girl might refuse. Then, with a reluctant 'Yes, Mamma,' she dropped a curtsy to Amy. After murmuring a brief apology she fled from the room.

Amy was hardly aware of the brevity of the expiation. She was looking at the matronly woman with something akin to awe. 'She called you "Mamma". Then you must be . . . the Duchess of Clarence?'

The woman gave an amused snort. 'Duchess, indeed. No, my dear. Royal dukes do not marry actresses – and that is what I was when Willie, the Duke, first saw me. Now after bearing ten of his children I am still Mrs Dorothea Jordan, the Duke's "companion".'

Dropping the cloth into the water, she said: 'There, that's stopped the bleeding. Some salve will ensure that it heals satisfactorily.'

Looking up from the bowl, Mrs Jordan caught Amy's expression and she laughed: 'Why! I do believe I've shocked you, child. Who are you that you don't already know of me? Where do you come from, pray?'

'I'm Amy Mizler. Mrs Mizler, ma'am. From Portgiskey, in Cornwall.'

'Are you, indeed? You seem hardly old enough to be married. But what is a little country girl doing coming to Bushy Park in a hackney carriage?'

'I've come to see the Duke of Clarence, ma'am. To beg a favour.'

'Indeed?' Mrs Jordan's expression hardened, and she stood up abruptly. 'And why do you think the Duke of Clarence might feel inclined to oblige you with a "favour"?'

'He helped a friend of mine, Nathan Jago, some time ago. He needs help again. It . . . it's very important.'

'Nathan Jago?' Mrs Jordan repeated the name. 'I've heard Willie and his friends talking of him. Isn't he the prize-fighter?'

'Yes, but at home he's a fisherman, with two boats of his own. Him and me are partners.'

Amy felt unusually inexperienced and awkward in the presence of this woman. Still blowzily attractive, Mrs Jordan was astonishingly down-to-earth. Yet this woman had given ten children to one of King George's sons. She must be intimately acquainted with the Prince Regent and everyone at the King's Court. Amy looked at her in awe.

But Mrs Jordan was smiling again now. 'Indeed, my dear. I like to tell the Duke that he and I are partners in the business of producing children. It's something we do rather well, I think. Now, do I sense an intrigue between you and this partner of yours?'

'An intrigue? Is this something I should know about?'

The Duke of Clarence had entered the room silently through a door behind the two women and he stood in the doorway beaming benevolently.

Amy attempted to get to her feet to curtsy to the Duke, but with a hand on Amy's shoulder Mrs Jordan pushed her firmly down in the chair again.

'Willie, dear. This child has travelled all the way from Cornwall to beg a favour – only to have Sophie frighten her horse and cause her to injure her poor face.'

Mrs Jordan twisted Amy's head so that the Duke of Clarence might see the graze.

The Duke dutifully looked at Amy's slightly grazed face, but it was not the injury that made him frown.

'You and I have met before, young lady. What's your name, eh?'

'Amy. Amy Mizler. We met when Nathan Jago fought in Bristol.'

'That's it. You watched the fight with me. But your name wasn't Mizler then. Are you related to Sammy Mizler, who runs the boxing club?'

Amy nodded. 'I'm his wife . . . but I've come to see you about Nathan Jago.'

'Have you, now?' William, Duke of Clarence looked at his mistress with a faint smile. 'Damned if you're not right, Dorothea. There *is* an intrigue here. Have someone bring a drink, then lock the door to keep the brats outside. I want to hear all about this.'

A servant was summoned, drinks were served, and

the Duke of Clarence and his mistress sat back to listen to Amy's story.

Hesitantly at first, but gaining in confidence as she went along, Amy told the story of Nathan's life at Portgiskey during the previous two years. She spoke of Preacher Josiah Jago's arrests, the death of Annie Jago, and why Nathan had wanted the Duke of Clarence to buy Venn Farm from the earnings of the Bristol fight. Amy described Nathan's struggle to earn a living from his fishing-boats, and choked on her emotion when she related the tragedy of his marriage to Elinor and his life at Polrudden. During the course of her story, Amy also touched briefly on her own disastrous marriage to Sammy Mizler.

When Amy had no more to tell, Dorothea Jordan dabbed at her eyes with a ridiculously flimsy lace handkerchief and looked questioningly at the Duke of Clarence.

'H'm! I had no idea Jago had been a naval man. Fought with Nelson, you say?' The Duke seized on an aspect of Amy's story of particular interest to him.

'He was Nelson's coxswain. My brother was in *Victory*, too. He died at Trafalgar, at the same time as Nathan was wounded.'

'Well, I'm damned . . .! Well, I'm damned!' For a full minute, the Duke of Clarence was lost in his own reminiscences. He, too, had spent a number of years in the Royal Navy, and one day, as William IV, he would be known as 'The Sailor King'. By mentioning Nathan's service in the King's navy, Amy had guaranteed him the Duke's fullest sympathy.

Bringing himself back to the present, the Duke said: 'You didn't come all this way to tell me a story, no matter how interesting it might be. What is it you want?'

Amy seized her opportunity eagerly. 'Before Nathan came to London he told me it was possible to get odds of five to one against him retaining the championship. Is this still so?'

Puzzled, the Duke of Clarence nodded. 'There was a time when they were quoting *six* to one at the club. But, yes, five to one sounds reasonable. Why?'

'I'd like you to bet some money on Nathan for me.'

Neither the Duke of Clarence nor Dorothea Jordan dared to look at each other. For years they had lived in a state of regal poverty, much of it brought about by the Duke's extravagance and his love of gambling. There had been many occasions when Dorothea Jordan had threatened to leave him unless he spent less of both time and borrowed money in the gaming clubs of St James's. Yet here was this unsophisticated young girl from a remote Cornish fishing hamlet asking the Duke of Clarence to place a bet for her!

Clearing his throat noisily, the Duke asked: 'How much money do you wish to bet on Nathan Jago?'

'Fifteen hundred pounds,' said Amy proudly. Oblivious of the incredulous looks that passed between the Duke of Clarence and his mistress, she opened the leather pouch she carried and took out a piece of paper, which she passed to the Duke. It was a note, drawn on the bank of Philip Ball & Son, of Mevagissey. It promised the sum of fifteen hundred pounds to whoever should present the note.

'My dear girl! This is a *vast* sum of money for you to risk on the outcome of a prize-fight! Are you quite certain you know what you're doing? I mean, if Jago *loses*, you've thrown away a considerable fortune . . .'

'He won't lose,' said Amy confidently. Then, doing her best to appear nonchalant, she added: 'Besides, the money really doesn't matter to me. It was left by my pa. I've already spent some to buy another boat for the partnership – Nathan's and mine. But Nathan wants Polrudden far more than anything I'll ever want to spend the money on.'

The Duke of Clarence looked in astonishment at Amy. 'You are a remarkable young lady. Don't you agree, Dorothea?'

'I think this Nathan Jago is a very fortunate young man,' replied Mrs Jordan, reaching out and squeezing Amy's hand affectionately. 'I would very much like to meet him. But tell me, dear. What does he want with a manor-house? You've told us that when the prize-fight is over he'll go back to fishing once more.'

There had been gaps in Amy's narrative. Dorothea Jordan was attempting to fill some of them.

'He wants it for his son, for Beville. It's his heritage. But now Sir Lewis Hearle has put it up for sale, even though he knows Beville will become the fourth baronet one day.'

Amy spoke proudly of Nathan's son. 'Beville can hardly have the title and no manor-house, can he?'

She smiled at the Duke of Clarence, who was having great difficulty in absorbing this latest astounding piece of information. 'That brings me to my second favour. You arranged for Venn Farm to be bought for Tom and Nell Quicke. Would you do the same with Polrudden? Buy it with my winnings, for Nathan. It might be better if you did it through a friend, though,' she added as an afterthought. 'Sir Lewis Hearle was very upset when he learned it was really Nathan who'd bought Venn Farm.'

The Duke of Clarence began spluttering uncontrollably. Amy was uncertain whether the cause was mirth or anger. His words did nothing to help her.

'Dammit! I asked Jago once before whether he regarded me as some sort of estate agent. Now I know! I'll soon have the whole of Prinny's blasted Duchy after me to buy and sell land for them!'

The Duke of Clarence was referring to the huge land holdings that came to every Prince of Wales, together with his hereditary title of 'Duke of Cornwall'.

Rising from his seat, the Duke of Clarence took a handkerchief from his sleeve. Putting it to his mouth, he hurried from the room, making sounds as though he were choking.

'Have I angered him?' Amy asked anxiously, as the door banged shut behind the departing Duke.

'My child, you are absolutely *priceless*,' declared Mrs Jordan, hugging Amy to her suddenly. She was having great difficulty controlling her own amusement. 'Willie will place your bet for you. Yes, and he'll purchase Polrudden for your gladiator. *I'll* see to that. But I doubt if I'll be able to bear the suspense on the day of the prize-fight. Willie will have to take both of us to watch from his carriage. Now, you must stay here at Bushy Park with me until the day of the fight. No, I'll take no argument from you. I am absolutely *starved* of company, so far away from town. Mind you, it's going to be a unique experience, having a guest give me *honest* replies to all my questions.'

14

The day of the fight dawned crisp and clear. Nathan drove from London to Bushy Park accompanied by John Gully and Ned Panter. Panter had insisted on acting as Nathan's second cornerman, even though he sported a swollen and colourful right eye as evidence of Nathan's powerful punching.

Nathan knew that, win or lose, he would be fighting in front of a huge crowd on such a day. This was confirmed by the time they came to within two miles of Bushy Park. People were streaming towards the scene of the prize-fight from all directions. Prize-fighting was unlawful, but here, where the Duke of Clarence sponsored prize-fights between the best boxers in the land, no magistrate would risk his standing in county society by invoking the law.

The crowds and the gentlemen in carriages were reluctant to give way to anyone, but the booming voice of the coachman calling 'Make way for the champion of the world' was enough to clear a path and bring resounding cheers from the crowds. The odds might be heavily against Nathan Jago, but he was an *English* champion. The people of England were strongly behind him.

Bushy Park itself was heaving with spectators. Some were forced to stand so far from the prize-fighting ring that they could not possibly have a clear view, even though the ring had been raised on a huge wooden platform. Around the ringside, in the area reserved for members of the 'Fancy', friends of the Duke of Clarence would watch from the comfort of their own carriages, obstructing the view of the spectators even more.

When Nathan and his seconds drove up, Abraham Dellow was already in the ring. Striking exaggerated poses to demonstrate his impressive muscles, he was drawing roars of approval from the throats of thousands of waiting spectators.

'We'll stay in the coach a while longer,' said the wily John Gully cheerfully. 'There's a cold wind out there, and it's well known that Dellow doesn't like the cold. It will stiffen his muscles and have him calling for strong drink to warm him before the fight's even started. Ned, do you have a pack of cards in your pocket?'

Ned Panter had no cards, so John Gully began pointing out well-known members of the 'Fancy' to Nathan. John Gully knew them all, their family backgrounds, mistresses and children. He also entertained Nathan and Ned Panter with a wealth of anecdotes of these men who promoted and encouraged the art of prize-fighting. John Gully was displaying the knowledge that was soon to earn him a fortune gambling on horse racing and prize-fighting, and take him to the House of Commons as a Member of Parliament.

When half an hour had passed, Abraham Dellow gave up exhibiting his body. He stood in his corner, wrapped in a large, warm overcoat and sipping from a silver brandy-flask. Beside him, peering peevishly along the road from which he expected Nathan to arrive, was Sammy Mizler.

The crowd was growing restless. Looking from the window of the carriage, John Gully said: 'Nathan, boy. There are two classes of people entitled to keep others waiting – brides and champions. They've had their waiting, out there. Now it's time for them to feast their eyes on you. Out we go.'

The three men climbed from the carriage, but for a few moments no one in the huge crowd recognised them. Then a mighty roar went up. Some of the spectators were angry that Nathan had deliberately kept them waiting. The remainder, realising why Nathan had remained in the carriage, roared noisy approval.

Climbing the short ladder to the wooden platform, John Gully was the first of the trio to duck beneath the single rope of the ring and he held it high for Nathan.

Once in his corner, Nathan acknowledged the shouts and cheers of the crowd. Stripped to the waist, he pranced about in his corner for a few minutes, slinging punches at imaginary opponents. It served to loosen a boxer's muscles and, over the years, the spectators had come to expect the brief exhibition.

In the far corner, Abraham Dellow was doing the same. Now both men were stripped, the discrepancy in their weights was evident. Dellow's black shoulders bulged heavily with muscle. Nathan's were hard and sinewy, and far less showy.

Sammy Mizler had not acknowledged Nathan and had given him only one brief glance. But that look was sufficient to tell him that Nathan was as fit as he had ever seen him. Abraham Dellow would win – but it would not be the walkover that many were expecting. Dellow *had* to win. Boasting incessantly that Nathan stood no chance, Sammy had taken money – a *lot* of money – from gamblers loyal to the champion, offering them odds that varied from four to one to six to one. One such gambler was the Prince Regent himself.

The referee called both men to the mark in the centre of the ring and satisfied himself they were ready. Then, signalling to the timekeepers, he hurried from the ring and called on the boxers to begin fighting.

Abraham Dellow came straight into the attack. Driving Nathan across the ring before him, he scorned the left jabs with which Nathan tried to keep him at a distance. Ducking and moving all the time, Nathan escaped most of the other man's blows for more than three minutes, until Dellow backed him against the rope. Crowding in on him, Dellow caught Nathan in a wrestling hold and threw him to the ground.

Immediately, a break was called. Nathan returned to his corner to perch on the knee provided by Ned Panter, while John Gully rubbed his body briskly with a rough towel to prevent him becoming chilled.

'You're doing fine, boy,' said Gully. 'Make him come to you. Hit him when you have the chance. But *keep out of trouble*. The longer you make him work, the better it will be for you. Dellow has never fought a long fight and he may not have the stamina.'

Abraham Dellow was not relying upon a second to keep out the cold. He had a flask to his lips and was pouring best smuggled brandy down his throat, while Sammy Mizler remonstrated with him.

Time was called for the second round and both prize-fighters met again in the centre of the ring. The pattern of the first round was repeated until Nathan caught Abraham Dellow with a blow to the face that stung the bigger man. Dellow came back with a speed and ferocity that took the champion by surprise. Nathan took a crashing blow to the left eye, and another to the side of the jaw that dropped him to his knees.

Back in his corner, Nathan's seconds worked hard to clear his mind before he needed to toe the mark for the next round. As Ned Panter sponged icy cold water on the back of the champion's neck, John Gully burned a fistful of feathers beneath his nose.

Nathan made the mark, but spent the whole of a long round retreating before Abraham Dellow, who was convinced he already had Nathan beaten. Dellow won this round also, but then lost the next two. However, by this time, Nathan's left eye had almost closed and his vision was severely restricted.

Taking advantage of Nathan's handicap, Abraham Dellow kept his attack coming from Nathan's blind side. On three occasions he succeeded in tripping him to the ground. The prize-fight had now settled into a punishing pattern. Nathan landed one or two good punches in every round, but in terms of knockdowns Dellow was winning three rounds out of every four.

Nathan had already absorbed more punishment than in any prize-fight he had taken part in before. His body was badly bruised, great red blotches standing out from the pale skin. But it was Nathan's face that caused John Gully to look anxiously at his fellow-second, over the top of Nathan's bowed head, during the interval after the twenty-sixth round.

Nathan rose from Ned Panter's knee for the twenty-seventh round – and thirty seconds later was back in his corner. Gasping with pain, he had been felled by a low blow that the referee had missed – or chosen to ignore. A minute and a half later, Nathan was back again, knocked to the boards of the ring in similar circumstances.

This time John Gully protested vehemently to the referee that the blow had been low, but the referee shook his head.

'I reckon he's got failing eyesight,' grumbled Ned Panter, as the disgruntled John Gully returned to the corner.

'More likely a small fortune riding on Abraham Dellow,' scowled John Gully. 'I've met him before. He refereed the last fight I lost. I swear to this day I was never given a full half-minute to come to the mark.'

Nathan said nothing. He ached in every limb. From his one sound eye he hazily saw Abraham Dellow grin at Sammy Mizler before taking another swig – from a bottle this time, the flask being long emptied.

Nathan closed his eyes and leaned his head back. He should never have agreed to this fight. He had been out of the prize-ring for too long. Then he was being pushed to his feet and led across the ring to the mark, to come face to face with Abraham Dellow once more.

The twenty-ninth, thirtieth and thirty-first rounds passed in a haze of pain. It seemed to the crowd that the big Negro was playing with Nathan now, using him to demonstrate his own boxing skill as he cut Nathan's face to ribbons with angled, slicing punches.

During the brief intervals, John Gully and Ned Panter tried to persuade Nathan not to come up to the mark for another round, but stubbornly Nathan lurched to his feet and plodded to the centre of the ring.

As Nathan slumped to Ned Panter's knee at the end of the thirty-first round, blood gushing from his nose, there was a sudden commotion outside the ring, only yards from the corner where he sat. Nathan was too weary to do more than register the disturbance until the shrill voice of a woman cried: 'Let me go. Let me get to Nathan.'

It was Amy!

Suddenly she was at the ringside, and he could see her expression of despair as she looked at his battered face.

'Nathan, give up. Please . . . Don't go on.'

At that moment the referee called for the two men to meet at the mark in the centre of the ring for the thirty-second round. Only John Gully escorted Nathan to the mark. When he glanced over his shoulder, Nathan saw Ned Panter forcibly preventing Amy from getting inside the ring.

His astonishment gave Nathan a new and unexpected strength. Abraham Dellow moved in, instructed by a grim-faced Sammy Mizler to end the fight quickly, only to be met by a barrage of blows that dropped him to one knee in the space of five seconds.

Almost before the referee had declared it to be a knockdown, Nathan was back in his corner.

'What are you doing here? Where's Beville?'

It was the first time Nathan had used his voice during the fight and his jaws moved stiffly, the muscles of his face battered and bruised.

'Beville's with Nell. I came to see you fight. But you've had enough, Nathan. End it now. Come back to Portgiskey . . . and Beville. Please. Please!'

As Amy talked of Portgiskey and Beville, it was as though she was pumping new strength into Nathan. He thought of the sea, of Portgiskey, and the small, unchanging village of Pentuan; of his life there as a fisherman. And he thought of his son. Today was Beville's first birthday. This was not the day to make him the son of a *defeated* prize-fighter, an *ex*-champion.

There was something else, too. Across the ring, Sammy Mizler had stared open-mouthed at his wife when she first fought her way to Nathan's corner. Now, ashen-faced, he glared across the ring, his lips drawn together in a tight, thin line. Amy was Sammy's wife. In the eyes of the law she was no more than a chattel – and the law was inclined to ignore what a man did with his own. If Nathan was beaten into the ground, here in this prize-ring, Sammy would reclaim his 'property'. No doubt he would then teach her a harsh lesson for shaming him in front of so many of his friends.

'Did you come all this way just to see me beaten?' Nathan mumbled painfully.

'That doesn't matter now. Just finish the fight, here and now. Let Dellow take the championship. What good is a prize-fighting title to a fisherman? You've got so many other things . . .'

Once again the shout of the referee brought the two prize-fighters to their feet. Nathan wasted no time getting to the mark, but he was no quicker than Abraham Dellow. The Negro fighter had been ordered to end the fight in this the thirty-third round.

For a full two minutes the two prize-fighters stood toe to toe, each throwing punches that would have felled most men. The action set the crowd roaring its approval. Then Nathan ducked low beneath Dellow's muscular arms and sank a mighty punch into his opponent's stomach, putting all his weight behind the blow.

A look of agony contorted Abraham Dellow's face. Clutching both hands to his stomach, he doubled up and sank to the boards, groaning.

The crowd went wild as Dellow's seconds hurried to treat him where he sat in the ring. Straightening him out, Sammy Mizler desperately rubbed and kneaded his fighter's tender stomach muscles while the other second tried to pour brandy down the suddenly reluctant throat of the challenger.

When the referee called for the men to step up to the mark, Dellow was still on the ground; but Sammy was equal to the occasion. Leaving his fighter, he turned to the referee. Protesting loudly, he called on him to declare that his man had been put down as the result of a low blow.

Before Nathan could say anything, John Gully had crossed the ring to denounce Sammy Mizler as a liar. As the two men argued heatedly, the crowd of spectators erupted in a roar of disapproval, calling for the fight to be continued.

It was a full minute before order was restored and both seconds ordered back to their respective corners. But Sammy Mizler's interruption had served its purpose. Abraham Dellow was on his feet. Although still hunched over with pain, he was able to toe the line.

It was a brief respite. As Sammy screamed instructions to the still-dazed challenger, Nathan repeated the last punch of the previous round; but this time he did not stand back to watch the result of his blow. As Dellow folded forwards, Nathan straightened him with two hard uppercuts. His final punch was a superb right cross that exploded on Dellow's chin and dropped him to the ground at Nathan's feet.

The challenger lay on the ground without so much as a muscle twitching, and Nathan knew he was still the champion.

The crowd knew it, too. They were going wild long before the referee performed the formality of calling the fighters to come to the mark. With Abraham Dellow still lying on his back, arms outstretched, the referee declared Nathan to be the winner.

Grinning as widely as his battered face would allow, Nathan returned to his corner to be hugged by John Gully, Ned Panter . . . and Amy. But there were many disgruntled losers in the crowd, and when they began to get out of hand John Gully suggested that they should leave the ring as quickly as possible.

Nathan agreed but, gripping Amy's arm, he said: 'On the way you can tell me exactly what you are doing here.'

Amy looked up at him, her concern for his injuries hidden beneath a happiness that, for the moment, supplanted all other feelings. Beyond her, across the ring, Nathan saw Sammy Mizler standing alone, his expression that of a man who was living out a nightmare.

'I think you'd better come with me, Nathan.' Amy was talking. 'There's someone here who can tell you better than I can.'

Amy guided the three men to where a liveried coachman stood beside a plum-coloured carriage. On the side was the motif of a ducal crown. Nathan knew to whom the carriage belonged before an aristocratic man with high forehead and a genial expression opened the carriage door and said: 'Come inside, Nathan. You'll be ready for a seat that's a sight steadier than Ned Panter's bony leg.'

It was William, Duke of Clarence.

The hours that followed the fight were cloaked in an air of unreality for Nathan. Even with Amy clinging to his arm he was so dazed and battered that he was still not certain she was really beside him. Nathan was introduced to Dorothea Jordan and was forced to endure her tearful ministrations as she smoothed balm on his badly battered face.

They drove to the home of the Duke. By the time they arrived, Nathan was so stiff and sore he had to be helped from the carriage by two of the Duke's footmen.

Once inside the house, Nathan had his battered face dressed yet again by Dorothea Jordan, while a whole series of awe-filled young faces swam in a vague sea of unreality about him, and a succession of huge brandies were forced upon him.

Then, ignoring Nathan's demands to be told what

was happening, Dorothea Jordan ushered him off to bed, telling him firmly there would be ample time for explanation when he was thoroughly rested.

Nathan was convinced he would lie awake for hours, going over the exciting events of the day, but within minutes of stretching his aching body on the soft bed he was fast asleep.

When he awoke, the room was in darkness, only a faint light coming from the square of dark grey sky filling the window. For a moment Nathan could not remember where he was. When everything came back to him, he sat up suddenly. All the aches and pains returned to his battered body and he sank backwards once more with a groan.

A tinder-box scraped in the room and moments later it was illuminated by the soft, yellow glow of a lamp. Then Amy was kneeling beside the bed.

'At last! I thought you were *never* going to wake.' She took his hand and hugged it to her, tangling his fingers in hers. 'I've got so much to tell you.'

Her happy excitement was contagious. Nathan grinned – and immediately regretted the facial movement. It would be many days before he would be able to change his expression without the muscles of his face reminding him of the battering they had taken at the hands of Abraham Dellow.

'I've got a few questions to ask you, too. What you're doing here, for instance.'

'I came to London to place a bet on you winning the prize-fight.'

'You did what . . . ?' Nathan repeated his earlier mistake and tried to sit up. This time he succeeded, but at great cost. When he turned his head he dis-

covered he had vision in only one eye. The other was
tight-closed. He put a hand up and carefully traced
the extent of the swelling with his fingertips.

'God, but I took a battering.'

'Yes, but you won the fight, Nathan. You're still the
champion – and I won my bet.'

'How much did you win?'

Nathan was puzzled that Amy should make so
much of a wager. Until he learned of the sum involved.

'I won seven thousand five hundred pounds.'

In an instant all aches and pains were forgotten.
Nathan's mouth dropped open in utter astonishment.
When he spoke again his voice came out as a hoarse
whisper of disbelief.

'Amy . . . How much did you wager on the fight?'

'Fifteen hundred pounds.'

'But that was all the money you had. The money
your father left you.'

Nathan felt sick when he thought how close he had
come to losing the fight. Then he remembered how
Amy had urged him to give the fight to Abraham
Dellow because he was being badly battered. As the
thoughts went through his mind, he squeezed Amy's
fingers so tight she winced painfully.

Nathan was immediately filled with concern. 'I'm
sorry, Amy. It's just . . . I don't know what to say.
What are you going to do with your fortune?'

This was the question for which Amy had been
waiting. She could not conceal her delight, as she said:
'It's already spent. Well, much of it. I've bought
Polrudden – for Beville.' Amy added the rider hastily,
as she saw Nathan's expression changing.

'You've . . . bought Polrudden?'

'Yes. Sir Lewis Hearle also bet on the fight. Only he thought Abraham Dellow was going to win. He owed five thousand guineas to a moneylender who would have sent him to Newgate Gaol had he not been able to pay him immediately. He was desperate for money. When a friend of the Duke of Clarence offered him five thousand guineas for Polrudden, he accepted immediately. Gratefully, too, I understand.'

Nathan sank back on his pillows again and tried to make sense of all that Amy had just told him. It was impossible. It all mattered far too much. If what Amy said was true . . .

'Amy, why should the Duke of Clarence be so kindly disposed towards me? He's Abraham Dellow's sponsor. He must have lost a lot of money on the fight.'

'He *would* have done had I not come to London. When I convinced him that *you* would win he managed to switch his money to you – or something like that. Whatever he did, he won a lot of money. Far more than I did.'

Nathan was silent for a while. Then he said: 'I can't take Polrudden from you, Amy. You can see that, surely?'

Amy shook her head vigorously. 'No, I *can't*. Anyway, I've told you. It's for Beville. You can't take it away from *him*.'

She gripped his hand tightly in hers and spoke in near-desperation. 'Nathan, listen to me. I haven't lost by this. Even after giving you Polrudden I'm going home much richer than when I arrived in London. Please don't refuse my gift, *please*. It means more to me than anything I've ever done before.'

Nathan withdrew his hand and, ignoring his complaining muscles, he put his arms out and pulled her to him. 'Amy, I know why you've done this, and I love you for it. You've saved Polrudden for Beville – and for me. All right, I'll live there – but as your tenant until I can raise the money to buy Polrudden from you.'

Amy was about to argue that she had bought the house for Nathan and his son, and would attach no conditions to the gift, but she bit back her reply. Nathan had said he would remain at Polrudden. It was enough for the moment.

15

Nathan and Amy spent that day and a further night at Bushy Park as guests of the Duke of Clarence and Mrs Dorothea Jordan. It was a warm and friendly stay, if somewhat hectic. Most of the children of the union seemed to be of an indeterminate age, caught between childhood and adulthood, and each had a crowd of friends who spent much time at the house. They passed through the room where Nathan rested continuously, pausing to chat with the easy-going Duke of Clarence, or just standing gazing admiringly at Nathan's battered face.

It soon became evident that the crowd of young people would not have been nearly so large had Nathan not been staying at the house. Dorothea Jordan was convinced her own children were charging their friends for admittance to see him.

When it was time to leave there was genuine warmth in the farewells said between Dorothea Jordan and Amy. The one-time actress had taken a great liking to Amy that was in sharp contrast to her manner towards most young women of the Duke's acquaintance. As she led her to the Duke's carriage, which was taking Amy and Nathan to London, Mrs Jordan gave her a few words of advice.

'You've got a fine young man there,' she told Amy, patting the arm that was linked through her own. 'Don't lose him because a few narrow-minded busy-bodies say it isn't right for you to love him.'

She looked back to ensure that the Duke of Clarence was not within hearing. 'Had I listened to the advice of others, I would never have spent so many happy years with Willie. They are coming to an end now, but I'll always have the children, and Willie is a kind man. He'll never take them from me.'

Amy looked at her new-found friend in some bewilderment. 'Take them away – but why should he? You are all so happy here together.'

Dorothea looked at Amy's face quickly but saw no guile there. She gave a wan smile. 'Forgive me, my dear. I keep forgetting you're an uncomplicated little girl from Cornwall, far away from the dreary intrigues of the Prince Regent's Court. Willie is the third of King George's fifteen children. Alfred never survived infancy, and poor Amelia died two years ago, but the remainder are tenacious survivors. The male members of the family are also prolific pro-creators of children – out of wedlock. As such, they are a serious drain on the funds of the poor old King, their father. Consequently, they are all under con-stant pressure to marry into money, especially poor Willie. Then, of course, there is the question of the accession to the throne. The Prince of Wales and Caroline have only their daughter, Princess Charlotte. They are unlikely to produce any more – at least, not by each other. If anything should happen to Charlotte, the succession to the British throne would be thrown wide open once again and there would be an unseemly scramble to make "suitable" marriages, and beget legal offspring.'

Dorothea Jordan laughed gaily, but Amy detected a deep bitterness in the sound. She was also aware that the Duke's mistress cared more for her royal lover than was good for any woman in such an uncertain situation.

At the coach Mrs Jordan kissed Amy and embraced her warmly. 'Goodbye, child. Promise you'll write and let me know how you and your champion are getting along.'

To Nathan she said: 'Take care of this young lady. She is rather special.' Then she kissed Nathan, too, adding: 'If I am ever in the West Country I will visit Polrudden – and I expect to see you *both* there.'

The Duke of Clarence was less emotional, but considerably more practical. At the last moment he pressed a weighty bag upon Nathan. 'Here's five hundred guineas. It's the money that would have gone to Abraham Dellow, had he won. It's yours, Nathan. You've earned it and proved yourself a great champion. Dammit! Can't I persuade you to defend the championship just once more? I'll give you the largest purse ever. *Two* thousand guineas . . . two thousand *five hundred*.'

The Duke had to shout his last offer. Mrs Jordan had given a signal to the coachman, and he had driven away before Nathan could give the Duke of Clarence an answer.

Nathan and Amy went to the Plough inn before returning home to Cornwall. Here, in the company of John Gully, Ned Panter and their friends, they enjoyed a riotous party. Nathan had trained at the inn and was well liked and respected there. In addition, many of the staff and customers had backed him to retain the championship. Now they had an opportunity to express their gratitude, and spend some of their considerable winnings.

The singing and dancing went on throughout the night, although Nathan and Amy left the party early. They were catching the morning coach. The hard springing of a mail coach and the potholed roads upon which it travelled made no concessions to a head heavy from an excess of brandy and porter.

Nathan and Amy were pleased they had not stayed to greet the dawn when they saw the state of John Gully, Ned Panter and the other revellers who came to see them on their way the next morning. Still far from sober, their bleary eyes and general air of fragility set them a world apart from those about them who shouted farewells to Nathan and Amy's fellow-travellers.

At Andover the coach stopped at an inn to allow the passengers to enjoy a meal before facing the wide open spaces of Salisbury Plain. It was here that the Duke of Clarence's emissary caught up with the coach. He bore a letter addressed to Amy and written in the Duke's own bold hand.

Puzzled, Amy broke the seals on the letter and

opened out the large sheet of paper. As she read a variety of expressions crossed her face. They ranged from shock and anguish to a sudden realisation of new hope.

'What does it say?' Nathan asked when he could contain his curiosity no longer.

Instead of replying, Amy handed the letter across the table to Nathan. Setting down her knife and fork, she left the dining-room hurriedly.

Nathan squinted through his one good eye to read the letter. His expressions followed the same course as had Amy's. When he had read the letter through twice, Nathan sat back in the chair and closed his one good eye, as a host of jumbled thoughts chased each other through his mind. The letter he held in his hand informed Amy of a tragedy that had taken place in London – one that would change the whole course of Nathan and Amy's lives. Aware of the importance of his news, the Duke of Clarence had penned the letter hurriedly and sent a horseman to overtake the coach.

It informed Amy that Sammy Mizler was dead – killed by his own hand.

Carried away by his own boasting, Sammy Mizler had convinced himself that Abraham Dellow was unbeatable and could not possibly lose to Nathan. Sammy's prize-fighting club was frequented by many of London's richest men, a few of whom favoured Nathan. Sammy had stupidly accepted wagers from these wealthy clients – almost twenty thousand pounds, at odds of up to six to one. In the belief that he was making himself a rich man, he had then taken the money to the gambling clubs of St James's and used it to back his own man to win the world championship.

When Abraham Dellow failed to reach the mark for the thirty-fifth round of the championship prize-fight, he left Sammy Mizler owing the gentlemen of London more money than he could ever hope to raise – six thousand guineas of it to the Prince Regent himself.

The situation was an impossible one for Sammy Mizler. Faced with social annihilation, and a lifetime in Newgate's debtors' gaol, Sammy returned to London's East End. Here, in the tiny Haggerston house tucked between the tallow works and the brewer's stable, he consumed a quart of brandy before cutting his throat inexpertly with a kitchen knife. He then bled to death on the cheap carpet.

Nathan thought it was a tragic end to the man who had been his friend and companion for many years, even though the friendship had turned sour for both of them.

But Sammy's death had set Amy free. She was no longer another man's wife . . .

Nathan found Amy outside the inn, where the newly harnessed coach-horses blew clouds of vapour high in the cold air, while driver and guard exchanged crude jokes with the inn's ostler and a tapman who had brought out brimming tankards of porter for the two coachmen.

Amy looked pale and taut, but there were no tears for her late husband. Nathan took her hand and they walked across the road from the inn to stand looking over a low wall at a fast-running stream.

Amy spoke first. 'It's awful to think of Sammy dying like that. No one should die so . . . so *alone*. I know I should feel sorrow for him, weep for him . . . but I *can't*. I'm sorry for the way he died, but all I can feel is a great relief. A tremendous weight has been taken from me. Nathan, help me. I'm so confused . . .'

Suddenly, in complete contradiction of all she had said, Amy burst into tears and turned to Nathan. He held her until she stopped crying, then dried her eyes, aware that the coachmen were watching them curiously from the innyard.

'Feel better now?'

Amy nodded. 'Yes. I'm glad I was able to cry for Sammy. Just once. I gave him little else.'

'You're wrong, Amy. Sammy gained the greatest victory of his life when you married him. But now he's given us back a future again. Let's think of him kindly.'

Amy nodded, saying nothing as from the innyard a coachman blew a long brass horn to summon passengers to the coach.

Nathan and Amy made their way across the road and climbed inside the coach. A few minutes later the creaking vehicle lurched from the innyard and gathered speed on the smooth stretch of road that linked town cobbles to country lane.

Amy's fingers slipped into Nathan's hand. Leaning against him, she whispered: 'Nathan? Will you accept Polrudden as my dowry . . . ?'

SOMEWHERE A BIRD
IS SINGING

E. V. Thompson

Sally is an orphan living in Plymouth's Barbican, a late 19th century dockside slum, where a vile trade flourishes in young girls, duped and shipped off to the brothels of Europe. Her sister, Ruth, is driven to prostitution in order to support them, until she becomes too ill to work.

Now, with her sick sister to take care of in their single room home, Sally finds employment delivering wares for a local shop, meeting fisherman Ethan and, through him, Eva, a captain in the local Salvation Army. Eva has dedicated her life to rescuing the endangered girls and bringing their procurers to justice.

When Ruth is brutally murdered, Sally finds the father she has never known, but he is to bring only trouble and unhappiness into her life. When Ethan, his father and brothers are reported missing at sea on a fishing trip, Sally volunteers to help Eva's crusade – with near-disastrous results.

The loves and tragedies of a young woman fighting to escape from her environment are vividly captured in *Somewhere a Bird is Singing*.

Other bestselling Time Warner Paperback titles available by mail: